IMPERIAL FIRE

Robert Lyndon

sphere

SPHERE

First published in Great Britain in 2014 by Sphere
This paperback edition published in 2015 by Sphere

1 3 5 7 9 10 8 6 4 2

Excerpts from
The Seafarer and *The Wanderer* copyright © Kevin Crossley-Holland 1982.
Reproduced by permission of the author c/o Rogers, Coleridge & White Ltd,
20 Powis Mews, London W11 1JN.

A CIP catalogue record for this book
is available from the British Library.

ISBN 978-0-7515-4776-4

Typeset in Sabon by M Rules
Printed and bound in Great Britain by
Clays Ltd, St Ives plc

Papers used by Sphere are from well-managed forests
and other responsible sources.

MIX
Paper from
responsible sources
FSC
www.fsc.org FSC® C104740

Sphere
An imprint of
Little, Brown Book Group
100 Victoria Embankment
London EC4Y 0DY

An Hachette UK Company
www.hachette.co.uk

www.littlebrown.co.uk

To Sam and Caoileann, Andrew
and Jane. And James ...

A BRIEF CHRONOLOGY

1044	First mention of 'gunpowder' in a Chinese military manual
1066	*October* Duke William of Normandy defeats the English army at Hastings and in December is crowned King of England. Some dispossessed English warriors travel to Constantinople and join the Varangian Guard, the Byzantine Emperor's elite bodyguards
1071	*August* A Seljuk Turk army routs the forces of the Byzantine Emperor at Manzikert, in what is now eastern Turkey
1076	China bans the export of sulphur and saltpetre, two of the ingredients of gunpowder
1077	Suleyman ibn Kutulmish, a Seljuk emir, establishes the independent Sultanate of Rum in western Anatolia
1078	In return for Suleyman's aid against the Byzantine Emperor, a rival for the imperial throne allows the Seljuks to settle in Nicaea (modern Iznik), less than a hundred miles from Constantinople
1081	*April* Alexius Comnenus usurps the Byzantine throne *May* Robert Guiscard, the Norman Duke of Apulia, invades Byzantine territories on the Adriatic coast, capturing Corfu and laying siege to the port city of Dyrrachium, in what is now Albania *October* Duke Robert defeats an army led by Emperor Alexius at Dyrrachium

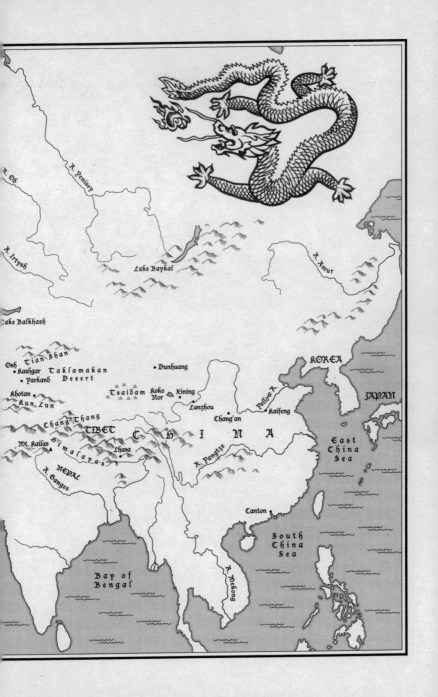

He who is used to the comforts of life
and, proud and flushed with wine, suffers
little hardship living in the city,
will scarcely believe how I, weary,
have had to make the ocean paths my home.
The night-shadow grew long, it snowed from the north,
frost fettered the earth; hail fell to the ground,
coldest of grain. But now my blood
is stirred that I should make trial
of the mountainous streams, the tossing salt waves;
my heart's longings always urge me
to undertake a journey, to visit the country
of a foreign people far across the sea.

(From 'The Seafarer' in the *Exeter Book*,
England, tenth century)

Dyrrachium, 1081

I

Vallon's squadron struck the Via Egnatia around noon and pounded on down the paved road towards the west. They rode with fierce determination, bloodshot eyes fixed straight ahead, and at sunset three days later – the sixteenth day of October – they pulled up their blown horses on a wooded ridge overlooking the Adriatic coast. Vallon leaned forward, squinting into the evening light. The sun had already sunk halfway beneath the sea, leaving a burnished copper fairway fanning back to the port of Dyrrachium. From this distance the city was just a tiny blur, too far away for him to make out the Norman positions or the damage inflicted by their siege weapons.

Shortening focus, Vallon studied the Byzantine encampment about four miles inland, entrenched in a broad rectangle along a meandering river. A pall of dust half a mile long drifted away from the camp.

He glanced at Josselin, one of his centurions. 'It would appear that we're the last scrapings of the imperial barrel.'

Josselin nodded. 'Judging by the size of those earthworks, I'd put our strength at more than fifteen thousand.'

Vallon conned the terrain, trying to work out where the battle would be fought. On the plain north of the city, he decided.

Only a sliver of sun remained above the horizon and the sea had darkened to deep violet and indigo. He looked back down the line. His Turkmen troops dozed in their saddles. Most of the rest of the squadron had dismounted and sat slumped against the cork oaks, their eyes raw hollows in faces masked with dust. In the last two weeks they'd ridden four hundred miles cross-grain through the Balkans from Bulgaria's Danube border, and now they looked more like the survivors of a battle rather than warriors about to go into action.

3

From the hillside below came the clanking of sheep bells and the sweet riffle of running water. Some of the soldiers were already ferrying skins and barrels back up to their comrades and their thirsty mounts. Vallon's three centurions sat their horses, waiting for his orders. He hawked to clear the dust from his throat. 'It will be hell if we arrive at the camp after dark. Endless questions, ordered from pillar to post. We'll be lucky to find a billet before dawn. We'll rest here tonight and ride in before sunrise. Dole out what's left of our provisions.' He turned to Conrad, his second-in-command, a German from Silesia. 'Captain, pick ten men, smarten them up and inform headquarters of our arrival. Take the wounded in one of the supply carts. Beg or borrow whatever food you can. Find out what's going on and send a report.'

'Yes, Count.'

Vallon's rank wasn't as grand as it sounded. As *Kome* of a *bandon*, he commanded a squadron of light and medium cavalry numbering two hundred and ninety-six men by this morning's muster. That was twenty fewer than when he'd left Constantinople for the Bulgarian marches seven months ago. The Outlanders they were called – mercenaries recruited from all over the Byzantine empire and beyond.

Shadows were pooling among the trees when Conrad's party left, the wheels of the wagon wobbling and squeaking on its worn axle, five bandaged casualties lying in its bed. Vallon led his horse towards the spring, limping slightly – the effect of a ligament torn in a swordfight nine years earlier. At the age of thirty-nine, he was beginning to count the cost of even the minor wounds and knocks he'd suffered in more than twenty years of campaigning.

The spring ran bubbling from the base of an ancient holm oak whose trunk parted from the roots to create a cleft housing a painted statue of the Virgin holding the baby Jesus. Icons, bells and wind chimes hung from the branches. An old man with a face like an empty purse sat beside the spring, his arms crossed tight over his chest. A boy attended him, one hand placed on the patriarch's shoulder.

4

Vallon nodded at him. 'God keep you, father.'

'Your men are stealing my water.'

Vallon dropped to his knees beside his horse. 'It seems to me that there's not one drop less than when we arrived.'

The old man rocked back and forth in resentment. His eyes were clouded. 'The spring is sacred. You should pay for it.'

Vallon leaned over the pool, pushed back his hair and scooped a handful of water into his parched mouth. His eyes closed in rapture at the delicious sensation of cool liquid sliding down his throat. 'All water's sacred to men who thirst. But who to pay? He who created it or the man who guards it? I'll gladly offer my prayers to both.'

The old man mumbled to himself.

Vallon wiped his mouth and nodded towards the plain, where fires were beginning to prick the rising tide of darkness. 'Do you know what's going on down there?'

The old man spat. 'Murder, rape, thievery – all the ills that follow in an army's train.'

Vallon smiled. 'I'll tell you what I will pay for.' He fished a few coins from his purse and pressed them into the wrinkled palm. 'Some of my men have the marsh sickness from spending too long on the Danube plain. They can't stomach rough rations. If you could spare a basket of eggs, some milk and fresh bread ... '

The boy took the coins and examined the imperial heads. 'They're good, Grandpa.'

The old man squinted sightlessly. 'You're not a Greek.'

'A Frank. Driven by life's tempests to this far shore.'

The man struggled to his feet. 'Franks, English, Russians, Turks ... The empire's infested with foreign soldiers.'

'Who are fighting to defend its borders while your native-born lords show off the latest fashions in the Hippodrome.'

The boy guided his grandfather away down the hillside. Vallon chewed a supper of raisins and hardtack, drew a blanket around his shoulders and dropped into sleep to the tinkling of bells.

The boy returning woke him. 'Here are eggs and bread, Lord.'

Vallon rubbed his eyes and faced uphill. 'Captain Josselin, some food for the invalids.'

When the officer left, Vallon hunched forward, examining the fires of the imperial army laid out in a grid, the flames of the Normans strung in a burning necklace around the beleaguered city. All he knew about the Norman force was that it was led by Robert Guiscard, the 'Crafty', Duke of Apulia and Calabria, a general of genius who'd ridden into Italy as a mere adventurer and within fifteen years had carved out a dukedom and made the pope his staunch ally.

A torch flickered through the trees, approaching up the road. Hooves clattered. By the light of the wind-torn brand, Vallon made out a rider leading a packhorse. The rider drew closer, a man of massive bulk. Tongues of flame fleeted across a braided vermilion beard, receding yellow hair, a red tunic medallioned in gold.

Shadows darted into the path of the rider. 'Halt! Who goes there?'

'Beorn the Bashful, *primikerios* in the Varangian Guard. Are you Count Vallon's men? Good. Lead me to him.'

Vallon grinned and stood. 'I'm up here by the spring.'

Beorn slid off his horse, lumbered through the trees and seized Vallon in a scented embrace. The impression of bulk wasn't false. The man had to walk sideways through doors and his chest was almost as deep as it was broad, yet in matters of grooming he was very dainty.

'What are you doing moping in the dark?'

'We've been riding hard for weeks and I fell asleep through sheer weariness.'

'You nearly missed the feast. Which reminds me. I ran into your German centurion and he said you've been living on worms for the last month. I brought some food. You can't fight on a hollow stomach.'

Vallon took Beorn's hands. 'My dear friend.'

Beorn was an exile like him, an English earl, a veteran of the battles at Stamford Bridge and Hastings who had lost his estate in

6

Kent to the Normans. Vallon had forged a friendship with him while campaigning in Anatolia. They had saved each other's lives and the bond was reinforced when Beorn discovered that Vallon had made a journey to England, spoke the language and had gone wayfaring in the far north with an English companion.

The Varangian turned to the sentries. 'Unsling those panniers. Bring them over here.'

The sentries doubled over under the weight of the loads. Beorn opened one of them and rummaged through its contents. 'Wrong one. Hand me the other.' He delved into it, gave a grunt of satisfaction and lifted out a roast chicken. 'Brought three of them.'

'I can't fill my belly with meat while my men gnaw stale biscuits.'

'Same old Vallon. I directed your German captain to the Master of the Camp. Your men will have all the food they can eat by midnight. We'll keep one fowl for ourselves and you can do what you like with the others.' He held up a flask. 'But this is just for the two of us. Finest Malmsey from Cyprus. Tell your men to light a fire. You and I have a lot to talk about and I want to see your face while I'm about it.'

Vallon laughed and called to his centurions. They carried off the food and soldiers bustled to lay kindling and branches.

Vallon held out his hands as the wood began to crackle. 'So we're definitely committed to battle.'

Beorn wrenched a leg off the chicken and passed it to Vallon. 'I pray God we are. The emperor arrived yesterday. Another two days and you would have missed the action.'

'Would that be the same emperor as when I left?' Vallon saw Beorn's brows bristle. 'Alexius is the fourth I've served under in nine years.'

Beorn tore off a piece of chicken with his teeth. 'The same, except that Alexius is different from the others. He's a soldier's emperor. Fought his first battle against the Seljuks when he was fourteen and has not been on the losing side since. Wily in war as he is in diplomacy.'

Vallon gestured at the fires winking on the plain. 'I'm not even sure what's led to this confrontation. I'd already left for the north when Alexius was crowned, and I only received orders to ride to Dyrrachium a fortnight ago. News is slow to reach the Danube.'

Beorn cocked a shaggy brow. 'Hard time of it on the frontier? I saw the wounded men in your wagon.'

'The Pechenegs harried us as we withdrew. Sending my squadron to defend the border against horse nomads is like setting a dog to catch flies. Most of our losses were due to sickness rather than action.'

Beorn gnawed a drumstick. 'It's been brewing for years, ever since the Emperor Michael was overthrown after offering the hand of his son to Duke Robert's daughter. Gave the duke the excuse he needed to invade. He sailed from Brindisi this May, took Corfu without a fight and marched on Dyrrachium. His fleet followed but was hit by a storm and lost several ships.'

'How big is his army?'

Beorn tossed the drumstick into the fire. 'Thirty thousand originally, mostly riff-raff scraped together without consideration of age or military experience. When Alexius heard about the invasion, he played a clever hand by forming an alliance with the Doge of Venice. The last thing the Doge wants is Normans controlling the approaches to the Adriatic. He took personal command of the Venetian fleet, caught the Norman ships napping and destroyed some and scattered the rest. Then he sailed into the harbour at Dyrrachium. When the Byzantine navy arrived, they joined with the Venetians and routed the blockading Norman fleet.'

'Not the most auspicious start to Robert's campaign.'

'There's more. Robert laid siege to the city, but it's well defended by *strategos* George Palaeologus.'

'I served under him in the east. As brave a commander as ever lived.'

'You're right. Not only has he held out against Robert's catapults and siege towers, he's also taken the fight to the enemy, mounting sallies from the city and destroying one of their siege engines. During one assault, he took an arrow in the head and fought all day with the point lodged in his skull.'

'Palaeologus threatening the Normans' rear will make our task easier, even facing twice our number.'

'Less than that. Pestilence struck Robert's army in the summer and carried off five thousand men, including hundreds of his best knights.'

Vallon laughed. 'You almost make me sorry for the man. How strong is the Byzantine force?'

'About seventeen thousand. Five thousand from the Macedonian and Thracian *tagmata*, a thousand *excubitores* and *vestiaritae*, and a thousand Varangians. As well as the native troops and a regiment of Serbian vassals, we've got about ten thousand Turkish auxiliaries, most of them supplied by your old friend, the Seljuk Sultan of Rum.'

Vallon pulled a face. 'I wouldn't place too much faith in them.'

'Don't worry. The contest will be settled by the heavy cavalry and my Varangians. We've waited a long time to avenge our defeat at Hastings.'

'Do you know the battle plan?'

Beorn pointed towards the distant fires. 'Dyrrachium stands on a spit running parallel to the coast and separated from it by a marsh. The citadel's at the end of the spit, connected to the plain by a bridge. From what I gather, the emperor intends to send part of his force across the marsh to attack the Normans from behind. The rest of the army will hold the plain opposite the bridge.'

Vallon sipped his wine. 'I hear that Guiscard's son is his second-in-command.'

'Bohemund,' said Beorn. 'A big, brawling bastard and another first-rate soldier. And he isn't the only kin who'll be fighting at Guiscard's side. His wife Sikelgaita rides into battle with him.'

Vallon coughed. 'You're jesting.'

'It's true as I live. She's taller than most men and fiercer than a lion. A love-tussle with her would be something to remember.'

Vallon thought of his wife, Caitlin, herself a redoubtable woman of fiery temperament.

'Have you any news of home?'

Beorn poured another cup. 'Forgive me. I should have delivered it first. I dined at your house in August. Lady Caitlin grows more queenly each time I see her, and your daughters will have no difficulty making favourable matches. Aiken thrives in their company and his accomplishments grow daily.'

Three years before, Beorn had asked Vallon if he would take his then thirteen-year-old son into his household as the Frank's squire or shield-bearer. Aiken's mother was dead, and Beorn wanted his son to grow up learning to speak Greek and adopt Greek ways. The Anglo-Saxon Varangians still held to their own language and customs, even addressing the emperor in English. It wasn't only Beorn's pleas that had made Vallon accept. Caitlin had seen how lonely the boy was and pressed Vallon to take him under his wing. He would be the son that she hadn't been able to give him.

Almost shyly, Beorn drew a letter from under his cloak and passed it across the flames.

Vallon read it and smiled. 'Poor Aiken. He's learning how to dance, with my eldest daughter as partner.'

'It's all right, isn't it – a warrior learning how to turn a fancy step?'

'Of course it is. Life isn't only about shearing the heads off your enemy. In any case, dancing isn't all that he's mastering. He writes a good Greek hand and says that his tutors are pleased with his progress in mathematics and logic.'

Beorn jabbed a finger. 'But soldiering is his birth destiny. He turned sixteen last month. When you ride out on your next campaign, you'll take Aiken with you.'

Vallon hesitated. 'Not all youths of sixteen have hardened to the same degree.'

Beorn leaned forward. 'And some don't harden until they're tempered by the heat of battle. Promise me you'll take Aiken on your next campaign. I know you won't expose him to serious hazard until he's ready to face it.'

'I'd like to talk to him first, hear what ambitions he harbours.'

10

Beorn waved aside this consideration. 'There's only one course for my son – the way of the oath-sworn warrior. Give me your pledge, Vallon. In two days we march into battle. I might be killed. I'll face that fate serenely if I know that Aiken will follow my calling.'

Vallon grimaced. 'In two days it might be me who lies dead and then it will be my lady calling on you for protection.'

Beorn's features set in complicated lines. He stared into the flames. 'I've been waiting a long time for this encounter. I still feel shame that I didn't die with my king at Hastings. This time we crush Duke Robert or perish in the attempt.'

Vallon reached out and touched Beorn's shoulder. 'That isn't the attitude that wins battles.'

Beorn looked up, his eyes red in the firelight. He laughed. 'You've always been the foxy one who lives to fight another day.' He shot out a hand. 'If I die, swear that you'll make a warrior of Aiken.'

Vallon extended his own hand. 'I swear it.'

Beorn sprang up and thumped him on the back. 'I've kept you too long from sleep. You aren't anxious about the battle, are you?'

'Not particularly.'

Beorn gave a booming laugh. 'Good. Fate always spares the undoomed warrior.'

Vallon managed a weak grin. 'My old friend Raul the German used to say the same.'

Beorn looked down, his brutish face gentled. 'And he spoke the truth.'

At break of day, Vallon led his squadron down to the Byzantine camp. Banners and standards glimmered through the dust kicked up by thousands of horses. Centurion Conrad met him at the outer rampart and guided him through the controlled chaos to the headquarters of the Grand Domestic, the emperor's field marshal. A Greek general received Vallon with ill-concealed suspicion.

'You cut it fine. You should have received your marching orders at the beginning of September.'

'They reached me only two weeks ago, and the Pechenegs were so sorry to see us leave that they chased us halfway to Nicopolis.'

The general narrowed his eyes in the face of Vallon's subtle insubordination. 'I trust that your squadron is in fit shape to fight.'

Vallon knew there was no point explaining that his men and horses were exhausted. 'I'll carry out my orders diligently.'

The general's slow, wagging nod conveyed a lack of conviction.

Vallon cleared his throat. 'I request permission to scout the enemy's positions. My squadron will be more effective if we know the lie of the land.'

The general kept Vallon under dark review. Like most native Byzantine commanders, he resented the fact that the empire's defenders were largely made up of foreign mercenaries. 'Very well. Make sure you're back well before dark. After sunset the camp will be sealed. No one leaves, no one enters.'

'Hear that?' said Conrad as they left. 'It must mean the emperor intends to give battle tomorrow.'

Vallon took his three centurions and a squad of horse archers on the reconnaissance, riding to a low ridge about a mile from the city. From here he could see the breaches pounded in the citadel's walls by the Norman trebuchets. He could also make out the marshy channel through which the emperor intended sending part of his army.

'If Alexius has thought of that ploy, you can be sure Guiscard has done the same. Gentlemen, I think we could be in for some hot action.'

He lingered a long time, committing the particulars of the terrain to mind. The season had been dry and the Byzantines had torched the fields to deny the invaders food, leaving a bare undulating plain ideal for cavalry.

He returned to the camp in a honeyed light and was still dismounting when Beorn ran up and seized his arm. 'Come. The emperor's holding his final council of war.'

They headed towards the double-headed eagle standard flying above the imperial headquarters, a large silk pavilion surrounded

12

by guards three lines deep. Another wall of guards sealed off a crowd of officers pressing around the inner cordon.

One of the guards held up his hand to stop Vallon.

'The count's with me,' said Beorn, the wall of soldiers giving way before his bulk.

Vallon followed him through the scrum of officers, ignoring their black looks, until he had a clear view of the emperor. Alexius I Comnenus stood on a platform engaged in discussion with his senior commanders. Not at first sight a particularly imposing figure – pale face almost eclipsed by a bristling black beard, a chest like a pouter pigeon. Strip him of his crown and parade uniform – a corselet of gilt lamellar armour over a purple and gold tunic – and no one would guess his exalted rank and title.

Vallon recognised a few of the generals. The blond man wearing a tunic of madder red and a cloak fastened by a jewelled fibula at one shoulder was Nabites, the 'Corpse Biter', the Swedish commander of the Varangians. The portly man to his right was the Grand Domestic. One of the generals, lean, haggard and serious, seemed to be arguing with the emperor.

Vallon nudged Beorn. 'That's Palaeologus, commander of the citadel.'

'Yes. He sneaked out of Dyrrachium when the emperor arrived and will make his way back tonight so that he can coordinate his attack on the Normans.' Beorn rubbed his hands. 'Everything's running in our favour.'

Vallon saw Palaeologus step back and shake his head in vexation. 'He doesn't share your optimism.'

Alexius turned and looked out over the crowd, his piercing blue gaze transforming Vallon's impression of the man. He raised a hand to command a hush, timing his delivery to perfection.

'The talking is over, our tactics agreed. Rest well tonight, for tomorrow we drive the invaders into the sea.' He smiled a disarming smile. 'Unless any of you have something to add that might sway my decision.'

Gusty sighs of relief or anxiety gave way to a heavy silence.

Vallon didn't know he was going to speak until the words left his mouth. 'I see no compelling reason to risk battle.'

Beorn gripped his arm. Faces spun with expressions of disbelief. A general pushed out of the crowd, his face puce with anger. 'Who the hell are you to question His Imperial Majesty?'

'It wasn't a question,' said Vallon.

'The emperor's not interested in the opinion of some lily-livered mercenary.'

Alexius raised his jewelled baton. 'Let him speak,' he said in refined Attic Greek. He leaned forward, black brows arched in polite enquiry. 'And you are?'

'Count Vallon, commander of the Outlander squadron.' He spoke in clumsy demotic and heard men utter the word *ethnikos*, 'foreigner', seasoned with a selection of insulting epithets.

Alexius leaned further. 'Explain the reason for your timidity.' He wafted his baton to still the angry jostle around Vallon. 'No, please. I would like to hear the Frank's answer.'

'It's not cowardice that compels me to speak,' Vallon said. He could see a scribe recording his words. He dragged in breath. 'Winter approaches. In a month the Normans won't be able to advance even if they capture the city. Nor can they retire to Italy. They've already suffered serious setbacks – the destruction of their fleet, the ravages of plague. Most of their army are unwilling conscripts. Leave them to wither on the vine.'

Palaeologus was nodding and Alexius glanced round to intercept the meaningful glances of other commanders before turning back to Vallon. He gave every impression of a man open to argument. 'Some of my generals share your opinion.' His expression hardened, his voice rose and his blue gaze seared the audience. 'I'll tell you – all of you – what I told them.' He allowed a strained hush to settle before breaking it. 'It's true that the Normans have suffered reverses. If we withdraw, it's quite possible that they'll try to return to Italy for the winter. But next spring they'll be back, with a larger navy and army and the whole campaigning season in which to make gains. As for us, we've already withdrawn the

14

armies from our remaining holdings in Anatolia, leaving them exposed to attack by the Seljuks. No, now is when we're at our strongest. Now is the time to attack.'

Hundreds of fists punched the air around Vallon. The roar of salutations to the emperor spread until the Normans four miles away could have had no doubt that the order to battle had been given.

Beorn dragged Vallon away, sweeping aside an officer who clawed at the Frank and spat in his face. When Beorn was clear of the crush, he swung Vallon round. 'What the devil possessed you to fly in the face of the emperor? You just ended your career and ruined my chances of promotion to commander of the Varangians.'

'I spoke the truth as I saw it. As Palaeologus knows it from months of experience.'

Beorn's jaw jutted. His breath came in gusts. 'Fool. The truth is whatever the emperor wants it to be.'

Still panting in disbelief, he disappeared into the crowd, leaving Vallon isolated. A Byzantine officer barged into him and others leaned in with muttered remarks about his craven character. Face set, hand on sword, he set out to rejoin his squadron, unaware that fate had settled its indifferent glance on Beorn and that he would not speak to him again.

II

No moon on the eve of battle. Nothing visible except the hazy glow of Norman campfires burning around the city. Only the chink of metal and creak of horse harness told Vallon that his squadron were drawn up around him. Hooves pummelled the ground ahead and then stopped. He heard an exchange of passwords and after a little while Conrad arrived at his side.

'You were right, Count. The Normans have left the city and advanced onto the plain.'

'Send word back to the Grand Domestic.'

Mist lay thick along the coast and daylight was slow to break through, tantalising shapes swimming out of the murk and then retreating until at last the sun rose above the hills behind and the vapours lifted, revealing the Norman army arrayed in formations spanning a mile of plain, drawn up in perfect stillness, their banners limp and their mail armour leaden in the dim light. Behind them Vallon could see the fleet of blockading Venetian and Byzantine ships anchored outside the bay south of Dyrrachium.

The spine-tingling tramp of thousands of feet and hooves announced the approach of the Byzantine army. In battle-proven tradition it was drawn up in three main formations, with the emperor in the centre and a regiment led by his brother-in-law to his right. On the left, nearest to Vallon, was the *tagma* commanded by the Grand Domestic, his troops clad in glittering iron cuirasses and greaves and helmets with mail aventails protecting their necks, their horses skirted with oxhide scale armour and helmed with iron masks, so that men and beasts looked more like machines than flesh and blood. Vallon's own men wore plain mail or leather armour rusted and stained by long exposure to the elements.

The imperial army halted in line with Vallon's position, less than a mile from the Norman front. The Grand Domestic had posted Vallon's squadron out on the left flank, close to the coast. Vallon's intervention the night before had marked him out as too unreliable to occupy a more central position. He wasn't concerned. His men were coursers and skirmishers. Whether the battle went well or badly, he might not see any action today. As Beorn had said, the encounter would be decided by the heavy cavalry and infantry.

A stirring in the Byzantine rear heralded the Varangian Guard arriving on horseback, their two-handed axes winking in the sunlight. They dismounted and formed into a square a hundred yards

16

in front of the emperor's standard. Grooms led their mounts away and a squadron of light cavalry cantered into the gap between the Varangians and the imperial centre. They were Vardariots, elite horse archers recruited from Christianised Magyars in Macedonia.

Priests blessed the regiments, the incense from their censers drifting across the plain. Vallon's squadron joined in the Trisagion, the Warriors' hymn. 'Holy God, Holy Mighty One, Holy Immortal One, have mercy on us' – his Muslim and pagan troopers singing as fervently as their Christian comrades.

Now the low autumn sun flashed off the lines of Normans and illuminated the brilliant standards borne by the Byzantine units. Vallon glanced at his own banner, its five triangular pennants stirring in the morning breeze. A bugle note prickled his blood. Trumpets blared and drums pounded, the notes resonating in his chest. With a shout that raised the hairs on his neck, the Varangians began their advance. The Normans' response drifted faint and eerie across the battlefield and above Vallon's head a flock of swallows heading south hawked for insects.

The Varangians swung along in full stride, singing their battle anthem, huge axes slung across their left shoulders, the shields on their backs redundant. Vallon couldn't suppress his admiration. Anxiety, too. How could infantry, however brave and skilled they might be, withstand a charge by mounted lancers? He pulled on his helmet, raised his hand and dropped it.

'Advance.'

They rode at walking pace, keeping level with the Varangians. When the distance between the two armies had narrowed by half, a detachment of Norman cavalry peeled off from the centre and charged the Varangians head on. The Guard halted, closing ranks.

'It's a feint,' said Vallon.

At a trumpet blast, the Varangian phalanx split in two, opening a corridor for the Vardariots. They galloped down it and when they reached the end they released their arrows at the cavalry before wheeling and riding back along the Varangians' flanks.

The square closed up again and resumed its advance. The Norman cavalry circled and made another charge, the Varangians and Vardariots countering with the same move as before. The Normans made one more feint and this time the Vardariots rode around the Varangians, discharging their arrows into the cavalry from a range of no more than fifty yards. Vallon saw riders tumble and horses go down.

'That stung them,' said Conrad.

Directly opposite Vallon's position, Guiscard's right wing urged their horses forward, spurring the beasts into a trot, angling across the battlefield.

'Now it comes,' said Vallon. Tight of throat, he watched the formation charge at an extended canter and then a gallop aimed at the Varangians' left flank. The horse archers' arrows couldn't stop them. Vallon winced as the mass of horses ploughed into the Varangian formation, clutched his head when he saw it buckle, leaned forward on his stirrups when he saw the cavalry slow and begin to mill. Across the dusty arena the tumult of war carried – the clash of iron, the meaty impact of heavy axes smashing into flesh and bone, blood-crazed yells, the shrieks of injured beasts and dying men.

He sat back in his saddle. 'They're holding their ground.'

'Skirmishing on the right,' said Conrad.

Vallon's attention flicked across the Byzantine front before returning to the grisly contest in the centre. The attack on the Varangians' left flank had ground to a halt. Those terrible axes had wreaked havoc, throwing up a wall of dead horses. The cavalry couldn't find a way through and while they wheeled and reared, the Vardariots poured arrows into them from close range.

Conrad turned. 'Why doesn't Guiscard throw his centre forward?'

Vallon rasped a knuckle along his teeth. 'I don't know. That's what worries me.'

Unable to break the Varangian square, defenceless against the archers, the Norman cavalry wrenched their horses round and began streaming away, at first in trickles and finally in a flood, kicking up dust that obscured the formations.

Vallon stood upright in his stirrups. 'No!'

Dim in the haze, the Varangians were pursuing their enemy, streaming like hounds after their hated foe. Vallon recognised Beorn by his vermilion beard, leading the reckless charge. Vallon kicked his horse and galloped towards the Grand Domestic's regiment, swinging his arm to signal that there was no time to lose. 'Follow them up!'

A few cavalrymen glanced at him before turning their attention back to the action, as if it were a drama staged for their benefit.

Vallon spurred back to his formation. 'After them!' he shouted. 'Don't engage without my order.'

His squadron clapped spurs to flanks and galloped after the fleeing Normans and the pursuing Varangians. Here and there pockets of cavalry had turned on their enemy and were surrounded and cut down.

Conrad drew level. 'It's not a feint. It's a rout.'

Vallon pounded on. 'For now it is.'

And for a while it was. In the panic of war, the Norman right wing fled back to the sea. Some of them stripped off their armour and plunged in, trying to reach their ships. The rest milled along the shore, not knowing which way to turn. A detachment of Norman cavalry and crossbowmen cut between them and the Varangians, led by a figure with blonde hair spilling below her helmet. Back and forth she rode, smiting the cowards, exhorting the rabble to regroup and unite against the enemy.

'It's true,' said Vallon. 'That's Sikelgaita, Guiscard's wife.'

Her intervention turned the tide. In ones and twos and then in tens and twenties, the cavalry regrouped and turned. The Varangians were scattered over half a mile of plain. They had fought a brutal battle and followed up in heavy armour to exterminate the old enemy. They were formationless and exhausted, unable to offer any concerted defence against the Norman counter-attack.

19

Vallon watched the ensuing slaughter in furious disbelief. Time and time again, Beorn had told him how the Normans' feigned retreat at Hastings had lured the English shield wall to their destruction. And now it was happening again.

Conrad pranced alongside Vallon. 'We could make the difference.'

'No.'

Some of the Varangians, including Nabites their commander, managed to escape back to the Byzantine lines. Others fought their way through the Normans, gathering other survivors, making for a tiny, isolated chapel not far from the sea. By the time they reached the building, they must have numbered about two hundred – a quarter of the strength that had stepped out so bravely less than an hour before.

The chapel was too small to accommodate them and so many were forced to take refuge on its roof that the structure collapsed, casting them down among their comrades. Already the Normans were at work firing the building, piling brushwood around the walls and hurling burning brands over the eaves. Flames licked and then rose in smoky banners. Timbers crackled and Vallon heard the screams of men being consumed alive.

The door burst open and a dozen Varangians crashed out, led by Beorn, his beard scorched to stubble and his forehead blistered and boiled. He sliced through one Norman with a stroke that folded him over like a hinge before ten men hacked him down, flailing at his body as if he were a rat driven out of a rick at harvest time.

'Here comes Palaeologus,' said Conrad.

Out from the citadel rode its garrison. Almost immediately it met fierce opposition and the sally petered out.

'Too little, too late,' said Vallon.

A chorus of war cries heralded a charge by Guiscard's regiment at the emperor's exposed centre.

'Back!' yelled Vallon.

Led by Guiscard, the Norman cavalry bore down on the

20

imperial standard, sweeping aside the Vardariot archers who contested their path. Clumsy in their layers of armour, the imperial force lumbered forward to meet the attack, the two sides colliding with a splintering crash.

Swirling dust obscured the fighting. Vallon drove his horse towards the cloud, straining to make out the two sides.

'The Normans have broken the centre,' he shouted.

They had split the Byzantine formation, driving a deep wedge into it.

Vallon checked that his squadron was with him and pulled his horse to the left. 'Closer! Keep formation!'

He aimed for the imperial standard, the only fixed point on the battlefield. But then he realised it wasn't fixed. It had been reversed and was withdrawing. And over on the right flank another Byzantine formation was streaming away.

'Treachery!' Conrad shouted. 'The Serbians are deserting.'

Nor were they the only ones. Behind the heavy Byzantine cavalry, the Seljuks – all ten thousand of them – turned tail and fled before they'd struck a single blow.

'Calamity,' Vallon groaned. 'Complete disaster.'

'Look out behind!' Conrad yelled, hauling his horse round.

Vallon spun to see a squadron of Norman lancers plunging out of the dust, hauberks flapping about their legs, lances couched.

'Stand and engage,' he yelled. 'Archers!'

With their first volley, they toppled more than ten of the enemy, the powerful compound bows driving arrows through plate and mail.

Vallon drew a mace. 'Javelins!'

Scores of missiles arced towards the pounding cavalry. Few reached their target. And then the enemy was on them. Vallon singled out an individual riding pell-mell towards him. His attacker jounced in the saddle, only his lance held steady. Waiting until the last moment, Vallon swerved away from the point and, leaning out with his weight on his right stirrup, smashed his mace into the

Norman's mailed head with a force that sent him somersaulting backwards over his horse's tail.

Blood and brain spattered Vallon's hand. Eyes darting right and left, he weighed up the situation. Some of the Normans had charged right through his squadron and were disappearing into the dust. Others had drawn their swords to engage at close quarters. While most of the squadron fought hand to hand, the horse archers circled the fray, shooting at targets as they presented themselves. The assault by sword and dart was more than the Normans could deal with and they broke off, one of them wrenching his horse around so violently that it lost its footing and collapsed, toppling on the rider with a force that broke his leg and made him scream. Falling, his helmet toppled off and his coif slid down his neck. One eye clenched in agony, he registered Vallon's approach and his own execution.

Vallon leaned down and shattered his skull. 'Mercy on your soul.'

Short as it was, the skirmish had left him disoriented. The billowing dust made it impossible to make sense of what was happening. The only thing he knew for certain was that the Byzantines had lost the day. If the emperor was dead, they might have lost an empire.

He brandished his mace. 'Follow me!'

Less than half his squadron responded, the rest unsighted by the dust or scattered by the skirmish. Vallon didn't catch up with the main Norman force until they'd overrun the imperial camp, riding roughshod over the place where only last night Alexius had promised victory.

Giving the Normans a wide berth, Vallon's force outpaced the enemy. A distraught Byzantine cavalryman fleeing from the fray cut across his path.

'Where's Alexius? Is he alive?'

'I don't know.'

Vallon must have ridden a mile further before he came upon the Byzantine rearguard engaged in a desperate struggle to stem the

Norman pursuit. The task was beyond them. Their role was to bear down on the enemy in close formation and crush them by weight of arms and armour. In retreat, that beautifully crafted material – the plated corselets, greaves, arm- and shoulder-bands – weighed twice as much as Norman mail, reducing them to lumbering targets.

Vallon rode through them and at last overtook a group of stragglers from the Imperial Guard. He drew level with an officer.

'Does the emperor live?'

The officer pointed ahead and Vallon spurred on, overtaking friend and foe alike. The Normans were so desperate to catch Alexius that they barely registered the Frank's passing until one of them, strappingly built, mounted on a particularly fine horse and wearing the sash of a senior commander, heard Vallon shout an order in French and steered towards him.

'You're a Frank. You must be regretting this day's employment.'

Vallon dug in his spurs. 'Fortunes of war.'

The knight couldn't match his pace. 'What's your name?'

'Vallon.'

'Not so fast, sir.'

Vallon cocked an eye back to see the man raise his helmet, revealing a handsome, ruddy face.

'I'm Bohemund. If you survive the slaughter, apply to me for a position. You'll find me in the palace at Constantinople.'

Vallon booted his horse on. The mob of horsemen ahead of him thinned to reveal a core of the Imperial Guard bunched around a horseman accoutred in splendid armour and quilted silk. About fifty Norman cavalry were trying to force their way through the cordon. Vallon galloped up behind them, slung his shield over his back, holstered his mace and drew both his swords – the beautiful Toledo blade he'd taken off a Moorish captain in Spain, the sabre-like paramerion slung at his left hip. The exultant and single-minded Normans never expected to be attacked from behind and didn't see him coming. Trained since childhood to wield weapons either-handed, he rode between two of the trailing

Normans, dropped his reins and cut down first one and then the other in the space of a heartbeat.

The audacious attack unbalanced him. He had to discard the paramerion in order to recover his seat and reins. He was no longer a limber youth and he wouldn't be trying that move again.

A Norman officer signalled with violent gestures and a dozen mailed horsemen converged on Vallon. He glanced back to see how many of his squadron were still with him. Not more than twenty.

'Hold them up,' Vallon shouted. His eye fell on Gorka, a Basque commander of five. 'You. Stay close.'

Now the ground ahead was almost clear and Vallon could see that the Normans had broken through the emperor's defensive screen. Three of them attacked the emperor simultaneously from the right. Alexius, mounted on the finest horse gold could buy, couldn't avoid their weapons. One of the Normans planted his lance in the horse's leather-shielded flank. The other two drove their weapons into the emperor's side, the force of the impact pitching him to the left at an angle impossible to sustain.

Fifty yards adrift, helpless to intervene, Vallon waited for the emperor to fall. *So ends the empire.*

But Alexius didn't fall. His right foot had become entangled in the stirrup and somehow he managed to cling on. Two more Normans charged in from the left to deliver the killing strike. They aimed with deliberation, both lances taking Alexius in the left side of his ribcage.

If Vallon hadn't seen it himself, he wouldn't have believed it. Like the previous attack, the points didn't penetrate the armour. Instead, the force of the blows jolted the emperor back into the saddle and he rode on, three lance shafts dangling from man and mount, the iron heads trapped between the lamellar plates.

Vallon didn't see the final attempt on the emperor's life until it was too late. A Norman angled across him, spiked mace held high, determined to win glory. Lashing his horse into greater effort,

24

Vallon strove to catch up. The emperor turned his bloody face as the Norman drew back his mace to crush it.

Gorka shot past with sword angled behind his shoulder. 'He's mine,' he shouted, and sent the Norman's head bouncing over the plain with one mighty swipe.

Vallon had outstripped the enemy and the river was less than a quarter of a mile away. He drew alongside the emperor. Blood flowed from a wound in Alexius's forehead.

'Cross the river and you'll be safe.'

Alexius raised a hand in acknowledgement and Vallon pressed close to the emperor. Together they crashed into the river and forged through the current. On the other side a Byzantine force large enough to repel the Norman pursuit coalesced around the emperor. Men who just a short time ago had thought only of their own lives lifted Alexius to the ground, exulting at his deliverance. Surgeons hurried forward to treat him. A piece of his forehead hung in a bloody flap. Vallon dismounted and stood back while the surgeons did their work.

An officer hurried past and clapped him on the back. 'Praise the Lord. The emperor will live.'

Vallon recognised the man who'd spat in his face the night before. After the hideous events of the day, reason snapped. He shot out an arm, seized the man and yanked him round. 'No thanks to you,' he said. And then, swamped by emotion, he slapped the man to the ground and stood over him, sword poised. 'Easy to prate about courage and honour in camp. Not so easy to convert words into action in the face of battle-hardened warriors who don't give a shit about your noble lineage.'

The officer struggled to his feet, drawing his sword. Vallon swatted it aside and crashed his shield against the officer's head, knocking him down again.

'Get up if you dare.'

Hands seized Vallon and dragged him away. A Greek soldier drew back his sword to strike.

'Stop this,' a voice shouted. 'Unhand that man.'

Into Vallon's view rode a Byzantine general, casting his gaze around. 'One of the mercenary captains assisted the emperor in his escape. Let him step forward.'

Vallon smiled at the officer he'd assaulted and shoved his sword back into the scabbard. 'I think he means me.'

When Vallon approached, Alexius raised his blanched face and laughed. 'I might have known it. It seems that you only came to my aid to tell me your judgement was vindicated.'

Vallon bowed. 'Not so. Your tactics would have worked if the Varangians hadn't suffered a rush of blood. I give thanks to God for sparing your life, and I pledge to continue serving in defence of the empire.'

Alexius pinned him with his disconcerting blue gaze, then allowed the surgeons to lower him back onto his cushions. He rotated one hand and closed his eyes. 'Vallon the Frank. Make a note of that name and strike everything else from the record.'

Constantinople

III

Vallon left his squadron at its winter quarters in Hebdomon, seven miles south of Constantinople, and set off alone for the ride home. He entered the city's triple line of defences through the Golden Gate, passing under a triumphal arch bristling with statues of emperors, sculptural reliefs and a chariot pulled by four colossal elephants. His route took him along the Mese, the wide marble-paved thoroughfare used by emperors embarking on or returning from campaigns. Snow had fallen and Vallon had the road almost to himself, the city muted and melancholy under a gloomy November sky. He jogged through empty plazas, horse and rider dwarfed by the lofty statues of dead emperors whose triumphant attitudes only made the defeat at Dyrrachium more humiliating. At the Forum of Constantine he turned left and made his way down to Prosphorion Harbour on the south side of the Golden Horn. Here he caught a ferry to the north shore, remounted his horse and rode up into the suburb of Galata.

His walled villa stood near the top of the hill. He frowned to see the courtyard door standing ajar. He pushed it open and entered, breathing a sigh of weary pleasure at being home again. For a few moments he stood absorbing the atmosphere. He'd owned the villa for four years and in all that time he'd spent only eleven months under its roof.

From a precinct behind the stable came the clatter of practice swords. Vallon led his horse over to find Aiken sparring with Wulfstan, his Viking watchman. Vallon watched, putting off the moment when he'd have to break the news to Aiken.

As always, he was struck by how little the boy resembled his father.

Aiken was slight, of medium height, with straight mousy hair and grey eyes. Two of him would comfortably have fitted into his father's massive frame. Even allowing for the blood inheritance on his mother's side, it wasn't credible that Beorn had sired him, yet the Varangian had never broached the subject and in all respects treated the lad as if he were flesh of his own flesh.

Wulfstan lowered his sword. 'No! You keep closing up. You're not a snail; you don't have a shell. All you're doing is showing your opponent that you're scared.'

'I *am* scared. Who wouldn't be?'

'Listen. There's no reason to fear being killed in battle. If you receive the death blow, the shock and pain will stop you thinking about death. And once you're dead, you won't be thinking about anything.'

'False dialectic. According to Plato—'

'Listen, lad, I might not have your book-learning, but I know one thing. A man who's scared of death is fearful of life, and a man who's fearful of life might as well be dead.'

Vallon cleared his throat.

Wulfstan whirled and his bruiser's whiskered face lit up. He freed the stump of his left hand from the socket attached to the back of his shield. 'Lord Vallon! Welcome home, sir.'

'It's good to be back,' Vallon said, not taking his eyes off Aiken.

Wulfstan knew that look and what it meant. 'Lord save us. Don't tell me ...'

Vallon handed him the reins of his horse. 'She's weary. Feed, water and groom her.'

'Yes, sir,' Wulfstan said in a downcast tone.

Aiken hurried over, a boyish smile lighting his face, then he registered Vallon's expression and the smile withered.

Vallon didn't soften the blow. 'I'm sorry to bring you woeful news. Your father perished at Dyrrachium. He died gallantly, leading a charge against the Normans, singing his battle hymn. He didn't suffer.'

Aiken swallowed. Something in his throat clicked.

Vallon took his hands. 'Before the battle, your father and I

30

spoke at length about you. He told me how proud he was of your achievements. So am I. We'll arrange a mass to pray for his ascent into heaven. You'll need a period of mourning and reflection, but after that it's my wish to adopt you as my son. I know you already hold that place in my Lady Caitlin's heart.'

A tear winked on Aiken's lashes. 'What a waste.' He pulled free and stumbled away.

The villa door opened and Vallon's daughters ran out, skidding on the slush. 'Daddy! Daddy!'

He caught them one in each arm and swung them up. 'Zoe! Helena! How you've grown. What beauties you've turned into.'

Over their heads he saw Caitlin hurry onto the veranda, followed by Peter, his house servant. Her lips trembled. His own mouth twitched and his heart distended. At thirty-three, she was as beautiful as the day he'd first seen her – more so, thanks to the ministrations of maids and hairdressers and seamstresses.

She held up the hem of her skirts and hurried towards him. 'You should have sent notice of your homecoming. I would have arranged a celebration.'

'I'm afraid there's nothing to celebrate.'

Only then did Caitlin notice Aiken leaning against the wall in the corner of the courtyard, his shoulders racking with sobs. Her eyes widened in horror. 'Beorn's dead?'

Vallon nodded. 'Along with most of the Varangian Guard.' He put out a restraining hand. 'Give him some time on his own.'

She batted aside his hand, ran to Aiken and squeezed his head to her bosom.

'What's wrong, Father?'

Vallon looked into the uplifted faces of his daughters. He tried to smile. 'I brought you some presents.'

Vallon's homecomings seldom went as joyously as he'd anticipated. Always there was distance to be bridged, a friction that took time to smooth away. Beorn's death and its consequences made this the most strained reunion yet. Over supper, Caitlin tried to show interest in Vallon's activities during his seven-month absence. He filled the silences with questions about domestic matters, the girls, Caitlin's social arrangements. Aiken had retired to his room.

When the servants had cleared the dishes, Caitlin looked at the empty table. 'What will become of him?'

'As I told you, we'll adopt the boy.'

'I meant, what does life hold for him?'

'He'll join the military under my tutelage.'

Caitlin screwed up her napkin. 'No!'

'Aiken is my squire, my shield-bearer. It's his duty.'

'The boy isn't a soldier. He has no aptitude for violence. Ask Wulfstan. What he does have is a gift for languages and philosophy.'

'Caitlin, I have no choice in the matter. I swore an oath to his father.'

'A loud-mouthed roaring idiot who got himself killed just like all those foolhardy warriors who perished at Hastings.'

'Beorn died defending the empire.'

'From what you told me, it sounds like he squandered his life to settle an old blood grudge.'

Vallon gritted his teeth. 'My lady, I think you've settled so comfortably into the luxurious ways of Constantinople that you forget what sacrifices have been made to safeguard your lifestyle.'

Both of them stared at the table. Caitlin eventually broke the silence. 'Surely you don't mean to take Aiken on your next campaign.'

'I do.'

'But he's only sixteen, just a boy.'

'He's the same age I was when I first saw military service. Don't worry. I'll lead him on gently.'

Caitlin stared through him, then rose and made for the door.

'Where are you going?'

She whirled, eyes ablaze. 'Where do you think?'

Vallon remained at the table, half articulating justifications for

32

his decision, his discomfort worsened by the knowledge that Caitlin probably was right. Sweet anticipation of returning home had soured. Smacking the board with his fist, he picked up the flagon of wine and two beakers and went to Wulfstan's lodgings by the gate.

'I'm not keeping you from sleep, am I?'

'God, no, sir.'

'I thought we might drink to my safe return and Beorn's voyage into the afterlife.'

The Viking swept a bench clean with his good hand. He quaffed his cup in one and leaned forward, eyes shining. 'Tell me about the battle, sir.'

Vallon sipped his wine and his gaze wandered back to that chaotic day. 'It was a complete mess ...'

Half-drunk by the time he'd finished his account, he looked up to see Wulfstan's gaze rapt and distant. The Viking's nostrils flared. 'God, I'd give anything to fight another battle.'

'Isn't the loss of one hand enough?'

Wulfstan looked at his stump and laughed. 'I can still hold a sword.'

Vallon sobered. 'Do you think Aiken will make a soldier?'

Wulfstan's manner grew circumspect. 'Under your tutelage, I think any lad would.'

'The truth now.'

'His sword-play is quite pretty.'

'But he lacks fire and fibre.'

Wulfstan had drunk twice as much as Vallon. 'The trouble with Aiken is that he thinks too much. Imagination is the enemy of action.'

'That suggests I think too little.'

Wulfstan gave a tipsy chuckle. 'Not at all. I remember the day you fought Thorfinn Wolfbreath in the forests north of Rus. Christ, what a contest that was.' He glugged his wine. 'At dawn before the contest, you were sitting alone at the edge of the arena and Thorfinn, who'd been pouring birch ale down his throat all night and boasting how he'd break his fast on your liver, spotted you and said, "Couldn't you sleep?" And you replied cool as autumn dew, "Only a fool lies awake brooding over his problems. When morning comes, he's tired out and the problems are the same as before."' Wulfstan thumped the table. 'I knew then that you'd beat him.'

'I don't remember,' Vallon said. He lurched to his feet. 'I swore an oath against my better judgement. I don't want to force Aiken down a path not of his own choosing. I'll wait a few weeks and let him decide for himself.'

Vallon and Caitlin made up, as they always did. They shared a bed, made love with mutual pleasure, sat together during the long evenings, easy in each other's company, occasionally breaking off from their private pursuits to exchange smiles.

Late one raw afternoon soon after the turn of the year, Vallon was working on his campaign report close to the hearth when the courtyard bell rang. Caitlin looked up from her embroidery. 'Are we expecting visitors?'

'No,' Vallon said. He went to a window overlooking the court-yard and parted the shutters. Wulfstan had opened the gate and through the gap Vallon could see a group of men armed with swords.

The Viking marched towards the house, followed by an officer. 'Soldiers of the Imperial Guard,' Vallon told Caitlin.

Wulfstan opened the door, admitting a gust of cold air. 'A squad of vestiaritae. Their captain wants to see you. Won't say why.'

'Show him in.'

Caitlin came close. 'What can they want?'

Vallon shook his head and faced the door. Boots slapped on the floor with military precision and a young officer entered, wearing a fur mantle against the cold. He snapped a salute at Vallon and made a bow to Caitlin. 'John Chlorus, commander of a fifty in the vestiaritae, with orders for Count Vallon the Frank.'

Vallon sketched a salute. 'I know your face.'

'I know yours, sir. We fought at Dyrrachium. You're one of the few mercenaries I do recognise. Most of the others I know only from their backs.'

'And the reason for your visit?'

'My orders are to escort you to the Great Palace. You'd better wrap up warm. We're travelling by boat.'

That was a two-mile journey. It would be dark before they reached the palace. 'What's the purpose of the summons?'

'That I can't tell you, Count.'

'Can't or won't?'

Chlorus hesitated. 'My orders are to accompany you to the palace. That's all.'

Caitlin stepped between them. 'Night is falling. Do you really think I'd let you carry my husband into the dark without knowing who he's meeting?'

Chlorus had been trying to keep his eyes off her since entering.

'Well?' Caitlin demanded.

'My orders were issued by the Logothete tou Dromou.'

Vallon's eyes narrowed. The title translated as something like the 'Auditor of the Roads', but the Logothete's responsibilities went much further than maintaining the empire's highways. He supervised the Byzantine government's postal service and diplomatic corps, monitored the activities of foreigners in Constantinople and ran an empire-wide network of spies and informers. He was in effect the emperor's foreign minister, a personal adviser who wielded great and covert influence.

'In that case I won't keep the minister a moment longer than necessary. You'll have to excuse me while I make myself presentable. My house guard will bring wine to warm you.' Vallon cast a loaded look at the Viking hovering behind the officer, his hand on his sword, his face glowering with mistrust. 'Wulfstan, the soldiers must be perishing. Invite them inside.'

Caitlin hurried after Vallon as he made for their sleeping chamber. She seized his elbow. 'What's going on?'

'I have no idea,' said Vallon, struggling out of his gown.

35

Caitlin watched him dress. 'It must have something to do with you saving the emperor's life.'

'Don't speak of it. According to the official accounts, Alexius fought his way to freedom after slaying twenty Normans and riding his horse up a hundred-foot precipice.'

With mounting impatience, Caitlin watched Vallon pull on a tunic. 'For heaven's sake, you can't wear that. Let me.'

He let her complete his costume and then he buckled on his sword. She stood back and appraised him. 'Well, you won't disgrace us. I'm sure the emperor intends to reward you.'

Vallon took her in his arms and kissed her. Their lips lingered. She stroked his neck. 'Return soon, dear husband. I want to show how much I love you.'

'As soon as I can,' he murmured. 'I'll hold you to your promise.'

He broke the clinch, turned and went to face his destiny with a neutral smile. 'Shall we go?'

A caique rowed by eight men carried them down the Bosporus, their passage speeded by a cutting northerly. Vallon's escort spoke little and only among themselves. Dreary dusk darkened to starless night. Shielded by a windbreak, Vallon watched the torches on the great sea walls sliding past to starboard. He wondered how he would return home, and then it occurred to him that this might be a one-way journey. Officers who'd distinguished themselves in battle weren't wrenched from the fireside on a cold winter night.

They passed the Pharos, its flame projected by mirrors far out to sea, and docked at the port of Bucoleon, the emperor's private harbour south of the Great Palace complex. Vallon's heart beat faster. The escort formed up around him and marched through a postern guarded by bronze lions. They crossed a series of open spaces lit by lanterns whose fitful flames illuminated gardens and fish ponds, pavilions and pleasure grounds. Vallon had never been inside the complex before and had no idea where the escort was taking him. They angled left towards a massy building with random lights showing at some of the windows.

'Which palace is this?'

'Daphne,' said Chlorus. He ran up a monumental flight of steps leading to the entrance. 'I'm afraid I'll have to ask you to hand over your sword and submit to a search.'

Vallon stood unmoving while the men patted him for secret weapons. Chlorus pounded on the doors and they opened into a blaze of candelabra. A chamberlain carrying a silver staff of office received them and led the way through aisles and halls supported by onyx and porphyry columns, through lofty chambers decorated with polychrome mosaics and tapestries, across pavements inset with gold peacocks and eagles, past fountains spouting water from the mouths of bronze dolphins. At each entrance guardsmen and eunuchs stood rooted at attention.

They entered a plain room with a door at the far end guarded by two soldiers. One of them threw the door open and Vallon found himself in a passage or tunnel lit by torches in sconces. His footsteps echoed off bare walls wringing with condensation. The passage must have been fifty yards long and the torches fluttered in an icy draught issuing from the far end.

The chamberlain halted at an entrance open to the night. 'Wait here.'

He went out and gave a deep bow, murmured something inaudible and received an even fainter response. He turned and beckoned Chlorus forward. The officer put every fibre of his being into his salute. 'Allagion Chlorus reporting with Count Vallon.'

'Admit the count,' a voice said, 'then you and your men withdraw.'

Vallon stepped onto a covered balcony overlooking a lake of darkness surrounded by the faint breathing glow of the city. It took a moment to realise that the U-shaped arena beneath him was the Hippodrome, and that he was looking down on it from the imperial box. His flesh seemed to congeal about his bones.

Three figures swathed in fur overgarments occupied the

37

balcony, seated around two braziers that cast only enough light to suggest form but not features. Vallon had the impression that one of them was veiled and possibly a woman.

One of the muffled shapes rose. 'An interesting perspective,' he said. 'Looking out over the city while it sleeps.'

Vallon struggled for words. 'Indeed.'

'I am Theoctistus Scylitzes, Logothete tou Dromou. I apologise for dragging you away from your hearth on such a bitter night.'

Vallon decided that a deep bow was sufficient response. No seat had been set out for him and the minister obviously had no intention of introducing the other figures. Vallon indicated the arena. 'It's strange to see it empty. The last time I was in the Hippodrome it must have held sixty thousand spectators.'

A breeze fanned the coals, throwing the Logothete's bearded face into relief. He held up what looked like a bound document. 'I've been telling the emperor about the travels that led you from the barbarian northlands to Constantinople.'

Vallon's nape crawled at that 'I've been telling'. His gaze darted to the other two figures. Was that the emperor? Surely not.

'Yes,' said the Logothete, 'I spent two days studying the report you wrote for my predecessor.'

Vallon found his voice. 'I didn't pen it myself. It was written nine years ago, before I'd mastered Greek. The account of our travels was set down by a companion, Hero of Syracuse.'

'Quite so. He seems to have a gift for literary exposition.'

'He has many gifts.'

'And a fertile imagination.'

'My Lord?'

The Logothete tapped the book. 'Most interesting, absolutely fascinating.' He paused. 'If true.'

'Tell me which part of the account rings false and I'll try to set your doubts to rest.'

Theoctistus laughed and smacked the document across his knee. 'The whole damn thing. Are you really telling me that you journeyed from France to England, then sailed north to Ultima

38

Thule before returning south through the land of Rus and crossing the Black Sea to Rum?'

'Yes, Lord.'

'And all to deliver a ransom of falcons demanded by that rogue Suleyman.'

'In essence, yes, Lord.'

The Logothete appraised him. 'You're a remarkable fellow, Vallon.'

'Remarkably lucky. If I succeeded, it was because I was well served by a brave and ingenious company.'

One of the other figures leaned towards the Logothete and whispered. The minister nodded.

'Vallon, I'll come to the point. I want you to undertake another journey on behalf of the empire.'

Vallon's guts constricted. 'May I ask where you propose to send me?'

The Logothete took a moment to answer. 'In your account you describe a former Byzantine diplomat, a noted traveller known as Cosmas Monopthalmos.'

Vallon saw the Greek's dark eye as if it were yesterday. 'Indeed I do, Lord. Although I only met him in his dying hours, he left a lasting impression.'

'Then you'll remember that Cosmas travelled as far east as Samarkand.'

'It's only a name to me.'

'Samarkand lies beyond the Oxus, in the wilderness that spawned the Seljuk Turks and all the other swarms of horse nomads who plague our eastern frontiers.'

'You want me to lead a mission to Samarkand?'

'You'll pass through it. I calculate that it marks the halfway point on your journey.'

Despite the cold, sweat filmed Vallon's forehead. 'I'm sorry, Lord. My knowledge of that part of the world is flimsy.'

The glow from the braziers cast the Logothete's face in sinister relief. 'Have you heard of an empire called China? It goes by other names, including Cathay, though some reports suggest that Cathay and China are separate empires. Its own citizens, subjects of the Song emperor, call it the Middle Kingdom or Celestial Empire, titles stemming from their belief that it occupies an exalted position between heaven and earth.'

'I've heard rumours of a rich kingdom at the eastern end of the world. I have no idea how to reach it.'

The Logothete pointed down the tunnel leading from the balcony. 'Quite simple. Follow the rising sun and you should reach it in about a year.'

About a year! Vallon was so shocked that he missed some of the Logothete's smooth exposition. He shook himself. 'Even Alexander the Great never travelled so far.'

'You'll be following the Silk Road, a well-trodden trade route, travelling in stages, stopping and resting at entrepôts and caravanserais.'

Vallon stiffened. A year felt like being saddled by a dead weight, but that represented only the period of outward travel. A year to reach China, a year returning, and God knows how long spent between the two termini. He felt old before he'd taken a single step.

'Might I ask the purpose of the expedition?'

The Logothete spread his hands. 'Constantinople is the mirror of Western civilisation. By all accounts, China enjoys the same glittering pre-eminence in the East.' He brought his hands together. 'It's only natural that the two poles of civilisation should establish diplomatic relations. Yours won't be the first Byzantine mission to China. I've examined the records and discovered that the empire has sent seven embassies to China in as many centuries.'

'Resulting in benefits to Byzantium. I trust.'

The Logothete's breath condensed in the chill air. 'They have created mutual recognition and respect.'

Achieved absolutely nothing, Vallon interpreted.

'Now is the time to build on this foundation,' the Logothete said. 'An alliance with China will yield practical rewards.' He pulled his cape tight over his shoulders. 'Vallon, you don't need me to tell you what a plight we're in. Seljuks within a day's ride of the Bosporus, Normans hammering at our Balkan possessions, Arabs threatening our sea lanes. Byzantium is under siege from all sides. We need allies; we need friends.'

'I agree, but I fail to see how a foreign power a year's journey to the east can offer any succour.'

'China is also threatened by the steppe barbarians. Form an alliance with them and we can squeeze our common enemy, allowing us to concentrate on foes closer to home. Other benefits will flow from establishing a conduit to the East. With our trade routes closed or under competition from Venice and Genoa, opening up a road to China will provide a much-needed lifeline.'

Vallon knew that he was on the rim of a whirlpool and would be sucked down if he didn't thrash clear. 'Lord, I'm not the man to accomplish these goals. Next year I turn forty. My health is not as robust as it was when I made the journey to the north. I have—'

The Logothete slapped the document. 'You're cunning and resourceful, steadfast and brave. Don't think your actions at Dyrrachium have gone unnoticed. You've had years of experience campaigning against the nomads. You employ Turkmen soldiers in your own squadron.'

Vallon opened his mouth and then shut it. A decision had been made at the highest level, and nothing he could say would change it.

The minister resumed his seat. 'There are other prizes to be sought in China.'

Vallon's response sounded dull in his ears. 'Such as?'

The Logothete looked over the empty arena. 'You know that silk is Constantinople's most valuable export.'

'Yes, Lord.'

'Do you know where we obtained the secret of its manufacture?'

'A place called Seres, somewhere in the East, beyond the River Oxus.'

41

The Logothete turned in some surprise. 'You're better informed than I imagined.'

'Hero of Syracuse told me, passing on information he obtained from Cosmas. Both men thirsted for knowledge about far-off places.'

'I'd like to meet this Hero of Syracuse.'

Vallon held his tongue, and after a few moments of interrogative silence, the Logothete continued. 'Seres and China are one and the same. Five hundred years ago, an official who held a post corresponding to mine sent a pair of Nestorian monks into a silk-making town east of Samarkand. They smuggled silk worms back in hollowed-out staffs.' The Logothete reached under his furs and stroked his gown. 'Silk has been the mainstay of our wealth ever since, but now the Arabs and others have learned how to produce it and broken our monopoly. It's time to discover fresh secrets in China – new metals, ingenious war engines.' The Logothete eyed Vallon. 'No doubt you've seen Greek Fire used in battle.'

'Yes. I've never employed it myself. I don't know its formula.'

'I'm glad to hear it. Greek Fire is the secret weapon that forms the bulwark between Byzantium and its enemies.'

'Long may it preserve us,' Vallon said, in the tone of someone reciting a response in a litany.

The Logothete stepped close and spoke in a scented whisper. 'Suppose I told you that China possesses a weapon more powerful than Greek Fire.'

Vallon resisted the instinct to step back. 'That would be a prize worth having.'

The Logothete withdrew. 'Three years ago slavers in Turkestan captured a Chinese merchant who eventually ended up in Constantinople. The man had been a soldier and engineer. Under questioning, he told his interrogators that Chinese alchemists had formulated a compound called Fire Drug, a substance that ignites with a spark and explodes when packed into a container. Now then, Vallon. You've seen a sealed bottle of oil burst in a fire. *Poof!*

42

Alarming and possibly injurious to those standing close by.' The Logothete's face ducked back into the firelight. 'In the same circumstances, a bottle of Fire Drug would blow everybody within twenty yards to shreds.'

Vallon massaged his throat. The Logothete swung away and tramped along the balcony, one hand slapping the rail.

'Packed into cylinders, Fire Drug propels arrows twice as far as any bow can shoot. Encased in iron spheres, it explodes with a force that can shatter a ship into splinters.'

'An army equipped with such a weapon wouldn't need knights, only engineers.'

'Precisely,' the Logothete said. 'But the strange thing is that the Chinese don't exploit this terrible incendiary for military purposes. Apparently, they use it to frighten away evil spirits.' The Logothete paused. 'We want you to obtain the formula for this devastating compound.'

'Lord, Byzantium has possessed Greek Fire for centuries, and during all that time we've kept the secret of its manufacture to ourselves. The engineers of Cathay will guard their formula just as closely.'

'I'm sure you'll find a way of discovering the secret.'

'Steal it, you mean. If the theft is discovered, it would wipe out any diplomatic gains at a stroke.'

'That won't do at all. You must use guile and ingenuity.'

Vallon recognised finality in the Logothete's tone. He drew a shuddering breath. 'When does the expedition set out?'

'Next spring, as early as wind and weather permit.'

'Lord, if the embassy is so important, I can't understand why you would choose a foreign count to lead it.'

'Not lead. Escort. Professional diplomats will head the mission. You'll meet them in due course. But you're right. Your rank must befit the importance of your commission.' The Logothete bowed. 'Congratulations, *Strategos*.'

General. Never had promotion been so unwished for. It was all Vallon could do to bow and acknowledge the honour.

'I should stress that the expedition is secret,' the minister said. 'Your promotion will be announced as recognition for your valour at Dyrrachium.'

'I understand,' said Vallon.

The Logothete resumed his seat. The braziers hummed in a swirl of air. A harsh female voice spoke. 'We've been told that your wife is a beauty.'

Vallon's night vision had sharpened. A veil covered the speaker's face, but he was sure that the woman was the Empress-Mother, Anna Dalassena, the most duplicitous schemer in Constantinople and the woman who'd plotted her son's seizure of the throne. Which meant that the third figure hunched over in his furs *must* be Alexius.

'My wife is from Iceland,' Vallon said. 'The island breeds a fair race.'

'You dwell in Galata, I understand. I've never been there. Of course, when you return, you must find a home closer to the palace.' Her hand described a circle. 'And perhaps a small estate on the Marmara coast.'

Vallon managed a bow before turning to the Logothete. 'How many men will I command?'

'One hundred cavalry, chosen from your own squadron, each man selected for his courage, loyalty and versatility in arms. Our ambassador will be accompanied by his personal guards and staff. With grooms, muleteers, surgeons, cooks – about two hundred men in all.'

'Two hundred is too few to fight a battle, too many to keep supplied on a year's land march.'

'I don't anticipate any serious fighting. I've already taken steps to arrange a safe conduct through the Seljuk territories in Armenia and Persia. Once you've passed through those lands, you won't face anybody more fearsome than nomad bandits.'

How do you know? Vallon wanted to shout. *That's how you dismissed the Seljuk Turks who defeated the cream of the Byzantine military and captured the emperor only ten years ago.*

44

He breathed deep. 'My men are mercenaries. I can't compel them to follow me to China.'

'You won't tell them until you've taken ship. Until then, you must convince them that they're bound for another spell on the Bulgarian border. Only when you're three days' sail from Constantinople will you reveal your orders. To soften any distress this might cause, you're authorised to tell your men that they'll be drawing double wages for the duration of the expedition.'

None of them would see a penny, Vallon thought. All of them would perish in a nameless desert with not even a coin to close their eyes against the sun.

'I'm sorry, Lord. I won't lie to my men. They're a rag-tag bunch drawn from many lands and my greatest pride is that they trust me. I won't betray that trust. I will take only volunteers who know what hazards they face.'

Outside the walls of the Hippodrome, dogs barked and a bell tolled from a distant church. Gases hissed in the braziers. The third figure – it had to be Alexius – reached out and took the Logothete's sleeve. The minister leaned and then straightened.

'Very well. You'll tell your squadron at the last moment, without informing them of their precise destination. That's a simple security precaution. You'll be carrying a great deal of treasure.'

Vallon drew himself up. 'I'm honoured that you regard me as equal to the task. I humbly submit that you overestimate my talents and I beg to be relieved of it.'

'Your request is denied, General. You have three months to prepare. During that time, you will meet with the diplomats and learn everything you can about China.'

'And if I refuse?'

'That would be treason, and the punishment for treason is to be blinded and whipped through the city sitting backwards on an ass.' The Logothete gave a signal and Chlorus emerged from the tunnel. 'His Imperial Majesty has promoted Vallon the Frank to a general's command, and an officer of such high rank shouldn't be

45

exposed to another choppy ride on the Bosporus. You'll find a carriage waiting at the Chalke Gate.'

Vallon's escort set him down outside his villa and rode back to the ferry. He hesitated before pulling the bell, aware that this might be one of the last times he entered his home. To the south the metropolis slept under a glowing bubble. Across the Bosporus only a few isolated lights marked the Asian shore. He wrenched the bell-pull and Wulfstan shepherded him inside, goggling with questions he didn't dare ask. Caitlin jumped up from the fireside.

'Was I right? Has the emperor rewarded your valour?'

Vallon sat down and massaged his eyes. 'In a way. I've been promoted to general.'

'Then why do you look like a man under sentence of death?'

'I've been ordered to lead an expedition to China.'

'Where's that?'

Vallon gave a curdled smile, aware that he would hear the same question many times in the months ahead. 'Already I face a problem. I have strict orders to tell no one about the mission.'

'Nonsense, Vallon. I'm not one of those Greek gossips. We've never let secrets divide us.'

'I'm merely warning you that you mustn't repeat anything I tell you.'

'Of course I won't.'

Vallon blew out his cheeks. 'China is an empire on the other side of the world, a year's journey away, a year back. I'll be old before I return. *If* I return.'

Caitlin took both his hands. 'You're frozen.' She turned and called. A maid appeared. 'Hot wine for the master.' Caitlin led him to a couch, sat him down and knelt before him, kneading his hands. 'I couldn't bear such a long separation.'

Vallon shrugged. 'The only way to avoid the mission would be to flee Byzantium.'

'Where would we go?'

Another shrug. 'I could take up the Seljuk Sultan's offer to join his army.' Vallon laughed. 'I encountered the Normans' second-in-command on the field of battle. He made a similar offer. I could go anywhere they'd employ an ageing mercenary.'

Caitlin looked around the comfortable apartment. 'It would mean giving up everything and starting afresh in a foreign land. The children would have to learn new languages.'

Vallon sat straight. 'No. I won't allow my family to be uprooted. I'll carry out my orders, even if I might never see my loved ones again. I'm sorry that you will have to make a similar sacrifice.'

The maid returned with the wine. Vallon turned the cup in both hands. Caitlin rose and sat beside him. 'If anyone can make the journey and return home safe, it's you.'

Vallon lifted the cup to his lips and knocked it back in one, aware that Caitlin had made only a token stand against what was effectively a death sentence delivered against her husband.

'How long until you leave?' she asked.

'Three months.'

'Then there's hope. The emperor might change his mind before then. Every week brings news of fresh alarms on the frontier. They won't send you on such a far-flung expedition if there's fighting to be done closer to home.'

Vallon summoned a smile. He squeezed Caitlin's hand. 'You're right.'

Her expression became pensive. 'If you do go, will you ask Hero to join you?'

Vallon swung round. 'Of course not. It didn't even occur to me. As for summoning him ... He's a distinguished physician in Italy. He wouldn't throw up his career to tag along on some reckless adventure. Heaven forbid.'

Caitlin leaned towards the fire. 'And Aiken?'

Vallon studied her face in profile, the firelight gilding her skin. He stroked a hand down her cheek. 'No. The challenge is too severe. The lad will stay here and continue his studies.'

Caitlin closed her eyes in relief and kissed Vallon on the lips.

'Thank you, husband.' She rose in one graceful movement and extended her hand. 'I think it's time we retired.'

Vallon pressed her hand to his lips. 'I fear my thoughts are too wrenched about to give you the consideration you deserve.'

Caitlin brushed her hand over Vallon's head and withdrew.

He watched her glide out of the room, his thoughts dark and rancid. Much later his servant found him staring into the fire, studying the pulsing embers as if they were a prefiguration of his destiny, open to any interpretation.

IV

Hero stood in the bow, a warm breeze from the south blowing his hair about his face. The first swallows of spring skimmed the surface around the ship, and high in the sky storks drifted in lazy gyrations on the way back to their nesting grounds. Ahead, the Sea of Marmara funnelled into the Bosporus, the mile-wide strait flecked with sails, the city of Constantinople beginning to shape itself out of the haze on the western shore. With swelling heart, Hero watched the metropolis draw nearer, its sea walls taking on massive form, mansions and palaces and tenements spilling over the promontory in a great upwelling of civilisation.

He glanced around smiling, wanting to share his pleasure, and his gaze fell on a youth watching the approaching city with a mixture of awe and apprehension. The lad was Frankish, only about sixteen, but tall and well-set with a face that reminded Hero of the young Emperor Augustus – the same jutting, high-bridged nose, curly hair, rather prominent ears and a mouth both truculent and sensitive. He'd caught Hero's attention soon after boarding the ship at Naples. Partly it was because he was alone and a Frank, a youth trying to project an image stern beyond his years. He was obviously poor, dressed in a patched tunic and crudely repaired shoes. For food all he had was a satchel of what looked like cold porridge that he cut with a knife and forced down with stolid revulsion. Hero had tried to engage him in conversation before and been rebuffed. The youth shunned all company, possibly because he spoke no Greek. Now, seeing the lad's scarcely disguised nervousness, Hero decided to make another attempt.

'A wonderful sight, but intimidating on first acquaintance. Imagine. Half a million souls dwell behind those walls.'

The young Frank glanced at him, surprised to be addressed in French, then looked away.

'This is my second visit,' said Hero, 'but the sight still quickens my pulse like no other. I'll point out the landmarks if you want. The land walls were built by Theodosius more than six hundred years ago. They're nearly four miles long and no army has ever breached them. Those splendid columns and façades above the sea walls are part of the Great Palace. Beyond is the dome of St Sophia. In a short while you'll be able to see the whole structure, the most beautiful cathedral in Christendom.'

'I'm not here to admire the views.'

'I didn't imagine you were. I assume you're travelling to Constantinople to join the military.'

'Assume what you like.'

St Sophia in all its glory glided into full view. 'My name is Hero of Syracuse. Some people think it's a girl's name.' He pointed back down the Sea of Marmara. 'Like the maiden whose lover Leander swam the Hellespont each night to be with his mistress. In fact my father named me after the inventor and mathematician, Hero of Alexandria.'

The youth ignored Hero's out-held hand. 'I've never heard the name and I'm not interested.'

Hero made one last effort. 'We still have some time before we reach harbour. This breeze sharpens my appetite. Will you share breakfast with me? Just some bread, figs and cheese. A flask of decent wine.'

The youth rounded on him. 'Look, I know your type. I've had to deal with them since I left Aquitaine.'

'Aquitaine? That's interesting. As it happens—'

'Don't tell me. You just happen to have a friend from Aquitaine, so why don't we all get together for a quiet supper. You're not the first who's tried that on.'

Hero stepped back. 'I can see you're wary of strangers. Do you know anyone in Constantinople? I have a friend in the city who could give you advice on joining the military. In fact I'm here to visit him.'

'You don't take no for an answer, do you? I don't want to share your food. I don't want to meet your friend.'

Hero coloured. 'You're too quick to twist motives. That's not a trait that will take you far in Constantinople. The city has a reputation for eating strangers.' The ship was approaching the Golden Horn. 'I won't impose on you any further.' He laid a few coins down. 'No, don't throw them back. I know you need them. I bid you goodbye and good fortune.'

Discomfited by the encounter, Hero gathered up his luggage and prepared to disembark. On landing, a customs official noted his name, place of origin and purpose of visit before waving him through onto the teeming quayside. A dozen porters surrounded him, clamouring to know where he wanted to go and offering competing fares even before he'd answered. He let the squall blow out before announcing his destination. 'I'm travelling to the home of Count Vallon, a Frankish officer in the imperial army.'

One of the porters thrust aside his competitors. 'I know Vallon. He's a general now.' The man pointed across the Golden Horn at a hilly suburb. 'He lives in Galata, right at the top.'

The porter took Hero's luggage and hurried towards a ferry-boat. At the water's edge, Hero looked back to see that the passengers had dispersed, leaving the Frankish youth alone on the quay. Their eyes met, then the porter took Hero's arm and assisted him into the boat. When the two oarsmen were into their stroke, Hero turned a last time to see the young Frank walking towards the city gate, pestered by touts. A laden cart shut him from view, and when it had passed, the Frank was gone, swallowed by the city.

Watching the shore approach, Hero experienced a tingle of pleasurable anticipation. Nine years had passed since he'd last seen Vallon, and though they had exchanged a few letters, he didn't know what changes time had wrought in his old companion. He was delighted to hear that Vallon was now a general – a promotion long overdue in Hero's opinion. Vallon's correspondence shed little light on his military career. His letters, written in laboured Greek, were mainly about his family and the observations he'd made on his travels.

Despite his pleasure at the prospect of meeting his friend again, Hero couldn't suppress a twinge of resentment. The request – more like a summons – to journey to Constantinople had meant leaving his prosperous medical practice and a comfortable tenure at the University of Salerno. What rankled most was the formality of the letter – not a personal request from Vallon himself, and therefore to be met without hesitation, but a stiff demand from the Logothete tou Dromou stating that Vallon was engaged on important imperial business and had insisted on Hero joining him without delay.

The ferry reached the opposite shore. The porter gestured at the hill. 'You'll be wanting a mule.'

'I've been at sea for two weeks. I'd prefer to walk.' Hero saw the porter's disappointment. 'Of course you must hire a mule to carry my bags.'

They entered Galata through a gate and climbed past handsome walled villas with feathery black cypresses and gnarled mulberry trees growing in courtyard gardens.

'Mind if I ask where you're from?' the porter said. 'You speak Greek like a proper gentleman, but you aren't from Constantinople. I can tell.'

'I grew up in Syracuse and now I live in Salerno.'

'Travelled a fair bit, I'd say. I heard you talking Arabic to one of the porters.'

Hero smiled. 'A fair bit.'

'Like where, sir? I enjoy hearing about different places. I've met people from all over – Spain, Egypt, Rus. Me, I've never been no further than the Black Sea.'

Hero bowed in passing to a respectable couple. 'Well, I've been to the land of the Franks and I've visited England.'

'Lord, that must have been a trial.'

Memory loosened Hero's tongue. 'From there I sailed to Iceland and then journeyed south to Anatolia and the court of Emir Suleyman, now the Sultan of Rum. That was nine years ago.'

The porter's eyes popped. 'You met that devil Suleyman? Well I never. Forgive me for asking, sir, but if it was that long ago, you must have been awful young.'

'I was eighteen.'

The porter had to wrench his gaze away. 'I'd love to hear more, sir, but here we are at General Vallon's residence.'

Hero faced the door and took a deep breath. The porter jangled the bell. Bolts scraped free. The gate opened and a thickset man with moustaches like wings stepped out. Both of them gaped, then Hero stumbled back.

'You!'

Wulfstan swept him up in an embrace. 'Hero, my old friend.'

Hero wrenched loose. 'You're no friend. What are you doing here? How did . . . ?' He broke off in confusion. The last time he'd seen Wulfstan had been on the River Dnieper, when the Viking and his companions had deserted Vallon's company to pursue a Russian slave ship. Shock made Hero pant. 'You left us to die. You promised to wait for us at the estuary.'

Wulfstan scratched his head and grimaced. 'I know it must have looked that way. We came back for you, found your campsite, the fire still warm. We missed you by hours.'

'But how did you find your way into Vallon's service?'

'Long story.' Wulfstan took Hero's luggage from the open-mouthed porter. Only then did the Sicilian register that the Viking had lost his left hand and his arm ended in a stump. This he threw across Hero's back before shepherding him into the courtyard. Hero took in his surroundings with dazed approval. The white-washed villa formed a square C, with a vine-clad loggia running the length of the main dwelling. In the garden, blossoms covered fruit trees in a haze of pink and white.

Wulfstan winked at Hero. 'I can't wait to see the general's face when he claps eyes on you.' The Viking cupped his hands around his mouth. 'General Vallon,' he called. 'Look who's here.'

Vallon emerged from the villa, followed by a young man. Vallon stopped stock still and his jaw dropped. 'Good lord,' he said. Then he ran down the steps. 'Hero, my dear Hero. What a delightful surprise.'

He seized Hero's hands and they stood smiling at each other, taking stock. Age had not been unkind to Vallon. The same lean and upright frame, the nose more aquiline and the face more lined, the auburn hair beginning to grey at the temples.

Vallon steered the youth forward. 'You've heard me speak of Hero many times. Well, here he is, and looking most distinguished. Hero, may I present Aiken, my English son by adoption. His father was a companion in arms.'

Hero shook Aiken's hand. The youth had a pleasant, intelligent countenance and a quiet and courteous manner. 'It's a great honour to meet you, sir.'

Vallon laughed. 'I still can't believe it. Caitlin will be devastated to have missed you. She and the girls are visiting friends in the country. They're due back tomorrow.' He draped an arm over Hero's shoulder. 'But what brings you to Constantinople? Why didn't you write to let us know you were coming?'

'A letter wouldn't have reached you in time. I sailed as soon as I received the summons.'

Vallon stopped. 'Summons? I sent no summons.'

'From the Logothete tou Dromou, asking me to join you in Constantinople with all haste.'

Vallon's hand dropped from Hero's shoulder. His gaze drifted away. He plucked at his mouth. 'Oh, God.'

'What's wrong?'

Vallon took a breath and braced himself. 'We'll talk at supper. You must be tired from your journey.' He turned to Wulfstan. 'Show Hero to his room.' Two servants – a middle-aged man and a young girl – had appeared on the veranda. 'Peter, Anna, attend to our guest's comfort. He's travelled all the way from Italy.'

Wulfstan talked non-stop as he led the way to an airy room overlooking the Bosporus. Peter began unpacking Hero's bags. 'Wulfstan, my arrival seems to have shocked Vallon.'

'Shocked us both.'

'In Vallon's case, not pleasantly.'

'What are you talking about? He's thrilled to see you.'

'Is anything troubling him?'

'Far from it. At last he's got the promotion he deserves. Know why? He saved the emperor's life at Dyrrachium.' Wulfstan's forehead wrinkled. 'What's the matter?'

Hero forced a smile. 'Nothing. Nothing at all. Meeting old friends after a long absence is always an emotional shock.'

'It's no strain for me. I never had nothing but respect for you – the way you used your healing arts on anybody who needed them, even if they were your enemy. If you need anything, just call me. Anything.'

'Thank you. Right now all I want is rest.'

Wulfstan grinned. 'What stories we have to tell.' He raised his hand and stole out of the room like a benign troll. The maid was still making up the bed, plumping the pillows. Peter was arranging Hero's luggage. A bowl of fruit had appeared on a table by the window and a ewer of water and clean cloths stood on a washstand. Peter bowed. 'A bath will be ready at your convenience. Is there anything else you require?'

'No. I'm much obliged.'

Alone at last, Hero went to the window and gazed down on the Bosporus, the sea-lane criss-crossed with barges and caiques and dromons and fishing boats. Over there on the Asian shore, no more than two weeks' ride to the south-east, Wayland and Syth were going about their lives. What had become of them? Did they still retain their English language and customs, or had they adopted Turkish manners? Fatigue smothered Hero's speculations. He plopped onto the bed, sat for some time in a slack-jawed trance, then undressed, slipped under the bedclothes and fell asleep the moment his head touched the pillow.

He woke muzzy-headed in the dark. A figure glided in and lit a lamp. Hero sat up and rubbed his eyes. 'What time is it?'

'The church bells have just rung vespers,' Peter said. 'The master says you mustn't stir yourself until you're fully rested. He was most insistent on that point. If you're hungry, I can bring supper to your room.'

'Tell General Vallon that I'd like to join him. Perhaps after a bath.'

'I've taken the liberty of preparing one.'

A mosaic of fanciful sea creatures decorated the bath-house. After a hot soak, Hero took a cold plunge and rose clear-headed to find Peter waiting with freshly laundered clothes. The servant led him into a salon painted with frescoes of pastoral scenes inspired by Ovid's stories. Vallon rose from the table. 'Are you hungry?'

'Ravenous.'

Over a simple meal of grilled red mullet and spring salad, Vallon explained how he had come to adopt Aiken. 'I'd be grateful if you spent some time with the boy. I think he'll find your company more congenial than mine. His teachers say that he has quite a gift for logic and rhetoric.'

Hero sensed stresses in the relationship. 'I'd be delighted.' He glanced round and lowered his voice. 'What's that treacherous ruffian Wulfstan doing here?'

Vallon smiled. 'I found him begging in the street. After reaching Constantinople, he and the rest of the Northmen joined the Byzantine navy and saw service against the Arabs in the Mediterranean. That's where he lost his hand.'

'Yes, but after abandoning us the way he did ...'

'If I'd been in his shoes, I might have done the same. And in the end his conscience did override his greed and made him return to the estuary. By then we'd already committed ourselves to the waves.'

Hero shuddered. 'The most hideous experience of my life. It was a miracle we were saved.'

Peter cleared away the dishes and left. Vallon swirled wine around his beaker. 'I can't apologise enough for you being dragged all this way on a wasted journey.'

'I don't count seeing you again as a waste.'

'You believe me when I say that I had nothing to do with the summons?'

'Of course. But what was the Logothete's purpose?'

'Since it doesn't concern you, it's better if you don't know.'

'That won't do. We didn't keep secrets from each other on our quest to carry the ransom hawks to Anatolia.'

Vallon laughed. 'Yes, we did.'

'Then this time let's start by being completely open.'

Vallon pursed his lips and stared into his glass. 'After I came to the emperor's attention at Dyrrachium, the Logothete examined the reasons that brought me to Constantinople. He read your account of our travels and on the strength of that document and my military record, he decided I was the right man to escort another expedition.'

'Where to?'

Vallon's jaw worked. 'Well, since the Logothete has deluded himself that you'll join me, he can hardly protest if I tell you our goal.' He glanced up, the lamplight hollowing out his features. 'China, the realm of the Song emperor.'

Hero let his breath go in a low whistle.

Vallon smiled after a fashion. 'My first reaction, too – or it would have been if I'd been at liberty to express myself. The Logothete conducted the interview in the presence of the Emperor Alexius and the Empress-Mother. On a cold winter's night in the imperial box at the Hippodrome.'

Hero straightened in his seat. 'Why does the emperor want to send you to China?'

'To establish relations with the Song court. Personally, I can't see what Byzantium will gain by exchanging niceties with a heathen potentate dwelling in a land a year's journey away.'

'An alliance must produce some benefits. News of it would certainly burnish the emperor's prestige.'

Vallon nodded. 'There's more. On his travels into the East, did Master Cosmas come across a compound called Fire Drug? It's an incendiary even more violent than Greek Fire. The Logothete believes it has important military applications and wants me to obtain the formula.'

Hero shook his head. 'Cosmas never mentioned such a compound.'

'It probably doesn't exist except in myth. Well, no matter.' Vallon raised his hand to forestall protest. 'You'll stay here for as long as you wish and then return to Italy at the Logothete's expense. I've already despatched a letter to the minister expressing my outrage at his deception.'

Hero traced a pattern on the tabletop. 'I assume that he thought I would be an asset on the enterprise. Obviously you don't share his opinion.'

'The journey there and back will take at least three years. I regard it as a death sentence.'

'I take it that you're not in a position to refuse the commission.'

'You're right. I face my fate knowing that if I perish, my family won't suffer.'

Hero mused for a while. 'Could I have another glass of that excellent wine?'

'Forgive me,' said Vallon, raising the flagon. 'The whole business has unsettled me. What grieves me most is the dissension it's caused between me and Caitlin. Imagine how she feels, knowing that I'll be gone for years, probably never to return.'

'When do you leave?'

'At the beginning of the sailing season. We sail to Trebizond on the Black Sea, cross Armenia and then strike through Seljuk Persia armed with a safe conduct from the Sultan.' Vallon uttered a sardonic laugh.

Hero raised the glass to his lips but didn't drink. 'Cosmas told me that the Chinese are a most ingenious race, with many inventions and wonders to their credit. It would be a singular privilege to study their arts and engineering.'

Vallon swallowed his wine and poured another cup, the neck of the flagon chattering on the rim.

'No, I won't allow you to come. Consider how I'd feel if you died on the journey.'

'Consider how *I'd* feel if I let you go without me.'

'I'm duty-bound. You aren't. I have family to consider. You don't.'

Hero's mouth tightened. 'Each of us has different motives. In my case, I'd accompany you out of choice, to satisfy my curiosity, to further my store of knowledge. An expedition to China would be the adventure of a lifetime.'

'Do you despise your profession so much that you'd throw it away for a land march into the unknown?'

'I'm still only twenty-seven. I have half a lifetime in which to practise medicine.'

Vallon knocked over his glass and swore. 'Hero, you're not coming. Let's talk of other matters. I insist.'

Hero drank no more than a couple of sips. 'Do you think Wayland has received a similar summons?'

Vallon glanced around as if he half-expected to find someone lurking in the shadows. 'No, thank God. Even if the Logothete's influence extended as far as Suleyman's court, Wayland wouldn't abandon Syth and the children to go traipsing to the end of the world on some unknown minister's say-so.'

'You said "children". That means an addition to the family.'

'A girl, born three years ago. I have the letter in my study. Bring your wine and we'll read it together.'

Vallon took Hero to a small room furnished with a table

overflowing with papers. Vallon waved at them in disgust. 'I'm still struggling to complete my report on the last campaign.' He rummaged in a casket that held his personal correspondence. 'Here it is,' he said. 'Wayland's command of written Arabic is as weak as mine.'

Hero smiled as he unravelled meaning from the letter. 'He says that in addition to holding the position of senior falconer to the Sultan, he's been honoured with the title of Master of the Hunt. I'm not surprised. Wayland can truly bewitch animals.'

A jangling at the gate made Vallon cross to the window.

Hero peered over his shoulder. 'Could that be Caitlin?'

'Most unlikely.'

Wulfstan entered. 'Letter for you, General. Delivered by imperial messenger. No answer required.'

Vallon broke the seal and read the missive. His lips drew back from his teeth. 'Another summons, ordering me to present myself at the Magnaura Palace in four days' time to meet the imperial ambassador I'll be escorting to China.' He turned his snarl on Hero. 'And guess what? The Logothete has learned of your arrival and requests most earnestly – in other words, demands – that you accompany me.'

V

Watching the ferry carry Hero away, Lucas felt a stirring of shame at his boorish behaviour. He suspected that he'd misjudged the man. Seeing him board the ship at Naples, he'd assumed from his sober dress and quiet manner that he was a monk. Perhaps he was, though he wasn't tonsured like the Roman priests or bearded like the eastern clerics. He wore his black hair long, brushed back from a high forehead. His protuberant eyes, quill-like nose and full, almost feminine mouth should have conveyed a comical effect, but in fact he projected a most dignified air. He was certainly a scholar with an uncanny command of languages. Lucas had heard him converse with his fellow passengers in Greek, French, Arabic, Italian and some unknown tongue that might have been English.

One of the touts pestering him tugged his sleeve. Lucas rounded on him. 'Take your hand off me.'

The tout gauged the level of resistance, flicked his fingers in front of Lucas's face and strode away muttering. Lucas drew a deep breath and walked through the port gate into a crowded street lined with tenements, picking his way past trundling carts and porters stooped under bales. The city assailed his senses. Tradesmen from a dozen lands shouted their wares. Spices and leather goods scented the air. Overhead, neighbours held bellowed conversations from adjoining balconies that nearly blocked off the sky, their voices almost drowned out by the din up ahead. A legless man scooted alongside on a trolley, begging for alms. Whores in dresses cut low to expose their breasts stuck out their hips and spread their lips in salacious Os.

The racket increased to a deafening pitch and Lucas found himself at the junction of a thoroughfare packed with a heaving mob – men, women and children all heading in one direction and chanting what sounded like battle cries. Some wore green or blue tabards and when the factions met, the faces of both parties contorted in fury and they stabbed fingers at each other and hurled abuse. Mounted soldiers brandished staves and whips to keep the rival groups apart.

Someone shoved him from behind, propelling him into the mob. It bore him away. Unable to go against the flow, he struggled into a colonnaded walkway on one side of the thoroughfare. Merchants had set up booths and stalls under the arches. A man waved a token in his face.

'I don't understand. Where's everyone going?'

The man pushed him away and plucked another passer-by out of the stream. A shoe barked Lucas's heel and he stumbled, almost falling. A hand pulled him upright and he turned to see a man carrying on his shoulders a little boy trumpeting through his hands in fierce ecstasy.

'What's going on?' Lucas shouted. 'Is this a religious procession?'

The man pointed ahead. Lucas heard the word 'Hippodrome' and understood: the crowd was on its way to the races.

He went with the flow, buildings sliding past on both sides. Some of them were fine mansions with draped balconies occupied by silk-clad figures who looked down on the stew of humanity with patrician disdain.

The mob must have borne Lucas nearly a mile before it disgorged into a forum, the river dividing around a lofty shaft of purple marble crowned with an imperial statue. The buildings on all sides were the most splendid he'd seen, with dazzling white façades and noble porticoes. The crowd spilled into an even wider thoroughfare. Over the packed heads rose a high arcaded wall similar to the ruined Colosseum he'd seen while passing through Rome. It extended away almost to vanishing point. Slowly the crush moved forward. A hand touched Lucas's waist, but when he whirled, the faces around him were blank. He patted his purse under his tunic.

The crowd funnelled towards a massive gate surmounted by four life-size rearing bronze horses. Stewards manned the entrance. Lucas thought he saw money changing hands and fumbled for his purse, was still fumbling to remove coins when the crush thrust him forward. A steward held out his hand, but Lucas didn't know the price of admission, didn't know the exchange rate for his Italian money, didn't know the value of the coins that Hero the Greek had given him. Didn't know *anything*.

'*Diploma*,' the steward kept shouting. Lucas held out a few coins. The steward threw up his hand in vexation.

'I don't understand,' Lucas shouted, bracing himself against the mob pressing from behind.

Unable to force Lucas back, the steward snatched the coins from his palm and propelled him forward. He stumbled through the gateway into a huge amphitheatre lit by dazzling sunshine. He'd never seen so many people in one place. The stadium could have held the population of Rome with room to spare. All the ringside seats were taken and the spectators spilled up the tiered stands. He climbed thirty steps and worked his way around the Hippodrome before finding a thinly occupied section, below the U-shaped curve at one end of the racetrack. The starting stalls were at the other end, almost a quarter of a mile away. Down the middle of the course, separating the two straights, ran a stone plinth crammed with obelisks, statues and bronze figures of animals and charioteers. Fitful music carried from an orchestra assembled in the centre of the arena. Peering hard, Lucas saw that some of the musicians were playing organs, the bellows operated by teams of children.

His neighbour noticed his astonishment and drew his companions' attention to it. They grinned with the good-natured condescension of cosmopolitans showing off their sophistication to a foreign hick. They had come prepared for the day, with cushions to pad the stone benches, parasols, baskets of food and flagons of wine. Lucas had to turn his face from all that plenty. He hadn't eaten a decent meal in three weeks and his stomach had shrunk so that it almost touched his backbone.

By now the Hippodrome was full, the crowd settling into an expectant buzz. Then the noise swelled to a roar that pulsed against Lucas's ear-drums. Everybody jumped to their feet. His neighbour pulled him upright, pointing at the eastern side of the Hippodrome. Out onto a covered balcony processed a line of god-like figures. The stall must have been more than two hundred yards away, but Lucas could make out the shimmer of silk, the glint of gold, the flash of jewels.

One of the figures, black-bearded and clad in red and purple, advanced to the edge of the box and raised a hand. The crowd bellowed a salutation.

Cupping his ear against the uproar, Lucas leaned towards his neighbour. 'Is that the emperor?'

The man crossed himself. 'Basileus Alexius, God preserve him.'

The emperor dropped a white cloth to signal that the games had begun. Out from the stables at the far end of the Hippodrome rolled six chariots, each pulled by four horses. Their riders punched the air and the crowd responded with cheers and boos. The chariots lined up in the stalls, a flag twirled and fell and the horses sprang forward. They galloped straight towards Lucas and it wasn't until they rounded the first turn directly below him that he appreciated their speed. The chariots drifted and skidded, wheels spraying sand, took the next curve on one rim and went weaving up the far straight.

Lucas's neighbour nudged him, holding out some nuts. Lucas wolfed them down, the morsels only aggravating his hunger.

On the third lap two of the chariots contested the inside line and collided. One of them kept going, but the other lost a wheel; its axle dug in and flipped it over, hurling its driver ten yards through the air. Stewards ran out, and while some carried the motionless figure away, others caught up the horses and raked the ruts smooth. By the time the chariots raced round again, the track was clear.

Lucas calculated that the race had gone more than two miles before the victorious driver crossed the finishing line below the imperial box to the applause of his supporters and the groans of the punters who'd backed the wrong team.

Between races, musicians and troupes of acrobats performed for the spectators. The sun beat down and Lucas felt increasingly light-headed. 'How many more races?' he mimed.

His neighbour held up seven fingers. Lucas couldn't face a whole day at the races. He had to eat or he would pass out. Touching his neighbour's shoulder in thanks, he rose on stiff legs and worked his way to the exit.

Outside, the street was nearly empty. He walked through the forum and was heading back towards the port when a waifish girl slipped in front of him, her pretty face screwed up in appeal. She spoke to him and fluttered her eyes, caressing his arms and chest.

She couldn't have been older than twelve, yet it was clear what she was offering. He shifted her aside and walked on. She whimpered and wheedled, matching his pace, then clutched his elbow and burst into tears.

From the odd word and gesture, Lucas understood she was an orphan and perishing of hunger. She wouldn't leave him alone. He reached inside his tunic and produced a coin. She took it and, overcome by his generosity, threw both hands around his neck and kissed him.

He disentangled himself. 'There's no need for that. I had a sister your age and I know what it's like to go hungry.'

She ran off and he forgot about her, intent on finding a food stall. A heavenly aroma drew him to a booth offering kebabs and flatbread. The fumes from the grilling lamb made him swoon. Ahead of him a customer collected his order, served in a pocket of bread and topped off with a helping of pungent fish sauce. The customer paid with two coins that looked similar to the ones the Greek had given Lucas. He stepped forward. 'I'll have the same.'

Watching the lamb sizzle, he could hardly contain his hunger, imagining sinking his teeth into meat and fresh-baked bread for the first time in weeks. When the vendor handed over the fragrant packet, he couldn't speak for the saliva flooding his mouth.

The vendor held out his other hand for payment.

Lucas felt for his purse, frowned, patted his waist and, with an increasing desperation that would have seemed comical to anyone who didn't know the reason for it, beat and probed every inch of his body.

'My purse,' he said. 'It's gone.'

The vendor snatched back the food.

Understanding hit Lucas and he looked down the road where the girl had vanished. 'I've been robbed.'

He ran into the road and scanned both ways. His hand went to his knife and that's when he discovered that she'd stolen that, too.

The vendor had followed him and was shoving him in the chest. Lucas in a sick daze put up no resistance. In a stupor of disbelief he began walking, so shocked that he didn't realise he'd taken the wrong direction until he saw a harbour below him and the Sea of Marmara widening out to the horizon.

He sat on a bench by a church and tried to work out what to do. No doubt about it, he was in a bad plight – penniless, friendless, unable to speak the language. Begging went against his nature, and from what he'd seen, the city's halt and lame practically formed a guild. No one would give alms to a fit and healthy foreign youth. He'd have to find work. That shouldn't be difficult in a city as large as Constantinople, and the harbour was the obvious place to look. Feeling more positive, he descended to the waterside and worked his way around the semi-circular quay, enquiring of any likely person where he might find employment. Most of them waved him away; some acted as if he were invisible.

He spotted a column of porters bent under bulky loads, ferrying grain from a ship to a granary. An overseer presided over the gang, tapping the side of his shoe with a stick. Lucas presented himself, pointed at the hurrying men, then pointed at himself. The overseer looked him up and down, assessing him as if he were a beast, then turned and shouted. One of the older stevedores set down his load and came over, cringing with anxiety. The foreman dismissed him with a flick of the hand, jerked his chin at Lucas and pointed at the load.

It must have been early afternoon when he began his labour, and he was tottering on caved legs, his back slick with sweat, his throat and eyes sore from the dust in the granary, when the overseer's whistle signalled the end of the shift. The gang ceased like a machine that had been turned off. At first, Lucas could only move in a tortured stoop. He approached the overseer and held out his hand. The overseer fended it off with his stick.

Lucas pointed towards his mouth and patted his stomach. 'Please. I haven't eaten all day.'

A remote smile passed over the overseer's face. He made to walk away.

Lucas pulled him back. 'Just give me what you owe.'

The overseer drew back his stick. Lucas kept his grip.

'What I've earned. That's all.'

Perhaps the overseer saw in Lucas's gaze the belligerence that had made the tout on the dock back off. With a kind of disgust, he handed over four tiny coins and swaggered away. The coins weighed next to nothing.

The sun was sinking behind the rooftops when Lucas left the harbour. He slaked his thirst at a public drinking fountain and made his way back to the centre, keeping an eye out for a food stall.

Night came down fast. One minute the streets were busy with home-goers and merchants dismantling their stalls, the next they were almost empty. Lucas took a wrong turning and found himself shut in by dark alleys that wound through canyons of solid masonry. The other pedestrians he met travelled in groups and moved at a hurry, as if fearful of overstepping some sinister deadline. The authorities must have imposed a curfew.

It wasn't completely dark. Here and there lamps glowed in windows and torches guttered in sconces above iron-barred posterns. Several times he encountered armed watchmen making their rounds in pairs.

Lucas was going the wrong way, heading downhill towards the sea walls. He turned left and stopped halfway down the alley, his passage blocked by a pack of bat-eared dogs snarling over carrion. He retreated, took another turning and halted, a vague sense of threat tickling his senses. The alley behind him crooked into darkness. A child cried and cooking pans clattered somewhere in a tenement apartment. He went on, ascending a lane that rose in shallow steps, glancing back occasionally.

He was almost at the end of the alley when a man stepped around the corner like someone meeting an appointment. What little light there was struck cold shards from his knife. Lucas whirled and saw another man pushing out of the shadows only fifteen yards behind him.

No doorways, nowhere to run or hide. Cursing the girl who'd

stolen his knife, Lucas stripped off his tunic and wrapped it around his left arm. He backed against the wall and sidled towards the edge of a step, his gaze darting between his assailants. They stopped a few yards short and one of them spoke, making beckoning gestures.

Lucas's voice shook. 'You're on the wrong trail. I haven't got any money.' He gave a cracked laugh. 'Somebody got to me before you.'

Very slowly the two men closed in, their knives steady, their eyes alert to any move. Lucas forced himself to stay still. Perhaps when they discovered he had only a scrap of loose change, they'd let him go. Wishful thinking. They'd slit his throat out of sheer vindictiveness. His breath rasped in his throat, impelled by rage as much as fear. Neither of the men matched him in height. The one behind him seemed hesitant, waiting for his accomplice to take the initiative. Go for him first. Use your training, use your feet.

Closer and closer. Lucas stood on the edge of the step, braced to spring, when a roar swung everyone around. A squat figure blocked the entrance to the alley, a huge blade in his hand. He roared again and came lumbering down the lane. The footpads exchanged glances and bolted, the uphill one sprinting past Lucas as if he'd ceased to exist. He sagged against the wall, legs fluttering, and blinked at his saviour.

'Thank you.'

The man said something, broken and cavernous teeth glinting in a shaggy black beard. He cradled Lucas's chin and his grin widened. He held up the blade for Lucas to admire. It was the sort of cleaver used in a slaughterhouse. The man stank of rancid flesh and sour wine.

'Come,' he said. That's what Lucas thought he said. The man didn't speak Greek or any other language Lucas recognised. He put a brawny arm around Lucas's waist. 'Come.'

The man talked continuously as they threaded the empty streets, Lucas too shocked to do anything but follow. He put on his tunic and stood rocking in a daze when the man stopped outside the entrance to a degraded tenement. The man opened it and beckoned. 'Come.'

Lucas followed him up a dirty stairway, hesitated when the man opened a door. 'Come.'

The room was filthy, the atmosphere so frowzy that Lucas fingered his throat. The man laid his cleaver on a table and lit a candle. In one corner stood a cot with rumpled linen that looked as if it had been stripped from a corpse a week in the grave. An icon hung at a wonky angle on the wall. Something stirred in a corner and Lucas saw eyes glowing red in a hole. Verminous feet scrabbled behind him. The man grinned at Lucas. It seemed to be the only expression he had. He unstoppered a bottle, filled two earthenware beakers and held one out.

Lucas grimaced. 'Wine on an empty stomach isn't a good idea.' He patted his belly to get his meaning across. The man's grin took on an expectant air. Lucas sipped, the sulphurous brew making him splutter.

The man laughed and tossed back his drink. He regarded Lucas afresh, his grin softening into something like ardent speculation. Lucas forced a smile.

The man tapped his chest. 'Krum,' he said, then gestured at Lucas with an enquiring expression.

'My name's Lucas.'

Krum or whatever his name was pointed at something behind Lucas. The Frank turned and saw that the man was indicating the cot. A cold feeling ran down Lucas's spine. 'I'm not tired. I'm hungry. Let's go and find something to eat.'

The man's expression changed again, fixed in yearning expectation. He reached out one hand, its back furred by black hairs, placed it on Lucas's shoulder and tried to guide him towards the cot. Lucas resisted, teetering on his heels. The man pushed harder. Lucas grabbed his hand and threw it off.

'Look, I'm grateful, but I have to be going.'

The man mumbled to himself and began loosening his breeches. Lucas measured the distance to the door and was gathering himself to make a bolt when the man caught his eye and saw his intention. Fast as thought, he picked up the cleaver and aimed the point between Lucas's eyes.

Lucas held up his hands. 'All right. But first, let's have another drink. Here, let me.'

He fought to keep his hands from shaking as he poured. The man watched, cleaver dangling. Lucas swallowed the contents of his beaker, coughed and grinned. The man reached out with tenderness and cupped Lucas's genitals with his free hand.

Lucas rammed his cup into the man's face, aimed a kick at his balls, made only glancing contact and followed up by hurling himself bodily against him, trying to get inside the arc of the cleaver and block the man's arm with his elbow. He didn't quite succeed and felt a searing pain in his scalp as the blade cut. He managed to grab the man's right wrist before he could deliver another blow and both of them went tumbling over the table. Lucas heard the cleaver clatter to the ground. His assailant scrambled after it. Lucas threw himself on him from behind, wrapped his left arm around his opponent's neck and formed a lock by gripping the biceps with his right hand. He applied pressure on the back of his foe's neck. Lucas felt blood running down his cheek. The man lay on his side, flailing his limbs to break the lock. Lucas knew that if he could apply pressure to the arteries, the man would soon pass out. His hold was wrong, though, most of the pressure against his opponent's Adam's apple. By an immense effort the man heaved himself to his feet and swung Lucas round. The Frank clung on and ran him head-first into the wall. The man spun, trying to fling Lucas off. Lucas hooked a foot under his ankle and both of them crashed to the floor. In his huge effort to maintain his grip, Lucas bit through his bottom lip. He clung on, eyes closed, squeezed against his opponent to deny him any purchase. The man made another gigantic effort, bucking and heaving like a beached fish. Lucas maintained his stranglehold. The man stopped struggling and gave a gurgling moan. Lucas couldn't see his face and kept his hold, squeezing after the man went limp beneath him and his muscles could no longer take the strain. When he released his grip, the man didn't move. Lucas staggered to his feet, his breath coming in great whoops. Blood ran down his chin and spattered on the floor. Chest heaving, he rolled the man over. He lay dead and horrible, eyes bulging out of his black face.

Fists pounded on the door. Voices shouted. Lucas picked up the cleaver, lurched to the door and unbolted it. Faces started back in terror. A woman screamed. He barged through the crowd and stumbled down the stairs into the street. He took the first turning he came to and when he'd put two more behind him he threw the cleaver away.

He slowed to an exhausted walk, holding his ribs, staggering as if one leg were longer than the other. His head was still bleeding. When he felt his scalp he could feel bone exposed by the gash. You've just killed a man, he thought. How does it feel? Disgusting. But so simple. Desperation is all it takes. The day's events galloped through his mind, all funnelling towards that foul deed in that foul room. If that girl hadn't robbed him, if that overseer hadn't cheated him, if those two thieves hadn't menaced him ... he would never have been able to summon the animal rage to throttle the man. He leaned and retched, coughing up strings of bile. He'd imagined killing, but only during a glorious encounter on the field of battle, trumpets blowing and banners whipping, a worthy opponent asking his name as they wheeled on their chargers.

Lucas slumped against a wall, threw back his head and groaned. His mind emptied. A shrill whistle brought him upright. It came again, from the vicinity of his crime. The man's neighbours had seen him; they had his description. His wound was all the evidence they'd need. He pushed away and went reeling down the empty streets, taking turns at random.

One of them led him into a market square lit by a single lamp at the far end. The sweet rot of decaying vegetables clogged his senses. Even injured and hurting, he couldn't deny his hunger. He advanced, scanning the ground, and then stopped, alerted by faint crepitations and squeaks. The place wasn't empty. It seethed with rats, a horde without number swarming in clots and clumps and streams.

Trapped in a waking nightmare, he ghost-walked through the silent city, the only living soul abroad in Constantinople. He must have gone half a mile when a shout behind him made him whirl. A watchman with a drawn sword and flaming torch straddled the path. Another silhouette appeared and Lucas took to his heels. Whistles shrilled and feet pattered in pursuit. He darted down an alley.

The wall on one side was about eight feet high, reinforced by buttresses with an angled step about three feet off the ground. The urgent slap of feet drew nearer. Bracing himself against the opposite wall, he sprang forward, leaped onto a step and crooked his arms over the top of the wall. With one heart-bursting heave he dragged himself up just as one of the watchmen ran past the entrance to the alley. Sobbing with effort, Lucas wriggled over the wall and dropped to the ground.

From the other side came voices and the clinking of metal. Lucas pressed against the wall. The voices faded. Lucas waited. He couldn't work out what manner of place he was in. Perhaps a private garden or paved courtyard. He shuffled into the blackness and had gone about twenty yards when the ground opened beneath him. He tripped down a couple of steps before recovering his balance. He was in pitch black, unable to see a hand before his face. Water dripped with cavernous echoes. He groped his way down the steps until he reached level ground. The atmosphere was cold and aqueous. He felt around until he found a pebble. He tossed it ahead and heard it plop into water.

He was in a cistern, one of Constantinople's underground reservoirs. He backed away and collided with a pillar. He slid down it, too exhausted to make another move. His bottom jaw juddered with cold. He wrapped his arms about his chest and stared into the dripping blackness.

He slept in fits and starts. When at last he opened his eyes, the cistern had filled with a spectral light just bright enough to show the lacquered surface of the water and colonnades soaring up to shadowy vaults.

His skull throbbed. He felt his scalp. The bleeding had stopped, leaving his hair a congealed and treacly mat. He knelt by the water's edge and ducked his head under. The pain made him cry out. Three times he immersed his head before he'd washed away the gore. The collar and shoulder of his tunic was stiff with the stuff. He took it off and rinsed it and wrung it out. Quaking with cold, he put it on wet then mounted the steps. Dawn had just broken. The yard around the cistern lay empty. A faint hum told him that the city was coming awake. On this side, the wall offered no footholds. Lucas's gaze fixed on a flat-roofed hut built into one of the angles of the yard. A window ledge gave him a step up. He crept towards the wall and looked over, ducking down as a man walked by. Next time he looked, the street was empty. He rolled over the parapet, dropped down and set off walking as soon as his feet hit the ground.

A workman walking towards him shied in alarm and gave him the widest berth possible. Lucas glanced back and saw the man staring after him. Lucas understood why when he looked down. His tunic was stained and blotched pink, his breeches smeared red. His wound had opened again. Blood wormed down his neck. He kept his head down.

He passed through a smiths' quarter where the workmen left off their hammering to watch him pass. He found himself in a thoroughfare where merchants were setting up stalls. He didn't meet their eye and kept walking. He climbed a hill and saw through a gap in the skyline the dome of St Sophia to the right. The traffic was growing heavier and he tried to blend into it – just another labourer off to a day's toil.

Three soldiers pushed through the crowd ahead of him. He stopped. They hadn't seen him yet, but when they did . . . By now news of the murder would have circulated. He swung on his heel and had retreated only a few yards when the gleam of iron revealed more soldiers. To his right was a taverna – a few tables under an awning and a shadowy room open to the street. He walked in. Faces looked up from platters and backgammon boards. As he walked to the counter, the proprietor watched him with a dark frown. Lucas smiled and grimaced, rubbing his head to indicate that his ruinous appearance was the consequence of a night's debauch gone wrong. He produced the four miserable coins he'd earned at the docks.

The keeper of the tavern looked at them, then transferred his disbelieving gaze to Lucas's face. He shook his head in slow finality.

'It's all I have. Christ, I worked hard enough for it.'

The taverner poked out his cheek with his tongue and studied Lucas afresh before motioning him towards a table in a corner. Lucas slumped with his back to the entrance. Two curvy young serving girls weaved between the tables, their arms piled with dishes, smiling and chatting to the regulars. After a long interval, one of them appeared before Lucas and set down half a loaf of white bread, an omelette and a jug of wine. Her smile was so pleasant that he almost burst into tears.

He abandoned himself to hunger. It was all he could do to resist tearing at the bread and cramming it down in throat-straining gobbets. When he'd finished, his head felt as if it were floating off his shoulders.

'I hope you gave the other fellow something to remember you by.'

Lucas started awake. A man had plonked himself down opposite. Lucas realised that the man had spoken in French.

The man waggled a toothpick between his lips. He nodded at Lucas's head. 'You've been in the wars, my friend.'

Lucas tried to frame a rueful smile, but his mouth just wobbled. 'I was set upon by thieves.'

'New to the city, I'll wager.'

'I landed yesterday,' Lucas said, his voice small.

The man was a veteran, his military calling evidenced by a scar from temple to eyebrow and a knot of gristle where his right eye had been. His pugnacious bearing was softened by the humorous set of his mouth.

'Come to go a-soldiering for the emperor?'

Lucas nodded.

'Got any friends in Constantinople?'

'No,' said Lucas, then looked up. 'I'm looking for a Frankish officer called Vallon.'

The veteran removed the toothpick from his mouth. 'Vallon?'

'You know him?'

'Know him by reputation. Never served under him. What's he to you?'

'Someone I met said he might find me a place in the ranks. Do you know where I can find him?'

The veteran placed one palm against his forehead. 'I think he lives in Galata.'

'Where's that?'

'Jesus, I can't believe it.' The veteran bracketed his hands on the table and stared at Lucas. 'Galata's the other side of the Horn. Right opposite where you docked.'

'Oh.'

The veteran regarded him. He shook his head. 'Vallon's too high and mighty to waste time on the likes of you. He's a general, got promoted after the do at Dyrrachium.'

'The man I met said Vallon's from Aquitaine. Same as me.'

The veteran laughed, scraped back the bench and stood. 'He'll be all over you. Go ahead, youngster. When Vallon gives you the bum's rush, come back here – the Bluebird Tavern – and ask for Pepin. If it's soldiering you want, I can find you all you bloody well want.'

'Thank you.'

Pepin the veteran looked him over. 'You can't go wandering the streets in that state. The watch will think you've murdered some-one.'

Lucas stared at him and gave a slow swallow. Pepin's good eye narrowed. 'You didn't, did you?'

'It was him or me. God's word.'

'Hell's teeth,' Pepin murmured. 'Stay here.'

He went into close conference with the taverner and the man glanced over, dismayed at being told he was harbouring a murderer. Certain that the proprietor would call the law, Lucas rose, intending to make a bolt for it. Pepin reeled him in just in time.

'Easy, lad. This way.'

He led Lucas into a backyard occupied by a few chickens scratching in the dust. 'Take your tunic off,' he said. He fetched a pail of water and began mopping Lucas's face and hair with a flannel. The water ran pink. Pepin changed it. 'That wound will need stitching by a doctor.' At last he rocked back and appraised his work. 'You'll do.'

When Lucas had towelled himself dry, Pepin held out a clean tunic and a cap. 'I don't know how to thank you,' Lucas whispered.

'Us *Frangoi* have to stick together. You got any money?'

Lucas shook his head.

Pepin dug into his purse. 'That'll keep you going for a couple of days.'

Lucas stared at the coins. 'I don't know how much they're worth.'

'There ain't no limit to your ignorance, is there? Those are folles. Two hundred and eighty folles buys one gold solidus. Two folles is what your meal should have cost. Those coins you handed over were nummi, not worth shit. But the landlord's an old soldier and took pity on you.'

'How much is the fare to Galata?'

'Four folles if you're the only passenger, less if you share.' Pepin squinted at Lucas. 'I don't suppose you've got anywhere to stay either.' He sighed. 'All right, when you've finished wasting your time with Vallon, come back here and we'll fix you up. Tomorrow, I'll introduce you to a couple of my old army mates.'

Awash with gratitude, Lucas went out into the street. In his clean tunic and with the hat hiding his wound, no one looked at him twice. He walked down to the harbour, approached a ferryman and pointed across the channel. He made only a feeble attempt to haggle and ended up paying twice the amount stipulated by Pepin. Crossing the Horn, his nerves began to jangle. What was he going to do if he did see Vallon? What would he say?

The ferry landed. Lucas looked up at the settlement, took a shaky breath and set off. Walls surrounded the suburb and a soldier stopped him at a gate and demanded his business. On hearing that Lucas was looking for Vallon, the soldier looked at him with blatant scepticism but let him through.

Warehouses gave way to clean wide streets lined by smart villas behind walls overhung with jasmine and wisteria. The higher Lucas climbed, the more his resolve leaked away until it was all he could do to put one foot in front of another. Pepin's right, he told himself. Vallon won't see a peasant from Aquitaine. I won't even get past his doorman. I'll find out where he lives and then go back to the taverna and work out what to do next.

Few people were abroad and none of them answered his pleas for directions. He came to a crossroads high on the hill and took the right-hand turning, past a green occupied by four idling youths. One of them nudged his companions' attention in Lucas's direction. They stood and pulled their tunics straight. From their smart costume, Lucas guessed they were Venetians, the sons of rich merchants. Their glances and grins suggested that in Lucas they'd found someone to liven up their day.

They drifted across his path in a pack. Lucas slowed for a moment before adopting a confident tread, shoulders rolling. 'Good morning,' he said, breaching the line.

A hand fell on his shoulder. The other three youths closed up. 'Where do you think you're going?' said the one holding his shoulder.

Lucas shook his head and kept walking. The youth pulled him back. 'I asked you a question.'

'I'm looking for General Vallon's house.'

That raised eyebrows. 'You're a Frank,' one said.

'From Aquitaine.'

They trailed him like dogs. One of them said something that provoked a burst of laughter. Another ran in front of Lucas, sketched an hour-glass shape, grabbed his crotch and thrust it in and out in lewd pantomime.

Lucas fended him off. 'I don't know what you're talking about.'

One of the youths snatched Lucas's hat off, spat into it and then invited Lucas to put it back on. Lucas stopped, blood rising in a tide that threatened to drown reason. He fought down his rage. 'I don't want any trouble.'

'I don't want any trouble,' they mimicked. Their laughter died and their quick glances and hardening expressions showed they were ready to attack. One of them flat-handed Lucas in the chest. 'We don't want Frankish beggar scum here.' He gave Lucas another shove. 'Fuck off back to Frankland.'

Lucas held his ground and tried to fend off his tormentors. 'Look, there's no need for this.'

A hand grabbed him and he snapped, driving his fist into the attacker's face with meaty impact.

'Get him!' someone shouted, and the rest dived in, punching and kicking. Lucas kept his feet for a few seconds before weight of numbers bore him to the ground. And then it started. A foot slammed into his nose, smashing bone and gristle. Another foot drove into his ribs and drew back to deliver another kick. Barely conscious, Lucas seized it by the ankle, sank his teeth into the tendon and sawed like a beast. An awful scream, followed by a blow to his eye that made him see the universe on the day of creation, before everything went black.

Consciousness returned. Gasping and spitting blood, he rolled over to register a vision of violence incarnate bearing down from above – a tawny-haired barbarian with moustaches like the wings of an avenging angel and a stump where his left hand should have been. He clamped his good hand on one of the attackers, nailing him to the spot. The others had fled and now they stopped, condemned to witness the final scene in the play they'd improvised so carelessly.

Lucas looked up through the blurred slot that was all that was left of vision. 'Vallon?'

The man glanced down. 'You came to find Vallon?'

Lucas nodded. Pain pulsed from the place where his nose had been.

The captured youth struggled to break loose. The man held him easily and his face took on a rapt expression. The youth whined. His captor drew him forward so they were standing eye to eye, and then with a beatific expression, like one lifting his eyes to a saint in exaltation, he drew back his head and butted the youth full in the face with a sound like a hard-fired pot cracking. When he let go, his victim dropped as if he'd been poleaxed and writhed about with blood squirting through his splayed hands.

Lucas was dimly aware of other people running towards him. He saw a young girl, a statuesque woman who clutched her hands to her throat and called to a steepling figure in clerical grey who bent over Lucas so that his familiar face blotted out everything else. The last thing Lucas remembered was hands lifting him and a jagged tearing in his chest as something vital parted.

He woke in lamplight, his head bursting. The moment he regained consciousness, he vomited. Hands guided a bowl under his mouth. He sank back. Figures drifted in and out. The tall red-headed lady who stared down at him without sympathy. The cleric from the ship who felt his pulse and peered into his eyes. A young man who covered his mouth when he saw the damage inflicted on Lucas's face. And then – he might have dreamed it – a tall grim man who studied him without expression before turning away. Lucas's own gaze was blank, the world spinning away down a tunnel, but in a last moment of lucidity, he knew that at long last he'd found what he'd come looking for.

That's him. Vallon, properly known as Guy de Crion. My father. The man who murdered my mother and brought ruin and death on my family.

VI

Lucas woke propped against pillows, his skull bandaged, nose taped, one hand splinted, vision reduced to one slitted eye. Light from a shuttered window diffused through the small bare room. A figure stood at the end of the bed, studying him with forensic detachment. It was the youth who'd helped carry him inside.

'Are you awake?'

Lucas blinked.

'Can you speak?'

Lucas unstuck his lips and made a swallowing sound.

The youth poured a beaker of water and held it to Lucas's mouth. Most of the contents dribbled down his chin. The youth set down the vessel. 'Your head's swollen to twice its normal size,' he said. 'Your own mother wouldn't recognise you.'

Lucas dabbed at his face. A grating pain in his side made him gasp.

'That's your ribs. Two of them are broken. So is your nose and one of your fingers. The wound in your scalp required sixteen stitches. Master Hero also put two stitches in your lip. You were unconscious and didn't feel a thing.'

'Where am I?'

'The gatehouse of General Vallon's residence.'

'How long have I been here?'

'Two days. You've been asleep most of that time. What's your name?'

'Lucas.'

'I'm Aiken, Vallon's son.'

Lucas squinted up, considering this claim. So far as he could tell, he and Aiken were about the same age. 'No, you're not.'

'Not his real son. Vallon adopted me after my father died.' Aiken sat on the edge of the bed, his movements almost prim. 'What brought you here?'

'I came east to join the Byzantine army.'

'I meant, what led you to Vallon's house? Wulfstan said you spoke the general's name.'

'I met a Frankish veteran in a taverna. When I told him I was from Aquitaine, he suggested I join Vallon's regiment.'

The bed creaked as Aiken rose. 'I don't expect the general will recruit someone who gets beaten up on his first day in Constantinople.'

'What's he like?'

'He's a general. What do you think he's like?'

Lucas took a risk. 'The veteran said that Vallon fled from France after being condemned as an outlaw.'

'Did he? If I were you, I'd keep such slanders to yourself.'

Aiken closed the door behind him. With geriatric slowness, Lucas extended a hand to the water. When he'd drunk, he lay back considering his situation. Since leaving France, he'd rehearsed his confrontation with Vallon countless times, imagining the shock on the man's face when he told him he was his son. Sometimes he got no further than that before plunging a sword into Vallon's belly – plunging it in time after time. *That's for my mother, and that's for my brother, and that's for my sister. And this last one's for me.*

Now, though, wasn't the time to exact revenge. He wanted to be in full health so that he could savour every detail. Time would season the dish, and he had plenty of time. Vallon had no idea that he was his son. No one did. Wait and learn and use the knowledge to inflict maximum pain. Settling into sleep, Lucas had an intimation that Aiken might prove to be a useful lever. Brief though their conversation had been, Lucas already hated him.

Awful dreams chased each other. Lucas started out of one smothering nightmare with a cry to find someone sponging his brow.

'Hush,' said Hero. 'Your body and soul are at war and we must let them make peace.' He held an aromatic pad under Lucas's nose. 'Do you remember me?'

Hero's volatile physic chased away the demons in Lucas's skull. He coughed and snorted.

'If you'd been less stiff-necked, you would have spared yourself a lot of trouble and a great deal of pain.'

'I'm sorry I rebuffed you on the boat.'

'I don't blame you for being wary of strangers. How are you feeling?'

'About how you'd expect.'

Hero took Lucas's pulse, examined his uncovered eye, listened to his chest. 'How's your vision?'

'I can see you.'

'How many fingers am I holding up?'

'One.'

'And now?'

'Four. You must be a physician?'

'Fortunately for you, I am.' Hero slid an arm under Lucas's shoulder and held a bitter infusion to his lips. 'Swallow it.'

Lucas forced it down, shuddering at the taste.

Hero lowered him back onto the pillows. 'Aiken says you're called Lucas.'

'Lucas of Osse.'

'It didn't take long for you to get into trouble, did it? More than once, it seems. Those Venetian louts didn't inflict your head wound.'

'I was attacked by thieves the night before.'

'How strange that only a day after we spoke, you ended up at the house of the very man to whom I was going to offer you an introduction.'

'A veteran I ran into—'

'I know. Lucas told me. It's still a remarkable coincidence.'

Lucas lay rigid under Hero's gaze and didn't relax until the physician rose.

'You'll have your chance to put your request to General Vallon tomorrow,' Hero said. 'Good night.'

Lucas's heart thumped. 'Before you go, sir, can I ask you something?'

Hero stopped with his hand on the latch.

Lucas wriggled into a semi-upright position. 'How did you become acquainted with Vallon?'

Hero laughed. 'That would take all night to tell and you'd be better off spending the time in sleep.'

'I'm not tired.'

Hero returned and sat at the foot of the bed. 'Nine years ago, when I was still a student, I was appointed travelling companion to a Byzantine diplomat carrying a ransom demand to the family of a Norman knight whose son had been captured at Manzikert.'

'I've heard of that battle.'

'My master died in the Alps and I would have turned back if I hadn't met Vallon. He was travelling south, intending to take service with the Varangian Guard.'

'Why? I mean, what made him leave France?'

'What's that to you?'

'I just wondered.'

'It's not your place to wonder about the man who gave you house space.' After a moment's wary contemplation, Hero continued. 'Vallon agreed to accompany me to the Norman knight's estate in Northumbria, where we delivered the ransom terms. I can still remember them: "four white gyrfalcons as pale as a virgin's breasts or the first snows of winter".'

'What's a gyrfalcon?'

'White falcons that live under the Pole Star, many weeks' voyage north of Britain. From there we carried them south through Rus and across the Black Sea to Anatolia. The journey took the best part of a year and many of the companions who accompanied us didn't reach the end.'

'But you did. You achieved your goal.'

'A part of me likes to think we did. Another part tells me that the sacrifice wasn't worth it.'

Lucas sagged back on his pillows. 'You're not telling me the half of it, are you?'

'No. I could never share the joy and heartache of that odyssey with anybody but Vallon and Wayland.'

'Who's Wayland?'

'A remarkable Englishman, a falconer who sleeps tonight in the court of the Sultan Suleyman with his wife, Syth, who travelled every mile of that long journey with us.'

Lucas wanted to know more about his father. 'Is General Vallon a good commander?'

Hero looked down. 'I'm not qualified to judge martial prowess. All I can say is that without Vallon's leadership, cunning and courage, I would be a heap of bones mouldering in some distant wilderness.'

'How would you rate his skill with arms?'

'I would say that in his prime, there wasn't a man alive who had the beating of him.'

Lucas lay still, digesting the claim. 'It sounds as if you admire him.'

'I abhor violence, but Vallon is a warrior of honour. I never saw him kill a man wantonly. And no one else could have led us through the wilderness of the world. He's the only man I'd follow to the ends of the earth.' Hero snuffed out the lamp. 'Except I've already done that.'

Tomorrow, Hero had said. All day, with rain lashing the shutters, Lucas held himself ready for Vallon's appearance. He was still waiting, nauseous with anticipation and dread, when the candle died, leaving him in darkness.

The door slamming against its hinges startled him awake. A figure sensed rather than seen forced the door shut, shielding a lamp from the draught. Its light steadied, half-illuminating Vallon's face.

'Did I wake you?'

Lucas gargled some response. Vallon beat rain from his cloak, seated himself on a stool too small for him and placed the lamp on a table. Its light threw his face into planes and grooves. Lucas could scarcely breathe. All his bravado leaked away. The general didn't resemble the blood-dripping monster branded on his memory, but he looked like a killer – a tired and careworn professional slayer. His deep-set gaze was direct, apparently indifferent until one corner of his mouth crooked in a manner that suggested bleak humour.

'So,' he said. 'I've come to learn more about the cuckoo in my nest. I understand you travelled from Aquitaine.'

Lucas was glad bandages hid his face. 'From Osse in the Pyrenees.'

'I recognise the accent. Your people would be farmers.'

'Shepherds and horsebreeders, my Lord.'

'Sir will do. You didn't have to come all this way to enlist in the military. Why didn't you find an army closer to home?'

'I ... I'd rather not say. Except that I couldn't stay in France.'

Another wry twist of the mouth. 'Well, you wouldn't be the first outlaw to seek employment in my command. How did you travel to Naples?'

'I walked, my Lord ... sir. It took six months, stopping many times to earn food by my labour.'

Vallon leaned forward, his shadow rearing up the wall. 'Unnecessary effort. If it's a soldier's life you crave, you could have found it in Italy. The Normans have been combing the peninsula for recruits. I'm surprised they didn't sweep you into their net.'

'What I saw of the Normans didn't endear them to me.'

Vallon rocked back. '"Endear"? Your speech is more polished than I would expect from a shepherd's son.'

'We weren't peasants, sir. One of my uncles was a priest and saw that I had an education.'

'Can you read and write?'

'Tolerably well. That's to say, poorly by your standards.'

'Hm. This veteran who pointed you in my direction. What's his name?'

'Pepin, sir. He spoke highly of you. He said that your regiment had gained a notable victory at Dyr ... at Dyr—'

'Dyrrachium, and it wasn't a regiment and we didn't win the battle.' Vallon raised his eyes to the ceiling. 'The only Pepin who served under me lost his life in Castile more than ten years ago.' Vallon looked down. 'Horsebreeders, you said.'

'Yes, sir. And I can break them.'

'Any experience with weapons? I expect you know how to use a slingshot.'

'I can handle a sword, sir.'

'Can you indeed? I don't suppose many shepherds from Osse can make that claim.'

'An old soldier who'd fought against the Moors instructed me. From a young age I've wanted to follow his calling.'

Vallon grunted. 'Well, we'll see how you handle the real thing when your ribs have mended. If you show promise, I'll find you a place in one of the infantry regiments.'

'My ambition is to serve in a cavalry unit.'

'You don't have the means. A war horse costs two years' wages, and then there are weapons and armour to purchase. No commander would outfit an unformed youth who's never seen action.'

'I'm not as raw as you think.'

'I take that to mean you've taken at least one man's life.'

Lucas pushed away the sordid image of Krum's death spasms. 'I thought I could start as your groom.'

Vallon's forehead pleated. 'What makes you think I'd find space for you in my squadron?'

'You took me into your household.'

'Not by choice. Why are you so keen to serve under me?'

'Master Hero described the expedition you led to the north. His account of the way you achieved your goal convinced me that I would like to serve in your Outlanders.'

Vallon picked up the lamp. 'No, you wouldn't. That was then. This is now.'

VII

Caitlin didn't look up from her needlework when Vallon returned from his visit to Lucas. Hero broke the awkward silence. 'What do you make of our invalid?'

'An odd case. In one breath he sounds like a bumptious peasant. With the next he gives the impression of someone from better-bred stock.'

Caitlin made a fierce stitch and put aside her embroidery. 'As soon as he's well enough, I want him out of here.'

'He's no trouble.'

'No trouble? The families of those boys he attacked are threatening to complain to the magistrate.'

'It was the Venetians who started the fight.'

'It doesn't matter. Their families are of good standing, while that lout is a nobody.' Caitlin's breathy voice threatened to break into a higher register. 'And what was Wulfstan thinking of, breaking Marco's nose?'

'He wasn't thinking of anything. Marco attacked a visitor to our house. He got what he deserved.'

'It's all very well for you to treat the matter lightly. You're hardly ever here. I have to live with my neighbours. I'm the one who has to cultivate friendships, make alliances, consider marriage matches.'

'Zoe is barely eight.'

'The same age as Theodora's daughter and she's already betrothed.'

Vallon closed his eyes briefly.

Hero had been following the exchanges, his eyes switching from Vallon to Caitlin. He cleared his throat. 'Lucas should be well enough to leave by Sunday.'

Vallon grunted. 'Good.'

'Will you take him into your squadron?'

Vallon shook his head. 'I need seasoned fighters who can supply their own horse and arms. The boy doesn't have a penny to his name.'

'He seems a very determined young man – proud, too. On the ship he ate food I wouldn't have given to a pig, yet he didn't beg. And anyone who can walk from Aquitaine to Naples must be resourceful.' Hero hesitated. 'How much does a horse cost?'

'The cheapest won't leave change from twenty solidi.' Vallon frowned. 'You're not thinking of setting him up, are you?'

Hero blushed. 'Somehow I feel responsible for him. If I'd approached him more tactfully on the ship, I might have spared him a beating.'

Vallon converted his surprise into a shrug. 'Well, it's not my place to advise you on how to spend your money. He claims he can master horses and knows how to swing a sword. We'll see.'

Caitlin rose in a swirl of silk. 'You don't listen to a word I say. You're about to set off on another journey, and all you can talk about is some stranger who means nothing to us.' Gathering up her skirts, she swept out of the room.

Vallon ran his tongue around his cheek and stared at the floor. 'My lady is taking my departure badly.'

'She has my sympathy.'

Vallon drew in his legs. 'Tomorrow the Logothete will introduce me to the imperial ambassador.'

'And I'm coming with you.'

'We've been through this,' Vallon said. 'There's no need for you to attend. You're not subject to the minister's dictates.'

'Vallon, I didn't travel all this way to turn down the chance of a visit to the Great Palace. There are princes who would pay for the privilege. Who's the ambassador?'

'Duke Michael Skleros, related to not one but two noble houses. His mother was a Phocas, a family that has produced two emperors, including the last one. His fortune doesn't match his rank, though. The family's estates were in Cappadocia and they lost them to the Seljuks after Manzikert. Oh, and I've been told that he's as ugly as sin. The odd thing is that the Logothete hasn't seen fit to introduce us until now. I can only deduce that Skleros isn't his first choice. I suspect he approached other nobles who quite sensibly refused the undertaking.'

'It will be an interesting encounter.'

'Promise me something. Don't commit yourself to the journey, and don't let the minister take you in with his flattery.'

'I trust I'm too mature for that.'

'You haven't met him. He's a spider. You step onto his web with never a thought for the creature that spun it. By the time you feel the strands tremble and tighten, it's too late.'

A carriage and splendidly accoutred cavalry escort awaited them on the Prosphorion quay. They rattled through the streets, the horsemen clearing the way, citizens peering into the carriage and bowing in a way that made Hero feel rather grand. The Chalke Gate opened before them as if by magic, its white-uniformed guards springing to attention, and they bowled through immaculate gardens before drawing up at the Magnaura entrance. A eunuch with the springy gait of an energetic stork led them through cavernous halls, Hero gawping at the lavish decoration and statuary. He grinned at Vallon.

'This alone makes my journey worthwhile.'

'Remember my warning.'

The eunuch flung open ivory-panelled doors and announced the visitors in a fluting alto. Twenty yards away across an exquisite mosaic floor, a dozen grandees broke off their conversations and eyed the newcomers with guarded interest or rank suspicion.

The Logothete, dressed in a blue and silver kaftan, advanced with open arms. He had a velvety white complexion and black serpentine brows that met over a fastidious nose and a fleshy red mouth framed by a silky beard. Hero wondered if he was one of the bearded eunuchs.

'General Vallon, what a pleasure to see you again.' He beamed at Hero. 'And I'm delighted to make the acquaintance of such a distinguished physician and scholar.'

Vallon butted in with no consideration for protocol. 'Hero has responded to your invitation only out of respect for your elevated rank. In no way does his presence signify any desire to join the enterprise.'

The Logothete made an ambiguous gesture and concentrated his liquid gaze on Hero. 'I apologise for any misunderstanding. From the enthusiastic way Vallon spoke about you when we discussed the mission, I assumed that he would be delighted to have you at his side.'

Vallon spoke through clenched teeth. 'My Lord, nothing I said could have given that impression.'

The Logothete kept his gaze on Hero. 'As a diplomat, it's my job to search for the true meaning behind words, and from what Vallon told me, I certainly formed the opinion that he would greatly value your presence on a venture of such importance.' He swivelled to face Vallon. 'Am I wrong?'

'You know how much I admire Hero, but—'

'Good. It seems my judgement was correct.' The Logothete turned back to Hero. 'Of course, the decision is yours alone. If you decline, we'll return you to Italy at our expense and with something to compensate you for the inconvenience you have suffered. On the other hand—'

Vallon interrupted in English. 'Accept the offer. You can be gone within a week.'

Murmurs rose from the craning onlookers. Whether or not the Logothete understood English, he seemed to gather Vallon's meaning and frowned in rebuke. 'If you'd allow me to finish ...' He smiled at Hero. 'Naturally, if you did decide to join the embassy, we would reward you well, more than making up for the income you would have earned from your practice.'

Vallon attempted to speak. 'My Lord—'

'General, a gentleman of Hero's intelligence can surely decide for himself.'

Hero avoided Vallon's eye. 'I would need to hear all the details before reaching a decision.'

'Excellent,' said the Logothete. 'And after our discussions, per-haps you'd favour us with your company at an informal meal. I'd very much like to question you on some details about your travels in the north, particularly the time you spent in Rus.'

'My pleasure.'

With a triumphant glance at Vallon, the Logothete turned to the other guests. 'His Excellency, Duke Michael Skleros, imperial ambassador to the court of the Song emperor. Allow me to present General Vallon, commander of your escort, and his companion, Hero of Syracuse.'

It was all Hero could do to hide his shock. 'Ugly' didn't do jus-tice to Skleros. His appearance was repulsive – a fat and stunted body with a disproportionately large head on no neck to speak of, tiny mole-like eyes and a sagging bottom lip, long in the hip and short in the shank. Hideous. Hero should have felt pity for some-one so ill-favoured, but somehow the man left him feeling obscurely menaced.

Vallon made a bow. 'I'm honoured to serve such a distinguished servant of the empire.'

Skleros extended a podgy, manicured hand as if he expected Vallon to kiss it. 'General,' he said. For Hero he managed only a nod and flutter of the fingers.

The Logothete massaged his palms. 'General, we haven't been idle since our last meeting. We've received the guarantees of safe conduct through Seljuk territory. We're gathering supplies and have requisi-tioned transport for the Black Sea voyage. You'll sail to Trebizond in four ships. One will carry your military escort, the second Duke Skleros and his entourage, and the others the horses and supplies.' At a click of the Logothete's fingers, a clerk hurried to press documents into the hands of Vallon and one of Duke Michael's retainers. 'Inventories. Examine them carefully. If you spot any omissions or deficiencies, bring them to my attention immediately.'

During the ensuing discussion, Vallon sidled up to Hero. 'I trust that your encounter with the ambassador has banished your illusions.'

'He certainly has a most unfortunate appearance. I can only assume that the emperor chose him for other qualities.'

'Such as? His sneering condescension. Imagine being stuck with that bloated snob for the next three years.'

The Logothete clapped his hands. Double doors opened. 'If you'd care to follow me.'

Trailing behind the duke's party, Hero entered an antechamber artfully lit to display a hoard of treasures heaped on a table.

'These are the gifts for the Song emperor.'

The company circled the table, murmuring their appreciation. Hero didn't know where to rest his eyes. Two gold goblets set with amethysts and cabochons. A silk gown dyed purple with murex and embroidered with precious metals and pearls. A water clock mounted in a gilt bronze case. Icons depicting Jesus Christ and the Virgin Mary painted in encaustic by a master. A silver dish bearing a niello monogram of the emperor. Two lustreware chargers, one painted with a dromon, the other with a hunting scene ...

The Logothete leaned towards Hero. 'Fit for an emperor, would you say?'

Hero passed a hand over his eyes. 'They're wonderful objects.'

The Logothete craned closer. 'But? Don't be scared to speak out.'

One by one all turned until Hero was the focus of attention. 'My worry is that the emperor of China already possesses treasures beyond price.' Hero stroked the gown, a fabric so gorgeous that a wealthy man might labour all his life and never earn enough to possess it. 'Silk? It was China that originated the craft of silkmaking.' He pointed at the icons. 'The Chinese worship their own gods and ancestors.' He picked up one of the goblets. 'Gold and jewels? Yes, no ruler can have enough of them. The problem is, are you prepared to lavish sufficient to satisfy the Cathay emperor's appetite? The clock is very fine, but if Master Cosmas is to be believed, the Chinese make their own timepieces, including water-powered chronometers that stand as tall as a house and can track the planets as well as telling the hours. Again, Cosmas told me that the Cathay nobility dine off ceramics fairer and finer than anything crafted by our potters.' Hero hesitated. 'I'm sorry if I belittle your treasures.'

The Logothete darted a tight smile at his guests. 'No, this is why I brought you here.' He expanded his chest. 'So, what does Byzantium have to offer an emperor who apparently possesses everything?'

'Envy?' said Vallon.

The Logothete managed a pained smile. 'I didn't know you had a sense of humour, General.'

Hero smothered a laugh. It wasn't often Vallon made a joke. He composed his features. 'It occurs to me that the Cathay emperor might appreciate gifts of a more practical nature.'

The Logothete's eyes widened. 'Name them.'

'Manuals on engineering and medicine, warfare and governance. 'Also . . . ' Hero slid a glance at Vallon. 'The general told me that you hoped to obtain from China the formula for an awesome incendiary.'

'Fire Drug. Do you know about it?'

'No, but if it's so important, perhaps you should consider obtaining it in exchange for Greek Fire.'

The Logothete shook his head, shutting his eyes for emphasis. 'Out of the question.'

'But you expect the Chinese to share their own military technology.'

'If they won't divulge it willingly, you might have to resort to other methods.' The Logothete made a dismissive wave. 'I've already been through this with Vallon.'

'And I share the general's doubts,' Skleros said. 'Any diplomatic benefits we might gain would be wiped out if the Chinese discover that one of our aims is to steal a state secret. Even our lives might be put in jeopardy.'

The Logothete flung up a hand as if warding off something obscene. 'I didn't say "steal". I simply urge you to use whatever stratagems you can devise to obtain the formula. No doubt it will involve the exchange of money.' The Logothete's dark eyes roamed across his audience. 'I have only this to add. Return with the secret of Fire Drug and the emperor will reward you with twenty thousand solidi, to be shared between the duke and the general in the portion of two parts to one.

The guests glanced at each other. Hero boggled. Twenty thousand solidi amounted to more than two hundred pounds of gold. He turned his gaze towards Vallon and found the general's expression as hard as stone.

'Will we be armed with Greek Fire?' Vallon asked.

'Only for the voyage across the Black Sea. I don't suppose you want to lug barrels and cauldrons and siphons all the way to China.'

Vallon turned to Skleros. 'I understand that your retinue will number about forty.'

Skleros flicked a look at him before addressing the Logothete. 'Since you've encouraged us to speak our minds, allow me to express mine. I mean no disrespect to General Vallon, but our embassy would carry greater prestige if the commander and his troops were Greek. After all, you as minister for foreign affairs would be less inclined to take an embassy seriously if the majority of the party were foreign mercenaries.'

The Logothete's mouth opened in anticipation. 'Do you have an alternative?'

A bubble formed on Skleros's lower lip. 'Yes, I do. Justin Bardanes is a noble lord with a distinguished military record and a subtle grasp of diplomacy.'

The Logothete seemed to sadden. 'Bardanes plotted against the emperor and has shown no distinction in the field except to demonstrate how smartly he can retreat. I can't discern any recommending feature except for the fact that he's your cousin.'

Skleros reddened. Giving him no time to protest, the Logothete stabbed a finger in Vallon's direction.

'Whereas the general's credentials are beyond question. You all know about his extraordinary travels and his exemplary valour at

Dyrrachium. If you have reservations about his appointment, voice them to His Imperial Majesty. I'll arrange an audience if you wish.' The Logothete's voice dropped. 'But know this: it was our emperor, the grand and hallowed Alexius Comnenus, who personally selected Vallon for the mission.'

Skleros slunk back. 'I'll say no more.'

The Logothete bestowed a wide smile on the company. 'Then let's go in to lunch.'

The Logothete seated Hero on his left and quizzed him on various matters pertaining to his journey to the far north, the minister displaying an impressive grasp of geography and foreign affairs. The conversation turned to medicine and science, and here again the minister demonstrated an admirable breadth of knowledge. After listening to Hero's account of his work as a physician, he made a gesture that took in part of the palace behind him.

'The Magnaura has a fine library containing many rare medical texts. Perhaps you'd like to explore its treasures.'

'It would be a dream come true.'

'Is there a particular author whose works you'd like to study?'

'One of the physicians I most admire is Hunayn ibn Ishaq. He wrote a text called *Ten Treatises of the Eye* that I've been trying to track down for years.'

The Logothete's eyebrow formed a sinuous line. 'The name is familiar. Excuse me while I enquire.' The merest tilt of the head brought a clerk hurrying to his side. Their quiet exchanges ended in a brilliant smile aimed at Hero.

'We have two copies – both in the original Arabic, one of them penned by Hunayn himself. You're welcome to copy it, or if you prefer, I can assign the task to one of my *antiquarii*.'

'I would prefer to translate it myself. Even the most sensitive of scribes tends to make errors of interpretation when dealing with specialist subjects.'

'I understand.'

Conversation turned to other matters. Hero found the

Logothete an engaging and stimulating host and was rather disappointed when the minister rose to signal that the occasion was over. The minister escorted him to the door.

'I would have liked to talk longer. Unfortunately, I have to rehearse a formal reception for the Venetian ambassador. Let us meet again at your convenience. In the meantime ...' The Logothete handed Hero a small codex volume bound in ivory.

Hero opened it. There on the title page was Hunayn ibn Ishaq's signature in flowing calligraphy on papyrus. His bemused gaze darted up.

'A gift,' said the Logothete. 'Consider it small recompense for any misunderstanding I might have caused.' He raised a hand. 'No, no. I insist.'

'Thank you,' Hero said. 'Thank you.' He looked around with delight, his smile withering under Vallon's jaundiced leer. He cupped a hand to his mouth and whispered in English, 'I know what I'm doing.'

'Said the fly to the spider.'

VIII

Hero moved his table to catch the early morning light and opened the book. He had long admired Hunayn ibn Ishaq for his breadth of scholarship, but until now he'd been able to read only a fraction of his work, and that in poor translations. Hunayn, a Nestorian Christian born in Iraq at the beginning of the ninth century, had studied medicine in Baghdad and mastered Greek and Persian in order to translate scientific treatises written in those languages. He was no mere copyist, though. He interpreted and refined, applying his own practical experience to the books he rendered into Arabic or Syriac, and he also wrote more than a score of original works, including the *Ten Treatises*. His reputation stood so high that the

95

caliph had appointed him his personal physician and placed him in charge of the House of Wisdom, a school dedicated to the transmission of classical knowledge.

Hero leafed through the pages and came upon a detailed drawing of the human eye, all its parts illustrated. He studied it for some time before turning back to the beginning.

Peter interrupted to ask if he would be joining the household for breakfast, but Hero was so absorbed that he declined the invitation without raising his eyes from the page. He had read about half of the book when someone knocked on the door. He covered the text with his hand.

'Come in.'

Vallon entered, bade Hero a good day and crossed to the window. He stared across the strait. 'I've arranged your return passage. A merchant ship sails in three days. You'll slip aboard just before she casts off. You'll be beyond the Logothete's reach before he discovers that you've gone.'

Hero rubbed his eyes. 'I'm sorry to have put you to unnecessary trouble. I hope you didn't pay the fare in advance.'

Vallon turned. 'You're going on that ship if I have to carry you aboard myself.'

Hero gave him a quick look. 'Have you noticed anything amiss with my eyes?'

Vallon's brow furrowed. 'I know your vision isn't sharp.'

'Examine my left eye. Closer. Do you see it – a veil over the iris? The clouding is caused by what the ancients called a "cataract", or "foaming water". Every month it grows thicker. The condition doesn't correct itself. It becomes more acute with time and usually spreads to the other eye. If left untreated, I calculate that in five years I'll be blind.'

Vallon's throat pulsed. 'All the more reason to spend those years in profitable study rather than wasting them on a foreign adventure.'

Hero continued as if he hadn't spoken. 'Apart from the company of friends, reading is my greatest delight. Without books I can't acquire the knowledge I need to advance my medical skills. Without clear vision, I won't be able to practise those skills. In short, if I lost my sight I would lose my purpose.'

Vallon splayed a hand across his face. 'Hero ...'

'I come to the point. The book the Logothete gave me discusses diseases of the eye and their treatment. Cosmas told me that physicians in China have perfected an operation to remove cataracts by surgery. There. Isn't that a good enough reason to make the journey?'

Vallon swallowed. 'I'm sorry. I hadn't realised.'

'So let's agree that my mind is settled. Actually, it was settled the day I arrived.'

'If you're sure,' Vallon said in a husky voice.

'Quite sure. My motives are selfish, but I hope that what skills I've learned as a physician will prove useful on what I know will be a difficult journey.'

Vallon hung his head. 'Oh, Hero. You don't know how much your ...' He broke off, his hand going to the hip where his sword should have hung. Hero heard a shout. Vallon wrenched open the door and Wulfstan appeared, almost falling over himself in glee.

'What the devil's got into you?' Vallon snapped.

'Beg pardon,' Wulfstan gasped. 'Some kid just arrived with a message. An Englishman and his family, all wearing Seljuk dress, have landed at the Harbour of Theodosius, claiming they know Vallon the Frank.'

Hero and Vallon gaped at each other. 'It can't be.'

'It is,' Wulfstan said. 'The lad didn't give a name but said the man had corn-coloured hair and his woman had hair as pale as flax. And they've got a giant dog with them and two kiddies. The harbour guards won't let them leave.'

Vallon pushed past Wulfstan and strode into the hallway. 'My lady, come quick. Amazing news.'

Caitlin bustled in. 'What now? I can't take any more alarms.'

'Wayland and Syth have arrived in the city. We're going to collect them.'

Caitlin steepled her hands in front of her mouth and screamed. 'I'm coming with you.' She ran for the door. 'What about the girls?'

'Bring them with you. Aiken, too. Wulfstan, order a caique. It will be quicker than riding.'

On the ride down the Bosporus they worked themselves into a fever of speculation over what could have brought Wayland and his family to Constantinople.

'The Logothete must have sent for him,' said Hero.

'No. Wayland wouldn't uproot his family on the minister's say-so.' Vallon gestured towards Wulfstan and put a finger against his lips. 'Let's wait and see.'

The Harbour of Theodosius on the Marmara coast was Constantinople's largest port, built to handle Byzantium's grain imports from its former Egyptian colony. Vallon's party hurried down the quay, dodging stevedores and fishermen unloading catches.

'That must be them,' Wulfstan cried, pointing at a cordon of soldiers.

Their officer strode forward and saluted. 'General Vallon?'

'I believe you've detained an English family.'

Behind the soldiers, a tall blond man with Viking blue eyes rose from a bale. Up darted a slim lady, holding in each hand a tow-haired boy and girl, the boy clutching a miniature bow, the girl with tear-swollen eyes folding a doll to her chest. Beside them stood a long-limbed Anatolian shepherd dog with a tucked-up waist and shaggy cream and grey pelt.

'Syth!' Caitlin shrieked, and ran forward and gathered the woman in her arms. Vallon advanced at a stroll, smiling from ear to ear.

'Wayland.'

The Englishman smiled a lazy smile. Years of staring into the sun had etched a fan of lines around his eyes. He looked weary and his quilted tunic was travel-stained.

Syth smiled the lovely smile that still glowed in Vallon's memory. Two children hadn't spoiled her figure, and her eyes remained as clear as northern skies.

Wayland kissed his old companions. 'Captain Vallon, it's good to see you again after all these years.'

'He's a general now,' said Hero.

'There are no ranks between us,' said Vallon.

'Hero, I've often thought of you and I'm delighted that you look even cleverer than when we parted.' Wayland noticed Wulfstan and laughed. 'You're the last person I expected to see.'

Wulfstan threw out his chest. 'I'm the general's houseguard. A reformed character. I even go to church. Come here, you bastard, and let me hug you.'

Vallon presented Aiken. 'This is my adoptive son. He's English. His father was an officer in the Varangian Guard.'

Aiken shook Wayland's hand. 'It's an honour to make your acquaintance.'

Hero put the question that everyone wanted answering. 'What brings you to Constantinople?'

'Later,' said Vallon. He put his arm around Wayland. 'Let's take you home and then we'll chase all the missing years.'

The officer intervened. 'I'm sorry, General. The Englishman served at the Sultan of Rum's court. I'm afraid I can't release them until they've been properly examined.'

'The devil with that. I can vouch for them.'

'I'll need more than your word, General.'

'If that isn't good enough, I can vouch for them before the Logothete tou Dromou.'

'It's his officials I'm waiting for.'

'Then tell them they can find us at my villa, but not before tomorrow at the earliest. My friends need rest.'

Caitlin was already leading Syth and the children to the ferry, brushing aside a soldier who made a half-hearted attempt to detain her.

'Very good,' said the officer.

Wulfstan jostled Vallon's arm as they boarded the caique. 'Now we're all together again. Like old times.'

Vallon's tone was sad. 'No. Those days are gone, and we'll never see them again.'

On the trip back up the Bosporus, Caitlin handed out snacks from a basket. The children were called Brecc and Averil and regarded their counterparts with silent fascination before falling asleep in their mother's arms. The whole family gave off an air of exhaustion.

'Your rooms have been prepared,' said Vallon when they reached the villa. 'Sleep as long as you like. If you feel like joining us for supper, we usually dine at sunset.'

Caitlin showed the guests to their room. Hero waited until they'd left before turning to Vallon.

'It will be hard to keep the expedition a secret.'

'We simply tell them that I'm leaving for another tour of duty, and that you're accompanying me to observe the customs of the natives.'

Hero said no more on the matter and he and Vallon went to the study to go over the inventory drawn up by the Logothete. It ran to sixteen pages – so many horses and mules, javelins, suits of mail and lamellar armour, sacks of hardtack ...

Vallon put pen to paper. 'We'll be taking about one hundred and thirty horses and pack animals, each needing twenty pounds of dry fodder a day. The voyage to Trebizond could take two weeks, so that means we'll need ...' He began his calculations, making frequent crossings out and brushing his hair up into spikes.

'About thirty-five thousand pounds,' said Hero.

Vallon looked up from under his brows. 'How do you do that in your head?'

'With the aid of the signifier zero. It's quite simple. I can teach you how it works in less than an hour.'

Vallon held up a hand. 'Not that again. You know it's beyond my grasp. I'm too old to learn new ways.'

'Actually, I introduced Aiken to the concept and he picked it up straight away. Why don't you let him help with the inventory?'

'That's not a bad idea. It will teach him that soldiering isn't just about slaughtering and being slaughtered.'

'What will we do for provisions once we reach Trebizond? Will the governor be expecting us?'

'No, and he's going to have an unpleasant shock when I show him the imperial orders demanding that he opens his granaries and warehouses to us. After that we'll have to pay for our provisions. We'll be carrying fifty pounds of gold solidi, which the Logothete assures me is acceptable currency all along the Silk Road. On top of that there's the squadron's pay – a hundred and thirty men averaging two solidi a man every month for a year, with the remainder to be paid in arrears to those lucky enough to see home again.' Vallon cocked an eye. 'What does that add up to?'

Hero half-closed his eyes for a few moments. 'Forty-five pounds.'

'So a hundred pounds of gold plus the gifts for the Song emperor. Let's hope pirates don't get wind of our fortune.'

They were still ploughing through the inventory in late afternoon when a child's cry broke into their calculations. They went to the veranda to find Zoe seated on the dog's back, being led around the courtyard by Brecc, Caitlin looking on in apprehension. Wayland stood beside her freshly bathed and wearing a smart tunic of blue shot silk borrowed from Vallon's wardrobe.

'Are you sure that dog's safe?' Caitlin demanded.

'Don't worry. If the children plague him too much, he'll take himself off somewhere quiet.'

'I'm not taking about the *dog's* welfare. I meant, are my children safe with that brute?'

'He grew up with my own youngsters and has never so much as nipped them.'

'What's his name?'

'Batu. It means "faithful".'

'Is it the dog Syth picked out at the emir's encampment?'

'His son. Old Burilgi was killed by a bear two years ago.'

Caitlin's voice came from high in her throat. 'I don't think I want to hear any more. Wulfstan, don't take your eyes off my girls for one moment. I'm going inside to see Syth.'

The women and children dined separately, as was the custom in Constantinople. The evening was warm and the men ate in the courtyard, bats cutting erratic paths through the lamplight.

Vallon waited until the first course had been served. 'You haven't told us the reason for your flight.'

A gust of feminine laughter carried from the house. Wayland composed his hands on the table. 'We lived comfortably in Rum, but we never really adjusted to Seljuk ways. The curbs they place on women are hard to tolerate for English folk. Matters came to a head when one of the sultan's nephews asked to take Averil as his bride. It wasn't a request we could refuse, but we determined that our daughter should make her own choice of husband when she came of suitable age. We talked about it at length, not knowing what to do, until the sultan himself ordered us to send Averil to his nephew's household. We forged papers and joined a caravan travelling to Sinop, where we took ship for Constantinople. It wasn't as simple as I make it sound.'

'I can tell that your journey was fraught.'

'It was hard for the children.'

'What will you do?'

'Return to England. We're not penniless. I have enough gold to pay for the journey and buy a decent holding of land.' Clearly uncomfortable, Wayland changed the subject. 'But you, Hero. What brings you to Constantinople?'

Vallon answered before Hero could speak. 'A happy coincidence. Hero decided to pay a visit, and when I told him that my next posting was to the Danube border, he insisted on accompanying me.'

Hero examined his plate. 'In a few weeks, Vallon and I leave on a mission to China.'

Vallon grabbed the edge of the table so hard that the crockery rattled. 'I told you not to say one word about that matter.'

'You can't keep it a secret. Caitlin has probably already told Syth. And how would Wayland feel after we slip off and he learns that we've gone to the other side of the world? Explain what we're up to, and make it plain that there's no place on the expedition for a husband with two young children. Anything less would be a betrayal of our friendship.'

Vallon subsided. 'You're right.' He smiled at Wayland. 'No man in his right mind would choose to accompany me. And as commander of the expedition, I would reject anyone who did volunteer as a fool.'

Wayland's response was mild. 'Hero's no fool.'

'Hero has his own good reasons for making the journey, and he doesn't have family.'

Wayland turned his slow gaze. 'Aiken, what about you? Will you be going?'

Aiken glanced at Vallon. 'Yes.'

Vallon choked in surprise. He coughed and thumped his chest. 'We agreed that you'd stay and continue your studies. I thought that's what you wanted.'

'I changed my mind.'

'Have you told Caitlin?'

'Not yet.'

Vallon ran a hand through his hair and looked around with a wild stare. 'We'll discuss this later.'

'In that case, will you excuse me? I have to finish a grammar exercise.'

Vallon watched in disbelief as the boy left. 'By the Virgin's bloody tears! I feel like the only full-witted man in an asylum.'

Hero filled the strenuous silence. 'Aiken is a promising scholar,' he told Wayland. 'He speaks Greek as well as I do and has an impressive flair for logic.'

'I don't doubt it,' Wayland said. 'I've only had one conversation with him, but I was struck by the way he leads you through

103

a sentence only to leave you in a place where you didn't expect to be.'

Vallon sat slumped over his drink, his expression blasted. 'Caitlin will never forgive me if I take him.'

'Why not?' said Wayland. His gaze drifted between Vallon and Hero. 'You'd better tell me more about this enterprise of fools.'

Vallon told him, stressing all the negative aspects. When he'd finished, Wayland sat with a half-smile. The house had fallen quiet, only one window lit. Wayland stifled a yawn. 'Well, that certainly sounds like a journey too far, but I'm too tired to take it all in.' He rose from his seat. 'Would you mind if I retire?'

Vallon stood. 'Before you go, let's drink a toast.' He hoisted his wine cup. 'To good friends and loyal companions. And here's to the next generation. May they be as blessed by fortune as their parents.'

Vallon followed Wayland into the house and barged into Aiken's room.

'What the hell are you playing at? First you don't want to go, then you do. Explain your fickleness.'

Aiken laid down his quill and seemed to consider a whole range of responses before selecting the one that best suited his purpose. 'I decided to see where an irrational decision would lead me.'

Vallon's face screwed up in incomprehension. 'What?'

'You're travelling to a distant empire. Your chances of returning are slim, so I would be foolish to go with you. At the same time, if I stay, not a day will pass without me worrying about you and feeling guilt that I wasn't at your side – a duty I swore to my father. I have to decide between logic and emotion. It should be easy, but it isn't. In this case, sentiment overrides reason. Or rather, they balance each other. What tips the scales is Hero's presence on the expedition. I know I can learn from him more than I can garner from my teachers at the academy and so I choose to throw in my lot with him.' Aiken picked up his pen. 'I trust that answers your question, General.'

'Call me "father".'

'I find that as awkward as it is for you to call me "son". I had the same problem with Beorn. I addressed him as "father", though I knew he wasn't anything of the sort.'

'He loved you and treated you as his son. That's all that matters.'

'And I'm eternally grateful.' Aiken stared away, smiling slightly. 'To satisfy your curiosity, my real father was an English priest at Canterbury. My mother told me before she died, and she also told me that she wasn't the only woman he seduced.'

Vallon rubbed the back of his neck. 'Have you told Lady Caitlin of your decision?'

'Not yet. I'll inform her before she goes to bed.'

Vallon's response was weak, almost pleading. 'Leave it until tomorrow. My lady has had an eventful day.'

'No, decisions are best announced as soon as they're made.' Aiken plied his pen. 'Now, I really do have to finish this exercise.'

Vallon's anxiety boiled into fury. 'From now on, the only exercises you'll perform will be on the field of Mars.' He pointed a trembling finger. 'You'll join my squadron at Hebdomon and you'll be treated like any other recruit.'

Aiken continued writing. 'I expect nothing else.'

'Pass me the wine,' Vallon said when he returned. He drank as if he couldn't force it down fast enough. 'I can't believe it,' he spluttered. 'Aiken says he's coming with us so that he can be with you.'

Hero made to rise. 'I'll have a word with him.'

'No,' Vallon snarled. 'He's made his decision. Let him live with it.'

Hero moved his cup in a circle. 'That still leaves Wayland.'

Vallon banged his cup down. 'No, it doesn't. I'm the commander of the expedition. I decide who joins it, and that doesn't include Wayland.'

A moth blundered into the lamp. Hero rescued it only to see it flutter back to the mantle and beat against the glass until its wings scorched and it fell twitching to the table. He looked up at the night sky.

'The stars are bright tonight. They remind me of the heavens above Iceland and the northern aurora in Rus.'

Vallon poured more wine. 'I remember puking my guts out in the North Sea and eating moss soup in the forests of Rus.'

'I remember floating down the Dnieper and seeing the city of Kiev appear through a golden dawn.'

'And I remember blistered hands and loose bowels and burying companions in shallow graves a thousand miles from home.'

'I know, and the strange thing is that I never felt more alive than when we were most imperilled.'

Vallon ducked his head. 'Don't.'

'Go to bed, sir. It's been a long day.'

'Yes. I apologise for my intemperate speech. You retire. I'd like to sit a while and contemplate.'

Hero's voice carried out of the dark. 'Wayland will make up his own mind.'

'No, he won't. I've already made it up for him.'

Vallon stayed in the courtyard after the lamp had burned out. The constellations cast a frosty glaze on the roof tiles. Somewhere in the distance a woman sang a sad refrain to a lute accompaniment. Vallon poured a last cup and looked round with a snarl. 'Wulfstan, stop lurking in the shadows and come and share what's left of this wine.'

The Viking approached out of the darkness most delicately and scuffed one foot on the ground. 'General, allow me to make a heartfelt request.'

'Request refused.'

'You haven't heard it yet.'

'Yes, I have. You want to join me, like the other lunatics. Well, you can't. Your place is here, attending to my family.'

Wulfstan drew himself up. 'With respect, sir, you could find a thousand men to guard the house and deal with tradesmen selling nick-nacks.'

Vallon slapped the bench. 'Sit down and fill a cup.' He drank from his own. 'My next assignment will be the most testing of my career.'

'All the more reason why I should be at your side.'

'You were at my side on the Dnieper and left me in the lurch.'

Wulfstan grimaced. 'I'll never desert you again. My word before God. Besides, Aiken will need me. I can't fathom the lad, but I've grown fond of him and want to be there to look out for him.' Vallon must have glanced at his stump. 'Don't worry about that. Even with one hand, I'm a better soldier than most.'

'It's not that. This campaign is no ordinary military venture.'

'I know.'

'How?'

'The troubled expression you've worn since you returned from the palace in winter. Your lady's tears. The way Hero turned up out of the blue. The hours you and him spend shut away. And now Wayland's arrival.'

Vallon made a violent fanning gesture. 'Wayland's no part of it. He has a family to look after.'

'But I don't – not one of my own.'

Vallon raised bleary eyes. 'You really want to come?'

'I do, sir. Much as I love your family, I'm going nuts guarding a door. I may be a Christian; I love the chanting in church. But I'm still a Viking.'

Vallon sighed. 'Oh, God. Why not?'

Wulfstan pumped Vallon's hands. 'Thank you, General. You won't find me wanting.'

'My lady will need another house minder.'

'I've already found one. Pepin, the veteran who steered Lucas to your door.'

Vallon glanced towards the gatehouse. 'I'd almost forgotten about Lucas. All right, arrange for Pepin to meet me.'

He walked rather unsteadily towards the house and found Peter

107

waiting inside the door with a cowled lamp. 'Everyone's asleep,' the servant whispered. 'Your English guests are quite worn out.'

Vallon followed Peter's light, stole into his bedchamber and in an agony of stealth slid under the covers. Caitlin's nightdress caressed his skin. He closed his eyes and was almost asleep when he realised from her tiny convulsions that she was weeping. He sat up and leaned over.

'Aiken told you.'

She swung round and threw her arms around him. Tears splashed on his cheek.

'I'm pregnant and this time I know it's a boy.'

'But that's marvellous, a cause for celebration.'

She swung her head, her hair swishing across Vallon's cheeks. 'I know you won't live to see either him or me, and Aiken tells me he means to go with you. You're robbing me of everything I hold dear.'

IX

Hero removed the bandage from Lucas's head and examined the wound. 'Those stitches can come out. You're a quick healer and you've got a thick skull. How are your ribs?'

'Knitting well. I've seen Wayland. He looks exactly as I imagined him. Eyes like blue flames.'

'Why are you grinning like that?'

Lucas reclined on his pillows. 'I've been thinking. First you arrive in Constantinople and then a week later Wayland turns up.'

'So?'

'It's obvious. You must be off on another adventure.'

Hero bridled. 'For an uninvited guest, you display unwarranted familiarity. In any case, you're wrong. Wayland's returning to England with his family.'

Lucas watched Hero make for the door. 'I know something's going on. I've never seen Wulfstan so cheerful, singing hymns all day long. And yesterday I saw him sharpening his sword and polishing his armour. He's preparing to go on campaign.'

Hero seemed about to speak, thought better of it, then exited, leaving Lucas grinning in his wake.

A few days later Lucas was staring, bored and fretful, through the window when Wulfstan stuck his head through the door. 'Are you up to riding a horse?'

'Of course I am. There isn't a steed I can't manage.'

'Don't be so cocky. The general doesn't like it and it's him you have to impress.'

'You mean ...'

'No promises, but demonstrate you're a good horseman and Vallon might find you a place in his squadron.'

For all Lucas's swagger, he approached the stable with churning trepidation. Vallon's casual glance struck like a blow. This was the first time the general had seen his face. Surely he'd spot some family resemblance.

Vallon barely registered his presence before nodding at a placid-looking bay mare.

'Let's see if your actions match your boasts.'

Lucas swung into the saddle with one move and waited for Vallon to mount with stiff decorum. They ambled out into the open country beyond Galata. Vallon drew rein.

'Show me your paces. Don't force it. Have consideration for your ribs.'

For the next half hour, Lucas trotted, cantered, wheeled, stopped and backed up, finally urging his horse into a circling gallop that brought him up short within three feet of the general.

'I'm used to more fiery mounts,' he gasped.

'When did you learn to ride?'

'Before I could walk.'

'That would explain your good seat. I like the way you don't rely too much on your stirrups.'

109

'I didn't ride with stirrups until I was eight.'

Vallon watched a buzzard rising on a thermal. 'Are you fit enough to wield a sword in earnest? If not, say so. I won't hold it against you.'

'I think I am, sir.'

Without another word, Vallon turned his horse and headed back to the villa. Lucas kept darting glances at him, words rising unbidden before choking in his throat.

'Is something bothering you?' Vallon said without looking round.

'No, sir.' Lucas's tongue felt thick. Now wasn't the time. He'd know the right moment when it came.

Next morning Wulfstan arrived with a suit of padded lint, a helmet and a wooden practice sword.

'Who am I fighting?'

'Aiken.'

'Aiken! He fights like a girl.'

Wulfstan's eyes widened alarmingly. 'Would you rather cross blades with me?'

'It would be a more even contest.'

The Viking clipped Lucas around the head. 'Cheeky bastard. Even with only one hand, I could spit you in six moves. That's for another day. Come on. Vallon's waiting.'

In the courtyard garden that served for an arena, Aiken mooched in nervous circles. Vallon and Hero stood at a distance.

'Don your helmets,' Wulfstan said.

'I don't need one,' said Lucas. 'It's not as if we're using real swords.'

Wulfstan bristled. 'I've seen men die from pates cracked by practice swords. Put it on.' He retreated a few paces. 'Bow, touch swords and engage.'

For a while Aiken held his own, countering with some elegant moves and even threatening a flank attack. Once Lucas broke through his guard, though, the English youth's defences collapsed. He fell apart, shrinking into a flat-footed cringe and wafting his

110

sword in a feeble attempt to keep his opponent at bay. Lucas rained blows on him, each stroke precisely delivered, one to each quarter and then a one-two to the head that staggered Aiken. Lucas began to play with his opponent, walking in a tight circle around him, naming the part he would strike next.

'That's enough,' said Wulfstan. He grabbed Lucas's arm. 'I said that's enough.'

Lucas lowered his sword and skipped from foot to foot, panting and sweating. 'I still haven't recovered my full strength.'

Aiken, scarlet with humiliation, swung his sword listlessly then walked away.

Wulfstan and Vallon conversed. Lucas waited for their verdict, smug in the knowledge that he'd trounced an opponent who'd received professional training. His grin died when Vallon beckoned him over.

'Your master taught you well, but you've got a lot to learn. For a start, you don't toy with an opponent. If he presents an opening, you go for the kill. That's your job. Showing off is unprofessional, vain and ugly. I won't allow it in my command.'

Lucas reddened and looked down. 'Does that mean you'll let me serve under your standard?'

'Tomorrow you join the Outlanders at Hebdomon. Aiken will be going with you. The two of you will be the youngest members of the squadron. I trust that you'll look out for each other, like true spear-companions.'

Lucas's chest fluttered with excitement. 'Thank you, sir.'

'There are only twenty Franks in the squadron. The rest are drawn from all over the empire and beyond. That's why we're called the Outlanders. You'll be serving alongside Thracians, Macedonians, Bulgarians, Serbs, Poles, Hungarians, Russians, Armenians, Pechenegs, Cumans, Seljuks … If God made him, he's in my squadron. And the thing is, they're a tight outfit, rough and ready but always loyal to each other. Fit in and they'll defend you to the death. Show them the contemptuous attitude you presented to Aiken and they'll smother you under your mattress on your first night.'

111

Lucas examined his feet.

'You'll be entering the tower of Babel,' Vallon continued. 'Greek is our common language. You'll take lessons daily and in two weeks I expect you to understand the basic commands. Do you have anything to say?'

Lucas raised his eyes. Vallon's expression conveyed professional impatience. Lucas contemplated the ground again.

'I won't disappoint you,' he said. Then, writhing at his betrayal of his slaughtered mother and dead siblings, he added 'sir' in a tone that made Vallon squint at him before turning away.

'Your manners could do with improving,' the general said. 'Look to them.'

Lucas and Aiken travelled to the barracks together on a caique, Aiken with his head in a book the entire journey, Lucas contemptuous yet intrigued that words on a page could be so absorbing.

'What are you reading?' he said at last.

'Euclid's *Geometry*.'

'What's that about?'

Aiken didn't look up. 'If you have to ask, you wouldn't understand.'

Lucas sucked in his cheeks and smiled around for the benefit of an invisible audience. He stretched out his legs. 'You think you're clever.'

Aiken transferred only part of his attention from the book. 'I know I am. It's one of the few things I'm certain of.'

Lucas pulled in his legs and leaned forward. 'Your book learning won't be of much use in the army.'

'I'm aware of that.'

Lucas sniffed. 'I expect you think that being Vallon's son will make things go easy for you.'

A contemptuous glance from Aiken. 'That shows how little you know the general.'

Lucas composed his next words with care. 'I've never heard you call him "father".'

'Because he isn't.'

'Do you wish he was?'

Aiken laid his book down. 'I wish I'd known my real father. He wasn't Beorn, as I expect you've heard.'

Aiken's frankness reduced Lucas to silence.

'What about your family?' Aiken said.

'Dead. All except my father. He disappeared on campaign when I was five.'

Aiken's quiet eyes engaged his. 'I'm sorry.'

For a moment the two youths faced each other across the voids in their lives. Lucas broke the bond with a ragged laugh. 'I know he's still alive. I've got proof of it. One day I'll catch up with him, and when I do ...' Lucas swung his head and stared into the wave glitter.

'I pray that the day will come soon,' said Aiken. He took up his book again. 'If you don't mind ... I suspect I won't have much time for reading in the barracks.'

Hebdomon Fort on the Marmara shore housed four squadrons, each occupying a square complex with three barracks, a bath house large enough to serve a hundred men, a stable block, a parade ground, granaries, storerooms and an armoury. Outside the perimeter an exercise field sloped down to the sea.

A guard at the gate marched Lucas and Aiken to the duty officer's quarters. Soldiers lounging outside their barracks followed their progress with mild curiosity. Vallon was right about them being drawn from all corners and cultures. Lucas saw blue-eyed, tattooed giants from realms of mist and snow, agate-eyed Turks as lean as whips, small dark men from unknown mountain fastnesses, warriors with tribal scars. Some wore beards; others were clean-shaven. The only thing they seemed to have in common was a drab green uniform and an unforced air of toughness.

The guard led the two youths inside one of the barracks, stopped outside an office and saluted. 'The new troopers reporting for duty, sir.'

113

A trim man of middling height rose from a table covered with papers. His fingers were ink-stained and his eyes strained from writing. An embroidered gold roundel on his tunic indicated his rank.

'My name's Josselin,' he said in French. 'Second Centurion in the Outlanders. You'll be attached to my *hekatontarchia*. Your pay is six solidi a year, rising to nine solidi after a year's service. Payment is made every four months. Trooper Lucas, half your pay will be withheld to pay off the cost of your horse and equipment. At that rate you'll clear the debt in three years – unless you win promotion or share in the spoils of war. It's important that you learn to speak Greek. I've arranged lessons for you – an hour a day after your ordinary duties.'

Centurion Josselin then lectured them about hygiene and warned them about the perils of gambling and intercourse with either sex. 'The punishment for minor offences ranges from withdrawal of your wine ration to a twenty-mile forced march in full kit. More serious offences merit a flogging. Vallon doesn't like seeing his men flogged; he'd rather dismiss the offender. For treachery or desertion, the sentence is death. In six years, we've had only two executions. Have you taken all that in?'

Lucas had listened in a daze. All he could think of was that he was in a cavalry unit and was even being paid and fed.

He and Aiken went through the swearing-in ceremony. 'We swear by God, Christ and the Holy Spirit, and by the Majesty of the Emperor – which second to God is to be loved and worshipped as His commander on Earth – that we will strenuously do all that the Emperor may command, will never desert the service, nor refuse to die for the Byzantine state.'

'You're now members of the Outlanders,' said Josselin. He nodded at the waiting guard. 'Show these men their billet.'

Eight men occupied two adjoining whitewashed rooms in one of the barracks. The outer chamber was a common room. Some off-duty troopers broke off games of dice. Three NCOs stood to receive the new recruits. A man with gap teeth laughed.

'Maybe we should change our name to the Baby-Snatchers.'

'That will do,' said the tall, slope-shouldered senior NCO. He studied the new recruits. 'I'm Aimery, your *dekarchos,* leader of ten.' He spoke softly and had a kindly manner. He gestured at the other soldiers. 'These are your squadmates. You'll eat, sleep and drill with them. On campaign you'll share a tent and in battle you'll fight as a unit. Your beds are in the next room. Keep them immaculate.'

'What happened to the men we're replacing?' said Aiken.

Aimery's expression didn't alter. 'One died of fever on the Danube, the other was killed by the Normans at Dyrrachium.'

He showed the recruits into the dormitory, its floor clean enough to eat off. Aiken dumped two heavy kitbags on his bed. Lucas possessed only a few personal items in a satchel.

Aimery turned to one of his NCOs. 'Gorka, take trooper Lucas to the stores. Gorka is my *pentarchos*, leader of five. He'll be in charge of your basic training.'

Even before the sergeant said the name, Lucas had guessed that Gorka was a Basque. The heavy brow forming a straight line, the long ear lobes, the barrel chest. On the walk to the quartermaster's store, Lucas wondered if he should tender some remark about their shared homeland, but decided from Gorka's expression that pleasantries weren't in order.

Gorka dumped himself on a bale of tents while the quartermaster outfitted Lucas. He handed him two knee-length tunics, two pairs of breeches, all in linen, and a wide leather belt. For cold weather he provided an ankle-length woollen tunic and a wool cloak fastened by a fibula in the shape of a flying falcon. The same motif was woven on the right chest of the tunics. A felt hat and two pairs of sandals completed Lucas's day-to-day wear.

'I expected the uniform to be more colourful,' Lucas said.

Gorka came off the bale. 'Colourful,' he said. He looked from side to side as if he doubted his hearing. 'We're scouts and raiders. We blend in. We don't flutter around like a bunch of butterflies.'

Lucas flinched from his gaze. Gorka's green-brown eyes suggested a capacity for infinite malice. He lurched towards the door with a wrestler's gait and Lucas followed, resolving to keep his mouth shut.

The armoury was the next stop – a hall surrounded by a warren of bays and alcoves exuding the odours of leather, iron and wax. A one-legged veteran and three assistants presided over the martial emporium. The armourer, propped on crutches, sized Lucas up and said something. An assistant rummaged in one of the bays and brought back a heavy quilted jacket that had seen better days. On it he placed a battered iron helmet with an aventail of boiled-leather lappets that gave some protection to the neck. He also produced a pair of knee-length leather boots. Lucas was disappointed. He'd dreamed of receiving a bodice of mail or, even better, a coat of lamellar armour.

Gorka read his mind. 'Forget it. You'd still be paying off mail or scale by the time you retire. The only way you'll come by decent armour is by stripping it off the enemy.'

The armourer's assistants had disappeared into the bowels of the depot. One came back with a short recurved bow, a canvas case and three coiled bowstrings. The second with a lance and two javelins. The third with a shield and sword.

Gorka picked up the bow. 'Ever used one of these?'

'Not a bow shaped like that.'

'It's Turkish, designed to be shot from horseback.'

Lucas opened his mouth.

So did Gorka. 'Got something to say?'

'I wasn't expecting to be deployed as an archer. The Normans don't—'

Gorka was chest to chest with him in a flash. 'We don't fight like Normans. Every man in our squadron must be skilled with sword, bow and lance.'

'Sir.'

'No need to "sir" me. Call me "boss".'

'Yessir ... boss.'

Gorka demonstrated how the bow fitted into its case. 'You keep the cover waterproofed with wax and tallow.' He patted a pocket

116

on the side. 'Strings go in there. No excuse for a limp bow or slack string.'

The armourer took hold of Lucas's right hand, examined the thumb and emptied a box of curious-looking horn rings onto the counter. A projection stuck out from the thick bands, curved on one side, flat on the other. He selected one and twisted it onto Lucas's thumb. Too large, apparently, the next too small. He tried three more before finding one that fitted neatly behind the first thumb joint.

'Your archery instructor will show you what it's for,' said Gorka. 'Don't lose it.'

Lucas regarded the scabbarded sword, the haft wrapped with scuffed and sweat-stained leather, the pommel a roughly worked iron finial. He looked for permission to handle it, and when Gorka nodded, he drew the blade. A workaday weapon that had seen a lot of use, the metal pitted and nicks along both edges. Even so, he grinned as he angled it to the light. He took up the circular shield, leather-covered on a wicker base, the front painted with a white falcon on a field of green. It looked magnificent. He fitted his hand in the grip and took guard.

'You keep your equipment spick and span,' Gorka said. 'Centurion Josselin holds a weekly inspection and woe betide if you fall short. You can start by polishing your helmet. And I see some of the stitching on the corselet is working loose. And those boots could do with a polish. Pick your kit up later. Now we'll see about a horse.'

'Why isn't Aiken with us?' Lucas asked on the way to the stables.

'Trooper Aiken's outfit was sent on ahead.'

Of course. Vallon would have supplied Aiken with brand-new equipment at his own expense, all of the best quality and of Aiken's choosing. The sour thought dissolved as Lucas approached the stables. Please God, he prayed, don't let them give me a broken-down nag.

The chief groom led them between two lines of stalls, Lucas breathing in the peppery scents of horse flesh, dung and tack. He hardly knew where to look. There wasn't a horse in the stable that he didn't admire. The groom stopped at a stall housing a dappled grey gelding. One look at its head, its full, intelligent eyes, and Lucas knew he hadn't been given second best. He looked over the stall and uttered a sort of moan before turning with shining eyes.

'For me?'

Gorka sniffed. 'The general says you're not a bad rider. His name's Aster. He's five years old. Treat him well.'

Lucas stroked Aster's muzzle and murmured his name. The horse blew in his face and his heart brimmed over. He spoke to cover his emotions. 'Do the officers ride stallions?'

Gorka snorted. 'Our horses are our friends. Unlike the Normans, we don't want to be forever fighting the brutes.'

On the walk back to his quarters, Lucas summoned up the courage to ask a question. 'Sir ... boss ... can I visit the stables in my free time?'

Gorka glanced at him. 'Free time? You won't see any of that, laddie.'

If that day was anything to go by, he was right. Lucas fell into bed long after the other troopers had given up their games, having spent an hour with his Greek tutor and two hours polishing his sword and helmet. Aiken slept next to him and over his bed hung a magnificent suit of armour.

'I could help you with your Greek,' Aiken said.

Lucas stirred from a doze. 'I can manage.'

'Do you like your horse?'

'He's not bad,' Lucas said. 'Better than I expected.'

'Hero bought him for you.'

'Hero? Why would he do that?'

'He's kind. He's the main reason why I decided to come.'

Lucas sank back. 'Do you know what we're doing tomorrow?'

'They're going to test our weapon skills.' Aiken shivered. 'I'm dreading it.'

*

After reveille and ablutions, Aimery inspected his unit before they headed for the mess hall and a breakfast of millet porridge, wheat bread and watered wine. Then they swept and scrubbed their quarters under Gorka's merciless scrutiny.

'Bring your weapons,' he said. 'Today I'll find out how much grief you're going to cause me.' He led the way to the exercise ground and halted in a space surrounded by dozens of other soldiers practising their martial skills. 'First, a sparring session with practice swords.' He frowned. 'Did I say something funny?'

Lucas knew he was taking a risk. 'I've already been tested against Aiken and trounced him. I should face a sterner match.'

Aiken reddened under Gorka's scrutiny. 'It's true.'

Gorka turned to Lucas with a dreamy smile. 'So you fancy yourself as a swordsman.'

'General Vallon himself said I showed promise.'

Gorka allowed himself a moment of malign speculation before scanning the arena. He cupped his hands around his mouth. 'Sergeant Stefan, I wonder if you could spare a moment.'

A hard-bitten little Serb wandered up, practice sword resting over his shoulder. Gorka cocked a finger at Lucas. 'Our new trooper thinks he needs tougher opposition than his spear-companion can offer. Perhaps you'd oblige.'

Stefan smiled a pleasant smile and raised his sword. Lucas took guard.

A blur of movement and he was looking cross-eyed down Stefan's blade, the point arrested a few inches short of his throat.

'I wasn't ready,' he said.

Gorka laughed. 'All Stefan's opponents would have said that if they were still alive to speak.'

Again Lucas took guard. Stefan crooked his brows in enquiry. Lucas nodded and shifted from foot to foot. This time he almost made contact with Stefan's sword before the blade threatened his head again.

He skipped back. 'It's not a style I'm used to.'

'Oh dear,' said Gorka. 'Not his style.' He lowered his head and shouted into Lucas's face. 'The enemy doesn't ask what style of swordplay you prefer before engaging in combat.' He smiled his evil smile. 'Still, the lad's young. Sergeant, let him fight the way he's used to.'

What followed was abject humiliation. Lucas managed a few counters but was always one move behind and on the back foot. Stefan landed two blows to the ribs that hurt even through the padding, followed up with a blow to the helmet that made Lucas see stars, and finished by chopping Lucas's wrist with a clip that numbed him to the elbow.

Almost weeping from pain and shame, he picked up his fallen sword.

'Thank you, Sergeant,' said Gorka. 'That was a pleasure to watch.' He squinted at Lucas. 'In future, you do exactly what I tell you.' He turned on his heel. 'Now collect your horses and we'll try you with lance and javelin.'

Lucas partly redeemed himself in these exercises, which involved throwing a javelin at a straw dummy from horseback and aiming a lance at the quintain. Aiken showed no aptitude at all, unable to strike either target even at a canter, while Lucas hit the quintain at his first pass and only missed by a whisker with the javelin.

Gorka regarded him with narrowed eyes. 'Again, at an extended canter.'

Lucas hit both targets. Aiken took a blow in the back from the quintain as it spun round from his half-hearted effort.

Gorka put his hands on his hips. 'This time at a gallop.'

Lucas trotted off, turned, patted Aster's neck and spurred him into a charge. He drew back the javelin and launched, the point taking the target square in the chest. He trotted back to pick up the lance, swung round and once more galloped up to the quintain, hitting it with a force that spun it twice on its axis.

Gorka eyed him. 'You've done that before.'

'Many times, but only in my imagination.'

*

Next it was archery under the supervision of a Pecheneg called Gan, a horse nomad recruited from the steppes north of the Danube. He wore his hair in long braids behind his ears and his eyes were crescent slivers above padded cheekbones. He didn't speak French and Gorka had to translate.

'Show Gan your draw,' he told the recruits.

Lucas demonstrated. He sneaked a glance at Gorka. 'I'm used to a heavier bow.'

'You need a light bow to develop the correct technique. You have to learn a new method of releasing. Have you got your thumb ring?'

Lucas fished it out. Gan produced one of his own and demonstrated how to use it, sliding it over the first thumb joint with the flat side of the projection facing back. Gorka relayed instructions. 'See how he hooks the ring onto the string and holds it in place by gripping the tip of his thumb with his forefinger. That way the string doesn't touch the finger – less strain and no finger-pinch, meaning greater accuracy.'

Three times Gan went through the sequence of preliminary moves before releasing the arrow. He swivelled at the hip, drawing with the bow above his head, then in an extension of the move, he lowered it and loosed without apparent aim at a butt about sixty yards away. Lucas blinked as it struck, blinked again as Gan shot another arrow. Nor did the archer stop there. In the space of a minute he released twelve arrows with breathtaking fluency. Every arrow hit the mark.

'Gan's as accurate on horseback at full gallop,' said Gorka. He stepped back. 'Now you try.'

The technique seemed pretty basic, yet no matter how hard Lucas concentrated, he couldn't master the knack. With his first few attempts, he couldn't even string the arrow. It kept dropping off. When he did draw, he couldn't time the release. On his sixth attempt, the bowstring caught the tip of his thumb, ripping off the end of his nail and leaving the nail bed bleeding.

'You're releasing too slow,' said Gorka. 'Imagine you're flicking a marble.'

By the time the session was over, Lucas had taken the skin off his left wrist and his best shot hadn't come within five feet of the target. What made it more galling was the fact that Aiken landed two arrows on the mark.

'It takes practice,' said Gorka. 'Practice, practice, practice.' He nodded at something Gan said and translated. 'If you ignore archery for one day, it will desert you for ten.'

Walking back to the dormitory, Lucas vowed to master all branches of weaponry. He knew he would never achieve the standard of the Turkish archers who had drawn their first bows at the age of five, but he would do his best.

'You impressed Gorka with your equestrian skills,' Aiken said.

Lucas decided he could afford a concession. 'You handled the bow better.'

Aiken shrugged. 'I've been using the thumb ring for years. Another week and you'll have left me behind.'

'You don't seem to care.'

'Not really.'

'Then why did you join the cavalry?'

'Because Beorn wished it and because Vallon insists I honour those wishes.'

'What would you prefer to be doing?'

'Studying philosophy and natural science.'

'You're weird.'

That was as close as Lucas came to unbending with Aiken. Over the following days he grew increasingly irked by the fact that though he surpassed Aiken in every branch of arms, Gorka overlooked the English youth's cack-handed deficiencies and treated him with a respect that bordered on deference – all because he was the adopted son of their commander. Meanwhile, he pounced on every mistake that Lucas made.

Rancour spilled over on the morning Josselin was due to inspect his century. Lucas pulled on his shabby armour. Not only was it second-hand, but it looked as if it had been stripped from a battle casualty, with two obstinate stains he was sure were blood. He picked up his helmet, eyeing the fresh dent Stefan had inflicted. All the polishing in the world wasn't going to make it look like anything other than a stew-pot. When he'd finished dressing, he watched with sour envy as Aiken donned his outfit. Over a patterned quilt undercoat he pulled on a corselet of lamellar armour made up of overlapping blued steel plates, the rounded ends facing upwards. He fitted shoulder guards and arm plates.

'That lot's wasted on you,' Lucas said.

Gorka stuck his head around the door. 'Aren't you ready yet? There'll be hell to pay if you're late.'

Red-faced and sweating, Aiken sat on his bed struggling to strap iron greaves to his calves. He threw Lucas a desperate look. 'Lend a hand, will you?'

Lucas almost refused. Let him be late for the inspection and suffer the consequences. With ill grace, Lucas knelt and buckled on the greaves. 'I suppose Vallon paid for all this.'

'With the money I inherited from my father.'

'I don't understand why he would waste so much gold on someone with so little military aptitude.'

'It's because I lack soldierly skills that I need the armour. It's the only thing protecting me.'

'And you expect me to fight at your side.'

Aiken looked down, smiling. 'Oh, I wouldn't rely on me. I'll probably run away as soon as I see the enemy.'

Lucas tightened the last strap with a savage jerk. 'You even boast of your cowardice.'

The *dekarchos* heard him. Aimery strolled up, a musing expression on his face. His thoughts always seemed to be miles away. 'You're looking fit today, trooper.'

Lucas scrambled to attention. 'Sir.'

'Have you seen much of our beautiful city?'

'Not a lot, sir. I only spent one night in it and somebody tried to kill me.'

123

'I wonder why I'm not surprised. Could it be that you have a knack for putting people's backs up?'

'Sir.'

Aimery stood with legs akimbo, hands behind his back. 'Since you've had no chance to enjoy the sights, I've got a treat for you. Run around the city walls as far as the Golden Horn. The Gate of Charisius is particularly fine, I'm told. I'd be interested to hear your description of it when you return.'

There and back was twenty miles and by the time Lucas hobbled into barracks after sunset, his calf muscles were so cramped that he was forced to walk backwards.

After washing his blistered feet, he fell onto his cot and lay staring at the ceiling.

'Here,' said Aiken, sliding across a hunk of bread.

Lucas didn't thank him. 'If it had been you who'd done the mocking, no one would have punished you.'

Aiken propped himself on one elbow. 'I don't understand your animosity. From the moment we met, you've had it in for me. What harm have I ever done you? Well? Answer.'

Lucas rolled over. 'You'll find out.'

Two days later Vallon rode into the barracks, provoking a scurry of activity.

'Everyone to the parade ground,' Aimery shouted. 'At the double.'

Lucas heard similar orders ringing out from the other barracks. 'What's all the excitement about?'

'It's the beginning of the campaign season,' Gorka said. 'Vallon's going to give us our marching orders.'

The unit marched out into a glorious April day. Vallon and his centurions sat their fine horses, the sea behind them the colour of hyacinths under an unclouded sky. For the first time Lucas laid eyes on the other centurions. Conrad, the shaven-headed and craggy German second-in command, looked as if he'd been hewn from rock. Otia, the Georgian, with his jet-black hair, wavy beard

124

and beautiful dark eyes, resembled a melancholy saint in an icon. Lucas had heard that in ordinary life, Otia was the most self-effacing of men, but that in battle he was a maniac.

'Squadron form ranks,' Conrad ordered.

The men formed up in three lines, Lucas's unit on the right of the rear rank.

Vallon pitched his voice to carry. 'Can everybody hear me?'

'Sir!' the squadron shouted.

A breeze blew a lock of hair across Vallon's face. He brushed it back. 'No doubt you've been wondering where your next tour of duty will take you. Well, I for one won't be returning to the Danube frontier.' Vallon raised a hand to quell the cheers. 'My commission takes me much further afield, on an expedition commissioned by His Imperial Majesty. I'm not at liberty to tell you where, only that it will be at least two years before I see my home and family again.'

Not a sound from the Outlanders, all of them straining for the general's next words.

'I'm not taking the whole squadron,' said Vallon. 'My orders are to select a hundred volunteers. We can whittle the number down by excluding all married men and those over forty. That still leaves almost two hundred of you. I hope I can find enough brave souls from that number to furnish a sufficient force.'

Lucas saw his excitement reflected on his companions' faces.

'Those who join me will receive double wages. Those of you fortunate enough to return will be paid the same again. For those who don't make it back, there will be generous pensions for your families. That tells you something about the dangers we'll be facing. I want you to dwell on that aspect before you make a decision.'

Excitement rippled through the squadron.

Conrad rode forward a pace. 'Silence in the ranks!'

The parade ground fell still. At its rooftop nest, a stork clacked its beak with a sound like the roll of a snare drum. Out to sea, ships heeled against the breeze.

'Front rank first,' Vallon said. 'All those who wish to join the expedition, take two steps forward.'

A grizzled Croat thrust up a hand. 'Permission to speak, General?'

'Granted.'

'What happens to the men you'll leave behind?'

'They'll be merged into a new squadron commanded by Centurion Conrad and posted to the Danube border.'

The front rank looked along their line, shook their heads and stepped forward as one.

Vallon rubbed his brow. 'I said I'm not taking married men.'

'Permission to speak again,' said the Croat.

'If you must. In your case, it won't make any difference. As I recall, you have at least one wife and four children you acknowledge as your own.'

The Croat glared at his chuckling companions. 'General, I'd rather risk the unknown than go back to those fever marshes. As for my wife and children, they know a soldier's fortunes are uncertain. For the last eight years they've lived every day with the fear that I won't be coming home.'

A murmur of agreement ran through the ranks.

'Silence!' shouted the three centurions.

Vallon's gaze raked over the faces. 'On this expedition, failure to return isn't a possibility. It's a probability.' He paused. 'I'm flattered that you put so much faith in me, but I don't demand loyalty for loyalty's sake. Let me repeat: the expedition will be extremely dangerous. Many of you who ride out with me won't return. Their bodies will be consumed by wild beasts in lands where no Christian has trod.' He left another resonant silence. 'We'll try the second rank, as before. All those who wish to volunteer, take ...'

With impressive timing, the second rank stepped forward.

Vallon conferred with his centurions before addressing the squadron again. 'Third rank.'

Lucas took two paces forward, face held high, chest straining. No, not every man had volunteered. Lucas glimpsed a gap to his left and realised that Aiken had held back. Vallon noticed it, too, and made the best of an embarrassing situation.

'Aiken has no need to volunteer. As my son and shield-bearer, his place is at my side.'

Otia the Georgian centurion stuck out his hand. 'That man there. What are you smirking about?'

Lucas jerked his head back. 'Nothing, sir.'

Vallon rubbed his forehead again and sighed. 'I see there's nothing for it but to choose for myself.'

He went into a huddle with the centurions and several minutes passed before he broke off and faced the squadron. 'I'd take all of you if I could. No man left behind must take it as a slight on his courage, loyalty and integrity.'

Vallon dismounted and began the long selection process. From where Lucas stood, he saw that the general had words with every man he came to, and warm gestures besides. After he'd passed by, some of the soldiers clutched their fists at their sides and some went grey with the shock of rejection. One man broke into sobs and Lucas saw gritted faces and the sparkle of tears on several others.

Vallon's progress meant that Lucas was the last to hear his fate. His tense stance made him tremble by the time the general stood in front of him.

'Trooper Lucas, by all reports you'll make a fine soldier in time. You handle weapons well and have a natural way with horses. But you're too young and green for this adventure. It would be a crime to expose you to dangers you're not ready to meet. Also, your Greek isn't up to standard.'

Rejection struck Lucas like a kick in the guts. Vallon had turned away before he found his voice.

'General, you said we might be away two years.'

'At least.'

Lucas's voice shook. 'In that time I'll have grown to manhood and acquired the necessary military skills. My training goes well and my Greek teacher is pleased with my progress.'

Vallon looked back. 'I'm sure that when I return, you won't disappoint me.'

'General!'

Gorka seized Lucas's arm. 'Shut up! Vallon's heard your plea. He's turned down many others more deserving.'

Lucas struggled, features contorting. 'You can't leave me behind!'

Gorka's hand dug into his arm. 'For your own sake, get a grip.'

Vallon turned, his face conveying puzzlement. Everyone within earshot was spectating. Over the sea, gulls wheeled and mewed.

'You took me into your home,' Lucas panted. 'You put me into your squadron with Aiken. To be spear-companions, you said. You can't separate us now.'

Centurion Josselin jerked his chin. 'Take him away. Put him on a charge. Failure to obey orders.'

'Wait,' Vallon said as Gorka lugged Lucas away. He moved closer and spoke only for the young Frank's benefit. 'Yes, I hoped you and Aiken would become companions. Unfortunately, I hear that your attitude towards him is anything but friendly. Spite isn't a quality I admire.' He swung on his heel. 'Dismiss the squadron.'

Lucas made a lunge, but Gorka yanked him back. 'You've said enough,' he snarled. 'It's a flogging for you.'

Blanched and dazed, Lucas knew what he had to do. *Vallon, I'm your son, the son of the wife you murdered, brother of your younger son and the daughter I held in my arms before she died two years ago. Sole survivor of a disgraced family reduced to rooting for acorns in the mountains.*

He opened his mouth, framing a shout. *Father!*

'Let Lucas come,' Aiken said. 'Unlike me, he acts as if his life depends on it. He doesn't like me. I don't like him. That doesn't matter. I'll be interested in seeing how he deals with the reality of life on campaign.'

Vallon waved away the bystanders. 'Gorka, you were in charge of Lucas's training. What do you think?'

Gorka slackened his grip. 'Well, General, it's like this. Trooper

128

Lucas has a long way to go before he can call himself a soldier, but I've dealt with worse raw material. The thing is, he gets up my nose, and what I hate is the thought of him twiddling his dick in some cushy billet while me and my mates are fighting whoever it is you're leading us against. So ... I agree with trooper Aiken. Let him come and take his chances.'

Lucas had been standing to attention for two hours. Vallon's face seemed to go into eclipse, the darkness not like the dark of night, but the absolute blackness of a world where no sun ever shone. He had no recollection of Gorka catching him just before he hit the ground.

All leave was cancelled. For the next ten days the expeditionary force laboured from dawn to dark. They spent most of the time in a cordoned-off section of the harbour loading supplies onto the dromons – *Stork* and *Pelican* – and the two cargo ships. Vallon and Hero sometimes appeared on the quay to monitor progress, and it was on one of these occasions that Lucas, trundling barrels up *Pelican*'s gangplank, crossed paths with the Sicilian. He wiped his brow.

'These barrels weigh as heavy as bullion. What's in them?'

Hero smiled. 'Nothing so precious as gold, I'm afraid. It's a mineral called cobalt, mined in Persia and used by potters to produce a blue glaze on ceramics.'

'Is it valuable?'

'I'm not sure. We don't know what our clients want from us.'

'Who are they? Where are we going?'

'Vallon will tell you once we're at sea. All I can say is that by the time you return, you'll be grown to man's estate.'

'Sir ...'

Hero had already turned away.

Lucas delivered his next statement in a flurry. 'Thank you for buying the horse. I'll repay you.'

Hero blushed. 'You weren't supposed to know.'

'It doesn't matter. I'm grateful – not just for Aster, but for the

129

way you treated my wounds. I crave your pardon for my churlish behaviour on the ship.'

Hero's expression gentled. 'Granted without reservation. I know what it's like to be a stranger in a strange land. I wasn't much older than you when I fell in with Vallon.' Seeing Lucas about to pursue the subject, he made his tone brisk. 'If you want to show your gratitude, bestow it on Aiken. These last few months haven't been easy for him.'

'Lucas,' Gorka shouted. 'No one gave you leave to chat. Get back to work.'

Lucas lay in bed that night, turning over what Hero had said, torn between the physician's request and his own resentment. Resentment won, rising like a bitter froth. So Aiken hasn't had an easy time of it these last few weeks. What about me? I've been carrying pain for ten years. Curdled memory dragged him back to the night when Vallon had lurched into the nursery splashed with his wife's blood, his sword raised to slay his children. Lucas had been six years old, and since then not a day or night had passed when the hideous image didn't rear up.

'Aargh!'

He bolted awake to find Gorka's face leering down, his features grotesque in the light of a candle.

'No more pleasant dreams, laddie. We're off to catch a ship and explore the world.'

'You mean—'

'That's right. By the time the city wakes, we'll be gone, and every one of us no more than a memory.'

The Black Sea and the Caucasus

X

Stars were multiplying in the east when Vallon's squadron began filing aboard *Pelican*. Midnight had passed before everyone had found a berth and stowed their kit. Still no sign of the duke. Vallon couldn't even send to find out what was delaying him because the Logothete had ordered the quay to be sealed. The general paced the dock with mounting impatience. The stars were paling before Skleros and his entourage trotted up with about as much urgency as a group of clubmen returning from a good dinner. Some of the ambassador's company were the worse for drink. It was all Vallon could do to contain his anger.

'My Lord, the minister gave clear instructions that we were to sail under cover of dark.'

The duke's bottom lip drooped. 'My dear general, do you really think our departure would have gone unnoticed after all the bustle of the last fortnight?'

'My Lord, we're carrying enough treasure to attract every pirate in the Black Sea. It's imperative we observe all security measures.'

'Oh, stop fussing,' Skleros said. He yawned and looked around. 'Now then, if you'd be so good, I'll need some men to see to our horses.'

Vallon's windpipe burned with suppressed rage. 'That gentleman will learn I'm not to be trifled with,' he told Josselin.

'Thank God we're sailing on separate vessels.'

Lucas was among the party who loaded the duke's mounts. Josselin had assigned him to one of the cargo ships because of his horse-handling skills, and even in his fuming temper, Vallon noticed how neatly the youth coaxed a high-strung steed up the gangplank.

The sun was sliding up over the rim of Asia when Josselin approached. 'Everybody aboard and everything loaded, sir.'

Vallon looked around at the empty quay. No one had come to see them off. No priest to bless the enterprise with holy water. No proud flags flying from the mainmast. Vallon had received his last instructions from the Logothete the morning before and bade farewell to his family after a private service in St Sophia. A last glance and he strode up the gangway. 'Cast off.'

Crew members drew up the plank. A gang of dockers began unhitching the mooring cables. *Pelican* was almost floating free when a commotion at the far end of the wharf drew Vallon's attention.

'Hold hard!' Wulfstan shouted.

But Vallon had already seen the tall blond man loping down the quay with a bow slung over his shoulder, a dog at his side and a porter pushing a hand cart scurrying in their wake. 'Get a move on,' he cried to the dockers.

'No, wait!' Hero shouted. 'We can't sail away without saying farewell.'

Wayland drew up beside the ship and smiled lopsidedly at Vallon. 'That was sneaky – telling me you wouldn't be sailing until next week.'

'I was acting in your best interests.'

'I'll decide what's good for me.'

'Who told you we were leaving?' Vallon demanded. He spun round. 'Wulfstan, was it you?'

'It was me,' Hero said.

Vallon growled low in his throat.

Wayland cocked his head. 'Are you going to lower the plank or do I have to jump? I'm not as agile as I used to be, and my swimming hasn't improved since I left England.'

'I don't want you to come out of any misplaced sense of obligation.'

'I'm coming of my own will.'

'Does Syth know?'

'We discussed it most of the night. She's not happy with my decision, but agrees it's the right one. There's no hurry to return to England. She and the children will remain in Constantinople with your family. They'll take comfort from each other in our absence.'

Someone on the duke's ship demanded to know the reason for the delay. Vallon looked at Hero. The smile and shining eyes said it all. Behind Hero Wulfstan was grinning like a loony.

Vallon turned to the waiting crewmen. 'Lower the plank.'

When Wayland arrived on deck, both men embraced. 'You always did go your own way,' Vallon muttered. 'I pray you haven't chosen the wrong path.' He broke off and walked blindly away.

The wind was against the flotilla and when *Pelican* had shoved off into open water, the two tiers of oar ports below deck on each side opened and one hundred and twenty rowers put out their oars. A drum beat a sonorous rhythm and the oars lifted. When the beat was established, a whistle shrilled and the oars dipped in unison. Up they rose again, water flashing in the sunlight, and down once more, the fifteen-foot-long shafts flexing under the strain. *Pelican* gathered way. The rhythm of the oars speeded up until water ran foaming past the prow.

Vallon looked back at *Stork*. *Pelican* was the larger of the dromons – a rakish fighting vessel almost one hundred and fifty feet from bow to stern, only twenty-five feet across the beam. Her crew numbered a hundred and forty, plus about seventy of Vallon's squadron standing in for the fifty marines she usually carried. Two masts supported the furled lateen sails that gave greater manoeuvrability than the square-rig Vallon had learned to handle on his northern voyage. For combat, she was equipped with a metal-clad ram projecting from her prow, and an armoured wooden castle amidships for archers and catapults. Bronze siphons for spraying Greek Fire had been fitted at bow and stern. The stern cabin, whose roof also functioned as a fighting platform, only accommodated a dozen passengers, including the captain and his senior officers, Vallon, his centurions and Hero. The rest of the

Outlanders, plus the off-duty sailors, slept under canvas awnings on deck.

The supply ships, *Thetis* and *Dolphin*, were a type of dromon called *chelandia*, with broad hulls adapted to carry horses and cargo. Crewed by a hundred men, they were slower than the fighting dromons under either sail or oar. Thirty of Vallon's squadron, together with the muleteers and other non-combatants, had been divided between the transports. The arrangement was to rendezvous at the northern end of the Bosporus before proceeding in convoy across the Black Sea. Already they were in the strait's southern mouth. Vallon watched Galata approach. He could even see his villa and knew that Caitlin would be up there holding the girls and telling them not to cry. *Hush now. Your father will be home soon.*

Three years!

He saw Wayland staring landwards with a bereft expression that flexed in a forced smile when he noticed Vallon's attention.

'I would have suffered more pain if I hadn't joined you.'

'And your pain softens mine. Wayland, I can't tell you how glad I am to have you and Hero at my side.'

'Don't forget me,' said Wulfstan.

Vallon's laugh sounded like a sob. 'You, too, you Viking rogue.'

Wayland made a fist, shoved it into Vallon's arm and turned away to watch Constantinople dropping away behind them.

Pelican and *Stork* reached the Black Sea in mid-afternoon and anchored off the Ancyraean Cape – so named, Hero told Vallon, because here Jason had taken on board a stone anchor for the *Argo* during his quest for the Golden Fleece. The supply ships didn't catch up until the sun was flaring behind the soft black contours of the Thracian coast. During the night the wind shifted full west and at dawn the fleet hoisted sail and set course for Trebizond. It was the twenty-sixth day of April.

When the coast had sunk from sight, Vallon assembled his squadron and told them their destination. They took the news calmly, unable to absorb the scale of the enterprise or the distances involved. For most of them, the realm of China was a destination as abstract as heaven – or hell. On that first day they were just glad to be away from barracks, bound for a mysterious empire where the natives talked like cats, concubines minced on bound feet and dragons were as common as crows.

Warm airs wafted them east all day and when Vallon woke next morning, the same favourable wind was pushing them along. He stood at the bow, watching flying fish skimming the waves.

Hero joined him. 'At this rate we'll reach Trebizond within a week.'

'And our journey will have hardly begun.'

'Admit it, part of you is thrilled to be off on such a grand venture.'

'That's what makes me feel guilty. It's always harder on the ones we leave behind. What about you, Hero? Is there anyone who grieves for your absence?'

'My colleagues will miss me, I expect. Apart from them, there are only my sisters.'

'The Five Furies, you used to call them.'

'Marriage has mellowed them. I'm the proud uncle of seven nephews and five nieces now. This journey will save me a fortune in presents.'

Vallon sensed that Hero felt awkward talking about personal matters and changed the subject. 'Let's take a closer look at the Greek Fire siphons. I've only seen them in action at a distance and I'd like a better understanding of how they work.'

Iannis the ship's captain was reluctant to stage a demonstration. 'General, the siphons are only used in battle, and even then only in extremis. Greek Fire poses almost as much danger to the ship that fires it as to the target.'

Vallon was insistent. 'As military commander, I need to know our fighting capabilities.'

While sailors reefed sails and a team readied the bow flame thrower, Vallon and Hero examined its mechanism. The incendiary compound was ejected from a swivel-mounted bronze barrel with a mouth cast in the shape of a roaring lion. From the rear of the flamethrower a copper tube, fitted with a valve to regulate the flow of oil, led to the fuel reservoir – a welded iron chamber pressurised by a bronze plunge pump. Underneath the reservoir, mounted on wheels, stood a bellows-fanned charcoal brazier to heat the fuel.

Ten men were required to operate the machine. They mustered in leather suits and aprons fire-proofed with vinegar and alum. Vallon noticed that several of the men's faces bore flame scars. Their leader explained their functions. One man's job was to tend the brazier and ignite the jet of hot oil at the muzzle. The squad leader aimed the siphon, while another man operated the valve, and two others manned the pressure pump. The rest were fire-fighters, equipped with buckets of sand and oxhide blankets. Before the team went to work, they spread a layer of sand around the weapon and crossed themselves.

They lit the brazier, and when the coals glowed red, its minder began pumping the bellows. The reservoir made ominous pinging sounds as the metal expanded.

'General, please stand well back,' said the captain. 'It's not unknown for the cauldron to explode.'

'I've seen it happen myself, sir,' Wulfstan said behind Vallon. 'Killed the entire firing crew. I can still smell them roasting.'

One look at the Viking's face and Vallon retreated half a dozen paces.

The team leader took control of the siphon and the two men at the pump began pressurising the reservoir. The firestarter took up position with a flaming torch. The valve operator stood ready. In their outlandish gear, they looked like agents of Satan preparing to incinerate sinners in the fiery pit.

The leader seemed to take his timing from the sounds produced by the fuel tank. His face knotted in concentration. The tank gave another high-pitched twang. The air around it pulsed and shimmered. Vallon took another backward step.

'Now!'

The valve operator turned on the oil supply and a jet of hot fuel spewed from the nozzle. The stink of the compound caught in Vallon's throat and stung his eyes. At full stretch the firestarter lit the stream with a torch. *Whoomph*. A smoky red and yellow jet of flame sprayed twenty feet from the barrel, the range increasing to more than thirty feet as the men working the pump increased their efforts. The jet formed a reverse arc, the partly vaporised fuel curving down before rising in a fan of roaring fire that fell to the sea and, still burning, drifted past the dromon's hull in fiery pools.

'That's enough,' shouted the captain, scissoring his arms.

The supply valve was turned off. The flame shortened and died, leaving blobs and dribbles of stinking oil sizzling on the carpet of sand. A sooty belch of cloud drifted away downwind. The team wheeled away the brazier and opened a pressure relief valve on the reservoir, while the rest of the crew stood ready with their fire blankets. When the contraption had been made safe, they looked at each other and puffed out their cheeks as if only divine grace had prevented a disaster.

Vallon bowed to the captain. 'That was most impressive, and more than a little terrifying. Now that I understand the power of the weapon, I won't imperil your ship again merely to satisfy my curiosity.'

When the weapon had cooled, Vallon and Hero inspected it more closely. 'Have you learned any more about the formula?' Vallon asked. In the wilderness north of Rus, Hero had improvised an incendiary to destroy a Viking longship.

'I think the main ingredient is a substance called rock oil that seeps from the ground in parts of Persia and the Caucasus. As for what makes it stick to whatever it touches ... I imagine they use plant resins – dragon's blood would be an appropriate choice. Quicklime might be involved, too. Did you notice how the fire burned more intensely when it hit the sea?'

Hero examined the pump. 'Very ingenious,' he said. 'It's double action, drawing air on the up-stroke as well as the down-stroke. I must make a drawing.'

Vallon laughed. 'There's not a branch of science you couldn't master if you set your mind to it.' He squeezed Hero's shoulder. 'It would have been a much lonelier command without your company.'

Vallon wandered down the deck, exchanging words with his men. They seemed to be in good heart, enjoying the fine weather after months cooped up in their winter quarters. He leaned his hands on the rail and surveyed the convoy, the dromons sailing under shortened canvas to allow the supply ships to keep pace. *Pelican* cut through the waves within forty yards of *Dolphin* and Vallon saw Lucas sparring with another trooper on the foredeck.

Wulfstan joined Vallon and watched the troopers cutting and thrusting. 'The lad's not bad.'

'He's better than that,' said Vallon. 'Look how sweetly he moves.'

Lucas evaded an attack, sprang back, dashed his opponent's shield to the right and then, with time to spare, hit him a backhanded inswinger from the left.

'What do you reckon?' Wulfstan said. 'Think he'd have the beating of you?

'Give it a year, and even you'll have the better of me. It's called growing old.' Vallon cupped his hands around his mouth. 'Nicely done,' he shouted, 'but don't rely too much on the edge of your sword. It's not a good one and against armour the chances are it will produce only a shallow cut or bruise. Use the point more.' Vallon drew his own blade and demonstrated a few tight moves. 'See? It delivers a more lethal thrust. Even your piece of scrap iron will punch through mail if you put enough weight behind it.' He caught his breath. 'Another thing. Fighting with the aim of killing with the point keeps your body more centred, exposes less arm and flank. Try it.'

Lucas backed away and raised his sword. Wulfstan chuckled. 'Compliments and advice from the master – he'll be made up for the day.'

Vallon turned back to Lucas on an afterthought. 'How's your Greek coming on?'

'*Etsi ki etsi, kyrie.*'

'Good. Keep it up.'

Wind and weather stayed so benign that even Vallon had to remind himself that the Black Sea crossing was only the first and shortest leg of their journey. Once they reached Trebizond, they faced a land march of four thousand miles through unknown and probably hostile territory. Would the horses and pack animals stand up to it? No, they would have to find new mounts and hire camels. Would the men's resolve and discipline hold in the face of boredom, sickness and the inevitable distractions of booze and women? Almost certainly not. The occasional scrap might even be a blessing, helping to maintain morale, but with a fighting force only a hundred strong, Vallon couldn't afford to lose any men in combat. And then there was the duke, a hideous liability. Concern after concern floated through his mind, only to dissolve in the flawless blue sky. If any expedition had been blessed with a favourable start, it was this one.

Around noon on the sixth day out of Constantinople – only one more day to Trebizond – *Stork* manoeuvred to within sixty feet of *Pelican* and one of the duke's men hailed Vallon through a speaking trumpet.

'His Excellency invites you and Master Hero to toast our good progress over a meal.'

'It's too soon to celebrate. I'd be delighted to raise a beaker when we reach Trebizond.'

Duke Skleros, dressed in layers of silk, took the trumpet. 'Vallon, we got off to a bad start and I fear the fault lay with me. In Trebizond it will be all formal banquets and empty speeches. Let's talk man to man. I promise a good luncheon.'

The swell was gentle, the breeze just strong enough to fill the sails. Vallon saw Captain Iannis spectating from the castle amidships. 'Can you transfer me safely?'

'Yes, General.'

Officers bawled orders and teams of sailors reefed sail until *Pelican* was making no more than steerage way. A gang lowered a gig over the side and dropped a rope ladder into it. Gingerly, favouring his stiff ankle, Vallon climbed down, glad of the strong hands that reached up to steady him.

On board *Stork*, Skleros ushered his guests into his cabin, where half a dozen of his entourage were assembled. Glass and silverware gleamed on the dining table. The chests containing the gifts for the Song emperor stood locked and chained in one corner.

'A toast before we dine,' Skleros said. 'To a safe and successful journey.'

Vallon and Hero raised their beakers. 'Safety and success.'

At table, stewards served a main dish of roast ortolans that had been netted on their spring migration, blinded, force-fed on millet and figs until they were four times their normal weight, drowned in wine and then cooked guts and all, only their feathers and feet removed. Skleros ate four of them, ravaging the carcasses and dabbing at the grease running down his chin. His conversation was inconsequential, mainly scurrilous gossip about court hangers-on. He kept plying his guests with strong Thracian wine.

After the second refill, Vallon placed a hand over his glass. 'No more, thank you. I'll need a steady head and legs to make my way back.'

'Now then, General,' Skleros said, spitting out the last beak. 'Tell us what you think of our chances.'

'Of reaching China?' Vallon glanced around at the company. 'There's no point worrying about the unknown perils. Time enough for that when we run into them – and we will. It's the logistics that most concern me – finding enough food, fodder and water. We have plenty of gold, but I'm not sure how far that will take us when we reach the deserts of Turkestan.'

Skleros began tucking into a spiced lemon custard flan, shovelling it over his pendulous lower lip. 'I have every faith in you and your men.'

'I must say, Your Excellency, that your own attitude is remarkably sanguine.'

Skleros rotated a hand, giving priority to another mouthful. Once he'd swallowed it – minimum chewing – he fixed Vallon with his tiny eyes. 'I'm a stoic, General. The vicissitudes I've suffered mean I can embrace no other philosophy.' He lifted a querying gaze past Vallon and seemed to nod. Vallon turned to glimpse a figure vanishing through the door. A servant shut it behind him.

Skleros had resumed talking. 'Yes, Vallon, fortune has dealt me some harsh blows. My estates in Cappadocia were so large you would have needed a good horse to cross them in a day. All gone, lost to the vile Seljuks. I can't look on those heathen mercenaries of yours without a shiver of rage. Have another slice of flan. I certainly mean to.'

Someone nudged Vallon's ankle under the table. Hero was pulling a face at him, indicating the door. 'I think you should take a look outside,' he said in English.

Skleros laughed. 'Speaking in a foreign tongue. Come, come. That's not polite. Share what you have to say with us.'

Vallon made an apologetic grimace. 'I'm sorry. Hero was reminding me that I'd arranged to test the ship's catapult this afternoon.'

'Cancel it. We'll be in Trebizond tomorrow.'

'No, my men will be waiting for me. I'm sorry to leave such a splendid meal, but I really must be getting back.'

Skleros's eyes sidled. His men seemed edgy, keyed up, as if waiting for a signal. 'I insist,' he said. 'We have important matters to discuss.'

Vallon rose. 'They'll have to wait until we reach Trebizond.'

Skleros screwed up his soiled napkin and tossed it on the table. 'Oh, very well, but I must say I find your manners somewhat wanting.'

Vallon stepped out into blinding sunlight to find *Pelican* cruising an arrow flight off *Stork*'s starboard beam. Wayland and Josselin stood on the tower, jabbing towards the south.

'What is it?' Skleros demanded.

'I don't know,' said Vallon. 'Bring me that speaking trumpet.'

Josselin had already found one. 'Ship to the south-west. Looks like one of ours.'

Vallon peered from under a shading palm and spotted the tip of a white thorn nicking the horizon. 'What course?'

'Heading our way.'

Wayland said something to Josselin. 'Two dromons,' the centurion shouted. 'Three-masters. Wayland thinks they're flying the imperial flag.'

'How long before they run up to us?'

Josselin consulted *Pelican*'s captain. 'Not more than half an hour. They must be making twice our speed.' Josselin pointed at the tubby transports wallowing in the dromons' wake.

The situation left Vallon vexed and uncertain. Almost certainly the approaching ships were Byzantine vessels, but that didn't mean they were friendly. Since the Seljuks had captured most of Anatolia, dispossessed Greeks had established several pirate bases on the Black Sea coast. If *Stork* and *Pelican* heaved to now, allowing him to return to his ship, the delay would enable the approaching vessels to catch up. On the other hand, after the duke's odd behaviour, he didn't want to be on *Stork* when they arrived. He glanced over his shoulder to see Skleros and his men arrayed outside the cabin, waiting to see which way he'd jump.

'Excuse me,' Vallon said. He steered Hero out of earshot. 'Do you think the duke was told about the ships while we were at table?'

'I don't see what else it could have been.'

'Then why didn't he share the news with us?'

'Perhaps he was enjoying stuffing himself too much.'

Vallon studied the approaching ships. Now the leading vessel was hull clear and its companion's sails notched the horizon.

'Or else he was expecting the ships and wanted to keep us on board until they intercepted.'

'He couldn't have known they'd be in this place at this time.'

'No, but if he'd posted a lookout at the masthead, he would have learned of the ships long before our men spotted them. Long enough to make sure we were still on his vessel when they ran up to us.'

'But why would he do that?'

'I don't know. Stay close.'

Josselin hailed him again. 'Definitely flying the double eagle.'

Vallon put the trumpet to his mouth. 'Maintain course. Keep close station with the supply ships. Have the men prepare for battle.'

'That's preposterous,' Skleros spluttered. 'Rescind your order.'

Vallon ignored him. Majestic under full sail, the leading battleships had closed to within two miles. Another flag ran rippling up the main masthead.

'Ordering us to heave to,' Josselin shouted.

'Do as they say,' Skleros said. He fluttered a hand at the captain. 'See to it.'

Vallon stepped forward. 'Wait.'

The captain hesitated, eyes switching between his two superiors.

'I'm under orders to stop for no one,' Vallon said.

'General, you can't ignore a signal from the admiral of the Black Sea. That's his flag flying from the foremast.' Skleros's tone hardened. 'Carry on, Captain.'

'As you were,' Vallon snapped. 'The Logothete assured me that the Black Sea fleet has orders not to hinder our passage.'

'Perhaps they're carrying messages that affect our mission.'

'We've had ideal sailing conditions since we left Constantinople. To catch up with us, those galleys would have had to leave port within a day of our own departure.'

'I know nothing about ships and sailing. Heave to and solve the mystery.'

'Why would the Logothete despatch two ships to carry a message?'

'General, I haven't got the faintest idea. I act on the evidence of

145

my eyes and not according to what affrights my imagination. I see an imperial dromon signalling us to stop and therefore, for the last time' – the duke rounded on the captain and purple blotches stained his cheeks – 'I demand that you obey without further delay.'

'Damn it,' Vallon shouted. 'I'm in charge of security.'

But the duke's title carried more weight, and the captain's orders to heave to were already being relayed. Ropes rattled, yards creaked, sails luffed.

'Hero and I are returning to *Pelican*,' Vallon told Skleros. He raised his voice. 'Lower a boat.'

No one moved. He swung round. 'Didn't you hear me?'

One of the duke's men fingered his sword hilt and that was all Vallon needed to confirm his fears of treachery. He had his own blade out before the man could even think of drawing. His eyes darted. 'What's going on?'

'You're behaving like a lunatic,' said Skleros. 'Show some dignity. The dromons will be alongside before you reach your ship.'

Josselin had noticed something was wrong. 'Do you need help, General?'

'Send two squads. Transfer all our men on to *Pelican*, then order the transports to make full sail. You stay where you are and be ready for my instructions.'

A rush of activity as two gigs were lowered. Twenty troopers piled into them and rowed flat out towards *Stork*. The supply ships began closing up on *Pelican*.

The duke flapped his arms. 'Order them back. I'm not having your thugs on my ship.'

'You don't have a choice,' Vallon said. 'Don't even think of resisting. You have no more than twenty soldiers in your company and I suspect it's been many a long year since any of them raised a sword in anger.'

Skleros appealed to *Stork*'s captain. 'This is mutiny. Call your soldiers to arms.'

Vallon's sword shot out. 'Captain, you've defied one of my

146

orders. Defy another and I swear you'll find my reaction most disappointing.'

Looking sick, the man retreated, muttering to his officers and waving his arms in dismay at the chaos that had engulfed his ship from a clear blue sky.

Aimery was first to pile aboard. Vallon gave him a helping hand and muttered in his ear, 'I suspect foul play. Take your lead from me.'

Gorka the Basque followed, with Wulfstan in the rear, climbing the ladder one-handed, a knife between his teeth. Vallon made for the ladder and then turned, smiling. 'Your Excellency, I forgot to thank you for your hospitality.' Still smiling, he advanced on the duke, seized his arm, swung him round and laid the edge of his sword across his throat. His men had no time to react before Vallon's troopers menaced them.

'Take as many as will fit in the boats,' Vallon ordered. He pointed with his free hand, singling out the most senior of the duke's entourage. 'That one, that one and that one there.'

'You'll go to the stake for this,' Skleros gurgled.

'Fetch the treasure,' Vallon told Gorka. 'It's in the cabin.'

One of the duke's men tried to block the door and Gorka clubbed him aside with his sword hilt. Vallon wrenched Skleros towards the side and handed him over to a squat Seljuk with a moon face all the more frightening for its impassivity. 'Guard him close.'

The leading battleship was less than a mile to starboard, foam curling from its prow. Gorka and his men staggered out of the cabin, burdened by the treasure chests. A collective failure of nerve rooted the duke's men to the spot.

'Josselin, order those ships to stand off. Tell their commanders that we're on imperial duty and will treat any attempt to close as an assault. Tell them I have the duke in my custody.'

Vallon waited until every man was in the boats before taking his place. They'd found space for six of the duke's company and the craft sat low in the water. Wulfstan balanced on one of them, exhorting the rowers to put their backs into it with a string of expletives almost poetic in their intensity. No hymn-singing now. He was back in his element and rejoicing in it.

Pelican's hull blocked Vallon's view of the oncoming battle-ships. 'Josselin, what are they doing?'

'Shortening sail, sir. They know something's amiss.'

Pelican's hull loomed over the boats. Hands stretched down. 'Take the duke first, then me.' Two men plucked Vallon on deck. Grabbing Skleros, he ran to the other side as an amplified voice drifted from the dromon.

'Dungarios of the Eastern Sea, carrying imperial despatches for Duke Michael Skleros.'

The duke wriggled in Vallon's grasp. 'I told you.'

'What orders?' Vallon bellowed.

'For the duke's eyes only.'

'Where did you sail from?'

'Trebizond.'

Vallon swung the duke round. 'Trebizond? There's not a ship built that could have sailed from Constantinople to Trebizond and then put back to sea in time to intercept us. The only reason they're expecting us is because they knew of our voyage in advance.'

Skleros had regained possession of himself. 'Very possibly,' he said. 'You've lived in Constantinople long enough to know how difficult it is to keep secrets. An imperial order whispered in a palace closet will be the talk of the taverns by midnight.'

'No,' said Vallon. 'This is your doing.'

The duke's face grew inflamed. 'How dare you! Remember who you're addressing.'

Vallon's manner was implacable. 'It was you.'

'Nonsense. Where's your evidence? I could make the same accusation against you.'

'I spoke to no one.'

'Not even your wife?'

Vallon flung him away. 'We'll settle who's to blame soon enough.'

The officer on the battleship raised his megaphone. 'Transfer the duke to the admiral's ship for instructions regarding your mission.'

'If you want him, you'll have to come and get him.'

Skleros tugged Vallon's sleeve. 'You're only making things worse for yourself. Those ships carry six hundred men and marines. Pointless to resist. You can't save your career, but you still have a chance to save your life.'

Vallon's lip curled. 'I thought you knew nothing of military matters, yet now you reel off the enemy's strength.'

The duke looked around, shaking his head, before fixing a tragic gaze on Vallon. He gave a weary sigh. 'You're a damn fool. If you'd stayed longer at table, we could have settled everything to everyone's satisfaction. But no. The first glimpse of a sail and you run around like a rabid dog.'

A chill closed around Vallon's spine. 'So I'm right. You've sabotaged our expedition.'

'Saved us from certain death,' Skleros hissed. He leaned back. 'Admit it, Vallon, you have no more appetite for this adventure than I do. I saw it on your face the day we met.' He brought his face closer. 'Only I have firm evidence of the emperor's folly.' He nodded, one plump finger wagging, his voice dropping to an intense whisper. 'We're not the first expedition to set out for China. The emperor deposed by Alexius sent a delegation last spring. A carrier pigeon brought news of their fate in December. They'd lost three-quarters of their men and run out of food and water. Nothing has been heard of them since. They're dead. Do you want to meet the same fate?'

Vallon stared at the war galleys. Hundreds of armed men lined their sides. 'Those ships aren't part of the Eastern Fleet and they're not carrying an admiral. Who commands them?'

'Close relatives and trustworthy friends.'

'What arrangement have you made?'

'Allow them to come alongside and escort us into Trebizond.'

'Then what? I'll be transported back to Constantinople and executed for treason.'

149

'Neither of us can return to the capital. You'll have to remain in Anatolia. The duchy is effectively independent. In Trebizond you'll be beyond the emperor's reach.'

The situation was spinning out of Vallon's control. 'My wife and family are in the capital.'

'So are mine, waiting for instructions to join us. As soon as we reach port, send a message to your lady. A ship will be waiting. I've arranged it. In a week or two you'll be reunited with your family.'

'Lose my home, my career?'

Skleros's carnal breath gusted into the general's face. 'I've lost much more. Both of us can build a new life in Trebizond. Better that than dying among barbarians a thousand miles from home.'

'And my men?'

'Trebizond has need of soldiers. They'll find employment.' Skleros had seized the initiative. 'Listen, Vallon. Why do you think the emperor chose you for this mission?'

'My experience of travel in hostile lands.'

Skleros tugged Vallon's arm. 'Yes, yes, all that. But something else.'

Vallon frowned. 'Because I saved the emperor's life?'

Skleros gave a gleeful laugh. 'And something before that. You stood up in front of his generals and told him that it would be foolhardy to engage the Normans. And you were right. And when you'd been proved right, you rubbed salt into the wound by rescuing the emperor from his own vainglory. You don't move in court circles as I do, but believe me, at private banquets and bath houses, important men whisper your name and smile at the irony. They haven't forgotten – and nor has Alexius – that Basil the Macedonian, one of our greatest emperors, began his career as a foreign general.'

'What's *your* crime?'

'My name. I'm a Phocas, cousin of the emperor deposed by Alexius and his scheming bitch of a mother.'

Vallon felt dull-witted. He shook his head. 'Alexius wouldn't spend a fortune just to get rid of one of his generals and a treacherous duke.'

When Skleros smiled, his eyes disappeared. 'How little you understand Byzantine politics.' He waved at the treasure chests. 'That gold amounts to less than what it cost Alexius to build a private chapel in which to confess his sins.' He held up a finger and his voice fell to a hush. 'But for us, General, a fortune, a solid foundation on which to rebuild our lives.'

Vallon's hopes, shakily constructed from the start, had collapsed in ruins. Skleros recognised his dismay and followed up. 'Another thing. You have a beautiful wife. You've spent longer on foreign service than you've been at home.' Skleros flinched and held up a placating hand. 'Don't misunderstand me. I've heard nothing to suggest that your lady is anything other than a faithful partner. But at dinner parties I've heard several wealthy and well-connected gentlemen who would like to separate you from your mistress.' He gripped harder. 'Three years, Vallon. That's how long we'll be away, maybe longer. That's how long your wife will have to endure an empty bed.'

Vallon felt cold. 'What part does the Logothete play in this?'

Skleros loosened his grip. 'Who knows? He spins and weaves, knotting saint and sinner into warp and weft.'

Vallon took a shuddering breath. 'I have to consult my officers.'

'There's nothing to consult about. The expedition's finished. Even if you could escape, you'll lose the supply ships.'

Vallon looked at Skleros as if seeing him for the first time. 'I thought you were a fool, a lazy glutton without a thought in your head except where your next meal would come from.'

The duke tittered. 'Cleverer men than you have made the same mistake.' He sobered and his eyes grew round with false sincerity. 'I won't hold it against you. You're just a simple soldier trying to do your duty.'

'Yes,' Vallon said. 'A simple soldier.'

'So I forgive the rough treatment you've subjected me to. Now then, do as I command and you'll receive a share of the gold and treasure.'

'How much?'

Skleros cocked his head like a bird about to spear a worm. 'A quarter would be fair, I think.'

Vallon stepped back. 'I'll weigh everything you've told me.'

His squadron watched in mystified silence as he made for the tower, summoning *Pelican*'s captain and Otia the Georgian centurion to join him. He climbed up to the platform and faced his officers. Wulfstan sneaked alongside.

Vallon's tone was wooden. 'Those are pirate ships and the duke is in league with them. He says that if we follow them into Trebizond, we'll be free to start afresh with a share of the gold.'

Wulfstan spat. 'Well, that was a short expedition.'

'I don't believe him. If they wanted us to go to Trebizond, they could simply have waited for us to arrive. I think they hoped to board us without raising suspicions, disarm us and slaughter us. They would have killed the crew and sunk the ships, leaving no trace of their crime.'

'Are we going to fight them?' Josselin asked.

Vallon cleared his throat and stood straighter. 'Only if we have to. Captain, can *Pelican* outrun those ships?'

'General, I'm not going to—'

'I asked you a question.'

Iannis swallowed. 'We're lighter and more nimble. I'd wager we have the beating of them as long as this breeze holds. If it fails, their speed under oars would be greater.'

'Where would we run to?' Josselin asked. 'Sinop is the nearest friendly harbour, but it must lie more than a day upwind. Voyage north and we'll fall into the hands of Rus warlords or steppe nomads. Sail east and we'll end up in Armenia or Georgia.'

Vallon's wits were beginning to fall into place. 'We won't find a safe haven in Armenia. It's in Seljuk hands and has close relations with Trebizond. Our documents guaranteeing safe passage wouldn't be worth the ink they're written in.' Vallon squinted east. 'Captain, how far are we from Georgia?'

'If this breeze holds, we should sight the coast tomorrow morning.'

Vallon looked for Otia. 'That's your country. What kind of reception can we expect?'

'Not a friendly one. It's only forty years since Byzantium went to war against Georgia, and my compatriots have long memories.'

'We're not going to invade the place, just make a safe landfall until we work out our next move. Captain, can you find a peaceful spot to put us ashore?'

Iannis eyed the eastern horizon. 'The mouth of the river Phasis. The coast there is flat and marshy, inhabited only by fishermen.'

'Make for it.'

Josselin indicated the warships to windward. 'How do we get away from them?'

Vallon's eye fell on the catapult – a trebuchet with a timber throwing arm twenty feet long, the short end counterweighted with a basket of sand that must have weighed close to a ton. He glanced at Wulfstan. 'You used catapults in the Mediterranean. What's that thing capable of?'

Wulfstan studied the machine with a professional eye. 'I'd say it could hurl a thirty-pound rock more than five hundred feet.'

'How far would it toss the duke?'

Wulfstan spluttered with laughter. Even Otia's face twitched in a smile. 'I calculate that he'd fall a way short of the galley, but he'd make a fair old splash.'

Hero was shocked. 'Vallon, I hope you're joking.'

'Fetch him.'

The Seljuk minder bundled Skleros up onto the roof. The duke looked around at the faces and found no comfort in them. His voice quavered. 'I trust that I've made you see sense.'

Vallon's nod had all the hallmarks of defeat. 'Yes, after considering all aspects of our situation, I realise our position is almost hopeless.'

Skleros exhaled in relief. 'Good. I knew you were a practical fellow at heart. Remember the—'

'*Almost* hopeless,' Vallon snapped. 'A position with which I'm depressingly familiar.' His gaze flicked towards Wulfstan. 'Lash him to the beam.' He turned to face the captain. 'Raise sail. Josselin, meet any move on the enemy's part with a volley of arrows.'

Four men dragged Skleros kicking and screaming to the trebuchet and hoisted him onto the beam. The officer on the battleship raised his megaphone. 'General, what are you doing? If any harm comes to the duke, you'll pay with your life.'

'What's your name?' Vallon shouted. 'When someone threatens me, I like to know who I'm dealing with.'

'Thraco,' the officer said. 'A cousin of Duke Skleros.'

'You asked me to transfer him to you, and since he's confessed his crimes and I have no more need of him, I'm returning him as promptly as I can.' He glanced sideways to see the duke held by arms and legs astride the beam, Wulfstan poised to release the trigger that would propel the human missile with the speed of a departing arrow. 'On my command.'

'No!' Skleros screamed. 'Please God.'

'Make it quick,' said Wulfstan. 'His nibs has shat himself.'

Vallon raised the megaphone again. 'It seems that the duke has changed his mind and wants to stay on *Pelican*. If you wish to save him, you'll let us sail away without hindrance. Remember, we have six more of his men to use for target practice. I'm sure you don't want to see so much blue blood wasted.'

'Vallon, if any harm comes to the duke ...'

Vallon lifted an arm as *Pelican* gathered way, her slopping motion smoothing into a glide. She was almost out of earshot before Thraco's final words reached him. 'Vallon, you're only delaying the inevitable. You're cornered. You can't defend your supply ships. Without food or horses ...' Distance swallowed the rest of his message.

Vallon let his breath go. 'Release the duke and clean him up.' He climbed down to the deck and the first face he saw was Aiken's, lips drawn back in a rictus of disgust.

'Don't look at me like that. You chose to come by outsmarting yourself. This is war and war doesn't know logic or reason.'

Aiken backed away and Vallon took up position in the bow. He was still standing there at dusk.

'The war galleys have captured the supply ships,' Josselin said behind him.

'I'm not blind.'

Josselin hovered. 'General, can you tell me your plans? The men are anxious and—'

'I'm still assessing our situation. As soon as I've found a way out, I'll tell you.'

'Very good, General.'

It was almost dark when Hero stepped up to Vallon's side. They watched night drawing down and Venus winking in the east.

Hero broke the silence. 'Would you really have shot the duke from the catapult?'

'If I'd had to,' said Vallon. 'Only a temporary reprieve, I fear. With the amount of treasure we're carrying, the pirates might decide that Skleros and all his other nobles are worth sacrificing.'

'You'll find a way out,' Hero said. 'I remember you telling me that a good commander is one who, confronted by a dead end, would hack out his own path.'

When Vallon turned, Hero had gone and he stood alone under the overarching night.

XI

In a desperate attempt to evade the warships, the crews of *Thetis* and *Dolphin* had taken to their oars, only for the galleys to race down on them, their armoured prows shearing off one bank apiece as if they were toothpicks. Boarding parties had seized the transports, and now they were hull down over the horizon, closely attended by one of the enemy dromons. The other war galley shadowed *Pelican* a mile astern. At one point she'd closed with intent to grapple and had only dropped back when Vallon threatened to dump the gold and treasure over the side, along with Duke Skleros.

Lucas watched the galley's sails flush red against the setting sun and then fade into the night before appearing again as parchment triangles under the light of a half moon.

He'd been mucking out in *Dolphin*'s hold when the dromons were sighted and clambered on deck to witness the spectacle of the ships bearing down on them. Like everyone else he assumed that Vallon had planned the rendezvous, and when the order came to evacuate, he had to be dragged kicking and shouting away from Aster. He was one of the last onto *Pelican*'s deck, and with his rudimentary Greek it took a long time to find out what was happening. Even after Josselin had assembled the men and told them about the duke's treachery, there were some who thought the warships were genuine Byzantine naval vessels sent to prevent the general from making off with the emperor's gold. Men spoke about Vallon's intention to establish a colony on some foreign shore. Rumour and counter-rumour swirled.

At midnight the enemy sails were still in sight. On either side of the stern, water slopped past the twin quarter rudders. Fatigue weighed on Lucas, but he couldn't sleep. He was still devastated by the loss of Aster, and Aimery had told him that tomorrow they'd make land and might have to fight a battle. Lucas gave a juddering yawn.

'So much for our great expedition. Over before it's hardly begun, and no chance of returning home.'

Lucas blinked round to find Aiken confronting him.

'I don't have a home.'

'We're as good as dead,' Aiken said. 'They outnumber us three to one and they have our horses.'

'I still don't understand why they would attack us. We're here on the emperor's orders.'

'So is the duke and did you see what Vallon did to him? Lashed him to the trebuchet and threatened to hurl him into the sea. What kind of man could contemplate that sort of cruelty?'

'Aimery told me it was a ruse to intimidate the enemy, a ploy to buy time.'

'You don't think Vallon would have done it?' Aiken said. He brought his face close. 'A man who murdered his own wife.'

Hearing it from another was like a cold blade inserted between Lucas's ribs. He could barely force words past his throat. 'Where did you hear that?'

'It was you who gabbled about Vallon having to flee France with a price on his head. I asked Hero and he admitted it was true. Shocks you, doesn't it? Not what you expected to hear about the great Vallon.'

Lucas grabbed Aiken's tunic. 'Tell me why.'

Aiken removed Lucas's hand and spoke in a matter-of-fact tone. 'His wife took a lover when he was campaigning in Spain. He slaughtered them in the marital bed.'

Lucas responded without thought. 'What happened to his children?'

Aiken was too wound up to wonder how Lucas knew that Vallon had children. 'He probably killed them, too. Even if he didn't, he condemned them to poverty and disgrace. The Duke of Aquitaine seized Vallon's estate and declared him an outlaw. That's the man you travelled so far to take service with.'

When Aiken left, Lucas slumped down, memories bubbling like foul vapours. The winter night two years ago when he held his dying sister in his arms, her breath coming in shallow gasps, the roads blocked by snow and not even a priest to administer the last rites. Two years before that and his brother poisoned by a blackthorn, threads of red running up his arm, the glands in his armpit swollen to the size of apples, delirious in his final hours and then so peaceful in death. And before that, long before that, the fiend reeling into the nursery like an ogre drunk on blood, gore dripping off his sword – the same blade Vallon carried to this day.

'Easy, lad. We're not done for yet.'

Lucas screwed tears from his eyes and looked up into Aimery's serene face. 'It isn't that.'

157

'Whatever fears haunt you, you'll face them better on a full stomach. Cook's made a thick broth. Get some inside you. Here,' Aimery said, extending a hand. 'I need you fit and strong. Today could be right lively.'

'Land ahead!' called the lookout.

Lucas ran with everyone else towards the bow. All he could see was a grey smear. By mid-morning, the sun hot and the air clammy, the prospect was no clearer. It was midday before the first contours began to take on form and colour. The coast was still miles away when Vallon addressed his squadron from the castle. Standing at the rear, Lucas strained to hear the general's words.

'I'll make this short. First, I assure you that the ships pursuing us aren't vessels of the Byzantine navy. They're pirates, and the only reason they haven't closed with us is because we hold the duke, the gold and the treasure. Guess which they covet most? As soon as we reach land, they'll press home an attack, so we have to disembark with all speed. I'll go first, together with a squad carrying the bullion. Next, a squad to escort the duke and the other hostages. Officers, work out a drill for an orderly evacuation. I want everyone to reach shore ready for combat. That's it. Any questions?'

Captain Iannis intervened before anyone else could respond. 'General, I can't land you directly on that shore. The water's too shallow and we're approaching on an ebb tide. *Pelican* will run aground.'

'That can't be helped and may be to our advantage. The enemy ships have deeper draughts than us.'

A trooper put up a hand. 'What about the horses, sir? Without them the enemy will mow us down.'

Vallon gauged distances. The leading war galley was less than a mile in arrears, its sister ship and the transports only just in sight. 'We'll have to fight without horses.'

Lucas spoke without thinking. 'I'm not leaving Aster.'

Vallon pointed. 'Put that man on a charge.'

158

Gorka elbowed Lucas. 'You twonk.'

Vallon raised a hand. 'Our situation's not as bleak as you might think. From what Otia and the captain tell me, horses won't be much use on that coast. It's marsh and lake for miles inland, only a few narrow causeways leading across it. I don't think the enemy will waste time getting the horses ashore. They're not cavalrymen and they'll be so keen to lay their hands on the gold that they'll come after us like hounds after a doe. Don't worry, though. I'm determined to get our horses and supplies back. Stand down. Get something to eat.'

Lucas dressed for battle in his cast-offs and watched the coast take on definition – a swampy littoral cut by sluggish creeks and lagoons, lush green hills beyond under a backdrop of cloud-swathed mountains, pockets of snow showing through rents in the overcast. South of the rivermouth a few small ships plied in and out of a port. The rest of the shoreline seemed to be empty.

'Steer to the north of the estuary,' Vallon ordered.

'Why don't we head for that port?' Lucas asked Gorka.

'Because the Georgians hate us. And even if they didn't, running into a foreign harbour carrying treasure and with pirates nibbling our heels isn't the brightest of moves.'

Josselin supervised the evacuation with his customary calm.

'Form up by squad both sides of the bow.'

Lucas found himself almost in the rearmost rank, only the muleteers and grooms behind him. In his padded armour his body ran with sweat.

'Enemy taking to their oars,' someone yelled.

Lucas looked behind to see foam creaming from the blades, a wave building at the dromon's bow.

'Order your men to do the same,' Vallon told *Pelican*'s captain.

'General, I'm not going to wreck my ship.'

'You, your dromon and your crew serve at my will and disposal.' When the captain hesitated, Vallon raised his voice. 'Otia, take two squads below and keep the rowers hard at it until I give the word.'

Troopers sprinted below and Lucas felt *Pelican* spring forward as the oars bit. A glance behind showed that the effort wouldn't be enough. The war galley was only half a mile astern and closing fast.

Vallon pointed at a huddle of shacks set back from a lagoon. 'Make for that village.'

Lucas saw people fleeing from the settlement. The coast was no more than a quarter of a mile away and the sea had taken on the colour of thin ale.

'Hold tight,' said a trooper. 'We're going to hit smack-bang and wallop.'

'Suits me,' said another. 'I can't swim.'

Vallon swung his sword down. 'Lower sails. Stop rowing.'

Oars crabbed and lifted. Before the sailors could reef sails, *Pelican* shoaled with a long skidding hiss, the deceleration sending Lucas lurching. Only fifty yards separated them from the shore.

'Boats away,' Otia shouted.

The two gigs splashed into the sea. 'Bullion and prisoner squads.'

When the boats had pulled clear, the next two squads jumped into the sea, one on each side of the bow, and waded chest deep towards the shore, holding their weapons above their heads. The war galley was only a long bowshot behind *Pelican*, still bowling along under sail and oar.

'Next two squads. Go! The rest move up.'

Lucas plucked at his mouth. 'We're not all going to get off in time.'

'Shut it,' Gorka snapped.

'The bastards are going to ram us,' said a trooper.

'Prepare for boarders,' someone shouted.

Lucas braced himself and watched the galley's onrush. By now only four squads remained on board *Pelican*. Forty men against hundreds.

'Next two squads. Go!'

The first men off had reached the shore and were running up

into the village. Lucas concentrated on the oncoming galley. It was still committed to a collision course, soldiers massed on her foredeck and beating on their shields.

They toppled like skittles as the hull ploughed into the seabed and the ship ground to a stop within its own length, the masts groaning with the strain, stays twanging apart.

'Enemy lowering boats.'

An arrow glanced off Lucas's helmet and buried its head in the deck. He looked around in bemusement. Gorka tugged his arm. 'What are you waiting for? Come on. We're next.'

Lucas faced the shore, sucked in breaths and prepared to jump. Josselin held him back.

'Not so hasty. We've already had a couple of accidents.' He waited for what seemed an age before thumping Lucas's back. 'Off you go.'

Lucas hit the sea, went under and surfaced spitting brine. He ploughed through the water, grunting like a beast, and staggered ashore, tripping over the two javelins he carried. Gorka pulled him upright. 'Who said you could take a rest?'

Weighed down by his weapons and waterlogged corselet, Lucas jogged through the hamlet onto a causeway elevated a couple of feet above the marsh.

'What's the plan?' he gasped.

Gorka flashed him a look. 'If I fucking knew, I'd be a general. Keep going.'

Lucas found his second wind. The wetlands stretched away to a mist-softened horizon. All around lay a waterworld of lakes, creeks, bogs, reedbeds and islands overgrown by stands of alder and willow, oak and ash. Beside him, Gorka grunted and clutched his ribcage.

'Need a hand, boss? I'll carry your shield if you want.'

Gorka's glance would have curdled milk.

Lucas lifted his knees and increased pace. 'Just say the word, boss.'

Half a mile up the causeway, Wayland and his dog stepped out

161

from a patch of boggy woodland. He nodded them past. 'Not far now.'

Where the causeway emerged from the wood, it made a sharp turn before crossing a wide and reedy lake. A furlong up the track, Vallon was organising two squads into a defensive formation. He held up his hand to halt Aimery's squad.

'How long have we got?'

Aimery bent over, hands on knees. 'Not sure, sir. They hadn't reached land when we left the coast.'

'Form up behind the wall. Did you see Wayland?'

'Yes, sir.'

'There are three squads hidden in the trees each side of him. We draw the enemy onto this wall and block them.' Vallon nodded towards a squad of Turkmen archers further along the causeway. 'They'll make your job easier. When you've halted the enemy attack, the squads in the wood will engage, cutting off the enemy's retreat.' He interlocked his fingers. 'We'll squeeze them between us.'

'Understood, sir.'

Vallon noticed Lucas. 'I didn't expect you to face action so soon. Are you sure you're up to it?'

'I want to stay with my squad.'

'Good lad. Acquit yourself bravely and I'll forget your insubordination.' He clapped his hands. 'Go to it!'

The foremost ten-man squad arranged themselves in a *foulkon*, a defensive formation usually used by infantry against cavalry. The first rank of five knelt on bended knee with their shields resting on the ground in front of them, their spear butts planted in the earth and the points angled upwards to resist a charge. They completely blocked the narrow causeway. The second rank remained standing, their shields locked with those of their companions and their spears held at chest height. To an attacker, the shieldwall would be an intimidating sight, the men behind it invisible and apparently invulnerable. Lucas had practised the formation only once, kneeling in the subordinate position, and had found it intensely uncomfortable, the shields above snagging against his, leaving him no room to manoeuvre.

The second and third squads formed up four ranks deep, shields overlapping, each man armed with two javelins, one in the hand, the other stuck butt down in the peaty soil.

Gorka hauled Lucas into position at the rear of the formation. 'Don't get carried away. Wait for Aimery's command before you hurl your javelins. I've seen men skewered by overexcited idiots standing behind them.'

Lucas waited, soaked in sweat and seawater. The muleteers and other non-combatants came wheezing up the track, scourged on by Josselin. Cursing their tardiness, the shieldwall shifted to let them pass.

Silence fell. The causeway stretched away empty. Lucas's heart knocked against his ribs. His craw was tight. He'd dreamed of battle many times, but never had he imagined combat in such a strange and constricted setting. What made it more unreal was the tranquillity – reeds whispering in a light breeze, frogs croaking and waterfowl babbling, a warbler carolling in the sedges. From the corner of his eye Lucas spotted a bright green snake undulating through a scum of weed. A heron flew a stately transit across the lake with an eel wriggling from its beak.

Gorka nudged him. 'Bearing up?'

'It's the waiting.'

Gorka laughed. 'If I had a solidus for every time I heard that, I'd be richer than the emperor.'

'Here they come,' said Aimery. 'Don't make a sound.'

Lucas tugged at his throat. He heard metallic clicks, the tread of cushioned feet and rasping breaths. And then around the corner at the edge of the wood the first of the enemy trotted into sight. The front runners stopped when they saw the shieldwall, the men following up barging into them. An officer raised a hand and shouted. The enemy mustered behind him, score upon score backing up along the causeway.

'Don't let their numbers dismay you,' Aimery said. 'They can only attack five or six abreast.'

The weight of men piling up behind the enemy's vanguard began to shove it forward. Those in the rear couldn't see the obstacle blocking their path and piled against the forward ranks. Yielding to the crush, the leader raised his sword, gave the order to advance and led his force forward at a brisk march.

Lucas watched them come, the mass resolving into individual faces contorted by fear and frenzy. A wordless cry welled in his throat. How could they just stand in silence while a hundred warriors strode forward to annihilate them?

'Steady,' Josselin said.

Arrows from the archers behind ripped low over Lucas's head. The attacking force seemed to give a collective twitch. The second flight stung them into a headlong charge. Attacking along a front only fifteen feet wide, they found it hard to maintain formation. Feet tangled and tripped. Elbows collided. Men on the flanks found themselves shoved off the causeway. Through the war cries Lucas heard curses and recriminations.

A third volley of arrows tore over in a shallow arc and the officer leading the charge staggered and ran himself into the ground until he pitched on all fours, spewing blood. The men directly behind hurdled him. One of them clipped him with a foot and tumbled flat on his face, bringing down a companion as he fell. Another man went careering into the water with windmilling arms. Now the enemy were too close for the archers to aim at the vanguard, and their next volley landed in the ranks behind.

Someone gave a thin squeal and was still squealing when the nearest attackers closed. Lucas stood rooted to the spot until the yell delivered in unison by his comrades released him from his paralysis. The roar that had been building in his belly erupted. His face knotted and his lips rucked. The squad ahead of him rocked back and launched their javelins, were reaching for their second darts before the first had landed. They ducked down and Gorka backhanded Lucas across the chest.

'Now!'

Lucas's first throw was a dismal misaim, his second truer. The javelin was still in flight when the enemy crashed into the shield-wall, the weight of their attack driving grunts from the defenders. The wall buckled but held. A trooper went down and a man from the third rank scrambled to fill the breach. The noise was horrendous – sword clashing against sword, shield on shield, vile obscenities and a formless baying from those not yet engaged in the fray.

'Stand your ground,' Vallon shouted from behind.

They did. The Outlanders' front rank, better trained than their enemy, fresh from the wars and hardened in battle, had slain the first narrow wave of attackers, laying them low so that those who took their place had to find their footing on fallen bodies, not all of them dead. Those in front were jammed between the shieldwall and the soldiers pressing from behind, with little room to wield their swords. Some took to the water in an attempt to get round the bottleneck. Turkish archers picked them off or speared them. The attackers were so tightly hemmed in that one soldier whose head had been split in two by a sword stood propped among the living like a swaying stump. Lucas glimpsed another with his back turned, his head hanging upside down between his shoulders, suspended by a flap of skin.

A trumpet blared, announcing the attack in the woods. When the threat communicated, panic swept the enemy, the rear peeling away first, followed by the front. What remained of the shieldwall was too exhausted to follow up, and when they slumped down, sobbing with exhaustion, Lucas saw what carnage they'd wreaked. In front of them lay a mound of bodies three deep, some still alive, limbs stirring. Lucas was used to the sight of blood, but nothing had prepared him for the atrocity of war – gore lying in thick pools, men clutching coils of viscera, a victim holding his severed leg with an expression that would rack Lucas's dreams for months.

With hideous whoops, the second squad began climbing over the carnage in pursuit.

'Follow up in good order,' Vallon bellowed. 'Don't engage unless you have to. I want them alive.'

Gorka wrenched Lucas's arm. 'Here we go. Don't let's miss out.'

'What?'

'Booty time, you idiot. Everything the enemy carries belongs to us.'

Lucas found himself quick-stepping down the causeway after the fleeing troops. When they found their way blocked by the formation in the woods, some of them stripped off their armour and tried to escape across the lake. Marshalled by an officer, a few determined souls turned at bay.

'Form up in close order,' Josselin shouted.

Before the enemy could organise a counter, Vallon barged to the front. 'Another attack will meet the same bloody end. You're trapped front and rear. Surrender and I promise to spare your lives.'

Further along the causeway, the same ultimatum rang out. The fighting down there continued for a while before the cries and clash of weapons died. The trapped soldiers cast about like frightened animals, waiting for someone to take the initiative. An officer pushed through the scrum and addressed Vallon.

'How can we trust you?'

'My word. It's minted in a currency less debased than the one the duke deals in.'

'You swear it?'

'On the cross.'

The enemy folded up, propping themselves on their swords, many weeping for shame and relief.

'Collect their weapons,' said Vallon. 'Offer no violence except in return.'

Gorka nudged Lucas's arm. 'You just won your first battle. Now it's time to reap your reward.'

So Lucas, who hadn't used his sword in anger, found himself gathering the blades from the foe and handing them back to the baggage servants. He found it hard to meet the prisoners' faces.

Taking a sword from one sobbing captive – a man old enough to be his father – it struck him how easily their positions could have been reversed. That's when he realised how fickle the fortunes of war could be, and that's when he resolved to be a soldier who would leave as little as possible to chance.

Like Vallon.

Altogether the squadron had trapped sixty soldiers and killed or injured more than thirty. After stripping the captives of their valuables, Gorka worked his way back along the dead, scavenging gold and jewels like a malign magpie. Lucas tagged along with loathing and didn't take a thing. This wasn't how he'd imagined war.

Gorka hopped knee-deep into water and levered up the head and torso of an officer clad in finely wrought lamellar armour who'd sprawled face down over the causeway. The Basque's hand swooped and he held up a bejewelled brooch. 'Worth forty solidi in Constantinople. Give me a hand.'

Lucas assisted Gorka onto firm ground while staring transfixed at the corpse. 'His armour must be worth a count's ransom.'

'Too bulky. Stick to the portable high-value stuff.' Gorka registered Lucas's queasy fascination. 'Do you want it? Looks about the right fit.'

Lucas glanced up the causeway.

'If you don't take it, someone else will.'

'I didn't do anything to deserve it. I never even blooded my sword.'

'You held your ground. That's good enough. Go on. He's got no further use for it.'

Lucas manipulated the lolling corpse onto the causeway and began easing the armour over its head. A porridge of brain matter leaked from the skull. Lucas's face took on the expression of a man straining shit through his teeth.

Gorka shoved him aside. 'You're not trying to grope a virgin on your first date. Like this.'

He removed the armour as if he were skinning a rabbit, swilled it in the lake and handed it over. Lucas regarded it with awe. 'It must be worth ten times the price of your armour.'

Gorka stroked his shabby iron corselet. 'Wear fancy armour and you become a target for every peasant with a billhook. In battle it's best not to stand out.'

Lucas slung the armour over his shoulder. 'I don't intend to be one of the herd. One day I'll be a general.'

'You? Listen, lad. Stick close, do what I say and in five years you might win promotion to commander of four.'

He was still chuckling at Lucas's fantasy when Vallon gave the order to escort the prisoners back to the coast.

'Did you kill the man who wore that armour?'

Lucas, herding a group of captives at sword point, swung round to see Aiken, ashen-faced but otherwise immaculate. He hadn't even got his feet wet.

'Suppose I did?'

'What's it like to kill a man?'

A prisoner stumbled against Lucas and he rounded on the man in fright. The prisoner cringed, begging mercy.

Aiken persisted. 'How do you feel now?'

Lucas began to pant. He flat-handed Aiken in the chest.

'Hey!' Gorka said.

Lucas shoved Aiken backwards. 'You skulk in the rear and then have the nerve to ask me how it feels to face the enemy. If you want to know, join the shieldwall yourself.' Spittle flew from Lucas's mouth. '*Daddy's boy!*'

Gorka almost wrenched him off his feet. 'You never learn, do you?'

Lucas went slack and a sob racked his body. He looked up to find Vallon's eyes boring into his. He gave an unhinged laugh.

'You don't scare me. You—'

Gorka's slap spun Lucas sideways. He stumbled away, clutched his knees and vomited a stream of throat-scalding puke.

'Shock,' Gorka told the general. 'It was his first taste of combat. I'll sort him out.'

Vallon gave a judicious nod. 'Even so, his behaviour is intolerable. Put him in the supply train for a month. Keep him away from Aiken and out of my sight. I don't want to set eyes on him again for the duration of our expedition.'

XII

The remainder of the enemy, still formidably strong, stood arrayed in battle formation with their backs to the sea. Both dromons had floated free on the rising tide and the other enemy galley had landed its complement of soldiers and was loitering offshore. Thraco, the Greek leader, stepped out of the front rank.

'We still have a crushing advantage in numbers and hold your ship, horses and supplies. Surrender the duke, the prisoners and the gold and we'll leave you to go your own way. That's my final offer.'

Vallon strolled forward, followed by two troopers dragging the duke by his bound hands. 'If you have the beating of us, why waste time talking?'

Thraco didn't answer. A muggy breeze rippled the Outlanders' banners. Thunder growled inland. Vallon advanced another step. 'Here are *my* terms. Land all our horses and supplies. When that's done, you'll let *Pelican* sail away without interference.'

'Once you're on board, any promise I make is void. There's no way back for you.'

'Who says we're going back? When *Pelican* has sailed over the horizon, I'll release all the prisoners except the duke. Refuse and I'll kill them one by one in front of you. You'd better be quick. I've lost five men to your treachery and my temper threatens to get the better of me.'

'Even if you kill them all, we'd still have the beating of you.'

'Hear that?' Vallon called to the Greek troops. 'That's how little your lords value the lives of your comrades.' He let silence stretch. 'So be it. Lead the first prisoner forward.'

Two Turkmen hustled a wounded officer out of the ranks, pushed him to his knees and slid swords from their scabbards. The prisoner raised his bloodied face towards Thraco. 'Is this how you reward the men who fought and died on your behalf? Are we just pawns in a game designed to line the pockets of the duke and his relatives?'

Ugly murmurs of agreement bubbled through the Greek ranks.

'Thraco, your men will die for nothing,' Vallon shouted. 'You'll never get the gold. It's cached miles inland. To reach it, you'll have to wade through the bodies of the prisoners and a hundred other soldiers we'll kill if you embark on that futile task. You'll be forced to sail away empty-handed in the company of three hundred armed men who watched you sacrifice their comrades to your greed. Believe me, you won't sleep easy on your voyage to Trebizond.'

'Give him what he wants,' yelled a prisoner, and two or three Greek marines echoed his demand before officers lashed them into silence.

Vallon laughed. 'You can stop their mouths, but you can't blow away that rank odour. Smell it? It's the stink of mutiny.'

Thraco pawed his mouth. 'Release the duke and then I'll consider your demands.'

Vallon shook his head with slow finality. 'Oh, no. The duke is never going home.'

Skleros lunged against his tethers. 'Let me go,' he begged. 'I'll plead your case.'

'You'll plead it from here,' Vallon said. 'And in the most abject terms.'

Skleros raised his hands. 'Do what he says.'

'Louder,' Vallon ordered.

Skleros made a last appeal to venality. 'I was too greedy. Half the gold for you.' He shrank from the flame in Vallon's eye. 'Three-quarters.'

'Kill him and have done with it,' Vallon said. He flexed his sword. 'No, by God, I'll shear his head from his neck myself!'

'Please!' Skleros shrieked. He pumped his bound hands. 'Accept the general's demands in full.'

Capitulation sat ill with Thraco but the duke's craven appeal and the troops' simmering dissent left him little choice.

'What I pledge today doesn't hold for tomorrow.'

'Right now I command my fate, and I order you to return to your ships, get your men off *Pelican* and allow her and my transports to tie up. I won't release the prisoners until we've secured all our supplies and all the horses – the duke's as well as our own.

Thraco's features writhed. He turned with an airy wave as if he'd just lost a trivial bet.

Foul weather was brewing and the afternoon was all but done by the time the ships had worked their way to shore. Vallon and his aides climbed aboard *Pelican* and handed Captain Iannis a sealed letter.

'Deliver it to the Logothete tou Dromou in person.'

'Aren't you returning with us?'

'No,' said Vallon. He measured the remaining daylight. 'Leave now and use the night and rain to put distance between yourself and the enemy.'

He was at the gangplank when he checked, his gaze stopping at the Greek Fire siphon in the bow. 'Take that,' he told Josselin, 'together with half a dozen barrels of the fire compound. And while you're about it, dismantle the trebuchet. That's coming with us, too.'

'General, we have only enough pack animals to carry a week's rations and other essentials.'

'We don't know what's essential on a journey such as ours. We can always discard unnecessary baggage.'

*

171

All through the twilight Vallon strode from ship to ship, exhorting his men to greater efforts. They landed the last barrels and bales in a drenching mizzle and it was full dark before they'd loaded the supplies and the baggage train stood ready to depart. Vallon walked down to the sea's edge.

'Can you hear me?'

Faint and far came Thraco's reply. 'I hear you.'

'We're leaving. You'll find the prisoners unharmed on the causeway.'

Thraco's response followed them into the soggy night. 'You're going nowhere. You'll never get through the Caucasus. Either the natives will slaughter you, or what's left of your squadron will straggle back to Trebizond. And we'll be waiting.'

The column crawled across the causeway in pelting rain, the flames of their torches reflected in the water and frogs croaking on all sides. Mosquitoes plagued them. Several times the wagons bogged down to their axles and had to be unloaded before they could be hauled free. Voices rose in complaint. Why hadn't they sailed back on *Pelican*? Where was Vallon leading them?

A warning shout at the head of the column heralded the return of a scout. It was Wayland. Vallon scuffed mosquitoes from his face. 'Where in Hades are we? How much further before we get out of this swamp?'

'Only about a mile, but it would be safer to camp in the marsh. The villagers who fled have probably raised the alarm. I've found a patch of firm ground where we can pitch tents. The wagons will have to remain on the causeway.'

He led the way to the site. Vallon slid stiff-limbed from his horse and handed the reins to Wulfstan. 'Tell the officers to report to my quarters when they've eaten.'

His own meal was hardtack soaked in wine, chewed outside in the rain while servants struggled to erect his command tent. It must have been around midnight before his centurions crammed in, along with Wayland, Hero and Wulfstan.

Vallon slapped his neck. 'Damn these blood-sucking fly-by-nights.' He settled on a camp stool. 'Well, let's hear what you have to say.' He indicated Hero and Wayland and managed to overlook Wulfstan. 'You know I respect their judgement as much as I value yours,' he told the officers.

Josselin spoke first. 'Why didn't you sail back to Constantinople on *Pelican*?'

Vallon's laugh could have come from a coffin. 'Even if we eluded the warships, I doubt that the emperor would shower us with honours for abandoning our mission after little more than a week.'

'Does that mean you intend to continue?'

Vallon stared into space for a moment. 'That's what we have to decide. In some ways, nothing has changed. We still have the treasure and the traitors haven't reduced our strength by much. I count myself better off without the duke in charge. He was only a figurehead, after all, and a damned unpleasant one at that. The Chinese won't know our rank or pedigree. We can give ourselves any titles we please.' He grinned at Otia. 'How would you like to be the Byzantine ambassador to the Song court?'

Otia's demeanour remained grave. 'What are you going to do with Duke Skleros?'

'I'll settle his fate in good time. I take it that he's well-guarded.'

'By four men, sir, night and day.'

Wulfstan sniffed. 'Kill the bastard, sir.'

Vallon eyed him asquint. 'I'm not sure in what capacity you're attending this meeting.'

'Right-hand man, sir. Loyal servant and bodyguard.'

Vallon let it pass. 'He certainly deserves to be executed, but he might still serve some purpose as a hostage.' He swivelled and looked around the cluttered interior. 'The maps,' he said. 'I need to establish our position.'

Hero rummaged in a chest and unearthed a goatskin scroll. Vallon unrolled it on a camp table, weighting the corners down with oil lamps. 'We're a long way north from our planned line of march through Persia.'

In tactful silence, Hero turned the chart the right way round. It was a copy of Ptolemy of Alexandria's map of the known world, updated with material borrowed from the best Arab cartographers. Hero tapped it. 'We're roughly here,' he said. 'North of Armenia, south of Rus, between the two main ranges of the Caucasus.' His finger slid south-east. 'Persia lies here.'

The others gathered round, trying to make sense of the world flattened into two dimensions. 'Otia,' said Vallon, 'which route would you recommend?'

It was apparent that the centurion couldn't make head or tail of the chart. He scratched his head. 'If I wanted to get to Persia, I wouldn't start from here. The easiest way is south, following the coast. The problem is that course would bring us to Armenia, only a few days' ride east of Trebizond. It's the route the duke's men will expect us to take and that's where they'll be waiting for us.' Giving up on the map, Otia pointed towards where he imagined Persia to lie. 'Take the direct route and we'd have to fight our way through mountains, a dead end every second turn and tribesmen contesting every mile.'

'He's right,' Hero said. 'That's the route Xenophon took on his retreat from Persia. He lost hundreds on the march.'

Vallon made an impatient gesture. 'Why can't we head east and follow the Caspian shore until we reach Persia? Surely that's the shortest way.'

'Yes, sir,' Otia said. 'But it would take us through Kutaisi, the Georgian capital. Even if the king granted us a safe conduct, we'd still have to pass through Tiflis and the eastern provinces – all of them held by the Seljuks.'

Vallon stirred in irritation. 'Are you saying there's no way off this coast?'

Otia hesitated. 'The only way to avoid the main Georgian and Seljuk strongholds would be to follow the Phasis upriver into Svaneti, deep in the Caucasus. From there we'd have to take mountain trails east and then cross the northern Caucasus by a high pass before descending towards the Caspian.'

174

'Anyone got any better ideas?' Vallon demanded. 'No? Then that's the route we'll take. Why didn't you say so before, Otia?'

The Georgian winced. 'General, the Caucasus is savage country inhabited by wild clans. Each valley is a world to itself, with its own language and customs. Blood feuds run like a spurting vein through society. The only thing the mountain men hold in common is a murderous hostility to outsiders – and that can mean folk from the next valley. Something else you should know. Many Georgians fleeing from the Seljuk invaders have taken refuge in the mountains. They won't look tenderly on a force containing so many Turkmen.'

The rain had hardened, falling on the tent with a steady hiss that eventually made its own silence.

Vallon scratched his neck. 'You wouldn't have suggested the route unless you thought it was passable. You know the country and you know the perils. That's a great advantage compared to the unknown alternatives. Now then, from this Svaneti can you lead us through the mountains – following some pass known only to a few shepherds?'

Otia shook his head. 'Not a path our baggage train could follow. There's only one way through the Caucasus for a force as heavily laden as ours. It's a high pass called the Daryal Gap – the Gate of the Alans.'

Hero nodded. 'Also known as the Caucasian Gates, Alexander's Gates and the Scythian Keyhole. Actually, Alexander never crossed that pass, but King Mithridates escaped from Pompey's legions through it. In legend, the country beyond the pass was the home of Gog and Magog.'

'Save the history till later,' said Vallon. He stared at the map. 'Who controls the pass?'

'The Georgians still held it when I left fourteen years ago,' said Otia. 'The Seljuks probably control it now. When I say "control", I mean they occupy the forts at the southern end. The higher reaches are in the hands of mountain tribes – brigands who exact tolls on travellers or simply rob and kill them.'

The muggy atmosphere and voracious insects were making Vallon tetchy. 'It can't be that hazardous if armies have been crossing it for centuries.' He stooped again over the map. 'The Gate of the Alans, you said. I take that to mean the land of Alania lies on the northern side.'

'Yes, sir.'

'Our last emperor was married to an Alan princess,' said Vallon. 'She adopted Alexius as her son – and her bedmate, say some. Whatever the case, Constantinople and Alania are allies. Reach Alania and we should be among friends.'

Otia pulled at his beard. 'Sir . . . '

Vallon looked up, his cheeks cavernous in the lamplight. 'Go on.'

'I fear you're underestimating the dangers. I've campaigned against the Caucasus tribes and learned from bloody experience how formidable they are. From the moment we leave this camp, we'll become targets for every brigand and warlord we encounter. If we fail to cross the mountains, they'll pursue us all the way back to the sea. To win any sanctuary, we'd have to capture it by force. Even the smallest villages are fortified with towers built to resist an army.'

Vallon straightened. 'Then we mustn't fail.' He ground his index finger into the map. 'When we reach Alania, what next?'

'Head east to the Caspian and try to find ships to carry us to the Persian coast. From there it's only a short journey south before we strike our planned route.'

Vallon might have left it at that, but Hero could read the map better than anyone else and had spent a considerable time consulting with the Logothete's geographers. 'Excuse me,' he said, easing Vallon aside. His hand traced a tentative course across the Caspian. 'Whatever route we take, we have to reach Turkestan and join the Silk Road in the lands across the Oxus. Even allowing for errors on its maker's part, the map shows that Transoxiana lies due east of the Caspian.' He glanced at Otia. 'How long would a sea voyage take?'

'I'm not sure,' said Otia. 'About a week.'

'Only a week? Even if the voyage was twice that length, it would be considerably shorter than a march across Persia.'

'There must be a good reason for avoiding the sea,' said Josselin. 'Otherwise the Logothete would have sent us that way.'

'Not with Georgia hostile to Byzantium and infested by Seljuks.'

'Some of our Turkmen troopers are from Transoxiana,' said Vallon. 'Fetch Yeke.'

The Turk entered the tent with his face shiny from the rain. He appeared a most affable fellow, but Vallon had seen him in battle engaging the enemy while holding between his teeth, suspended by its hair, the severed head of an opponent he'd slain moments earlier. His grasp of Greek only extended to military commands, and Vallon left the intelligence gathering to Wayland. The exchanges lasted a long time, with much hesitation and head-scratching on Yeke's part.

At last Wayland made his report. 'Yeke says there are no ports on the Caspian's eastern coast. The hinterland is virtually uninhabited, nothing but desert for hundreds of miles – one desert called the Red Sands, the other the Black Sands. We'd never find our way through without guides who know where the wells lie, and we'd have to move fast to cross the deserts before the heat of summer makes them impassable.'

'But it's possible,' Vallon said.

Wayland glanced at Yeke. 'If we don't perish of thirst, a month's hard travelling should bring us to the city of Khiva on the River Oxus. It's called the Amu Darya in Turkic and lies on the caravan trails to Bukhara and Samarkand.'

Vallon pondered. 'Say three weeks to reach the Caspian, a week to sail across it and a month to reach Khiva.' He frowned. 'Hero, we calculated that it would take three months to reach Bukhara by way of Armenia and Persia.'

'At least.'

'Plus another month just to make our way through Armenia.

Four months in total, compared to only two if we take the Caspian route.'

'The sea-road's the road for me,' said Wulfstan.

'Forgive me, sir,' Josselin said. 'It seems to me that you're placing too much reliance on this map and our ability to conjure up several ships.'

'I trust Hero's interpretation and Yeke's first-hand knowledge. There's another consideration. During the journey through Persia, our lives will be dependent on the safe conduct negotiated with the Seljuks. Flimsy protection to be sure. I'd put more faith in a clipping of our Lord's toenails purchased for four solidi from a tout in the Neorian Market.' Vallon placed both hands on the table. 'Gentlemen, I believe the duke has done us a favour by forcing us to diverge from our original course. Otia, I'm putting you in command of the advance party. You'll be our pathfinder and negotiator. Take three squads.' Vallon switched to French. 'Wayland, I'd be obliged if you accompany Otia's squad.'

The rain had increased in intensity, drubbing on the tent with a force that discouraged speech. Vallon didn't need his officers to tell him what they thought. Their expressions made it plain that he was taking an appalling gamble on the flimsiest of intelligence, the wildest of hopes.

XIII

Wayland sprinted through the downpour and dived into his tent, the dog plunging in after him. He lit a lamp, mopped himself dry and lay down on his pallet. Water ran in streams across the ground and the dog heaved up and flopped onto his chest with a groan. Somehow he managed to make room for it and lay half on, half off his bed, listening to the rain on the roof. Water dripped onto his head. Mosquitoes bit.

He'd told Vallon that he hadn't joined the expedition out of a sense of obligation, but that was untrue. After sharing the trials and triumphs of the northern voyage, he'd felt duty-bound to hazard this new venture. And he couldn't deny that the prospect of exploring new lands had made his blood tingle.

The duke's treachery changed everything, relegating the expedition to a madcap quest manned by soldiers who had no idea what they were up against. Wayland knew the risks better than most. During his long sojourn among the Seljuks, he'd learned something about the territory they'd be passing through – tracts of scorching desert where every oasis lay under the control of a warlord. A hundred men were but a mite in that wilderness, infidel prey sent by Allah to be plucked and bled by the faithful.

Also – he was reluctant to admit it – his relationship with Vallon had changed. On their northern adventures, they'd been a close-knit band who shared everything – food, shelter, decisions. On this journey he was just an individual attached to a small army with its established hierarchy, its own way of doing things. Since leaving Constantinople, he'd had only a dozen conversations with Vallon. Wayland didn't resent that. The general's main responsibilities were to his men, some of whom had served under him for almost a decade. Even so . . .

Wayland grunted as the dog sat up, planting a bony paw in his stomach. Hero stuck his dripping head through the tent flap. 'What a foul night. Can I come in?'

Wayland shoved the dog off. 'If you can find somewhere to sit.'

Hero managed to take perch on the edge of the bed and screwed rain from his eyes with both hands. The dog licked his face. Hero laughed and pushed it away. 'Your hound is certainly kinder than the brute that accompanied us on our first journey. I never dared approach within ten feet of it.'

'That dog's temper was framed by years of living in the wild.'

'So was yours,' said Hero. 'You were such a fierce youth when we first met.'

'Man or dog, we all mellow with time.'

'I expected you to say more at the meeting.'

'I don't speak much Greek. A lot of the discussion went over my head, but I didn't want to waste Vallon's time by asking for a translation.'

'It isn't just that. You're not happy with his decision.'

'It's not my place to tell him what he should do.'

'Vallon values your opinion and you know the Turkmen better than anybody. What would you have advised?'

Wayland hesitated. 'Go back. Vallon wouldn't be punished for failure. It wasn't him who chose the duke as ambassador. The Logothete or the emperor is responsible for this mess.'

'You don't understand Byzantine politics. The powerful don't punish themselves for their failures.'

'What's the worst they could have done to Vallon? Strip him of his general's rank. At least he'd be back with his family.'

'Where you'd rather be.'

Wayland didn't answer. Hero absentmindedly stroked the dog's head. 'Vallon feels the same way, though he has to hide it. He resisted this command with all his will. He even considered fleeing with his family and taking service with the Normans. But now he's accepted the mission, his sense of honour won't allow him to abandon it at the first setback.'

'Being forced onto a hostile shore with no clear way ahead and enemies behind us isn't a setback. It's a disaster.'

Hero smiled. 'The night we first met at that castle in Northumbria, Vallon told Count Olbec that the leader of our quest would have to be a man brave enough to cut through the known hazards and resourceful enough to navigate perils as yet unseen. A man who, if he couldn't find a path, would make his own. Vallon's still that man.'

'I know. It's me who's changed.' Wayland sat up. 'Don't misunderstand me. I'll serve Vallon to the best of my abilities. Just don't expect me to be at the centre of his councils.'

After a moment's pause, a question framed but left unspoken, Hero crawled towards the entrance. 'Sleep well, dear friend.'

Fat chance of that. The dog took advantage of Hero's departure to stretch out on the bed. Wayland shoved up against it, the rain leaking on him in fat drops. 'Ah, Syth,' he sighed.

At the sound of her name, the dog sprang up in an ecstasy of expectation that threatened to collapse the flimsy shelter. Wayland grabbed its scruff. 'Lie down, you soft fool.'

The dog subsided with a whimper and fixed a mournful gaze on Wayland's face. He quenched the lamp, but darkness couldn't extinguish his imaginings. A dread echo from the past lodged in his soul – a voice sounding across a fog-bound sea.

You're all bound for hell.

'Wake up, Master Wayland. It's not like you to play the slug-a-bed.'

Wayland heaved himself round and shielded his eyes from the sunlight dazzling behind Wulfstan's grinning face.

'What are you so cheerful about?'

'Rain's stopped, sun's shining, and we're off on an adventure worthy of the heroes of old. What else could you ask for except breakfast? I saved you some pancakes. Stir yourself while they're still warm.'

Wayland dragged himself out and stood swaying slightly, dizzied by the steamy heat and stunning landscape. A bank of pearlescent mist girdled the foothills to the north. Above it, peaks soared in flutes and folds, fresh snow trailing down the lower slopes. So far as Wayland could gauge, the mountain barrier was no more than three days distant.

He ate the pancakes spread with honey and eavesdropped on the troopers. No grumbles this morning, only the bustle and banter of a well-disciplined army striking camp. But Wayland was sensitive to mood and knew that the men's joshing disguised apprehension.

He washed his face and brushed his teeth with a twig bashed into a fuzz at one end.

'Lord?'

Wayland lowered his gaze to bring the speaker's face into sight.

A delicate-featured boy looked up in an agony of shyness. Wayland smiled. 'Hello, who might you be?'

The boy's voice quavered between treble and alto. 'Atam, your Lordship. Master Hero said you needed an interpreter. I speak Greek, Georgian and Turkic. I was born in Armenia and captured by the Seljuks when I was five.'

Wayland had encountered a hundred Atams during his employment with the Seljuks – children taken in war, sometimes wrenched from their dead mothers' arms, usually treated kindly by their captors, but scarred forever by cruel separation from their families.

'I'm not a lord, so call me Wayland. How old are you?'

'Fifteen?' Atam said after a moment.

Thirteen at most, Wayland decided. 'Where did you spring from? I haven't seen you before.'

'I was a cook's assistant, Lord.'

'Have you got a horse?'

'Master Hero found me a mule.'

'You'll need a swifter mount if you're to keep up with me. I'll arrange it.' The lad made Wayland feel protective. 'I'm sure you'll do very well and I'm obliged to Hero for his thoughtfulness. You can start proving your worth right away. The column will soon depart and I must discuss my duties with Otia.'

His little squire approached the centurion with such timidity that the officer didn't notice him.

'Speak up,' said Wayland. 'Tell the centurion that Wayland the Englishman is reporting for duty.'

After listening to Atam's piping announcement, Otia shook Wayland's hand.

'He's pleased to have you in his unit,' said Atam. 'General Vallon told him that nobody can scout a trail or sniff out danger as well as you.' Atam pointed at the mountains. 'Lord Otia says you'll need all your cunning to spot the snares and pitfalls waiting for us up there.'

*

Menials had stirred themselves well before dawn to prepare the baggage train. It was a long process and the squadron didn't move out until the sun stood halfway up the sky, the troopers riding with short reins to match the supply column's pace. Atam at his side, Wayland trotted in company with the reconnaissance squad, the dog loping with lolling tongue in the shadow cast by his horse.

Wayland allowed the hound to make the occasional foray for game. There was much to excite its hunting instincts, including long-tailed fowl with bronze and green plumage and enamelled red heads that stalked the thickets with autocratic tread. Wayland hadn't seen such birds before. Otia told him they were called pheasants and took their name from the river Phasis and its province.

There rode in the scouting party three Turkmen who snapped shots at the pheasants as the dog flushed them. One of the bowmen – a Cuman from the steppes north of the Black Sea – brought down a bird as it burst into flight and invited Wayland to bend his bow in friendly competition, saying that he'd heard the Englishman was a match for the finest Turkish archers. Wayland kept his bow slung and his challenger whirled away with a disparaging laugh. Watching him, Wayland remembered the Cuman youth he'd slain in an archery duel by the Dnieper nine years before. Since that expedition he'd never shed another man's blood.

They left the marshlands and struck north on a road leading through pastures and orchards drenched in blossom. They passed wattle-and-daub hamlets thatched with reed, and Otia called out reassurance to the inhabitants clustered at a safe distance. The women wore colourful smocks, pantaloons and head scarves. Some of them half-raised their hands in response to Otia's greetings. Most crossed themselves or made signs to ward off the evil eye. Their menfolk just peered in hard-eyed suspicion until the invaders passed from sight.

Wayland kneed his horse alongside the Georgian. 'A handsome race. Proud, too.'

'Wait until we get into the mountains. Then you'll see pride.'

With the sun dissolving into the horizon, they made camp by a river called the Inguri and on the day following they reached the highlands. As the road steepened and began to twist, the scouts ceased their idle pursuits and watched the rolling hills and forest margins for signs of ambush. Nor was it long before their caution was justified. On a rise commanding the road, the river hard to the left, a line of armed horsemen reared up. Otia ordered his men to keep their swords sheathed and stood in his stirrups to announce who they were and where they were going, stressing that a larger force was following and that they were just passing through with no hostile designs on this place.

It was like that all day, potential belligerents ghosting out of trees or staring down with bristling hostility from the heights, Otia shouting assurances until his voice had been abraded to a husky croak.

At one pinch point in a sunken way, a sling-stone thrummed past Wayland and struck one of the troopers' horses on the rump, stinging it into a wild gavotte. The men drew their bows and scattered, searching for their attacker.

'Leave it,' Otia ordered. 'Probably a boy acting on a dare.'

Wayland passed the sweating centurion a leather water bottle. 'If we didn't have you to smooth our passage, I think we'd have had a sharp encounter today.'

Otia tilted the bottle and drank deep before handing it back. He wiped his mouth. 'When I told the general I couldn't guarantee safe passage, I spoke the truth. I'm a lowlander and the Svans despise lowlanders. For my part, I hate the highland tribes. Every winter they descend from their mountain keeps to steal cattle. The folk hereabouts would love to hang me and burn me hanging, and given the chance, I'd mete out the same fate to them.'

Next day Vallon ordered the scouts to stay close to the main party, the whole force and its supply train climbing at a mule's plod. The tumbling river carved a path through a beech forest with trees so massive that it took five men with linked hands to encircle one mighty bole. Leaving the wood, the column advanced up a green glen and entered a highland basin that might have been the park and pleasure ground of a wilderness prince. Stands of walnut and oak curved up to grassy ridges overlooked by fanged peaks. On the other side of the river, pines showed as dark cones in a dense deciduous forest. Wayland spotted bears browsing high up in a clearing. Two eagles soared on splayed wings, tuning their pinions to the air currents, the sun striking gold from their heads. One of them gave a yelping cry and locked talons with its mate, the pair pinwheeling through the air.

Otia pointed to the north-east. 'Over there stands Elbruz, the loftiest mountain in the world. Where Prometheus endured his torment.'

Hero explained the myth, recounting how Prometheus, a Titan, had enraged Zeus by first creating man out of clay and breathing life into him, and then stealing the gift of fire from the gods and giving it to man. For his crime, Zeus had chained him to the icy slopes of Elbruz and condemned him to have his liver pecked out by an eagle in perpetuity.

Warming to his tale-telling, Hero added that it was in the Caucasus kingdom of Colchis that Jason had fulfilled his quest for the Golden Fleece belonging to a magical ram sent by Zeus to rescue Phrixus and Helle.

Otia leaned to touch Hero's wrist. 'I'm sorry to spoil your story, my learned friend, but the Golden Fleece has nothing to do with gods. In these mountains the people use fleeces to trap gold in the rivers, weighting them down underwater. Sometimes, after a land-slide or flood, the prospectors retrieve the fleece with so much precious dust caught in the wool that the skin appears to be made of solid gold.

At that point the squad cantered over a rise and Wayland reined in, taken aback by the sight of a distant fortified settlement that looked like something from fairyland. Lofty square stone towers capped with turrets clustered around the houses, the limewashed keeps brilliant against the intense green slopes. In a valley to the north, a glacier descended from the mountain chain like a silver staircase.

'I prefer Hero's version,' said Wayland.

The trees thinned to a stippling of firs, the green curve of the valley replicating the blue arc of the sky. The wayfarers passed shrines painted with frescos of four-winged seraphim with wheels for feet, and other oddities rendered in a vigorous folk style. Of the inhabitants of this lofty land, the squadron saw nothing.

'Where is everybody?' Wayland asked Otia.

'Waiting for us,' the centurion said, pointing at four fortified settlements clumped near the end of the valley. 'Ushguli. It means "heart without fear".'

Wayland absorbed the scene – the river cascading through hay meadows, larks trilling overhead, the scent of pine resin wafting on an updraught. The towers – there must have been more than fifty – made the settlements look like miniature cities.

'A man could live content in such a beautiful place.'

'Come back in winter, when the snow drifts over the eaves and the wolves howl outside your door and you have to check before you enter a byre in case a bear has forced its way inside.'

Wayland scanned the slopes. 'So everybody's inside the towers.'

Otia nodded. 'News of our coming probably reached them more than a day ago. In Svaneti, all strangers are potential enemies and every home is a castle.'

The centurion directed the force towards one of the settlements. The closer Wayland approached, the more impressed he was. Some of the towers stood a hundred feet high, tapering up to shallow-pitched roofs with arched loopholes at their eaves. But the houses and byres huddled around their bases were squat and windowless, roofed with crude slate tiles and surrounded by dry-stone walls.

'See how the village forms a compound like a hive,' Otia said. 'Any army trying to take it would have to fight house by house, the inhabitants retreating before them, the defenders in the towers pouring down a rain of arrows and rocks.'

Wayland spotted arrows trained on them from every machicolation. Otia identified the defenders' spokesman and began negotiations, questions and answers drifting back and forth.

Vallon rode up. 'Is that the chief?'

'First among a council of leading men. His name's Mochila and he refuses to admit us. He says we can camp at the end of the valley and he'll call on us before dark.'

The campsite offered a view of a mountain wall hung with a glacier. By the time the squadron had secured their position, the snow glimmered cold blue and the gold tracery outlining the summits was fading. A sentry called a warning and Wayland turned to see thirty men cantering out of the dusk. At their head Mochila rode a splendid black stallion. He was clad in a felt cape with square shoulder pads as wide as wings. Under this he wore ring mail, his outfit capped by a pointed iron helmet so archaic that it might have been salvaged from a Scythian grave barrow.

He and Otia greeted each other with solemn ceremony, touching hand to heart. The centurion introduced Mochila to Vallon, both men appraising each other for signs of strength, weakness or sinister intent. Mochila had the features of a starved eagle.

'Victory to you,' he said.

'And to you,' Vallon repeated.

Otia addressed Vallon. 'General, I think I've convinced Mochila that we pose no threat. He invites you and your senior men to a feast. I suggest you take no more than half a dozen.'

'I know *we're* no threat. I'm not so sure about these Svans.'

'Mochila would treat a refusal as an insult.'

'I'd rather risk offending the man than handing myself over as a hostage.'

'General, we won't get through his domain without his consent. Even if we fight our way through, he'll raise the next clan against us.'

'He'll want payment.'

'Leave that to me. I think I can negotiate a safe passage without digging too deep into our coffers.'

Vallon and Mochila locked gazes, each looking for a tell-tale blink. Vallon inclined his head in a finely calibrated bow. 'Tell Mochila that I'm delighted to accept his invitation. You'll accompany me, of course, together with Wayland and Hero.'

A shout made everyone whirl. 'Those men are traitors and felons. I'm Duke Skleros Phocas, appointed leader of this expedition by the Emperor Alexius Comnenus. A thousand gold solidi to anyone who—'

The duke's guards smothered his outburst. Mochila stroked one finger along his top lip.

'Who's that?' he asked.

'A prisoner,' Vallon replied. 'Tell him it's none of his business.'

Mochila nodded in contemplation, made a last appraisal of the Outlanders and led his party into the darkness.

Vallon watched them go. 'Do you think they understood?'

'The duke mentioned solidi,' said Josselin. 'Even up here they know what that's worth. I advise you not to put yourself in jeopardy. If the Svans take you captive, we'll have the devil of a job to get you back. Let me go in your stead.'

Vallon trained his gaze on Ushguli. Stars wreathed its towers and a tilted moon cast inky contours across the pastures. 'This won't be the only time we'll have to throw ourselves on the mercy of strangers. You stay here. If I don't return, you're in command.'

A guide holding a tallow torch led them through lanes ankle-deep in cow shit. Chained mastiffs snarled and lunged from dark entrances. Wayland glimpsed eyes tracking them through shuttered windows. The guide climbed a wooden gallery, opened a door and ushered them into a large and sooty chamber fogged with smoke from a dung-fed hearth. Eyes and teeth glimmered in the light of a dozen lamps. As his vision adjusted, Wayland counted two dozen faces, old and young, many of the countenances as hard as spades. His gaze roamed over carved panels and chests painted with celestial symbols and other arcana. Crosses and icons shared wall space with trophy horns of aurochs, bison and ibex, hanging next to saddles and bridles inlaid with turquoise and silver. Mochila and his attendants had shed their armour and wore loose shirts with crosses or triangles embroidered over the heart. Mother of pearl embellished the seams of their trousers.

Servants showed the guests to their places on shaggy rugs. Wayland folded his legs and sat, placing Atam at his side.

'What's the procedure?' Vallon asked Otia.

'A long one, I'm afraid. We begin with a formal exchange of toasts, then we feast. Only after that do we get down to business. Mochila will try and get us drunk.'

Wayland put his mouth to Atam's ear. 'Tell me everything's that's said.'

A steward brought the guests beer. After the second cup, an elderly man rose and struck a theatrical pose.

'He's the *tamada*,' Atam whispered. 'The clan's toastmaster.'

The man declaimed at length, lifting his cup at each toast. Atam summarised. 'He says how honoured his community is to welcome distinguished travellers to their motherland. He asks you to drink to their motherland. Now he raises his cup in blessings on *your* motherland.'

The ceremony was interminable and confusing, the toastmaster sometimes raising his cup in invitation to drink, sometimes hoisting it as a prelude to another long-winded speech. Wayland refused the fourth refill, but the steward pulled away his protecting hand and slopped beer to the brim. When he tilted the jug over Atam's beaker, Wayland wrenched the steward's arm aside. 'Enough. He's too young to take strong drink.'

After the *tamada* had finished, it was Otia's turn. Shedding his usual taciturnity, he spoke with a poet's flourish, thanking the Svans for their hospitality, rejoicing in his return to Georgia, and lamenting the prospect of leaving Ushguli so soon.

As soon as he'd finished, another Svan stood and delivered a tipsy peroration on universal friendship under God. Atam's voice grew squeaky with the effort of translating. Wayland tapped his arm. 'Rest your voice for the important part.'

Service with the Seljuk sultan had trained Wayland to endure lengthy audiences, but even he was half asleep when Atam prodded his ribs. 'Now it's your turn.'

'Me?'

Eyes bored expectantly through the fug. He climbed to his feet and appealed to Vallon. 'What am I supposed to say?'

'Whatever takes your tongue. I gave them the twenty-third psalm. "Yea, though I walk through the valley of the shadow of death ..."'

Wayland managed only a few halting platitudes before his voice dribbled away.

'Recite one of your English poems,' Vallon prompted.

'They don't understand English.'

'Then you needn't be shy.'

Wayland remembered a poem called *The Wanderer* he'd first heard seated on his grandfather's knee, a January storm moaning through the wildwood outside. His throat loosened.

> Storms crash against these rocky slopes,
> Sleet and snow fall and fetter the world,
> Winter howls, then darkness draws on,
> The night-shadow casts gloom and brings
> Fierce hailstorms from the earth to frighten men.
> Nothing is ever easy in the kingdom of earth,
> The world beneath the heavens is in the hands of fate.

Wayland struck his palm with his right hand.

> Here possessions are fleeting, here friends are fleeting,
> Here man is fleeting, here kinsman is fleeting,
> The whole world becomes a wilderness.

He lowered his head and paused. The room hung on his next

190

utterance. He pointed at a gilt cross at the rear of the chamber.

'It is best for a man to seek mercy and comfort from the Father in heaven where security stands for us all.'

Fierce applause and hoisted cups rewarded his recitation. Vallon patted his arm. 'That was well done. Do you think our hosts are drinking watered ale?'

Wayland took a glug of beer to ease his throat. 'I've been watching. They're drinking the same piss as us.'

One more speech delivered by Mochila followed before women sashayed in with the food. Most of them were handsome matrons, strong of feature and weighted with heavy silver ornaments and head-dresses studded with cowrie shells. The one who served Wayland was a maid with slender arched eyebrows and a face as oval as an almond. Her breasts jostled under her homespun shift. A crescent of gold in one ear emphasised the perfection of her features. When her grey-green eyes met his, he had to avert his gaze. Only two weeks since he'd parted from Syth and already he was making eyes at another woman. How could he remain faithful to his wife for two years? How could she remain true to him?

Eyes downcast under long lashes, the girl served him a mess of baked cheese and butter topped with a crust of mixed meal. The sweet-sour mixture stuck to the roof of Wayland's mouth, but it was a delicious change from twice-baked bread as hard as brick, and he trowelled up the mess with gusto, following his hosts' example by using his knife to scrape the treacly bits stuck on the pan. Next, the women bore in a smoke-blackened cauldron of broth holding hunks of beef. The room filled with the sounds of tearing and slurping. Mochila personally served Vallon the choicest pieces. All the time the beer kept circulating.

At last the men set aside their bowls, belched, loosened their belts and slumped back. Mochila placed his hands on his knees and inclined his face towards Vallon, his features skull-like in the smoky light.

Atam translated in a forceful whisper. 'He asks how he can assist our mission.'

Vallon massaged his stomach. 'You've already transformed our journey from painful toil to luxurious pleasure. The only help I require is advice on how to reach the Daryal Gorge.' He allowed a pause. 'And if you could provide a man to show us the way ...'

Mochila rotated a hand in a dismissive half-circle. 'You'll never reach the Daryal. The passes ahead are difficult enough for lightly laden horses. Impossible for your carts.'

'I have no intention of abandoning our wagons,' Vallon said. 'If necessary, we'll strip them down and carry them over the mountains plank by plank, wheel by wheel. Of course, our task would be made easier if we had extra hands.'

Mochila sucked in his cheeks and shook his head. 'It's spring. All our sons are tending the herds in the high pastures, and our women are busy in the fields from dawn to dark. You've arrived during our busiest season. In Svaneti, the snows allow only six months to sow and reap.'

'Naturally, we'll compensate you.'

Wayland knew the Svans had scented prey by the way they licked their lips, pushed out their cheeks with their tongues and glanced at each other without quite making eye contact. Mochila remained immobile. 'What are you offering?'

'For you, my Lord – I'd rather discuss that in private.'

Mochila stilled a buzz of discontent with an upheld finger and resumed his discussion with Vallon. Wayland sensed tension growing.

'I'll make allowances for your ignorance of our customs. In Svaneti we don't strike deals behind our kinsmen's backs.'

'Forgive me, Lord. As a general appointed by the emperor, I'm used to treating with great men and rewarding them according to their station and influence.'

Wayland saw a gleam of avarice come and go in Mochila's eyes. The Svan leader turned his horn drinking cup and looked at it. His tone when he spoke was thoughtful.

'I ask nothing for myself, but it's only proper that men diverted from their livelihood should be recompensed.' Mochila relaxed on his cushions. 'An expedition as large as yours must be carrying a great deal of gold.'

Vallon uttered a rueful laugh. 'If only we had enough to spare. Alas, we're at the beginning of our journey and can't afford to shed a single coin. I have to pay the men's wages. They're mercenaries,' he continued before Mochila could respond, 'warriors hardened in some of Byzantium's bloodiest battles. They serve only for gain, not out of personal loyalty. Dip into their wages and they'll vent their anger first on me and then on the people they hold responsible for depriving them of their due.'

Mochila's expression turned malevolent. 'Then what are you prepared to offer?'

'Salt.'

'Salt!' Mochila's mouth formed a tube. 'What makes you think we want salt?'

'I understand it's a scarce commodity in these mountains. I've seen for myself how your curs follow us and lick our piss. Of course, we have other goods you might find more to your liking – cloth, oil, grain ...'

Wayland registered Mochila making complicated calculations. 'How much salt?'

Vallon consulted with Otia before answering. 'Enough to furnish your needs for half a year.'

Mochila smacked one hand on his knee. 'You ask me to provide human labour and in return you offer to reward cattle. No, my honoured guest. Let us go back to the beginning.'

But the deadlock was broken. Wayland dozed through the rest of the haggling. So far as he could tell, when the bargaining was over the Svans were better off to the tune of salt, cloth and cowrie shells – the last a condition imposed by an old woman who'd been lurking by a door throughout the negotiations.

Starlight glazed the summits when Wayland stepped into the night, the grass underfoot crisp with frost. He swallowed breath after breath of pure cold air. A hand gripped his elbow.

'What did you make of that?' Vallon said. 'I know from old experience how sensitive you are to treachery. If Mochila makes you itch, we'd all better get scratching.'

Wayland looked back at the turreted settlement. 'He wants our gold but doesn't command enough men to take it by force.'

'I found a moment to tell him that I'd line his purse as well as giving him the pick of two of the duke's horses.'

'It will only sharpen his appetite. I think he intends to exact more than a few bags of salt and a fistful of gold.'

'I've put the squadron on maximum alert.' Vallon said.

'Even if we get through Svaneti, we still have to deal with the leeches in the next valley – and the one after that. If Mochila's the measure of the highlanders, they could bleed us dry before we reach the Caspian.'

Vallon squeezed Wayland's arm. 'With God's grace, we'll find a way through.'

With that he was gone, issuing orders to his lieutenants. Wayland tilted his face towards the firmament, struck by the thought that the same stars he was viewing shone down on his family.

A husky cough brought him back to earth. He laid a hand on Atam's shoulder.

'You did well,' said Wayland. His dog stood at Atam's side with ears pricked and eyes bright. 'You really have no family left?'

Atam scuffed a foot across the ground. 'None.'

'We have a long way to go, and all of us will find the going easier if we have friends we can depend on. I'm too young to be your father, but not too old to be your brother.'

Atam's eyes grew round and the dog wagged its tail.

Wayland cupped a hand around the orphan's shoulder. 'It's late. The sun will soon peep over the mountains, and I suspect a hard day will follow. Stay close to me at all times.'

XIV

It took the squadron all the next day and most of the night to dismantle the carts and portion out the loads among the Svan porters. Mochila had mobilised most of Ushguli's population, including women and children. The first rays of the sun were splaying through the mountain gaps when the column set off. Mochila and his entourage accompanied it to the end of the last home pasture and showered blessings on the travellers with every sign of sincerity. He looked too pleased by half, Wayland decided.

A bend and dip in the valley hid the farewell party and Wayland turned his attention to the route. Abram their guide was a stringy mountain man – sixty if he was a day – wearing two fleece jackets and with eyes so fogged by exposure to wind and ice glare that he appeared half-blind. He led the way on foot, a staff yoked behind his shoulders and his head bowed like a mendicant deep in contemplation.

They followed a brawling torrent of meltwater flowing from the glacial tongue under the mountain wall. The ice-hung massif loomed overhead and Abram appeared to be leading them into a dead end until he struck off east up a tributary. A little further on, the trail divided, one well-trodden path making an easy ascent to a broad col, the other little more than a goat track that kept to the stream, climbing in steps towards a valley hemmed in by precipices.

Wayland and Atam caught up with the guide and asked him why he'd chosen the harder route.

'He says the Zagar Pass will be blocked by snow,' Atam told Wayland. 'This way is steeper, but the snow will be less deep.'

Wayland studied the wizened pathfinder, but Abram's clouded gaze was unfathomable. It was true that storms had blacked out the mountains since they'd left the coast, depositing a good six feet of snow on the upper slopes. Wayland glanced back down the column, the tail already a mile adrift, then took another look at the ascent. He couldn't believe that the Svans would lay an ambush in such difficult terrain against a force so widely dispersed.

Even so, he kept close to the guide and a wary eye on the crags. The stream leaped and jostled over rust-red boulders and he lost count of the times they crossed the current, sometimes on log bridges, sometimes on spans of ice, sometimes by fording the icy water. In places the track rose a hundred feet above the stream and in others it dipped below levees of boulders piled up by floods.

The valley narrowed into a gorge, huge scarps of naked rock reducing the sky to a ragged slit. They rode through a pine forest rooted among house-sized boulders carpeted with moss. Azaleas and rhododendrons bloomed in the shadows.

The trail climbed above the stream and steepened, slanting along a cliff. It wasn't an ascent for the faint of heart or head. Landslips had swept away sections of the trail, leaving steep scree slopes that had to be crossed on a rut only a few inches wide. The Svans set their horses at these places in a rattle of shale, while the more cautious tip-toed after with a lot of balletic arm movements. Wayland stayed in the saddle, glancing down at the stream muttering hundreds of feet below.

The Svans pointed out shrines to travellers who'd lost their lives on the route, Atam translating with unseemly relish. This wayfarer had met a bear on the track and the beast had asserted its right of way. That poor fellow had fallen three hundred feet, yet when his brother had recovered the corpse, he'd found the body completely unmarked, its bones so pulverised that it could be bundled up into a saddle bag.

Wayland wiped his brow and shed his cloak. The Svans had boasted that their settlement was the highest in Georgia, and he estimated that they must have climbed at least two thousand feet, yet the atmosphere was oppressively warm. Meltwater splattered from the heights, and stones released from a melting lobe of ice whistled past. He saw tattered black clouds streaming across the dulling sky. Abram shouted a warning and Wayland pulled Atam into the lee of the cliff.

The sky went dark and hailstones as big as grapes rattled down, bouncing knee-high off the ground and laying two inches of ice before the clouds shredded and daylight returned. Sunlight dazzled on the mantle of hail and a bird sang. The guide set off again as if committed to some eternal task.

On they climbed, turning this way and that up a rock staircase until Wayland hardly knew whether he was coming or going. Choughs spiralled in the void, their witchy cries echoing between the cliffs.

At one spot the track made a tight turn around a knife-edged outcrop, the trail no more than three feet wide and a stomach-swooping drop below. Wayland led Atam's horse around it and waited, the Svan horsemen negotiating the danger point with swaggering indifference. A squad of Turkmen followed. Not to be outfaced, they stayed mounted, allowing their horses to negotiate the hazard unsupervised.

'Take care,' Wayland said. The Turkmen were superb horse-men, but for most of them, this was their first experience of mountains.

A Seljuk trooper came round the corner, chatting over his shoulder to a companion. Wayland anticipated the accident a moment before it happened and lunged forward.

Too late. The tip of the Seljuk's bow nudged the cliff – the glancing touch enough to unbalance the horse. Pushed sideways, it put its hind legs over the drop and flailed for purchase, its rider throwing his weight forward.

'Jump!' Wayland shouted.

The horse made a last frantic lunge to regain its footing, then slid with a terrified whinny over the edge. Wayland grabbed the rider's arm as he toppled and was nearly dragged into the depths himself. He smacked face first against the ledge, cheek sawing against its edge, his arm half-wrenched out of its socket by the Seljuk's weight. From this ghastly perspective, he saw the horse cartwheel into the abyss, strike a ledge with a sickening smack, spin down and burst in a bloom of gore on the bottom of the gorge.

He would have followed if the Seljuk's companions hadn't pinned his legs and relieved the strain on his arm. They hauled him and the Seljuk to safe ground. He sagged against the cliff, gulping air and massaging his wrenched shoulder. The man he'd rescued sat with his arms clasped around his knees, grinning like a lunatic. Wayland converted a slap into a gentle touch. He held thumb and forefinger a whisker apart.

'We were that close.'

The Seljuk seized his hand and kissed it. The Turkmen touched hands to lips and bestowed thanks on Wayland before leading their companion away.

'You nearly died because of that silly man,' Atam said.

Wayland rotated his arm to check that he hadn't torn ligaments. He dabbed at his flayed cheek. 'Come on. We can't be far from the top.'

They crossed a shallow basin, the horses ploughing through mushy snow, and emerged onto a col flanked by frost-shattered spires sheathed with lichens. Reaching the other side, Wayland looked out over frozen chaos, the Great Caucasus range stretching east and west for as far as the eye could see. At this height most of the peaks appeared level with his eye, but a few distant mountains were so lofty that only their summits showed, floating in the ether. Below, the route descended to a frozen tarn like a glaucous eye before spilling down into canted planes of forest and alpine meadow.

Otia drew alongside and surveyed the scene, hands crossed on his pommel. 'Now we come to the country of the Ratchuelians.'

'What are they like?'

Otia laughed without mirth. 'I'll tell you. A stranger travelling to Oni, the main town, fell in with a native of Ratcha. "Are we far from Oni?" the stranger asked. "No, not far," the native replied. They walked for another two hours and again the stranger asked, "Are we far from Oni?" "Now we are," said the Ratchuelian.'

Otia clicked his tongue and began his descent. Wayland and

Atam found a resting place against a sun-soaked boulder and Wayland divided a small truckle of smoked cheese and a loaf. They ate while the column trudged past. A clump of dwarf daffodils growing on a rocky seep reminded Wayland of Northumberland. A vulture scribing a lonely circle in the sky made him aware that he'd probably never see home again.

All the while the soldiers and porters kept filing past. The train must have been strung out over three miles. It had been mid-afternoon when Wayland reached the col, and now the sun stood balanced on the western peaks and shadows were filling the valleys. It would be dark before the last of the column reached camp.

Lucas strode by, leading his horse and driving three mules with staccato cries. Wayland nodded at him and the Frank took this as an invitation to come over.

'Master Wayland, can I ask a favour of you?'

Wayland cocked a suspicious eye.

Lucas dropped to his haunches. 'What happened to your face?'

'Say what you have to say.'

'You and Vallon are old companions.'

'You're not, so call him "General".'

Lucas scratched his nose. 'You heard he put me in the baggage train.'

'You got off lightly. Most commanders would have had you flogged or hanged for abusing their son.'

'Adopted son, and he deserved it. Anyway, I don't want to spend the rest of this journey staring up a mule's arse. I was thinking—'

'No, you're not, or you wouldn't waste your breath. I'm not going to plead your case with General Vallon.'

'Yes, but—'

'Didn't you hear me? The general sentenced you to a month in the baggage train. Stay out of trouble and you'll be back with your squad before we reach the Caspian.'

'Everyone expects the highlanders to ambush us before then. I don't want to be stuck with shit-shovelling muleteers if there's a

199

fight. That's another thing. The captain of the baggage train is a thief. Him and his pals have been selling off our supplies on the sly. I can give Vallon proof.'

Wayland closed his eyes in disbelief. When he opened them, they were cold with anger. 'You don't understand a thing, do you? All baggage captains are thieves. I know it, you know it, the general knows it. Report the thieving and he'll be forced to take action. The result? One baggage captain with a stretched neck and deep resentment among his men.'

Lucas pushed up and looked down on Wayland. 'It seems to me that Vallon punishes the innocent and turns a blind eye to the guilty.'

Wayland kept his temper – just. 'You have a strange way of showing gratitude to a man who took you into his home.' He jerked his chin in dismissal. 'Look to your beast.'

Lucas stood and whistled. Aster whinnied, trotted towards him and shoved his muzzle into his master's hands. Lucas laid his face against Aster's head and the horse whickered with pleasure. Lucas squinted at Wayland. 'Admit it. I'm clever with horses.'

'I meant that mule,' said Wayland.

The beast, burdened with a cartwheel on each flank, was dangerously unbalanced, trying to reach a clump of herbage in a steep gulley. Lucas stooped, picked up a stone and from a range of thirty yards sent it whirring on a flat trajectory to hit the mule in the crupper. With a triumphant glance at Wayland, he gathered his charges and disappeared down the other side of the col, singing a Pyrenean shepherd song. He held a tune pretty well.

Wayland shook his head. 'I don't know what to make of that lad.'

Atam groped for a response. 'He's a very naughty fellow.'

Wayland threw back his head and laughed. 'Yes, he is.'

Cold clamped the summit by the time the tailenders came plodding past, a squad of disgruntled Outlanders shepherding a group of puffing porters and snorting mules burdened with the dismantled trebuchet. The siege engine's arm was slung between two pairs of mules and it was beyond Wayland's comprehension how they had manoeuvred it around the steep hairpins. He stood and dusted off the seat of his breeches.

'Are you the last?'

'We are.'

'Make haste, then.'

When the sound of chinking hooves and sliding shale had faded, Wayland mounted and prepared to follow. He was on the brink when he glanced back.

'Did you see the duke come past?'

Atam shook his head.

Wayland spurred his horse down the slope, shouting at the troopers to stop.

'The duke,' he panted. 'Where's the duke?'

They eyed each other and shrugged. 'How would I know?' one said.

Wayland's gaze shimmied. Had the duke and his guards passed while he was talking to Lucas? No. Wayland registered things even if they didn't lodge at the forefront of his consciousness. He kept his voice calm. 'The duke and his escort rode not far in front of you. When did you last see them?'

The troopers knew something was amiss and tried to distance themselves from any consequences. 'We haven't seen the duke since we left Ushguli,' one of them muttered. 'We've been too busy herding these sluggards.'

'Think hard,' Wayland insisted. 'No blame attaches to you.'

A Thracian trooper spoke up. 'The last time I saw the duke's party was before the hailstorm.'

That must have been around midday. Pointless to backtrack. The first stars already shone and it would be impossible to follow the trail by night. If the duke had escaped during the storm, he could be back in Ushguli by now.

'Look after Atam,' Wayland said, and rowelled his horse, riding

201

helter-skelter down the trail, demanding of every soldier he passed if they'd seen the duke. No one had, and what little hope he had was all but gone when he galloped into camp.

'Duke Skleros,' he shouted. 'Is he here?'

Vallon stepped out of his tent. 'He's in the rear.'

'No, he's not. I counted the whole column past. He's gone.'

'Are you sure?'

'I'm telling you.'

Vallon clawed aside the entrance to his tent and crooked a finger for his officers to follow. Wulfstan inveigled himself into the company.

Vallon stood with his back to them. 'How?' he demanded.

'Simple,' said Wayland. 'The column was scattered, each man concentrating on the next step. There were dozens of places where the duke could have slipped out of sight. He probably did it under cover of the storm, and then all he had to do was wait until everybody had passed.'

Vallon's hand tapped his thigh with ominous slowness. 'I know how he did it. I want to know who allowed him to disappear.'

Otia fingered his throat. 'The guards must have aided him.'

Vallon didn't turn. 'Who were they? Who selected them?'

Josselin stood rigid. 'I did, sir. I chose two four-man shifts, all from different squads to reduce the risk of any conniving.'

Vallon threw out a hand. 'Call a muster. See who's missing.' He pivoted. 'Skleros wouldn't have escaped unless he was certain that Mochila would offer him sanctuary.'

'Ride back to Ushguli and demand the duke's return,' Josselin said. 'Lay the place under siege if necessary.'

'You've seen its defences,' said Otia. 'We'd go hungry long before the Svans feel the pinch.'

'Destroy a tower or two with the trebuchet. That would bring Mochila to his senses.'

'Do that,' said Otia, 'and we'll make foes of every mountain tribe we meet.'

Wulfstan stroked his moustaches. 'General, if I was you—'

202

Vallon lashed out. 'You're not, damn it, and if you tell me one more time that I should have killed the duke, I'll cut off your other hand and choke you with it.'

Wulfstan assumed a martyr's air. 'I wasn't going to say that, General. The way I see it, we have a hundred Svans at our mercy. Hold them hostage against the Duke's return.'

'Otia?' said Vallon. 'Would that work?'

The centurion breathed out. 'You have to consider how the Svans regard us. To them we're unwelcome foreigners carrying rich cargo – sheep ripe for fleecing as far as Mochila's concerned. If the duke escaped because of our negligence, we have only ourselves to blame.'

Wulfstan made to spit and only just remembered the company he kept. 'He won't feel so cunning if we hang a dozen of his kinsmen outside Ushguli.'

Wayland saw Vallon giving serious consideration to the suggestion and weighed in. 'Our mission isn't ruined if we don't get the duke back. He must have promised gold in exchange for freedom, but the gold isn't in his gift.'

Vallon stared through him. 'Allow the Svans to go unpunished and every tribe we encounter will take it as licence to attack us.'

'And if we exact revenge, every tribe will treat us as enemies.'

Vallon pondered. 'The duke will tell the Svans how much wealth we're carrying. What I don't understand is how Mochila expects to lay his hands on it. We're out of his territory and I can't imagine he'd want to share any spoils with his neighbours.'

'I think he'll deliver Skleros to the Georgians,' Otia said. 'For a hefty price, of course. That's the only outcome that would benefit the duke. Without Georgian help, he'll never reach Trebizond. He'll pay for that passage by reporting our route and telling the Georgians how much wealth we're carrying. If I'm right, we can expect a bloody reception on the road to the Daryal Gorge.'

'Mochila will be aware of the mischief Skleros can do to us and might offer to eliminate it by returning him for a ransom.'

'A price worth paying,' Otia said. 'We're not strong enough to take on the Georgian army.'

Aimery entered to confirm that the duke and his guards were gone.

Vallon paced back and forth in the confined space. He stopped and everybody held their breath. 'Bring me Mochila's leading man.'

The general waited, legs akimbo. Two troopers shoved a Svan warrior into the tent. He smirked around at the company, his smile fraying when it settled on Vallon.

'Ask him what price Mochila demands for the duke's return.'

'He claims to have no idea what you're talking about,' Otia said.

Vallon's sword came out with a slither. 'Ask him again.'

A long wrangle ensued before Otia delivered the terms. 'He swears that Mochila isn't harbouring the duke, but says that the Svans will do everything they can to hunt him down and return him to our custody. Naturally, Mochila would expect a reward.'

'How much?'

'Half our gold and treasure.'

Vallon considered the demand as if it were a reasonable basis for negotiation. He pointed at the Svan. 'Take him out and hang him. Keep as many of his clan as we need to transport our supplies to the next settlement, and drive the rest away.'

Otia grimaced. 'Executing him would be seen as a declaration of war by all the mountain tribes. It's a war we can't win. They'll winnow us away by ones and twos until nothing is left of us except a highlander's proud memory and a rusty Byzantine corselet nailed to a wall.'

'And if we don't exact justice, every petty lord will take it as an invitation to gnaw on our bones.' Vallon's forefinger jabbed. 'Even if we paid the ransom, Mochila would still betray us to the Georgians. I'm damned if I'll let him line his pockets twice over at our expense.' Vallon caught his breath and spoke with calm finality. 'The sentence stands. Execute it forthwith.'

XV

At the first Ratcha village, Vallon dismissed the remaining Svan porters and ordered Otia to negotiate with the Ratchuelians for replacements. The highlanders remained in their towers, rejecting all inducements, scorning all threats. The one-sided parleying went on until afternoon of the next day before Otia gave up.

'We have to press on, General. The longer we delay, the more time we give our enemies to lay ambushes.'

'We can't go forward without beasts and men to carry our baggage.'

Otia exchanged a glance with Josselin. 'Sir, the only way we'll reach the Caspian is by travelling light. Abandon the trebuchet and the fire siphon.'

'Not before I give these mountain men a taste of my wrath.' Vallon's gaze fell on Wulfstan. 'You know how to operate the trebuchet.'

'Yes, sir.'

'And you've used it to deliver Greek Fire.'

'I have, sir, with devastating results.'

'I'm promoting you to captain of ordnance. Assemble the siege engine and drill a crew in its operation.' He gauged the distance to the settlement and pointed at a patch of ground about three hundred feet in front of it. 'That's the spot you'll be aiming from.'

'Right away, sir.'

Vallon pointed at a thatched byre lying outside the settlement. 'And that's your mark.' He stalked off. 'Josselin, give Wulfstan the men he requires.'

Under the apprehensive gazes of the highlanders, Wulfstan supervised the recommissioning of the trebuchet, fitting the arm to an axle running through the frame uprights, attaching a leather sling to the long end of the throwing arm, and weighting the cradle on the short counterpoise end with rocks. Shadows were pleating the snowfields when the Viking reported that the machine was ready.

'Use water barrels to find the range,' Vallon said. 'When you're sure of hitting the target, destroy it with Greek Fire. Can you do that?'

'I can.'

Wulfstan sighted on the target and made a few minor adjustments before pulling the release lever. The counterpoise dropped and the throwing arm swung up in a lazy arc, pulling the sling after it. As the sling whipped into the vertical position, the barrel flew out, sailing in a high curve to burst thirty yards behind the target and slightly to the right. Wulfstan removed some rocks, corrected his aim and delivered another shot. Three times the arm swung and threw before a cask of water burst through the byre's roof. The defenders in the towers vented their nervousness with catcalls and flights of arrows. Only a lemon streak of light remained in the sky.

'This time with Greek Fire,' Vallon said.

A gang of troopers stripped to the waist heaved on a windlass to crank the arm down. Wulfstan laid a bed of kindling in the sling, placed a barrel of Greek Fire on top like an infernal egg, poured more of the incendiary over the barrel and ignited the kindling. Smoky flames licked into the dusky sky.

Half-crouching, eyes mad in the hellish glow, Wulfstan bided his time. 'Not yet. Wait for the fire to bite.'

Vallon watched, wincing as the flames charred the staves. 'Wulfstan, if you don't release, it will be us who—'

'Now!' Wulfstan yelled.

Up into the sky the blazing barrel flew, the flames roaring with the speed of its passage and then extinguished by the rush of air. It fell to ground God knows where. Vallon clamped both hands to his cheeks.

The roof of the byre erupted in a gout of flame that went rolling into the night like the hellfire conjured up by preachers to frighten the wicked. After the first burst, the roof burned in a steady conflagration, sparks whirling in vortices fifty feet high.

Vallon waited for the flames to settle. 'Turn the engine on the village. Light torches so that its defenders have no doubt where the fireball will fall.'

Men heaved and prised the trebuchet around until its arm pointed towards the heart of the village. They began hauling on the windlass. Again, Wulfstan primed the sling with kindling before adding a barrel of Greek Fire. As he raised his burning brand, a voice drifted from one of the towers.

'Wait,' Otia said. 'They're prepared to consider our demands.'

Vallon turned away. 'You make the arrangements.'

The Outlanders pitched camp next day below the treeline in a shepherd's summer camp occupied by a log cabin and four primitive dwellings that looked like flattened stone beehives roofed with sods. The shepherds had made a corral from tree trunks and into this the muleteers drove the pack animals and stowed the baggage.

It was a lovely spot – a long wildflower meadow divided by a burbling stream. Down one side of the valley a waterfall cascaded in a lazy plume, spray drifting in veils across the dark haze of pine forest. On the other side the walls shot up to dizzying scree slopes and beetling crags overlooked by peaks with wisps of snow curling off them.

With an hour of daylight left after he'd finished his duties, Lucas wandered upstream. It looked trouty. At the first pool he came to a fish dived into the milky green depths. Eyes narrowed in concentration, he stalked up the next pool, searching for likely lies. A smooth boulder projected into an eddy below a rapid. He slid belly first across the rock and peered over. Two feet beneath him, only its head showing, a trout hung on fanning fins.

Lucas dipped his right hand into the water behind the fish. Hand cupped, fingers upheld, he brought it forward until he contacted the trout's tail. Tickling with his fingers, he worked along the fish's belly until he reached its gills. A gasp, a grasp and a scoop and he wrenched the fish from its element, juggling to keep hold of it. He clapped it in both hands and gave a whoop of triumph. He examined his catch – only about eight inches long with a moss-green back speckled with coral pink spots. A beauty.

He despatched it and made his way to the next pool. This one was more tricky to work and he had to wade, feeling under every likely rock or fallen tree. He lost the next trout but added another two to his bag, and by the time the light was almost gone he'd caught six fish weighing in total something over two pounds.

'You're not a bad guddler,' a voice said behind him.

It was Wayland and his dog, accompanied by Atam and Aiken.

Lucas sploshed to the bank. 'I've been tickling trout since I was five. The technique's easy. What counts is knowing where the fish are hiding.'

Wayland nodded. 'I used to guddle when I was a boy. One September I lived on nothing but trout, wild raspberries and chanterelles. A king never dined better.' He laughed. 'I'll never forget the time I thought I'd teased a trout and pulled out a water rat. I don't know who was more shocked.'

Lucas laughed, too, delighted to be speaking to Wayland on equal terms. 'Hero told me that you grew up alone in the wilderness. One day I'd like to hear about your experiences.'

'There's not much to tell. I found the summers easy and the winters hard. I wouldn't choose to return to that way of life.'

'How do you catch them?' Aiken asked. 'What's the trick?'

Lucas ignored him. He gestured at the peaks. 'These mountains remind me of the Pyrenees.' He pointed at a lammergeir quartering a slope in the last light. 'I've seen them drop tortoises onto rocks to break their shells and get at the meat.'

Wayland glanced at the vulture. 'I doubt you have leopards at home.'

'You saw a leopard?'

'About a mile back.'

Lucas whistled. 'I wish I'd been there. A leopard.' On impulse he hefted his string of trout. 'I have too many for my own supper and they're best eaten with the taste of the river still on them.'

Wayland inclined his head. 'Thank you. Share them with your mess-mates.'

Lucas scowled in the direction of the camp. 'I've been separated from my mates, haven't I? Trout would be wasted on the mule-teers. Your dog would appreciate them more than those brutes.' He pushed four of the fish at Wayland. 'Go on, take them.'

'Thank you. I promise the dog will get only the scraps.' Wayland glanced at the sky. 'You'd better get out of those wet breeches. A cold night is coming and I wouldn't be surprised if we see snow before dawn.'

Watching him leave, one hand placed on Atam's shoulder, the other on Aiken's, the dog waving its tail like a flag, Lucas felt at first admiration and then desolation. He should be walking beside Wayland, not Aiken.

He stiffened when Aiken headed back, the youth's face set in painful resolve. Lucas breathed in through his nose and braced to meet him.

'What do you want?'

Aiken spoke with his head down. 'I'm sorry my outburst led to your punishment. I spoke out of fear and excitement. Watching you fight on the causeway, I was sure you'd be killed.'

Lucas scuffed one sodden foot against a rock. 'Yes, well, easy to say now.'

'I asked the general to restore you to your squad. He refused on grounds of discipline, but he holds no grudge against you. On the contrary, he says you have the makings of an excellent swords-man. Even Gorka said that he was just about getting used to you when the general demoted you. He used very impolite language, but he's clearly fond of you.'

Both of them raised their heads and for a moment they were looking into each other's eyes. In that instant Lucas could have cast aside his enmity. He knew the Englishman wasn't the agent of his misfortunes and it was Aiken, not he, who'd lost a father. But out of Lucas's churning emotions, it was the troll squatting at his core that made itself heard. 'I don't need your sympathy. Another

209

week and I'll be back with my squad – a proper soldier – while you'll still be skulking in the rear.'

Aiken's features pinched. 'I don't understand your hostility. It's as if you hated me from before we met.' He gulped. 'So be it. I won't offer another olive branch.' He hurried away.

Lucas slumped on the riverbank and watched the stream glide past in the dusk. You could end it now, he told himself. Simply march into Vallon's tent and tell him who you are. His entire being cringed at the prospect. He could imagine the look of horror on Vallon's face. The general had a new wife and two daughters. So far as he was concerned, his son was dead, and that's the way he wanted things to stay.

'Are you still out there?' Wayland cried. 'The fish are asleep on the riverbed and it's time for supper. Remember, leopards stalk these mountains.'

It was nearly dark, campfires branded on the ground and the bustle of the squadron subsiding to the appreciative murmur of men about to fill their stomachs.

'Coming,' Lucas cried, and swaggered into camp, showing off his catch to everyone he passed.

Livestock and baggage were housed in the centre of the camp, surrounded by the beehive-shaped koshes. Lucas was billeted in one of these huts and didn't consider it a privileged berth. Its roof was only four feet from the ground, coated with tar quarter of an inch thick. Lice plagued him and he could hardly sleep for the mice – or were they rats? – scurrying over him in the dark. It was almost a relief when sometime in the small hours Gorka's voice cut into his wakeful sleep.

'Lucas, your watch. Get your arse out there.'

He rose scratching and yawning and pulled his cape over his shoulders. Demotion to the supply train didn't mean he'd been let off sentry duty.

Crawling out into darkness, he blinked at the gossamer touch of snow on his eyelashes. Gorka tugged his arm. 'This way.'

Lucas blundered behind, the only lights in the blackout a few beds of ashes sizzling in the snow and a pitch lamp burning outside the command tent.

The camp formed a square with one side protected by the river. At the upstream corner the trail crossed a log bridge. Here Gorka tugged down on Lucas's arm, fixing him to the spot. 'Arides?' he called.

A muffled voice answered from somewhere to the right. Gorka leaned in that direction. 'I hope you weren't asleep.'

'No, boss, just frozen.'

Gorka gripped Lucas's arm. 'Before your watch is over, I'm going to check that you're alert. If I can sneak up on you unawares, you'll find yourself in a world of pain.'

Lucas's teeth chattered. 'Better be careful, boss. If I hear you coming, I might think you're the enemy and take a swipe at you.'

Gorka's rank breath fanned Lucas's face. 'Don't get smart with me, you useless piece of Frankish piss. It's because you can't control that flapping tongue that you're with those sheep-shaggers in the baggage train.'

'Only for another week, boss.'

'Do you know, Lucas – every night before I go to sleep, I fall to my knees and give thanks to our eternal Father that it's one day less until I'm reunited with that noble trooper, fucking Lucas of fucking Osse, the Frankish fuckwit who's fucked up so many fucking times I've lost fucking count.'

'Glad to hear you're missing me.'

With a rumbling growl, Gorka was gone. Lucas hunched his shoulders against the cold, wishing he had the money to buy warmer garments than the hand-me-downs he'd been given. He blinked into the snow flurries. Flakes found their way down his neck. The river hissing and spitting under the bridge would have drowned the sounds of an approaching war host. The watch was pointless. Nobody would attack the camp on a night as dark and drear as this.

'Hey,' Arides called. 'You're Lucas, ain't you – the trooper Vallon put in the baggage train?'

'Can't really blame him after thumping his son.'

Muted laughter. 'Ain't this hell? I don't know about you, but I'm fucking perishing.'

'Won't be long before light.'

'I'll tell you one thing. If I'd known I'd be freezing my balls off in these mountains, I wouldn't have been so quick to step forward when the general asked for volunteers. I'm beginning to think I'd be better off back on the Danube. What say you?'

Some perverse sense of loyalty asserted itself. 'Cold doesn't bother me. I've spent many a winter night guarding sheep and horses against bears and wolves.'

'I've got a skin of wine. Step over and warm your stomach.'

The prospect was tempting. 'Thanks, but if Gorka finds me away from my post, he'll murder me.'

Arides spat. 'He's all piss and wind. I saw him run like a frightened girl at a skirmish in Bulgaria.'

Lucas bristled. Gorka might be the bane of his existence, but he was a member of Lucas's squad, and that counted for a lot. 'Oh, yes? That's not how I heard it. Aimery told me that Gorka rode at Vallon's side when the general saved the emperor at Dyrrachium.'

'You're young and green, lad. Don't be taken in by campfire tales.' A long glugging sound and a sniff. 'Damn good wine. Tell you what. If you're too frit to leave your post, I'll bring the wine to you. Where are you – on the bridge?'

'Yes.'

'I'll be right over.'

'No, really. I'm on duty.'

'To hell with you, then.'

Lucas's face and feet grew numb. He nestled his hands in his armpits and jogged up and down. He blew like a horse through fluttering lips. Time dragged like a millstone.

He whirled, alerted by a sound. Hard to tell where it came from. He rubbed his eyes. 'Arides?' he whispered.

No answer. Another faint noise sent his heart into spasm. It

212

sounded like horse harness. He drew his sword, searched behind him and gave a nervous laugh. 'I'm wise to you, boss. You'll have to tread more lightly if you want to catch me dozing.'

No answer and no more movement. Lucas strained through the dark. 'Gorka?'

A crow called, heralding the approach of dawn. Lucas peered to his right. 'Arides? I heard a sound.' He raised his voice. 'Arides? Where are you?'

'Right here,' Arides whispered, grabbing his arm.

Lucas was so keyed up that he skipped back at Arides' touch, wrenching free. In the next instant something went *swish* and cold flame seared his forearm. 'God,' he said in disbelief, staggering backwards and tripping on the bridge's logs. That slip saved his life. Another hiss cut a savage semicircle inches above his head and he knew it was a sword blade but couldn't believe Arides was wielding it or imagine why. He scrambled backwards onto the far bank, still too choked with shock to cry out.

Arides cursed and followed him, feeling his way across the span, his sword slashing right and left. Gripping his injured arm, Lucas stumbled downriver.

'Arides?' another voice hissed. 'Have you dealt with him?'

'I don't know. I cut him but he got away.'

'Find him, you useless idiot.'

'You find him. I can't see a thing.'

'Forget him, then. Mount up before he raises the alarm.'

'No, we've blown our chance.'

'We can't go back now. Come on!'

Muffled hooves trembled the bridge and rancorous voices faded away upstream.

'Enemy attack,' Lucas gurgled. He massaged his throat, recrossed the bridge and stumbled towards the beacon at the centre of the camp. 'To arms!' he shouted. 'Enemy attack!'

Voices took up the alarm and pandemonium ensued, cries and counter-cries merging with the sounds of men drawing weapons and running blind through the snow.

'Over here!' Lucas shouted.

Spectral figures erupted out of the dawn. One of them raised his sword and would have slashed at Lucas if he hadn't called out his name. Troopers milled, searching for the enemy. A riderless horse galloped past.

Vallon's voice cut through the mayhem. 'Everyone stay where they are!'

Movement ceased. A weird silence fell. Lucas touched his right forearm and felt warm blood welling.

Torches had been lit. 'What's the cause of this panic?' Vallon demanded. 'Who raised the alarm?'

Lucas felt sick and his wounded arm ached to the bone. 'Me,' he croaked. 'Lucas.'

'Ah, Christ,' Gorka groaned. 'I might have known it.'

A clump of torches drew close and Vallon appeared, his face ruddy in the flames.

'Who attacked us? Who cut you?'

'Arides, sir. He tried to kill me.' Lucas held up his wounded arm, the blood black and glossy on his sleeve.

'Are you out of your mind? Why would Arides try to kill you?'

Lucas's voice broke. 'I don't know, sir.'

Josselin twisted in his stirrups and fanned snow from his eyes. 'Arides?' he shouted. 'Arides?'

The only sound was the sputtering of the torches. Vallon bent over Lucas like a claw. 'If you've murdered Arides in some squabble, you'll hang.'

'On my oath, sir,' Lucas said, close to tears.

'Hold,' Josselin said. 'Someone's approaching.'

Silent as shadows, Wayland and his dog ran back into the torchlight. 'No trails approaching the camp. Three horses heading north. We weren't attacked. The enemy was from within.'

Vallon sat rigid, his face writhing. 'Deserters.' He clicked his fingers. 'Send a squad after them. Ten solidi for each traitor. Bring one back alive.'

Josselin wrenched his horse round and disappeared. Hero

stepped forward, took Lucas's arm and examined the wound. 'Can you move your hand?'

Lucas flexed it.

'Good. No sinews severed. It requires attention, though.'

Supported by Gorka and Wayland, Lucas followed Hero into his tent. He dropped onto a pallet while Hero prepared his instruments. He swabbed the wound with a resinous ointment whose volatile vapours caught in the back of Lucas's throat. 'That will help clean the wound and dull the pain while I stitch. Are you ready?'

Lucas stretched out his right arm and gripped the edge of a camp table. Gorka pinned his wrist. 'Typical. Your first wound and it's inflicted by your own side.' He made a bob to Hero. 'Stitch away, Master.'

Hero was spoon-feeding Lucas broth when Wayland entered the tent. He acknowledged Hero before turning his gaze on Lucas. 'Are you able to ride?'

Hero rose. 'I'll be the judge of that.'

'I'm afraid not. Scouts report trouble ahead. Vallon wants us over the next pass before sunset.'

'I can ride,' Lucas said, swinging upright. Immediately his surroundings spun into a kaleidoscope and he would have collapsed if Wayland hadn't caught him. Lucas stretched his eyes wide and blinked until his surroundings came back into focus. 'I'm all right,' he said, his voice reaching him from far away.

Wayland patted his shoulder. 'You've got pluck. I'll give you that.'

'What happened?' Lucas asked.

Wayland paused. 'Arides and two other Outlanders deserted. They're riding back in the hope of finding their way to the coast. Vallon's sent a squad after them. They won't escape. Even if they outpace their hunters, last night's snow will have closed the pass. And if they manage to cross it, the Svans will be waiting for them.'

A flick of the tent flap and Wayland was gone. Lucas fixed his woozy gaze on Hero. 'They're mad if they think they can get back to the Black Sea.'

'Hush,' Hero said. 'You'll need all your strength for tomorrow's journey.'

Long after darkness had fallen, Lucas woke in Hero's tent to hear orders being cried and feet shuffling to attention. Then silence fell. Hero went to the entrance, looked out and returned with a forced smile.

'Nothing that need trouble you,' he said. 'Go back to sleep.'

Lucas heard a voice intoning what sounded like a solemn mass. It was Vallon, his words too indistinct to make out. Lucas threw off his blankets and swung his legs to the floor. Hero tried to push him back.

'Don't go out there. I mean it.'

'The scouts have caught the deserters, haven't they?'

Hero closed his eyes briefly. 'Yes. They killed all but Arides. They brought him back for summary trial and execution. Stay here. There are some sights a young man shouldn't witness. In a tender mind foul weeds take root.'

Lucas shoved past. 'I've witnessed crueller sights than the hanging of the bastard who tried to kill me.'

He emerged blinking against leaping flames that silhouetted a gibbet. Beneath the gallows, Arides sat astride a horse, hands bound behind his back and a noose around his neck. He grinned at the assembled company. 'Well, comrades, we've ridden a long way together and now my journey is done. We're all heading down the same road. The only difference is that when you reach the end, I'll be there waiting for you. If there's wine in hell, the first round's on me.'

Someone gave a caustic laugh. 'That will be a first.'

At an order from Josselin, two troopers lashed the horse's rump. It plunged forward and Arides dropped from its back and swung in convulsions, feet kicking only inches from the ground. The squadron waited in silence until his body stopped twitching and dangled, rotating first one way, then the other.

'See that,' Vallon said. 'Now that Arides has left us, he doesn't know which way to turn. Let that be a lesson to you all. The only way we'll crown our journey with success is the same way we began it – as a company loyal to each other and to your commander. The way back is more dangerous than the way forward, and grows more so with each passing day. We're on a bridge that's collapsing behind us. Our only hope is to advance faster than it crumbles. Dismiss.'

Lucas returned to the tent to find Hero writing in a fierce flurry.

'Satisfied?' the Sicilian said, without looking up.

'He got what he deserved.'

Hero dug the point of his pen into the parchment. 'Arides had a wife and three children. All the deserters had families. They acted out of desperation. They were convinced that Vallon was leading them to certain death.'

Lucas hadn't given much thought to the mission. Its scale was so large that he could only absorb it one day at a time. And his obsession with Vallon's crimes meant he'd given little thought to where they were going or what purpose the journey was supposed to serve. He felt a bit stupid.

'Is he?'

Hero resumed writing. 'Possibly. Probably. I've studied the accounts without finding any record of a party reaching China from Byzantium.'

'But you and Vallon and Wayland made an impossible voyage to the ends of the earth.'

Hero laid down his pen. 'I was your age when I travelled to the northlands, and though I saw friends die on that journey, I was too callow to believe death would lay its grip on me. Since then I've learned that death is indiscriminate, taking the young as well as the old, innocents as often as the guilty.'

Lucas stroked the soft stubble on his jaw. 'I know how cruel life can be.'

Hero sifted sand over his page. 'Which is why I prefer to explore it through books. Unlike our own utterances, the written word doesn't die.'

'What are you writing?'

'A journal. A record of our journey.'

'In case none of us survive.'

'I told you that watching the hanging would plant morbid thoughts. Rest now. Tomorrow you'll rejoin your squad. Report to me morning and evening so that I can check your wound. It's healing well.'

Lucas allowed Hero to help him to his pallet. He managed a weak smile as the Sicilian drew the covers up. 'That's the second time you've saved my life.'

Hero laughed. 'You exaggerate. You're as tough as the cats that prowled the Syracuse docks where I grew up.' He prodded Lucas's chest. 'Still, you've used at least three of your lives since we met, so you'd better take more care.'

XVI

Ten days and five passes later, Lucas trotted Aster out onto the military highway winding north to the Daryal Gorge. In dribs and drabs the rest of the column followed. They camped that night in a pine forest and spent the next day reassembling the carts. Lucas was polishing the suit of armour he'd stripped from the Greek officer when Josselin strolled by.

'I'm looking for Aimery.' His eye fell on the armour. 'Good Lord, that corselet's more splendid than the general's *klivanion*.'

Lucas swallowed, fearful that the centurion would confiscate the outfit. 'I don't intend wearing it until I've distinguished myself in battle.'

'Quite right. We don't want you outshining your superiors before you've shed a drop of enemy blood. How's your arm?'

Lucas flexed it. 'As good as new, sir.'

'No bluster now.'

'Really, sir,' Lucas said. He drew his sword and made a pass, cut a smart parabola and sheathed the weapon with precision. 'See?'

The rest of his squad had drifted over. 'Tomorrow you'll be riding reconnaissance,' Josselin told them. 'About ten miles further on, the road's guarded by a Georgian fort. Approach with the utmost caution.'

'Are we going to storm it?' Aimery asked.

'Vallon hopes to creep past at night.'

'It ain't going to happen,' said Gorka. 'Too many folk have spotted us.'

Josselin ignored him. 'The fort's the last Georgian stronghold against invaders from the north. Once past it, we'll be back among highlanders. Ossetians this time. Four marches should bring us to the Daryal Gorge. After that, our path makes an easy descent towards the Caspian.'

When Josselin left, Gorka took Lucas aside. 'What did the captain say about the armour?'

Lucas extemporised. 'He said I'll be entitled to wear it once I've killed five men in battle.'

Gorka grinned. 'That'll be the day. I'll have retired to a monastery by then.'

'You in a monastery!'

'Only because they won't let me into a nunnery.'

Fog wreathed the trees when the squad moved out at dawn. Condensation beaded on Lucas's clothes and face. They rode in silence, eyes panning across the forest margins. Miles floated past. Lucas's padded corselet was soaked through when he hauled back on Aster's reins and drew his sword.

'Enemy ahead!'

Faces turned in anger. 'Did you learn to whisper in a smithy?' Gorka growled.

Two silhouettes advanced through the murk. One mounted figure lifted an outspread hand and only then did Lucas spot the dog trotting at his side.

'It's Wayland.'

The Englishman rode up in the company of a Seljuk. Lacking Greek, Wayland relayed his intelligence through Lucas.

'The fort's about a mile ahead. It's built on a spur to the right, with no way round it except by road. I estimate its garrison outnumbers us two to one.'

'Are they expecting us?' Lucas said, proud to be discussing martial matters.

'Did you meet anyone on the road today?'

'Not a soul.'

'There's your answer, then. The garrison commander has cleared the route for action. I spied on the lookouts and they didn't strike me as men twiddling their thumbs in the hope of something turning up.'

Vallon and Otia arrived, shunting Lucas into the background. They went into convocation with Wayland before Vallon squinted at the weeping sky, flapped a hand in frustration and rode back down the column.

'What's the plan?' Lucas asked Gorka.

'The weather's too foul for us to sneak through by night. Vallon's ordered us to lie up in the woods and be ready to advance at a moment's notice. No tents or fires. No hot food or dry clothes.'

The squadron and its train took cover under the dripping trees and bedded down as best they could. Lucas forced down a piece of hardtack and a wodge of rancid salt pork coated with pickle. None of the muted voices reaching him through the dark spoke of the next day's encounter. They moaned about the cold and wet, blistered feet and vile rations – anything except the possibility of meeting a violent death before another day had rolled round.

Lucas's jaw juddered. He cowled his head in his cape and sank into an uncomfortable slumber.

A foot ground into his ribs. 'Rise and shine,' Gorka said.

Lucas woke shivering into soggy blackness. He coughed and

groaned. The muted sounds of men arming themselves carried through the dark.

'What's the time?'

'Coming towards dawn.'

Lucas rose and stretched his limbs. Turning to gather Aster, he walked into a tree. He wiped his nose, licked his fingers and tasted salt-sweet blood. 'I don't feel like fighting today.'

Gorka laughed. 'That's my lad.'

By feel and sound, the squadron formed up on the road, two-thirds of the fighting men ahead of the baggage train, the rest guarding the rear. With a collective lurch, like a sluggish beast goaded into reluctant motion, the column plodded forward.

The road could only accommodate five horsemen riding abreast. Troopers tangled stirrups or blundered onto the verges. Behind them carts creaked and rumbled.

'Do something about that squeaking hub,' someone said.

Blind and disoriented, the force crept on. Lucas started at the sound of footsteps splashing towards them through puddles.

'Hold back,' Otia said. 'It's a scout.'

The scout delivered his report in an intense murmur.

'We're almost on top of them,' Otia said. 'Hold your positions.'

Lucas waited. Thump, thump went his heart. Night faded to grey and the tops of the pine trees formed out of the fog, the road still an opaque channel.

Shade by shade the gloom relented until Lucas could make out the shapes of his companions. A crow cawed in the woods and a breeze shook flurries of spray from the treetops. The light grew and the fog receded as if drawn down a tunnel.

'There they are,' Gorka said.

Lucas's mouth dried. A cordon of soldiers two ranks deep blocked the road where it broadened at a junction an over-ambitious bowshot ahead. Infantry in front, cavalry behind, shape-shifting in the vapours.

'Mend your lines,' Otia said.

Lucas found himself in the fourth rank. Vallon trotted up and studied the enemy position.

'I put their strength no greater than ours,' he told Otia. 'Wayland made them twice as many.'

'So much the better,' said Otia.

'So much the worse. Where are the rest of them?'

The mist rolled past in veils, offering glimpses of the Georgians and their castle perched on a promontory east of the main highway. Neither side made a move or sound.

'Have you kept your bowstring dry?' Gorka asked.

Lucas patted the waterproofed pocket. 'Why don't we attack? One charge and we'd smash through the centre.'

'Leaving the baggage carriers to be cut to shreds. Since returning to your mates, you've done nothing but bitch and moan about the muleteers and wagoners. But remember that if we're forced to abandon them, we'll have nothing to put into our mouths come tomorrow.'

Lucas watched the enemy coming and going in the mist. A scrambling in the forest made everybody whirl.

'It's me,' a voice cried, and the troopers relaxed their sword arms as Wayland and his dog came bounding down through the trees. Vallon swung out of the saddle and the two men held a discussion. When their exchanges were over, the general issued an order and two troopers spurred away down the column.

'Hear that?' Gorka said. 'The Georgians have sent half their force to attack our rear.'

Flanked by two cavalrymen carrying a flag of truce, a Georgian officer on a high-stepping stallion sallied into the ground separating the opposing forces. Vallon sent Otia to negotiate.

Gorka spat. 'Whatever deal they offer, ten solidi to a counterfeit nummus that Vallon tells them to shove it up their arse.'

Otia cantered back and went into another confabulation with Vallon.

The delay was driving Lucas mad. 'What are we waiting for?'

Vallon separated from Otia and heeled his horse to face the

squadron. 'As I feared, Duke Skleros has found his way to the Georgians and whetted their greed with tales of the treasures we carry. His hosts offer generous terms. Hand over every last scrap of gold and they'll grant us passage forward or back without the least encumbrance. After what we've been through, that doesn't sound equable. What say you? Fight for what's yours or submit like curs?'

Swords pounded on shields. 'Fight!'

Vallon stilled the outburst and faced the enemy. The Georgian negotiator returned to his lines. The breeze was beginning to shred the fog.

'Look there!' Gorka cried. 'It's the duke.'

Lucas spotted the traitor, clad in furs and silks, mounted on a grey at the centre of the Georgian cavalry.

'Spit the fat bastard,' someone shouted

'A long shot,' Vallon said. 'Three hundred paces at least. Worth a try, though, if only to demonstrate how far our bowmen out-range theirs. Bring up half a dozen of our best archers.'

Six Turkmen hurried forward and assessed the challenge. From the faces they pulled, it was clear that they judged it lay beyond them. Even though they'd shielded their weapons from the rain, creeping damp had sapped torsion from their bows and slackened the strings.

'General, this isn't a day for accurate bowmanship,' said Gan, the Pecheneg archer who'd demonstrated his remarkable skills on Lucas's second day at Hebdomon barracks.

'Use your sipers,' Vallon said.

Lucas had only seen these devices used at the practice butts. Strapped over the archer's wrist and bowhand, a siper was a pad with a channel of bone on top that allowed the arrow to be drawn back behind the stave, increasing range. Lucas was still struggling to master the Turkish draw and hadn't graduated to such advanced techniques. Get it wrong and you could put an arrow through your hand.

Gan fitted his siper. Not for him a leather pad and bone

223

groove. His overdraw device was crafted from shagreen and ivory. The other archers took their timing from him and six arrows flew high to splinter on the road fifty yards ahead of the enemy.

'Again,' Vallon ordered.

Four times the archers bent their bows, each volley falling shorter than the one before. The enemy jeered and Duke Skleros, emboldened, rode forward to add his taunts and threats.

'A month's pay if you puncture that bladder,' someone called, and another ragged flight of arrows hissed through the overcast. One of them shattered only a few feet in front of the duke, sending him hurrying back to the safety of the ranks.

'That will do,' Vallon said. He lifted an arm to signal the advance. Lucas's chest tightened in excitement.

'Let me try a shot.'

Lucas swung round to see Wayland dismount and hold out a hand to Atam. Wayland rode equipped with three bows – a light one, much knocked about, that he used for game; a short, powerful war bow designed to be shot from horseback; and a target bow crafted to his own design. It was the target bow that he drew from its protective sheath. Lucas had seen it once before and Wayland had even allowed him to handle it and marvel at its workmanship. It was a cross between a war bow and a flight bow, forming a crescent when unstrung rather than the boat shape of the weapons used by horse archers. Its composite construction – sinew on the back, wood for the core, horn on the belly facing the archer – was nothing unusual, but Wayland had selected the best and rarest materials. Instead of cow sinew, the tension face was sheathed with the sinews of an elk he had shot himself. Instead of maple for the core, Wayland had cut a yew branch in the Taurus Mountains. For the compression face he'd used water buffalo horn rather than cow horn. And to bond these materials, he'd chosen fish glue. Not any old fish glue, but glue imported from the Danube, rendered from the roof of a sturgeon's mouth. The bow's maker had decorated its belly with a repeat design known as 'flower bud', painted with pigment ground from the finest Persian lapis lazuli and lacquered with damar resin. On the back of the bowgrip he'd signed his name and inscribed a flowing motto in gold calligraphy under a flake of sea turtle. *In God not arms.*

'How far can it shoot?' Vallon asked.

'Six hundred yards on a good day. This isn't one of them.'

'Make it quick and God guide your aim.'

Wayland's movements were almost too fast to follow. He strung the bow with a dry silk string – the draw weight equivalent to that of a strapping youth – nocked an arrow, bobbed his head at the target like a hunting hawk sighting on prey, then tensed into a fluent draw that made bow and archer as one. Open-mouthed in admiration, Lucas knew he could never emulate such skill no matter how long he practised.

As Wayland released, a skein of fog floated across the road, hiding the target. Lucas strained, waiting for a cry to announce that the dart had bitten. No sound carried from the Georgian line and when the fog cleared, everything looked exactly as it had been before.

Everything the same until the duke toppled sideways off his horse to the mute astonishment of the officers around him.

'I don't fucking believe it,' Gorka said.

The Outlanders close to Wayland pummelled his back or just touched him as if a bit of his magic might rub off on them.

'Bravo!' Vallon called. 'A shot made in heaven.'

Wayland gave a sheepish smile. 'I missed. I was aiming for the Georgian commander.'

In that moment Lucas's respect for Wayland surged into worship.

'Squadron advance,' Vallon said. 'When you reach broader ground, form ranks one squad wide. Hit the centre.'

Lucas was in motion before he was ready, trying to curb his excitement and hold back his horse. Vallon set the pace, his right hand raised.

'Steady. Charge on my word. If we break through, turn and attack again. On no account lose contact with the supply train.'

He urged his horse into an extended canter, the squadron flowing behind him like a river gathering strength before plunging over a fall.

He dropped his arm. 'Charge!'

Swept along in the current, Lucas saw the enemy lines surge closer. This was how he'd imagined battle. This was the real thing. In a few heartbeats he'd be one step closer to wearing the gorgeous suit of armour. It never occurred to him that within those few pulsations he might be dead.

He reached full gallop and couched his lance. He'd singled out his target and nothing else existed. The Georgians held their line. He was less than fifty yards from it when the enemy broke and scattered, the infantry bolting for the trees, the cavalry skeltering up the road to the castle. Where moments earlier death or glory had been waiting, only one figure remained – the tubby corpse of Duke Skleros Phocas, late imperial ambassador to the Chinese court.

'Don't pursue them,' Vallon yelled. 'Otia, send two squads to bolster the rearguard. The rest of you hold yourselves ready for a counter-attack.'

Lucas howled in frustration. 'Cowards,' he shouted after the Georgians.

He wasn't the only one disgusted by the enemy's flight. Gorka drew his sword and hacked at the duke's corpse. Every trooper who followed did the same, bending over and slashing with offhand formality, almost in the same manner that they'd acknowledge a roadside shrine. Turkmen mashed the body under their horses' hooves. Cartwheels rolled over what was left, and by the time Josselin ushered the rearguard past, the traitor was just pulp. Turning for a last look, Lucas saw a pair of crows hopping towards the carrion, bright-eyed in a sudden shaft of sunlight.

XVII

The Outlanders pressed on until dark and established a defensive position in a wooded gorge. Wayland grew weary of the praise and handshakes and took himself and Atam off up to the ridge-line. The sky had cleared and stars massed in gassy swirls. To the north, snow peaks jutted like fangs. Wayland lay back and looked up through the cross-hatched branches, watching the constellations' almost imperceptible drift.

'You did aim for the duke,' Atam said.

Wayland smiled. 'It was pure luck.'

'Will you teach me how to bend a bow?'

'You don't want to be a soldier.'

'What else can I be?'

'When we return home, you'll go to school.'

'Home,' Atam said, as if it were a destination as remote as heaven.

'That's right. My wife is minding it as I speak. You'll like her.'

'Tell me about her.'

Wayland closed his eyes to picture Syth better. 'In form, tall, fair and slender – taller than you and with a carriage that would put most queens to shame. In manner, kind and cheerful, but she knows her own mind and isn't slow to voice it. Talking around the fire-side – I don't mind admitting it – my Syth often has the better of me. She has a way of uttering things that seem nonsensical until you screw your head around and look at the world from her direction.'

Atam laughed. 'Your children wouldn't welcome a strangeling into their nest.'

'Why not? My dog has adopted you as my own. My children will do the same.'

Atam rubbed his cheek against the dog's head. It wagged its tail and flicked its tongue across his face.

A lookout cried a warning. A smudge of flame glowered in the south, growing brighter.

'A signal fire,' Wayland said. 'We're not out of danger yet.'

Sure enough, a smear of flame appeared to the north, and then another one, deeper into the mountains.

Wayland helped Atam to his feet and led him down to the camp.

'You did mean it,' the boy said. 'About taking me home.'

Wayland squeezed his hand. 'As God is my judge.'

They continued up the road under a blue sky stippled with lambs'-fleece clouds. Watching the landscape unfold, Wayland was struck by the thought that every day would be like this – a new patch of world revealed and then left behind, forgotten or fixed in memory forever.

Like this stretch of road. To the right a verge of wildflowers sagging under the weight of bees. Above it a rocky slope matted with rhododendrons running up to a vertical scarp capped with trees. To the left, a great green swoop of valley threaded by a river like a milky vein. The rhododendron blossoms filled the air with a rich honeysuckle scent. A cuckoo cried its drowsy note from the undercliff.

A falcon's harsh cry drowned the cuckoo's song. Wayland spotted the strung-bow profile of a peregrine defending its eyrie, patrolling back and forth above the cliff. It checked and half-stooped towards a wooded outcrop. Wayland's eyes narrowed. The falcon wasn't alarmed by the commotion on the road. The threat came from above.

He was still swivelling to cry a warning when the first arrows whistled past. A trooper thirty yards behind him clutched his ribs and folded over his horse's neck.

A dozen more arrows flighted down, one of them nicking Wayland's sleeve. He snatched the reins of Atam's horse and dragged it over the downhill slope, pulled the boy to the ground and pushed him flat.

'Stay down,' he ordered. He seized his dog's head in both hands. 'Guard Atam and the horses.'

Crouched below the road's rim, he scrambled down the highway. A horse squealed somewhere above him. A trooper threw himself off the road and looked back, wiping dirt from his mouth.

Wayland ducked his head above the verge. Half the force had sought cover on the uphill slope. The rest had flung themselves on this side and were wriggling back up to assess the threat. The baggage train stood abandoned, one mule dead, another kicking in its traces. A single driver remaining at his station with his hands clasped over his head. Wayland sprinted forward, grabbed him and dragged him to cover. He propped himself on one elbow and cupped a hand to his mouth.

'Vallon!'

'Down here!'

Wayland slip-slided towards the general, negotiating a muleteer drumming his feet in a death spasm. He threw himself down beside Vallon. 'They chose the site well,' he panted. 'It would take a day to find a way up those cliffs and our archers won't trouble the ambushers from below.'

'I know. And the Georgians are threatening our rear.'

'If we ride into the valley, we'll get round the ambush.'

'Carts can't negotiate the slope. Lose the baggage and we lose everything.'

Wayland squirmed up for another look. The scarp contoured north for another mile, its cliffs broken by fissures and wooded ledges that could have harboured an army of marksmen.

'We're just going to have to take our chances,' Vallon said. He raised his voice. 'Centurions, pick forty men to get the carts and mules out of danger. The rest of you, work your way up the road, keeping out of sight.' He sank down while his captains made their choice.

'Ready!' Josselin cried.

'Go!' said Vallon, leading the way. The troopers sprinted after him and Wayland felt he had no choice but to follow. Vallon organised the men, delegating some to cut the dead animals from their traces and replace them, ordering the others to form a defensive screen with their shields. Wayland lent his strength to one heaving group. Arrows sprayed down.

Safe from counter-attack, the ambushers began to show themselves. Some of them were armed with heavy bows which they drew by sitting down and bracing their left foot against the stave. Wayland saw one seated archer hauling back a three-foot-long arrow two-handed, with both feet straining against a bow as thick as a wrist. The man seemed to be aiming straight at him. He ducked and a trooper toiling beside him collapsed, the arrow punching through both shield and armour.

The troopers got the train moving. Wayland jogged beside the wagons, trying to ignore the lethal hail. A trooper ahead of him buckled with a barb in his calf. Wayland bore his weight and helped him peg-leg along. 'Not far now.'

He wasn't lying. The cliffs curved away from the highway and the assault tailed off. Wayland handed the wounded trooper over to Hero and found Atam and the dog unscathed. Men called out, searching for missing comrades. Four of them would never answer an earthly summons again, and the same number of baggage men had perished.

Vallon, reunited with his horse, pounded over, his face running with sweat. 'See that,' he cried.

Up the valley light winked from the top of a watchtower pitched on a high ridge. 'The brigands haven't done with us. Unless we find another path, they'll kill us by a hundred cuts.' Vallon dragged his hand across his brow. 'Our attackers have won an easy victory and will follow up. Wayland, hide with half a dozen men and grab some of them.'

Vallon was so incensed that he'd forgotten Wayland wasn't subject to his command.

Wayland pushed out his cheek with his tongue and nodded. He turned and singled out a Bulgarian freebooter who'd impressed him with his calm during the assault. He pointed at another man. 'And you.'

'And me,' said Lucas.

'You,' Wayland said, selecting Gan the archery instructor. Three times more he pointed. 'Seven should be enough,' he told Vallon.

'Make it eight,' said Lucas.

Vallon swiped the air. 'Take the fool. If he dies, it's no great loss.' The general quirted his mount and rode off.

Wayland watched him go with an ambivalent smile before organising his squad. For the ambush site, he chose a birch spinney along an innocuous stretch of road just past a tight bend. He divided his force on each side of the road and nestled into a dell with his dog. Lucas found his way beside him. The expedition laboured out of sight, dust settling in its wake.

'Can I ask you something?' Lucas said.

'I suppose so.'

'How many men have you killed?'

'I've never counted.'

'You must have some idea.'

'That's between me and my confessor.'

Lucas rolled a halm of grass between thumb and forefinger. 'I've made a resolution. If I kill five men in battle, I'll consider I've earned the right to wear the armour I took on the causeway.'

'It didn't do its original owner any good.'

Lucas was straining out an answer when Wayland cut him off. The dog had cocked its ears.

'They're coming.'

'What if they arrive in a horde?'

'Let fly an arrow and then run as if Old Horny were trying to pin your tail. Take your lead from me.'

Lucas tensioned his bow. Wayland made him relax it. They waited. A striped hyena trotted into the road, looked down it and galloped into the undergrowth as the first highlanders came loping around the bend.

They advanced in a loose pack, running in cleated sandals that made hardly a sound.

'Don't shoot until I do,' Wayland said.

He waited until the nearest highlander was forty yards away before rising and dropping him in his tracks.

Lucas's bow discharged with a wonky twang. 'I missed!'

Two more highlanders went down. One of the front runners, bearded to the waist and waving a strange-looking fluted sword, urged his men on. Wayland released his fourth arrow at the same moment Lucas shot his second and the shaman sat down in the road with a most tragic expression.

'Whose shot?' Lucas cried. 'Yours or mine?'

'Neither. It came from the other side.'

The highlanders hadn't expected opposition on this scale and turned tail with woeful cries.

'After them!' Wayland shouted.

Two troopers caught one of the highlanders before he'd gone fifty yards, hurling him down in a swirl of dust. Wayland's target jinked off the road, scrambling up rocks and shoving through shrubs.

Wayland followed, branches whipping his face. The slope was steep and tangled. His breath came in painful gasps. Lucas overtook him and closed on the quarry. Ahead of him the dog brought the runaway to bay. It wasn't a man-killer, but the fugitive didn't know that. He backed against a tree and swiped a knife from side to side.

Lucas kicked it out of his hand, seized a hank of his hair and dragged his head down.

'Alive,' Wayland shouted with the last of his breath. He staggered up, grasped the prisoner and hoisted his head up to reveal the face of a boy, reared in a harsh school to be sure, but not much older than Atam.

Wayland lashed out at Lucas. 'Do you think killing a kid entitles you to wear fancy armour?'

Lucas made an idle swipe at a shrub. 'I got carried away.'

Wayland grabbed Lucas by his tunic. 'Learn to bridle your temper, or I'll never have truck with you again.' He released him. 'Now take him down.'

Wayland watched the young Frank escort his captive back to the road as if he were a geriatric relative. Wayland smarted. Never before had someone outpaced him in the chase. He stroked the dog. 'I'm getting too old for this,' he said.

With their prisoners at heel, the snatch squad caught up with the main force at a bridge over a rushing burn. The Georgians had given up their pursuit, but that suggested they were more intimidated by the mountain tribesmen than by the Outlanders.

Vallon sat his horse. 'You know what to do,' he said to Otia.

Soldiers dragged one of the prisoners before the centurion. The man was middle-aged, a shepherd or hunter with faded blue eyes in a sun-darkened face. Under Otia's interrogation, he grew increasingly agitated, pointing at the peaks and throwing up his hands.

Otia turned to Vallon. 'He says the Daryal Gorge is the only road through the mountains.'

'There must be another way. Tell him that if he doesn't reveal it, we'll execute him.'

Otia resumed his interrogation. The prisoner spoke fervently at first, but then faltered and halted, resigned to his fate. He took a cross from his tunic and kissed it.

'He says there's no other path,' Otia said.

'Kill him.'

Otia handed over the prisoner to an Armenian trooper who'd lost a friend in the ambush. He forced the highlander into a kneeling position and hacked off his head, taking four strokes and making such a bloody mess that the Outlander veterans winced and averted their gaze.

The youth Wayland had captured trembled in his grasp and piss stained his crotch.

Vallon crooked a finger.

'The boy will give you the same answer,' Wayland said in French. 'This road is the only road.'

'I'll be the judge of that.'

Tears squeezed out of the prisoner's eyes when Otia questioned him. The centurion turned to Vallon. 'He swears there isn't another path through the mountains.'

Vallon pointed at a trooper. 'Kill him.'

The other Outlanders, who not much earlier would have slaughtered every highlander they met – from white-haired matriarchs to suckling babes – spectated in a queasy silence.

Wayland stepped out under the executioner's sword.

'Stand back,' Vallon ordered.

'I didn't join this expedition to watch youngsters being slaughtered.'

'Don't waste your sympathy. If our situations were reversed, I warrant that this stripling would be gouging out our eyes and boiling our brains above a fire.' Vallon half-stood in his stirrups. 'Kill him.'

Wayland turned away the executioner's sword. Again he spoke in French. 'Killing him won't achieve a thing. You're asking the wrong question.'

Vallon struck his saddle. 'I won't have you interfering with my command.'

'You were happy for me to interfere when I took that shot at the duke. You were happy for me to interfere when I captured the prisoners – even though I don't serve in your ranks. This youth can't show us a safe passage because it doesn't exist. What he can do is warn us of the other perils waiting on this road.'

'Trust Wayland,' Hero said.

Vallon's jaw jutted. His head hunted about. He spoke through gritted teeth. 'Make one thing clear. If the boy doesn't give us useful intelligence, I'll carry out the death sentence myself.'

Wayland waved Otia over and they began questioning the boy. The sun was low over the mountains when Wayland reported to Vallon.

He pointed north. 'The highlanders will spring their next trap from up there. A score of them are waiting to roll rocks down on us.'

A few miles up the valley, the eastern side fell in three gigantic steps, the lowest falling almost plumb to the road, above it two bands of cliffs separating scree slopes angled at the limits of stability. The road cut into the mountain and there was no way to avoid the ambush.

'I'll send a squad of mountain men to take the position,' Vallon said.

'I'll lead them,' Wayland said.

'I thought ...' said Vallon, and left it at that. He managed a short bow. 'Arrange the attack as you see fit.'

Mellow evening sunshine bathed the mountains as the convoy approached the ambush site. They had climbed above the treeline and long shadows threw the valley into wild relief. Vallon halted his force well short of the site and Wayland used what remained of daylight to plot a route. A direct ascent was impossible. Even if they climbed the cliff by a more devious line, the scree slope above the crag was so bald that the ambushers would spot the squad long before they could engage. To command the enemy position without being seen would involve a lengthy detour that would bring them above the second step before traversing left to take up position behind the ambushers. Then they would have to descend the cliff before falling on the enemy. Judging by the great apron of scree beneath it, the strata were rotten. Not a descent to be undertaken by night.

He'd chosen his squad – all men who'd grown up in mountains. That included Gorka and Lucas. The youth might be a windmill to emotion, but any man who could outstrip Wayland in an uphill dash was fit for the task.

He was eating supper with Atam when a hideous braying raised the hairs on his neck. The dog lifted its head and bayed at the moon.

Wayland heard Vallon laugh. 'We know how to answer that.'

Troopers rose and bellowed into the hollows of their shields, the amplified cries and countercries merging and echoing between the valley walls. When the noise stopped, two distant wolf packs continued howling in melancholy counterpoint.

Wayland retired to his tent and woke around midnight. Stars burned in the windless sky. His ten-man squad stood ready. He shouldered his war bow, eyed the crag where the enemy waited and sighted on the moon.

'Careful with your feet. On a night as still as this, the enemy will hear a stumble half a mile off.'

They set off, plugging up the tortuous route. Most of the night had passed before they reached the second band of cliffs. Wayland looked for a route up, his brow sheened with sweat.

'This way,' he said, leading up a gulley lined with rock that came away in his hands.

Behind him a trooper dislodged a hundredweight of rotten stone that went clattering down the mountain.

Wayland hissed. 'The enemy may put that down to chance. Make a second clumsy move and they'll know we're up here.'

Dawn still stood below the peaks when the squad reached the cliff top above the ambush site. All around the sky was awash with stars. A shower of meteorites glided overhead in a shallow arc. The troopers dozed or talked quietly among themselves.

'I've got a question for you,' Wayland said to Lucas.

'Ask away.'

'If Vallon had ordered you to kill that boy, would you have?'

'I was wondering that myself. I don't know. If I had, it would have poisoned my dreams.'

'Good. That means you have a conscience.'

'Are you saying that Vallon doesn't?'

'Far from it. His conscience is more troubled than most because of the decisions he's forced to make.' Wayland lay down and wrapped himself in his cloak. 'Wake me between dawn and dark.'

The stars were dimming when Wayland prepared to make the descent. He leaned out from the cliff top as far as he dared. It was higher and steeper than he'd expected.

'Search for a way down,' he told the troopers.

Light outlined the eastern ranges when the pathfinders returned. 'Only a cat could find safe footing on that debris,' said one. Another panted in agreement. 'I got halfway down and reached a sheer drop.'

'We'll have to use ropes,' Gorka said.

Lucas trotted up. 'I think I've found a way. It's a bit of a scramble.'

'Show us.'

Lucas led him to a fissure and lowered himself down it, bracing hands and feet against the sides. Wayland followed, cramping himself against the narrow walls. Even moving carefully, he couldn't avoid dislodging rocks.

'Careful,' said Lucas from below. 'You nearly brained me.'

Dawn was in full flush when they reached a ledge hanging out more than twenty feet above the base of the cliff.

Wayland peered over. 'Too steep to descend unaided.'

The men began to uncoil the ropes. There was enough light now for Wayland to make out the shapes of the ambushers crouched beside cairns of rocks. Not much imagination was required to envisage the devastation the boulders would wreak on a slow-moving column hundreds of feet below.

'Look out!' one of the troopers cried.

A rock he'd dislodged whirred past Wayland's head, struck the ledge a sharp crack and flew into space. It hit the scree slope and bounded away towards the ambushers.

'That's torn it,' Gorka said.

The ambushers turned and stared up at the cliffs.

'We're in shadow,' a trooper said. 'They might not spot us.'

Even as he spoke, a group of highlanders began struggling up the slope. Gorka threw his rope over the drop.

'Not enough time,' Wayland said. 'They'll reach us before everyone gets down.'

Lucas stepped to the tip of the drop. 'We don't need ropes. Just jump.'

237

'Are you fucking mad?' Gorka said.

'The scree's so steep and loose it will cushion our fall. I used to jump off cliffs like this in the Pyrenees. Look.' With that, Lucas launched off. He hit the slope and skidded twenty yards before flailing to a halt. He grinned. 'The trick is to land at the same angle as the slope.'

Gorka wiped a finger under his nose. 'Fuck.'

By now the highlanders had gained more than a hundred feet, advancing at an indefatigable trudge.

'I'll go next,' Wayland said.

He shut his eyes in brief prayer and jumped. A long rush of weightlessness before he struck the scree and careered down. Lucas managed to arrest his descent. Wayland looked back at the remaining troopers. 'It's not as bad as it looks.'

Seven of them summoned up the courage to jump, all landing without injury. The last held back and spoke in a wheedling tone. 'I can't. I twisted an ankle on the way up.'

'Then find your own way down,' Wayland said.

The highlanders were already a third of the way up the slope. 'Do we meet them or wait for them?' Gorka said.

'We can tear straight through them,' Lucas said.

'He's right,' Wayland said. 'Spread out in a line. Ready? Go!'

The squad set off down the slope, running with staccato steps and leaning back for balance and traction. The scree began to move beneath them, forcing them to take longer and longer strides, the surface sliding faster and faster until it threatened to overtake their whirling legs.

'Ride it,' Lucas cried, bending his knees and spreading his arms.

Wayland balanced on the wave of rocky surf and accelerated at an alarming rate, his hair blowing straight back and tears whipping from his eyes. The squad glissaded past the band of highlanders as if they were stumps. The hiss of scree behind the human toboggans harshened into an ominous rattle. They'd set off a landslide, a lobe of debris that grew coarser the further they descended. Stones as big as a fist bounded past Wayland. The ambush site rushed up and he saw that he had no more than fifty feet of runout before he went over the precipice.

'How do we stop?' he shouted.

'Like this,' Lucas yelled, slaloming to the right.

Wayland skidded to the left and just made it off the hurtling shale, tearing the skin of one palm in the process. Somehow the other troopers also found safe ground. Six of the ambushers scattered before the landslide engulfed them. The other four left it too late and the mass of scree crashed into them and swept them over the cliff like woodlice carried down a drain.

The hellish rattling died to a dribble. A single stone trickled and fell. Troopers groaned and laughed. 'That was better than sex,' Gorka said.

Wayland sucked shards from his lacerated palm and saw Lucas giving futile chase to the fleeing ambushers.

'Get back here,' he shouted.

Lucas gave up, flailing back at a pace that suggested he had enough energy to do it all again. He dumped himself down beside Wayland.

'What do you think? Four men dead and an ambush foiled. Does that count towards my armour?'

'No. It wasn't proper combat.'

Lucas appealed to Gorka. 'What say you, boss?'

With a beckoning gesture that boded ill, Gorka enticed Lucas into range and grasped him in a head lock. 'You came close to wiping all of us out,' he said. He hurled Lucas away and chuckled. 'Mad idiot.'

Wayland smiled. He stood and touched Lucas in passing. 'You did well.'

He went to the edge of the cliff, pulled out an Outlanders pennant and waved it to signal that the way was clear. The column strained into motion. From his vantage, Wayland could see what they couldn't – the road strangled by a yawning chasm, precipices shooting up to white peaks on every side.

*

239

Nobody molested them on the journey though the pass. Beyond it the road descended in wild zigzags and Wayland spotted Ossetian settlements on the other side of the valley, some of the houses no more than heaps of stones, recognisable as habitation only by wisps of smoke escaping from their roofs.

The road began climbing again and the twin summits of Mount Kazbeg appeared above the lesser peaks like a bishop's mitre. A quilt of grey clouds settled, obliterating the summits. This was the gloomiest and most savage section of the route, immense iron-grey walls squeezing in on both sides, the river smoking a thousand feet below and wicked gleams of ice directly above. Banks of snow lay heaped in the shadows, some of them blocking the track. At one place the convoy had to dig through a landslide before the carts could pass.

Afternoon found them stretched out single file on a section of road hacked out of the cliffs. A headwind smelling like cold iron funnelled through the pass. Vallon rode up alongside Wayland.

'Snow's coming. A double march should see us clear.'

Wayland eyed the precipices louring under the cloud mantle. 'Wait until dark.'

'If we delay, the snow could block the road.'

'The highlanders haven't finished with us.'

Vallon looked up the cloud-draped cliffs. 'Even if they're waiting, they won't be able to see us.'

'They've probably posted spotters. Let's wait until night.'

'A storm could delay us for days.' Vallon swung his arm at the column. 'Keep moving. Don't stop until we're through.'

Twilight and overcast created a ghastly netherworld. Wayland advanced with his nerves strung tight. The column lit torches to show the road and had gone perhaps another mile when a horn blew from somewhere close by. Wayland looked up into the dark clouds. He heard a groaning sound and then the grating of stone. Moments later an infernal crack shattered the silence.

He wrenched his horse towards the cliff. 'Take cover!'

A boulder boomed down the precipice and exploded on the

road in a shower of sparks, sending splinters flying in all directions. An acrid stink drifted downwind. The second missile crashed to earth, shattering into pieces with enough force to breach a city wall.

'Back!' someone shouted. 'Forward!' cried another.

It didn't matter which way they turned. The enemy had judged their attack perfectly, catching the Outlanders at the point between no advance and no retreat. They'd had days to prepare and they levered over boulders as big as huts that burst on impact, shooting out fragments with enough force to reduce a body to mush. One rock scored a direct hit on a horse and rider, squashing them like bugs. A sliver of stone no bigger than a nail paring slit Wayland's cheek. He clung on to his terrified horse.

'Atam!'

Someone screamed and went on screaming, the sound horrible enough to tear gristle.

Wayland gripped his dog's nape. 'Find Atam.'

It didn't hesitate, running uphill through the deluge of boulders. Wayland abandoned his horse and followed.

'Atam! Where are you?'

The boy drifted out of the mayhem, his face freckled with blood.

'Oh my God,' Wayland said, skidding to his knees.

A fearful impact had torn Atam's left arm off below the shoulder. He clutched the stump. 'I've lost my arm,' he said in the tone of a child who'd mislaid something important and feared punishment.

Wayland dragged him under an overhang. The boy's eyes were sinking into his face. The dog whimpered. 'Good boy,' Atam whispered.

Wayland choked back his horror and examined the wound. The force of the impact had effectively cauterised the blood vessels. 'Hero,' he shouted. 'Hero, I need you.'

'He's down there,' said a trooper hunched over a few yards away.

'Stay with the boy,' Wayland said. He sprang up. 'Hero!'

241

Wayland found the physician treating a soldier with a smashed jaw. 'Atam's dreadfully hurt. Hurry!'

Hero's glance was measured. 'I'll come as soon as I've finished treating this patient.'

Wayland wrenched him away. 'He's not going to die soon, but Atam won't live unless you attend to him straight away.'

The trooper tending Atam looked up as they approached and sniffed away a tear. 'Poor little bastard.'

Hero crouched and touched Atam's cheek. 'The shock alone would have killed him. I don't think he felt any pain.'

'He can't be dead,' Wayland shouted. 'Only two days ago I swore to bring him home to my family.'

Hero took Wayland's hands. 'I'm sorry,' he said. Horrid cries carried through the dark. 'I must attend to the living.'

The dog had couched its head on Atam's lap. Wayland brushed back his hair and clutched the back of his skull. 'Did he speak? Did he say anything?'

The trooper laughed away tears. 'He called for his mother. I expect I'll do the same when my turn comes.'

Wayland slumped beside Atam and cried tears from a well that seemed bottomless. Hollowed out by grief, he looked up when someone shook his shoulder.

'We'd best be getting on,' Wulfstan said,

The bombardment had stopped and the storm had arrived, whirling wet flakes sticking to Wayland's face. The column drifted past, cartwheels muffled on the cold blanket.

'I'm not leaving Atam here,' Wayland said.

A teamster drove by, urging on his mules with shouts and lashes. Wulfstan stepped out. 'Hold up while we load a casualty.'

The driver registered Atam, one side of his body already plastered by snow. He flicked his whip. 'I'm overladen as it is. Let the dead look after the dead.'

Wayland sprang up, leaped onto the cart and held a knife to the driver's throat. 'You'll go down among them if you don't take the boy.'

They laid Atam on the cart and walked behind the crude hearse, leaning their weight against it to force it through the deepening snow. They were at this labour until dawn, when snow and slope relented and they stood looking down on foothills emerging under a clearing sky.

At the first camp below the Daryal Gate the officers tallied up the losses. Of the hundred troopers who'd boarded *Pelican* and *Stork*, twenty were dead, another eight injured. Wayland waited until the expedition had reached gentler ground before burying Atam. The trooper who'd watched the orphan's life drain away joined Hero, Aiken and Wulfstan in the mourning party. Vallon didn't attend.

'I hadn't realised how much he meant to you,' Hero said to Wayland.

'Nor did I until he was gone. I don't know why except that he had no one else in the world.'

'Come away now. We'll talk later.'

'Give me a while alone.'

He kneeled beside the grave and prayed that Atam would find a kinder existence in the afterworld. The dog whined and pawed at the turned earth. Wayland rose as the sun broke through the clouds, revealing the peaks stepping away in splendour.

The Caspian Sea and Turkestan

XVIII

On a muggy afternoon towards the end of May, Vallon stood looking across a corridor of coastal steppe to the Caspian Sea merging into the sky like a misted mirror.

Otia pointed at a tiny stain on the shore. 'That must be Tarki.'

'It doesn't look like much of a place.'

'It's the only port between the Volga and Derbent.'

Vallon reviewed the squadron ranged along the ridge. 'Take three squads and secure the town. Offer no violence unless necessary. Make it clear that we'll pay for our passage.'

'We'll be lucky to charter a fishing smack in that back-of-beyond hole,' Josselin muttered.

'Mind your tongue,' Vallon snapped. 'I won't have my officers voicing doubts in front of the men.' He turned back to Otia. 'Signal if you're successful. The usual system.'

Vallon retreated to his tent after the force had left. Since breaking through the Caucasus he'd kept much to his own company, only communicating to his men through terse orders.

Night fell, and with it, rain. Vallon was penning a letter to Caitlin that she'd never receive when his servant announced Wayland. Not long before, the Englishman would have entered the commander's tent without ceremony and they would have exchanged pleasantries as a prelude to business. This time Wayland presented himself with a formal bow.

'No signal yet,' he said.

'I don't expect any before morning. Keep lookout from first light.'

'Very good, General.'

Vallon cast down his pen. 'What's this "General"? Even as a youth you weren't afraid to call me by my name.'

'I think it would be better for discipline if I addressed you by your rank.'

'Even in private? Oh, to hell with it, then.'

At the entrance, Wayland paused and Vallon opened his mouth in anticipation. The moment passed. Wayland was gone and Vallon was alone again. He read the letter he would never send – the words no more than an outlet for the heartsickness he couldn't confide or cure. He crumpled the letter into a ball and flung it across the tent.

He buried his face in his hands and was still sunk in that position when his servant stole in to enquire if he needed anything for the night.

'No, nothing, thank you,' Vallon said. 'You can take your rest now.'

The servant noticed the screwed-up letter and stooped to retrieve it.

'It's not important,' said Vallon. 'Burn it.'

At dawn he tracked the sun rising in a baleful red swell. The pall thinned and the brassy orb bored through the haze. Still no signal from Otia's men. Sweat trickled down Vallon's neck. He rubbed his chapped lips. If the force failed to take the port, he had no idea which way to turn.

'There's the signal,' Wayland said.

'Where?'

Wayland jostled his horse alongside. 'There.'

Through the overcast a mirror flashed dully – once, twice, thrice. Vallon curbed a cry of triumph. 'They've taken the port. One squad accompany me. The rest follow with the baggage train.'

A ragged cheer went up and Vallon's squad swept down to the coast. Otia rode out to meet them. 'No casualties on either side, sir. The inhabitants are sheltering in the church. I've told the priest and elders that we'll pay for anything we take.'

'Good work,' said Vallon, but he could tell from Otia's expression that the capture of the port hadn't solved all their problems.

He understood why when he rode through the settlement of daub walls and tousled thatch and saw four small fishing boats and two shabby coastal freighters riding the listless tide. One glance told him the vessels couldn't carry all his men and freight.

He feigned cheerfulness. 'The worst is behind us,' he said. 'If we can come through the Caucasus, we can cross this millpond. Organise a feast for the men.'

Vallon examined the vessels with Wulfstan. 'How many can we pack into them?'

'Most of the men, but that will leave little room for horses and cargo. And none of the vessels is fit for deep-water voyaging.'

Vallon surveyed the Caspian's oily calm. 'It's just a big lake. Why, the tide's so feeble there's barely a foot between ebb and flow.'

'It's a lot wider than the North Sea and a storm in shallow waters can whip up waves before you can reef sails.' The Viking pointed at one of the freighters listing like a weary drunk. 'I wouldn't risk sailing out of land-shot in that wreck.'

'We need to rest and recover. There's a good chance that a trading ship will dock in the next two or three days. Meanwhile, do what's necessary to make the vessels seaworthy.'

Returning to camp, he had to skip aside as a gang of troopers chased a squealing pig through the muddy lanes. He shut himself in his tent while the men feasted and they were still sleeping it off when he went down to the strand next morning. Not a sail showed all day, nor did the morrow bring any relief. Vallon waited by the slopping waves, wiping sweat from his eyes, and was still scanning the horizon with his shadow lying long before him. He turned to face the blue wall of the Caucasus. Returning through the mountains meant certain death. North lay nothing but empty grassland and the marshes of the Volga delta. The only large harbours were in Georgia to the south, reached along a coastal strip that pinched shut at the Iron Gates of Derbent. Follow that corridor and in a few days they would be among Seljuks or Arabs.

Otia had been hovering and seemed to read his commander's mind. 'I suggest we go south, the squadron travelling by land, the baggage train staying in close touch on the ships. Derbent's the only city where we'll find vessels large enough to transport all the men and supplies.'

'We'll give it one more day.'

Vallon was trudging back to camp when Wayland called out.

'Sails to the north-east. Two of them, close together, halfway below the horizon and bearing south.'

Vallon ran over. 'Show me.'

'Out there, heading away from land.'

The light was draining fast and Vallon couldn't spot anything against the upwelling night. He knuckled his eyes.

'Are you sure you didn't imagine it?'

Wayland looked at him.

Vallon backed away. 'Light a fire,' he ordered. 'Pile it high.'

The men ran in search of firewood. Wulfstan hurried over. 'If you want to attract their attention, burn that.'

He was pointing at a haystack capped with a wooden roof. Vallon glanced at the settlement.

'An inferno is as likely to repel as attract.'

'They ain't going to see us any other way.'

'You're right. Use Greek Fire to quicken the blaze.'

Wulfstan ran into the night. Stars twinkled in the east. Wulfstan returned, climbed a ladder leaning against the stack and poured incendiary compound over the hay. He sprinkled more around the base. Troopers lobbed firebrands onto the stack and flames licked into the sky.

Fifty feet away, Vallon shielded his face from the singeing heat. The fire illuminated Wayland. 'That's someone's precious fodder we're burning. I hope your eyes didn't deceive you.'

'They didn't,' Wayland said. 'There was something odd about the sails, something . . .'

'Yes?'

'Wait until dawn. If I'm right, the blaze will have lured the ships closer. Keep a fire burning on the foreshore and have some of the men blow trumpets and act as if pirates have taken the port.'

250

'Damn it, Wayland. Aren't you going to tell me what you suspect?'

'I'll come for you early.'

'Wayland's here,' Vallon's servant whispered, holding up a lamp.

Vallon rubbed his eyes and threw off his bed covers. He dressed and went out. Stars outlined the Caucasus and the eastern horizon was invisible.

'It's still the middle of the night,' he said, tetchy from having been kept awake by the racket of trumpets and war cries.

Wayland guided him towards the bonfire on the foreshore. Three troopers pulled themselves to attention. Wayland stationed himself at the waterline. Vallon sat beside the crackling logs with a blanket draped over his shoulders.

'See anything?'

'It's still too dark.'

'Why did you drag me from my bed, then?'

'Because if I'm right, we'll need to act fast.'

Vallon mouthed an oath and fell into a doze. Wayland woke him by squeezing a shoulder. Vallon still couldn't separate sea from sky.

'They're out there,' Wayland said.

Vallon stumbled to his feet and peered into the pre-dawn gloom. 'If I didn't know your eyes were as keen as a hawk's, I'd swear you were making sport of me.'

Wayland's teeth glimmered in the fireglow. 'Cover your eyes for a time. You'll see all the better.'

Like a child playing a game, Vallon shielded his eyes.

'I can make them out now,' Wayland said. 'Not far to the south of us, about a mile out.'

Vallon probed the semi-darkness. His gaze kept returning to two motes of matter that remained dark while the world around them grew ever paler.

'Is that them?'

'That's them.'

At this season of the year, the light came fast. Birds were in full song when the ships took on solid form. Vallon advanced a step, rubbed his eyes and gave a husky laugh. 'By God, I don't believe it.'

'Nor did I when I first spotted them, but the cut of the sails looked familiar. It's like when you see someone from afar. Even though you can't make out their features, something about their posture, the way they move, tells you it's an old friend.'

Vallon laid an arm around Wayland's shoulder. 'Or enemy.'

Side by side they stood looking out to sea until the sun's first flush silhouetted two Viking longships, the carved dragons on their stem- and stern-posts rearing up in black snarls.

The entire squadron stood along the shoreline watching the Vikings watching them.

'What do you make of them?' Vallon said.

'They must be Swedes,' Wulfstan said. 'The only way they could have reached the Caspian is down the Volga. I never heard of a Norwegian crew taking that route.'

During the night, the ships had crept to within half a mile of the coast, still well out of hailing distance. They drifted together, roped stern to bow.

'I count only forty-two crew,' Wulfstan said. 'They must have lost a fair few men on the way south. From Sweden to the Caspian is more than a year's voyaging.'

Vallon swung his arm in a come-hither gesture. 'Call them again.'

'Waste of breath,' said Wulfstan. 'They ain't going to risk landing in the teeth of a well-armed force.'

One of the Vikings gave a loose wave and his comrades separated and began to take their positions on the thwarts.

'They're leaving,' said Vallon in exasperation. 'Well, if they won't come to us, I'll send someone to them. Wulfstan, you're the man for the job. Off you go.'

Wulfstan cast a dubious look at the longships.

'What are you waiting for?' said Vallon. 'They're not going to carry off an old pirate with only one hand.'

Wulfstan spat. 'That's what worries me. They might just knock me on the head and drop me in the sea.'

Vallon shoved him. 'You're wasting time. Don't tell them any more of our business than you have to. Say nothing about my voyage to the north.' He pointed at a grassy spit curving into the sea half a mile to the south. 'Tell their leader to meet us there – four in each party. Everyone else to stand well clear.'

Wulfstan ran towards the harbour. The Vikings had begun to stroke away when he took to the sea in a skiff rowed by two oarsmen. Vallon shielded his eyes against the glare. The longships slowed and stopped. The skiff came alongside in a twinkling of oars and a Viking reached out to help Wulfstan aboard.

There followed a long hot wait before Wulfstan returned to the skiff and pulled for shore. Vallon met him at the water's edge.

'Well?'

'They've agreed to talk. They're Swedish all right. Their leader's called Hauk.'

'Anything else?'

'They've been in a bad scrap, but Hauk's too proud to admit it. He doesn't give much away. If it wasn't for the empty thwarts and half a dozen men groaning from wounds, you'd think he was on a spring cruise.'

'Join me for the negotiations,' Vallon said. He addressed his centurions. 'Remain here with the men in clear sight. Any threatening move and the Vikings will be off.'

Josselin clearly would have been happy to see the back of them. He indicated Vallon's splendid armour, his superb sword in its finely chased scabbard. 'With respect, sir, you shouldn't put yourself in jeopardy. Let me go in your place.'

'You don't speak Norse and this won't be the first time I've negotiated with Vikings.' Vallon grinned at Wayland. 'Do you remember balancing on a rock in a wilderness river while we parleyed with Thorfinn Wolfbreath?'

'That didn't turn out too well.'

'Not for Thorfinn it didn't. I want you at my side again.'

Hero took a tentative step. 'And if the Vikings are carrying wounded men, perhaps my presence might be useful.'

An hour after the sun had started its descent, Vallon and his team were still standing on the promontory, blasted by heat, while the longships lolled offshore.

Hero fanned away flies. 'Do you think he's changed his mind?'

Wulfstan removed a pebble from his mouth and spat a fleck of white spittle. 'He's softening us up by letting us stew while he lounges in the shade. I'll send for water.'

'Wait,' said Vallon. A stirring at the side of one of the longships had caught his attention. The Vikings lowered a skiff and four men climbed into it. 'At last.'

The boat rowed towards them, its occupants elongating and dwarfing in the heat waves. They ran the boat aground and stepped out – three yellow- and russet-haired warriors standing half a head taller than their commander, all of them wearing woollen cloaks over rusty mail shirts, linen kirtles and leggings or trousers.

'Hauk, you said.'

'That's the fellow.'

Vallon studied him as he approached. Neat of foot and well-made, clean-shaven and with sun-faded brown hair trimmed short. Small only by comparison with his brawny companions. Not a heathen either, judging by the crucifix at his throat.

The delegation halted ten yards away and Hauk appraised the general. He had eyes like a jackdaw's – silvery grey pupils ringed by dark irises, a quick unsmiling gaze. His eyes dwelt on Vallon's armour, lingered on Wayland and glanced over Hero.

He gave a dismissive sniff. 'Your commander has chosen a strange set of lieutenants,' he said to Wulfstan. 'I expected something more formidable than a one-armed soldier, a holy water clerk and a man with a dog.'

'You can speak to me directly,' Vallon said. 'I'm Vallon the Frank, general in the army of His Imperial Majesty Alexius

Comnenus. And Hero isn't a priest. He's a physician. Wayland's an Englishman, a former hawkmaster to the Sultan of Rum.'

A slight widening of Hauk's eyes betrayed his surprise at being addressed in his own language.

'Where did you learn to speak such bad Norse?'

'On a journey to Iceland and Greenland. We travelled the Road to the Greeks with Norwegian Vikings before going our separate ways. I continued to Miklagard where I took service with the Byzantine army.'

'I'm Hauk Eiriksson, a prince of Uppland, grandson of a Viking who travelled to the Caspian with Ingvar the Far-Traveller some forty years ago. If you voyaged down the Dnieper, you might have heard of his exploits.'

'By the time we ran the Dnieper, the Varangians were a fading memory.'

'My countrymen still honour their venture. More than thirty runestones commemorate the men who made that voyage.'

'I hope they returned home laden with riches.'

'Six ships began that journey and only one returned. My grand-father died in Serkland with Ingvar. I hope to discover how he went to his doom.'

Vallon found Hauk's lack of bombast encouraging. 'Yet you've chosen to repeat the enterprise. I thought the days of the Viking raider were over.'

'The king of Svealand exiled me after I killed one of his sons. I've won fame in my country, but not fortune. I intend to gain both in Serkland.'

'He means Persia,' Wulfstan said.

'And you,' said Hauk. 'I understand you're on a mission to the East.'

'To a land called China. My orders are to establish friendly rela-tions with its ruler. Tell me, Hauk Eiriksson, how you reached the Caspian.'

'We crossed the Baltic last spring and travelled by way of Novgorod to Vladimir on the Volga.'

'Surely you didn't carry those drakkars across the portage.'

'Of course not. We built them on the Volga last winter and sailed downriver when the ice broke up.'

Vallon's gaze strayed to the longships. 'Forgive me if I aggravate a sore, but I'd say you have many fewer men than you started with.' He splayed a placating hand. 'I speak as one with bitter experience of setbacks and losses. Our journey through the Caucasus has cost me nearly quarter of my force.'

Hauk relaxed. 'Sickness claimed twenty of my men during the winter and I lost another dozen in a battle near the mouth of the Volga.'

'I'm glad we speak so frankly. It seems to me that this meeting might breathe fresh wind into both our endeavours.' Vallon waved at the sorry little fleet in the harbour. 'We don't have enough ships to cross the Caspian. You, on the other hand, have empty berths. Perhaps we can—'

'I'm not a ferryman. I steer my own course.'

'Hear me out. I'm not calling on your charity. Transport us to the eastern shore – a week's sail at most – and I'll pay you for each man you carry.'

Hauk's eyes narrowed. 'In silver.'

'No.'

Hauk snorted.

Vallon held up a solidus. 'In gold.' He held it out. 'Take it. Go on, take it.'

Hauk reached out and handed the coin to one of his lieutenants without looking at it. The man turned away like a dog concealing the theft of some dainty and assayed it by taste, texture and weight, his companions craning for his verdict.

A grin split the man's face. Hauk plucked the coin from his hand and stuffed it into his purse. The sun struck silver flecks from his eyes. 'One gold coin doesn't persuade me of your honesty. You outnumber us two to one. If I take your soldiers on my ships, how do I know you won't try to seize them?'

'My word, for a start.'

Hauk's laugh rang harsh.

'If that isn't enough, we can make some practical accommodation. Suppose you transport my muleteers and grooms, leaving my fighting men to take their chances on the freighters and fishing boats.'

'You sound desperate.'

'I can only go east. Even if I could bring my force back to Miklagard, I would face certain disgrace and probable death. There you have it.'

While they'd been talking, intermittent wails had drifted from the longships.

'Some of your companions are wounded,' Vallon said. 'Whatever you decide, allow Hero to treat them. He'll minister to them for no reward.'

'Why?'

'Treating the sick is his vocation, as tending men's souls is a priest's sacred calling.'

Hauk took another look at Hero. 'I'll discuss your proposition with my comrades.'

'While you're talking, I'll send for water. I can hardly speak for thirst.'

Hauk's party withdrew to the skiff and huddled together, punctuating their exchanges with emphatic gestures.

'What do you think?' said Hero.

'I wouldn't trust him as far as I could spit him,' Wulfstan said. 'I expect he feels the same about us.'

A trooper hurried up with goatskin bags of water. Vallon drank in long glugs, the liquid spilling down his chin. He took off his helmet and poured the rest over his head.

'Here comes the answer,' Wayland said.

Hauk advanced at the head of his men. 'It's not enough.'

'Then name your own terms.'

'I don't have to. I could seize you here and now and hold you for ransom.'

Wulfstan laughed. 'I'd like to see you try.' He cocked a finger at Vallon. 'The general's the finest swordsman I've met.'

'Hush,' said Vallon.

Hauk's escort fingered their swords. One Viking, his face disfigured by a purple cicatrice running from temple to jaw, partly unsheathed his blade. Vallon made no move.

'Fighting would be stupid before we've finished negotiating. I've stated my terms. Now let's hear yours.'

Hauk's nostrils dilated. 'Three solidi for each man we carry, plus another solidus for each beast of burden.'

'Agreed.'

Hauk's features froze. 'What?'

'I said I agree to your terms.'

Wulfstan hid a snigger. Hauk ground his teeth. 'To be paid in advance.'

'You'll receive half the gold when we quit this shore. The rest when we make landfall on the other side.'

Hauk looked at the ground and then raised his face with a pensive smile.

Another gargling cry from the longships broke the impasse. 'Your wounded need treatment,' Hero said. 'Let me collect my medicines and return to the ships with you.'

'Wulfstan and I will come too,' said Vallon. He half-inclined his head. 'With your permission.'

Hauk gave a curt nod. 'Come in your own boat,' he said. In parting, his gaze lingered on Wayland. 'He doesn't speak much.'

'He speaks when he has something important to say.' Vallon smiled at Wayland and spoke in French. 'Have I made a bargain with the devil?'

'I don't know. Hauk's a lot smarter than Thorfinn. He reminds me of someone.'

'Oh, yes. Who?'

'You.'

Conditions on board the dragonships were worse than Vallon had expected. The Vikings were famished, dull eyes cupped in mauve sockets, sores on their faces. They were a mixed band, some of

258

them barely into their teens and some old enough to have made their first raids when the men of the northlands still ruled the seas.

Hero took charge. 'These men need food and fresh water.'

'We have plenty to spare,' Vallon said.

Hauk's jawline tightened. He dipped his head a fraction.

'Fetch them,' Vallon told Wulfstan. 'Don't stint.'

Vallon and Hauk trailed after Hero while he examined the six wounded men, probing their injuries with an unflinching delicacy that both repulsed Vallon and filled him with admiration.

One man had taken a stab to the gut and was rotting from inside. Another, barely conscious with an indented skull, drooled and gibbered to old gods. A third, with no apparent sign of injury, clasped his stomach and implored Hero to put him out of his pain. The fourth stoically proffered an arm severed at the elbow and wrapped in a filthy bandage crawling with flies. The fifth had taken two deep slashes, one to the ribs and one to the shoulder, both exposing bone. And the last – one glimpse of the smashed leg, splintered bone sticking out of seeping, stinking flesh, made Vallon giddy. Dear Lord, he prayed, when death comes for me, let it be swift.

Hero rose, flicked a maggot from his hands and rinsed them in seawater. His expression was strained and distant. So far as he was concerned, Vallon, Hauk and the others didn't exist.

'You'd better go ashore,' he said. 'I'll be at work all night.'

'They're as good as dead,' Vallon said. 'When they die, their companions will lay the blame on you.'

Hero towelled his hands dry. 'Since when were you a physician? I might be able to save two of them if I attend to their wounds straight away. As for the others, I have physic to make their last hours bearable.'

Awkwardly, like a sinner reaching for a holy relic, Vallon touched Hero's arm. 'You're a good man.'

He was climbing into the boat when he noticed the girl sitting alone in the stern of the second longship. From a distance and in the shallow evening light he formed an impression of dark hair and pale hieratic features.

'Who's that?' he asked.

Hauk didn't look round. 'A slave.'

'Why is she tethered?'

'To stop her throwing herself into the sea. She's already done it once.'

Vallon nodded at the oarsmen to begin rowing. He chuckled as they found their rhythm. 'A year's voyaging and all Hauk has to show for it is one wild slave girl.'

Wayland sat facing him in the bow, framed by the sun's aura. 'I'm not travelling in the company of slavers.'

Vallon yawned. 'We'll meet precious little else in the East.'

'I mean it. If you recall, when we met, I was a slave in all but name. So was Syth.'

One startled glance and Vallon knew that Wayland spoke in earnest. 'What do you expect me to do about it?'

'Buy her freedom. I'll pay.'

Vallon remembered how Wayland had fought tooth and nail to keep Syth with him on the northern voyage.

'Wayland, I hope—'

'The girl means nothing to me. I set her value at no more than a few of those coins you've been throwing around.'

Vallon's mouth worked. 'Stop rowing,' he ordered. He looked over his shoulder. 'Hauk Eiriksson.'

The Viking leaned over the side, his features burnished by the sun.

'The slave girl,' Vallon called. 'Where did you get her?'

'In a village near the Volga Bend. What's it to you?'

'Have your men used her?'

'That would halve her value. In Serkland they employ witches to tell if a girl still has her maidenhead.'

'What will she fetch? I only ask because I'll be dabbling in the slave trade myself.'

'A girl as rare as that one – at least five solidi.'

'You overestimate her worth.'

'I told you I'll pay,' Wayland muttered.

'Row us back,' Vallon told the oarsmen

Hauk received them with mild surprise. Vallon extended a hand. 'Five solidi, you said. Here's six.'

'I didn't say she was for sale.'

'Yes, you did.'

Hauk laughed. 'I wouldn't have put a lust for virgins among your weaknesses.'

Vallon slid a glance at Wayland. 'She's not for me.'

Hauk regarded the Englishman in a new light before whisking the money from Vallon's hand. 'Take her and good riddance. A word of warning,' he said to Wayland. 'After you've taken your pleasure, stay awake unless you want to feel her teeth closing about your throat.'

A huge Viking hoisted the girl kicking and scratching over the side and dropped her into the skiff. Her struggles threw her ragged clothing into disarray, giving Vallon a glimpse of the dark triangle above her thighs. He tugged his cloak tight over his shoulder and set his sights on shore.

'You'll rue that purchase,' the Viking said. 'She'll cut your balls off while you sleep.'

The skiff rowed towards shore.

'What's her name?' Wayland asked.

Vallon stared past him. 'How would I know?'

Wayland sprang forward to stop the girl throwing herself into the sea. Her struggles threatened to capsize the boat. Raucous jeers billowed from the longships.

'Oh, for Christ's sake,' Vallon said.

Wayland pinned the girl down. 'Find out what tongue she speaks.'

'I'm not your go-between, damn it.'

'Just try her.'

'Anyone else . . . ' Vallon growled. He turned and addressed the girl in Greek. Her expression didn't change. Vallon tossed a hand and faced forward again. 'She doesn't understand Greek.'

'She must be a long way from home.'

'Aren't we all?'

Wayland spoke to her in Persian, one of the languages he'd learned at the Seljuk court. 'What's your name?'

Vallon glanced round when the girl answered in a gush of words, first pointing south, then north.

'She's called Zuleyka,' Wayland said. 'The Vikings weren't the first to carry her off. Khazar raiders captured her in Persia five years ago. She claims to be a daughter of the King of the Gypsies.'

Vallon gave a scoffing laugh.

Wayland stepped past Vallon and resumed his place in the bow. The sun had sunk into a bank of cloud and Vallon no longer had to squint to make out Wayland's expression. 'Why are you looking at her like that?'

'See for yourself.'

'I'm not interested.'

'Her head hangs like a wild hawk hooded for the first time. Touch her however lightly and she'll spit and bate.'

Vallon pointed a finger. 'Wayland, if I thought you intended to man her ...'

'I don't.'

'Good,' Vallon said. The skiff grounded and he clambered past Wayland. 'Because she's not coming with us.'

'Thanks to you, she's a free woman. She can go where she pleases.'

Vallon stalked up the shore. 'Anywhere except in my company.'

XIX

One look at the girl and Lucas was smitten. He was collecting firewood when she landed, moving as gracefully as a cat walking along a fence. The wood dropped in a heap from his hands. He goggled, her filthy and ragged camisole flashing glimpses of slim, shapely legs and accentuating her breasts and hips. Her neck was as elegant as a swan's, her face crowned by a nest of dark curls, her large hooded eyes the green of ilex leaves. Her long, delicately arched nose only emphasised her aristocratic bearing.

Gorka elbowed him. 'Don't even think about it. The general paid six solidi for her.'

'What for? I mean, is she his woman?'

Gorka pushed back his hat, somewhat at a loss. 'He doesn't allow us to take sweethearts on campaign, and he wouldn't break the rules to suit himself. In all the years I've served with the Outlanders, I've never seen him so much as glance at a woman – and believe me, it wasn't for lack of opportunity. Some real beauties, too. Better than that stringy witch.' Fond memories softened his expression, then his mouth set like a trap. 'Get on with your work, trooper.'

In a squadron as close as the Outlanders, rumours about the girl crept and multiplied, mixing fact with speculation, some of it prurient.

'She ain't here by the general's doing,' Gorka said. 'It was the Englishman who bought her. He's warmer-blooded than he lets on.'

'I heard he bought her to set her free,' said a trooper.

Gorka flicked a bone into the fire. 'Only after he's taken his pleasure with her. Lucky bastard. The rest of us won't dip our wicks until we reach Samarkand, wherever that is.'

'She's a Luri,' said another. 'A gypsy. She was a dancer in a troupe of singers and performers.'

Gorka hawked and spat. 'Gypsies are bad cess. They can read the future and put the hex on you. I saw it with my own eyes this very day.' He patted Lucas's knee. 'One glance from that witch and Lucas's bones melted. Am I right, lad?'

Lucas wriggled. 'Give it a rest, boss.'

A man crossed himself. 'What's her name?'

'Zuleyka. Something like that.'

Zuleyka. The name expanded in Lucas's mind.

Gorka laughed. 'See? She's enchanted him.' He prodded Lucas's thigh. 'You'll need a priest to drive out her magic.'

Lucas twisted away and spoke in a rough manner. 'Don't be daft. It's only because I haven't seen a woman for weeks.'

The troopers' laughter tailed off. 'The lad's right,' said one. 'At least on the Danube watch there was always a village girl to pleasure you and darn your socks.'

'You and your bloody socks.'

A tall shape against the fireglow made them scramble up.

'As you were,' said Vallon. 'Everything all right?'

'No complaints,' said Aimery. 'We were wondering what arrangements you'd made with the Vikings.'

'They've agreed to transport us across the Caspian.'

'For gold?'

'It won't come out of your wages.' Vallon cleared his throat. 'I want to be off tomorrow, so you'll need to start loading before first light. You'll have plenty of time to catch up on sleep during the crossing. Good night.'

Aimery broke the dragging silence. 'You heard him. Turn in.'

Gorka stirred the cinders as if to shape them into auguries. 'Vallon made a deal with the Svans and they broke it. Now he gets cosy with a gang of Vikings . . . '

The sizzling of spit in the embers was more eloquent than words.

Even with a night start, the task of distributing the men and cargo among the vessels took until afternoon. Lucas was loading the last string of horses onto the lopsided freighter when a trooper at the top of the ramp shouted and pointed.

Lucas whirled to see the slave girl galloping away. His mouth went slack. His eyes bolted. 'Hey, that's my horse!'

He sprinted down the line of horses and leaped bareback onto a fine bay. Grabbing its mane with his left hand, he lashed it into pursuit with his right. A trooper flung himself out of his way. Shouts faded behind him. He rode crouched over the horse's neck, the steppe streaming back in a green blur. The girl had a furlong start, an excellent mount and weighed fifty pounds less than him. Also, he realised, she was a superb rider with perfect balance. Stride by stride she increased her lead until by the time he'd covered two miles she was the best part of half a mile ahead. He couldn't maintain the pace. The effort of managing his horse by hand and thigh was too much to sustain. A swerve as his mount switched direction to avoid an anthill almost spilled him onto the steppe.

Hooves drubbed behind him and two Seljuks swept past, apparently seated on cushions of air. Their saddles and stirrups gave them an advantage and yard by yard they ran the girl down, coming up on her one on each side. One of them transferred his weight to his left stirrup, leaned out and snatched Aster's reins. The gelding crabbed to a stop and the Seljuks' horses squealed and nipped around him.

Lucas caught up, hot and furious. The girl's camisole had ridden up to her waist. He tried to drag her off and she backhanded him across the nose, bringing tears to his eyes. 'God damn you,' he shouted. He seized her and they tumbled to the ground. She was first up and when he pulled her back she ran a clawed hand down his cheek.

Warding off her flailing hands, he wrestled her to the ground. Still she struggled. He straddled her hips and pinned her wrists. She went still only for long enough to spit into his eyes.

A buffet to his head knocked him sideways. Blinking up, he saw the universe rearrange itself around Wayland. The girl seized her chance and lunged for Aster. One of the Seljuks ran the horse out of her reach and the other rode tight circles around the girl, giving strange high-pitched cries.

Lucas shook his head to restore vision. 'What did you do that for?'

'Fetch your horse.'

Lucas darted poisonous glances at the girl while he examined Aster. 'If you've lamed him . . .'

He was blown and lathered, but had suffered no serious harm. Lucas dabbed at his leaking cheek. The Seljuks sat their horses with impassivity. Wayland nudged his chin in the direction of the horse Lucas had appropriated. 'You know who that belongs to?'

Lucas managed a grin. 'No, but she's a good one.'

'So she should be. She's the general's spare mount.'

Lucas swung his arm as if hurling something into the ground. 'Ah, hell.'

Wayland took Vallon's horse and led it away, the Seljuks jogging after him. 'Get going. You're holding up the convoy.'

'Hey,' Lucas shouted. 'What am I supposed to do with *her*?'

'Nothing,' Wayland said. 'She can go wherever she pleases provided it's not on one of the company's mounts.'

Lucas slumped. He pulled Zuleyka away from Aster. 'You're free. Understand?' He shoved her. 'Go on. Get lost.'

She began walking south.

Lucas's lips curled. Stupid bitch, he thought. 'You're going the wrong way.'

'No, she isn't,' Wayland called back. 'She's from Persia. Khazar pirates captured her when she was twelve.'

Lucas dragged himself onto Aster. 'She's not going to reach Persia on her own. Look at her. She won't last a day.'

'That's not my problem.'

'Nor mine.'

Wayland kicked his horse into a canter. 'Don't make matters worse by delaying the convoy any longer.'

Lucas urged Aster into a trot. His face smarted and his thighs ached. Tomorrow he'd hardly be able to walk. Wayland and the Seljuks were already silhouettes and the girl was just a blip on the hot grassland. He swore and caught up, slowing his pace to match hers. She strode on, slim calves flashing, her eyes fixed ahead.

'You're crazy,' he said. 'You'll only be captured by another bunch of pirates.'

She ignored him.

266

'Go on, then. See if I care.'

But Lucas couldn't leave her. Grass halms had already cut her feet. 'Come on, Zuleyka. Say something.' He rode ahead of her and turned. 'Listen, I'm sorry I handled you roughly, but you can't blame me. Aster's the only thing I have.'

She stopped and he melted at the sight of tears flooding her eyes. He held out a hand and his voice dropped into a deeper register. 'Get on behind me.'

She looked at him properly for the first time and he wished with all his heart that he could have undone his hot-blooded actions. He stretched towards her as if trying to bridge a gulf, and after a moment she took his fingers and sprang up behind him.

They plodded back, Lucas aware of Zuleyka's breasts against his back. He eased his throat.

'You ride pretty well.'

He might not have existed for all the attention she paid him.

He tapped his chest. 'I'm Lucas.' He craned over his shoulder. 'Lucas.'

Her strange green eyes looked straight through him.

Love, lust and guilt made a curdled brew. Lucas clapped his heels against Aster's flanks. 'To hell with you, then.'

Jeers and catcalls greeted his return. Vallon stood planted in his path, his face frozen in rage he wouldn't express to a mere trooper. Lucas felt a spurt of self-pity at the injustice of it.

'What was I supposed to do?' he muttered.

Wulfstan took Aster's reins. 'Get aboard.'

Lucas slid off. 'What about the girl?'

Wulfstan shoved him towards the freighter. 'Just do what you're told.'

Gorka met him at the top of the plank, shaking his head at Lucas's latest transgression. 'Oh dear,' he said. 'Oh dear, oh fucking dear. You attract trouble like shit draws flies.'

'It wasn't my fault.'

Gorka's face grew choleric. 'Not your fault? You're in the

267

fucking army. It's always someone's fault.' He cuffed Lucas's back. 'Now pretend you don't exist.'

Lucas flung himself down, wrapped his arms around his chest and didn't stir until the freighter had cast off. Rising on stiffening joints, he saw the mountains receding behind them in a pastel haze, the ships drawn out in line under the oncoming night. Hungry, he joined his squad for supper.

'Anyone know what happened to the girl?' he said, trying to make his tone casual.

'It was awful,' Gorka said. 'Vallon executed her. Stealing imperial property's a capital offence.'

Lucas sprang up. 'No!'

One of the troopers took pity on him. 'Gorka's making sport of you. Vallon and Wayland had a flaming row over her. The general insisted she be left behind and Wayland told him they couldn't just ditch her on the steppe. They were shouting into each other's faces right in front of us and I thought for one moment they'd come to blows. Anyway, the Englishman won the argument. The girl's coming with us until we reach Turkestan and can find a caravan that will take her back to Persia.'

Lucas subsided in relief. 'Where is she?'

'On one of the baggage boats.'

'Those unnatural brutes!' Lucas glared around. 'On my first night with them I woke to find one of them snuggling up under my blanket.'

The troopers laughed and slapped their thighs. One of them flicked a tear from his eye. 'Her maidenhead's safe. Wayland's dog is guarding it.'

'What?'

'Wayland has set his dog to watch over her. He trained it to protect his children.'

Another trooper shook his head. 'A hundred men, one girl. That can only lead to one thing.'

Gorka nodded. 'Well said, Petrocles.' He aimed a knife in the general direction of Lucas's throat. 'I'll say this once so you'd

268

better listen good. Flirt with the gypsy girl and two soldiers will end up dead – the man stabbed by his rival and the murderer Vallon leaves hanging from some wayside gallows. Believe it. I've looked back at more than one trooper whose neck was stretched because he couldn't wait to dip his wick at the next town for a few baubles.'

Lucas flushed. 'I only chased her because she stole my horse.'

Gorka kept his knife aimed. 'I think she stole more than that.'

Aimery deflected the blade. 'You've made your point. It's been a tiring day and we'll all feel better after a night's sleep.'

When Lucas lay down, he looked up at the stars, remembering the feel of the horse between his thighs, the hot wind in his face, the girl's breasts stirring under her gown, the creamy smoothness of her thighs.

Zuleyka.

Gorka elbowed him. 'Are you dreaming of diddling the gypsy girl?'

'No, boss.'

Gorka pounced. 'Why not? Are you a fucking *homo*?'

XX

A hot and thirsty crossing they had of it. Each day at noon the sky curved over them like a brazen shield, the sun a molten boss. Even though they'd filled all their water barrels, supplies dwindled so fast that Vallon imposed rationing on the fourth day.

Dawn on the sixth day found them tacking into a scorching headwind off the Turkestan coast. By mid-morning even Hero could make out its black and naked hills broiling under a urine-coloured sky. The air had an unpleasant sweetish taste that caught in the throat, making the men spit and hawk in defiance of the captain's warnings that insulting the sea would make it angry. At midday, with the sun hot enough to melt pitch, the lead longship shortened sail half a mile offshore and the convoy hove to.

'What's that noise?' said Vallon.

Hero raised his head, listening. It sounded like water sliding down a distant millrace.

Aiken pointed at a rocky inlet. 'It's coming from over there.'

Vallon shaded his eyes and examined the bight. 'I can't make out what's happening.'

Nor could Hero until they rowed close to the channel. Men crossed themselves and exchanged apprehensive glances. The water wasn't flowing into the sea. Instead, unnatural and terrifying, the sea was pouring into the land.

'Mother of God,' a trooper whispered. 'It's the throat into hell.'

The captain of the freighter knew what it was and had contrived to make landfall with maximum dramatic effect. '*Kara Bogaz*,' he said. 'The Black Maw.'

'What is it?' Vallon demanded. 'Where does it lead?'

'It's a waterfall flowing the wrong way, descending from sea to land. It runs into a great bay said by the Turkmen to be the child of the Caspian and the Black Sea. Because the Caspian deserted her husband, God decreed that the *Kara Bogaz Gol* would never cut its umbilical cord, and so the Caspian must feed it with water until the end of time.'

'Steer clear and put us ashore.'

They stepped onto baking rock crawling with insects and scrambled along the shoreline in a haze of stinging flies. From the mouth of the channel Hero saw what had been hidden from the sea. The Caspian slid through a rocky channel only a hundred yards wide and spilled into a huge lagoon ringed by ribbons of salt. Under a glittering sky hurtful to his eyes, Hero could see no end to the bay.

'I believe I can explain the mystery,' he said. 'This bay, being smaller than its progenitor and lying in a more desiccated region, loses water to the sun at a greater rate than the Caspian can supply it. Hence the difference in level.'

'Aye,' said the captain. 'At this time of the year, the drop is no more than six or seven feet. In high summer it's twice as steep.'

Hero's gaze hunted over the cauterised landscape without finding any traces of man. No vegetation except spindly shrubs that rattled like bones in the stifling breeze. They seemed to have made landfall on God's most neglected patch of creation.

'Where will we find water?' Vallon asked the captain.

'I don't know. Even the nomads shun this coast.'

'Then why did you land us in this Godforsaken spot?'

'You demanded that I steer the shortest course.'

'Where's the nearest fresh water, damn it?'

The captain quailed under Vallon's anger. 'There's a river about three days to the south, but it's been many years since its waters reached the sea. You might have to travel far inland before you find a well.'

Vallon squinted through the piss-coloured light. 'How far does the bay extend?'

'From hearsay, two days with a following wind.'

'Will we find water on the other side?'

The captain cringed. 'General, I've never ventured that far. I didn't choose to make this voyage.'

Vallon muttered something vile and then spoke as if to himself. 'Only three days' water left and no certainty that we'll find fresh supplies whatever direction we take.' He closed his eyes. Everyone hung on his decision, aware that it might make the difference between life and death.

Vallon clicked his fingers. 'That Seljuk trooper who advised us on the route through Transoxiana. Yeke. Ask him what we can expect to find.'

Troopers relayed Yeke's response from ship to ship until it reached Otia's ears, the intelligence no doubt distorted in transmission. 'He says we should cross the Black Lake to its utmost shore. From there not many days separate us from a caravan trail supplied by wells.'

Wayland sounded a note of caution. 'I wouldn't place too much

271

faith in Yeke's directions. The Seljuks don't measure distance the same way we do.'

Vallon's shoulders relaxed – a sign that he'd reached a decision. 'Order everyone ashore. Lash the ships together and guard them. Post a screen of archers behind me.'

The Outlanders on the cargo ships and fishing boats disembarked, leaving the rest of Vallon's force on the longships. Hauk's drakkar rowed to within hailing distance.

'Put my men ashore,' Vallon called.

'First give us our gold.'

'Only when you've landed my men.'

Hauk waited until the bulk of the Outlanders had withdrawn inland before his ship nosed ashore and allowed most of the hostages off. Then he had his men row a hundred yards out to sea.

'I said *all* of them,' Vallon shouted.

'I'm keeping ten back until I count the gold.'

'Your greed blinds you to our predicament.'

'Ours?'

'Release my men, come ashore and I'll explain.'

Hero was light-headed from the heat when the last of Vallon's men waded to land. Hauk and eight bodyguards lounged up, hands on swords.

Vallon indicated the waterfall. 'I imagine you can take your ships down that.'

'Can and will aren't the same thing,' Hauk said. 'Deliver you to the eastern shore, you asked. Well, now you're here and I'll take my due before bidding you farewell.'

Vallon pointed at Josselin. 'Send for the gold. All of it.'

'General ...'

'Just bring it.'

Four men accompanied by Aiken lugged the coffer to the strand. 'Open it,' said Vallon.

The Vikings gasped when the lid yawned back, exposing its trove of bullion. Vallon slithered the surface. Hauk made a small gesture to still his companions' excitement.

Aiken counted out the coins while the Vikings grinned and jostled, licking their lips and nudging each other. Their good humour faded somewhat when they saw that their portion had hardly dented the chest's contents.

Hauk trickled coins through his hands. 'If I'd known you were carrying so much treasure, I'd have struck a harder bargain.'

Vallon slammed the lid shut. 'Take it away. Our account's settled.'

Hauk watched the troopers bear away the treasure. 'You're a man of your word, Vallon. The only favour I ask is sufficient food and water to last us until we reach a source. If you insist, I'll pay you in your own coin.'

'There isn't any.'

Hauk's brow creased. 'No food or source?'

'I have no water to spare and no idea where you'll be able to fill your casks.'

Hauk quelled his men's ugly mutters. 'I observed our agreement to the letter.'

'So have I. I don't recall it included any obligation to provide you with water.'

A Viking half-unsheathed his sword and in the same moment the screen of archers behind Vallon bent their bows.

Hauk fanned away a snarling coil of flies. 'I can carry you off before your men can do a thing.'

'Don't be so sure. The Turkish bow is a terrible weapon.' Vallon lifted a hand and dropped it. Thirty arrows ripped into the sky with the sound of tearing cloth and fell fizzing into the sea beyond the furthest longship. Hauk glanced round to measure the threat before turning a tight smile on Vallon.

'We'd still hold you prisoner.'

'A pretty worthless prize. I'm too tough and stringy to tempt slavers. Let me speak candidly of your prospects, Hauk Eiriksson. You're on a mission to nowhere. The days when a shipload of Varangians could exact tribute from rich coastal settlements are over. Persia and Anatolia are ruled by the Seljuks – a warrior race

273

who've fought their way almost up to the walls of Constantinople. Chase booty in the south or west and you'll meet the same dismal fate as your grandfather.'

Hauk's gaze travelled down the monotony of grey and dun hills. 'I'll shape my own destiny. As for water, I'll replenish my casks from the other ships once you've left.'

'Wrong. They won't return until they've delivered us to the far side of this stinking stewpot.'

Hauk's composure deserted him. 'You're taking them down the fall?' He laughed.

Wulfstan puffed up like a bantam cock. 'Me and the general lowered a fleet down the Dnieper Rapids. You've heard of them – the Gulper, the Insatiable, the Sleepless One ... Compared to those bastards, this is just a ripple.'

Hauk's pale eyes flickered between the two men. 'I smell a proposition.'

'You're right,' Vallon said. 'I still need your longships. Continue with us to the end of the Black Bay. You'll share the same rations as my own men, the same dangers.'

Hauk squinted across the bay. 'Then what? We might not find water over there.'

'At least we'll be in the same boat.'

Hauk ran his tongue over his lips. 'I'll want more than water in return.'

'You can't drink gold.'

'No, but if we perish, at least I'll die rich.'

'Deliver my men to the far side and I'll pay you the same again.'

'I won't do it for less than double.'

'Then you won't do it at all. If necessary, I'll make room by abandoning the pack animals. As you've seen, we don't lack money to pay for fresh mounts.'

The whining of flies filled the silence. A cautious smile crept across Hauk's face. 'Double and not a penny less.'

Vallon spun on his heel. 'Come.'

'Vallon!'

The general took several more paces before turning. 'This heat fries my wits and parches my tongue. Unless you have something useful to say, sail away.'

Brushing aside his bodyguards, Hauk approached. The Outlander archers stood only a hundred yards behind the general, their forms wavering in the heat.

'Half as much gold again and it's a deal.'

'My offer was final. Farewell, Hauk Eiriksson.'

'Vallon!'

With infinite slowness, Vallon faced the Viking. 'Last chance.'

Hauk crooked his forefinger and brought it down as if he'd like to claw the general's heart out. 'Consider yourself lucky.'

'I take that for a "yes",' Vallon said. 'Good.'

Stranded in Vallon's wake, Hero saw Hauk's lips compress in a silent vow to take revenge for this humiliation.

Hero caught up with the general to find him telling the fleet's masters that their work wasn't done. They couldn't return until they'd ferried the Outlanders across the Black Lake.

'How will we return?' one of the captains wailed. 'How will we haul our ships back up to the Caspian?'

'You should have thought of that before landing us on this infernal griddle.'

A gust of parching wind carried away the captain's response. A vortex of dust skated past. Hero eased his arid throat.

Wayland appeared at his side. 'I preferred it when there was only the three of us.'

'We were more than three,' Hero said.

'Yes.'

Despite the intolerable heat, Hero shivered. 'I always knew that a sliver of ice was lodged in Vallon's heart, but with every day of our journeying it's grown until it freezes out all warmer feelings.'

'Command forces harsh decisions.'

'I don't understand why he showed off our wealth to the sea pirates.'

'He intends to make good our losses by recruiting the Vikings.

275

Having seen how much gold we're carrying, they won't need much persuading. Why quarter hostile shores for a few slaves and a scrap of gold when a king's ransom lies right under their nose?'

'I'm glad I don't have to make the decisions,' Hero said. He took a step, stumbled over a rock and rubbed his eyes. 'Oh, damn it.'

'Take my arm,' Wayland said. 'The ground is treacherous.'

Vallon left Wulfstan to organise the lowering of the ramshackle convoy down the Black Maw. The freighters' keels chattered and scraped over ledges before bobbing into slack water. When all the vessels had descended, the Vikings rowed down the rapids with casual aplomb.

Wulfstan tramped up to Vallon. 'Ready to depart.' He grinned. 'You've got to hand it to the Vikings. No one handles ships as tidily as a Norseman.'

'You're not tempted to change sides,' Vallon said. It wasn't a question or a jest.

'Sir, how could you?'

Vallon wagged a finger. 'Before our journey is over, some of my most trusted lieutenants will desert me.'

'Not me,' Wulfstan said. 'I'll follow you into the mouth of hell.'

'We're already in it.'

Vallon boarded his ship and signalled for the convoy to get under way. Slowly the ships gathered headway.

With the wind against them, the men heaved to make progress through the lead-coloured waters. Fish sucked in from the Caspian floated dead among pillows of grey scum, seagulls hovering and dipping on pliant wings. Away from the fall, a muffling silence descended. The shore fell away on both sides until the voyagers could only separate sea from land by the band of minerals rimming its shore.

The sea was poisonous. After the cook used brine to make porridge, the men came down with stomach cramps and diarrhoea. One of the wounded Vikings died, and when his comrades cast him overboard he stayed afloat, bobbing in their wake with one arm upheld in a jaunty farewell.

The very air was toxic, bringing men's flesh out in boils and weeping lesions. When their shifts at the oars ended, the troopers hunched in what little shade they could find, hands crossed over their shoulders, heads wrapped in wet rags. They only showed animation when their water rations came round, greedily swallowing the liquid before sinking back into apathy, measuring out their lives by how much water was left.

On the third day into the crucible, Vallon cut the daily ration by half for man and beast alike. One trooper – a younger man from Thessalonika – snatched a waterskin from the man serving the ration and sucked greedily at the source before guards wrenched it away.

'A flogging for that man when we reach land,' Vallon said.

That provoked hollow laughter. What land? They would all be dead of thirst within two days.

But next day around noon a trooper called out to his companions. 'Hey, lads, take a look at this.'

The men hauled themselves to their feet and rubbed their eyes to better witness their salvation.

'Jesus,' a voice said in the awed tones of someone witnessing the Second Coming.

Dead ahead a rusty pall slanted across the sky, thunderheads roiling above it like monstrous fungi. Jagged daggers of lightning stabbed between the cloud mountains and thunder crackled. Down at sea level, the world sank into dusk.

Vallon stood at the bow. 'It looks like the storm will break above us. Be ready to collect the rain.'

The men scrambled to rig up sailcloth containers and waited, mouths moving in supplication. A flash of lightning seared their eyes and thunder loud enough to rattle their brainpans followed. Darkness blotted out all but the nearest ships. Blue flames fizzled along the rigging. At the third thunderclap, hot brown raindrops as fat as grapes splattered on the deck. And then the heavens

277

discharged their burden in one swoop, the deluge so intense that it was an effort to breathe. The men ran about to collect the rain, spilling more than they decanted. It didn't matter. The downpour was so heavy that they filled the casks within minutes. The men stripped off their salt-stiffened clothes and cavorted on the spray-stung deck before standing naked with faces uplifted, eyes closed against the drubbing rain.

The storm passed and the clouds shredded like rotten shrouds and the sun broke through, etching the contours of a coast against a sky purged of dust. They had no way of knowing that more rain had fallen in the last half hour than would fall for the rest of the year.

They surged onto the foredeck, craning to see what awaited them.

Wayland brushed back his damp hair. 'Kara Kum,' he said. 'The Black Desert.'

Vallon heard him. 'I can see fresh green growth. The storm has brought the desert to life and saved our own.'

Seeing the glitter in Vallon's eyes, Hero wondered if mania had gripped the general. 'We were lucky. If it hadn't been for the storm, we would all have perished from thirst.'

Vallon lolled against the bow, his hair plastered about his face. 'I don't leave everything to fortune. We still have four days' water hidden away.'

'You denied your men even though we have supplies?'

Vallon laughed. 'A soldier always keeps a reserve. Remember?'

Hero did and was transported back to a freezing February night in England when Vallon had handed over the last of his rations and gone hungry himself.

'Wayland says you hope to recruit the Vikings.'

'Turkmen make up more than a quarter of my squadron. Like the other Outlanders, they're beginning to dread the journey. Unlike the Christians, they'll be on familiar territory once we land. I expect many to desert.'

'You can't employ pirates.'

'Nature will blunt their avarice. They've already learned that gold is a poor substitute for food and water.' Vallon shoved up from the gunwale. 'Your eyes look sore.'

'They're much soothed by the rain,' Hero said. That much was true, but the mist over his right eye had thickened to the extent that it created a permanent fog.

'Good,' said Vallon. 'These last few weeks I haven't seen as much of you as I would have liked. Don't let distance come between us.'

XXI

Evening had fallen before the Outlanders disembarked, leaving the animals and stores to be unloaded in daylight. Vallon paid off Hauk and the Viking returned to their ships moored half a mile down the coast. During the night the sounds of a fierce argument carried from the Norsemen's camp. At dawn both longships still rode at anchor. By then Vallon had despatched Yeke and two other Turkmen to scout for water and a trail.

If it hadn't been for the storm, the country they'd landed on would have been as malignant as the coast around the Black Maw. It looked like a sea bed heaved high and dry – a scabrous waste of salt pans and bald domes of sun-shattered sediments gouged by gulleys that ran out into drains and sinkholes. But the cloudburst had germinated long-dormant seeds and water still lay in pockets and hollows. Once the squadron had unloaded the ships, they set to work digging pits lined with tarred sailcloth.

Vallon settled up with the Tarki shipmasters and provided them with more than enough water for the return voyage. The skippers reacted to the money as if they'd been paid in turds.

'What use is gold to us?' one said. 'We don't have enough men to haul the freighters up the Black Maw.'

'You'll find strength in desperation, and if that isn't enough, you can drag one of the fishing boats up the rapids. It will be large enough to carry you back across the Caspian.' Vallon dismissed the shipmasters with a curt farewell. 'You'll be back with your families in a fortnight, while we'll be lucky to see our loved ones again. I hope that when you're back at your hearths you find room for us in your prayers.'

The squadron left off their labours to watch the little fleet sail away, and there wasn't a man among them who didn't suffer a clutch of dread at seeing their last line of retreat severed. Glancing down the coast at the Viking camp, they envied the Norsemen with their longships and voiced their discontent until officers ordered them to hold their tongues and get on with their work.

After supper Vallon called a conference attended by his centurions and Hero. The officers lost no time in relaying the troopers' anxieties and adding their own.

'The ground's drying by the hour,' said Josselin. 'We can carry only enough water for two or three days. If we don't find wells inland ...'

Vallon sat behind his camp table. 'I trust the scouts will return with positive news.'

'Your optimism might be misplaced,' Otia said. 'It was a mistake to release the ships before establishing what lies ahead.'

Vallon fiddled with a quill pen. 'We have no more need of ships. Our path lies east, so stop looking back.'

The centurions traded glances, neither wishing to be first to speak his mind.

Vallon eased back. 'I see,' he said. 'You have an alternative plan.'

Josselin's voice was tight. 'I agree we can't return to Constantinople.'

'So where?'

Josselin stared over Vallon's head. 'We have enough men and gold to found a colony. Once we've established a settlement, we can send for our families.'

Vallon was neither surprised nor angry. He tapped on the table with the quill. 'And where do you intend to found this colony?'

'There's rich land in the Volga delta.'

Vallon threw down his pen. 'Oh, for heaven's sake. We're not living in the days of Homer. Every scrap of fertile land between here and the Bosporus has been claimed and ploughed for scores of generations, as the Vikings discovered to their cost.' He narrowed his eyes. 'I trust you haven't dangled this crack-brained idea in front of the men. If you have ...'

'Of course not,' said Otia. 'But you know as well as I do that they've lost all relish for the journey.'

Vallon placed both hands on the table. 'Now listen. In a month we'll reach the Silk Road – the greatest trade route in the word, blessed with rich cities and caravanserais all the way to China. There'll be wine and whores for the men at every stop.'

'As for that claim,' said Josselin, 'you have only the word of a scholar who construes the world from squiggles on parchment.'

'If you're referring to Hero,' Vallon said, 'know that he spent weeks consulting the best geographers and the most reliable maps. That isn't all. As a youth he was employed by Cosmas Monopthalmos, a great traveller who explored the Silk Road as far as Samarkand. Unlike us, Cosmas followed the road there and back alone and unarmed.' Vallon's voice rose. 'I've always encouraged my officers to speak freely, but I won't tolerate you inventing perils like a pair of timid—' His head snapped up. 'Yes?'

'Excuse me, sir,' his servant said. 'The Viking commander requests an audience.'

Vallon stood. 'Admit him.' He noticed his centurions' grimaces. 'We'll continue our discussion later. Hero, I'd like you to stay.'

The two officers brushed past Hauk as he entered and he turned to watch them depart. 'Your officers don't look happy.'

'Take a seat,' Vallon said. He nodded at his servant. 'Bring us wine.'

Hauk perched on a folding stool and examined the interior of Vallon's tent. When the servant poured the wine, neither commander would drink before the other. It was Vallon who spoke first.

'You gauge my officers' mood correctly. Neither they nor my men have any more appetite for this adventure.'

Hauk sipped. 'Nor mine. You probably heard them last night. Half of them are for returning home.'

Vallon raised his beaker. 'And given the chance, half of mine would go with them.'

'But you intend to drive them on.'

Vallon drank. 'If I reach China and establish amicable relations with its ruler, I'll return home to riches and titles. If I fail, but die in the attempting ... well, at least my honour will remain unsullied and my family will receive a pension. But if I turn back simply because of fears and rumours, I'll be vilified and my family ruined.' Vallon drained his beaker and held it out for a refill. 'What about you?'

Hauk smiled into his cup. 'Wealth wastes, fortune turns, we ourselves must die. Only one thing lives on – the dead man's reputation.' He emptied his drink in one and wiped his lips. 'Still, there's no merit in making a name by throwing your life away on a hopeless quest.' Hauk nodded in Hero's direction. 'This learned fellow told me a little about the journey. I confess that until we met, I'd never heard of China. What are your chances of reaching it?'

'Slim to vanishing point,' Vallon said. He hunched forward. 'I'll tell you something I haven't even confided to my officers. Last year the former Byzantine emperor despatched another China mission. It vanished into the sands before it had got halfway to its goal.'

Hauk held Vallon's gaze. 'I'd appreciate your frankness even more if you tell me how you intend avoiding the same fate.'

'My expedition is better manned, better equipped and – dare I say it – better led. With those advantages, I'm confident we can deal with any hazards that present themselves. Right now, though, I have too many immediate concerns to worry about dangers that might lie months in the future. As you Vikings say, "A man who doesn't know his fate in advance is free of care."'

Hauk threw back his head in unaffected laughter. 'You learned some good Norse wisdom in the northlands.' He shifted on the stool. 'Even so, it's a foolish leader who marches into the unknown, never sure from one day to the next what lies ahead.'

Vallon gestured at Hero. 'Tell Hauk where our route will take us.'

Hero stepped into the lamplight. 'The next month will be the hardest – a desert crossing with few if any permanent settlements. Survive that and we'll reach the fertile lands of Chorezm, watered by the Oxus, a river followed by Alexander the Great.'

Hauk's interest quickened. 'A river. Is it navigable?'

'Alas, no. It wastes itself in an inland sea. The capital of Chorezm is a city called Khiva.'

'A rich town?'

'Passably rich, but not as wealthy as Bukhara and Samarkand further along the Silk Road. *Their* wealth rivals that of Constantinople.'

Hauk nuzzled the rim of his wine cup. 'Could a small, well-disciplined force impose itself on these centres?'

Hero's eyes drifted in Vallon's direction. 'If you mean, could you exact tribute by superiority of arms, I'd say the answer is no. The emirs who rule the trading centres defend their interests by maintaining large standing armies.'

Hauk hoisted his sword onto his lap. 'Slaves, then. Do these cities deal in slaves?'

'Yes, they do, but I suspect you'll find the natives have cornered the market in that commodity.'

Hauk frowned at Vallon. 'You told me you intended to dabble in the slave trade.'

'That was a lie. A man who treats his fellows as beasts is no better than a beast himself.'

Hauk set down his beaker. 'I promised my men riches. You claim I can find them in the East, yet offer no clue as to how I can obtain them.'

'Trade,' Hero said. 'Along the Silk Road you can buy goods for a penny and sell them a month later for a shilling. Take coral for example. In Samarkand its value is set at five solidi a pound, but in Khotan it will fetch four times that sum, enough to purchase an equal weight of jade. Carry that as far as China and you'll sell it for ten times what it cost.'

'We don't have coral or jade,' Hauk said. 'The only trade goods we have left are a few fragments of Baltic amber.' He placed his hand on his knees and made to stand. 'I hoped to carry more encouraging news back to my men. Thank you for the wine.'

'Stay and have another cup,' Vallon said. 'There are other avenues to wealth.'

Hauk resumed his seat with feigned reluctance. 'Lead me through them.'

Vallon waited until his servant had replenished their cups. 'Some of the Silk Road caravans contain as many as a thousand camels laden with trade stuffs. That much wealth requires protection – which comes at a price determined by the value of the goods and the dangers to which it's exposed. Suppose a caravan carrying goods to the value of ten thousand solidi is approaching a pass where bandits have robbed the last three trains down to the last scrap of horse harness. How much do you think the merchants would pay for guaranteed protection – a tenth of their goods' value, a fifth?'

'Hmm,' Hauk said. 'Yes, I can see profit in that line of business.'

Vallon cocked his elbows on the table. 'Unfortunately, neither of us commands enough soldiers to take advantage of those opportunities. If we were to combine our forces, however ...'

Hauk stuck up a hand. 'Hold on, General. These opportunities might not fall into our paths for months. My men won't proceed unless they can see the reward for their labours within close grasp.'

Vallon spoke softly. 'They've already earned from us by cooperation more than they would have gained by piracy. Stay with us until we reach the Oxus and I promise to pay the least of your men the same wages as my troopers receive. I'll reward your officers according to rank. In your case, I'm happy to pay you the same rate as my centurions.'

'I'm not a kept man.'

'Yes, you are. If we hadn't fed and watered you, you'd be food for crows by now. Don't bridle. Better a reclaimed hawk well nourished by its keeper than a free bird starving for lack of prey.' Vallon half-rose as Hauk stood and made for the door. 'Hear me out.'

'There's nothing more to say,' Hauk said. 'I'm not a sword for hire.'

Vallon's servant whisked aside the entrance for the Viking to exit.

Vallon stood to full height. 'Cross that threshold and I won't allow you back.'

Hauk stopped at the last moment, his hands bunched against his thighs. 'What about our ships?' His hands splayed. 'Without them ...'

'They'll be safe enough if you leave them here,' Vallon said. 'Nobody visits this coast except for a few nomads who wouldn't know what to do with a sailing vessel.'

Hauk turned. 'We don't have horses. I'm not walking to China.'

'We have a few spare mounts for you and your lieutenants. The rest of your men can ride on the carts if they're that lazy. We'll purchase horses for them at the first opportunity.'

'Let me get it clear. If we accompany you as far as the trade road, you'll pay us in gold. A month's wages.'

'Two months. Serve my purpose as I trust you will, and I'll pay for your return journey. You'll not only profit from the gold, but also gain experience and knowledge.'

Hauk sneered. 'I'm beginning to see how you deal with problems – by throwing money at them.' He pushed off into the dark. 'I'll return with my decision before midnight.'

'Don't leave it too late,' Vallon called. 'A man of my age needs his sleep.'

Hauk's laugh rang with good humour or mockery.

'He'll agree,' Hero said. 'He has no choice.'

'That's the problem,' Vallon said. 'Drive a wolf into a corner and he'll go for your throat.' He sat. 'On your way out, summon my centurions.'

Vallon didn't mince words when they marched in. 'I've asked Hauk to throw in his lot with us as far as Khiva. I don't want to hear any more about retreats or colonies. Understand?'

'Yes, sir.'

'Try to sound more wholehearted.'

Josselin waggled his Adam's apple. 'There's a rumour running through the ranks that a previous expedition to China disappeared without trace.'

'It's fact, not rumour. I'm determined we won't meet the same fate. Good night.'

XXII

In the brief cool after dawn, Wayland was out hunting game on a badlands ridge when he spied a swirl of dust to the east. A rider approaching hard, kicking up a cloud that trailed back in a long plume. Wayland scrambled down to the track and the horseman pulled up in a squirt of gravel. It was one of the Turkmen trail-blazers, unrecognisable beneath a carapace of grime, his eyes red wounds and his lips like roasted leather.

'Yeke?'

'Good news, my friend, blessings be upon you. We found the caravan trail after two days and reached wells a day later.' Yeke struck his chest. 'Didn't I say I'd find water?'

'I never doubted you,' Wayland said. He lobbed up his water bottle and Yeke swallowed half its contents before emptying the rest over his head. The runnels carved through the dust made him look like a disinterred ghoul.

'Where are your companions?'

'Back at the encampment, eating, drinking and making eyes at the lovely ladies. I left them yesterday evening and rode all night, so keen was I to bring the news to Lord Vallon.'

Wayland stroked the exhausted horse's neck. 'Don't expect much rest after your long ride. Vallon frets to be on his way.'

Yeke punched his left shoulder with his right fist. 'Pah! A Seljuk doesn't need a bed if he has a saddle.'

His horse turned beneath him and Yeke, only half-conscious, began drifting back the way he'd come. Wayland took the horse's bridle and steered it in the right direction. He had to shake Yeke awake when they entered the camp.

On receiving the Seljuk's report, Vallon ordered a night march that set out as the sun squatted on the Black Lake's horizon. Turning their backs on that sunset, none of the men thought that this might be their last sight of the sea. Even if such an intimation had crossed their minds, there was no way of forecasting which of them would survive the coming months to stand in wonderment on the shore of an ocean across the other side of the world.

Each trooper carried water for three days and a week's reserve slopped in the casks aboard the wagons. Wayland jogged along at the head of the column, invigorated by being on the move again, dreamy in the small hours as the landscape floated past in a mist of starlight.

At night the temperature fell close to freezing. Dawn came up in steely blues before the sun rose in a molten ball and the horizons began to wobble. When the landscape dissolved in white heat, the column halted to seek shelter under skeletal saxaul shrubs. When the sun touched the contours again, the men rose to face the next stage with resignation leavened by coarse humour and flashes of fantasy.

'Imagine if we were to ride over that next ridge and find ourselves looking down at a splendid city surrounded by vineyards and orchards and pleasure gardens.'

'Why stop there? Imagine it's a city without men, ruled by Amazons who yearn for bold soldiers with big dicks.'

'That rules you out on both counts.'

'Let a fellow dream. Did I tell you that in this city they serve wine that transports you to paradise, where every wish comes true?'

'I'd settle for a bath house and a clean bed.'

'Don't listen to Lucien. He'd bitch if he was seated in heaven at the right hand of the archangel Gabriel.'

'Not much fornicating while Gabriel's got his eye on you. Anyway, it's not sex I crave. It's decent food. What does this city have to make my mouth water?'

'Ambrosia, my friend. Food for the gods.'

Wayland drifted past this exchange and others like it, the troopers acknowledging his passing with lofted hands, looking after him with speculative expressions.

'He's a strange one,' a soldier said. 'Comes and goes like a ghost.'

'Be grateful he rides with us. You saw how well he shoots a bow, and he can read the trail of man or beast better than the Turkmen. As a child he ran wild with wolves. Don't take my word for it. Ask Hero.'

'He's another odd chap. Blinks and bumbles and mutters like a man in his dotage.'

'Hey, I won't hear a word against Master Hero. He salved a boil in my bum crack and didn't turn a hair. I'll never forget it.'

'Now you've shared that image, neither will I.'

'He's a proper surgeon, not the usual sawbones. Teaches at the university in Salerno. God knows why he gave up such a cushy berth to join this adventure.'

'Don't be fooled by his gentle manners. He's as tough as whip-cord. They say he drew an arrow from a friend shot through the lungs.'

'Did the fellow live?'

'Doesn't matter. Speaking personally, though I've spilled a fair amount of blood in combat, I could never wield a surgeon's knife. Hell, I come over faint if I cut myself shaving.'

'Well, here we are on the ridge and there ain't no city nor gardens nor maidens lining up to greet us.'

'Next one, or the one after that. On a journey as long as ours, we're bound to strike it lucky sooner or later. Stands to reason.'

'You want to bet?'

The column crawled through a clay desert eroded into fantastic shapes before entering a region of sand dunes. Rain was only a fading memory, but around brackish waterholes the land still grew green, the oases criss-crossed by the slots of gazelles and the pads of the lions and wolves that preyed on them. Humans dwelt here, too. Several times the troopers saw shining dust palls stirred up by nomads driving their flocks away from the invaders.

It took four days to reach the caravan trail. Wagons had broken down, their axles snapped or their hubs ground to wonky ovals. Vallon wouldn't abandon them and ordered the mechanics to carry out makeshift repairs with iron sleeves, leather washers and wooden wedges.

Wayland was first to spot the nomad encampment – a score of yurts along the shore of a dried-up lake surrounded by groaning camels and three flocks of bawling sheep guarded by dogs and youngsters.

One of the Turkmen outriders galloped out to greet the column. 'We'd almost given up on your coming.'

'Where's the water?' Wayland said, scratching the back of his neck where the rubbing of his filthy collar had produced sores.

The Turkman wheeled his horse and cocked his hand.

Wayland rode into the camp, breathing in the bitter-sweet smell of dung fires. Dogs flew at him and Wayland's hound locked jaws with one in a brief tussle before driving it away cowed and bleeding. Moments later the hound stood wagging its tail in front of a nomad child.

The herders had observed the hound's imposition of its dominance with curiously inert expressions, as if their struggle with nature had taught them that it was pointless to take sides. The men wore goat-hair caps and cotton robes over baggy trousers. The women appeared to be either young and sappy or old and withered – no middle age.

A nomad guided the advance party to a well rimmed with paving stones. Wayland peered into the black bore. He dropped a stone into it and waited for it to hit the bottom. Not a sound. The nomad grinned and lowered a leather bucket attached to a braided wool rope with its free end coiled in a stack three feet high. Grinning all the while, he paid out the rope, a process that took so long half the force had ridden in before the rope went slack. Gathering up the free end, the nomad tossed it over a wooden crossbar and tied it to a camel. A boy drove the beast away with a stick and both were small in the distance before the bucket rose swaying from the depths with its load of bitter water. Hero had joined Wayland and in the spirit of curiosity he paced out the length of rope.

'More than seven hundred feet,' he said. 'How did they sink a well so deep without engines or proper tools?'

On receiving the question, the nomad looked at both foreigners as if they were simpletons and made energetic digging gestures.

'Good Lord,' said Hero. 'It must have taken decades. Imagine sitting in a cradle hundreds of feet below ground, chipping away with bits of flint and iron.'

The nomad pointed north-east and Wayland translated: 'He says some wells are sunk more than a thousand feet.'

Hero shook his head in wonder. 'I must set down these particulars while they're fresh in my mind. Why are you laughing?'

For a few bolts of cloth and a bag of faience beads, the expedition purchased half a dozen sheep which they roasted in firepits over glowing beds of saxaul branches. After feasting, the troopers sat talking quietly under the stars until a three-man orchestra drawn from their company struck up an impromptu tune on syrinx, flute and zither. Well fed, pleasantly drowsy, Wayland flicked a finger in time to the melody.

The music faltered and the audience stirred. Wayland opened his eyes to find Zuleyka occupying the space in front of the ensemble. Since landing, he'd kept out of her way, but she hadn't stayed out of his thoughts. She took the flautist's instrument and blew an air that seemed to have been playing in Wayland's head all his life. She handed back the flute, spread her arms wide and tapped one foot while the musicians struck up. She looked at the ground, nodding until they'd found their tempo, and then tossed back her head, clicked her fingers and went into a rapture.

Wayland rose and so did every other man. It was as if the music travelled up Zuleyka's body. First her feet seemed to levitate, then her hips shivered before the current reached her arms. They waved in graceful articulations, suggesting all manner of images, sacred and profane. She dropped her arms to her side and swayed like a flame, her shoulders performing a dance of their own. A sharp cry from her, a lover's exhortation, quickened the music and Zuleyka's movements grew more ecstatic.

She wore only a pair of thin bloomers and a top cropped below her breasts, leaving her midriff bare. She began to rotate her belly, at the same time fluttering her hips. Both gyrations settled into voluptuous undulations that left nothing to the imagination.

Outlanders and Vikings both drew closer like moths to a lamp.

'Imagine a night with her,' said a trooper. 'She'd suck out your soul.'

Wayland shot an angry glance at the speaker. Zuleyka's performance amazed him more than it aroused. How could she move one part of her body independently of the rest?

The audience beat time, more than a hundred warriors exhorting Zuleyka to a climax.

'She's looking at me,' said a man to Wayland's right.

'No, she isn't. Her eyes are fixed on the Englishman.'

Wayland's skin tightened. The gypsy girl's eyes were indeed looking in his direction.

'*Stop this obscene display!*'

Vallon strode into the circle, rigid with anger. The music ceased and a sigh went up from the audience. Zuleyka relaxed, sucked in breaths and walked away on quick feet, the dog appointed to protect her virtue ambling at her side with its tail wagging like a banner.

'Get to your beds,' Vallon ordered. His gaze scoured around and settled on Wayland. There could be no doubt who he blamed for this assault on discipline, this flagrant undermining of the Outlanders' moral health.

With so many men and beasts to be supplied from a single source, the drawers of water were still labouring next morning to replenish the expedition's vessels. Vallon negotiated for a dozen camels and their drivers to accompany the force as far as the Oxus, with more beasts and helpers to be recruited along the way. Their guide was an old man who told the general, his voice whistling around a single tooth, that brigands infested the trail, falling on caravans as wolves descended on sheepfolds.

So the expedition's next encounter with the inhabitants came as a benign surprise. On a track beaten out of nowhere a wedding party passed from the opposite direction, a dozen two-humped camels shuffling along draped with flatweave trappings and harness jingling with bells of beaten silver, the women's faces hidden under horsehair veils, the bride crowned with a magnificent silver headdress, her long black tresses hanging to the end of her camisole. The Outlanders drew aside to let the procession pass and watched it diminish and disappear into the shrivelled landscape.

That evening Wayland was resoling a shoe in the sun's last radiance when a tall silhouette passed across the light.

'Vallon,' he said, pulling a stitch tight. 'I've been thinking about arranging a hunting party.'

The figure stopped and for a moment Wayland thought the general had taken offence at his casual address.

'Are you speaking to me?' Lucas said. There was no one else within earshot.

Wayland shielded his eyes and laughed. 'The sun was in my eyes. At first glance I took you for the general.'

'I never thought eyes as sharp as yours could trick you,' Lucas said. He seemed to be pinned to the spot.

Wayland rose smiling. 'Actually, there is a resemblance. Something about the jawline, your nose. I don't know. Something.'

Lucas scrubbed his hand down his face. 'My nose is bust. I don't look anything like the general.'

If he'd walked away then, Wayland would have forgotten the minor embarrassment. As it was, Lucas remained transfixed and had to wrench himself round by conscious effort. When he'd walked some distance, he stopped, shoulders tense, before hurrying on his way.

Wayland's forehead furrowed. No, it couldn't be, he told himself. Yet his eyes rarely deceived him. From a mile off he could distinguish a pigeon from a hawk, and if it were the latter, he could tell by the rhythm of its wings whether it was cruising or hunting.

Not long after this encounter he happened upon Gorka grilling skewered mutton over a fire.

Wayland massaged his hands in the heat. 'Lucas,' he said. 'I believe he's from your part of the world.'

Gorka grew guarded. 'What's he done now?'

Wayland dropped to his haunches. 'Nothing as far as I know. I'm just curious why a lad from the back of beyond would travel all the way to Byzantium to take military service.'

Gorka turned the skewer. Fat flared into flame. 'Plenty of recruits have travelled further. For a lad who wants to get on in life, there ain't many opportunities in a place like Osse. I should know. I grew up two valleys away.'

'Is Osse in Aquitaine?'

Gorka spat. 'It's Basque, whatever the Duke of Aquitaine says.'

Wayland straightened. 'Enjoy your supper.'

Most evenings he dropped in on Hero and talked over the day's events while the Sicilian wrote up his journal. Both men found the chats pleasant, cementing the bond they'd established over many months on the northern voyage. After exchanging news, Wayland rose with a yawn before pausing at the entrance.

'Vallon had three children by his first wife, didn't he?'

Hero continued writing. 'Yes. Two boys and a girl if I remember right. The eldest would have been about five when—' He laid down his pen.

'Do you know what happened to the children? Has Vallon tried to make contact with them?'

Hero rubbed his eyes. 'I don't know. I've never asked.'

'But his children – some of them – could still be alive.'

'I suppose so.'

'You don't happen to know their names.'

Hero shook his head. 'Vallon never told me. He wouldn't even speak his wife's name. I asked him on our flight from England and he made it plain that so far as he was concerned, she never existed.'

'Before Vallon fled France, he had a rank and title – Guy de Crion. A Frankish commander with hopes of advancement might have passed on his name to his first-born son.'

'Very likely,' Hero said.

Wayland forestalled the obvious question. 'The reason I ask is that I think a lot about my own family, and it occurred to me that Vallon must do the same.'

'Not that family,' Hero said. 'Caitlin and his daughters are all that matter to him now.'

'You're right,' Wayland said. He pulled the tent flap closed. 'Don't strain your eyes writing down the commonplace.'

He'd gone three or four yards when the flap opened, emitting a fan of lamplight. 'Commonplace to you,' Hero said. 'Rare and strange to folk who'll sleep tonight within familiar walls.'

*

A couple of days passed before Wayland crossed paths with Lucas again. Much of that time he spent in a state of somnolent stupefaction, riding into an infinity of horizontals, trotting across alkali flats as silky as talc, wading through tongues of sand that overflowed the track, the horizon fanning past in an endless wake.

Life flourished here, though. Sand grouse flushed from waterholes in flocks large enough to obscure the sun. Tortoises dragged themselves over the desert and lizards four feet long switched their tails and bared fangs oozing venom. These reptiles hunted kitten-sized hedgehogs with soft fur and desert rats that hopped on hind legs and tails. At night Wayland checked the ground for scorpions and cobras before settling to sleep. One evening he saw a cheetah course a gazelle, hunter and hunted sprinting across the skyline in spurts of dust that steadily converged until they merged into one violent swirl.

Herds of wild asses or kulans ranged over the desert – elegant creatures with cream and tawny-gold coats and a black stripe running from mane to tail. The Turkmen scouts tried riding them down, but the short-coupled kulans were deceptively fleet, outpacing the horses and galloping off to a safe distance before bunching up to look back. Wayland watched a couple of these fruitless chases before calling the Turkmen together and suggesting tactics. The only way to get within range was to post a screen of bowmen behind the kulans and then drive the beasts towards the ambush. They tried it next day, Wayland assessing the lie of the land for a long time before directing half a dozen men in a wide circle to a point behind the kulans' likely line of flight.

On the third sally they bagged two kulans and at the next attempt they killed three. Vallon was delighted. Fresh meat was a godsend to men with appetites jaded by double-baked biscuits hard enough to chip teeth, and the hunts were a fillip to morale, providing a welcome diversion for the troopers. He asked Aiken to draw up a rota that would give every Outlander an opportunity to join the chase.

Two days later Lucas confronted Wayland after reveille. 'When do I get my turn?'

Wayland checked Aiken's list. 'Sorry, but your bowmanship isn't good enough.'

'Who says? Aiken?' Lucas gave a scornful laugh.

'Cut it out,' Wayland said.

'Look,' Lucas said. 'I know my archery doesn't compare with yours, but I practise every day and my aim's improving.'

That was true. Every evening after the Outlanders made camp, Lucas took himself off and shot arrows until it grew too dark to see where they landed.

'Shooting at a standing target isn't the same as loosing at live prey. I don't want to waste half a day tracking a beast you've wounded in the haunch.'

'I know I've only shot at targets. That's why I need to try my hand at a moving object. And you can't deny I handle a horse well.'

Wayland relented. 'One of the troopers has an upset stomach. You can take his place.'

Lucas flashed his teeth and strode off before stopping as if struck by a brilliant afterthought. 'Can Zuleyka come too?'

That was typical of him, always pushing too far. Wayland shook his head. 'No, she can't.'

'It's not what you're thinking,' Lucas said. 'She might not know how to bend a bow, but she rides as if she'd been born on a horse.'

'I'll have to ask Vallon,' Wayland said. 'After her performance the other night, don't get your hopes up.'

In fact the general agreed to the request with the briefest of nods. 'Just make it clear that I won't tolerate any ... any ...'

'Hanky-panky?' Wayland suggested.

He reinforced the general's injunction by grinding a knuckle into Lucas's sternum. 'If you lay a hand on Zuleyka, if you so much as make eyes at her, the general will have you whipped until your backbone bleeds.'

Lucas's clenched fist shot up. 'On my word.'

Wayland watched him strut away, shoulders rolling. 'Guy,' he said.

Lucas stopped as if he'd taken an arrow in the back, stood

frozen for a moment then turned, his face straining for nonchalance. 'Who's Guy?'

Wayland strolled up. 'You.'

Lucas gave a cracked laugh. 'You're crazy.'

Wayland tapped him on the shoulder. 'When are you going to tell Vallon that you're his son?'

Lucas blenched. 'I'm not his son. I don't know what you're talking about.'

'Yes, you do.'

Lucas flung his head about in desperation. 'The men are ready for the hunt. Let me join them. Please.'

The hunting party was indeed chafing to be off. 'We'll discuss this further on our return,' Wayland said. 'Don't worry. I won't say anything to Vallon.'

It was late afternoon before Wayland spotted a herd of kulans grazing on an incline to the north. He assessed the situation, checking wind direction and studying the paths trodden by the animals before summoning the hunting party. He delegated eight of them to spring an ambush.

'See that pass,' he said, pointing at a shallow cup in the skyline. 'That's where the kulans will make for. Circle around the herd, keeping at least half a mile distant. Once you're over the ridge, take up positions in the pass and stay out of sight. It might be some time before we drive the game within range, so be patient.'

'Can me and Zuleyka join them?' Lucas said.' I want to be in at the kill.' He twanged his bowstring for emphasis.

Wayland regarded him with a jaundiced eye, then glanced at Zuleyka. She looked straight back at him – deep green irises against startlingly clear whites, her eyes framed by long black lashes. Dark as Syth was fair, she somehow reminded him of his wife – both of them not quite of this world. He'd intended to include the girl in his own party to keep her away from Lucas, but for reasons he didn't care to examine, he decided her proximity would be too unsettling.

He gestured at the leader of the ambushers. 'Keep Lucas and Zuleyka well apart.' He clapped his hands. 'Off you go. We don't have much light left.'

The ambush party followed his instructions and the kulans looked up only long enough to decide that the horsemen posed no threat before they resumed grazing. Wayland winced and clutched his stomach. All afternoon he'd had to clench his sphincter against squitters. The turmoil in his guts couldn't be checked except by a violent discharge, and he returned to his post, brow clammy, as the last of the ambushers popped over the ridge.

When they'd disappeared, he formed the eight remaining troopers into a crescent and led them towards the kulans at a jog. They allowed him to approach within two arrow flights before tossing their heads and galloping away. Wayland followed up, not pressing too hard, giving them every chance to take the natural line of escape that would bring them to the saddle. The sun was boiling on the desert floor by the time the kulans streamed over the ridge.

He swung his arm and his party rowelled their horses into flat-out pursuit to close the line of retreat. They emerged onto the saddle just in time to see the tailenders skeltering up a gulley on one side of the pass, chased by Lucas, Zuleyka and Yeke. They reached the skyline and dropped out of sight. The remaining troopers rode up to Wayland shaking their heads in disgust.

'What went wrong?'

One of the hunters pinched his nose and snorted snot. 'That idiot Frank didn't wait for the herd to enter the trap. As soon as the first kulan appeared, he tried to cut it off, sending the rest stampeding up there.'

'What's he doing chasing them?'

The trooper smeared mucus on his breeches. 'He fluked a shot to the beast's belly. If he thinks he'll return in glory, he's going to be disappointed. I'll murder him.'

'I'll do it for you,' Wayland said. 'Return to camp. I'll wait for Lucas.'

They slouched away. Wayland waited while the desert settled

into its evening hush and the sands grew cold around him. All that remained of the sun was a crimson slash. His stomach upset had left him too enervated to go chasing after Lucas. Perhaps the riders had killed and were now butchering their prey. It wasn't until Venus flickered into life that he began to grow worried. He clicked his tongue and his horse and dog advanced to the edge of the ridge.

Shadows flooded the world beyond. He scanned the emptiness without picking up any sign of movement. His cries dispersed into space. He told himself that the hunters must have killed the kulan in a gulley out of sight or hearing. The light had almost drained when a flame pricked the plain below the ridge. Relief turned to puzzlement. Surely the hunters hadn't stopped to cook their prey. His mind ranged over all kinds of possibilities without fixing on anything solid.

The flame went out. The hunters must be on their way back. Wayland waited and was still waiting long after the riders should have returned. Without further delay he set out to track them. Even in near darkness, he soon spotted the bloodstains left by the wounded kulan.

He'd left it too late, though. Night hid the trail before he reached its end. 'Find them,' he told the dog.

He followed, checking the dog when it got too far ahead. Anger at Lucas's indiscipline shaded into concern and then deepened into dread. Something bad had happened. Perhaps the girl had tried to escape. Perhaps Lucas and the Seljuk had fought over her. Perhaps they'd raped her . . .

The dog growled, bringing Wayland to a stop. He strung an arrow, slid from his horse and strained into the darkness. The idiot laughter of hyenas raised the hairs on the back of his neck. A nighthawk flitting past made him flinch. He made a swallowing sound and led his horse forward.

He smelt the tarry tang of embers and found the remains of the fire, the branches half-burned and roughly scattered. The dog led him up a draw to the right. At the top he came upon the dead kulan, one of its hind legs hacked off. A few yards further on he found a body, sprawled face down, two arrows in the back. Wayland rolled it over and recognised Yeke's face, his throat slit with a butcher's precision. Wayland dropped to one knee, his eyes evaluating every surrounding shape and angle.

'Lucas? Zuleyka?'

He didn't expect any response. His senses, preternaturally heightened in childhood, had absorbed the scents of strange men and horses.

He lit a scrub brand and quartered the ground, building up a picture of what had happened. Then he mounted and made his way back to camp.

A squad of troopers bearing torches intercepted him before he reached it. Vallon rode at their centre and placed a hand over his mouth when he saw Wayland's expression.

'Dead?'

'Yeke is. Five horse archers slew him and captured Lucas and the girl.'

Vallon turned his horse. 'A full report back in camp.'

Wayland washed and ate before presenting himself before the general. Vallon shook his head. 'I should have known that allowing Lucas to join the hunt would end in disaster.'

'He wasn't to know that bandits were lying in wait. If anyone's to blame, it's me. I should have checked the site more carefully.'

Vallon rolled his shoulders as if trying to dislodge a heavy weight. 'The hunters told me that Lucas loosed an arrow in defiance of your instructions. As a result, one of my men – my main pathfinder – is lying dead in the wilderness. Well, Lucas and the girl can pay for their stupidity.'

'Are you saying that you're throwing them to the wolves?'

'Yes.'

'Lucas is a trooper in your squadron.'

'Not through any wish on my part. As for the girl ...'

'Let me take four men and search for them.'

'No. I'm not risking any more lives.'

'Then I'll go myself.'

300

Vallon exploded. 'I forbid you!'

Wayland looked at the ground. 'I'm going with or without your consent.'

He'd left the tent before Vallon answered. 'Come back, damn you.'

Wayland exhaled all the air in his lungs before returning. He didn't meet Vallon's gaze.

The general laughed without mirth. 'Same old Wayland. Running counter to every order.' His shoulders hunched. 'I'll make my decision when I've examined the site.'

Two squads left the camp while it was still dark and reached the murder scene in the gloomy light of pre-dawn. Hyenas and jackals had already partly eaten the dead Seljuk and wild ass. Wayland followed the nomads' trail before returning to report.

'They met up with the rest of the clan about two miles to the north. Sixteen in total, including women and children, plus twenty horses and four camels.'

Vallon pinched his lips and stared across the huge landscape. He flicked a hand towards the guide. 'Ask him what's out there.'

The old man replied with eloquent hand movements.

Wayland half-smiled. 'He says nothing but djinns live in the desert.'

Vallon's gaze remained fixed on the awful vista. 'There's no need to give chase. The nomads will take them to the nearest slave market. That's Khiva. We'll look for them there.'

'The nomads will be travelling light on familiar ground,' Wayland said. 'They'll reach Khiva long before we do.'

'The same holds true if you pursue them. They already have half a day's start.'

'They'll be travelling at a camel's pace. Horsemen can ride twice as fast.'

Vallon squinted at Wayland. 'You really mean it.'

'I was in charge of the hunt. Lucas and Zuleyka are my responsibility.'

The desert was already beginning to quake under the sun's heat.

'You won't survive two days on your own. Select six men hardened to these conditions. If you haven't caught up with your quarry by sunset tomorrow, you must return.'

Wayland nodded. 'Sunset tomorrow.'

He and his men left carrying three gallons of water apiece, with more on two spare mounts. They rode as hard as conditions allowed, the trail easy to follow at first, the nomads moving at a good pace. Wayland's hopes of catching up by nightfall were dashed when the sand ran out into gravel fields and rock shelves. All he had left to go on were scattered clues – pellets of camel dung, a saxaul branch snapped by a pannier, discarded pistachio shells. Unless the nomads eased up tomorrow, he wouldn't overtake them before Vallon's deadline.

Next morning they faced a fitful headwind and went on over glazed clay pans so hard that hooves made no impression. Spurts of sand skittered over the polished surface as if gliding on ice. All day they rode, the sun glowing like a great ashen coal, the horsemen treading their indigo shadows until at last they came to the shores of a dry lake where all signs that man had passed vanished. The wind stiffened, forcing the squad to ride with faces masked, and at sunset the dust whipped up by the gusts painted the sky startling shades of rose, amber and purple.

Wayland had no choice but to turn back. The search party had used up more than half their water and knew they wouldn't find any more before they returned to the caravan trail. Some of the horses were lame. Wayland's dog had worn its pads raw. On the morning following, Wayland mounted up, cast one last look over the arid wastes and led his team south.

Six days it took them to catch up with the expedition, and if they'd had to endure a seventh, not all of them would have survived. Hero salved Wayland's blistered face and bathed his eyes before the Englishman reported to Vallon.

The general assisted Wayland onto a stool. 'You did your best.'

Wayland kneaded his eyes. 'I haven't given up all hope. As you said, the slavers will probably take Lucas and Zuleyka to Khiva.'

'We're not going to Khiva,' Vallon said.

Wayland stared.

'I've changed our plans,' Vallon said. 'We can cut a week off our journey by aiming for Bukhara, further up the Oxus.'

'You can't just abandon—'

Vallon's voice was gentle yet firm. 'I'm responsible for the lives of more than a hundred men. The Vikings grow more disenchanted with every day that passes.'

'I told you not to throw in your lot with them.'

'Vikings or no Vikings, I'm not in a position to divert my force. We ride for Bukhara.'

Wayland spoke through a fog of weariness. 'You might come to regret that decision.'

'Meaning?'

Wayland opened his mouth and found that the words wouldn't come.

'Well?' Vallon said.

Wayland knew he couldn't voice his suspicions. Suppose he was wrong about Lucas and the general rode to Khiva only to discover that the lad was what he claimed to be – a Pyrenean horse-breeder's son. Or, Wayland thought, suppose he was right and Vallon journeyed to Khiva to find that Lucas wasn't there.

'Nothing,' Wayland said. 'I'm too tired to think straight.'

XXIII

Yeke had shot his fourth arrow at full gallop, bringing the kulan staggering to its knees in a gulley more than a mile from the start of the hunt. He leaped off his horse and stabbed his knife into the beast's jugular. Blood spouted in a jet and the kulan thrashed, a horrible whistling issuing from its neck. Lucas caught up as the beast's spasms relaxed into death.

'Well aimed, Yeke, but don't forget who lodged the first arrow.'

The Seljuk was collecting the kulan's blood in a leather bowl he seemed to carry for just that purpose. He jabbed his blade towards the ridge. 'Fetch help,' he said in his limited Greek.

'You go,' Lucas told Zuleyka.

She rode away into the dusk. With one deep stroke, Yeke unseamed the carcass and began to pull out its intestines.

'Let me help,' said Lucas.

Yeke waved him away and pointed towards the mouth of the gulley. 'Light a fire.'

Lucas kindled shrub into life and tossed a couple of stout branches on the fire before making his way back to Yeke. It was almost too dark to see the ground beneath his feet and he took his direction from the keening song the Seljuk was singing over the kulan.

Something whirred in the night, cutting off Yeke's lament. Gravel rasped and the hairs on the back of Lucas's neck stood up. Drawing his sword, he peered about, unable to make out anything except the fire.

'Yeke?'

Sword held ready, he crept forward. A clatter ahead of him made him lunge around. 'Who's that?'

Shrieks from behind obliterated his senses. He whirled and registered two onrushing shapes before a blow to the temple dropped him cold.

He recovered consciousness to find a ratty face staring down at him with a smile of the utmost satisfaction. He fumbled for his sword and couldn't find it. Hands pinioned him from behind and frogmarched him towards the carcass. Behind him he could hear other men kicking out the fire.

He glimpsed Yeke sprawled face-down, two arrows sprouting from his back and a black stain spreading around his head. A nomad crouched by the kulan, butchering its hindquarters. Two more surged past, driving Zuleyka and her horse between them.

His captors heaved him into the saddle, bound his hands so that he could only just manage the reins, and tied his legs under Aster's belly. The leader gave a shrill command and one of his men whipped Aster into motion.

With the back of his hands, Lucas felt the lump swelling on his temple. He was too sick and dazed to work out what was happening. The attack had come from nowhere, that grating the only warning.

'Zuleyka,' he said in a slurred voice. 'Are you all right? Who are they? What do they want with us?'

The only word he understood from her reply was 'slave'.

'I'm no one's slave.'

A nomad backhanded him in the mouth and wagged his finger in admonition.

Lucas threw up and wiped blood and vomit from his mouth. 'Wag away, you black-hearted heathen. I'm slave to no man, and I'll prove it by cutting your heart out and feeding it down your throat.'

The man couldn't have understood but laughed as if he'd heard such empty claims before.

The nomads met up with three generations of their kin at a waterhole. Women ululated and fell to their knees and kissed the raiders' hands and wrung their knuckles in thanks to Almighty God who'd delivered these tender infidels into their hands. The leader cut short their celebrations and ordered them to strike camp with all haste. Judging by the looks they kept throwing back, they expected pursuit.

They rode all night without stopping, some of the nomads veering off to lay false trails, the constellations wheeling one way then the other. Twice, one of Lucas's captors shoved a waterbottle to his mouth. The first time he refused; the second he drank all he could and would have drunk more if the slaver hadn't pulled the bottle away.

Sunrise exposed the extent of the captives' plight, the shrivelled landscape spreading away to the uttermost rim of the earth. The leader drove his clan on with birdlike cries, sparing neither women, children nor prisoners. They negotiated a withered forest of shrubs that looked like they'd been consumed by fire and then bleached by a thousand years of drought. They rode through other trees with stubby trunks capped with a rim of branches like broken parasol frames, every third or fourth tree a perch for small owls with pupils slotted against the sun.

They crossed fly-specked barrens and mineral flats polished like mica, the sun's reflected rays boring into Lucas's skull. A boy relieved his suffering by daubing his eye sockets with a mixture of soot and tallow. The lad also hooded Aster's head. Afterwards he rode alongside Lucas, pulling grotesque faces in an attempt to elicit a response.

Lucas regarded his tormentor through smarting eyes. 'Young as you are, I'll stake you out in the midday sun with your eyes pinned open until they coddle like eggs.'

Another night fell and still they continued, riding in silence over a parched inland sea as white as bone. Lucas read the stars and concluded that the slavers were heading north-east – to Khiva.

It must have been getting towards dawn when two riders caught up from the south, delivering information that sent the clan into another paroxysm of prayer and thanks.

Lucas rubbed his cracked lips. 'The search party has turned back,' he told Zuleyka. He spat to relieve the gummy dryness in his mouth. 'It doesn't matter. I don't need anyone's help to escape.'

Zuleyka pointed into the vast emptiness. *Where to?*

Only now did the leader relax the pace. Soon after sunrise the raiders halted and fell to digging a pit in the sand. Four feet down they came to water where no one else would have thought to look for it. The men rigged homespun awnings and dragged Lucas under one of them. From its shade he watched while a mother and daughter pegged together a loom and began knotting a rug, exchanging domestic chit-chat.

A kick brought him out of a sickly doze. He shielded his eyes against another sunset to find the leader and his men grinning down at him. The clan chief was nondescript, pinched features framed by a scraggy beard.

'What are you looking at?'

The man cupped Lucas's chin and turned his head about for the benefit of the onlookers. They nodded and muttered in appreciation.

'Get your filthy hands off me.'

At an order from the leader, two of the nomads hauled Lucas to his feet and stripped him bare. As he struggled, he heard Zuleyka scream and saw a party of older women hustling her behind a screen. A blade against his windpipe silenced his protests.

His captors examined him in every particular, the clan leader squatting at a distance to assess his prisoner's worth. So far as Lucas could tell from the nomads' guffaws, they considered him a prime specimen who'd fetch a good price at market and bring pleasure to his next master's maids.

The leader ordered his men to cover Lucas. A crone tottered up, and from her unrestrained delight, Lucas gathered that Zuleyka had also passed the most intimate examination and been judged a prize commodity.

He'd eaten only crusts since capture and was ravenous. The acrid smell of firewood sweetened into the aroma of roasting meat. A nomad brought him a skewer and he sank his teeth into the charred flesh, the juices squirting in his mouth.

After eating he called Zuleyka's name and received no answer. She'd been segregated into the women's care and from that time on he'd only glimpse her at a distance, with no chance to exchange words.

The camp fell still and he lay looking up at the stars, spinning lurid fantasies of escape and revenge.

*

307

Days of desert travel stretched into weeks and Lucas's flame-hard certainty of escaping dwindled to a spark. His captors watched over him night and day, even at stool. It didn't matter if they let him go. Zuleyka was right. The wilderness offered no refuge.

Hope flared anew when his abductors struck a trail and they began encountering other travellers. Far from hiding their crime, Lucas's captors exulted in it, showing off their prizes to everyone they met. One fleshy merchant riding a white mule with fine saddlebags pulled up with his bevy of guards and negotiated to buy Lucas. The ratty brigand leader broke off the prolonged haggling, telling the merchant that the Frank would fetch twice the offered price in the slave mart.

Lucas had picked up enough of the Turkmen's language to understand that they'd decided to sell their captives in Bukhara. Another four days' ride brought them to the shores of the Oxus and they followed the south bank eastward, along a fringe of reedy jungle. The leader spent a day negotiating with a ferryman to take them across the river. Lucas tried to tell the bandit that whatever value he set on his captives, Vallon would pay three times as much to get them back. The desert bandit didn't seem to understand the concept of money. He'd probably never handled a coin in his life.

Beyond the Oxus, the road to the capital led through rolling savannah dotted with pistachio trees and fields of wild poppies. The arid lands softened into a fertile plain watered by a grid of canals. Lucas rode through melon fields and groves of pomegranates and at noon one day he saw the walls of the Bukhara oasis spread forty miles across the plain. Another two days' riding and he entered the city proper through walls that bulged out every hundred yards in watchtowers.

Once inside its ramparts, threading the crowded thoroughfares, the nomad bandits shrank into bumpkin status, riding in a huddle and casting nervous glances and half-hearted blows at the touts who plucked at their stirrups.

A dizzying sortie through the metropolis ended in a walled plaza surrounded by windowless barracks. Guards drew the

308

studded gate shut and the city's clamour fell to a murmur. An agent and his men came out and listened with feigned boredom while the sand-dwelling brigand extolled his captives' qualities. When he'd finished his pitch, the agent despatched a man who returned with a bolt of cotton and a few small strips of copper which he pitched at the brigand's feet.

The man wailed and stamped his feet. He appealed to God to right this injustice. But in the world of merchants, the law of Mammon stands paramount, and the official's bully boys drove the bandit away with goods lower in value than Vallon would have exchanged for a sheep.

In the empty square the official appraised his purchases before ordering his men to lead Lucas and Zuleyka away in opposite directions.

Lucas's keepers pushed him into a stinking vaulted dungeon and shoved him onto a low shelf cut into the walls. They fettered one leg to an iron ring set into the floor and then left. A few tapers cast a dismal glow over at least thirty other prisoners slouched in hopeless postures. None of them took more than dull and fleeting notice of the newcomer.

'Does anyone here speak French?'

Other than a witless gibbering, no one answered.

'Greek, then. Anyone speak Greek?'

'What do you want?' a voice said from the shadows.

'What is this place?'

'It's the antechamber to heaven. What do you think it is?'

Lucas slumped against the greasy wall. 'When do they take us to market?'

'Not long. They don't want us eating away their profits.'

'Is there any way out?'

A harrowed laugh. 'Oh, yes. Only this morning, one of us escaped and is now at rest in the bosom of our Lord. How did you end up in this hellhole?'

'I was a trooper in a Byzantine expedition to China. I was out hunting when—' Lucas broke off. 'What's so funny?'

'I can't believe those fools in Constantinople would throw good troops after bad. I was roped into the same mission more than a year ago and it was a disaster from beginning to end. Our commander was a ninny who thought he could order Turkmen about as if they were dogs.'

'What happened?'

'Most of my comrades were killed in an ambush, the survivors sold into slavery. I'm one of the last to go to market. In a month this pit will be full of your comrades.'

Lucas lunged against his fetters. 'You're wrong there. My commander is no fool or coward. He's ...'

'Yes? What?'

Lucas dissolved. 'He's my father.'

Lucas woke to find himself under lamplit review by an elegant gentleman with spotless robes and a snow-white beard cut along the oval of his chin. He spoke in Greek from behind a silver pomander.

'Who are you and where do you hail from?'

'I'm Lucas of Osse, trooper in the army of General Vallon, leader of a diplomatic mission commissioned by His Imperial Majesty Alexius Comnenus, ruler of the West. If my companions haven't arrived by now, expect them any day. They'll be looking for me, and if they discover that you've sold me into slavery, expect a savage reckoning. I'm General Vallon's son. Do you hear me? His son.'

The slaver elevated an eyebrow and withdrew. A tear squeezed from Lucas's eye. When Wayland had challenged him, he'd denied his kinship with Vallon. Wayland wouldn't take his suspicions to the general. Vallon would never know that for three months his own son had been riding in his company.

Food when it came was rusks served in thin gruel. On the third day, warders washed Lucas, cut his hair and dressed him in a coarse clean gown. The attendants led him and a dozen other shackled men into blinding sunlight. The square had been thrown open to traders who'd set up booths and stalls around the auction ring. Citizens going about their business observed the clanking file of slaves with no more interest than they would have eyed a herd of sheep on its way to slaughter. Lucas tried to square his shoulders. Whoever bought him would rue the day he laid claim on Lucas of Osse.

XXIV

Minarets and domes under an eggshell moon gave Hero his first sight of Bukhara the Noble. The expedition camped in an orchard two miles from the capital and left at dawn, faces scrubbed, clothes laundered and armour polished. They hadn't ridden a mile when a troop of lancers and archers blocked their way.

Vallon passed Hero letters in Arabic and Persian penned by the Logothete's department. 'I'll leave you to negotiate.'

The commander wore a coif and mantle of fish-scale armour over silk robes. After listening to Hero's address, he despatched a lieutenant to the emir's palace with the documents and then withdrew his troops a distance, leaving Vallon's expedition to simmer on the highway. A smog of smoke and dust hung over the city. Behind its dun walls a mosque's sea-green dome floated in the pall like a polyp, a gold cupola shining dully behind it and minarets like slim phalluses receding into the haze.

Permission to proceed arrived from the emir's secretariat in late afternoon. The soldiers formed up on each flank of the convoy and escorted it through a gate set in a fortified tower rising forty feet above the ramparts. Immediately inside lay a suburb favoured by the city's elite, a few open gateways offering glimpses of courtyards and well-watered gardens. The escort led the expedition to a *ribat* or caravanserai built against the ramparts. From the outside it resembled a prison, with blind mud walls and towers at each corner, the inner towers forming part of the city's defences. The company entered through a set of carved wooden doors let into a keep constructed of bricks plaited in knotwork designs. Inside lay a serene courtyard centred on a rectangular pool shaded by mulberry trees and surrounded by cloistered accommodation that included airy dormitories and apartments built above stables, kitchens and a bath house. A staff of servants stood ready to attend the foreign guests and a stooped gardener and his boy went about their work, watering rose beds.

The escort's commander informed Hero that the emir's representative would call on the expedition after morning prayers the next day. In the meantime, the cooks, launderers and ostlers stood ready to service the travellers' needs. The moment the gates closed behind the escort, soldiers armed with bows filed onto the parapet and took up position ten yards apart, facing inwards.

When Vallon had found his quarters and arranged his chattels, he summoned his leading men to a council in the caravanserai's *iwan*, a vaulted three-sided hall open to cooling breezes from the north. He swept out his gown and looked over the courtyard.

'I've seen worse billets.'

Hauk eyed the guards. 'A jail scented with roses is still a jail.'

Vallon half-raised a hand. 'Patience.'

That was a quality whose tensile properties the Vikings had stretched to breaking point. They were sea rovers hundreds of miles from their element, fair-skinned northerners who wilted under the fierce Asian sun.

'Remind us who we're dealing with,' Vallon said to Hero.

'Bukhara is ruled by Karakhanids, a Turkish tribe related to the Seljuks and opposed to them. Like the Seljuks, they're Muslim converts who have adopted Arab and Persian culture while retaining some of their nomad ways. The ruler styles himself both Sultan and Khan; his governor in Bukhara carries the titles Emir and Beg. The present khan is called Ahmad, grandson of Ibrahim, a lord of the horizons who considered walls to be a prison and ruled the city from a nomad encampment. Despite their wilderness origins, the dynasty are generous patrons of religion and the arts, endowing many madrasahs and burnishing Bukhara's reputation as "the dome of learning in the east". Avicenna, the great historian and physician, was born in the city. As a young man, Omar Khayyam, the brilliant mathematician, astronomer, philosopher and poet, studied algebra here.'

Hauk wasn't interested in the Karakhanids' cultural heritage. 'How do we milk the bastards?'

Vallon winced. 'We're fewer than two hundred surrounded by thousands. Act the pirate here and you'll die like a pirate. I should warn you the Turkmen have ingenious methods for executing malefactors. The blunted and barbed stake inserted up the rectum is one. A night cast into a pit with venomous serpents and scorpions is another. And I'm sure that doesn't exhaust their cruel inventiveness.'

One of Hauk's lieutenants, a hulking specimen with bleached eyes, a snub nose and a plaited beard, leaned forward and spat insultingly close to Vallon's feet.

'We're only here because you denied us a few barrels of water.'

Vallon touched the hilt of his sword. 'The only reason you're alive is because I took pity on you.'

Hauk put out a restraining hand. 'Peace, Rorik. We command our own destinies now and have enough gold to pursue our ambitions.'

Vallon smoothed out his gown. 'Precisely. You can follow any wind you find favourable.'

Hero watched the Vikings leave. 'I'm glad we've seen the last of that gang.'

Vallon nodded, but something about the general's expression suggested that a clean break with the northern marauders wasn't a foregone conclusion.

It wasn't just the heat stored in the sun-baked walls that kept Hero from sleep. He couldn't stop marvelling at the fact that he'd travelled further east than almost any man before him, further even than Alexander, the conqueror of the known world. Once he passed Samarkand, only a week's journey away, he'd be treading ground even Master Cosmas Monopthalmos hadn't stepped on. He threw back his sheet, lit a lamp and took a copy of the Logothete's itinerarium onto the balcony. Unrolling the scroll, he traced their progress sea by sea, city by city. He calculated that they'd covered between a third and a half of the distance to China. After Samarkand, the landmarks were no more than names – Kashgar, Khotan, Cherchen, Chang'an and, in a blank space at the end of the scroll, Kaifeng, capital of Song China.

A cock crowed. The first call to prayer rose and was answered from all directions, the sounds overlapping, one voice rising as another faded out, blending into a clamorous, melodious hubbub.

Hero turned and smiled. 'Couldn't you sleep either?'

'I'm too excited,' Aiken said.

'Let's go up and watch the sun rise.'

They climbed a twisting staircase built into one of the towers and emerged onto a high platform. Birds flocked past, black shapes winnowing across the peach and lilac sky. Hero rested his hands on the parapet and watched the sun swell above the metropolis, striking lustre from the green and blue tiles cladding mosques, minarets, mausoleums and madrasahs.

The sun rose and the clamour of the waking city rose with it. Flat-roofed houses, ribbed melon-shaped domes and feathery treetops faded into the smoke and dust of another day.

'Are you glad you came?' Hero said.

'Oh yes. I feel as if I'm treading in the path of emperors.'

After breakfast Hero visited the bath house where a taciturn giant laid him on a slab and pummelled and thumped him, cracking each joint in turn and finishing by lifting up his head and bending it forward until something inside gave. On the slab next to him another masseur trod Vallon's backbone with his feet.

Clad in a shot grey silk kaftan, Hero stood at Vallon's side to receive the emir's representative. The double doors opened and a mounted column high-stepped into the yard, preceded by a band playing fifes, trumpets and kettledrums. Behind the vanguard rode a young aristocrat with features so finely etched they should have been struck on coins. Only the suggestion of an epicanthic fold hinted at steppe origins. In his right hand he carried a gold-inlaid axe as badge of office. His spirited horse also commanded attention – small, chiselled head sprung on a long powerful neck, sturdy crupper and shortish straight front legs. Its flowing mane and tail suggested that at full gallop it would give the impression of flying.

Hero presented the official to Vallon. 'His Eminence Yusuf ad-Dawlah, Second Secretary in the Office of Foreign Affairs. His Eminence trusts that our accommodation meets our expectations and assures us that this house is our house for the duration of our stay.'

'I should hope so,' Vallon said. 'We're paying enough for it.'

Yusuf sat his horse, exuding authority and the faint scent of amber. A tattered mob of crows flew cackling overhead.

Hero explained their mission, stressing the benefits that would accrue to all centres of civilisation from an alliance with the Song emperor.

Yusuf didn't seem impressed. 'God above is closer to us than the emperor of China. Nevertheless, it's not our intention to deny you progress. You may proceed east with the emir's blessing and at your own risk.'

'We'll need guides and fresh pack animals.'

'That will be arranged.'

'Ask him to arrange an audience with the emir,' Vallon said.

Yusuf's response was silky. 'His Excellency would love to receive you. Alas, the emir is making a progress through the provinces, ensuring the peace and prosperity of the great khan's dominion.'

Hero decoded the lie. 'I suspect the emir doesn't want to be associated with us if we fail – not after the last embassy perished.'

'Ask the minister what he knows of their fate.'

Yusuf's expression veiled. 'They passed through Bukhara Sherif last summer and we afforded them every courtesy while warning them of the dangers they faced. They paid no attention. If I may say so, they struck me as arrogant and ill-prepared.'

'That's not a failing you'll find in us,' Hero said. 'We've suffered setbacks and know that more await. We would welcome any advice you can offer.'

'My advice? Turn back. Our khan, may God the exalted show mercy on him, can guarantee you safe passage only as far as Kashgar. Beyond that the roads to China unravel. Forts lie empty and crumbling. Gangs of deserters lie in wait for the few caravans desperate enough to risk the journey.'

At a prompt from Vallon, Hero indicated the troopers and Vikings. 'Our soldiers have been denied contact with society for months. They long to resume intercourse with it.'

At the thought of letting loose the lecherous soldiery on the city, a twinge of migraine seemed to cross Yusuf's face. 'No more than six men are allowed out at any one time, and then only under armed escort. Any crimes they commit will be punished under Bukhara's laws. I understand that your men have human needs.' Yusuf nodded at one of his retinue. 'Arrange it.' He made to turn.

'One last thing,' Hero said. 'I gather that you record the arrival of every traveller who enters the city.'

'We welcome the righteous and try to turn away the lawless. Why do you ask?'

'A month ago, nomads seized one of our troopers in the Kara Kum. We suspect his abductors intend to sell him in the slave market.'

'If he was taken a month ago, you should have looked for him in Khiva.'

That brought the minister's visit to an end. His orchestra struck up and he followed it out, the gates crashing shut behind him.

Next morning Hero and Aiken set out to explore the city under the protection of a minder called Arslan. They passed through an inner wall surrounding the medina and threaded narrow lanes tunnelling between windowless mud walls. Arslan forced a passage through the jostling crowd and strings of donkeys and camels heaped with country produce.

All God's tribes seemed to be represented on the streets – moon-faced Turkmen with apple cheeks and green eyes, hawk-nosed Arabs with iron-grey beards, Persians with features that might have been copied from miniatures. Most of the Turkmen gentry wore skull caps and striped gowns called *khatans* gathered at the waist by sashes broad enough to hold scimitars. The more rustic element favoured padded jackets and riding breeches and cone-shaped helmets of white felt with upturned brims. Hero observed a man wearing kohl eye-shadow and a rose behind one ear leading a tribe of wives and daughters so smothered in horse-hair veils that they resembled beehives with a narrow window at the top. Other exotic elements included Manichean monks clad all in white, wearing tall cloches; and Jews in hats of tight-curled karakul wool, obeying the sumptuary laws that decreed they tie their gowns with cords too thin to hold weapons.

Leaving the sunlight, Arslan plunged into the semi-darkness of a multi-vaulted bazaar that from outside looked like a clutch of giant eggs. Hero and Aiken followed him along labyrinthine aisles, past piles of saddlebags and prayer mats, between the stalls of cobblers, ropemakers, confectioners and goldsmiths, assistants crying the wares while the owners bargained with their customers and slandered their competitors.

Sunlight dazzled and shadows blinded. They had debouched into an open market offering everyday goods. Rose-coloured rock salt stood in piles like pink ice. Flies swarmed over racks of meat. Poultry scrabbled in wicker cages. A stallholder insisted that the foreigners sample melon with flesh as white as milk, as sweet as honey. Metalsmiths beat out household utensils on the spot, inviting passers-by to observe the quality of their workmanship.

Hero squeezed through a gate into a noisy square where the

atmosphere was as much festive as commercial. Groups of bumpkins watched artistes perform stunts with snakes and nimble dogs.

A pimp with a wall eye accosted them. 'Do you like bad girls?'

'Certainly not,' said Hero.

'Naughty boys. Hey!'

Hero tugged Arslan's sleeve. 'I think that's enough for the first day.'

Exiting the square into a quieter quarter, Hero noticed several drinking houses open to the street, their clientele lounging on rugs under awnings while musicians plucked lutes in the background.

'What are they drinking?' he asked Arslan.

'*Chai*, sir, from China. It's all the fashion among the gentry. Would you care to try some?'

'Yes, I would,' said Hero. He turned to Aiken. 'Master Cosmas sampled the beverage and claimed it had many sovereign qualities.'

At a word from Arslan, the owner of the next chai-khana hurried to prepare a place on a fine rug dyed with precious lac. He showed his guests a block of chai stamped with Chinese characters, explaining that it was called Longevity Dragon Sprout, reserved for the emperor's court.

He officiated while a waiter poured the chai from a silver pot into shallow white bowls. The proprietor held one of the vessels to the light to demonstrate its translucence and flicked its rim, producing a clear ringing sound.

'Porcelain,' said Hero. 'Also from China.'

He breathed in the chai's smoky scent and sipped, rolling the astringent beverage around his mouth. A servitor set down a platter of pancakes smothered in black liquid honey.

'No charge, sir,' said the proprietor. 'An honour to serve such distinguished guests.'

Hero smacked his lips and set down his bowl. 'It agrees with me,' he said. 'It refreshes and soothes at the same time. Do you think it would find a market in Constantinople?'

Aiken's lips puckered. 'Men nourished by strong wine wouldn't choose to drink something as insipid as this.'

'I expect you're right,' Hero said. He yawned, drowsy in the dappled shade, and reviewed the clientele. One gentleman seated with his legs folded beneath him was reading a book between sips of chai. From his faint smiles, Hero deduced that the codex wasn't a holy text, and when the gentleman laid the book down and stared away, his chai growing cold in front of him, Hero couldn't contain his curiosity. He rose and soft-footed over.

'Forgive me, Aga. I too am a slave to the written word, and I see that the book you're reading has laid a trance on you. May I enquire who wrote it?'

The scholar weighed the manuscript in both hands. 'It's a collection of the rubaiyat penned by Omar the tent-maker's son, God bless his posterity.'

'Omar Khayyam,' Hero breathed. 'I've heard of that great polymath's achievements in natural science, but I've never read his poems.'

The scholar leafed through the pages. 'Here's the one I was reading.

'Consider, in this battered caravanserai
Whose doorways are alternate night and day
How sultan after sultan in his pomp
Lived his destined hour and went his way.'

Hero allowed a silence. 'I'm lodging in a caravanserai near the western gate. I travel with a company bound for China.'

'My favourite nephew left for China with a mercenary force last winter. Three days ago I received news that he'd died at the Jade Gate fort.'

'Oh, my commiserations.' Hero turned in a whirl of confusion. 'Please forgive my thoughtless intrusion.'

'Wait,' said the cleric, 'Tell me where you come from and why you're journeying to China.' He arched a finger and a waiter hurried over to refresh their bowls.

Aiken joined them while they conversed. 'I can't believe it,' Hero told him. 'This learned imam met Master Cosmas Monopthalmos here in Bukhara twenty years ago. Imagine.'

The cleric stood. 'I have to attend a mosque council.' He picked up the book, hesitated, then held it out to Hero. 'For you, my friend.'

'I couldn't possibly.'

'Take it. You face a long and dangerous journey. Omar Khayyam's poetry might solace, inform and inspire you during the lonely desert nights.'

Hero sprang up. 'At least let me pay you what it's worth.'

The cleric was already leaving. 'Please don't offend me with money. I'm not a shopkeeper and wisdom can't be weighed in silver.'

Hero and Aiken watched him walk down the street, somehow remote from the bustling crowd. When he disappeared, Hero opened the book to its title page and read the dedication in Arabic. *To Kwaja imam, the most glorious, most honoured proof of the nation and the religion, sword of Islam and scimitar of the imams, lord of the religious laws ... From the least of slaves, Omar Khayyam.* Hero's hand flew to his mouth. 'Oh my goodness. Look. It's signed by the poet. I can't possibly keep it. Here,' he said, thrusting the book into Aiken's hands. 'Run after the gentleman and return it.'

Hero was still fanning himself when Aiken jogged back out of breath. 'I couldn't find him.'

Hero appealed to the proprietor for help, but the man could not or would not divulge the imam's address.

Walking back to their lodgings, Hero dipped into Omar Khayyam's quatrains. 'How ingenious they are. The tentmaker's son can distil a world of meaning into four lines.'

Aiken tried to steer Hero around a heap of human ordure. 'Careful. Too late. Never mind.'

Hero wiped the turd off against the dust without raising his gaze from the page. 'Here's a good one, containing a truth for both of us.

'Myself when young did eagerly frequent
Doctor and Saint and heard great argument
About this and that and everything.
Yet though I listened, I returned by the same door as in I went.'

'I saw Lucas,' Aiken said.

Hero stumbled. 'What?'

'In the slave market.'

'What, just now?'

'No. Before we stopped at the chai-khana. The trade minister lied to us. Lucas is here and is being sold into slavery as I speak.'

Hero gawped. 'Why didn't you ...?' Understanding dawned. 'Oh, Aiken. Well, we'll leave that for later.' Hero had grasped the implications and spoke as rapidly as thought could run. 'Tell Vallon. No, not Vallon. Fetch Wayland and bring money. Lots of it.' He tugged Arslan's sleeve. 'Take Aiken back to the caravanserai. Quick. As quick as you can.'

Hero trotted back up the road. Everywhere he looked, his dim sight revealed animated gatherings. Hurrying towards one crowd, he discovered that a storyteller was treating them to a tale of Rustam's exploits. Tacking towards another, he came up against a wall of spectators wagering on fighting partridges. He clutched a passer-by's sleeve. 'The slave market. Where is it?'

The man didn't understand and detached himself.

'Someone show me to the slave market,' Hero cried. His distraught gaze fell on a sober elder observing him with mild alarm. Hero latched onto him. 'Sir, please help me. I must get to the slave market.'

The elder called out in an authoritative voice and two touts homed in on Hero and commenced fighting over who had the right to bleed this wealthy foreigner. 'I don't have time for this,' Hero said, grabbing one of them and taking a glancing blow to the jaw in the process. 'You,' he said. 'Take me to the slave market. Not a moment's delay.'

The tout waded through the crowd until he reached a dense picket of prospective purchasers, casual spectators and, no doubt, a few pickpockets and prostitutes. He barged through the crush, the promise of gold proof against any amount of protests and indignant buffets.

'The man I'm looking for is a young Frank,' Hero panted.

His guide winked.

'Hurry!'

Even the tout's bullish efforts weren't enough to penetrate the crush. Three ranks from the front an armed man slapped him around the face and harangued him for his coarse manners. Hemmed in on all sides, Hero stood on tiptoe to find the podium bare.

'Too late,' he groaned. 'Oh, Aiken.'

The tout dug an elbow into his ribs and bared his teeth to their sallow roots. 'Frankish.'

Hero craned up to see two men manhandling Lucas onto the stage. The auctioneer followed and after an aloof survey of the audience launched into his pitch, pointing a baton at Lucas while his assistants showed off the young Frank's selling points, shoving him about as if he were livestock.

Hero heaved against the crowd. 'Let me through. There's been a dreadful misunderstanding. That young man is a member of a diplomatic mission.'

But the crowd held firm and bidding had already started, the auctioneer playing the crowd like a practised showman.

'What's he saying?' Hero demanded.

'This slave is the pick of the bunch,' the tout told him. 'Young and healthy. Very strong and lusty.'

'Tell the auctioneer I'm interested in buying the Frank. Ask him to speak in Greek or Arabic for my benefit.'

At the tout's bellowed request, the auctioneer leaned forward to evaluate Hero. Having gauged his worth, he acknowledged the request with a flick of fingers before resuming in both Turkic and Arabic.

Now Hero could follow the bidding, and it was brisk, half a dozen hopefuls in the market for Lucas. At forty dirhams – roughly one solidus – the bargain hunters fell out, and at one hundred dirhams only four were left in the bidding.

The tout prodded Hero. 'Why don't you bid, sir?'

'I don't have any money.'

'No money? Sir.'

'Hush,' Hero said. The bidding had slowed to a drip, each advance squeezed out. Hero couldn't see his competitors.

The auctioneer raised his baton. 'I have one hundred and eighty dirhams. Any advance on one hundred and eighty. No?' he said, staring at Hero. 'Then going once, twice and ...'

'Ten gold solidi,' Hero blurted.

Space opened up around him as the astonished audience drew back to view this profligate infidel. A voice launched an angry protest that rolled off the auctioneer like water off oil. Delighted, he raised his baton to conduct the finale.

'I have a bid of ten solidi from the Greek gentleman.'

'Twelve,' a voice said.

'Fifteen,' Hero responded.

'Twenty.'

'And another five,' Hero said, feeling sick and elated.

A disturbance around him, an aggressive pressing-in warned him that his rival wasn't taking Hero's intervention lightly. A man with a brutal face shoved the tout aside and confronted Hero.

'Stop bidding, you foreign dog.'

'On the contrary,' Hero said, and gave an airy wave. 'Thirty.'

The man went for his knife and drew it back. Some force wrenched him into reverse and suddenly Wulfstan appeared, his good hand clamped around the assassin's neck. Wulfstan kneed him in the groin and the man fell cross-eyed to the ground. Wayland and Gorka burst through the crowd, followed by red-faced and sweating Aiken.

Wulfstan picked up the knife, dragged the wretch to his feet and booted him away.

'Shall I proceed?' the auctioneer said, baton poised. 'I have a bid of thirty solidi.'

'*How* much?' Wayland said.

'Thirty-five,' said the auctioneer. His head darted. 'And five.'

'Ssh,' Hero said. He stuck up a hand. 'Fifty.' He gave Wayland an inane smile. 'It's not our money.'

'Fifty-five,' said the auctioneer, registering a counterbid.

A drawn-out interval, the auctioneer swinging his head around. 'I'll accept fifty-seven,' he said. 'Yes, you sir. I have fifty-seven,' he told the crowd.

'Sixty,' someone shouted.

'Seventy,' Hero countered.

Wayland groaned. Wulfstan laughed and slapped Gorka's back.

You could have heard the hush a hundred yards away. People from that distance had wandered over to see who was on sale for a sum they could never raise in a lifetime.

'Any advance on seventy Byzantine solidi?' Kites wheeled above the square. 'Asking once. Asking twice.' The auctioneer's gavel smacked down. 'Sold to the Greek gentleman, and I hope he derives a lifetime's satisfaction from his purchase.'

Hero stood in a daze while Aiken settled up with the auctioneer, leaving Wulfstan and Gorka clasped in speechless hilarity and Wayland shaking his head in disbelief. The assistants who'd forced Lucas up the steps as if he were meat on the hoof led him down as if he were a prince of the realm. Wayland took charge of him.

Lucas blinked around and his blasted gaze fixed on Gorka. 'Thanks, boss.'

'I only came because I couldn't bear the idea of someone else making your life a misery.'

Lucas tried to smile. 'How much did I cost?'

'A fortune,' said Wayland. 'You'll be paying for yourself all the way to China and back.'

'How did you find me?'

'Aiken spotted you.'

Lucas stared at his saviour.

'You needn't thank me,' Aiken said. 'I nearly left you there. After the way you treated me, it would have been no more than you deserved.'

'What happened to Zuleyka?' Wayland said in the silence.

'I don't know. They separated us when we arrived in Bukhara. We have to find her.'

'We'd better scarper,' Wulfstan said. 'We're attracting a lot of filthy looks.'

He and Gorka underpinned Lucas's armpits. The youth dragged his heels. 'No, we have to find her.'

Gorka grinned. 'He's a piece of work, ain't he? Next he'll be asking us to get his horse back.'

'Yes, and then I'll go after the pack who murdered Yeke and sold me into slavery.'

'Forget it,' Gorka said, tightening his grip. 'Time to get you back to your mates before someone else takes a fancy to you.'

'Wait,' said Wayland. 'The auctioneer will know what happened to Zuleyka. Have we got any money left?'

'About ten solidi,' said Aiken.

Wayland held out his hand for them and began making for the auctioneer.

'I'm coming with you,' Lucas said.

'Keep him right there.'

Lucas had been the last lot and the auctioneer's expansive manner had fallen into a kind of post-coital blank. Watching from a distance, Hero was certain that Wayland would get nothing out of him. The auctioneer tried to brush the Englishman aside and then, when pressed, he summoned his assistants to rid him of this pestering infidel. Before they could lay hands on him, Wayland said something that seemed to drip like honey into the man's ears and made him stare at the Outlanders in a calculating manner.

His superficial smile flashed and he draped an arm over Wayland's shoulder and walked him up and down, conversing cheek to cheek. Money passed by sleight of hand before Wayland returned.

'Did you find out where she is?' Lucas demanded.

'He sold her yesterday.'

'We'd better tell Vallon,' Hero said.

'I think not. Her owner is the same man who bid for Lucas and set his thug on Hero. After today's disappointment, neither gold nor threats will prise Zuleyka from his grasp.'

'All the more reason to lay the matter before Vallon,' Aiken said.

'Lucas means very little to Vallon, and the girl even less. He's not going to kick up hell to rescue her.'

'She means a lot to me,' Lucas cried.

'Take him back to the caravanserai,' Wayland said.

Hero had sobered and was appalled by his reckless bidding 'We don't have to tell Vallon how much we paid for Lucas.'

'Yes, we do,' said Aiken, 'The general has entrusted me with the accounts. I can't fiddle them.'

'Seventy solidi,' Hero groaned. 'Vallon will be furious.'

'I'll tell him,' Wayland said. 'Don't say a word about the girl.'

XXV

Vallon's jaw dropped. 'Seventy solidi!'

Wayland focused slightly beyond the general. 'More like eighty if you include the auctioneer's commission and other disbursements.'

'God's veins! That's more than most troopers earn in an entire career. It's more than my annual salary.'

'Hero bid only what was necessary. It's the underbidder who determines the selling price.

'Why didn't you seek my permission before throwing so much gold around?'

'There wasn't time. The bidding had already started. Hero couldn't just stand and watch Lucas sold into slavery.'

Vallon sagged in weary disbelief. 'That youth is the curse of my life. I'd pay seventy solidi to get rid of him.'

'He'll come good in time. The underbidder obviously saw something worthwhile in him.'

A last angry surge impelled Vallon to his feet. 'He's made me an object of ridicule.'

'On the contrary. Lucas's comrades are treating him as something of a charm. Naturally, I've spread the word that it was you who arranged his rescue.'

Vallon felt for his seat. 'Where is he?'

'In the sanatorium. He had a hard time in the desert.'

'Wonderful,' said Vallon. 'A count's ransom to redeem a broken-down peasant captured because of his own folly.'

'I have a feeling that one day Lucas will reward you for your generosity.'

'I want nothing from that lout except good discipline – and a decent respect for Aiken.'

'It was Aiken who spotted him. He could have left him there and I wouldn't have blamed him. I'll make it plain to Lucas where he must show his gratitude.'

Leaving Vallon to mull over this twist, Wayland made his escape, encountering Wulfstan in the courtyard. 'I think deep down he's pleased,' Wayland said.

'The gypsy girl?'

'Vallon didn't mention her and nor did I.'

Wulfstan cackled. 'How are you going to get her back?'

Wayland kept walking.

'Where are you going?'

'To call on a friend.'

Wayland ducked into a dormitory occupied by Turkmen troopers. He rubbed the dazzle from his eyes. 'Toghan?'

A Seljuk sprang up, the same trooper Wayland had saved from plunging into a gorge in the Caucasus. He was a good-natured and high-spirited young man. His name meant 'Falcon'.

They kissed and exchanged blessings. Wayland led Toghan outside. 'I have a favour to ask.'

'Everything my lord commands his slave, I will endeavour to perform.'

Wayland reached the shade around the pool. 'You heard that we rescued Lucas.'

'Of course. The favour of God was on him.'

'God didn't show His favour to Zuleyka. She was sold into slavery the day before.'

Toghan giggled. 'Her master is a fortunate gentleman.' His hips rotated in a sinuous pantomime. 'There will be a baby in the spring, God willing.'

'Not if I can help it,' Wayland said.

Toghan's hand flew to his mouth. 'Ah, Lord, I understand. You desire her for yourself.'

Wayland didn't waste time denying it. 'The man who bought her is a wealthy Arab merchant called Sa'id al-Qushair. He owns a house near the citadel and a country mansion about ten miles from Bukhara, just beyond Ramitan on the Golden Road to Samarkand. That's where he's taken Zuleyka.'

Toghan pressed a fist against his heart. 'You want me to rescue her. Of course I will. May I be your sacrifice.'

'I want you to ride out and scout the house, discover where the girl is kept and look for a way in. If possible, enter the property and commit the layout to memory. Dress shabbily and call at the gate, saying you're an ex-soldier looking for work in return for a meal.'

Toghan stuck out his elbows and brought them down like a bird springing into flight. 'At once.'

Wayland hauled him back. 'Wait until tomorrow. Leave the city as soon as the gates open, ride to the mansion and return before the curfew. I don't want you getting into trouble.'

Toghan leaned forward and gave a grotesque wink.

'What's that supposed to mean?'

Toghan tittered and placed a finger to his lips. 'I understand, Lord. You cherish this lady as your own and cannot bear to see her innocence defiled by a wealthy old greybeard.' Still holding a finger to his lips, he backed away.

Wayland lingered in the shade, considering with falling heart the possible consequences of a rescue attempt. Succeed or fail, it might jeopardise the mission and would certainly deepen the wedge between himself and Vallon. A fish in the pond surfaced and gulped down an insect. Wayland pushed off through the heat and entered the sanatorium.

'It's hot enough to bake an egg out there.'

Hero looked round. 'Drink some of Lucas's sherbet.'

The prodigal lay sprawled on a cot, his legs wrapped in poultices.

Wayland drank the cool liquor and watched Hero unwind the bandages, exposing Lucas's ulcerated calves. It occurred to Wayland that Zuleyka would be in a similar state and would require treatment and convalescence before her owner judged her fit to share the conjugal bed. He chased the thought away.

'How is he?' he said.

'This is the fourth time I've doctored him. That means he has only five lives left.'

'How long before he's back on his feet?'

'I can answer for myself,' said Lucas. 'I'm ready to leave now.'

Hero pushed him back down. 'You'll get up when I say so.'

Wayland watched Hero apply fresh bandages. 'Can I have a word with him in private?'

'Of course,' Hero said. He put away his dressing and lotions and went out, leaving Wayland and Lucas contemplating each other through the latticed sunlight.

'Wipe that smirk off your face,' Wayland said.

Lucas pulled his mouth down. 'It's just nervousness. You're going after Zuleyka, aren't you? Please take me with you.'

Wayland shook his head. 'You're in enough shit as it is.'

'I know. Whatever I do, I can't sink any deeper.'

Wayland sat at the end of the bed. 'We didn't have a chance to finish our discussion ...' He tapped Lucas's chest. '... Guy.'

Lucas laughed after a fashion. 'Don't tell me you still fancy I'm Vallon's son.'

329

'Sometimes I fancy you are, and sometimes I think not. Only you can tell me the truth.'

'You're wrong, so let that put an end to it.'

Wayland nodded in a pensive way, stood and made for the door.

'Is that it?' Lucas said.

'If you're not Vallon's son, there's nothing more to discuss.'

'What about Zuleyka?'

'She's none of your business. Troopers don't have sweethearts.'

Wayland was on the threshold when Lucas spoke again.

'Have you told anyone else?'

'No one.'

'What made you fancy I was Vallon's son?'

'At first only the fleeting resemblance. Then I fell to thinking and I wondered why a Frankish peasant youth appearing from nowhere would be so jealous of Aiken, the son of one of Vallon's closest comrades. Anyone else in your position would have tried to curry favour with the boy. Not you. Instead you treated him like a hated rival.'

Lucas gave a juddering sigh. 'It's true. I am the son of the man who calls himself Vallon.'

Wayland closed his eyes and breathed deep.

Lucas spoke in a voice just loud enough to be heard. 'I was six when he murdered my mother. After he'd fled I ran to her chamber and found her and her lover twined together on a bloody mattress.'

Wayland squinted out though the sunlight. 'His name was Roland.'

'He used to bring me toys. My favourite was a puppet carved in the shape of a Moorish soldier. He used to sing to my mother and I'd creep close to their door to listen. I hardly knew Vallon and thought of Roland as my real father.'

'He was a warped coward who contrived to have Vallon cast into a Moorish dungeon.'

'A boy of six can't interpret character. Roland was charming and

330

generous. Guy de Crion was absent for most of my childhood, and when he returned home he was stern and aloof. He scared me.'

Wayland turned, blinded by the change from light to dark. 'You showed great determination travelling all the way to Constantinople. I imagine your motive was murder.'

'At first, yes. Not a day passed when I didn't imagine twisting a sword in Vallon's guts.'

'And now?'

'I don't know. I really don't. It gnaws into my sleep.'

Wayland strode up to Lucas. 'Ask yourself who you'd rather serve – the general who sacrificed everything to lead this mission, or the popinjay who betrayed his commander in order to lie with that man's wife. A wretched cuckoo who insinuated himself into the family nest by giving toys to fledglings and singing merry airs. I've had my differences with Vallon, and at many points our personalities jar. But I'll tell you one thing. The general is a man of principle and honour who only shaves the edges of those virtues to protect his men.'

Sweat popped on Lucas's brow.

Wayland unclenched his hands. 'The sooner you tell him the better. Suppose Hero hadn't redeemed you? Vallon would have gone to his grave not knowing that his son and heir lived.'

'And died happier in his ignorance.'

'What do you mean?'

'The last thing he wants is for a forgotten son to confront him with his crimes.'

'Do you want me to tell him?'

'No!'

Wayland sat down on the bedside. 'One day you're going to have to own up.'

'Yes, but at a time of my own choosing.'

'Time has a way of running out faster than you think. Hero said you've already used up half a cat's lives. I don't want to be the one who has to inform Vallon that the trooper we tipped into a shallow grave in some desert was the blood of his blood.'

Lucas's head rolled on the pillow. 'I've wrestled with the dilemma since the day I laid eyes on him, and now I've decided. Vallon made his name as a warrior when he was the same age as me. Remember I told you I'd be entitled to wear the armour I stole when I'd killed five men in fair combat? On the day I achieve that, I'll reveal my lineage before Vallon.'

'That might be a long day coming.'

Lucas gripped Wayland's hands. 'The time must be of my choosing. Grant me that. I beg you.'

Wayland nodded. 'As you wish.'

'Anyway,' said Lucas. 'Right now, it's Zuleyka I'm worried about.'

'Leave that problem to me.'

'Let me join you. I swore I'd set her free, and if you don't let me help you, it will stain my honour.'

Wayland hid a smile at hearing such a high-flown statement. 'On two conditions. First, you do what I say without question.'

'Of course.'

'Second, you seek out Aiken and beg forgiveness for the slights you've dealt him. You don't have to give the reason, but you must be sincere.'

'Yes, I'll do that for you.'

'Not for me. For Hero who's cared for you and for Vallon who's put up with you and for Gorka who's spoken in your defence despite your ingrate behaviour.'

'I'll do it.'

Wayland rose. 'You know what they'll do if they catch us. They'll bury Zuleyka up to her neck and hurl stones at her, the stones selected for size to ensure she doesn't die quickly. As for you, once they learn how thick-skulled you are, they'll take out their revenge on your tenderer parts.'

'If you're prepared to risk it, so am I.'

Wayland gave a dry laugh. 'If it goes wrong and Vallon condemns you to the scaffold, you can win a reprieve by declaring his parentage as the noose kisses your throat.'

'Wayland.'

'Yes.'

'During my captivity, I had plenty of time to think. I'm not the same man I was.'

'I hope not.'

Moths brushed and tapped the lamp in Wayland's chamber when Toghan returned two evenings later, fizzing with excitement. Wayland sat him down and served him a bowl of curds.

'I expected you back yesterday.'

'Lord, what a story I have to tell.'

'You found the house?'

'Yes. A grand house. Bigger than this ribat.'

'Describe it.'

'A mansion on the Golden Road, just as you said. High walls all round, the road on one side and a canal on another. I told the porter I was a poor soldier seeking work in return for a meal. The man would have driven me away but by chance his master's overseer happened by and told him to set me labouring in the vegetable garden. That was not long before noon and I dug shit into the soil until there was no light left to see. My reward? A bowl of noodles and a cup of stale water. When I told those brutes I had to be back in Bukhara before the curfew, they threatened me with whips, saying I hadn't exhausted my obligations. Lord, the master of that house – a plague on his soul – believes every man who lacks might and wealth belongs to him to do with what he likes. Before light next day, his overseer drove me into the estate to resume my drudgery. I'd entered the mansion as an honest day labourer; they treated me like a slave. Me. Toghan son of Chaghri son of Tughril son of . . .'

Wayland walked the room. 'How did you get away?'

'I drew the knife hidden in my boot and held it to the overseer's windpipe, threatening to feed him his balls if he didn't return my horse and open the gate for me.'

'Couldn't you have devised a subtler means of escape?'

Toghan began lapping up the curds. 'If a man doesn't protect his honour, he's but a husk, an empty shell. I would have killed the overseer and sent him to hell better prepared to endure its torments if you hadn't made me promise to leave that ungodly household as peacefully as I'd arrived. I rode back with all haste.' Toghan half-stood. 'May God consecrate the souls of your ancestors.'

Wayland fell onto his seat and regarded Toghan through splayed fingers. 'After you took your leave in such a rough fashion, they might suspect you had other designs.'

Toghan licked his fingers one by one. 'They regarded me as no more significant than a fly. How do you find a fly after it bites? Here? There? No, too late. Gone.'

Wayland pulled up his stool. 'Did you find Zuleyka?'

'She's in the harem of course. I heard the servants talking about her.'

Wayland resigned himself for a long interrogation. 'Where is the harem?'

Toghan indicated right. 'On that side.'

Wayland stood, lifted Toghan from his seat and placed him by the door. 'Start from the moment you entered the property. What did you see?'

'A luscious garden and the mansion behind it, slave quarters and stables to the left, the harem to the right.'

'Separated by walls.'

'Yes. The harem has its own courtyard.'

'How will we enter?'

'Over the outer walls.'

'What's beyond them? You mentioned a canal.'

'No canal on that side. Just fields.'

'How high are the walls?'

'Not so big.'

One thing Wayland had learned during his employment in the sultan's court was that the Turkmen had no common scale for measuring. They could spot an enemy two miles away, but they couldn't agree on the exact distance. Point out a falcon seen close up and they'd declare it was an eagle. Show them an eagle a mile away and it was a hawk or falcon. Wayland had a dozen words for raptors, whereas the Turkmen had only three, meaning big, middling and small respectively.

'Are the walls higher than the ones surrounding this ribat?'

'Smaller.'

'Twice my height?'

Toghan's gaze roamed. 'Yes. Twice as tall.'

So any height between ten and twenty feet. Ropes and grappling hooks would be needed.

'You said the approach was clear.'

Toghan's manner became evasive. 'I couldn't ride all the way around the house. It would have made the guards suspicious.'

'That was going to be my next question. How many armed men?'

Toghan didn't hesitate. 'About a dozen.' He tossed a hand. 'Flabby bullies. Three of us could slaughter the whole household.'

'Killing isn't our intention. Our goal is to get Zuleyka away without hurting a soul. You're right about one thing, though. There'll be three of us. You, me and Lucas. Plus the dog. We'll do it tomorrow.'

Toghan's laugh drifted into a wistful register. 'Can't I kill the overseer?'

'No, you can't. Steal Zuleyka from under his nose and you'll inflict a sore that will never heal. Rub more dirt into the wound by suggesting that we bribed him to turn a blind eye to our entry.'

Toghan doubled over in husky laughter. 'How clever you are.'

How stupid, Wayland thought.

The guard at the Samarkand Gate watched Wayland and his two conspirators as they approached, leading a spare horse and with the dog tucked in behind. Wayland continued talking to Toghan in Turkic, sitting his horse in the slouched yet elegant posture that signified a lifetime spent in the saddle. The Turkmen clothes he wore and the indigo turban swathing his yellow hair couldn't disguise his foreign ancestry. His eyes, blue as the hottest part of a candle flame, betrayed his northern origins.

The guard stopped them. 'Who are you and where are you going?'

Wayland answered, running a rosary through his fingers. 'We are the trusted agents of Mohamed ibn Zufar of Samarkand, may the blessings of God be upon him.' He cocked his finger at Lucas. 'We're escorting this infidel to his new owner. I purchased him at the slave market four days ago, along with that horse.'

The guard walked around all three riders before facing Wayland again. 'When did you join your master's household?'

'Eleven years ago. I was captured at Manzikert aged sixteen. Defeat in that battle was my spiritual salvation. Through my master's teachings I embraced the true religion, thanks and praise be to God the most high exalted, the creator of the world and the knower of hidden things.'

The guard looked at Toghan.

'He's very religious,' the Seljuk confided.

The guard stepped back as if piety might be contagious. 'Pass in peace and may your journey be an easy one.'

Toghan burst into laughter when they reached the open road. 'That was a cunning touch.'

Wayland urged his horse into a trot. 'We're leaving a trail. He'll remember our passing and will testify against us when the time comes.'

The evening sky had separated into charcoal and vermilion when they rode past the mansion. Wayland took in the salient features of the compound with a couple of glances. Its walls were higher and thicker than Toghan had described, and there was no cover to hide their approach. They trotted on until the sun went down and then they lay up in a mulberry grove. Bats flickered through the branches. A rind of moon hung low in the south. Out on the plain a lion's roar shivered the night.

Wayland settled himself. 'Muffle the horses' hooves,' he told Toghan. 'Wake me at the deadest hour.'

He watched the stars in their orbits, wondering what Syth would make of this crazy adventure. That wasn't hard to answer. He flinched as he imagined her batting her hands against his chest. *You left me and our children to imperil yourself for a gypsy dancer.*

'It's not like that!'

He gasped against a muffling hand. 'Hush, Lord. There's no space on earth so distant that a cry doesn't enter.'

Wayland prised Toghan's hand away and blinked awake.

'Time to go,' Lucas said.

On padded hooves the horses approached the mansion. A furlong short of it, Wayland left the road and detoured through a field of alfalfa until the compound bulked over him. He slid to the ground, listening. Frogs burped in the waterway behind the house. Jackals snarled and yipped in the distance.

He crept up to the wall. Eighteen feet high at least. 'You're sure we're at the right spot,' he murmured.

'Yes,' Toghan hissed.

'Let me go in,' Lucas whispered.

'Watch the horses,' Wayland said.

'But I should be the one who sets her free.'

Wayland grabbed a bunch of Lucas's tunic. 'You promised to do what I told you.'

'Sorry.'

From his saddlebag Wayland drew a rope with two iron claws spliced to one end. He swung it in circles and lobbed it over the ramparts. The clatter when the claws hit the baked mud on the far side made him wince. He listened for sounds of alarm. The frogs went on croaking. The dog looked at him, panting.

He drew in the rope and the claws bit into the parapet. He pulled with all his strength and the anchor didn't shift. 'Keep it taut,' he told Toghan.

He spat into his palms and walked himself up the wall, reaching the top with chest heaving and arms burning. He lay flat on the parapet and conned the layout. Toghan hadn't got it wrong. The space below was a garden courtyard, the women's quarters to the right. Not a light showed in the building or anywhere else. Somewhere a fountain tinkled.

He craned back. 'Toghan.'

'Lord.'

'We'll need you to help haul us up.'

The rope jarred as Toghan heaved himself to the top. Wayland produced another clawed rope from his pack, hooked it over the outer face of the wall and dropped the free end into the courtyard.

'Make sure it doesn't work loose.'

He let himself down the rope. His confidence grew when he reached solid ground. He listened again then stalked towards the door of the harem. This was the part he couldn't plan for. Zuleyka might be confined in a cell deep within the compound. If she was, he wouldn't have time to find her before his forced entry roused the whole household.

He prowled the harem walls, listening at each shuttered window, picking up no sound at one, a pleasant female purring from another.

Looking back, he could just discern Toghan clamped on the wall – a malevolent incubus primed to descend on sleeping maidens and ravish them. Wayland tested the lock on the door and established that it wouldn't yield to tinkering.

From his pack he pulled an iron ram weighing twenty pounds. He drew it back and hesitated.

'Attack the citadel while it sleeps,' Toghan hissed.

Wayland smashed the lock with two blows, kicked the door open and stumbled inside.

'Zuleyka!'

Women screamed.

'Zuleyka!'

Wayland heard a terrific slap and a pained cry.

'I'm coming.'

Zuleyka threw herself into Wayland's arms wearing only a sheer silk shift, its luxurious texture not lost on him as he ran her towards the wall. A bugle's discordant note sounded through the caterwauling from the harem.

'Grab the rope,' Wayland said. 'Toghan will pull you up.'

Holding the free end, he turned to see what forces his invasion had unleashed. The whole establishment was in turmoil, women's squeals and men's cries mingling with the shrieks of peacocks. Zuleyka yelped and fell from the rope, knocking him flat. He yanked her up and put her hands to the rope again.

'Just hold on and let Toghan pull you clear.'

A chubby woman in a nightgown, clamping a wig cockeyed over her head, advanced as if propelled on castors. Gibbering with fury, hands crooked into talons, she made straight for Zuleyka. The gypsy girl took one look at her, released the rope and with a harsh cry launched herself at her jailer, gouging and kicking.

'Oh, great,' Wayland said.

He tore them apart, holding off the hellcat and suffering a lacerated cheek in the process.

'Get up the damned rope!'

He flung the harridan into the dust, where she lay mouthing imprecations to curdle the blood. 'The same to you,' he said, watching the gate into the main courtyard.

It burst open a moment after Toghan shouted that he had Zuleyka safe.

'Don't wait for me.'

Wayland went up the rope as if Satan's imps were jabbing from below with pitchforks. A hand brushed his ankle. He kicked it away and climbed hand over fist. Halfway to the top, he heard a falling wail and saw the hooks anchoring the rope on the other side spring loose and whip out of sight. He gained the top and glanced back to see a mob of armed men running towards him.

Toghan swung the rope. 'Here.'

Wayland glimpsed from the corner of his eye an archer drawing a bow. 'No time for that.'

He sat on the wall, drew a deep breath, and threw himself off. A fall of nearly twenty feet allowed a surprising amount of time to contemplate the injuries he might suffer. The impact knocked him witless, but he'd landed on soft sand and sprang up, pushing away his ecstatic dog. He hobbled towards his horse and mounted at the second attempt.

He kissed his horse between its ears and clapped his heels against its flanks. 'Fly!'

They reached the road and galloped down it in a windswept blur. Two miles from the mansion Wayland's horse stumbled and its rhythm faltered. He eased up. 'Wait!'

Zuleyka and Lucas returned from the darkness.

Wayland dismounted and lifted his horse's right foreleg. 'She's lame. You two go on. Wait for us outside the Gate of the Spice Sellers.' He rooted in his pack and lobbed a suit of men's clothes at Zuleyka. 'Put them on. Off you go.'

Toghan lay prostrate on the trackway behind him, one ear to the ground. 'Six riders at least.'

Wayland could already hear the drubbing hooves. 'We can't outride them. We have to get off the road.'

Toghan pulled his horse to the right. 'This way.'

Before they'd ridden a hundred yards a yell told them that they'd been spotted. Wayland cranked a glance across his shoulder to see a rider lashing his horse in pursuit.

'Split up,' he shouted.

'Never,' Toghan cried. In the next instant he demonstrated what Wayland had witnessed many times but had never been able to accomplish himself – the horse archer's rearward delivery, the Parthian shot.

Toghan dropped his reins, swivelled until he was facing his horse's tail, drew his bow and loosed. His arrow hit the pursuing horse square in the chest. It squealed and lurched to the left, spilling its rider over its neck. Five more riders crashed out of

340

the dark. The fallen horseman urged them to continue their pursuit.

Wayland spurred on, the concussions behind him drawing closer, his dog flowing alongside in an easy gallop.

'Hound them,' Wayland told it.

It swung round and ran towards the pursuing riders, giving tongue as if it had spotted a fox or jackal. Wayland glimpsed it bounding around a horse before a black canal opened up in front of him. He set his horse at the water and hit it with a mighty splash. His horse flailed to climb the opposite bank but couldn't find purchase. Wayland leaped off and, with Toghan's help, dragged it up. Three riders skidded to a halt on the other side and tried to aim their bows. The dog wouldn't let them. Jaws popping, it nipped their horses' heels, driving them in circles.

Wayland sprang back into the saddle and flogged his mount on. The yells and barks behind him faded away.

'Stop,' he said after covering a mile or so.

He listened through his pumping heart, Toghan panting beside him.

'I think we've lost them.'

Toghan threw back his head. 'Oh, what fine sport.'

Together they cantered back to Bukhara. Its domes were just beginning to show against the dark when the dog caught up, barely out of breath and very pleased with itself. They made a wide circuit of the walls and approached the western gate as dawn fanned up in pistachio green behind the city's minarets. Lucas and Zuleyka were waiting, the girl in nomad garb. Lucas gasped in relief.

'Did you have to fight?'

Wayland swigged from a water bottle. 'We didn't have to shed human blood, thank God.'

Not long after the first call to prayer, the gates opened. Wayland rode up to the three guards, his clothes wet and muddied, his turban unravelling. There was no point trying to hide his identity.

'I'm with the Byzantine mission.'

'Where have you been?'

341

'We were returning from Samarkand when thieves attacked us. To escape them we had to ride cross-country and got lost. We left Bukhara without the general's permission and must return to the caravanserai before he finds us gone.'

'Not before you tell us more about these thieves.'

Wayland rolled a gold solidus between thumb and forefinger. 'There's one for each of you.'

He placed the coin in a grasping palm and lobbed the other two into the dust.

The guards were still scrapping for the gold when Wayland and his companions rode through the gates.

He pushed Zuleyka into an empty cell and made for the door. 'Lie low until I say otherwise.'

'Wayland.'

His blood tingled at the first sound of his name from her mouth. He stopped.

'Come here,' she said in Persian.

'I don't have time,' he said in the same tongue.

'I want to thank you.'

He turned. 'Make it quick.'

She did, pulling his face towards hers and kissing him in one passionate movement.

She pulled back. 'I knew you'd come.'

He swallowed. 'Don't be daft.'

'You don't understand the power of dreams.'

With the lightest of touches, like a marble setting a boulder into motion, she propelled him towards the door. She yawned.

'Return soon.'

He crossed the courtyard with his lips still tingling and jumped when a voice spoke close by.

'You're up early if you slept at all. Where have you been?'

It was Vallon, off to the bath house, frowning at Wayland's dishevelled appearance.

'I went hunting.'

'Catch anything?'

'Only a wild dove.'

XXVI

'Hauk Eiriksson,' Vallon's servant announced.

Vallon broke off his discussion with his officers.

Hauk entered the *iwan* with a swagger, cutting a smart figure in a new costume of Viking design tailored from Bukhara silk, the hems brocaded with gold in the Arab fashion. He acknowledged the company with bows and smiles.

'I won't keep you long. I've come to announce my leave-taking. In two days I'll lead my men back to our ships.'

'You must have done good business,' Vallon said. 'What trade stuffs will you be carrying?'

'Carpets of incomparable workmanship, five hundred knots to the inch and dyed in gorgeous reds with a compound extracted from insects ...'

'Cochineal,' said Hero.

'Fine silks and muslins,' Hauk continued. 'Silver and cornelian and tourmaline jewellery. If I bring back only a quarter of the goods, I'll be the richest man in Svealand.'

'That's quite a large "if",' Vallon said. 'The Kara Kum will roast you alive at this time of year. Even if you cross it, you might find someone has stolen your ships. You could wait a long time on that shore before someone rescued you. And deliverance wouldn't be on your terms.'

Hauk grinned. 'I have your measure by now. You're loath to weaken your fighting force and hope to persuade me to remain with you all the way to China.'

'I'd certainly feel more confident embarking on the hardest part of our journey with your warriors at our side.'

Hauk shook his head. 'My men have had enough of deserts. They long to smell salt water again.'

Vallon extended his hand. 'Then I'll thank you for your service and wish you a safe journey and a happy homecoming.' He kept hold of Hauk's hand. 'I'm only sorry that our passage to Bukhara didn't throw up opportunities to see your men display their war skills. If you stayed another month, I expect I'd see their mettle tested to the limit.' He released Hauk's hand. 'Still ... so far as it's gone, our alliance has been useful.'

Hauk stiffened at the implied slight. 'There remains the matter of outstanding wages.'

Vallon cast a bored look at Aiken. 'Settle the account.'

Hauk laughed. 'I'll say this for you, Vallon. You're not a stinter. Perhaps you'll dine with me tomorrow evening.'

'Time presses. I'm afraid I'll have to forgo the pleasure.' Vallon bowed with finality. 'God speed you and keep you.'

Hauk bowed back. 'And you.'

He was almost at the door when Vallon's servant stepped through it again.

'The guides, General.'

Hauk made to step around the servant.

'Stay a while,' said Vallon. 'Even though our paths take us in different directions, these gentlemen might give you some useful information. They're Sogdians, experts on Silk Road trading, fellows of a guild that's been advising and leading merchants for more than five hundred years.'

Two men advanced through the door in close step – a strange-looking pair whose strangeness wasn't readily apparent. All Vallon could tell at first sight was that they looked remarkably alike and didn't fit either the Asian or Western mould. They had straight reddish hair as fine as an infant's and raisin-coloured eyes in curiously ageless faces. They wore conical hats tilted forward at the crown and knee-length silk brocade jackets flared below the waist and embroidered with roundels enclosing deer each side of a stylised tree. Their close-fitting trousers were tucked into calf-length kid boots worked with silver thread in a fish-scale pattern.

They bowed as one, courteous yet not at all subservient. 'An Yexi and An Shennu at your service,' said the left-hand one in passable Greek. 'Those are our Chinese names. People who don't speak our tongue find it difficult to pronounce our given names. His Eminence the Trade Secretary sent word that you're travelling to China and seek guides with expert knowledge of the routes and the conditions you're likely to encounter. If his recommendation isn't sufficient, allow me to present references from previous clients.'

Judging by the stack of yellowed pages, some of the documents dated back to the early days of Christianity. Vallon handed the pile to Hero. 'We'll study them with interest. For now, tell us your qualifications in your own words.'

'We're Sogdians, members of a brotherhood that has been guiding trains to and from China for thirty generations. Unlike local guides, who will take you only as far as the next oasis, we'll accompany you for the entire journey, smoothing your passage at every stage and ensuring that you make the most favourable transactions. We have relatives, business partners and agents in all the Silk Road centres, including Chang'an, the former Chinese capital. My cousin and I are fluent in all the principal languages you'll encounter – Arabic, Persian, Chinese, Tibetan and Uighur. We can also communicate in Khitan and the tongues of peoples you've never heard of.'

'What's he saying?' Hauk demanded.

Hero supplied a summary while Vallon continued his questioning.

'How many times have you made the journey?'

'I was twelve when I travelled to Chang'an for the first time, fifteen when I returned. Since then I've followed the Silk Road more than a dozen times.' An Yexi saw Vallon's eyes narrow in calculation. 'I'm older than I look. Sixty-three to be precise. We're a long-lived race. My father celebrated his hundredth birthday last year, having made his last journey to China at the age of seventy-eight.'

'Did you have dealings with the Byzantine mission that passed through Bukhara last year?'

'We offered our services to their commander. He declined, saying our rates of commission were too high.'

Vallon crossed his arms. 'Name them.'

'One fifth of the value of your merchandise in the Bukhara market. We'll need to make a detailed inventory.'

Vallon hunched forward. 'A fifth! That's outrageous.'

'I'll present the same facts I laid before your predecessor. If you make your own way, recruiting guides and camel trains at every oasis, expect to lose more than a tenth of your treasury in bribes, tolls and taxes. Add another tenth for goods pilfered and supplies overcharged. Throw in the time you'll lose haggling and I guarantee you'll reach China half as wealthy as when you left Bukhara. *If* you reach it. Employ us and there's every chance that you'll arrive in Kaifeng richer than you started. Through our network of agents, we know which goods command the highest prices.'

'Give me an example.'

'The fashion among the Song court ladies this year is for Afghan tortoiseshell and Arabian coral. Buy shell in the Bukhara mart and I guarantee that in Kaifeng your investment will reap a ten-fold reward.'

'A bold claim.'

An Shennu tapped the documents. 'Supported by the testimonials.'

'What happened to the last Byzantine expedition?'

'Reports and rumours agree that they perished in the Taklamakan Desert, east of Khotan. Bandits ambushed them after their guides deserted.'

Vallon had worked out what was so unsettling about the Sogdians. They answered as if they were one and the same person, each picking up from where his counterpart had left off, mirroring each other's gestures. 'Are you twins?'

'We're cousins, as I've already said. We're a close-knit race.'

'Christians? Muslims? What?'

'Manicheans.'

Hero explained. 'The Manicheans view the universe as the conflict between light and dark, good and evil. They believe that all earthly things contain various amounts of light particles trapped in dark matter, except for the sun and moon which were created from undefiled light. The Prince of Darkness created man from the copulation of devils in order—'

'Heretics or heathens,' said Vallon. He scrutinised the Sogdians again. Even now it was difficult to tell them apart. 'So you've made the journey to Kaifeng.'

'No,' said An Yexi. Or possibly it was An Shennu. 'The furthest we've travelled is Chang'an. The new capital lies a month's journey further east, on the Yellow River.'

'When was the last time you guided a caravan to China?'

'Four years ago.'

Vallon lolled back. 'I'm not surprised business is slow. I suggest you lower your commission.'

'Our rates have little to do with our lack of employment. Silk Road trade has withered under competition from the new sea routes. Demand for Chinese silk has declined as Western lands have established their own factories. Today, China's main exports are chai and porcelain – bulk goods more easily transported by sea than by land. A single vessel can carry as much porcelain as a caravan, with a better chance of delivering its cargo undamaged.'

'You're saying there's a sea route between China and the West?'

'From the Chinese port of Canton, cargoes are sent by stages as far as India, Persia and Egypt. Perhaps further. That far west my speculations give way to your certain knowledge.'

'The sea route doesn't reach Constantinople.'

'But if it goes as far as Persia,' Hero said, 'perhaps we might return along it.'

'Let's concentrate on our immediate goal,' Vallon said in French. 'Do we employ these guides on such stiff terms?'

'I say we must. Master Cosmas used Sogdian guides to escort him to Samarkand and spoke highly of their integrity.'

Vallon faced the cousins. 'I'll consider what you've told us and make a decision soon.'

'Don't delay. Even if we left tomorrow, we would be crossing the Taklamakan at the height of summer, and we wouldn't reach China until midwinter.'

A trumpet blew outside the caravanserai and Vallon heard heated voices. He strode onto the balcony as the gate swung open to admit a Karakhanid column led by the officer who'd intercepted the expedition outside Bukhara.

'This doesn't look like a courtesy call,' Josselin said.

Heralded by two trumpeters, the commander halted under the *iwan* and looked up at Vallon, tapping a sealed document against his wrist. 'I carry a summons commanding you to appear before the chief justice.'

'On what charge?'

'The court is convened. Your presence is demanded forthwith.' The commander turned his horse. 'I'll be waiting outside.'

Vallon watched the cavalry trot back through the gates. 'Does anyone know what this is about?'

'Some of the troopers must have been involved in an affray,' said Josselin. 'Or taken liberties with a woman.'

'It's more serious than that,' Wayland said.

Vallon looked at him.

'Two nights ago I rescued Zuleyka.'

Vallon boggled. 'You did *what*?'

'I entered her owner's house at night and took her from the harem. Nobody was hurt.'

The blood drained from Vallon's face. 'You broke into a man's house at night and made off with his property? My God, do you realise the seriousness of your crime? It could sabotage the entire enterprise, jeopardise our lives. And for what?' Spittle flew from his mouth. 'A slave girl, a dancing whore ...' He lunged at Wayland.

348

Hero threw himself between them. 'Now isn't the time. We're expected in court.'

Vallon backed off, ugly with rage. 'I thought I could forgive you anything, but not this. Not this.' Sick with anger, he allowed his servant to lead him away and smarten him up for the hearing.

On descending to the courtyard, he ordered Otia and Josselin to remain behind and put the troopers on maximum alert. 'Don't admit any soldiers without my orders. Hero, I need you with me. As for you,' he said to Wayland. 'You'll join me to answer the charges.'

'I'm coming too,' Hauk said.

'The affair doesn't concern you.'

'Yes, it does. The Karakhanids won't make any distinction between your force and mine.'

Vallon didn't speak again until they entered the Registan, a huge ceremonial square that stretched away empty except for a few soldiers scattered around its margins. On the far side, erected on an artificial mountain, stood the Ark, a brutal walled complex housing the citadel, palace, treasury, barracks, court of law and prison.

'You must have had accomplices,' Vallon said to Wayland.

'I acted alone.'

'Don't lie. I smell Lucas in this stinking mess, and you probably enlisted help from your Turkmen friends. I'll root them out, believe me.'

'It's my responsibility alone. If the court decides against us, I'll admit my part and pay the price.'

'Yes, you will. If I have to see you swing in order to save my mission, then so be it.'

They were in the middle of the Registan, the entrance to the Ark a dark slot in the blinding sunlight.

'Suppose I'd asked you to take action to save Zuleyka?' Wayland said.

Vallon ground his jaws. 'I would have negotiated for her

release. Reluctantly, but I would have done it. You must have known I would, so why didn't you come to me?'

'Because your intervention would have been fruitless. The merchant who bought Zuleyka is the same man who bid for Lucas, the man who set one of his thugs on Hero with a knife.'

'I would have appealed to the trade secretary.'

'And if he'd refused to take our side?'

Vallon didn't answer.

'I understand the Turkmen better than you do,' Wayland said. 'I've lived with them for nine years and know that the glue binding them together is allegiance to a strong leader. You're our commander, yet you ignored the first slight—'

'The loss of the gypsy girl wasn't a slight. It was a relief.'

'I'm not talking about Zuleyka. Bandits snatched Lucas and sold him in Bukhara without you lifting a finger to save him. If Aiken hadn't spotted him, if Hero hadn't bought him, he would have faded from your memory by now.'

Vallon set his face at the approaching arch.

'Hero asked the secretary if one of our troopers had been consigned to the slave market. He denied any knowledge and you didn't press the issue. Scores of Bukharans must know that Lucas was one of your soldiers and that you did nothing to claim him. The message that brigands can take any one of us without fear of reprisal will outrun us.'

'Wayland makes a fair point,' Hero said.

'Who asked your opinion?' Vallon snapped.

'Another thing,' Wayland said. 'I bought Zuleyka on the Caspian coast. Legally she's mine.'

'I've yet to see your money.'

'In which case, the gypsy maiden remains your property. Consider that.'

Vallon glanced at Wayland and as quickly looked away. 'One thing's for certain. That girl's no maiden.'

The Ark's massive inward-sloping walls discouraged further speech. They ascended a ramp and passed through a huge portal bastioned on each side with towers connected by walkways. Beyond it a long passage bored towards a sunlit court. The walls amplified the clopping hooves. Chains and manacles lay coiled in cell-like recesses on each side.

They emerged onto a terrace of dazzling white marble and the Bukharan commander led his charges on a diagonal to one of the façades fronting the courtyard. Guards relieved Vallon of his sword.

'I want a receipt.'

The commander began to demur. Vallon spoke through his teeth. 'I represent His Imperial Majesty Alexius Comnenus. Give me a receipt.'

A scribe hastily summoned penned the document and then the commander hurried Vallon and his co-defendants into the court. The vaulted chamber must have been thirty yards long and as many feet high. At the far end, on a throne behind a rank of guards, sat the Kazi Kalan or chief justice, holding in his lap an axe of office larger and more splendid than the one the trade secretary had carried. Vallon marched towards him and didn't halt until the guards blocked his progress with a wall of pikes. Vallon glared at the justice – a glandular man with a beard cut like an axe and sad fish-like eyes above sacs the colour of plums. He sat half-sideways swathed in a white silk gown voluminous enough to make a caique's sail, its folds so artfully hung that it must have taken a team of dressers half a morning to arrange.

To the right of the chief justice and his legal team stood Yusuf the trade secretary, looking uncomfortable. To the left a knot of scowling men surrounded the plaintiff, a tall cadaverous figure whose hennaed beard bore an unfortunate resemblance to pubic hair. Vallon loathed him at first sight.

He pointed at him. 'Is this the thief? Is this the rogue?'

The prosecuting team twitched in surprise. One of them, with a face like the crack of doom, stepped forward. 'Sa'id al-Qushair is the plaintiff, the gentleman who has brought serious charges against you. The men attending him are his witnesses.'

'What charges?'

'Trespass, assault, theft and other gross violations.'

Vallon snorted. 'Completely baseless.'

'That is for this court to establish.'

For the rest of the morning, the prosecutor laid out the case against Vallon, calling one witness after the other. All agreed that two days ago, in the early hours, three armed men – soldiers under Vallon's command – had entered the plaintiff's residence by stealth, breaking into the harem quarters and injuring one of the plaintiff's senior wives before carrying away by force a young slave woman recently acquired by the plaintiff. The men of the household had given pursuit, but the kidnappers had escaped after killing one of the plaintiff's horses. A savage hound had been involved, too.

Vallon stood tapping his empty scabbard while the evidence mounted up, occasionally darting evil looks at the plaintiff, who responded with appeals to God or mock lunges at Vallon.

The last witness stood down and the prosecutor turned to Vallon.

'Those are the charges. Do you deny them?'

'I deny them all. My men didn't steal Zuleyka. How could I steal my own property?' Vallon pointed at Hauk. 'I purchased the girl from this gentleman two months ago on the west coast of the Caspian Sea. Ask him.'

They did, and Hauk established that he had indeed sold Zuleyka to Vallon.

The chief justice summoned his legal team and there followed a lengthy conference concerning laws criminal and civil, tort, points of jurisprudence and nomology as they bore on the case of slaves who escaped from one owner only to find themselves under another's bondage – citing precedents going back to the time of Muhammad.

By the time the group separated – like spiders having sucked the life from a fly, Vallon thought – the shadows had shifted a long way round the chamber. By then he'd decided that the chief justice wasn't a healthy man. He looked as if he wanted nothing more than to lie down. A servant fanned him with osprey feathers.

The prosecutor approached Vallon. 'While no one doubts your claim that you bought the slave, the fact that you lost her several weeks ago is a significant factor. The plaintiff bought her in good faith. He had no idea that the girl had once been your property.'

'He does now and I have no intention of relinquishing my title. I note that you refer to the girl not as his slave, but as "that which his right hand owns". If he wants to contest my title, let him do it with his right hand at a time and place of his choosing.'

The prosecutor thumped his staff. 'General, this is a court of law and won't be mocked.'

Vallon pointed. 'If I stole that jewel in your hat and sold it to a merchant who then sold it to a third party, who would be the rightful owner?'

'Me of course.'

'Precisely.'

'But that doesn't mean I would be entitled to take it back by force. I would have sought redress in law, knowing that . . .' a bow to the chief justice '. . . it would be administered impartially.'

'I wish to question His Eminence the Trade Secretary.'

Yusuf stepped forward in a guarded manner.

Vallon went straight for the throat. 'The day we arrived at Bukhara, I informed you that one of my men, together with a slave girl, had been carried off by sand dwellers and might at that very moment be languishing in the slave market. I beseeched you to enquire after them and restore them to their rightful place.'

'I have a vague memory of your request. I don't recall you mentioning a slave girl.'

'Did you or didn't you follow up my request?'

'I did, with no success.'

Vallon smiled at the audience. 'You couldn't have been trying very hard. You only had to despatch an underling to the slave dormitory to find that my trooper was being held there pending his sale in a public auction.'

'General—'

Vallon's voice rose. 'It took my men two days – two days – to track down my trooper in the very act of being sold off in full view of the populace.' Vallon hoisted Hero's arm. 'The man who found him – this gentleman here – was obliged to pay the sum of seventy solidi to restore one of my own soldiers to my ranks. And who was the bidder who pushed the price up to such a ridiculous level?' Vallon flung out a hand. 'Him. The so-called plaintiff, the same man who only the day before had illegally deprived me of my mistress. Not content with stealing one item of my property, he wanted to steal two.'

'General—'

'Let me make clear how heinous this man's crimes are. He went to desperate lengths to enslave a man he knew full well was a trooper in my command, a soldier pledged to serve your ally, His Imperial Majesty Alexius Comnenus. As I understand Islamic law, taking slaves in war is a right sanctioned by God. Is Bukhara at war with Constantinople? Shall I warn my men to guard against imminent attack?'

'General, I must protest—'

'I haven't finished. And this only two days after stealing my mistress. Yes, my noble friends. My mistress. Unlike the plaintiff, who apparently herds women as a peasant farms goats, Zuleyka is the only love of my life. My heart broke in two the day those sand devils ripped her from my side.' Vallon kissed his hands and cupped them to heaven. 'I give thanks to your Divine Glory that in your infinite favour you restored my beloved.'

The prosecutor turned a sickly look on the chief justice. That august official beckoned the lawyers with a wave of his axe. When they'd finished their deliberations, the prosecutor addressed Vallon.

'His Excellency concedes that the case has some complicating features and adjourns it for one week until certain facts can be

354

established and case law examined. Until then, you and your men are restricted to barracks and you will hand over the slave girl to this court.'

Vallon glanced at Wayland. 'Do you have her?'

'Yes.'

Vallon drew breath. 'Having suffered heartbreak before being reunited with my beloved, I won't part with her again. Never!' He struck his empty scabbard. 'You'll have to tear her from across my dead body.'

Very clearly in the shocked silence, the chief justice's stomach rumbled.

'Keep going,' Hero murmured.

Vallon advanced a step. 'As for confining my men to barracks, I'll comply until we leave – in three days' time.'

'General, the chief justice has ruled that you remain in Bukhara until the next hearing.'

'In three days' time, I'll lead my men out of Bukhara, fulfilling the trust placed on me by my imperial master. I can't believe you'll oppose my departure with force just to satisfy the vanity and venality of that thieving scoundrel.'

The chief justice sagged; the trade secretary scuffed a palm over his mouth and spoke to the prosecutor. The prosecutor led the plaintiff around the chamber, yanking his elbow and hissing into his ear. Learning that the trial was not going his way, the man gave vent to awful tantrums – not at all the behaviour to endear himself to the learned advocates. The prosecutor returned him weeping and tearing his beard to his friends before approaching Vallon with a pasted-on smile.

'We can settle the dispute.'

'Dispute? A moment ago it was a serious crime.'

'General, don't throw away your advantage. Offer the plaintiff money by way of restitution.'

'Pay the rogue for my own property?'

'It's the only way to end the case quickly.'

'If I pay the thief, you'll let my expedition leave?'

'Yes. The sooner the better.'

Vallon put on a mulish look. 'How much?'

'Sixty solidi for the girl, twenty for the horse, ten for the assault. Call it a round hundred.'

'Ridiculous! What about recompense for the wrongs that wretch has done me? If he's defiled my mistress, how much compensation does that entitle me to? There isn't enough gold in Bukhara to outweigh the insult.'

The trade secretary intervened. 'You want to leave. We want you gone. It's a small price to pay.'

Vallon looked at the roof, now dimming in evening light. 'Out of my duty to the emperor and for the sake of my men, I concede.' He snapped a finger at Hero. 'Pay the devil.'

Before whirling on his heel, Vallon thanked the chief justice. 'Your Excellency, I withdraw any aspersions I might have cast on Bukharan justice. You have fulfilled the function of a judge in a manner that sets you on a pinnacle as an example of impartiality, justice and kindness to the people of God the Exalted.'

'That's enough,' the prosecutor snarled.

The trade secretary caught up with Vallon at the door. 'In the unlikely event that you survive your journey to China, I advise you not to return by way of Bukhara. You'll find the gates closed against you.'

Hero managed to contain his laughter until they were in the Registan. 'I didn't know you had so many words in you. You would have been a match for Cicero.'

Vallon didn't laugh. He directed a venomous glare at Wayland. 'We escaped by the skin of our teeth. More than once you've told me that you're not subject to my command. Very well. Since you don't feel loyalty to me, don't expect me to offer you my protection. You may as well leave, taking your slut with you.'

He raked spurs down his horse's flanks.

'You don't mean that,' Hero called. 'Hey, stop.'

Vallon kept going.

XXVII

Word of Wayland's raid and Vallon's courtroom theatrics spread through the squadron, producing much merriment. Lucas's comrades greeted him with a kind of dazed admiration and told him that he was the most expensive trooper in the history of the Byzantine army. They were pleased to have Zuleyka back, too. What particularly tickled them was that this was the third time she'd been delivered from bondage. It reinforced their suspicions that she possessed uncanny powers and made them keep a respectful distance. Besides, they believed that Wayland had laid claim to the girl – or perhaps, said some, it was the other way round.

The trial had another outcome. Fearing retaliation by the vengeful plaintiff or the smarting Bukharan high-ups, Hauk decided to postpone his journey back to the Caspian and throw his lot in with Vallon for one more stage. His men would accompany the expedition as far as Samarkand, where they'd add to their trade stuffs before returning to the ships by a route that avoided Bukhara.

With only three days to make ready the caravan, the men worked night and day laying in stores. Many of the troopers' mounts and pack animals were used up and had to be traded in against fresh stock. Here the Sogdians demonstrated their worth. Shennu – Vallon had dropped the 'An', a Chinese surname meaning 'from Bukhara' – accompanied the general to a horse fair in the Registan.

'They're ugly brutes,' Wulfstan said, surveying the shaggy, mallet-headed, crested-mane, mouse-coloured beasts. 'I've drowned better-looking dogs.'

'They're bred for desert travel,' Shennu said. 'Wild tarpans crossed with Turkmen stock. They'll survive for weeks in conditions that would kill your Greek horses in days. Their hooves are so hard they don't even need shoeing.'

Vallon eyed the horses. 'Even so, I don't intend to ride into Kaifeng with my spurs dragging in the dust.'

Shennu sized him up. 'If you have deep pockets, you can buy the finest steeds on earth right now, right here.'

'Show me.'

Shennu led Vallon's party to a corral ringed by a more affluent class of buyer. Wulfstan whistled when he saw the horses. Mainly grey or bay in colour, they matched Byzantine cavalry mounts in size and, but for a rather large head and very straight forelegs, they were splendidly proportioned, with eyes radiating spirit and intelligence.

'Ferghana horses,' Shennu said. The Chinese believe they are half-dragon, born in water and capable of carrying their riders to heaven. They're reserved for the aristocracy.'

Vallon pointed at a sweating gelding. 'How much will that one fetch?'

'You have a good eye for horses.'

'So I should. I'm a cavalryman.'

'It won't come cheap.'

'Pay whatever it takes.'

'That might be more than you bargained for, but if you bring the horse to Kaifeng in sound condition, you'll sell it for many times the price you pay today.'

Vallon folded his arms over his chest while a groom put the Ferghana through its paces. Hands shot up, registering bids. Shennu didn't make any gesture that went beyond his eyebrows.

'Are we in the bidding?' Vallon demanded.

'Of course. The agent for a rich dealer is driving the price up.'

Vallon wiped his palms on his thighs. 'Match him.'

Shennu stood calm while the other bidders shouted and waved their hands. Finally the crowd fell quiet and the auctioneer swung his head left and right before, like a pendulum coming to rest, he fixed his eyes on Vallon.

'The horse is yours,' Shennu said. 'Congratulations.'

'How much?'

'Forty-seven solidi.'

'Christ,' Vallon said.

'It's not as much as we paid for Lucas,' Aiken pointed out.

At midnight before the dawn departure, everyone in the cara-vanserai was up, saddling horses, greasing cart axles, attending to the scores of tasks required to get the caravan underway. One hundred and seventy-four Bactrian camels sat couched in the courtyard, submitting with haughty indifference while twenty-nine native handlers, including women and children, lashed loads onto them. Each camel could carry forty pounds more than a horse and could travel twice as far at half the pace on quarter as much water.

Shennu came over to Vallon. 'We're ready.'

It was still dark, the storks' nests crowning the ribat's towers ragged silhouettes against the greying stars. Vallon mounted his heavenly horse, rode to the gate and stood in his stirrups.

'Men, we're on our way to China. Stay faithful to our mission and to each other and you can look forward to returning home laden with riches and honours.'

His troops cheered. Vallon gestured to the gatekeepers to open up. 'And God save us,' he said, passing through.

The camels travelled in strings up to ten strong and the last of them were still pacing out of the city when Vallon heard the first call to prayer rising faint behind them on the plain.

Josselin caught up. 'It looks like three Turkmen have deserted.'

'I expected to lose more.'

'After a week's whoring and feasting, the men have forgotten the misery of desert travel. They're excited to be riding the Silk Road.'

Vallon grunted. 'They won't be so eager in a month's time.' He glanced back down the column. 'Is Master Wayland still with us?'

'He is, sir, riding in the rear with the gypsy girl. Do you want to send a message?'

Vallon hadn't exchanged a word with the Englishman since the trial. Working in his quarters late at night, he'd often looked up at the sound of approaching footsteps, hoping it was Wayland come

359

to make peace. He never did. Vallon shortened rein and headed for the rising sun. 'No.'

A week later the expedition camped five miles outside Samarkand. After the dramas in Bukhara, Vallon had no intention of letting his men inside another city so soon. Hauk entered the general's tent after supper and sat for some time in silence, nursing a beaker of wine.

'This really is our last meeting,' he said at last. 'A part of me wishes I was going with you, but my men are homesick. It's been nearly two years since they left their hearths.'

'Do you have a family?'

'My foes killed them.'

'I have a wife and two daughters in Constantinople.'

'I'll pray for your safe return. Farewell.'

Vallon looked up when the Viking was at the door. 'Farewell to you, Hauk Eiriksson.'

From Samarkand they travelled east by way of the Ferghana Valley, sweating in humid heat. They halted for two days at Osh to re-provision and then climbed through an outlier of the Pamirs, passing fields where horse-breeding nomads had taken to cultivating lucerne for their herds. The path steepened and narrowed. Four days' climbing brought the caravan gasping in the thin air to a rocky pass strewn with rags of snow and littered with the bones of animals and men who'd gambled on a fair-weather crossing and paid with their lives.

The path switchbacked over the ranges, gradually descending, at one point squeezing through a marble gorge so narrow that the camels' loads brushed the sides of walls polished smooth as silk by the traffic of centuries.

Seven days after leaving Osh, Vallon looked out from the last pass across the rust-coloured wastes of the Taklamakan, the desert that had swallowed the previous expedition. Shennu told him that its name meant 'you go in, but you don't come out'.

A trooper shouted and Vallon turned and spotted horsemen rising over the shoulder. They were too few to be a threat and were riding in a way that told him they were fleeing rather than following.

'It's Hauk and his men,' Wulfstan said.

Vallon counted twenty-eight, eight fewer than the number who'd gone their own way at Samarkand.

The Viking leader rode up, his silk suit torn and stained with dried blood.

'What happened?' Vallon said.

'An argument over a trinket whose value I wouldn't set at five dirhams turned into a battle.'

'Are they pursuing you?'

Hauk spat. 'Not unless they want more of the same. For every man I've lost, those bastards lost three.'

'What are you going to do?'

'It seems that fate conspires to prevent me returning home,' Hauk said. He peered into the dust-filtered wastes of the vast in-between. 'How far is it to China?'

'At least four months to the border, probably another two to the capital.'

'Hero told me there's a sea route from China to the western seas.'

'I wouldn't stake my life on its existence.'

Hauk glanced back. 'And I wouldn't hazard it returning through Samarkand and Bukhara.'

Three of his men were wounded, two seriously. One had taken an arrow through his lungs and died within the day. The other casualty was Rorik, Hauk's giant lieutenant. Hero examined him and decided there was nothing he could do to save him. A soldier had rammed a spear into the back of his thigh, auguring the barbed blade and ripping out a hole large enough to accommodate a child's fist.

Pus oozed from the blackened and fly-blown flesh. Hero shook his head at Aiken standing at a distance with one hand over his nose to ward off the stench.

'Gangrene.'

'I'm not done for yet,' Rorik said. 'The memory of my attacker's eyes when I popped them out of his head will keep me going.'

Each day for the next six days Hero cleaned and dressed the wound, astonished that someone so corrupted by death wouldn't yield to its embrace. By the time the expedition approached Yarkand, he almost wished that the Viking would die. Rorik's foul rantings offended almost as much as his rotting ham.

The next day, certain it must be Rorik's last, Hero went through the motions of bathing the wound when it seemed to quiver like a diabolical hatchling. He threw himself back in disgust as Rorik's thigh ruptured, expelling a mess of rotting flesh and a shard of iron. A trickle of clean blood followed.

Rorik opened one bloodshot eye. Already it looked less crazed.

'You have no right to be alive,' Hero said.

'Yes, I have. The coward attacked me when I wasn't looking.'

At Kashgar Shennu hired new camels and drivers. Here the Silk Road divided, one branch winding north of the desert under the Tian Shan Mountains, the other skirting the southern rim within sight of the Kun Lun range. A hundred rivers flowed into the Taklamakan and none flowed out. Shennu told Vallon that in the middle of the desert lay cities buried under sand, the mummified corpses of their fair-haired citizens dead a thousand years.

They took the southern route. The July sun, dull with the ash of its own burning, bored down, making travel by day intolerable. Each evening the caravan master waited until shadows overtook the lingering blue of the desert sky before giving the signal to depart. The handlers climbed to their feet, collected their hobbled beasts and drove them towards their loads where, by jerking on their head-ropes, they forced them to their knees. Then two men lifted the load onto the pack saddle and secured it with two loops and a peg. They struck the tents and stowed them on the beasts that carried the camp equipment, then string by string, the caravan moved off, the bells of the camels clonking and the drivers picking up a song that might last all night or stop for no reason, leaving only the *shush-shush* of the camels' pads brushing through sand.

At daybreak or soon after, the long procession would reach the next oasis or well and the drivers would lead the camels forward in lines to drink from troughs filled with water hauled up in caulked wicker baskets. Then they would drive the camels out to forage on the spiky vegetation and the camp would fall into fitful sleep until the sun sank to the western horizon. So it continued, day after day, night after night, week after week.

Riding half asleep at night through the desert, Vallon sometimes imagined that he was treading a path above the earth, the stars lying awash beneath him. Other nights the moon-blanched sands closed in until he was travelling down a lane bounded by high hedges and overhanging trees. His eyes focused on some destination that never arrived, drifting further and further into unconsciousness until a sudden jolt jerked him back to a reality almost as outlandish as his dreams.

One night Vallon and Aiken fell in with Hero and the two Sogdians. 'Shennu says we should reach Khotan within a week,' Hero said.

'The day we met I said that a journey was just a tiresome passage between one place and another. I wasn't wrong.'

Hero laughed. 'Admit it. A part of you is beginning to believe that we'll really reach China.'

Vallon turned to Shennu. 'Tell us more about its people.'

'They are a contradictory race. Deeply conservative, revering their ancestors and traditions, yet inventive beyond belief. They believe their emperor is appointed by the Mandate of Heaven. At the same time they consider him mortal and therefore fallible, which gives his subjects the right to overthrow him if disaster strikes the empire. That's why, though they value harmony, the empire has suffered so many upheavals. The real power lies with the scholar officials, civil servants selected by examination. In theory, competition is open to all and promotion is by merit.

In practice, most candidates and top officials are the sons of aristocrats.'

'What position do the military occupy?'

'The ruling class regard them as a necessary evil. To be frank, they despise them. Many of the commanders are foreigners and the rank and file are largely drawn from the dispossessed and criminals. The imperial circle prefers to pay off enemies rather than confront them. China is like a large honey pot surrounded by swarms of flies. The Chinese can't swat every fly, so they drip honey into the mouths of the flies' masters and hope that will satisfy them. Of course having tasted drips of honey, the flies want to drink deep from the source.'

'Who are these flies?' Vallon said.

'Horse nomads. Tanguts in the west, Khitans to the north. To placate them, the emperor lavishes wealth on them at the expense of his subjects.'

Vallon gave Hero a jaundiced smile. 'That sounds familiar.'

They rode on in silence for a while. 'Will you teach us Chinese?' Aiken asked.

'An excellent idea,' said Hero.

'It's a difficult language,' Shennu said. 'The Western tongue isn't shaped to speak it.'

Vallon indicated the night stretching ahead. 'It's not as if we lack leisure to learn. Let's fill these long nights in a practical pursuit.'

'Very well,' Shennu said. He pointed at Vallon's horse. '*Ma*.'

'*Ma*.'

'No. *Ma*.'

'That's what I said.'

'You said *ma*, which means "mother". Such a mistake could cast you into a most embarrassing situation. Suppose you asked a Chinese nobleman if you could mount his mother?'

Aiken suppressed a laugh. '*Ma*.'

'Very good,' said Shennu.

'*Ma*,' Vallon repeated.

'Now you pronounce the word for "linen". In a different context, the same pronunciation would mean "scold".'

'What a ridiculous language,' said Vallon. '*Ma*.'

'Like this,' Shennu said, stretching his mouth. '*Ma*. Do you hear the difference?'

'*Ma*,' Vallon and Hero said.

Wayland cantered past with Zuleyka, the dog loping behind. Hero hailed him. 'We're learning Chinese. Will you join our class?'

Wayland answered without turning. 'Thank you. I won't need Chinese.'

Hero watched him ride away. 'Did you hear that? Unless you and Wayland mend your differences, he's going to leave us.'

Aiken and Shennu exchanged glances and went on.

Vallon reined in. 'It's not for me to make the first move. If Wayland apologises for his irresponsible actions, I'll gladly welcome him back into my heart.'

'I've talked to him. He doesn't think he did anything wrong.'

Vallon's jaws worked.

'You're angry because he's taken up with the gypsy girl.'

Vallon erupted. 'He's married to a woman who's as dear to me as my own daughters. It offends me to the core to see him riding around with that strumpet.'

'I don't think they ... I don't think ... Even if they did ... Syth has made a hole in Wayland's heart large enough for any other woman to pass through.'

'That's what hurts. I never thought Wayland would so much as look at another woman.' Vallon wrapped his reins around his hands. 'I thought that Wayland and Syth had discovered what I could never find – true love.'

'But you and Caitlin love each other. I know that sometimes you strike sparks off each other, but that's what happens when iron and flame collide.'

Vallon didn't answer for some time. 'My wife is unfaithful.'

'Oh no, sir. Don't say that.'

'For the last nine years I've spent one season in four at home. Caitlin's a passionate woman, I think you'll agree. I can hardly blame her if she seeks solace in the arms of another man.'

'Are you sure? Do you have proof?'

'She wears jewellery too expensive to have been paid for out of my shallow purse. Once, soon after I returned from the frontier without warning, a Byzantine lord's servant arrived at the house with a letter for my lady. She said the message came from the man's wife, a woman she claimed to have befriended. A few weeks later we met the lady outside St Sophia. She didn't so much as glance at Caitlin. They were complete strangers to each other.'

Two stages later they reached an oasis surrounded by a forest of tamarisks, the trees growing out of sand cones, their spindly branches and grey leaves lashing in a roasting wind. At the evening reveille, Josselin called a trooper's name and received no response. His squad mates hadn't seen him since making camp. He wouldn't have deserted in such a hostile place, and foul play was unlikely. He must have wandered away from the oasis and lost his way. The search parties realised how easy that was when they set out to look for him. The tamarisks sprouted from the sand at ten- to twenty-yard intervals. Turn in any direction and the view was identical. Walk the wrong way for a few hundred yards and you lost all bearings. Vallon ordered a bonfire to be lit and left behind a squad to trumpet their whereabouts. In the morning the trooper still hadn't returned and Wayland set out to find his trail. Too many people and animals had criss-crossed the oasis for his dog to pick up the trooper's scent. Wayland rode north calling out until he reached the end of the tamarisks and climbed a huge wave of sand and looked over an ocean of red dunes overlapping each other like shields. He guessed that the trooper must have perished within half a mile of the camp.

Shennu had warned them of the black wind that could strike from nowhere. It attacked next day while the men lay scratching and sleepless in the noonday heat. The camels began to bellow and buried their muzzles in the sand. A few curs that followed the caravan whimpered and fled for shelter. The drivers shouted and ran about tightening saddle-straps and double-pegging tent ropes.

Emerging from his tent, Vallon saw that the sky had taken on a glassy look. A dirty yellow stain advanced from the east, thickening into a grey column, its spinning base spawning dust devils that waltzed through the tamarisks with a scuttling noise. The storm wobbled closer and semi-darkness obscured the sky.

'Take shelter,' Shennu cried. 'Hurry!'

Vallon ran for the lee of a low dune.

'Cover your head!' Shennu shouted.

Face down, head mantled, Vallon heard the rustling and clacking increase to a hungry roar and then a shriek as the storm hit, driving a wave of sand and gravel across the ground. Stones stung Vallon's hands. Dust forced its way into his mouth and under his eyelids. Peeping from under his cape he glimpsed trees, dunes and tents looming like spectres in the howling blackout. He held his breath and his lungs were close to bursting when his ears popped and silence fell. He thought he must have lost his hearing. Shennu shook him and he looked out from under his cape at a clearing sky. Spitting grit from his mouth he tottered to his feet to see the sandstorm spinning away to the west.

Mounds of sand heaved up, reconstituting themselves as men, slapping at their clothes and blinking around through dust-reddened eyes. The tents that had stood up to the storm sagged under the weight of driven sand. The caravan master gave an order and his men salvaged the tents and gathered the animals. Fine dust had found its way into the most tightly sealed containers. The caravan moved on as the sun sank into a bed of clouds, leaving the western horizon aflame, the red fading into violet dotted with a few smoky clouds.

The caravan made the last two stages to Khotan by day, advancing under a shining veil of dust kicked up by the animals. On the evening before they reached the oasis town, Aiken was in Vallon's tent reciting Virgil's *Aeneid*. They had begun reading poetry to help while away the night marches, and Vallon found the ritual soothing. Aiken had reached a passage concerning the tragedy of Dido, queen of the Phoenicians.

'"It was night, and weary bodies throughout the land were reaping the harvest of peaceful sleep. Forests and harsh seas lay at rest as the circling stars glided in their midnight course. The whole landscape was soundless – flocks and herds and painted birds, the ones that live far and wide on the glimmering lake-waters, and those that dwell in the wilds of prickly brambles – all laid to rest beneath the silent night.

'"But not so the Phoenician queen. Her wretched spirit could not relax into sleep . . ."'

Vallon opened his eyes to find his servant hovering at the entrance.

'Sorry to disturb you, sir. That young trooper Lucas is outside. He wishes to speak to you.'

'What about?'

'A personal matter, it would seem. He appears rather agitated.'

'I'll leave you,' said Aiken, making to get up.

Vallon waved him back into his seat. Troopers didn't speak to their commanding officer in his personal quarters unless summoned. Channels and procedures existed to allow them to bring their concerns to their superiors' attention.

'If, God forbid, Lucas is in more trouble, tell him to take his problems to his squad leader. I'm surprised you didn't point him in that direction yourself.'

'Yes, sir. I wouldn't have intruded unless . . . Very good, sir. I'll send him away.'

Aiken waited for the man to leave. 'I meant to tell you. Lucas apologised for his boorish behaviour. He sounded sincere.'

'I'm glad to hear it.'

'I still don't understand why he took against me so violently.'

Vallon wasn't interested in Lucas. He sank back. 'Read that last bit again.'

XXVIII

Pomegranate groves and fields of cotton surrounded Khotan, a walled town on the eastern frontier of the Karakhanid empire. It was an important Silk Road trading centre, famed for the quality of its silks and for the green and white jadestone gathered by prospectors in the two rivers that watered the oasis. After settling into the caravanserai, the expedition went into town – Hauk and his Vikings in search of precious nephrite jade, Aiken and Hero to visit an important madrasah. Cities didn't hold much allure for Wayland and he remained behind. He tended to agree with the Turkmen who said that men who built walls to protect themselves didn't realise that they were creating prisons.

Raucous cries at evening drew him into the courtyard. Hauk swayed past on horseback, drunk on wine.

'Feast your eyes on this,' he said in a slurred voice, holding out a chunk of pale mineral.

'It looks like a shiny lump of rock.'

Hauk took a long pull from a bottle and hiccupped. 'That's all you know.' He slapped the stone. 'It's white jade. Not any old white jade. It's mutton-fat jade. Only the Chinese emperor is allowed to wear it. Forget the carpets we had to leave behind in Samarkand.' He slapped the stone again, almost unseating himself. 'This, my friend, will make me rich if I don't make another purchase between here and China.'

'Let me take a look,' said Shennu, appearing out of the dusk. The Sogdian hefted the lump, held it against the light and rapped it with a pebble. Wayland knew what he was going to say before he said it.

'You've been cheated. It's serpentine from Afghanistan.'

'What!' Hauk bellowed. He snatched at the stone, toppled into the dust and staggered to his feet. 'Come on, men. We're going back to the bazaar. I'll cut the thieving bastard's liver out.'

Vallon blocked his path. 'Close the gates,' he ordered.

Hauk fumbled for his sword. 'Out of my way.'

Vallon stood his ground and one of Hauk's more sober lieutenants led the Viking struggling and swearing to his quarters. Wayland hadn't seen this side of Hauk before and it fed his forebodings. He returned to his cell and was meditating on this and other matters when someone tapped on the door.

'It's me. Wulfstan.'

Wayland let him in and fumbled a lamp alight. Wulfstan held what looked like a bolt of whitish cloth in his hands.

'You'll never guess what this is,' he said.

Wayland stroked the textile. It felt cold, heavy and inert. 'Some kind of coarse silk?'

'Salamander skin, born in fire and immune to flame.'

'Hauk showed me his jade. A fool's born every moment.'

'All right, it's not salamander skin. That was just the merchant's patter. Shennu says it's a textile spun from rock fibres. The Greeks call it asbestos, meaning "pure" or "unquenchable". Something like that. It's used to make royal burial shrouds.' Wulfstan picked up the lamp and held its flame to the fabric. The material didn't burn or melt or smoulder. When he took the flame away, it left only a sooty halo. Wulfstan brushed the lampblack away.

'You see? Flame doesn't harm it. The hotter the fire, the brighter the fabric.'

'Are you planning to wear it for your funeral?'

'Don't talk soft. I was thinking it might provide protection against Greek Fire. You know what a fickle friend that can be.'

Wayland suppressed a yawn. 'You made a better bargain than Hauk struck.'

Wulfstan stowed the material under one arm. 'I didn't call on you just to show my salamander skin. Hero told me that you mean to quit. That ain't no surprise. I've seen you moping ever since we left Bukhara.'

'Leave, not quit. I nearly went my own path at Kashgar, where a turning leads south to Afghanistan.'

'Don't take it. If the general's too proud to admit it, I ain't. We need you.'

'I suspect Hero put you up to this.'

'No, he didn't. It's the talk of the caravan.'

Wayland lay on his pallet after Wulfstan had left. He didn't latch the entrance and a breeze slapped the door against its hinges. Zuleyka appeared in the gap, her gown rippling against her body. She beckoned.

'Come away now. We must leave soon.'

Wayland jerked awake to find the doorway dark and empty.

Next day he explored Khotan. The Muslim Karakhanids had captured it less than a century before and were building mosques on the levelled foundations of Buddhist temples and monasteries. It was still a frontier town, though. Walking down one of the wider streets, Wayland gave way to a mob of Tibetans swinging along like pirates on shore leave – big, black-haired ruffians wearing boat-shaped felt boots and homespun red or black gowns hanging in pleats below the waist, baggy right sleeves dangling loose to leave unwashed arms and chests exposed. Crudely forged swords jostled at their hips and chunky coral and turquoise necklaces chinked against silver amulets containing charms certified by lamas. The Tibetans examined the blue-eyed stranger with unabashed curiosity and went on their way with earth-shaking tread.

In the next street he passed a depot where a Chinese overseer with hands tucked into the sleeves of his gown looked on while a gang of pigtailed menials in short black jackets and baggy trousers gathered at the ankles stacked loads for a caravan. Neither master nor workmen paid him a second glance.

Negotiating a bazaar, Wayland passed through the rancid butchers' quarter, fanning away flies when something glimpsed to his left swung him round. There on the pestilential counter, legs trussed and fledgling wings brailed, lay a young eagle.

'What on earth ... ?'

'You want to buy?'

'Where did you get it?'

The butcher pointed towards the Kun Lun range. 'Shepherds took it from its nest in the mountains.' He scooped it up. 'Good price.'

When he set it back down, it fell over before squatting right way up, propped on its elbows with its legs stuck out, head sunk on its balled-up feet. Wayland's lips curled. 'Why would anyone buy an eagle in that condition?'

'For soup.'

'You eat eagles?'

Like many citizens of Khotan, the vendor was afflicted by goitre. 'Oh yes, sir. Berkut meat makes men strong.'

Wayland exhaled a fluffing breath and studied the creature. It was close to death, its mouth agape, indifferent to the flies walking over its slitted eyes.

'What have you been feeding it on?'

'Bread.'

'Dear God.'

'Excuse me?'

Wayland stifled his anger. 'When did the shepherds take it?'

The butcher raised his shoulders. 'One week perhaps.'

'How long have you had it?'

'Fresh this morning.'

Wayland swung away. 'It will be dead before the day is out.'

'For you, one solidus.'

Wayland halted despite himself. The butcher cocked his head like a bird about to spear a worm.

'Nobody in their right mind would pay that much for carrion.'

'You belong to the Greek caravan. I hear you spend gold coins as if they were horn buttons.' The butcher held up a finger as if bestowing a benediction. 'One solidus.'

'To hell with you.'

'Not so fast, my friend. Let us talk. Let us bargain. We're gentlemen.'

Wayland stabbed a finger at the eagle. 'I'll give you a dirham just to save it from the cooking pot.'

The butcher clapped his hands at an attentive urchin. 'Chai for our honoured client. Or perhaps the gentleman would prefer wine. Please, sir. Step this way.'

Wayland entered the caravanserai cradling the sickly foundling, two live cockerels dangling around his neck. Lucas spotted him and hurried over.

'A young eagle, by heaven.'

'Find Hero and ask him for some eye balm.'

Wayland barged into his quarters and dumped the eagle on the ground. Even for a tenth of the asking price – cockerels included – the bird was worthless. What galled him was the knowledge that if the bird had been healthy, Sultan Suleyman's falconers would have paid as much as they would have laid out for a prize stallion. The berkut was the largest race of golden eagle, capable of killing gazelles, foxes and even wolves. Under Wayland's quizzing, the butcher had told him that no one in the Khotan oasis practised falconry.

Wayland's dog glanced at him, requesting permission to investigate the eaglet. It sniffed the soiled plumage, wrinkled its nose and backed off.

'I know,' Wayland said.

Lucas crashed in with Hero's potions and watched while Wayland swabbed the eagle's eyes.

'That doesn't look like a well bird,' he said.

'Cut one of the cockerel's throats and collect the blood. Fetch fresh water.'

Zuleyka entered. 'What are you doing?'

'Step out of my light. No, stay. I might need your help.'

'Here,' Lucas said, offering Wayland a bowl of warm blood.

'Grip her by the shoulders. Not too tight.'

Lucas clasped the eagle's wing butts. 'How do you know it's a "she"?'

'Because she is,' Wayland said.

He took from his bag of hawking furniture a thin gut tube and a horn funnel.

'Hold her beak open,' he told Zuleyka.

'She might bite me.'

'She's only a baby.'

Zuleyka prised the mouth apart. The eagle gave a pathetic mew and seemed to collapse from within.

'I think it's dead,' Lucas whispered.

Wayland inserted the tube above the eagle's pallid tongue, eased it down into its crop and fitted the funnel to the free end. He half-filled it with diluted blood, jiggled the tube and registered the level of the liquid sink.

'If you ask me, you're wasting your time,' Lucas said.

'You waste yours. I'll waste mine.'

Drop by drop Wayland emptied the funnel. He swayed back and scrubbed his brow with his forearm. 'Find a basket.'

Zuleyka left and the dog followed her.

Wayland slumped on a stool and looked at his purchase. The kindest thing would be to wring its neck.

'Anything else I can do?' Lucas said.

'No. Thank you for your assistance.'

'Call if you need me.'

'Yes,' Wayland said. 'There is something you can do. You can end this nonsense with Vallon.'

Lucas cramped up. 'I tried. I requested an audience a few nights ago and he wouldn't admit me.'

'You're not an ambassador seeking admission to a foreign court. You're his son. Just say the words or let me say them for you.'

'Aah,' Lucas groaned. 'It's not as easy as you think. Imagine yourself in Vallon's place. What sort of reception would you give to a son you gave up for dead ten years ago?'

They were strung on each other's stares when Zuleyka returned with a fleece-lined wicker basket. Wayland placed the eaglet in the cradle and levelled his gaze at Lucas.

'The eagle will be dead by dawn. Life is fleeting. We have only one chance to cast our shadows against the sun. The previous expedition was wiped out between here and the next oasis. When I'm gone, nobody else will know who you are.'

'You gone?'

Zuleyka stamped a foot. 'He tells you to go.'

She crouched before Wayland and took his hand.

Wayland snatched it away. 'I've told you. I'm not interested. I have a wife and children.'

Zuleyka rubbed her face against his hands. He jumped up.

'Get away from me.'

She flounced out, stopping at the door to crook two fingers at him in some kind of spell or malediction.

'Not you,' Wayland said to the dog.

It slunk after Zuleyka with a hang-dog look, leaving Wayland alone with the dying eagle.

During the night the fledgling produced a horrible squelching sound as it vented the noxious matter that had been clogging its gut. Wayland pushed up on one elbow and stared through the dark before sinking back. He'd already wasted too much time on the bird.

He woke by dawn, lit a lamp and stole over to the eagle. It lay in a heap, an inanimate bundle of flesh and feather. He steeled himself to handle the corpse.

At his touch the eaglet opened its eyes and blinked. *Kewp*, it said. It wobbled upright. *Kewp*, it repeated in a more insistent tone. *Kewp*.

Wayland ran to the door. The poplars surrounding the cara-vanserai were just beginning to brush the sky. 'Lucas!'

He was holding the eagle on his lap when Lucas burst in. Wayland smiled like a proud father. 'Baby wants her breakfast.'

Another feed of the nourishing liquor only sharpened its appetite and lent strength to its voice. 'Cut up a chicken breast. Chop it fine.'

By the time the sun had cleared the walls, the eagle had gorged and lay asleep on Wayland's lap with its crop distended to the size of an apple. His dog slunk in, looking guilty.

'Are you going to train her?' Lucas asked.

Wayland placed the eaglet in its cradle. 'I don't know. She's been taken too young. Now her cries tug at your heartstrings, but in a month her squalling will drive you mad. By then she won't be a helpless infant. She'll be full-grown and dangerous, with no respect for her handler or anyone else. I knew a Seljuk falconer who reared a goshawk from a ball of fluff. Six months later that hawk – a quarter of the size of a full-grown berkut – plucked out one of his eyes and laid his face open from brow to jaw.'

Lucas rubbed his hands. 'What are you going to call her?'

'I'm no good at names. Wait. What about Freya, the Norse goddess?'

'Freya sounds good.'

When Lucas left, Wayland studied the fledgling properly for the first time. He guessed she was about six weeks old, an infant with a gawky out-at-elbows look, her flight feathers still in blood and her head downy. But already she weighed more than any other bird of prey he'd trained. Her smoky hazel eyes, billhook beak and saffron feet armed with black talons hinted at her latent powers. Her hind claws were already as long and thick as his little finger. When fully grown, each extended foot would be wider than a hand's span and powerful enough to drive through a deer's skull.

He left Khotan with the eaglet travelling loose in a basket placed in front of his saddle. She wolfed down her rations and grew daily, metamorphosing from avian toad into Jove's winged avenger in the space of a fortnight. By then she was hard-penned, only a few traces of down on her head, her plumage an autumnal blend of greys, tans, cinnamon, plum brown and burnt ochre. Wayland had worried that her traumatic experiences would have left hunger traces on her flight feathers – thin lines marking arrested development and points of weakness. Instead, her feathers grew straight and sound. She began to exercise her wings and peer about with the curiosity of a youngster exploring the world and its wonders.

She'd outgrown her basket by then and he jessed her legs and carried her unleashed on his gloved fist. A morning of supporting her with his arm crooked left it so numb that he could hardly move it. At Keriya, the next oasis, he weighed the eagle on a corn merchant's balance. She tilted the scales at eleven catties, equivalent to fourteen English pounds – and she hadn't stopped growing. Wayland commissioned a carpenter to make a T-perch four feet high, its base footed in a leather socket stitched to his saddle.

He rode forth on the next stage with the eagle clutching her perch, wings spread in an eight-foot span, her eyes fastening on everything that flowed into her vision. The troopers liked to see her at the head of the column, imagining that she was the flesh-and-blood equivalent of the standards carried by their military forebears, the Roman legions of old.

One of the Sogdians added an intriguing twist. 'This isn't the first time the Roman eagle has travelled the Silk Road,' he told Wayland. 'Long ago a Roman army fought a battle with a race called the Parthians at Carrhae in Afghanistan. The Parthians defeated the legions and sold the survivors. Many of them were transported east, even as far as China, where they founded a colony that retained their language and customs for centuries. One of my ancestors encountered them on his first journey to China. They're only a memory now, but you can still find Roman armour on sale in bazaars.'

'How do you Sogdians preserve such long memories, Shennu?'

'From the day we can understand speech, our elders teach us our history. What happened here? Who can you trust in this oasis? Who to avoid? Which wells supply water fit only for camels and which wells provide water sweet enough for men? What time of day does the river freeze in the mountains, lowering the level and making it safe to cross? It's a father's duty to pass on such knowledge. I remember my grandfather telling me about the first Chinese traveller to reach Afghanistan. His name was Zhang Qian and he made the journey a thousand years ago, but to hear my grandfather tell the tale, you'd have thought the two of them travelled together. By the way, I'm Yexi. My cousin is riding with the general.'

Later that day the eagle launched into her first clumsy flight. Buoyed up by a gust of wind, she let go of her perch and flapped away south into sand country, feet dangling and scuffing the ground in an attempt to land. She hadn't learned how to stop. A hundred-foot-high dune blocked her path. She tried to clear it, ran out of strength and tumbled tail over beak not far below the top. Wayland jumped off his horse and climbed after her.

The eagle had scrabbled up to the crest and stood looking about as if she owned the wilderness. Wayland picked her up and laid his cheek against her head, breathing in her scent, wondering not for the first time why a creature with such a carnal appetite exhaled the odour of spring gorse.

'That's enough liberty for now,' he said. 'From now on you wear a leash and hood and only fly at my bidding.' He rested a while, the sweat on his forehead drying in a hot headwind that blew a yellow mist from the tops of the sandhills. To the south the haze that had hidden the Kun Lun range for weeks drew aside, exposing a panorama of icy peaks.

Lucas flogged up. 'I thought you'd lost her.'

'She has a long way to go before she finds independence. My task is to teach her to hunt before casting her loose.'

'You intend letting her go?'

Wayland didn't answer.

'What are you looking at?'

Wayland had stood, peering at a flock of vultures spiralling about half a mile to the south. One of them dropped out of the formation and fell on cupped wings. Another followed. Three more joined the carousel from different directions and more dots were converging.

Lucas followed his gaze. 'Probably a camel or wild ass.'

'A dead camel doesn't attract fifty vultures. That's a scene of slaughter.'

They laboured over four dunes before running down to a gravel terrace cut by an arid stream bed. Wayland followed the course, guided by the vortex of carrion birds and the occasional whiff of putrid flesh. Around the next bend twenty vultures trundled into clumsy flight.

'Christ,' Lucas said.

Twelve bloated and blackened bodies lay strewn over the stony bench on one side of the watercourse. Their murderers had decapitated some of them and the heads lay at hideous angles, glaucous eyes staring sightless at the sun and a droning fog of flies hovering over the carnage. Two wolves were feasting on the decomposing corpses. One of them fled when Wayland shouted. The other, riddled with mange, chopped its teeth at him and continued tugging at a baby clasped in the arms of its dead mother until Lucas ran at it with drawn sword. It abandoned its prey and crabbed humpbacked into the dunes.

Lucas smothered his nose against the stench. 'Who were they?'

Wayland squinted around. 'Tibetan traders or pilgrims to judge from their costume.'

'Who killed them?'

'Bandits. Perhaps the same gang who wiped out the last Greek expedition.'

'We'd better warn Vallon.'

'You go. I'll try to make sense of these tracks.'

Wayland quartered the ground, reading the clues. Lucas had dropped from sight when the dog came pattering up. 'Faithless hound,' Wayland said. He bent its head towards a faint impression. 'One member of the party escaped. Seek.'

With a yelp the dog ran down the stream bed, pausing to pick up scent and looking back at Wayland for encouragement.

'You're on the right track. Keep going,'

Quarter of a mile down the gulley the dog flung itself round and froze, its muzzle pointing towards a hole in the bank. A wolf's den. Wayland slid into the stream bed and squatted before the entrance.

379

'You can come out. The bandits have gone. I won't hurt you.'

Nothing stirred.

'I know you're in there. It's a lot cooler inside than out. I'm burning up. Put me out of my torment.'

The dog pranced around the hole, barking. Wayland called it off and slung a goatskin waterbottle through the entrance. 'You have to come out some time.'

He was holding the eagle on his left fist, his dog panting by his side when two hands gripped each side of the entrance and a dust-smothered head emerged. Wayland dragged the survivor clear and stood him upright. His eyes were deranged by shock and tears had carved channels through his dust mask.

'Let's get you back.'

A voice called and Wayland turned to see a squad of troopers crest the nearest dune. Lucas plunged down, lost his balance and tumbled the last thirty feet.

Wayland rolled his eyes. 'Do you always have to be so impetuous?'

Lucas shook his head and blinked. 'Who is he?'

'Take his other arm and we'll find out when we return to the caravan.'

A night under Hero's care restored the survivor. Washed, watered, fed and rested, he turned out to be a young Tibetan with features Greek sculptors would have loved to carve in marble. Raven-black hair hung down to his shoulders. His name was Yonden and he told his story in a ruined caravanserai while rats scuttled and chittered in the shadows.

At the age of sixteen, he'd entered a Buddhist monastery in the south of Tibet, within sight of a mountain range called the Himalayas. Two years before, an elderly monk had professed a wish to make a last pilgrimage to a shrine in a Buddhist cave complex called Dunyuang, on the northern branch of the Silk Road. The abbot had chosen Yonden to accompany the monk as his servant and secretary. They'd been two years on the journey, seeking alms and hospitality in return for prayers, horoscopes and medicines. When they reached Dunyuang, the monk told Yonden that he'd reached his last destination on earth and wouldn't be returning to Tibet. He gave himself up to prayer and fasting and within a week his spirit left him so peacefully that the closest observer couldn't have decided the moment when his soul slipped from his human shell into divine nothingness.

Shennu translated, conveying Yonden's conflicted emotions – his grief at his master's death, his awe at the manner in which the monk had sloughed off his mortal mantle, his resentment that the holy man had left him penniless to make the journey back to the Tibetan monastery.

'It was a test and I failed it,' Yonden said. 'Without my spiritual guardian, I fell into bad habits. I gambled and succumbed to temptations of the flesh.'

'Tell us more about them,' Wulfstan said, savaging a mutton shank. 'I'm partial to tales of sin and redemption.' He looked around the company. 'What?'

'Excuse me,' Vallon said. 'I have to discuss tomorrow's stage with the centurions.'

'I had nothing but the clothes on my back when I reached Keriya,' Yonden continued. 'Not even that. For my last meal I'd scraped the tallow off my boots and boiled it for soup. At the cheapest lodging I could find I met a party of Tibetan traders returning to the Chang Thang after exchanging yak tails and medicinal herbs for copper and iron. Three gold prospectors had joined them and offered to guide us. They led us with the sole intention of slaughtering every soul in a place where no one would see their crime.' Yonden put his hands together and bowed at Wayland. 'If this gentleman hadn't found me, their evil would have gone unnoticed on earth.'

Wulfstan prodded Shennu. 'I want to hear more about his sinning.'

'What will you do now?' Wayland asked.

'Thanks to you, I can return to my monastery and seek the true path.'

Wayland stood and pulled his gown over his shoulders. Even in summer, the Taklamakan nights were cold.

'Don't you want to hear the end of Yonden's story?' Hero said. 'It hasn't ended yet.'

Wayland made a hood for Freya out of antelope hide, stitching the seams together through their thickness, then soaking the leather and moulding it to shape on a wooden block he carved himself. The hood fitted well, shutting out alarming sights. Not that Freya was fearful of the world. She'd been wrenched from the wild so young that she regarded the strange environment into which she'd been plunged as natural. Unlike every other hawk that Wayland had trained, she didn't need manning to make her tame. After being scooped out of an eyrie, stuffed into a sack and displayed on a butcher's stall, there was little left to frighten her.

That made her the easiest bird Wayland had ever trained and the most dangerous. Long after she would have been driven away by her parents, she quivered her wings at Wayland and piped for food like a baby. At the same time she'd learned to guard her territory. This encompassed a narrow circle around her perch. If anyone but Wayland trespassed within a dozen feet, she puffed up, raised her hackles and dared the intruder to advance closer. No one did.

Another thing. She hated dogs, Wayland's included. At the sight of it, her plumage flattened like mail and then distended until she appeared twice her actual size. One day Wayland's hound strayed into her territory. Freya flew at him and raked his shoulder, hooking one hind talon under the skin. The dog would have killed her if Wayland hadn't grabbed its muzzle and ripped the talon out. From that day on, dog and eagle regarded each other with cautious hatred.

Having seen how dangerous Freya could be, Wayland shouldn't have let his guard slip. He was feeding her on a hare's hind leg, riding alongside Lucas and exchanging idle conversation, when he judged that the eagle had eaten enough and pulled the meat away.

He didn't see her foot flash out, didn't register anything until four talons locked on his right hand with a force that seemed to pump all the blood in his body through his head. The shock dashed Freya's food from his hand. The eagle, conditioned to think that her rations came directly from Wayland, paid no attention to the meat and tightened her grip.

He didn't panic or struggle. Hands manacled, eyes watering, he waited until the homicidal light in Freya's eyes dimmed and she relaxed her hold and stepped back onto his gauntlet. *Kewp*, she said, and scratched the underside of her neck with the delicacy of a dowager.

Lucas stared at him. 'Your face has gone as pale as clay.'

Wayland groaned and flexed his hand. Freya's talons hadn't even punctured flesh, but they'd left deep blue-black indentations and his hand was puffing up.

By evening it was swollen to twice its normal size and he was nursing it while he sat around a campfire, paying little attention to the conversation until Hero put a question to Shennu.

'On our journey to the northlands, we found a letter written by a man who called himself Prester John, ruler of a Christian kingdom somewhere in the East. Have you heard the legend?'

Shennu inhaled the smoke from a shrub he'd picked in the desert. 'I know the name, know the story and have heard of men who followed it to their deaths.'

'It doesn't exist, then.'

Shennu blew smoke at the stars. 'I can't say. There are strange realms hidden in the mountains to the south and west. Everyone has heard of Shambhala, a Buddhist paradise whose inhabitants live forever unless they leave their kingdom. My grandfather told me that the path to it is easy to follow at first, but the closer you approach, the more uncertain the way until at last you find yourself in an icy valley with no way forward and no possibility of returning.'

Vallon, silent until then, looked up. 'I told you ten years ago that Prester John's letter was a hoax. We've travelled further than almost any man who's lived and none of us has seen the unicorns and dragons and Cyclops the priest king describes.'

Shennu raised a hand for silence. 'The young lama has more to say.' The Sogdian listened, nodding and clarifying before translating.

'This is a story I've never heard before. Yonden says that many generations ago, a Christian hermit sought enlightenment in a Buddhist monastery deep within the Himalayas.'

'A Nestorian, no doubt,' Vallon said. 'We've seen their communities all along the Silk Road. Heresy breeds like rats.'

'Hush,' Hero said. 'I want to hear more.'

Shennu's questioning ended with Yonden sketching the sign of the cross. Wayland and Hero exchanged stares, then pulled closer.

'Has Yonden ever met a Christian?' Hero asked.

'You're the first he's encountered. He says that when his grandfather was a young man, he went south with a salt caravan and crossed the Himalayas into the land called Nepal. That country lies between Tibet and India. Dorje – that was the grandfather's name – passed through a valley where the lamas venerated a Christian priest who had studied in their temple many years before.'

'How long?'

'Before we Sogdians began recording our history. Before the Buddha's teachings reached Tibet.'

'What was the priest's name?'

'Oussu. Yonden's grandfather told him that he'd seen *thankas* – holy paintings – of Oussu in the temple. The hermit had also left scrolls written in his own language. The lama told Dorje that not long after Oussu left to return to his own land, a party of pilgrims or disciples arrived in the valley seeking their master's works. Since then, no Christian has enquired about Oussu until you.'

Wayland had forgotten his throbbing hand. 'Ask Yonden to describe the valley.'

If the Tibetan had described an Eden with palaces of gold and rivers cobbled with jewels, Wayland would have dismissed the tale as myth.

'A bleak place at the uppermost limit of settlement. So poor that its inhabitants have to overwinter in lower settlements, leaving only their lamas in the temple.'

'How long would it take us to reach it?' Hero asked.

'Three months,' Shennu said.

Hero hissed in disappointment. 'Too far out of our way.'

'Three days would be too far,' Vallon said. 'Even if it was Prester John's kingdom, it doesn't lie on our march. Our mission is to reach China by the most direct route.'

The fire had died to coals, the embers writhing and squeaking. 'Never mind,' Hero said. 'My vision is now so impaired that I couldn't make a worthwhile investigation.'

Wayland reached out and touched Hero's shoulder. 'I could be your eyes.'

Hero blinked at him.

'If my path takes me close enough, I'll visit Oussu's temple.'

'What do you mean?' Vallon said, frozen in the act of rising.

Wayland looked up. 'I'm going home.'

A flake of incandescent ash separated from the coals and wafted up like a glowing leaf. Vallon sank down.

'Everyone leave us.'

Sitting alone before the general, Wayland found himself trembling.

'Why?' Vallon said.

'You know why. You don't need me and we keep crabbing against each other.'

'You can't go,' Vallon said.

'You can't stop me.'

'If it's my harsh words that have driven you from my side, then I withdraw them and ask for your understanding. I need you, Wayland. And you know how high you stand in my affections.'

Wayland's throat constricted. 'I didn't reach my decision lightly.'

385

Vallon kneaded his brows. 'You'll never return home on your own.'

'The wilderness and I are old friends.'

'I expect the gypsy girl's behind this.'

Wayland shook his head. 'She's one of the reasons I'm going.'

Vallon rose like an old man and tugged his cape over his shoulders. 'I can't spare any men to accompany you.'

Wayland stood, too. 'Of course not.' He watched Vallon walk off.

He was settling back, drained by his decision, when Vallon came back.

'I'm not letting you traipse through the wilderness on your own. You can take three men and two spare horses.' Vallon overrode Wayland's protests. 'Leave before first light to avoid upsetting my men. God protect you. I don't suppose we'll meet again.'

Wayland tried to smile. 'Yes, we will. If not here, in the hereafter.'

Vallon paused, a black flapping shape in the night. 'I'll look for you in the hereafter, then.'

Tibet

XXIX

Only Hero was up to see Wayland leave in the deep dead dark.

'Won't you reconsider? Leaving Vallon has wounded him as grievously as if he'd lost a son.'

'Sons make their own way in the world.' Wayland leaned from his saddle. Above him on the crosspiece the hooded eagle sat perched like an idol. 'Take this,' he said, handing over a letter.

Hero balanced it in his hands, as a man would who knew words carried weight. 'Is it your last will and testament?'

'Quite the opposite. It raises the dead to life.'

'It's not like you to talk in riddles.'

'Read it when I've gone and all will become clear. I trust you'll observe the conditions set out at the end.'

Toghan and two other Turkmen leading the spare mounts rode up with Yonden. Hero made a last effort to dissuade Wayland.

'Winter will trap you on the wrong side of the mountains. I can't bear the thought of you dying far from your friends in some howling wilderness.'

Wayland massaged Hero's shoulder. 'So long as you live, I'll never travel alone.' He dug his heels into his horse's flanks. 'God bless you, Hero of Syracuse, the best companion a man could have.'

Hero ran in his wake. 'What about Zuleyka?'

Wayland tossed a hand. 'She's someone else's problem now.'

Three days' riding brought them to the first of five passes that led to the Chang Thang, Tibet's great northern plateau. Behind them and far below, a section of the Taklamakan glowed like a bed of coals through swathes of black dust. Westward the sun was settling into a gash of mountains, a golden thread separating the peaks from the falling night.

Labouring over the third pass, nauseous in the thin air, Wayland squinted back and spotted a lone rider following their trail.

'I'll catch you up,' he told his companions.

Watching the approaching rider, his dog began to wag its tail, uncertainly at first. Then as the rider drew near, it threw its head back and yodelled its delight.

'I might have known it,' Wayland muttered.

It was nearly dark when Zuleyka reached him, grinning like a naughty child. Wayland's expression was bleak.

'You want to go home,' she said. 'So do I. I know you won't send me back.'

Wayland considered. 'Only because it would cost me a fortnight's travelling.' He turned his horse. 'I can't stop you following me, but don't look to me for help if you weaken.' He glanced back in sudden dismay. 'You don't have anything but the clothes on your back. Where do you think you'll sleep?'

She regarded him as if he were a dolt – one she held in kindly affection. 'With you, of course.'

Once they breached the mountains, their path took them across a soda plain, the snow-white surface combed into furrows. The riders made masks to protect their eyes from the dazzle and rode cowed into silence by the huge distances and overwhelming sky. Here and there they came upon patches of scraggy grass that collapsed into powder under the horses' hooves.

They descended an escarpment into country rolling away in low undulations that followed one after the other like the ocean swell. The endless vista was monotonous yet exerted an irresistible fascination. Pinned in the middle of horizons, Wayland felt he was remote from everything, at the limits of his own being, while at the same time occupying the centre of the universe. He tried to describe the sensation to Yonden and the young monk put his hands together and stared into distance.

'Emptiness concentrates the soul. By the time you leave Tibet, you'll be a different màn from the one who entered it.'

The terrain changed imperceptibly, softening into high steppeland broken by grey ridges marked with cairns like fossilised gnomes. The waymarks were the only sign that any human had passed this way. In three weeks' travelling, they hadn't met another living soul.

For all its apparent sterility the plateau abounded with wildlife. Marmots whistled outside their burrows. Herds of kulans galloped away, pausing on the ridges to look back at the interlopers. Wild sheep with spiral horns filed over the mountain slopes. Wayland tried without success to stalk the antelopes that roamed the steppe. Hardly a day passed when he didn't see a wolf pack – dingy yellowish predators that sometimes trailed the riders in the hope of finding discarded scraps. One morning, having staked out a waterhole, Wayland shot a kulan, tracked the wounded beast and despatched it three or four miles from where he'd launched his arrow. Unable to carry the carcass, he rode back for help. By the time he returned, a pack of wolves had demolished the prey and were contesting for the hooves and hide.

It was the drong or wild yaks that fascinated Wayland most – enormous creatures, as large as the aurochs he'd encountered in Rus, but looking even more massive with their curtained black pelts.

Yonden advised him to give them a wide berth, saying that they were the most dangerous beast on the Chang Thang.

'Their coat is so thick that it can take fifty arrows to penetrate a vital organ.'

'Some Tibetans must kill them,' Wayland said. 'I've seen their horns decorating cairns.'

Yonden observed the Buddhist reverence for all living things to the extent that he removed lice from his body and sent the parasites on their way with blessings. He pulled himself closer to the fire.

'I'll tell you how hunters kill them. They dig a hole in a pasture where the yaks graze and lie in it until a drong comes within range. Then they shoot arrows as fast as they can. The drong attacks but can't reach the hunters, who let fly more arrows. Back comes the drong, bellowing with rage, gouging the ground with his horns. The hunters need brave hearts to continue their assault, and even if they deliver a mortal wound, sometimes with his dying effort the drong collapses over their hiding place, entombing them under his bulk.'

Wayland tested Yonden's claims, riding as close to the yaks as he judged prudent. Unless he approached downwind, when they picked up his scent half a mile away and galloped off, they seemed pretty stupid – short-sighted and dull of hearing. Approaching them upwind, he found that they didn't respond to the threat with a headlong charge. They rushed forward a short distance, tasselled tail held erect, relying on their bulk to intimidate. Hold your ground and they would back off; advance and they would make another high-tailed, ground-pawing feint. Wayland decided that Yonden had exaggerated their danger. Stay out of their way and they would stay out of yours.

'Let's hunt one,' Toghan said, gnawing on the thighbone of a hare Wayland had shot that morning.

Wayland looked across the fire. 'Am I such a poor provider? Does your belly shrink to your backbone?'

Toghan whinnied with laughter. 'Listen to him.' He hitched himself forward. 'You're a great hunter. No, it's not for food that I'd kill those giants. Hunting one with bow and arrow would make exciting sport.'

Wayland paused in his chewing. 'I'm not going to kill such a grand beast and leave most of it to rot.'

Toghan shrugged and produced a zither. 'Now I will sing.'

'If you must.'

Toghan plucked the strings. 'I'll continue with the epic of Oghuz, the founder of the Seljuk empire, blessed be his memory.'

'Toghan, you've been droning on about Oghuz since we left the desert. Don't you know any other songs?'

Toghan ignored him. 'We have reached the time when the Seljuks cross the Oxus and the emperor of Ghazni declares war on them, ordering his soldiers to cut off every Seljuk boy's thumb so they can't draw a bow.' Toghan shut his eyes and produced a nasal wailing that drove the dog whimpering from the fireside. The Seljuk's compatriots listened attentively, beating time and occasionally ululating in triumph. When he'd finished, wolves howled on the horizons.

Toghan's countrymen muttered their approval. The minstrel grinned. 'Now I'll sing a song of my own composition describing how my ancestors—'

Zuleyka rose in a swirl and snatched the instrument. Backlit by stars, she launched into a ballad, not a word of which Wayland understood, but delivered with such sweet melancholy that his heart overflowed.

Toghan had fallen asleep, snores rattling through his throat. Zuleyka placed the zither beside him, stepped past Wayland and brushed his hair.

Wildfire seemed to dart over his scalp. He rose and checked that the eagle was securely tethered, ordered his dog to stay alert for wolves and followed Zuleyka into their shared tent. After a month sleeping next to her, he'd decided he was immune to her attractions. The rigours of the journey would have made anyone celibate. After a day riding at high altitude, watching your companions empty loose bowels, dropping exhausted and filthy into bed under blankets infested by bugs and lice, scratching the parasites that gorged on your flesh ... The thought of conjoining with someone as dirty and verminous as you was repellent.

Tonight, though, he lay sleepless in the dark, aware that Zuleyka was also awake. He cleared his throat, adjusted his position and thought of Syth. That only increased his confusion. He rolled on to his other side.

'You seem restless,' Zuleyka whispered.

'Something's bothering the horses. I'd better check.'

He crawled out. A full moon and fields of stars lit the plateau almost as bright as day. The horses fretted against their tethers. The dog quested in an anxious fashion and rubbed its head against Wayland's legs.

'It's not wolves,' Toghan said from his bedroll by the fire. 'It must be the moon.'

Back in his tent, Wayland decided the Seljuk was right. Lunatic fancies flitted through his mind. An energy welled in him, demanding release. He became painfully aware of Zuleyka lying just a tiny way apart from him, yet linked by a current.

'You feel it too,' she said.

He rolled over and pressed his lips to hers, his hand tugging at her breeches. She arched up and he pulled them down.

'Not so fast.'

Clamped to her mouth, Wayland felt as if he were being sucked into a soft tunnel. His hand caressed Zuleyka's breasts. She clasped his neck tighter. His hand slid down her belly.

The earth wobbled and Zuleyka moaned.

The ground rocked beneath them. Wayland splayed his hands to steady himself. Horses whinnied and the Turkmen cried out in alarm. Zuleyka screamed.

'What's happening?'

'It's an earthquake.'

They clung to each other while the rocks beneath them seemed to dissolve. Wayland prised himself loose and staggered out to see a horse snap its tether and gallop away. The natural order had been reversed. The turning stars were fixed in their orbits, while the solid ground slopped like mud.

It was daylight before the aftershocks stopped and evening before he returned to the camp with the runaway horse. Zuleyka met him under a sky coloured with soft pigeon tints.

'You take the tent,' he told her. 'From now on, I'll sleep under the stars.'

Freya was now more than three months old, of an age when a wild eagle would have learned to hunt for itself. Wayland hadn't neglected her education. Each afternoon before the party made camp he fed her on his fist, trying to strike the fine balance between satisfying her appetite and keeping her obedient. After being footed by her, he always let her eat her full ration and never picked her up without offering her a titbit or tiring. She greeted him each morning with affectionate cries. To the dog and anyone who trespassed into her territory, she remained aggressive.

He cut her weight back by feeding her washed meat for five days. Hunger made her more vocal and freer with her feet. Although adult in stature, she hadn't grown out of her fledgling bad manners. Only the winds of freedom would refine her nature.

He began her training by making her jump from her perch to his fist for food. That went well enough and after three days he set her down on a rock and called her off, increasing the distance daily until she would fly two hundred yards without hesitation. Half a dozen flaps and she would set her wings. Watching her huge span fill his vision as she glided the last few feet was a rather unnerving experience. Once she misjudged her aim and landed with one foot on his shoulder and the other on his head, drawing so much blood that he couldn't comb his hair for days.

Next he made her to the lure, throwing her off his fist at a stuffed hareskin baited with meat dragged on a cord behind Toghan's horse. Freya learned fast and in four days she would bob her head in search of the lure the instant Wayland struck her hood and chase it for half a mile.

'Fly her at game,' Toghan pleaded.

Wayland palped Freya's chest and wing muscles. 'She isn't fit enough. Feel. She's as soft as dough.'

The only way to build up her muscles was to let her fly free and far. He gave her her liberty next morning, feeding her half her rations before placing her untethered on her perch. They were on a plain with the nearest horizon twenty miles away, mountains a month's ride off floating in the sky like islands. She launched off around noon, flapping heavily to a boulder and calling for food.

'You'll have to work for it,' Wayland said. Her querulous cries faded behind him. She was still seated on her perch after he'd ridden a mile. It was mid-afternoon when she caught up, making a clumsy pass at him before settling on the ground.

Wayland dismounted, held up his gloved fist and she ran towards him like a drunken hobgoblin before thrashing up to claim her reward.

He repeated the exercise over the next three days and on the last flight she flogged after him for half a mile before alighting on his fist. Good progress, but she still hadn't taken to the upper air and learned to command her element. Wayland wasn't surprised. Until they were confident in their ability to kill, few trained hawks flew for the pleasure of it. Wayland had flown falcons that would wait on a thousand feet above his head if they expected quarry to be served. Cast the same birds loose without the prospect of prey and they would sit hunched on a branch for hours while high above them their wild kin played on thermals.

He rode next morning into a gusting headwind, cloud racks scudding across shattered ridges. Not a good day to fly an apprentice eagle. His determination to stick to his regime wavered and it wasn't until the wind abated that he removed Freya's leash. She tested the breeze, hopping off her perch and floating before dropping back and clasping the familiar pole. The lull was brief. A blast of wind caught her and blew her away like a giant leaf. Wayland galloped after her, swinging his lure until she disappeared. He searched all afternoon before giving up.

The wind had strengthened to a gale, driving grit into Wayland's face and making his horse walk crabbed. He caught up with his companions and Toghan rode over, shouting to make himself heard. 'I told you not to risk it.'

At sunset the wind dropped and the sky ran with colours of such depth and clarity that a soothsayer would have interpreted the patterns as portents of war or disaster, the rise of an empire or its fall. Not a breath of air stirred when Wayland looked up and saw an eagle hanging above him at an immense height, the last of the sun striking bronze from its plumage and the first star twinkling above.

'That can't be her,' Toghan said.

Wayland watched the eagle and dismounted. 'Hold my horse.'

He walked out into the wilderness and swung a lure, whistling and calling. The eagle swung away until Wayland could barely keep it in sight. The sun sank. Shadows veiled the earth.

Wayland was about to give up when the speck in the sky vanished. He squinted and picked up a mote dropping through the atmosphere. It swung up in a pothook, unfurling into eagle shape as it reached the top of its arc, contracting again as it closed its wings for another plunge. In this fashion it fell in three giant steps before descending into the shadow of night.

'Lost her,' Wayland said.

Toghan whistled. 'Listen.'

The sound started as a flutter, reminding Wayland of the noise made by a leaf clinging to a wind-swept branch. It increased to the roar of a storm surging through a forest. He ran into the dark with upheld hand.

'Freya!'

Silence and then a drawn-out hiss. Wayland raised his gloved hand and waited with pounding heart.

Thump.

One instant Freya was lost and the next she was on Wayland's glove, grown from infant to adult in a day. She glared into the gathering night, adjusted her stance and lowered her head to eat. She didn't utter a sound, and when Wayland placed her on her perch, she gave a sort of chortle, rotated her neck to settle her crop and tucked her head under one wing. Wayland swelled with pride.

'You pretend you love that bird more than you love me.'

Turning, Wayland made out Zuleyka. She was slapping her hip and stamping the ground.

'There's no pretence. Freya means more to me than you do, yet when I thought she'd gone I felt relief. One less thing to worry about. I chose to bring the eagle with me. I didn't choose you for company. I'll be happy to see the back of you.'

She flew at him, mouthing imprecations. Toghan wrested her away. There was a moment of silence and then her voice carried through the dark.

'I love you, Wayland the English with the shining hair. What I love I own.'

A slap rang out.

'There's no need for that,' Wayland told Toghan.

'That was her hitting me,' the Seljuk said.

It was time to enter Freya to quarry. Feeding her half-rations for a couple of days brought her into the condition the Turkmen called *yarak* – a frantic urge to kill, manifested by her raised crest, loose plumage and maniacal stare. When Wayland sucked through his lips to imitate a rabbit's squeak, her feet convulsed so tight on his glove that he groaned.

He had to manage the flight so that she had every chance of success, and that meant selecting the right quarry. At this stage of her development, the wild sheep and antelopes were beyond her, the marmots and pikas not challenge enough. That left hares, which abounded on the steppe. Thicker-coated than their distant English cousins, they were every bit as fast and wily.

Wayland left the party and rode through a promising expanse of grassland, holding Freya hooded on his fist and keeping his dog to heel. He hadn't gone far when he spotted a hare lolloping about half a bowshot away. As he approached, the hare flattened itself to the ground. He ordered the dog to lie down, unhooded Freya and homed in. He was no more than forty yards away when the hare bolted. Almost in the same instant Freya reacted.

It was farcical, Freya's actions outrunning thought. She gripped Wayland's glove, imagining she'd already bound to her prey, at the same time flapping her wings. Wayland was left with a heavy, crazy bundle sagging from his fist, making his horse jibe while the hare made good its escape.

The next flight wasn't much better. This time Freya managed to disengage, only to fly into the ground, skidding to an undignified halt twenty yards in front of Wayland. He didn't pick her up until she'd composed herself. He'd learned that birds of prey understood humiliation and took it out on those who had witnessed it.

Turkmen falconers had told him that a thwarted eagle would sometimes attack men or even horses.

It was evening next day when he spotted a hare's ears pricked up on a gravel flat with no cover for miles. Wayland unhooded Freya. By now she knew the action heralded a hunt and her gaze darted in search of prey.

The hare had vanished. Freya glared around. Wayland hoisted her above his head. 'You're looking the wrong way.'

He didn't know which moved first. The weight on his arm lifted and the hare bounded away. Freya was off, rowing through the air with movements that seemed lethargic compared to the hare's efforts. Yet without apparent effort she caught up, extended her talons and braced back for the impact.

When Wayland made in, she was clutching a hank of grass, looking around with a baffled expression.

'That's life,' Wayland said, offering her food.

Freya learned fast from her failures. Next day she wasn't sticky-footed and weighed up her chances before deciding whether to attack. Even so she missed. This time, though, she returned to the fist and stared around in search of fresh quarry.

Wayland's arm was sagging under her weight when three hares erupted under his feet, each hare streaking off on a different path. Freya beat after one, gaining some height before sweeping down to bind to her quarry.

Hunter and hunted were small in the distance when they converged. One speck leaped and the other disappeared. The hare had anticipated Freya's attack and evaded it by flinging itself into the air.

A flurry of wings showed that Freya hadn't given up. Wayland stood in his stirrups and watched the eagle close the gap.

The hare ran in a circle and was less than a furlong from Wayland when Freya smashed into it, predator and prey rolling over in a cloud of dust. Wayland galloped up to lend assistance, but by the time he reached the spot the hare was dead. Freya mantled at him and he waited until she'd calmed down and broken into her prey before making in to her. He extended his glove, holding fresh meat at Freya's feet. She pulled at it and as soon as he made to withdraw it she released her grip on the hare and stepped onto his fist.

He rewarded her well and let two days pass before flying her again. They'd reached stonier terrain broken by gulleys and Wayland's search for hares drew a blank. Since Freya's vision was sharper than his, he unhooded her and transferred her to the T-perch. They hadn't gone more than a mile when she began to bob her head at something away to the left. She was undecided, half spreading her wings and then scissoring them shut.

'What is it?' Wayland said. He guessed it wasn't a hare and was about to take hold of Freya's jesses when she took off, powering thirty feet into the air before setting course.

Quarter of a mile away a russet shape broke cover and streaked off. A fox. Freya closed on it. Wayland rode after the chase with mingled excitement and apprehension. Tibetan foxes were big animals, twice Freya's weight. This one made for a sheer ridge riven with fissures. It bounded up a steep rock face and was nearly at the top when Freya took it side on. Eagle and fox tumbled down and Wayland knew Freya hadn't secured a killing grip. When he reached them, they were caught in a deadlock, Freya holding her quarry by shoulder and rump, leaning back on her tail to avoid the fox's jaws. Wayland despatched it with a knife and looked at the panting and dishevelled eagle.

'You won't tackle one of them again in a hurry.'

Two days later she caught her second fox. This time Wayland was close enough to see her slow down during her final approach and then, as the fox turned at bay, shoot forward, seizing its mask with one foot and grabbing its back with the other. When Wayland made in, he found she'd killed the fox by breaking its neck.

'You're almost ready to take your place in the wild.'

XXX

They reached grazing grounds streaming with flocks of sheep and herds of domesticated yaks, the black-hair tents of the nomads dotted on the pastures like pinned spiders. Running the gauntlet of fierce mastiffs, the travellers sought food and shelter at one *drokpa* encampment. Its occupants were unfriendly until Yonden told them he was a monk at the Palace of Perfect Emancipation, and then the nomads plied their guests with food and drink. Wayland had already sampled tsampa – barley meal ground as fine as sawdust, the staple diet of Tibet. This was the first time he'd eaten it in tea with rancid yak butter. It wasn't too unpalatable if you thought of it as soup and avoided looking at the hairs floating among the winking beads of grease.

A cheerful woman, two men and three children occupied a pair of smoke-blackened tents pitched on stone slabs. The woman wore a full-length sheepskin gown with the fleece turned inwards, but during the day she let the garment hang from her waist, revealing her naked torso. The men were two of the woman's three husbands and their relationships seemed not at all strained. The third husband, brother of the other two, was away trading in Nepal. Every spring one of the men would load up a sheep caravan with salt and journey across the Himalayas, returning in the autumn with rice and barley. Usually the second husband was away in the summer pastures. Wayland gave up trying to work out how the ménage worked when all four spouses were together in winter.

He rested three days at the encampment. Mornings and evenings the children milked the sheep into a wild yak's horn, tying the animals together in two rows facing each other and so closely packed that the head of each animal appeared to be growing backwards out of its opposite number. Before leaving, Wayland exchanged a lame horse for a yak. After two months on the Chang Thang, some of their mounts were so thin that they looked like skeletons sewn into skin.

'Who's going to handle the yak,' Toghan asked.

Wayland cocked a finger at Zuleyka.

Summer was ending. While the sun at noon was still hot enough to burn skin, water in the shade only a few feet away remained frozen. Even with sheepskins piled on top of him, Wayland couldn't sleep soundly in the open. One night, chilled to the bone by a moaning northerly, he took cover in the tent occupied by Zuleyka. The dog was already inside, curled nose to tail beside her.

'What are you doing?' she demanded.

'What does it look like? It's freezing out there.'

She tried to push him back through the entrance. 'I don't want you here.'

'It's my tent. If you don't want to share it, *you* sleep outside.'

Zuleyka muttered to herself.

'What's that?' Wayland said.

'I said I have a knife and I'll stab you if you lay a hand on me.'

Wayland's laugh was slightly crazed. 'A man would have to be desperate to molest you. You look like a witch and you smell like a polecat.' He wasn't exaggerating by much. Zuleyka's lips were black and scabby, her nose sore and flaking, her curls a matted grey rat's nest.

He settled down and was almost asleep when he registered her tiny rhythmic convulsions. He half-raised himself. Zuleyka was crying. 'What's wrong now?'

'It's true,' she wailed. 'This awful journey has destroyed my charms. Who would marry a hag so aged and coarsened by sun and cold? I should have killed myself when the Vikings captured me.' She drew her knife. 'I can still do it. What's the point of living?'

Wayland grabbed for the weapon, batting his hands against hers before finding her wrists. 'Stop that! I spoke in spite. If you must know, you're still beautiful. Too beautiful for your own good or mine.'

Zuleyka settled back and gave a throaty chuckle 'I know, Master English. I like to tease.'

'You're mad.'

Zuleyka yawned and rolled over. 'Sleep well and meet me in your dreams. I'll be waiting.'

A day came when Wayland heard the haunting song of geese migrating south, the chevrons passing overhead in squadrons so large they looked from a distance like rain squalls.

Below him spread a shallow grassland basin so wide that its far side was hidden beneath the curve of the horizon. A few clouds cast coloured shadows on a steppe that seemed to emit its own light. A river wandered across the basin in braids more than half a mile wide. On the other bank, etched by the clarity of the atmosphere, a herd of wild yak grazed, arresting in their blackness. At a distance from the herd, two bulls fought like beasts out of a fable, the impact of their collisions carrying as faint concussions through the still air.

The wayfarers rode down to the river. There were at least six main channels to ford, separated by gravel bars and islands. Wayland noticed that the yaks had stopped grazing and fixed their attention upstream, where the river emerged through a gap in the highland rim. He tried to work out what had alarmed them. Probably the pack of wolves stitching themselves into the landscape a mile away. A flock of cranes sprang into clanging flight on the far side and the yaks wheeled, tails upright, galloping away from the river.

Wayland had registered that the current was well below its maximum height, with some channels almost dry. That wasn't unusual. At this altitude rivers froze at night in their headwaters, only flowing when the sun had melted the ice, sometime late in the day. Wayland had learned not to pitch camp in a dry watercourse after being forced to evacuate a gulley that flooded not long after they'd pitched tents.

He coaxed his horse into the current, the eagle riding on its perch, Yonden close behind and Zuleyka following, leading the loaded yak by a rope tied to its wooden nose ring. The Seljuks tarried on the bank, foraging for dry yak dung – the only fuel on the plateau.

Even with the river so low, progress was slow, the fast-flowing current up to the horses' bellies in places, the cobbled bottom making it difficult for them to find secure footing. Some of the boulders were two feet across, separated by narrow gaps that could have snapped a horse's leg if negotiated carelessly. Wayland picked his way across to the first island and waited for Yonden and Zuleyka to join him before fording the next channel. Toghan had just set his horse at the water and the other two Turkmen were making for the bank.

Wayland lurched up onto the next gravel bar and looked back to see the Turkmen strung out, the rearmost rider hampered by the spare mount. Wayland's horse whinnied and laid back his ears. His dog whimpered, staring upstream.

'What's wrong?' Yonden said.

'I don't know,' Wayland said. He swung his hand at the stragglers. 'Hurry up.'

Nervousness had begun to infect the other animals. Yonden's horse balked at entering the water. The yak dug in its heels. The spare horse in the rear tried to break back to the far bank, almost unseating its handler.

Wayland had to kick his horse's flanks before it would tackle the next channel. This was the widest stream, about seventy yards across, strewn with boulders sunk deep in water that creamed between them, making it difficult to find a path. In one place he found his way blocked and had to detour upstream, forging against the current.

He was two-thirds of the way across the river when he saw it – a white deckled band foaming down the river, its contours frayed and constantly changing, flinging up into spouts of spray. It wasn't just water. Slabs of ice jostled on the wave.

'Dear God,' he murmured. He swung round. 'Ride for your lives!'

'What about the yak?' Zuleyka shouted.

'Let it go.'

He ploughed through the current, measuring his progress against the oncoming flood. He estimated that it was no more than a quarter of a mile away, surging down at the speed of a cantering horse. He could hear it over the riffling of the current – a malign hissing broken by dull shocks as slabs of ice smashed into obstacles. With only one more channel to cross, he knew he would make it, but when he looked back he realised with visceral horror that two of the Turkmen were doomed. The rearmost of them abandoned the pack horse. It stampeded and fell on its side, thrashing to regain its feet.

The wave was so close that its onrush blotted out all other sounds, the liquid roaring underscored by grating ice and the rumbling of boulders bowled along the riverbed. It sounded like subterranean gates being wrenched open.

Wayland leaped off his horse and dragged it snorting with terror to shore. The bank was undercut and he lost precious time finding a way up. Zuleyka was flogging her horse towards him, Yonden not far behind. Toghan was a long way adrift and the other Turkmen were still in mid-river. Wayland helped Zuleyka and Yonden on to the bank.

'Keep going,' he told them.

The torrent had spilled out of its course, swilling a hundred yards beyond the bank. Toghan whipped his horse through the boulders. It stumbled and went down on its knees before recovering its footing.

'Stay calm,' Wayland yelled. 'You can still make it.'

Those last moments stretched into infinity, Wayland measuring the Seljuk's progress against the surge. Sometimes the wave slowed, backing up in a bulging swell before bursting forward with renewed violence.

Toghan cast a desperate glance. 'Save yourself.'

Wayland stretched out a hand. 'Come on. You're nearly there.'

Their hands linked moments before the wave struck. Toghan drove his horse up onto the bank and dragged Wayland after him.

Reaching higher ground, Wayland looked back at the moment the wave of ice and water smashed into the yak and one of the Turkmen and swept them away.

His legs gave way beneath him. He was too stunned by the speed of the disaster to take it in.

'What caused it?' Yonden said.

Wayland pointed back with shaking hand. 'The earthquake must have set off a landslide that blocked the river. The water backed up until ...' He clutched his face. 'I should have known something was wrong from the yaks' behaviour.'

'Nobody could have foreseen it,' Zuleyka said.

Toghan was beside himself. 'We must search for our friends.'

Wayland raised his head. 'They're dead. We'll look for them when the river has abated.'

It was still ripping past in full spate, the torrent burdened with ice debris. Shadows were lengthening when the survivors began their search. By nightfall they'd found the battered and shapeless body of the yak, its packs torn off and lost. Of the two Turkmen and the three missing horses, they found no trace.

Over a campfire they took stock of their losses and reached a sober reckoning. The yak had been carrying their tents and most of their food. They had rations for three days.

'We won't starve,' Toghan said. 'My bow and your eagle will keep us fed until we reach another nomad camp.'

'How far before we reach your monastery?' Wayland asked Yonden.

'One more month.'

Overnight the river shrank to its normal size. The survivors went on, refugees rather than wayfinders, the least regarded of all the creatures in that wilderness. They ate only what they could catch, feeling the pinch of hunger when their arrows missed or the weather was too stormy to risk flying the eagle. Wayland had to take care about Freya's slips, making sure there were no foxes about before releasing her. She'd become wedded to them, sometimes ignoring a hare and beating after a fox a mile away. Once she checked at a half-grown wolf and might have bound to it if it hadn't taken cover in a lair.

Camps were sombre occasions, with little conversation to leaven the oppressive mood. Wayland kept thinking about the disaster at the river, berating himself for not interpreting the warning signs. Soft living had dulled his instincts. It was as if some sense amounting to a virtue had deserted him.

Nor was he prepared for the tragedy that would befall them on the next stage. A keening wind from the north blew snow parallel to the ground, sculpting icy arrow heads in the lee of each tussock. Toghan rode ahead, humming a tuneless song. Wayland swayed in his wake, half-frozen, sunk in a torpor.

He snapped awake as what looked like a blur of black smoke erupted through the streaking flakes. It was a wild yak bull charging at Toghan. In the instant of recognition, Wayland registered arrows stuck in its flank.

'Toghan!'

The Seljuk hadn't seen the yak and wrenched his horse right into its path. The horse went over as if hit by a wall, flinging Toghan backwards onto a boulder. The yak, blood drooling from its mouth, mashed the screaming horse with its horns, tossing it about as if it weighed no more than straw. One last gouge spun the horse around its axis and the yak trotted away, spotting the snow with the blood dripping from its flanks.

Wayland saw all this while fighting to control his crazed mount. Somewhere Zuleyka was screaming. He jumped off and dragged his horse over to Toghan. The Seljuk lay splayed across the boulder, his face the colour of putrid cheese and something unnatural about the way he was lying.

Wayland took his hands. 'You're a lucky fellow.'

'My back's broken.'

Everything went dark inside Wayland. He turned to glimpse Zuleyka in the whirling snow. She shook her head.

He knelt by Toghan. The Seljuk's eyes projected weary

resignation, as if he were already looking across death's door. 'I can't move. My back's broken.'

'Close your eyes.'

Toghan's lids slid shut. Wayland squeezed the Seljuk's hands. 'Do you feel that?'

'It's my legs I can't feel. Everything's dead below my waist.'

Wayland thumped Toghan's knee. He twisted his ankle and prodded it with the tip of a knife. The Seljuk didn't react.

Toghan's eyes flickered. 'When I was a boy, a friend broke his back in a horse race. An elder smothered him as an act of mercy. I don't want to die like that. Cut my throat so that I have one last glimpse of this earth.'

'I can't do that.'

'You'd do it for your dog.'

'You're not a dog. You're my friend, even though your singing drives me mad.'

Toghan tried to smile. 'Then end the tune. I don't want to be singing it when you've left me and a bear claws my face.'

'We won't leave you.' Wayland said. He rocked back on his haunches. 'Keep talking to him,' he told Yonden.

He opened his pack and pulled out a flask Hero had given him. It contained a liquid the Greek called 'drowsy mixture', formulated to dull pain during surgery. Hero had cautioned him about the dosage – more than three or four spoonfuls and the patient might not wake up. With shaking hands Wayland emptied half the contents into a beaker and bore the lethal chalice to Toghan.

'Drink it,' Wayland said. 'It's a cure-all prepared by our friend Hero.'

Toghan managed a crooked smile. 'I enjoyed our time together,' he said, and swallowed the mixture.

Wayland stroked the Seljuk's brow. 'There,' he murmured. 'I'll watch over you until you fall asleep. When you wake, you'll find yourself in paradise.'

Toghan would have died in the night anyway, but this way was much faster. His eyes wandered and he whispered a halting air before his eyes glazed and closed. Yonden was chanting prayers for a good rebirth. Wayland hauled him upright and spoke through chattering teeth.

'Toghan's gone. We'll follow him if we don't get out of the cold.'

That night Wayland lay wide-eyed in the dark, thinking about death and the infinite variety of ways it could strike. He recoiled from Zuleyka's gentle touch.

'Don't.'

Burial wasn't possible in the frozen barrens. Wayland and Yonden interred Toghan's corpse under a cairn of stones facing the rising sun.

'You go on,' Wayland told the others.

The words he struggled to articulate were directed at himself more than Toghan. He'd challenged the wilderness and lost, just as Vallon had predicted, and his pride had cost three men their lives.

Wayland rose and stood looking towards the north, wondering where his companions were and heartsick that he would never see them again.

Four days later he checked his horse, amazed at the sight of a moon rising in the south while another moon slid to rest in the west. A rub of his eyes showed that the rising moon was a snow pyramid isolated against a slaty sky.

Yonden dismounted and prostrated himself. 'The Precious Snow Jewel,' he said. 'Our journey's nearly over.'

Wayland learned that the mountain was sacred to Buddhists, Bon-pos, Hindus and Jains. To Buddhists it was the centre of the universe, the axis on which the world turned and the fount of four great rivers – the Indus, the Tsangpo or Brahmaputra, the Karnali and the Sutlej, all of which breached the Himalayan range. To the Bon-pos, who had grafted the teachings of Lord Buddha onto their shamanistic traditions, it was the Nine-Stacked Swastika Mountain. Hindus called it Mount Kailas or Meru and believed that Shiva resided on its summit. For Jains it was the place where the founder of their faith achieved liberation from the endless cycle of death and rebirth.

It took three days to reach the sacred mountain. The huge clefts that isolated it from the other peaks formed a pilgrim trail marked by shrines called chortens and walls constructed from slabs incised with holy texts and planted with prayer flags. The travellers encountered hundreds of pilgrims circumambulating the mountain, the Buddhists keeping it to their right, the Bon-pos taking the opposite direction. Some of the pilgrims had spent years journeying to their goal and made their final devotions by dragging themselves around the circuit on bleeding hands and knees.

From the south the mountain was even more beautiful, its chiselled mass rising above two huge lakes, its vertical banded walls inscribed by slashes that did indeed resemble a swastika. What dispelled its aura of spirituality was the squalid settlement thrown up by merchants to milk the pilgrims of every last penny. Wandering through a bazaar, fending off touts offering charms, medicines and souvenirs for unholy prices, Wayland emerged to see the Himalayas filling the southern sky.

They stayed only long enough to buy provisions before turning east. After a week following the Tsangpo along a road that led to Lhasa, Yonden struck south through shattered hills. Three days later he led the way up onto a ridge.

Wayland doffed his hat. Before him spread a grassland plain stirred into gentle waves by a breeze. On the other side clouds rising up from dark and hidden valleys smoked about the golden roofs and white walls of a monastery built on a spur jutting over a precipice. Above the fastness rose mountain walls with three tremendous ice summits soaring behind them. Dhaulagiri, Manaslu and Annapurna, Yonden said. Peaks no mortal could scale.

The way to the monastery had been hacked out of rock and it was nearly dark by the time the party reached the top of the mountain staircase. Yonden tugged on a bell and a monk opened a door with timbers six inches thick.

'I've returned,' Yonden said.

'We were expecting you,' said the monk.

He led the way into the monastery, the lugubrious blast of conch shells and the clash of cymbals echoing off the cliffs.

XXXI

Yonden pleaded with Wayland to remain in the monastery over winter. 'The Himalayan passes will be blocked by snow. Also, this is the season when gangs of bandits prey on travellers returning from pilgrimage.'

'I can't wait six months. If I leave now I could be home by spring. Tell me what route to take.'

Yonden led him to the top of a high wall and pointed west across copper and ochre hills. 'Travel two days in that direction and you'll reach a road used by salt traders.' He faced the other way. 'Three days' east there's a pilgrim trail leading to the kingdom of Mustang and the flaming shrine at Muktinath. I advise you to take the salt road. It's easier.'

'Which path will take me to the temple of the Christian hermit?'

'Neither. None of the monks has ever been there. It's just a place my grandfather told me about.'

'You mean it might not exist?'

'No, it lies in a valley a few days' east of Mustang, reached by a pass used only by the people who live in that wild settlement. The pass will already be closed. It's almost as high as the peaks that surround it and is open for only a few weeks in summer.'

Wayland scanned the range. The sky above the peaks was indigo, so dark it looked like the far reaches of space.

'It would be a pity to come so near to the temple and not visit it.'

Yonden summoned an elderly monk. 'Tsosang used to buy herbal medicines from traders in the valley. They sold a rare plant called "summer grass, winter insect", a remedy against diseases of the chest. Tsosang says it's been three years since they called at the monastery. Avalanches must have blocked the pass. There are no guides to lead you. Please don't attempt the journey on your own.'

'I would only satisfy my curiosity for Hero's sake. I have no intention of risking my life. I'll take a look at the route and if it's too difficult I'll follow the path through Mustang.'

On the eve of departure Wayland visited Zuleyka. Since arriving at the monastery he'd hardly seen her. He handed her a pile of clothes, including a full-length sheepskin robe.

'Take these. It will be bitter cold in the mountains.'

'I thought you were going to leave me behind.'

'I considered it. I don't want another death on my conscience.'

'I'd never have been able to find my own way out of Tibet.'

'I'm not travelling with you to Persia. Once we're across the Himalayas, that's it.'

'I'll be safe once I reach India. Luri communities live there. It's where my people came from.'

Wayland nodded but didn't answer.

Zuleyka blushed. 'You're looking at me in a strange way.'

'Am I? Sorry. It's time we went to our beds. We have an early start.'

She caught his sleeve as he turned. 'No, tell me what that look meant.'

Wayland stared at the ground. 'You don't need me to tell you.'

'I want to hear it in your own words.'

Wayland wrenched away. 'I was thinking how lovely you are.'

Yonden and a dozen other monks saw them off. 'Promise you won't allow your fascination with the temple to lure you into danger. Remember what I said about the land of Shambhala. By the time you realise you'll never reach it, it's too late to turn back.'

412

'I promise,' Wayland said. He heaved himself into the saddle. 'I haven't asked what life holds for you now.'

The monks chanted blessings and spun hand-held prayer wheels. Yonden smiled. 'Tomorrow I'll be immured in a cell and won't see another being for a year.'

'I've seen you breathe in the scent of flowers and admire a shapely woman. You'll go mad cut off from the world.'

'I'll have holy texts to study and the cell has a window facing east. Whenever I look through it, I'll be with you in spirit.'

Yonden's last act was to drape white silk scarves around Wayland and Zuleyka's necks. 'Farewell, my friends. Buddha and all the good spirits go with you.'

The monastery had provided them with fresh horses and three yaks, each with a handler. Horses couldn't cross the pass into Mustang. Once they reached the final approach, the handlers would take them back to the monastery, together with two of the yaks.

Fearful of bandit attack, the Tibetan escort sought safety in company, joining groups of traders and pilgrims travelling the highway to Lhasa. An uneventful journey brought them to the trail leading to Mustang, and then they struck off the beaten track, heading south into wild and uninhabited country.

Two days later they came upon a solitary shrine by the faint impression of a track leading into the mountains.

'It's the way to the temple,' one of the Tibetans said.

Wayland looked up into a cauldron of boiling clouds that swirled apart to reveal glimpses of glaciers, tumbled ice-falls and knife-edged buttresses. Thunder rolled and lightning clawed between summits. It was like staring into an aerial abyss inhabited by warring gods and titans.

'Christ,' Wayland breathed. 'I'm not going up there.' He turned to the leader of the escort. 'We'll take the Mustang trail.'

Returning towards the highway, they spotted a terminal of smoke rising from nowhere and made a wide detour before pitching camp on a desolate tableland. Wayland fed Freya a full crop.

413

'Tomorrow I'll release her,' he told Zuleyka.

The dog's growls woke him late in the night. He untied the entrance to his tent and looked out. The moon drifting through clouds cast light just bright enough to show Freya seated on her perch. He could tell from her tense, two-footed stance that she was nervous.

'What is it?' Zuleyka whispered behind him.

'Probably wolves,' he said, not really believing it.

He crawled out. The dog faced upwind, jaws rucked back and a snarl bubbling deep in its throat.

Wayland caught a whiff of tallow and mildewed wool. He squirmed back into the tent.

'Our visitors walk on two legs,' he said.

To her credit, Zuleyka didn't panic. 'Bandits?'

'Nobody else would sneak up on a lonely camp at dead of night. Wait here.'

Zuleyka threw off her coverings. 'I'm coming with you.'

They waited until the moon disappeared behind clouds before creeping to the Tibetans' tent. Wayland's news threw them into panic.

'Keep your voices down,' he hissed.

'How many are there?' one said.

'I don't know. I assume they outnumber us.'

The Tibetans gabbled like frightened geese. 'The devils never travel in gangs of less than a dozen. We're too few to fight them. Let's escape now, under the cloak of night.'

Wayland shook the man. 'They'll hear us loading and saddling.'

'We'll have to go on foot and leave the beasts.'

Wayland argued in vain for them to stay. Terror had seized the Tibetans and headlong flight was the only way to put it behind them. They delayed only long enough to throw a few possessions together before creeping out of the tent.

Wayland grabbed one of them. 'If you're going to flee, at least do it properly. Wait for the moon to hide.' He gripped tight until the earth went into eclipse, then gave a push. 'That way. Run and keep on running.'

Zuleyka fumbled for him. 'Why aren't we going with them?'

'We're safer on our own.'

'Wayland!'

'Hush.' His finger traced her mouth. 'It will soon be light. If the bandits find an empty camp they'll come after us. On foot we'll never get away. They'll catch us and kill us.'

'They'll kill us if we stay here.'

'I think I can talk our way out.'

Clouds covered the moon. Wayland took Zuleyka's hand and ran for their tent. He pulled the bed covers over both of them.

'Are we just going to sit here?'

'The dog will warn us if they attack. They won't, though.'

'Why not?'

'Because it's dark and they don't know how many they're facing.'

Zuleyka shivered against him. 'I'm scared. You know what they'll do to me.'

He put an arm around her and nestled her face on his chest. Her shudders subsided.

'This is the first time you've shown tenderness to me.'

'It's the first time I'm certain that tenderness won't flare into passion.'

He could feel her heart beating as fast as a bird's. He stroked her hair. Outside, the eagle roused and adjusted its position. He thought Zuleyka was asleep when she whispered his name.

'Tell me about your wife.'

'No.'

'I don't even know her name.'

'I'd rather keep it to myself.'

'You're scared that I'll put the evil eye on her.'

'Would you?'

'Perhaps. Is she beautiful?'

'I knew you were going to say that.'

415

'Well, is she?'

'Yes.'

'More beautiful than me?'

'You're opposites. She's as fair as you're dark.'

'Tell me about your children.'

'Why do you keep asking questions?'

'It helps keeps fear away. Also, I want to know more about you before I die.'

'My son's eight, my daughter's four.'

'You must have been very young when you became a father.'

'I was about your age.'

'Does that mean you haven't known another woman?'

Wayland gave a husky laugh. 'This is the closest I've come.'

Zuleyka rose up and peered at him though the dark before settling again.

'What about you?' he said. 'I don't believe you're a virgin.'

'I am when I want to be.'

Wayland's chuckle began in his belly and worked up through his chest.

'What's so funny?'

The dog barked. Wayland threw off the covers and reached for his war bow.

'Time to prepare for our guests.'

He waited beside the dog, an arrow nocked and another dozen close to hand. Zuleyka crouched behind him. The dog growled continuously and the eagle bated from its perch. Wayland stood.

'Ho! Who approaches from behind the curtain of night?'

'Harmless travellers,' a voice said. 'We saw your fire last night and wondered who was camping in such a lonely place.'

'I'm surprised you took so long to show yourselves. I hope it wasn't fear that held you back.'

The dog ran stiff-legged towards the bandits and stood with mane raised, barking defiance. Wayland called it back.

Dawn when it came was just a pale version of night, the landscape leached of colour and the mountains smothered under clouds.

'Now I see you. Welcome, untamed sons.'

Fourteen mounted shapes materialised out of the half-light. Zuleyka muffled a scream. 'They're demons.'

Moulded leather masks hid the bandits' faces, giving them a terrifying aspect. Apart from the masks, there was little agreement in their costume or weaponry. Some wore black or wine-red chubas, one sleeve dangling like wrinkled trunks, exposing their hairless chests to the freezing air. Some were bare-headed, their ropy black locks set off with eagle feathers and cowrie shells. Others wore sheepskin helmets or fox fur hats. Most carried swords of various designs, a crude sabre being the most fashionable. Others made do with lances or clubs. All had short bows slung over their shoulders.

At the centre of the band a man distinguished by a corselet of fine but distressed mail raised a hand and gave an oddly girlish little wave.

'I was about to prepare breakfast,' Wayland said. 'Please join us.'

The gang halted. 'Where are your companions?' said the mail-clad leader.

'They fled in the night. They thought you might be bandits.'

The masked men looked at each other through their leather peepholes and then advanced. One of them slashed the yak herders' tent before peering inside.

'Where did they go?'

Wayland shrugged. 'Back to the road.'

The leader looked down on Wayland from his saddle. 'Where have you come from?'

'The Palace of Perfect Emancipation.'

'Ah. Where are you going?'

Wayland pointed. 'Nepal.'

'Ah. You won't reach it that way.'

Wayland crouched and kindled a dung fire into flame. The leader watched him, then leaned down and lifted his blond hair.

He gave it a tug, testing to see if it was a wig.

'What country are you from?'

'England,' said Wayland. He reached up in turn and raised the bandit's mask. Bloodshot eyes looked at him from a face coated with soot, grease and dust. One scarred eyelid sagged in a squint. He wore his hair piled-up in ribboned braids that unbound would have hung to his waist. At odds with his cut-throat countenance, he wore around his neck an amulet showing an image of Buddha wearing a tranquil smile that represented his compassion for all living things.

'No wonder you wear a mask,' Wayland said.

He was quick at languages, and in the three months spent with Yonden, he'd become a proficient Tibetan speaker, unwittingly picking up an aristocratic dialect.

One of the bandits tittered. The leader scowled round, then turned back to Wayland and bared rust-coloured fangs the shape of tombstones.

'All of you show your faces,' Wayland said. 'You can't drink tea wearing masks.'

The bandits exchanged glances. At their leader's command, they uncovered themselves. Masked or bare, they were as complete a set of villains as Wayland had encountered in all his wanderings – wolf-faced and filthy, their faces coated with greasy dirt like a second skin.

The yak dung burned hot and bright, giving off no smoke. Wayland set a pot of water to boil. 'My name's Wayland. Who are you?'

The leader hesitated. 'Osher.' He pointed at Zuleyka. 'Your wife?'

'A nun. We're making a pilgrimage to the shrine of one of our saints.'

'Why didn't you run away with the others?'

'Unlike them, we're not cowards.'

Osher seemed nonplussed. 'Aren't you frightened that we might be bandits?'

'I *know* you're bandits. Sit.'

'Aren't you scared that we'll kill you?'

'We can talk about that when you've drunk your tea. Before *I* kill anyone, I like to know as much about them as I can.'

Osher fanned out his chuba and subsided cross-legged on the ground. Half a dozen of his men joined him, the rest remaining mounted, some staring with vicious intent, some wearing loopy grins, others gawping and slack-jawed.

'You have a fine pair of boots,' Wayland said to Osher.

The leader looked at his footwear with some pride. 'They were made by my brother-in-law, the best bootmaker in Kham.'

'Ah, you're Khampas. The monks warned me about your tribe. You're a long way from home.'

Zuleyka made the tea Tibetan-style, hacking a lump off a brick of chai and dropping it into the boiling water. After letting it stew, she poured the liquor into a brass-bound wooden cylinder fitted with a plunger. She added butter and worked the plunger, producing slurping sounds that made some of the Khampas exchange lewd guffaws. Osher stilled their antics with a gesture. Lazy-eyed, he watched as Zuleyka, the picture of pious modesty, decanted the liquid into the pot. The bandits took bowls from inside their robes.

Wayland produced a bag of tsampa. 'Help yourselves.'

The Khampas dug into the barley and trickled it into their cups, kneading it with filthy fingers until it was the consistency of stiff dough.

Osher shovelled a handful into his mouth. 'This country you come from. Is it in India?'

'Further.'

Osher's gaze wandered as he racked his memory for geographical references. 'Persia?'

Wayland drank. 'Further. Much further. I come from the land where the sun sinks at the end of the world.'

'How did you reach Tibet?'

'We crossed the Chang Thang from Khotan.'

Osher regarded the dog, sitting fifty yards away in an alert attitude. He took another scoop of meal. 'Call your hound over.'

'It won't come.'

'Why not?'

'Because it knows you'll kill it. Have some more chai.'

Osher dashed the pot from Wayland's hands. He drew his sword and pointed at the dog. Four horsemen spurred forwards and it turned tail and fled. Screaming like banshees, the Khampas galloped in pursuit.

The rest of them began rifling through the travellers' goods. One of them snatched up Wayland's target bow, showing off the gilt inscriptions to his companions as if they were cabbalistic signs. He flexed the weapon, his grin contorting when he realised he couldn't pull the bow to half draw. A comrade took the weapon from him, heaved with all his strength and shattered an arrow, taking the skin off his left wrist as he released.

The bandits went still and watched Wayland. He held out a hand and at a word from Osher the archer returned the bow. Wayland indicated a cairn about two hundred yards away.

'Let's have a friendly competition. Whoever lands an arrow closest to the target wins.'

The Khampas jostled like children trying to impress. Their bows were short, made from inferior materials degraded by age and exposure to the elements. The closest shot fell more than twenty yards short of the mark.

Wayland nocked an arrow. 'That will be difficult to match.' He rocked backwards against the draw and loosed. The arrow had just reached the top of its arc when it passed high over the cairn, falling to earth a furlong beyond the target.

'Lost,' Wayland said. 'In this thin air it's hard to calculate range.'

A bandit broke the silence with a laugh. Someone else laughed and then they were all laughing. Wayland offered his bow to Osher. 'Do you want to try?'

The Khampa extended a hand and dug fingernails as hard as

chisels into Wayland's cheek. 'You like to play tricks. Don't play tricks on me.' He stepped back and turned his attention on the eagle. Until now the Khampas had overlooked the bird or simply refused to believe their eyes. Freya had regained her perch and stood unhooded with her gnarled feet firmly planted, body held horizontal and feathers tight.

'*Ko-wo*,' said Osher.

Wayland nodded. 'I trapped her in the Taklamakan.'

At a gesture from Osher, one of the Khampas went to investigate. Freya watched him. As he approached, she swelled into hump-backed aggression, head thrown back, beak agape, feathers raised in a ruff.

'I wouldn't go any closer,' Wayland said.

One more step and Freya flung herself at the Khampa, lunging against her leash. The man hesitated, drew his sword and raised it.

Voices on all sides shouted at him to leave the eagle alone. Osher called him back and harangued him.

'The eagle is the spirit of our clan,' he told Wayland. 'Is it the same with you?'

'Yes,' said Wayland. 'Also I hunt game with her.'

'Hunt?'

It became clear that the Khampas had no knowledge of falconry. 'I've trained her to catch animals.'

'When you let her loose,' Osher said, 'why doesn't she fly away?'

'I've cast a spell on her.'

The Khampas crowded round, agog with curiosity. 'What does she hunt?' said one.

'Hares, foxes ... '

'Will she kill a wolf?'

Wayland could see from the way the Khampas hung on his answer that the wolf held some significance for them. 'I don't know. I've never tried her at one. Why do you ask?'

'The wolf is the totem of a rival clan,' Osher said. He stared at Freya. 'Show me her hunting.'

'Today the clouds are too thick,' Wayland said. He picked up his saddle. 'It's time we were going.'

Osher pointed at the mountains. 'You won't reach Nepal that way. There isn't a path.'

'Yes, there is.'

'Why do you want to go up there?'

'I told you. We're making a pilgrimage to a temple where a holy man of my religion once studied.'

'What's his name?'

'Oussu.'

Osher's gaze wandered past Wayland. The Khampas who'd chased the dog out of sight were returning on lathered horses. One of them spread his hands in a gesture of defeat. Wayland began to saddle up. Osher laid his sword across the saddle. His men waited.

'We only need one yak,' Wayland said. 'You can keep the other animals. Take the spare tent as well.'

Once again Osher studied the mountains. 'We'll ride with you a little way. I want to see your eagle hunt.'

Zuleyka drew level with Wayland. 'I thought you said the way was too dangerous.'

'It is, but if we go back the Khampas will kill us.'

'Then we'll die whatever direction we take.'

The dog returned and kept pace at a distance. The Khampas looked to Osher for a lead. He waved a hand and laughed.

Around the campfire that evening Wayland told tales of his travels, and Zuleyka sang Luri songs that reduced the brigands to moist-eyed silence. On the morning following they reached the mountain wall, the climb to the pass still hidden by clouds pouring down from the summits.

The Khampas kept pestering Wayland to fly the eagle. He refused. Because he'd intended releasing Freya, he'd allowed her to gorge and she wasn't sharp set enough to hunt.

'This isn't good country,' he told Osher, pointing at the cliffs and chasms.

The Khampa menaced him with his drooping eye. 'Tomorrow we leave you, and we're not leaving until we see the eagle hunt.'

Next day they laboured up a gorge and emerged onto a bare plateau. The occasional cairn, shredded prayer flag or fire-blackened hearth were the only waymarks. Nobody had passed this way for years.

In the late afternoon the sky cleared and the plateau glowed blood red. The travellers and their escort trod the rim of the plateau.

'*Chang-ku*,' shouted one of the Khampas. '*Chang-ku*.'

'What's he saying?' Zuleyka asked.

'He's spotted a wolf,' Wayland said. He rode towards a group of Khampas pointing excitedly into a wild amphitheatre walled in by cliffs tortured into weird folds and striations.

The wolf had stopped when it heard human cries and sat on a rocky bench a thousand feet below, looking up at the figures on the skyline.

Osher grinned at Wayland. 'Fly the eagle.'

Wayland indicated the precipices. 'If she kills, how will I get her back?'

'We'll find a way down. Fly the eagle.'

This was as good a chance as Freya would get, Wayland decided. He didn't think she would tackle the wolf, but letting her fly free and then calling her back to the fist might impress the Khampas.

'Everyone stand back,' he said.

A hush fell. He took Freya from her perch, stroked her back and unhooded her.

She'd never looked more beautiful, the westering sun lighting up her mantle and striking fire from her eyes. They raked around the cliffs.

'Why doesn't she fly?' someone whispered.

'She hasn't seen the wolf. She won't until it moves.'

He waited in the waning light.

'There it goes.'

Freya's feet grasped when she spotted the wolf and she leaned forward, unfurling her wings. Wayland rolled his fist, encouraging her to fly.

With one great waft she beat away. Her wings rose and fell like oars as she gained height, apparently indifferent to the wolf loping through the shadows. Out above the amphitheatre, a gilded speck, Freya drew back her wings and fell. She didn't plunge in the teardrop shape of a stooping falcon. She formed an anchor, the speed of her descent making the wind tear through her splayed pinions. The wolf heard her coming and put on a spurt before disappearing among a jumble of boulders. Moments later Freya dived into the gulf of shadows.

The Khampas had been shouting encouragement. They peered into the bowl, some swearing that they'd seen Freya carry the wolf aloft, others insisting that the wolf had caught her in its jaws. The outcome was important to them and arguments led to blows.

Osher's voice was soft. 'Tell me how it ended.'

'I don't know,' Wayland said. 'I think the wolf escaped.'

'Let's search,' a Khampa cried, skittering down a breakneck defile.

By the time they reached the bottom, the light was so dim that Wayland could have passed within ten yards of Freya without seeing her. She carried no bells and if she'd killed, she would freeze over her prey at any approach.

'Keep back,' he told the Khampas. 'Let the dog search for her.'

It picked up the wolf's trail and followed, sucking up scent, Wayland stumbling after it. He was certain that the wolf had escaped and the eagle was either marooned on the ground or perched somewhere high on the cliffs.

The dog checked, cast about and then backtracked. A pair of ravens flew by, uttering harsh cries. They circled overhead, dipped at something to the right and took stand on an enormous boulder. Muzzle close to the ground, the dog headed in that direction. The ravens took off and disappeared into the dark.

Wayland dragged himself over boulders. One of them was so

large that he had to take a run at it before teetering on the top. On the other side the darkness was too deep to penetrate. He looked back.

'Light a torch.'

Osher bore the brand and together they slid down the other side of the boulder.

'There!' Osher said, holding the flame high.

Twin sparks reflected. Wayland dropped to his knees. 'It's her,' he said. 'She's killed. Stay back or she might kill you too.'

Freya straddled the wolf. She'd made no attempt to break into it and stepped onto his fist as soon as he offered her food. He secured her jesses and let her feed, the Khampas crowding around the wolf with exclamations of astonishment, exclamations of awe.

It was a healthy adult male and Wayland couldn't work out how Freya had killed it until the Khampas skinned it and he discovered a deep puncture wound in its spinal cord just below the skull.

Over bowls of chang drunk around a fire, the Khampas recounted the details of the hunt with ever greater degrees of elaboration. Some of them placed offerings before Freya where she sat hooded at the edge of the fireglow. The moon hung high above, striking a silvery light from the precipices.

Somewhere a wolf howled and another answered, the cry so chilling it almost stopped the blood in Wayland's veins. The mournful sound rose until it filled the amphitheatre, then slowly faded away into a dying sob.

XXXII

Morning broke clear, giving Wayland his first sight of the pass. It was just a blue nick between two peaks washed yellow by the rising sun. He had to tilt his head back to view it. His gaze travelled back down over icefalls and glaciers and immense scalloped walls overhung by cornices.

The Khampas looked on as he and Zuleyka packed their supplies on one of the yaks, a cinnamon-and-cream beast with a placid disposition and tragic gaze. Its name was Waludong. Wayland took Freya from her perch and approached Osher.

'This is where we part.'

'Give me the eagle.'

'She won't fly for you.'

'Give it to me.'

'If you want her, you'll have to kill me.'

Osher appeared to give serious consideration to the proposition, one hand stroking the hilt of his sword. He broke the tension with his tombstone grin and hugged Wayland.

'Go slowly, my friend. Return soon.'

'Go slowly yourself,' Wayland said. He smacked the yak's rump with a switch to sting it into motion. The Khampas watched him and Zuleyka leave. They were still watching when a spur hid them from sight.

Wayland led the way through cold shadows until he reached a sunlit step. Down below he could see the amphitheatre where Freya had killed the wolf. Before unhooding her, he cut off her jesses. He'd let her gorge last night and her crop still bulged. She sat on his fist, taking in the landscape, a breeze ruffling her flank feathers. She spread her wings and held them at full stretch, her weight transferring from Wayland to the air until he could hold her aloft with his hand at full reach. Light as thistledown she left him, setting her wings in a swift glide. Wayland watched her go until she passed out of sight.

'Are you sorry she's gone?' Zuleyka said.

'I'm not losing her. I'm returning her.'

The monks had told him they had to make the crossing in one stage or risk being benighted at the top, with no shelter from the elements. The other side was as steep as the approach, they said, plunging thousands of feet down to the temple and its village.

At first Wayland thought they would reach the pass with time to spare, but by midday the notch in the mountain wall seemed scarcely any closer. Zuleyka made chai and Wayland noticed that the boiling water was cool enough to drink straight from the pot. He'd been travelling for months across a plateau where the lowest valleys were higher than most mountains in other lands and had thought he was acclimatised to altitude. Now, though, his breath grew short and his temples throbbed.

On they climbed, the yak ploughing a path through snow up to its knees. Wayland looked back to see the Tibetan plateau spreading away to the curve of the world. Sweat chilled on him as he rested.

The sun was dipping towards the summits when he emerged from an ice corridor and saw the pass directly above. The final approach was up a steep and tilted snowfield where a slip would have sent them spinning a thousand feet onto a glacier. The yak forged ahead, snorting steam from its nostrils and throwing up powder snow as fine as diamond dust. The pain in Wayland's head had intensified and it felt like an iron band was tightening around his skull. He had to stop every fifty yards or so, hands on knees, dragging in lungfuls of parched air. Zuleyka was suffering too but made no complaint.

Distances were deceptive in the rarefied air. The col seemed to recede as fast as he advanced. Looking back, he had a god's eye view of ranges aligned in no particular direction, saw-toothed ridges shooting up from bowls of ice and glaciers striped with rock debris. Looking up he felt the first prickle of anxiety. The sky behind the pass was beginning to dull over and a wind from the south drove licks of snow from the gap.

He dragged himself on, pushing through the limits of pain. Heart bursting, head pounding, he felt the slope begin to relent. Another few hundred feet and he reached the pass. At the moment of triumph clouds streamed up ahead like grey phantoms and the headwind strengthened, blowing spindrift into his face. Soon it would be dark and they still had to make the descent.

They stumbled across the col and it was dusk when they reached a cairn marking the highest point of the ascent. A little way further on the ground fell away at their feet. They were standing on the rim of an immense corrie, looking down thousands of feet into a horseshoe-shaped cockpit that flattened and narrowed at the far end. That was where they had to make for, but Wayland couldn't work out how to reach it. The direct route led down a snowfield pitched at an acute angle. To his left the snow was broken by crevasses. To his right a gap opened between a massive outcrop and a wall of cliffs.

'How do we get down?' Zuleyka said.

'It must be this way,' he said, traversing right. He moved fast, aware that time was running out. The wind whipped up a ground blizzard, blowing with a force that cut through his clothes. They would never survive a night up here.

For a while it seemed that he had guessed correctly, a ramshackle staircase of rock and ice descending between the cliffs. It was nearly dark. His foot pawed air and he stopped, one step from falling into space. Below him the stairway dropped into a couloir, a slipway of ice jammed in a gulley.

'This can't be the right way,' Zuleyka called.

Wayland climbed up to her, blew on his frozen fingers and unlooped a rope. He tied it to the yak's pack saddle.

'Hold Waludong,' he told Zuleyka.

He tossed the free end of the rope into the gulley and lowered himself down it hand by hand. He was wearing Tibetan boots soled with yak hide that gave little grip and he was only halfway down the chute when he slipped. He clung to the rope but it didn't arrest his slide. Feet first, he shot down the gulley. He knew he was going to die, yet he felt no fear and didn't panic. He even had time to loop the rope around his right wrist before his descent was arrested with a jar that almost wrenched his shoulder out of its socket.

He hung with his feet dangling in space. He opened his eyes, not daring to move. The rope went slack again and he slipped another couple of feet before another violent braking brought him up short halfway over the lip. Clinging to the rope, he looked back over his shoulder to see nothing but darkness below.

Zuleyka was shouting, her voice almost blown away by the wind. 'You nearly pulled Waludong over. I can't hold him much longer.'

Wayland raised his head. 'I'm coming back up.'

He strained against the rope, half-expecting it to give. It held and he hauled himself to safety. When he reached Zuleyka, he saw that the margin had been very small indeed. The yak was inches from losing its footing, Zuleyka braced back on her heels to hold it. If he'd fallen another foot, all three of them would have toppled to their deaths.

'I thought you were gone,' Zuleyka cried. 'Oh, Wayland, what are we going to do?'

Wayland's lips were so frozen he could hardly articulate. 'We have to return to the cairn.'

It was night now. If the wind hadn't eased and if a few stars hadn't appeared, they might not have found their way back. The way down was no clearer than before.

Zuleyka's teeth chattered. 'I'm freezing.'

So was Wayland – not just his face and hands. His blood was thickening, beginning to congeal around the functioning part of his brain.

Below him a robed figure appeared, floating above the snow.

Wayland leaned towards it. 'Yonden?' he said in a slurred voice. The apparition faded.

'We have to go straight down,' Wayland said. 'We'll die if we wait any longer.'

He'd taken only a few steps when the cornice hidden from above collapsed under his weight and he fell. He clawed his hands into the snow in a forlorn attempt to slow his descent. He tobogganed down on his back at breakneck speed and his only thought

429

was that if he went over a precipice or hit a boulder, the impact would kill him outright.

He hurtled into a drift, almost burying himself. He lay gasping and coughing before dragging himself out. He must have slid a thousand feet and he couldn't see Zuleyka and the yak. Then he spotted the dog bounding down the snowface. It flung itself against him, licking his face.

He cupped his numb hands around his mouth. 'Zuleyka, follow my path.'

She couldn't have heard him. A terrible decision had to be made. Use the last of his strength to climb back to her, or abandon her and try to save himself.

He'd dragged himself only a short way up the snowfield when he heard a faint cry and saw two dark dots inching down. With her dancer's balance, Zuleyka managed to reach him without losing her footing, the yak following in a manner part-comic, part-majestic, sitting back on its haunches.

From here the way was visible, but they were a long way from safety. Wayland's boots were full of snow and a poultice of ice chilled his back. If he didn't reach shelter soon, he would lose fingers and toes to frostbite.

'How are your hands and feet?' he asked Zuleyka.

Her reply was apathetic. 'I can't feel them.'

They tottered down the trail, each wrapped in a private world of pain. It began to snow again – big soft flakes that stuck to the face. They followed the yak, Wayland encouraging it with cries copied from Tibetan nomads. '*Ka, ka, ka. Bri, bri, bri.* Get on.'

The beast maintained its plodding pace.

'Look out for a cave or sheltered ledge,' Wayland stuttered. 'Somewhere we can light a fire.'

No haven appeared and the snow was falling more heavily, obliterating the view ahead. Zuleyka stumbled and fell.

'I can't go on,' she said in a matter-of-fact tone.

Wayland pulled her upright. 'It can't be far now.'

'It doesn't matter.'

Wayland took her weight with one hand and gripped the dog by its scruff. 'Find shelter. Go on, find it.'

It bounded away. Wayland followed, supporting Zuleyka, his feet like clods of ice. His mind was so deranged by cold that at first he thought he was dreaming when he heard the dog giving tongue in the distance.

He stood swaying. 'Hear that? Come on.'

Dragging Zuleyka beside him, he increased pace, barging into rocks, tripping over. He stopped and rubbed his eyes. Out of the darkness and flowing snow emerged a building, looking as if it lay in a white cave or at the far end of a tunnel. He staggered forward, unable to believe the building was real until his hands contacted stone.

It was a two-storey house, the entrance to the byre on the ground floor drifted over. Wayland found a notched log ladder leading up to the flat roof. He unloaded the yak, then pushed Zuleyka up the ladder and dragged the dog after. One side of the roof was occupied by a lean-to stacked with firewood. The shed had acted as a weathershield and Wayland made out a square impression on the roof. He scraped the snow away to reveal a trapdoor. He hacked at the ice sealing its edges and heaved it open. A ladder descended into darkness.

'Anyone there?' he called.

He dropped two bundles of firewood through the trap and climbed down. Cursing his useless hands, he managed after many attempts to light a lamp. Its flame threw shadows across a chamber about twenty feet long and ten wide. A fireplace was sunk into the floor at one end and at the other stood an altar bearing offerings to the gods. Stalactites of soot and ice hung from the beams.

He lit kindling with the lamp and heaped branches on the fire until the flames leaped halfway to the roof. Zuleyka sat slumped on the floor. He fumbled off her boots and felt her feet. Stiff as wood. His own feet were in the same state. He stretched them out to the blaze and waited for the pain to start. It began as a tingle that turned into an itch and swelled to a bloated throb. The pain came in colours, pulsing black and red. His fingers felt as if they were filled with splinters and were being squeezed in a vice. They felt swollen to twice their normal size, ready to split like rotten fruit, but when he inspected them they were merely puffy and mottled. Zuleyka sobbed to herself on the other side of the fire. The dog lay rasping at its pads.

Eventually the pain ate itself up, leaving Wayland sick and light-headed. A raging thirst consumed him. He made chai from melted snow and they drank four bowls apiece before stretching out by the fire and falling into a chasm of sleep.

The room was oppressively warm when he woke. Meltwater from the icicles dropped hissing on the ashes. Zuleyka slept on. He opened the trapdoor and climbed out into a day of ineffable brilliance, the mountains on all sides soaring like vast monuments of chiselled white marble. He'd slept past noon and the sun beat hot on his face. The dwelling was one of five scattered over the flat floor of a bowl walled by vertical precipices. A few thorny bushes stippled the snow. To the south the path divided around a chorten so that Buddhist travellers coming both ways could keep it on their right.

Wayland stuck his head through the trap. 'Wake up. We're nearly there.'

Zuleyka joined him on the roof, blinking and yawning. 'What's this place, then? Why isn't anyone here?'

'It must be a summer settlement.'

Wayland blew the fire back into life and made breakfast. They stuffed themselves on buckwheat pancakes cooked in butter. Wayland's fingers and toes were still sore to the lightest touch, several of the pads grey and dead-looking. He rubbed butter into them.

'My nose feels funny,' Zuleyka said.

Frost had nipped the tip. Wayland kissed it. 'It's not going to fall off.'

*

They rested another night and left in mid-morning, following a path beside a half-frozen stream. By the time they passed through a gateway marking the territory around the main settlement, the river had vanished into a deep gorge to their right. Down the valley Wayland spotted a few straight lines among the chaos of rocks.

'Fields. The village must be close.'

To reach it they had to pick their way along a track only a foot-print wide scribed into a scree slope. Wayland negotiated a tight bend under a shattered cliff and held out his hand to Zuleyka.

'We're here.'

Set inside the entrance to a valley on the other side of the gorge, the village resembled a fortress-citadel built on a plug of rock a hundred feet high, the two- and three-storey houses clinging like swallow's nests to the summit. Many of the houses were caved in or lay in piles of rubble at the base of the outcrop. A gulley with terraced fields climbed around the back of the settlement.

'It's empty,' Wayland said.

'The earthquake that blocked the river must have destroyed it.'

'It's been deserted for longer than that. The monks told me it's been years since the villagers crossed the pass. What I don't under-stand is why they didn't rebuild it.' Wayland pointed towards the other side of the gulley. 'That must be Oussu's temple.'

It stood in lofty isolation on a bluff under a cliff eroded into fluted columns and honeycombed with caves. From this distance it appeared intact. Tattered prayer flags on its roof fluttered defiance to demons at the four corners of the world.

'You'll never reach it,' Zuleyka said.

Where the lips of the gorge almost met, a bridge had once stood, its ends marked by stone pillars erected on a foundation of slabs and timber. The span was less than thirty feet and, so far as Wayland could tell, the bridge had been the only connection between the villagers and the rest of the world. He advanced to the edge and looked over. The view into the abyss made his head spin. Working over aeons, the river had cut down through the rocks at different angles and was now invisible below the crooks. Wayland couldn't even hear it.

He made his way back to Zuleyka. 'We'll camp here tonight. Tomorrow we should be below the treeline.'

In the evening he sat watching the temple recede into shadows. A flock of wild sheep inched down a cliff behind the village.

'Supper's ready,' Zuleyka called.

'In a moment,' Wayland said.

He tasted bitter dregs of disappointment at being balked so close to reaching the temple. Less than thirty feet, damn it.

'Wayland!'

Stars formed a mesh of quicksilver. The moon had risen. Wayland slapped his knees and rose. 'Coming.'

XXXIII

Dawn light set fire to the peaks as Wayland and Zuleyka strapped the pack saddle onto Waludong. Where they stood the light was a cold and cheerless blue. A breeze shivered the stunted bushes. The wild sheep were filing back up the cliffs.

'You're very quiet,' Zuleyka said.

Wayland tightened a cinch, then stopped, looking towards the gorge. On this side, the two pillars that had once formed a gateway onto the bridge still stood. On the other side only one remained standing.

'I'm going across,' he said.

Horror swept Zuleyka's face. 'But there's nobody there.'

'I'm looking for something.'

'What?'

'I don't know. A Christian hermit once lived in that temple. I told Hero I'd try to find out who he was and why he came here.'

'Hero wouldn't want you to throw away your life.'

Wayland indicated the gorge. 'It's not much more than twenty feet. In my youth I could have jumped it.'

'But how?'

'I'll make my own bridge.'

He took a spool of twine from his pack, cut two notches in an arrow – one above the tip, the other below the fletching – and tied two sixty-foot lengths of twine to the notches. He led the twine tied to the blade end of the arrow over the stave of his bow, nocked arrow to string, glanced at the pillar on the far side and tried to lob the arrow behind it. The trailing lengths of twine skewed his aim. He retrieved the arrow and tried again, attempting to drop it so that the strands fell on each side of the pillar. He couldn't do it. In flight the lines drew together. He must have made thirty attempts before he landed an arrow ten yards behind the pillar, the lines lying on top of it.

He jiggled one line and established that it was attached to the tip of the arrow. Holding the free end, he walked out to his left until the line slid off the top of the pillar. He tried to ease the other line down the right-hand side and almost succeeded before it snagged halfway down.

He went back to the left-hand line and drew it in, teasing the arrow around the pillar. When it was free, he pulled it back across the gorge. To the end of the other line he lashed a yak-hair rope about a hundred feet long. He dragged on the left-hand line, drawing the rope across the gorge and around the pillar. It was too high. He rolled it as if it were a whip. It fell another couple of feet and there it stuck.

'That's as good as I can get it.'

He hauled the rope back across the gorge. Once he'd retrieved it he spliced the ends together and tossed the loop over one of the pillars on his side. The joined rope dangled into the gorge, the left-hand side several feet lower than the right-hand side.

'You'll never get across on that,' Zuleyka said.

'I haven't finished.'

He took another rope, spliced one end to the rope encircling the

435

pillars and drew on it to pull the second rope around the opposite pillar and back to his side.

'Do you see what I'm doing?' he asked Zuleyka.

'No.'

As with the first rope, he spliced the ends together and threw it over the pillar on his side. Now two pairs of ropes about three feet apart bridged the gorge.

His work wasn't done. The ropes were too slack and he tensioned them by winding them up with a stout pole salvaged from the foundations of the bridge.

Zuleyka watched him with her arms crossed over her chest. 'Don't do it.'

Wayland was less confident than he appeared. The ropes were by no means symmetrical and under strain they would stretch and chafe against the pillars. He wiped his hands, took hold of one of the paired ropes and prepared to step onto the other.

'Here goes.'

'Please, Wayland. If you die I'll never forgive you.'

He shuffled off the edge of the gorge. Under his weight, the rope on which he stood dropped and only his hold on the other saved him from falling at the first step. He stayed where he was, flexing the rope under his feet, getting the feel of it, and then he began edging across.

'I'm going to be sick,' Zuleyka said.

Inch by inch Wayland shuffled across. The rope stretched much more than he'd anticipated, so that by the time he reached midspan he was hanging seven or eight feet below the rim of the gorge. He rested a while and before he set off again he looked down into the abyss. A glance behind showed Zuleyka watching through splayed fingers. To climb out he had to transfer most of his weight and effort to the upper rope. He was only a few feet from the other side when it slipped down the pillar and he fell, his feet coming off the lower rope. He managed to cling on, found his footing again and hung between the ropes at a steep angle, his face slick with sweat.

Only another few feet to go. He did it in one effort and fell to the ground. He kissed it and wormed around.

Zuleyka stood weeping on the other side. 'You could have died. You might still die.'

Wayland swallowed bile. 'If I don't make it back, I've sewn money into the sheath of my target bow. It should be enough to get you home.'

Snow devils spiralled up the gulley, almost as if they were leading him on. Brushing death had made him acutely aware of being alive. Climbing to the temple he noticed everything – an alpine plant that smelled of strawberries when crushed underfoot, snow pigeons circling the settlement on rocking wings, the scent of juniper borne on the breeze.

A high wall surrounded the temple. Wayland circled it and entered the precinct through a breach. The building was more substantial than he'd expected. Two recumbent stone lions guarded its entrance and the door was barred from inside. On one side of it panelled wooden shutters painted with wrathful gods wearing necklaces of skulls sealed a small window. One of the panels was missing. Wayland inserted an arm and unlatched the shutters.

'Sorry,' he said to the guardians before dragging himself through the opening.

Only the light from the window lit the interior. Wayland waited for his eyes to adjust. On the other side of the chamber three gilded statues of the Buddha seemed to float in space. Below them and to one side another statue sat enthroned on a dais in front of an altar. Beside the altar stood a hideous figure with bulging eyes in a black face and a mouth gaping in rage. In front of the seated statue was a basket containing effigies trapped in what looked like a web of coloured silk. Brass trumpets and cymbals glinted on the floor. Butter lamps stood on almost every available surface

Scarcely breathing, Wayland lit one and advanced. The effigies in the basket were made of dough joined by coloured threads. He raised the lamp and gasped. The figure seated on the throne wasn't a statue. It was the mummified corpse of a lama holding ritual instruments – a *dorje* or thunderbolt in one withered hand, a bell in the other.

Wayland held the lamp out, illuminating the lama's features. In death if not in life he'd found serenity. If he *was* dead. Yonden had told him there were holy men who by profound meditation could induce a state of suspended animation. Wayland didn't dare touch the lama.

A door slammed somewhere and he spun.

'Who's there?'

Only the wind, moaning through gaps in the windows. Wayland explored the chamber. One wall was lined with cubbyholes containing books wrapped in wooden bindings. Hero might have been able to make sense of them, but Wayland didn't know where to start. He passed on, images of gods and demons emerging in the light of the lamp and then sinking back into the dark. Wayland shivered, unable to shake off the thought that he was waking the dead.

He stopped, peering at a *thanka* – a painting that depicted a god or saint seated in a meditative posture, one hand raised in blessing and a rainbow forming a halo around his head. What struck Wayland was the saint's appearance. It didn't look oriental. Long reddish hair curled down each side of his pale face and his melancholy eyes were rounder than the eyes of the saints portrayed on the other *thankas*.

Wayland looked behind him before removing the painting and rolling it up.

The shutter slamming made him jump. The urge to escape into sunlight and fresh air was almost overwhelming. He resisted it by thinking of Hero, imagining him at his side peering through the shadows, his sharp mind compensating for his dull vision.

A ladder led to a gallery that ran round the ground floor. Wayland climbed it. Up here the gods seemed to be deities from an older age, more malevolent. The images drifting past in the lamplight were vengeful demons trampling on the dead, copulating with the damned in the depths of hell.

Wayland crossed himself and in almost the same moment he cried out and stabbed at a monster that leaned forward to engulf him. His knife drove deep. The yellow claws around his head didn't make contact. Something grainy sifted from the wound, trickling onto the floor with a noise that sounded like the sands of time running out. Forever fixed in an attitude of frightful menace, a stuffed bear loomed over Wayland.

He'd had enough. Knees knocking he descended to the ground floor and was back at the window before he realised that he hadn't explored the whole temple complex. He steeled his nerves and lit another dozen lamps. By their buttery glow he saw three doors leading off the main chamber. He tried them one by one, heart in mouth. From the moment he'd entered the temple, something had told him he wasn't the only living occupant.

He opened the first door on a room containing ceremonial robes and headdresses that suggested shamanistic rituals. The second was a chapel furnished with an altar and three gilt statues seated on lotus flowers. The third door creaked on its leather hinges as he opened it. A sigh of relief escaped him. The room was a kitchen, stacked with cooking paraphernalia.

He was closing the door behind him when he heard a rustle from inside. Probably a rat. Then it occurred to him that if rats infested the temple, they would have eaten the dough and butter effigies. He forced himself to open the door again and went in, negotiating the clutter. A pot clattered on the other side of the room.

'Don't be scared,' Wayland said. 'I won't hurt you.'

He tiptoed towards the far end. It was blocked by a pile of clay vessels. He swept them aside, gasped and jumped back. 'Holy Christ,' he said, hand on heart.

A man deranged by fear cowered against the wall. He was elderly and spindly and completely defenceless.

'I'm sorry I frightened you,' Wayland panted. 'Forgive me for breaking into your temple. I thought it was empty.'

The poor fellow shook and gibbered.

'I'm a pilgrim,' Wayland said in Tibetan. 'I came here because I heard that a Christian hermit once studied in the temple. His name was Oussu. Do you know the name?'

The little old man showed no comprehension. Whatever wits he'd possessed, Wayland's invasion had unstrung them.

Wayland unrolled the *thanka*. 'Oussu,' he said. 'Is this him?'

The man stopped shaking. He looked from the painting to Wayland, reached out a tentative finger and made the sign of the cross. 'Oussu.'

Relief flooded through Wayland. 'Thank God!'

The shutter flogged in a strengthening wind. He took the man's arm. 'Do you mind if we talk outside. I find the atmosphere inside overwhelming.'

He unbarred the entrance and went out, dragging gusts of air into his lungs. His legs felt so sappy that he had to sit down on the temple steps.

'Who are you?' he said. 'What are you doing here on your own?'

The man was the temple's sacristan. He'd stayed on to serve the lama after an earthquake destroyed the village four years ago. The lama had died two years later, but the sacristan hadn't deserted him. He wasn't left entirely solitary. Each summer a few villagers brought him food and other provisions. He pointed at a trail curving around a mountain shoulder. They came that way, over a pass open for only a few months in summer.

'Why don't they come by the main valley?'

'Closed,' said the sacristan. 'A mountain fell on it.'

Wayland put aside this disturbing news. 'Who was Oussu? Where did he come from?'

The sacristan couldn't say – only that the saint had travelled from India.

'How long ago?'

'One thousand years.'

Wayland smiled. 'That can't be right. The man who founded Oussu's faith and mine died a thousand years ago.'

The sacristan was insistent. 'He came in the reign of Nyima Kesang, the second lama. Wait.' He went into the temple and returned with a book. He opened it and pointed at a line. 'Nyima Kesang.' Running a finger down the pages, he recited the names of the lama's successors to the present day. There must have been more than fifty of them. He closed the book and held it to his chest. 'One thousand years.'

'I was told that after Oussu's death Christian pilgrims visited the temple.'

The sacristan nodded and made the sign of the cross again.

'How long after his death did they come?'

'Not long. One hundred years.'

'Why did they come?'

'To worship at the place where their master found enlightenment. They wanted to take away relics, but the lama wouldn't part with them.'

'Where did the pilgrims go?'

The sacristan gestured down the main valley. 'They died when a bridge collapsed.'

'What did Oussu study here?'

The sacristan pointed at a cave in the cliff behind the temple. 'The *dharma*, the laws of Buddha. He meditated for many days and nights and when his spirit was clear, he left to spread the light.'

'Where to?'

The sacristan pointed west. 'Home.'

Wayland eyed the cave. 'Can I take a look?'

The sacristan was too frail to accompany him. Wayland reached the cave up a staircase tunnelled through the rock and emerged into a room-sized chamber with a stone sleeping platform. From the entrance he could see a narrow, ice-scabbarded peak hidden from the ground. Niches hacked into the walls of the cave contained scrolls. Wayland pulled one out and unrolled it.

The writing wasn't in Tibetan or any other language he recognised.

He heard a faint cry. It came from Zuleyka, looking tiny and forlorn on the other side of the gorge. He descended the staircase and found the sacristan waiting for him. He showed him the scroll.

'Did Oussu write this?'

The old man nodded.

'Listen, I know it might seem like sacrilege, but I'm taking it with me.'

The sacristan looked at him with rheumy eyes and reached for the scroll. 'Leave it where it belongs. There's no way out of the valley.'

'You said a mountain had fallen. Has it blocked the route?'

'Yes. That's why the village is empty. They've all left except me. When I die, the village dies too.'

'You said the villagers brought you food across a pass.'

'It's winter. The pass is closed.'

The sacristan was still holding out his hand for the scroll. Wayland placed it in his pack. 'I'm taking it. If I can find a way into this valley, I can find a way out.' He made the sign of the cross. 'I hope your remaining days aren't too lonely. Goodbye and God bless you.'

The sacristan didn't answer. When Wayland reached the gap in the wall and turned for a last look, the old man was gone.

Wayland ran down the gulley, glad to get away from the temple. His speculations about Oussu stopped when he reached the gorge. He remembered what the sacristan had said about the Christian pilgrims dying when a bridge collapsed under them. Zuleyka stood on the other side, her face smudged by tears. Wayland committed his soul to God, stepped onto the rope and made the crossing without incident. Never had a man been more relieved to step back onto solid ground.

He and Zuleyka embraced in a wordless clinch. Wayland buried his face in her hair. It smelt of woodsmoke and sweat and butter and the scent filled him with a strange feeling of longing and loss. He soothed her back.

'There, there.'

'Waludong's gone,' she said through hiccupping sobs. 'Two yaks appeared and he ran away with them, taking our tent and food. If you'd been here, you could have caught him.'

'We've got a few days' supplies in my backpack. Anyway, Waludong won't be of much use to us now. I'm glad he's found company.'

She stepped back. 'What do you mean?'

'The old man in the temple told me that there's no way out of the valley.'

'What old man?'

'I'll tell you later.'

XXXIV

A hard road still lay ahead, but once they reached the treeline two days later, they dropped back a season in a morning, descending through birches burning with the last flames of summer, walking under cloud-forests of fir and rhododendron. Flocks of tiny birds flew through the trees, trailing a song like tinkling bells. Sections of the path were missing, obliterated by seismic convulsions that had swept away bridges and collapsed the stone ramps the villagers had erected to span awkward gaps in the side of the gorge. Using ropes, it took Wayland and Zuleyka a day to travel half a mile.

The track descended to the river and they camped where it raced past the remains of a bridge.

'We'll wait until morning,' Wayland said. 'The river will be lower then.'

It fell three feet overnight, still too high to ford. Wayland searched upstream and down, looking for an alternative crossing point. The villagers had built the bridge on the only practicable site and he returned with a fatalistic shrug.

'We'll just have to swim across.'

'I can't swim.'

He tied a rope around his waist and handed the free end to Zuleyka. A hundred yards downstream the river plunged through rapids. 'Don't let go.'

He stripped to his breeches and launched off into water not far above freezing point, beating his arms and legs like a frantic frog before reaching the other side forty yards below his starting point. After a lot of coaxing he persuaded Zuleyka to enter the water and hauled her across. The dog followed unassisted. He lit a fire and they drank scalding chai.

'We've got only enough food for one more day,' he said.

Naked under a blanket, Zuleyka regarded him with a look that seemed to catalogue all his faults. 'I came with you because I thought you'd keep me safe. If I'd known that you'd drag me over stormy mountains and icy rivers, I would have chosen another companion.'

'Like Lucas?'

'Why not,' Zuleyka said. She snapped her fingers. 'At least he would have put my wishes above his own.'

Wayland considered the claim. 'You're right and wrong. Wrong because Lucas could never have found a way through the mountains. Right because he could have offered you a brighter future than I could ever give you.'

Zuleyka's interest was piqued. 'Oh,' she said, squiggling forward. 'How so?'

Wayland stirred the fire with a stick. 'Lucas is Vallon's son.'

Zuleyka leaped up, inadvertently exposing one breast. 'No!'

'Yes.'

'But Vallon . . .'

'He doesn't know.'

'Why didn't you tell me?'

'Because it's none of your business. I'm only telling you now because it makes no difference.' Wayland coughed and indicated Zuleyka's nakedness.

She looked down. 'I can't believe you're shocked by a glimpse of a woman's breast. You piss in front of me and I don't complain.'

'I don't waggle my cock about.'

'If you did, I might be able to see it better.'

'Ha, ha.'

Zuleyka pulled the blanket apart. 'There. Take a good look.' She undulated her pelvis. 'I bet your wife can't do that.'

'Grow up,' Wayland said.

She ran off and the dog followed. Her laugh rang witchy among the trees. 'At least your dog loves me.'

That much was true. Batu – 'Faithful' – had grown up with Wayland's daughter and was happiest in the company of women.

Zuleyka returned as if nothing had happened. 'I didn't mean it,' she said.

Wayland regarded her with tired resignation. She was like a child, her emotions swinging this way and that. 'Didn't mean what? Your disappointment in my manhood or your insults to my wife.'

'I didn't mean it when I said I regretted coming with you.'

'I don't regret having you along.'

That night he told her about Syth – how they'd met, wooed and wed. Zuleyka sat quiet for a while.

'You'd never leave her for me, would you?'

'Not for anyone.'

'What if you weren't married?'

'I don't know. You and I are too different from each other – like ice and fire, two elements perpetually at war.'

'Fire melts ice; ice douses fire.'

Wayland laughed. 'Chalk and cheese, then.'

They picked their way across the wreckage of a landslide that had swept away a swathe of forest, scattering trees like toothpicks over masses of broken rock. Wayland came round a corner and halted, at first unable to take in what lay ahead.

The valley had narrowed to a gash blocked by a thousand-foot-high slab of mountain that had split away from the right wall and toppled against the opposite face. Wayland spent a day searching for a way over the rock door and returned to tell Zuleyka that it was unclimbable.

'Are you saying we have to go back?' Zuleyka said. Her voice broke. 'Go back where?'

Wayland contemplated the river. Down here the current crashed against rocks and threw up welters of spray, whirlpools sliding over the surface as if searching for prey. The strongest of swimmers wouldn't last a minute in that torrent. He looked at the tunnel into which the river disappeared.

'The river has found a way through.'

Zuleyka pointed at the tunnel. 'I'm not going into that.'

'The only alternative is to return to the settlement and wait until the pass opens next summer.'

Wayland climbed down to the torrent and worked his way over slippery rocks towards the entrance of the tunnel. It formed a right-angled triangle about twenty feet high, and God knows what obstructions and hazards lay inside. He squirmed across a mossy slab and flexed up on his hands, peering into the interior. He could see about forty yards before the light ran out. The tunnel might be a hundred yards long or a mile. There might be rapids and waterfalls.

He climbed back to Zuleyka. 'I think we can do it.'

Zuleyka crammed her fingers between her teeth. 'Darkness and drowning are my worst nightmares.'

'Tomorrow we'll make a raft.'

All next day they searched for trunks of the right size. The landslide had stripped the trees of most of their branches, which was just as well because Wayland had no edged tool bigger than a knife. They selected eight saplings about twelve feet long and six inches in diameter, dragging them by rope back down the path and then lowering them one by one onto the river bank upstream of the tunnel.

Wayland lashed the trunks together with rope. When the raft was finished, he tethered one end to a boulder, slid the craft into the river and stepped aboard. 'See,' he said, rocking from side to side. 'It's unsinkable.'

Zuleyka summoned a tepid smile. The dog retreated, tail curled under its belly.

It was growing dark by the time they made camp and ate the remaining scraps of food. Somewhere in the forests above them a tiger roared and monkeys chattered. The dog whimpered and stared into the darkness. Wayland threw another log on the fire and kept it burning bright all night.

The sun hadn't appeared above the cliffs when he led Zuleyka down to the raft. He gauged by the waterline that the river was more than two feet lower than it had been the evening before. He stepped onto the raft and held out a hand to Zuleyka. She hung back.

'Surely there's another way.'

'No, there isn't.'

Shaking with fear, she scrambled onto the raft. The dog refused to come and Wayland ended up dragging it aboard and tethering it. He'd given some thought to safety and had tied loops to the trunks as handholds. He'd considered fitting safety lines but decided that if the raft broke up, they'd stand a better chance floating free.

He looked at the tunnel. 'Here we go,' he said, casting off. 'Lie flat and hold tight.'

The raft slid towards the entrance. The walls closed around them and the raft bucked in a wave. Wayland knelt at the front, peering into the gathering darkness. The raft nudged a boulder and swung round so that he was facing backwards, looking at the rapidly disappearing triangle of daylight. Before he could face front again, the raft hit the wall with a force that threw him on his side. Without the handhold, he'd have been tossed into the river. It was pitch black now, with no way of anticipating when or where the next shock would come. He lay flat on the raft, one hand across Zuleyka's back. The dog was howling and flinging itself against its tether.

'Stay still, you dumb—'

Another collision drove the words back down his throat. He felt the trunks give beneath him.

They glided down a calm reach before picking up speed. The slop and gurgle of water echoed against the tunnel walls, the noise building to a roar.

'Waterfall,' Wayland shouted. 'Hang on.'

The raft shot forward and plunged nose-first into the river. Water washed over Wayland and then they were back on an even keel. He checked that Zuleyka was still with him, then felt for the dog. It had gone. The booming of the fall receded behind them.

'I can see daylight,' Wayland shouted.

Against the grey haze he made out two rocks dividing the current. The raft spun towards them and struck broadside, the current canting it against the rocks and holding it there. Wayland tried to push it free but couldn't exert enough leverage. He was soaked through and cold to the core.

He struggled onto one of the rocks and shoved against the raft with his feet. Slowly it began to swing around. A last effort and it came free, the current whisking it away too fast for him to scramble aboard. He threw himself after it and just managed to cling on to the trunks as it sped downstream.

The light grew. A few gyrations carried them out of the tunnel. An eddy spun them towards the bank and Wayland found his footing. Zuleyka sprang onto land and helped him climb out. He crawled a few feet and collapsed.

'Good girl.'

He came round to find the dog licking his face and Zuleyka chafing his back. A warm sun beat down into a glade bright with butterflies.

'I'm all right,' he said.

*

They hiked down a well-trodden path cushioned with pine needles, passing through pockets of sunlight and shadow. Magpies with azure wings scolded overhead. The trees opened up ahead of them, the path falling away down a steep wooded slope. Wayland and Zuleyka stopped at the top. Neither of them spoke.

They were back in the world. The torrent they'd been following was a tributary of a broad river flowing south through a valley covered in dense forest. Far below them a suspension bridge crossed to a road. Wayland could see a few travellers on it. Smoke drifted up from houses in cultivated clearings. Above the ridge on the other side of the valley the sky was curtained by a majestic range of snow mountains.

By noon they were eating dumplings in a hostelry for merchants and pilgrims travelling between the burning shrine at Muktinath and the lowlands of Nepal and India. Wayland purchased clothes for himself and Zuleyka. A local directed them to an inn standing high above the river. The innkeeper gave them a room with a wooden balcony overlooking the road and asked if they wanted to eat.

When Wayland woke next day, the food they'd ordered lay untouched inside the door and Zuleyka lay in purring sleep. The purple bloom of twilight filled the valley when she woke.

'I'm not putting on new clothes until I've bathed,' she said.

The innkeeper told them that they could wash in hot springs that welled out of rocks not far upriver. His son showed them the way, bowing to a Hindu couple seated naked in an alcove above a spring of hot bubbling water.

Wayland and Zuleyka stripped off at the next thermal spring and slid into the water. It was almost too hot to bear. They wriggled onto stone shelves, gasping in the steamy atmosphere.

Looking at Zuleyka, Wayland remembered that he'd first made love to Syth after they'd cleansed themselves in a makeshift sauna on the shore of a Greenland fjord.

'You look sad,' Zuleyka said.

'Just tired.'

It was another two days before they made love. For Zuleyka it was a painful experience. It turned out that she really was a virgin.

She dabbed blood on Wayland's forehead. 'By Luri custom, that makes us husband and wife.'

They stayed in the inn for a week, regaining their strength, growing comfortable with each other's bodies.

On the seventh morning, Wayland was sitting on the balcony, watching Zuleyka brush out her hair, when he heard music in the distance. Zuleyka jumped up. Wayland stood.

Around the bend to the north strode a man leading a white mule sporting a red plume and trappings covered with silver bells and tassels. A file of men and women followed, the men in high-waisted white coats, the women wearing bloomers and tunics in a riot of colours, bangles on their wrists and hoops in their ears. One of the men played some kind of wind instrument, the women singing and keeping time with tambourines. Padding behind the ensemble came a bear on a leash.

'Luri?' Wayland said.

Zuleyka nodded, her face radiant. She called out and the procession halted. The man leading the column looked up, shading his swarthy face. Zuleyka called again and ran down the hillside. The Luri clustered around her and they conversed for a long time before she made her way back.

'They're returning to India for the winter,' she panted. 'We can go with them.'

Wayland watched her pack her few possessions.

'Hurry up,' she said.

'I'm not coming with you.'

Her face fell. 'There's only one road south. At least stay with me until we reach the lowlands.'

Wayland took her in his arms. 'Have you been happy these last few days?'

She nodded.

'So have I,' Wayland said. 'Let's part while the memories are still sweet.'

'We can make more happy memories.'

'Your people will never accept me as one of their own, will they?'

Her eyes flickered.

'You see,' he said. 'It's better this way.'

She stood before him. 'Good bye, then. Thank you, Wayland.'

He kissed her. 'Good bye, Zuleyka.'

She flicked a tear away. 'I can't believe that's all. Not after everything we've been through.'

'It isn't all. I won't forget you.'

Zuleyka reserved her tears for the dog, spilling them onto its rough head. 'Good bye, Batu. Look after your master.'

The leader of the Luri troupe called out. Zuleyka squared her shoulders and walked away.

'That song you sang to the troopers in the Kara Kum,' Wayland called. 'Does it have a name?'

Zuleyka sniffled, half-crying, half-laughing. 'It's called "When we meet".'

'Sing it as you go, will you?'

He watched her hurry down the hill, so fleet of foot, so graceful. The leader of the troupe lifted her onto the mule. She looked up at Wayland, raised her hand to him and faced the road ahead. The musicians took up their instruments and struck up the air that had so captivated Wayland.

The dog lifted its head and howled.

'You can go with her if you want,' Wayland said.

The dog looked at him and ran forward a few yards before stopping and looking back, its tail wagging uncertainly.

'Go on,' Wayland said.

The dog bounded down the hill and streaked after the Luri. Wayland listened as the song grew faint with distance, climbing up the hill to keep the cavalcade in sight. The music faded away and Zuleyka rode around a bend in the road, out of his life and into memory.

China

XXXV

Early November found Vallon's expedition deep in the Tsaidam, a salt marsh basin extending for hundreds of miles to the Chinese border. The wells were brackish, and though the Sogdians rendered the water more potable by boiling strings of dough that absorbed much of the salt, the men suffered from perpetual thirst.

The days grew shorter and colder, the nights longer and freezing. The caravan had taken to leaving at midnight and travelling until noon, giving the camels enough daylight to forage. Disease had claimed three men. Aimery, Lucas's squad leader, had been one of the victims, dying in a pool of foul black effluent. Vallon's servant had also died. Hero had treated the sick as best he could, heedless of picking up the contagion himself.

These were grim days. One night march blurred into the next, Vallon riding in a haze of weariness, guided along a faint dappled track by bleached bones that lined the way like a tidal wrack. For two nights they rode through a waste of clay dunes eroded into bizarre shapes like grave barrows or giant termite mounds or the hulls of upturned boats. Each time Vallon nodded off in the saddle he was jerked awake by his horse reacting to an unpredictable drop or an unforeseen rise.

With lacklustre eyes he saw at daybreak a squat excrescence emerge from the drab and empty horizon. It was the next caravanserai, still almost two stages away. By morning next day he could make out the walls of a lonely fort. A detachment of cavalry galloped out from its gate. Vallon ordered his men to look to their arms and waited for the riders to approach.

Faced with a strong military force, they drew up short. One of them leaned forward, ordering them to go back.

'He says there's no room in the fort,' Shennu said. 'It's already occupied by two camel trains.'

'Tell him to kick them out. Why should they squat in comfort while we famish and thirst?'

'They refuse to leave. A gang of bandits menaces the road a few days to the east. They massacred the last caravan that tried to cross their territory.'

Vallon rode forward. 'Tell the fool that we're on a mission to the imperial court and won't be delayed by frightened merchants or a band of cut-throats.'

The Chinese cavalry, wretchedly equipped, gave way before force of arms and galloped back to the fort. Set on a stony plain stretching like a rule to every horizon, it didn't serve any strategic purpose that Vallon could think of. During the time it took the Outlanders to enter the fortifications, its garrison had suffered a change of heart, falling on the foreigners as if they were saviours come to relieve a siege.

Every space was occupied by camels and their handlers. More than two hundred men, women and children had taken refuge behind the walls, and after two weeks the yards were heaped with filth. There could be no doubting their fear, and the garrison commander told Vallon that their terror was justified. This was no ordinary bandit gang that terrorised travellers into handing over their possessions, perhaps slaying a few souls to speed up the transaction. It was led by a Chinese deserter called Two-Swords Lu, a former arms instructor who'd recruited a hundred Tangut tribesmen. Lu was a monster, a drinker of blood. Booty seemed to be of secondary interest to him. He killed for pleasure, sparing no one, his followers raping young and old of either sex before putting them to the sword or worse.

'Why doesn't he eradicate the vermin?' Vallon asked Shennu.

'His garrison numbers less than eighty, mainly criminals who chose military service on the frontier rather than execution. He doesn't even have enough horses to mount them. He's sent a message imploring help from the provincial governor at Lanzhou, but troops won't arrive until spring. Even if they come, he doubts they can destroy the bandits. They dwell in mountain caves to the south, venturing out only when they scent prey. Lu has spies in the staging posts who alert him to the passage of a caravan.' Shennu cocked his head, listening to the commander's next words. 'He says Lu is protected by charms and can't be killed by mortal means.'

Vallon looked at the commander across the globe of lamplight. The man was on the edge of a breakdown, fingering a rosary and staring at the general in frenetic expectation.

'I know what's coming next.'

'The garrison is running out of food. Unless the camel trains leave within the next few days, everyone in the fort will starve. He begs you to escort the caravans east.'

Vallon spoke softly. 'Tell him I sympathise with his plight. Tell him I can't help him. If I'd answered every plea for armed assistance, I'd still be back in Khotan.'

He rose and the commander stood and put hands together before reeling away.

'You were his last hope,' Shennu murmured. 'I wouldn't be surprised if he ends his shame tonight.'

'It doesn't sway my decision. We have to reach Kaifeng before winter freezes us in our tracks.'

'If you won't escort the caravans, I will,' said a voice behind him.

Vallon turned as Hauk pushed off from the wall he'd been leaning against.

'You enticed me into this adventure by telling me what profits I could make by hiring out my men's sword arms.'

'You've accumulated enough wealth by trade.'

'Not enough and not of the right kind. In Khotan I paid good money for fake jade. In Miran I ended up with a pile of forged religious paintings.' Hauk rubbed thumb and forefinger together. 'Silver and gold is the only currency I trust.' He cocked a thumb at the window of the commander's billet. 'Down there are two hundred souls in fear of their lives. How much do you think they'd pay to a man who would lead them to safety? You suggested the price yourself. One tenth of all their wealth.'

'I forbid it.'

'That's the other thing you forget. We agreed I would follow your commands only when they coincided with my own interests. For the last three months you've acted only in your own interests. It's time I redressed the balance.'

'You heard the garrison commander. The bandits outnumber your Vikings by three to one.'

Hauk made a contemptuous sound. 'They attack plump meat, not firm muscle.'

'Don't be so sure. Their leader is a former officer. The last caravan had an armed escort, and it didn't save them.'

'Join forces with me, then. Our camels walk no faster than theirs. If you want to speed your march, get rid of the catapult and fire siphon.'

'I'm not worried by the merchants slowing us down. You're right about the bandits avoiding a well-armed force. On our own we'll probably get through unscathed. Attach ourselves to the caravan and we become a target that can't be ignored.'

'Scared of fighting?' Hauk said. 'Since we joined the Silk Road you've wasted weeks haggling with petty chieftains and greedy officials, squandering precious gold on broken-down camels instead of speeding our passage with some judiciously spilled blood.'

Vallon touched his sword. 'Careful what you say.'

Hauk was beyond caring what actions his words might provoke. He and his men were sick of this soul-sapping journey.

'Allow me to speak,' Hero said. 'If we travel on our own, my relief at avoiding the brigands would soon be overtaken by guilt at the knowledge we condemned every other traveller in this fort to death.'

Vallon's temper broke. 'If the positions were reversed, those traders would abandon us without a backward thought. You've seen how they treat their camels, loading them so crudely that

458

their saddles dig maggot-filled holes, then lighting fires under their haunches to goad them on before finally leaving them in the desert for the wolves. Not even kind enough to give the beasts they depend on a swift death.'

'I agree with Hero,' Aiken added.

The stench from the multitude below filled the room.

'Trapped between an irresponsible pirate and two tender consciences,' Vallon snarled. He stalked towards the door. 'Summon the commander before he slits his wrists. Tell him we'll take his human baggage.' Vallon whirled and pointed at Hauk. 'That's the last concession I'll make. When we reach China, our partnership is dissolved.'

From a high pass between the Tsaidam and the Hexi Corridor, Lucas looked north-east into a depression occupied by a lake blurring into the horizon. To the south weak sunshine lit a monochrome backdrop of mountains. A steely wind nagged. Lucas sniffed and blew into his hands.

Vallon and Shennu rode up. 'Koko Nor,' Shennu said, indicating the lake. 'It means "Teal Sea". A community of monks live on an island. They have no boats and can communicate with the world only in winter, when the lake freezes over. It's salt, of course.'

Vallon rubbed his cracked lips. 'I'm tempted to join them.'

Lucas heard him speak without feeling any connection. Worn down by the journey, he no longer thought of Vallon as his father in anything but abstract terms. If anybody had been a father-figure on this voyage it had been kind and quiet Aimery, unofficial chaplain and confessor, who each evening said grace before the squad ate supper. His death had taken something out of Lucas. He looked at Vallon, wondering dully why God let the wicked thrive and allowed the good to die.

The sun blazed in a clear sky when the Outlanders made their first camp by the lake. Under bright light the waters were a deep and transcendent blue. Across them beat a squadron of swans, flying so low that Lucas could see their breast muscles flexing and hear the neck-prickling song created by the wind soughing through their pinions. Whether they were flying home or leaving home didn't matter. Lucas wished he was going with them, and by the way the other troopers turned and watched the formation beat south until their cries faded, he wasn't the only one.

Snow squalls interrupted the rhythm of the march, forcing the caravan to camp overnight by a creek dribbling into Koko Nor. Vallon ordered the Outlanders to pitch their tents in a defensive square around the horses and baggage, leaving the camels and the two merchant trains unprotected. The horses were left saddled and pickets posted. Lucas's squad stood the last watch.

Sometime in the small hours the snow stopped and freezing mist fell. Lucas shivered in his cape, pulled the hood down and willed away the hours until dawn. The light when it came was opaque, rising from the ground like a cold emanation. Lucas couldn't even see Gorka posted twenty yards to his right.

'You still there, boss?'

'I ain't sure. I couldn't find my dick in this fog.'

Lucas drew his sword. 'I thought I heard something.'

Gorka spat. 'Relax. A wolf doesn't attack guard dogs when it has a pen of sheep at its mercy.'

The light grew without illuminating anything solid. Fatigue conjured up phantoms in the mist. Peering into the whiteout, Lucas fancied he could see figures of vaguely human form – two of them, advancing at a bandy-legged trot and then halting. Lucas stared at the apparitions without really believing in them. Behind him the horses began to whicker and tread.

'Gorka ... ' he said on a rising note of apprehension.

With a scream that froze his blood one of the figures sprang at him. He raised his shield just in time to block the bandit's sword. His assailant didn't pause to engage. Both bandits ran past into the camp.

'Get after them,' Gorka shouted. 'They want the horses.'

Lucas set off in pursuit and gained on the bandit who'd cut at him. Sensing his presence, the bandit turned and skidded on the snow, falling to one knee. Lucas hesitated and the bandit sprang up, his face cruel beyond measure, a braid of hair hanging from the back of his otherwise shaven pate. He seemed to grin and his sword flicked out, probing for an opening. Lucas darted back.

The bandit followed up, hissing, his sword flickering.

The fear clogging Lucas's brain cleared. This was what he'd trained for. He parried the bandit's lunge, smashed his shield into the man's face and kicked him as hard as he could in the groin. The bandit went down in a heap. Lucas hefted his sword, held it at full height.

'Don't just fucking stand there,' Gorka bellowed. 'Kill him.'

Lucas brought his sword down as if he were trying to split a log and hacked halfway through the bandit's skull. Brain spilled out, steaming in the icy air. Lucas skipped back as if he feared being engulfed in a tide of blood.

'I've just killed a man,' he said.

He took one last look at the dead man and ran towards a scene of utter confusion at the centre of the camp. Shouts and screams, strangely muffled by the mist, mingled with the whinnying of horses and the blast of trumpets. Pale figures milled in the mist and Lucas couldn't tell if they were friend or foe until he was within a sword's length.

A horse galloped towards him – one of the Ferghanas that Vallon had bought in Bukhara. Lucas threw himself in front of it and lunged for its reins as it dashed past. Still holding his bloodied sword, he managed to get a one-handed grip and clung on while he was dragged twenty yards before bringing the horse to a halt. He heaved himself into the saddle as two more mounted bandits galloped past. One of the horses carried two riders – a bandit clutching in front of him a figure with a pale face that turned towards Lucas before the horse bore him away.

'Aiken!' Lucas shouted. 'They've got Aiken!'

No one responded. In the clamour of battle no one heard him, or they were too fiercely engaged.

Lucas wheeled the Ferghana in pursuit, the two horses already indistinct. The land sloped up from the river and the higher he climbed the lighter it grew until he broke out of the mist to see the riders only a hundred yards ahead, galloping towards a line of horses the other bandits had left tethered and untended before creeping into the camp.

One of them, directly in Lucas's path, was haring back on foot towards the mounts. Either he didn't hear Lucas's approach on the snow-covered ground or he assumed the rider was a companion. He paid no notice until the thudding hooves alerted him to danger, and then he cast a backward glance. He must have had just enough time to register the blade swinging down before it sliced through his neck in a welter of blood.

Lucas fixed his gaze on Aiken's captor and drubbed the Ferghana's flanks. The two mounted bandits swept past the tethered horses. The one holding Aiken shot a glance over his shoulder. Encumbered as he was, he knew Lucas would outpace him and he called out to his companion. Both spun to meet the threat and the unhampered rider screamed and set his horse in a headlong attack.

Lucas didn't falter. Gaze locked on his target, he drove the Ferghana on, calculating how and where to strike. The enemy came at him headlong until it seemed inevitable that they would collide.

The bandit's mount lost its nerve at the last instant and sheered away. At full gallop and full stretch Lucas struck its rider in the throat and when he looked back he saw the bandit galloping away with two fountains of blood gushing from his neck and his head bobbling over the ground.

Lucas faced forward. The other bandit threw Aiken off the horse, unslung a bow, drew an arrow and concentrated on his aim. Lucas drove at him and saw the bow spring open, felt the wind of the arrow sting his cheek. The bandit was still fumbling for his sword when Lucas fell on him, swinging his sword in a shallow sweep that caught him at waist height. Momentum carried Lucas past and when he wheeled, the bandit still sat his saddle, a gory stain spreading on his side and bright red flowers blossoming on the snow beneath him. Lucas drew breath and moved in for the kill. Before he closed, the bandit slid out of his saddle and toppled to the ground. Lucas didn't waste time on him. He caught the horse and led it back to where Aiken stood shocked and speechless.

'You all right?' Lucas said in a thick voice.

Aiken raised a trembling finger.

What Lucas hadn't seen was the main bandit force drawn up on a ridge and now sweeping down like a wave.

'Mount up and ride like hell!'

Aiken made two efforts before getting into the saddle. Lucas slapped the horse's rump with the flat of his sword.

'Faster! They're catching us.'

The leading edge of the wave was a hundred yards behind them when a score of Outlanders burst out of the fogbank ahead. The bandits divided, spilling away on each side, baying like a pack of hounds.

Vallon hauled up his horse in front of Aiken. 'Thank God you're safe.'

Aiken gave a strangled laugh. 'Lucas had more to do with it than the Almighty.'

Vallon turned his gaze on Lucas. He pulled his horse around. 'Return and secure the camp. That was only the first thrust.'

On the ride back, Gorka approached Lucas and addressed him in an uncharacteristically tentative manner. 'How many did you kill?'

'Four, I think. One of them was running away and doesn't count.'

Gorka planted a wet kiss on Lucas's cheek. 'They all count, lad. One more and you get to wear that fancy Greek armour.'

XXXVI

The Outlanders and Vikings advanced in close order across a dazzling snowscape, the lake about three miles to their left, low hills to the south and beyond them mountains smothered in cloud.

They'd covered perhaps four miles, the caravan trailing back another mile, when one of the Turkmen shouted and pointed. All eyes turned south. On a bluff about half a mile away sat a solitary horseman wearing scarlet armour and a horned helmet.

'That must be Two-Swords Lu,' Vallon said.

The lone rider raised his hand, as if preparing to orchestrate events only he could foresee.

'What's he doing?' Otia said.

'I think he's trying to intimidate us into abandoning the caravans,' Josselin said.

'He doesn't have to wait for us to leave,' said Vallon. 'He can fall on them any time he chooses. They're too scattered and we're too few to stop him.'

Wailing and weeping, the caravanners drove their beasts towards the Outlanders' position.

Vallon cast a malign look at Hauk. 'You took their gold and silver under false pretences.'

Hauk slapped his saddlebag. 'I've got it and that's all that matters.' He raised a hand. 'Ride on, men.'

'Then you ride alone,' Vallon said. He stood in his stirrups. 'Outlanders. We stand our ground. Form a tight square.'

'Leave the caravans,' Hauk said. 'You said yourself that in other circumstances the traders would abandon us without a qualm.'

'You pledged to protect them. As commander of the expedition, I'm the guarantor of your word. If you won't keep it, I will. Now run away and leave the fighting to proper soldiers.'

Flushed with anger, Hauk capered on his horse. 'I'll make a stand with you, but I won't forget your insults.'

The Outlanders waited on the plain. The figure on the bluff brought his hand down and somewhere a whistle shrilled. The troopers glanced around uneasily.

'Sir,' someone shouted at the rear of the square.

Vallon and Otia rode back. Out on the salt flats around the lake a tremble of movement had appeared, shaping into horsemen strung out in a frieze, the figures stretched thin by the warping light, the horses apparently treading on air.

'At least forty,' Vallon said.

By now many of the merchants and camel drivers had deserted their cargos and were besieging the Outlanders' position, begging to be granted sanctuary. The soldiers ignored them or beat away the more importunate. Vallon saw a mother with two children kneeling in front of the troopers, shrieking and rending her clothes.

'Open ranks and admit them,' Vallon said.

Otia winced. 'They'll get in the way.'

'They're in the way now.'

The formation enlarged to accommodate the terrified civilians. Some of the men were armed and Vallon's officers posted them to plug gaps in the perimeter. The bandits attacking from the lake were metamorphosing from phantoms to flesh.

'Take charge of the rear,' Vallon told Otia.

He returned to the front and had just taken up position when Two-Swords Lu swung his hand down a second time. The rest of his force poured out of the gulleys on each side of the bluff, fifty to the left, fifty to the right.

'Hold your lines,' Vallon said. 'They'll sack the caravans before tackling us.'

The horse archers at front and rear fanned out around the Outlanders' position and fell on the abandoned animals and loads. Some merchants hadn't been able to part with their goods and died as their belongings were ransacked before their eyes. Vallon averted his gaze from the sight of a group of bandits gang-raping a woman while one of their colleagues sodomised her husband before cutting his throat.

Presented with such bounty, the brigands didn't know which way to turn. They ran about, slashing saddlebags, kicking over the contents before darting to the next animal. A group of them fell to fighting over a pack of choice goods.

'They've lost all discipline,' Josselin said. 'Let me lead a sortie.'

Vallon looked at Two-Swords Lu on the bluff. 'It's a ruse. He's trying to make us break ranks. The moment we do, his men will recover good order.'

A whistle blew and the bandits left off their looting and coalesced in a single force in front of the Outlanders. Another blast and they peeled off right and left, riding rings around the square, lofting arrows flighted to produce an eerie whistling sound.

'Don't shoot back,' Vallon shouted. 'Let them think we have no teeth.'

Growing bolder, the bandits drew closer with each circuit, riding within fifty yards before loosing.

'Kill them,' Vallon said.

At such close range the bandits made easy targets for the Turkmen archers. Twenty arrows hissed in a nearly flat trajectory and half a dozen riders tumbled to the ground.

'More of the same,' Vallon said.

Another volley killed three brigands and brought down two horses.

'Keep shooting.'

Badly stung, the horde drew back out of range. Two-Swords Lu lashed his horse down from the bluff in puffs of snow. He reached his force and Vallon heard him haranguing the bandits. They formed up in three lines of fifty facing the Outlanders. Silence strained between the two positions.

With tremendous screams the bandits attacked, throwing all their weight against the Outlanders' front. Archers in the rear dropped several of the attackers during their charge, and a volley of javelins killed several more before they struck.

The bandits had no idea of the quality of soldiers they were up against. Well-armed, -armoured and -mounted, veterans of a dozen battles and a hundred skirmishes, the Outlanders absorbed the first shock, held their ground and chopped the bandits' first rank to pieces while the brigands behind them pranced and wheeled, unable to bear on the action.

The Outlanders must have slain twenty of the enemy before the bandits broke and withdrew.

'Follow up,' Vallon shouted. 'Smash them.'

He led the charge, Josselin galloping at his side. 'It could be a feint,' the centurion shouted. 'They still outnumber us.'

'That's why we have to destroy them now. If we don't, Two-Swords will keep biting at us all the way to China.'

Vallon had already selected the bandit chief as his target. Lu rode in front of a screen of horsemen and judging by the way he hurled orders left and right, he still imagined that he could organise a counter.

Vallon closed on him. His Ferghana horse was everything he'd hoped for. Strong, brave and swift, it cleaved through the enemy. Forty pounds of mail armour made him almost invulnerable to the bandits' shoddy swords. He swept through the foe, scything left and right.

The enemy flared away in front of him. Only half a dozen bandits stood between him and Lu. Ten Turkmen archers shot them down like jackals and then it was just Vallon and Two-Swords Lu.

And Otia. Somehow the centurion had outstripped his general and was only fifty yards behind Lu. Vallon swore. Calling on Otia to give way would be a waste of breath. Slow to wrath, Otia was implacable when roused.

Lu rode into one of the gulleys under the bluff, closely followed by Otia. By the time Vallon entered the defile, both men had disappeared around a bend. Broken ground slowed Vallon. The gulley twisted upwards and around each turn he expected to find Otia engaged with Lu. Vallon rode round another bend and saw the centurion, but he was alone and lurching back down the trail, a javelin sticking out of his belly.

Vallon reined in and knew from one glance that the wound was mortal. Otia gave a rueful smile.

'I hit his horse. He hit me.'

Two more troopers pounded up the gulley. 'Take care of Otia,' Vallon shouted.

He drove his horse onwards, following Lu's blood-spotted trail. The gulley narrowed and steepened, running into a dead end. Before the cliffs closed in, Lu had urged his horse up a spill of loose rock, making a traverse to the crest. Vallon could only follow at a plod, and before he reached the top he had to dismount and lead his horse.

He emerged onto a plateau cut away on three sides by canyons, the mountains to the south rearing up in a serrated wall. Lu's horse stood at a distance, legs straddled, head down, its neck and chest glossy with blood. Vallon searched around for the bandit chief, wondering how he could have disappeared on that bald summit. When he looked back at the horse, Lu was standing beside it, a squat figure planted on the ground with legs set wide apart.

Vallon waited, gathering his breath. He rejected the idea of riding into the attack. Snow and rocks made the going treacherous, and he knew from experience that a skilful warrior on foot could evade a mounted charge and use the momentum of his opponent to his own advantage.

Lu hadn't moved. There was something uncanny about his stillness. Vallon began his advance, moving like a man heading towards an urgent appointment – not hurrying, but composed and direct. Approach your enemy as if you were walking in the street, his swordmaster had taught him all those years ago. Neither fast nor slow, neither floating nor heavy-footed.

His teacher had taught him many other things that he'd tried to master. Keep a clear mind. Don't plan how you're going to fight the enemy. If he's any good, he'll read your thoughts. The only thing that should be in your mind is the determination to kill, to cut through your enemy as if he isn't there. He'll read that thought too and will be unnerved. Kill with one move if you can. The warrior who jumps about displaying fancy footwork and neat thrusts and fucking taradiddles would be better off taking up dancing.

Lu still hadn't moved. Cheek pieces on his helmet fell in lappets protecting his face and neck. For body armour he wore a shirt of lacquered red leather and a short skirt of the same. Two curved swords hung from his left hip. He carried no shield.

Vallon was close enough to make out Lu's eyes, black slits fixed in an unblinking gaze. Still walking, Vallon adjusted his grip on sword and shield.

Fifteen feet away Lu charged. From a standing start he seemed to shoot forwards at an astonishing pace, at the same time drawing both swords to present their single edges. Vallon had only time to notice that the sword in Lu's left hand was shorter than the other before the bandit was on him.

Lu trapped Vallon's parry in the angle of a cross made by both his blades. Before Vallon could disengage, he registered that Lu had somehow managed to reverse his swords to present the unsharpened thick edge. A lesser sword than Vallon's might have bent or broken with the force of the impact.

A whir, a flurry and Lu's right-hand sword hit Vallon's right ribs a slashing blow. He knew immediately that the cut had broken at least one rib.

From that moment he was on the back foot, parrying with sword and shield strokes almost too fast to see, Lu somehow managing to change the direction of his blows in mid-delivery, so that the right-hand sword struck where Vallon expected the left sword to land and vice versa. It was like fighting a fast and fanged spider, and if he hadn't been wearing such high-quality armour over a wadded cotton *kavadion*, Lu would have killed him in less than a minute. That was the time it took Two-Swords to make two more potentially lethal attacks – a reverse slice that cut through Vallon's nose guard as if it were tin, and a thrust to the heart that pierced the mail above his sternum and penetrated padding and flesh.

Vallon managed to block the next half-seen slash with the edge of his shield. It was made of linden wood, soft and light, constructed without a reinforcing metal rim. Lu's long sword caught just long enough in the fibres for Vallon to make his first threatening counter, a downswinging blow that glanced off Lu's armoured shoulder.

Vallon used the fleeting respite to take stock. He was letting Lu dictate the contest. He was trying to fight him on his terms and he wasn't a match. Vallon had to play to his own strengths, and they weren't negligible. He outstripped his opponent by half a head in height, reach and blade length. He wore superior armour that had already resisted blows that would have killed if delivered by his straight-edged longsword. The curved blades wielded by Lu were designed to slash more weakly armoured opponents. There were only eight basic moves in swordplay, and Lu's single-edged blades gave him sixteen lines of attack. But that was no more than Vallon's double-edged sword could deliver, and its straight edges made it a more versatile weapon than the curved blade, better suited for hacking and thrusting, giving better penetration at longer range. Plus he had a shield that could be used both defensively and offensively. What he couldn't match was Lu's speed and stamina. Vallon wasn't the man he'd been ten years before, and during the journey he'd had little time to practise his sword skills.

The contest had settled into an asymmetrical rhythm, Lu wielding his swords in quick-flowing arcs, much of the impetus coming from his hips, his feet sometimes gliding, sometimes moving with short, quick, stuttering steps. By contrast, Vallon delivered his counters primarily from the elbow and shoulder and moved with wide passing steps. It was as uneven a contest as a fight between a leopard and a bear.

Lu's curved blades delivered more fluent slashing cuts than the less oblique cuts Vallon could manage with his longsword. He countered with fast-jabbing thrusts aimed at head and chest, the straight edge and tapered point making it hard to see and the longer blade holding Lu out of effective killing range. If you face a lion, his swordmaster had told him, become a castle.

Little things can determine the outcome of great clashes. A slip or stumble and the greatest swordsman can die at the hands of a peasant armed with a billhook. What swung the contest in Vallon's favour was his cruciform sword hilt. Lu made a two-pronged crossing attack at Vallon's head and Vallon managed to trap both blades under his hilt. Only for a split second. In that instant Vallon brought his shield round with all his weight behind it, jarring Lu off balance. In the next instant, he unlocked his sword, cocked his wrist back to reverse the blade, then rammed the pommel into Lu's face. The bandit staggered back and Vallon followed, swinging shield and sword, imposing his weight to batter his opponent. Even giving ground Lu managed to land more blows than Vallon dealt. None of them penetrated. None of them deflected Vallon's bullish charge. Ignoring the stroke he could see Lu preparing to deliver, he drew back his sword and drove through the attack, plunging his sword into his opponent's chest.

Lu didn't fall. He jumped back like a cat, almost wrenching Vallon's sword from his grasp. Vallon put all his weight behind the hilt and ran the bandit twenty feet before Lu's legs went and he tumbled onto his back. Vallon didn't let up. He bore down as if trying to mash his opponent into the earth, strings of bloody snot dangling from his nose, his lips drawn back from his teeth.

'Die, you bastard.'

Lu went limp and his swords dropped from his hands. He was still alive and looking at Vallon with the same inert gaze he'd worn throughout the contest. Vallon pulled off the bandit's helmet.

'On second thoughts, take all the time in the world.'

When Vallon was sure that Two-Swords was dead, he rose and turned and saw Lucas standing at a distance.

'How long have you been there?'

'Almost since you locked swords.'

'Why didn't you lend a hand?'

'An apprentice doesn't meddle in a master's work.'

Vallon wiped the blood off his sword with snow. 'You've got a lot to learn, boy.'

Hero dressed Vallon's wounds and strapped his chest. He'd suffered a brutal pounding and his torso was already taking on the baleful hues of a thundercloud. Hero was worried that internal organs had been damaged.

'Have you passed water since the fight?'

'I have and saw no blood in it.'

'Do you hurt inside?'

'Are you jesting? I feel like I've been trampled by a herd of horses.'

'I advise that you abstain from fighting for a month.'

Pain like a twisting sawblade cut Vallon's laugh to one gasp. He crooked over, holding his ribs. Josselin helped him to a stool.

'Pour me a cup of wine,' he said. He directed a squint at Hero. 'I trust my physician will allow me that small comfort.'

'I would prescribe it myself – in moderate measure, together with all the rest our journey allows.'

Vallon sipped from the beaker and tilted his head back – empty of all thought except relief that he was alive.

'Before you leave me, summon Lucas.'

Josselin frowned. 'I trust you won't chastise him for standing by while you fought single-handed. In his mind there would have been no doubt about the outcome.'

Vallon waved a reassuring hand. 'I mustn't let the sun go down without thanking him for saving Aiken.'

Hero forestalled the centurion's move to the entrance. 'I'll fetch him.'

Vallon drank his wine, trying to keep at bay images of dead-eyed Two-Swords Lu reducing him to a lumbering brute. It was as close a contest as he'd ever fought, and by all the rules of martial law, it should have been him who lay in the snow while the sky darkened into everlasting night. He refilled his beaker. Outside, his troops were celebrating their victory around a bonfire.

He set down his wine when Lucas entered in a suit of armour that not only outshone his own bloodied mail, but which was superior to the trappings presented to him as a gift from the emperor. He beckoned Lucas closer and cleared his throat. 'You did good service

472

today. I thank you with all my heart for saving Aiken. I know we've had our differences, but I consign them to the dump of the past. I understand you're still in debt for the outlay I've incurred as a result of your indiscretions. Well, consider your debts written off.'

Lucas held himself very stiff. 'Thank you, sir.'

Wine and fatigue made Vallon expansive. 'I was about your age when I killed my first enemy. I didn't slay four in a day until I'd come to full manhood.'

'Five,' Lucas muttered.

'He killed another during our charge,' Josselin said.

Vallon raised his wine in a wordless toast. 'Learn to think before you act and you'll make a good soldier – a captain before your twentieth birthday, I dare say.'

Lucas held himself even stiffer. 'Thank you, sir. I'll do my best to repay your faith in me.'

He was turning to leave when Hero spoke. 'It comes as no surprise to me that Lucas should acquit himself so well on the battlefield. He comes from a warlike lineage. The blood of warriors runs in his veins.'

Vallon thought this was a bit rich. Right now Lucas looked more like a nervous schoolboy than a future general. Vallon made his tone polite yet dismissive. 'I'm sure he stems from brave stock.' He massaged his throat. 'Just one thing. That armour. Don't you think it's rather grand for a trooper?'

'Yes, sir. I was just trying it on for size.'

Vallon rubbed his hands, indicating beyond any doubt that the audience was over. 'You'll want to be getting back to your comrades and a cup of well-deserved wine.'

Lucas remained stuck in a wooden posture, facing neither Vallon nor the entrance. Hero nudged him and Lucas said something that Vallon strained to hear.

'I didn't catch that.'

'My name's not Lucas,' the youth mumbled, staring at the ground.

Vallon relaxed. 'That doesn't matter. Whatever crimes you

473

might have committed in the past are of no interest to me. In the Outlanders every man starts life afresh. Even I once went under a different name.'

'Guy,' said Lucas.

Vallon knocked over his beaker. 'What was that?

'Guy. The same name as mine. Guy de Crion.'

The blood in Vallon's head seemed to drain away. 'What?'

Lucas looked up. 'I'm your son. I'm sorry if it upsets you. It upsets me, too.'

Vallon couldn't breathe. He pawed the table and would have fallen if Josselin hadn't borne his weight. He clawed at the centurion, struggling to speak. 'Is this some terrible falsehood?'

'I don't know. I'm as shocked as you.'

'It's true,' Hero said. 'Lucas is your first-born son.'

Vallon looked in dawning horror at the youth, awful implications rising. 'That means . . . that means you were there on the night . . . '

'. . . you killed my mother. Yes, I was there.'

Vallon covered his eyes. 'Oh my God.' He sat, guts writhing. He breathed in through his nose and tried to recover his composure. 'How did you find me?'

'I met a soldier in Aquitaine who told me you were serving in the Byzantine army. The day after, I set off walking. By chance I sailed from Naples to Constantinople on the same ship as Hero. I almost told him who I was looking for. If I had, you would have known from the start. It was Pepin who directed me to your house.'

Vallon panted. 'That was more than six months ago. Why didn't you tell me when I took you in?'

'I wasn't sure what your reaction would be. I was uncertain about my own feelings and . . . No, that's not true. I hated you. I wanted to take revenge. Then . . . I didn't know what to think, so I kept the secret to myself.'

'You told Hero.'

'No, he didn't,' said Hero. 'Wayland did, in a letter he gave me before he left us.'

474

Vallon looked at Lucas. 'You confided in Wayland?'

'He guessed who I was, but I made him swear to keep it to himself.' Lucas slurred his feet. 'I don't expect you to treat me as your son. I find it hard to look on you as my father. The whole situation is very strange and painful.'

Vallon swallowed. 'I'm not sure what to call you.'

Lucas squared his shoulders. 'I'm more comfortable with "Lucas". And I would feel more comfortable addressing you as "sir".'

Vallon realised that he was only just uncovering the surface of the pit. 'Your brother and sister?'

'Dead.'

Vallon covered his eyes. 'I'll have to tell Aiken. God knows how he'll take it. I've been a poor enough father to him as it is.'

'We'll come with you,' Hero said.

Vallon walked in a sick daze to Aiken's tent and found the youth reading. He set down his book and stood. 'Who's dead?'

Vallon could find no way of varnishing the truth. 'Lucas has just told me he's my son. I haven't investigated the claim, but I have no reason to doubt it.'

Aiken looked from Lucas to Vallon and back again, then burst into cackling laughter.

'It's not a matter for levity.'

Aiken wiped his eyes. 'That's not laughter. That's the male equivalent of hysteria.' He shook Lucas's hand. 'Congratulations. Now your harsh behaviour makes sense.'

'Of course I still consider you as my son,' Vallon mumbled.

Aiken looked away. 'Actually, I'd rather end the pretence. I know I'll never live up to your aspirations for me, and I ... my feeling for you is one of respect rather than filial devotion.'

'You still need a guardian until you come of age.'

'Let me assume that privilege,' said Hero. 'With your agreement, and Aiken's of course.'

'I accept with pleasure,' Aiken said.

Vallon couldn't bring himself to look at Lucas. 'If the prospect isn't too painful, perhaps you would accompany me to my quarters. I don't know if we can mend such a bloody rift, but I'm prepared to try if you are.'

'Yes, sir.'

The news spread through the camp, causing great astonishment and glee. Wine flowed and many a cup was raised in celebration.

Gorka was drunk. 'I knew the lad was better bred than he let on. As soon as I saw him, I said to myself, Gorka, here we have an officer in the making. That's why I took him under my wing and gave him my special attention.'

'Ran him ragged you mean. He'll make you pay for all that "Yes, boss. No, boss. Kiss your arse, boss."'

'Well-forged steel needs tempering in a hot flame.'

'I seem to remember you telling him that you'd be mewed up in a monastery before he killed five men.'

'It was my way of encouraging him to achieve his goal. And he did. Today, with me riding at his side like I did with his father at Dyrrachium.'

Wulfstan joined them.

'Are they still talking?' Gorka asked in a hushed tone.

'Ten years is a lot of time to make up. And there's more than time to bridge. You've probably heard that Vallon killed Lucas's mother.'

'To protect his honour,' Gorka said.

'I know,' said Wulfstan, 'but the boy might not see it like that.'

A trooper broke the brief silence. 'The general will have to promote him. He can't have his son slumming in the ranks.'

'Don't be so sure. The general doesn't have favourites.'

'He'll make him his shield bearer at the very least.'

'I thought that was Aiken's rank.'

'Come on, the only weapon that lad can wield is a pen. Don't get me wrong. I like Aiken, but he'll never make a soldier.' Gorka poured another cup. 'What a day. Here's to victory over our enemies, and Vallon and Lucas reunited by the grace of God.'

XXXVII

From Xining, a Tibetan-controlled outpost in the Hexi Corridor, the Outlanders travelled by stages to Lanzhou, a Chinese frontier town and provincial capital on a bend in the Yellow River. They drew up before a battalion of soldiers waiting to meet them outside the city's western gate. Vallon wore his suit of lamellar armour and his men had polished their equipment until it dazzled. Above them, rippling in a cutting wind, flew the black two-headed eagle of the Byzantine imperial banner.

A corpulent general acknowledged Vallon's bow. His uniform seemed better suited to the theatre than the battlefield, consisting of a moulded bronze breastplate emblazoned with a fire-breathing dragon, a calf-length plate apron worn over three martial petti-coats, the ensemble topped off by a plumed and winged helmet and a spiked ruff at the back of the neck.

The general bowed again. Shennu translated. 'He asks if we have travel permits.'

Vallon was tired and cold. He caught Gorka's eye and the cor-poral rode up, reached for a cotton bag, untied it and dropped a black and rotting head on the frozen ground in front of the Chinese general. The commander's horse stepped back.

'Old Two-Swords don't improve with keeping,' Gorka said.

'Two-Swords Lu,' Vallon said. 'The garrison he was terrorising requested your help in bringing him to heel. We saved you the trouble.'

The general exchanged wondering looks with his officers before turning back to Vallon. 'Can I see the sword that slew this devil?'

Vallon handed it over with both hands. The general tested its edges, held it to the light, made a few trial swishes.

'I imagine it's one of a pair – male and female – worked by a virgin boy and girl who forge blades as dragon spirits and pro-ducers of lightning that can cut through jade.'

Vallon reclaimed his battered weapon. 'I don't know about that. It does its job, and that's good enough for me.'

The general with all formality bade Vallon to accompany him into the city. The column rode through streets under the gazes of an amazed citizenry, chased by grubby children with pates shaven to the crown or wearing pigtails sticking out at right angles.

The Outlanders fetched up at a dismal barracks. Before leaving them, the Chinese general promised to arrange an audience with the provincial prefect. Snow swirled from a stone-coloured sky and Vallon took refuge in his quarters – a room furnished with a clay-brick sleeping platform called a k'ang, heated by a brazier from beneath. After months of sleeping on frozen ground swaddled in as many layers as he could pile on, he had to shed most of his garments to make himself comfortable.

During his wait for the summons to the prefect's residence, Vallon saw Lucas only in passing, both of them exchanging stilted greetings. What was there to say? What kind of memories could you share with a son who remembered you best from the night you murdered his mother? Tossing and turning in the small hours, Vallon sometimes wished that Lucas had never found him, almost wished that the youth had died along with his brother and sister, leaving only an indelible stain on the conscience. In some ways, that would have been easier to live with.

Four days passed before the prefect granted Vallon an audience. Shennu told the general that the delay wasn't meant as a slight. The Chinese bureaucracy passed memoranda up from one tier of officialdom to another, the response then filtering back down, usually with requests for additional information or clarification.

The prefect, a distinguished-looking aristocrat with ascetic features, questioned Vallon in a courtly, rather cooing tone, asking him about Byzantium, the journey, the nature and temper of the people he'd met on the way. Shennu spoke for the general, but Vallon had worked hard on his Chinese and found he could understand much of what the prefect said. Once or twice he answered before Shennu could speak, eliciting smiles from the prefect's staff.

'I applaud your efforts to learn our language,' the gentleman said.

'Thank you for making the most out of little. I made the effort out of respect for your ancient civilisation. The Chinese empire is a counterweight to our own, twin mirrors at the ends of the earth, separated by sea, deserts and barbarians, yet united by reverence for good governance. I've told you why my emperor despatched me on this mission. Having come so far and lost so many men, I implore you to use your office to send us on to the capital with all speed.'

Groups of officials conferred, knots of bureaucrats forming in one place before unravelling and gathering in another. Finally they assembled behind the prefect.

'Do you have the emissary's bronze fish?' he asked.

Vallon looked to Shennu for enlightenment.

'It's one of the twelve diplomatic credentials,' the Sogdian said, 'taking the form of a fish in two parts. The Chinese government despatches one half to the country wishing to send an envoy, and retains the other. Both halves have a number specifying the month in which the envoys are permitted to enter the capital. If an envoy arrives in the third moon with a tally denoting the second moon, the emperor would refuse to receive him. If he arrives too early, he's obliged to wait until the specified time.'

Vallon ground his teeth. 'It's worse than Byzantine bureaucracy. Tell the prefect I don't have half a bronze fish. State my credentials as follows. First, I'm the ambassador of His Majesty the Emperor of Byzantium, God's representative on earth. Second, I brought the head of Two-Swords Lu, which is worth a bucket of bronze fish.'

The prefect deliberated with his officials before announcing his decision.

'I will forward your request, together with copies of your credentials to the Court of Diplomatic Reception. Until I receive a reply, you and your men will remain in Lanzhou as honoured guests. We will see to all your needs, providing lodging, food and fodder, sleeping mats and medicine – even funerals should any of your men pass away.'

'How long do you expect a reply to take?'

'It's winter. Even if the court decides to admit your embassy, you won't be able to travel before next spring.'

Vallon couldn't restrain his dismay. 'Having crossed the world in eight months, I'm not going to kick my heels for the next three. I'll go on without permission if necessary.'

'General, you're a brave and resourceful man, but I must point out that you're now in the Celestial Kingdom and therefore subject to its laws. I have stated my conditions and you would be wise to observe them. Your party numbers less than one hundred. The Chinese imperial army is more than a million strong. You will not leave Lanzhou until the court has examined your request and informed me of their decision.'

Vallon stormed out of the residence to be met by a group of his men.

'We have to wait for pen-scratchers in Kaifeng to decide if we can proceed,' he told them.

Waving away the palanquins set at his disposal, he strode fuming through the streets.

'A season in Lanzhou might not be time wasted,' Hero said. 'It will give us time to polish our Chinese and learn more about their culture.'

'I for one would appreciate a rest,' Aiken added.

'The devil with that. I didn't come all this way to be stalled on the border.'

Vallon's blind march took him through the North Gate and onto the south bank of the Yellow River, about a hundred yards wide at this point.

Hero advanced to the water margin and peered across the cold and slatey current. 'It doesn't look yellow to me.'

'The river still has two-thirds of its course to run,' Shennu said. 'It gathers sediment as it flows. By the time it passes Chang'an, it resembles liquid mud.'

On the other side of the river a temple complex climbed a cliff

480

capped by a pagoda. Downstream three waterwheels as tall as churches rotated with stately slowness, the foreshortening effect of distance making them look like meshed gears. A few fishermen cast their nets in the shallows. The Outlanders watched the river roll past.

'You wouldn't get me on one of them things,' Wulfstan said, nodding at a primitive craft bobbling along in mid-channel. It was some sort of raft lashed together from what looked like four giant udders with elongated teats uppermost. Three men crewed it, one of them plying a large steering oar.

'They're made of ox skins stuffed with straw,' Shennu said.

Wulfstan spat. 'I thought the Chinese were a clever race. Why don't they build proper ships with tight clinkers and a sail?'

'They build very fine ships where the water suits navigation. Up here the winds won't take you where you want to go, and the current is too strong to row against. Those rafts aren't as primitive as you think. The men who ride them drift downriver until they reach a market and then they dismantle the rafts, pack the hides on a donkey and return to their villages with the profit they've earned.'

'What do they carry?' Hero asked.

'Fleeces, hides, timber, coal – goods too bulky to be transported overland.'

'What's coal?' Aiken said.

'A rock the Chinese burn as fuel.'

The Outlanders pondered this oddity without following it up. Hero tracked the raft diminishing downriver and spoke without knowing where his question would lead. 'How far do they travel?'

'Only a few days downstream, until they reach a trading post. From there another crew carry the goods to the next landing, and so it goes on, stage by stage, until one day, months later, the goods reach Kaifeng.'

'A lot of effort for a small return.'

Shennu pointed at the bobbling craft. 'That one's tiny. They can be any size to suit your purpose. I've seen some as large as a field, constructed from hundreds of skins with a platform laid on top and huts for the sailors to sleep and cook in.'

All this Vallon had been taking in. He raised his head and looked at Wulfstan. The Viking massaged his stump and chuckled.

Shennu interpreted the looks. 'Oh no. You won't reach Kaifeng that way.'

'You said the rafts travelled all the way to the capital,' Vallon pointed out.

'By short stages. You can't just follow the river and hope it will take you to Kaifeng. No.' Shennu cast about and picked up a driftwood branch. 'The Yellow River is China's water dragon.' He drew a squiggly line on the foreshore. 'Here's its tail, wriggling down from Tibet.' He jabbed with the branch at the base of the tail. 'Lanzhou. From here its back arches north and then east for thousands of *li* before descending to the neck. Kaifeng lies half way along the neck, the dragon's jaws gaping towards the Yellow Sea. The river passage must be twice as long as the land route.'

Vallon looked at the hide raft, now only a distant blip. He addressed himself to Wulfstan. 'I'd say the current's flowing at two or three miles an hour. If we travel for all the hours of daylight, that means at least twenty miles a day – every day, without effort.'

'Why stop at nightfall?' Wulfstan said. 'The river doesn't. We could cover fifty miles between sunrise and sunset.'

In his anxiety, Shennu almost ran on the spot. 'You don't know the dangers. The river flows north beyond the Great Wall through deserts controlled by Khitan nomads. Somewhere along its course it plunges over a terrible waterfall.'

Wulfstan's expression grew dreamy. 'Like old times, General.'

Vallon took Shennu's arm. 'Where do the rafts come from?'

Shennu shook himself loose. 'The prefect has forbidden you to advance without permission.'

'I'm paying for your services, not the Chinese.'

'The river freezes in the New Year.'

'Then the sooner we get underway, the better. Where can we find a raft?'

Shennu kicked over his tracing. 'A village two days west, at the confluence of two tributaries that flow into the Yellow River.

That's where goods from the highlands are brought before being shipped on.'

'Look into it,' Vallon said. 'Take Wulfstan and a squad of troopers. We'll tell the Chinese that you're returning to pick up a sick comrade we left in a monastery.'

'What about Hauk and his Vikings?' Wulfstan said.

'I'd rather leave them behind, but since they've come this far, they might as well go all the way. Try to buy or charter two rafts large enough to carry all the men, horses and baggage.'

Six days passed before the party returned, wearing such long faces that Vallon winced in disappointment. Wulfstan's mask slipped first.

'It's fixed. At night the day after tomorrow, two rafts big enough to take every man, horse and sack will put in at a quiet spot about fifteen miles upriver.'

'The Chinese watch us too closely to permit a secret embarkation,' Josselin said.

Vallon's shadow stalked across the walls of his quarters. 'Shennu, arrange an urgent meeting with the prefect.'

Next morning Vallon told the governor that he couldn't remain in Lanzhou. He'd promised his men that they would reach journey's end before the turn of the year, and he feared they would mutiny or desert if left in limbo for another three or four months. He'd decided to turn back.

The prefect was horrified. 'You can't. I've already despatched couriers carrying my personal recommendation that the court receives your embassy. If, as I hope and suspect, the court sends a positive reply and you have left before it arrives, the government will hold me responsible. Please reconsider. Remember that during your stay in Lanzhou, we will meet all your needs. I understand that your men are far from home and miss domestic pleasures. Be assured they will be provided with all comforts.'

Vallon pretended to be mollified – up to a point. 'I appreciate your offer. The problem is that the more I satisfy my soldiers' wants, the harder it will be to dig them out of slothful habits.

Lanzhou offers too many attractions for men who haven't tasted civilisation for the best part of a year. If they have to sit out the winter, I'd rather they did it in a place that offered fewer temptations. Such as Xining.'

The prefect could barely contain his relief. 'You're prepared to take up winter quarters in Xining?'

'Being billeted close to enemy territory will help maintain discipline. The sooner we leave the better. Tomorrow preferably.'

Delighted to shed responsibility for the Outlanders, the prefect turned to his staff. 'Arrange an escort.'

'Please don't,' Vallon said. 'It will only reinforce the impression that we're unwanted barbarians. We reached Lanzhou without any help. We can certainly leave it on our own.'

It was afternoon when they rode out, accompanied by a token escort of a dozen Chinese soldiers and a camel train carrying sufficient supplies to last all winter. Retracing their steps, they followed a tributary of the Yellow River and pitched camp on a tongue of land at the bottom of a gorge. Vallon had cultivated good terms with the escort and they didn't hesitate when he invited them into his tent to share food and wine.

They were mellow drunk when two squads of Outlanders burst in, overpowered them and tied them up. Vallon went down to the riverbank with Wulfstan and Shennu.

Midnight passed. A capsized moon slid across the gorge. Vallon shivered in his cape.

'Do you think they'll come?'

'We're paying enough,' Wulfstan said. 'Put me in their boots and I'd keep my end of the bargain.'

Somewhere in the small hours Vallon woke to see a lantern winking up the river. He stood, sloughing off blankets, and made out a boat rowing downstream. It drew level and backed water. A man hailed the shore party.

'That's the fellow I dealt with,' Wulfstan said. 'He knows he doesn't get the rest of the money until we're on the rafts.'

He whistled and the boat put in. Wulfstan handed over a bag of silver. The boat pushed off.

'We might have kissed goodbye to a fortune,' Vallon said.

The lantern blinked five times and around the bend floated two flat masses, oarsmen straining to row the lumpen craft into slack water. They nudged the bank and Wulfstan leaped onto one of the rafts. He held out his hand to Vallon.

'Welcome aboard, sir.'

Before the first rooster carolled, the rafts drifted through Lanzhou without so much as a dog registering their passage. Dawn broke over terraced farmland and four days later, heading north, the Outlanders saw a stone wall tracking the eastern bank, unmanned watchtowers drifting past as regular as heartbeats. The wall appeared again on the opposite shore before wandering away.

It was a strange journey, the landscape sliding past as if in a dream. Vallon would fix his eyes on a distant landmark thinking it would never arrive, only to wake from a trance to find that the landmark had passed and another had taken its place. The country grew more arid. Dawns broke in acid blues and citron yellows before the wind rose and cast a sickly yellow haze over everything. Towards evening the wind dropped and the sky cleared, heralding glorious sunsets and nights frigid with stars. On the rafts the men hibernated around braziers and pondered where the voyage would lead them.

Vallon had learned that Greek would be useless in the Celestial Empire and Shennu spent part of the day refining his students' Chinese. Thirty native oarsmen crewed the two rafts and the foreigners tested their language skills on them with mixed results. Vallon also kept his men busy with daily drills and exercises in arms. The rest of the time they passed playing *shatranj*, chequers and dice.

The current bore them north into a desert of dunes salted with snow. Then the river swung east and the landscape flattened into icy steppe where the sun before daybreak threw the earth's shadow in a dark sphere above the horizon.

The north wind blew cold enough to weld flesh to metal and the river began to freeze over, lobes of ice creeping out from the banks, winter tightening its clutch so that only a narrow channel remained open. With the channel constricting daily, Vallon ordered his men to row, plying oars constructed from whatever material they could lay hands on.

A day dawned when the sun didn't rise in their faces. The river had turned south and the rafts drifted into clearer water. The wall appeared again, winding east like a yellow-grey snake.

The weather turned milder and for a week the Outlanders continued south without the fear that come morning they would wake to find themselves frozen into the landscape.

A cry one afternoon brought Vallon out of his makeshift cabin. Every man was rowing the raft to shore.

'It's the waterfall Shennu warned us about,' Wulfstan said. 'The Chinese call it the Kettle's Spout.'

Vallon could hear its bass undertones from a mile away and when he'd landed and picked his way onto a headland overlooking the fall, the roar was loud enough to scramble thought. Compressed into a channel only thirty yards wide, the river spewed over a step fifty feet high. A rainbow arched over the torrent and spray freezing as it rose matted Vallon's eyebrows. He took hold of Wulfstan and shouted to make himself heard.

'We'll never get down that.'

Two days later they were on their way again. The Chinese crew, with help from the Outlanders and Vikings, simply dismantled the rafts down to the last ox hide and reassembled them below the cataract.

The country grew more settled. They passed subterranean towns dug into hillsides of soft loess. Giant waterwheels irrigated fields on both banks. One evening Vallon saw a lamplit boat crewed by three men using trained cormorants to catch fish.

It must have been soon after the turn of the year when Josselin summoned Vallon late at night to observe a fire burning in the western darkness.

'A signal fire,' Vallon said 'And I imagine the only intelligence worth transmitting concerns us. Double the watch.'

All next day the men scanned the shorelines for any threat. None showed itself. The river widened into a slow-flowing lake. It was very cold that night and at sunrise mist drifted low across the water. Overhead the sky was eggshell blue. On each bank thick hoar frost covered the vegetation, making the landscape look as if it were carved from alabaster.

A light breeze wafted the mist away.

'Sailing ship putting out from the west bank,' Gorka shouted.

Vallon had already spotted it – a two-masted junk with a low bluff bow and a high canted stern.

'Another one heading out from the other shore.'

A smaller vessel with a single mast.

Wulfstan appeared at Vallon's side. 'That's a pincer closing on us if I ain't mistook.'

'Order the men to arms,' Vallon told Josselin. The Vikings on the other raft were already struggling into their armour. 'What can we expect?' he asked Shennu.

'River pirates are well-armed and ruthless. They leave no witnesses.'

Vallon's lips compressed. The enemy ships were still more than a mile away, heeling over in the breeze. There was no getting past them and no time to make shore. He looked for Josselin. 'Tell the men to cover their armour and hide themselves among the horses and baggage. Make the pirates think we're poorly defended merchants.' He strode to the edge of the raft and hailed Hauk. 'Hide your men. We'll take the right-hand ship; you seize the other.'

Hauk raised a hand and his Vikings disappeared behind bales and sacks. Vallon's men had done the same. The pirate ships were close enough to make out men clustered along their sides.

Wulfstan trembled like a hunting dog scenting game. Vallon turned an amused glance on him.

487

'You're looking forward to a bit of action, aren't you?'

'Oh yes, sir. When you took me in I was grateful that I'd found a comfortable berth, sad that my warring days were over.'

'We'll need grappling irons. I want to capture those ships, not beat them off.'

Wulfstan hurried away and returned with two hooked ropes. He handed one to Gorka. Vallon knelt behind a bale of yak hides and watched the ships draw closer. He judged from the pirates' attitudes that they weren't expecting serious opposition.

'Are the archers ready?'

'Yes, sir.'

The Chinese crew had commenced a terrified wailing that wasn't feigned. The sight cheered the pirates and they jeered and beckoned the rafts into their clutches.

'Wait for my order,' Vallon said.

The distance had narrowed to three hundred yards and silence fell, magnifying the sounds of slurping water and creaking ropes. Vallon raised his hand. The pirates, dressed in the cast-offs of half a dozen armies, trained small crossbows on the rafts. The captain of the junk Vallon was aiming for stalked the stern deck. A long banner rippled from the vessel's masthead.

Vallon dropped his arm and his archers loosed a volley of arrows. Before they could draw again, the pirates responded with crossbow bolts. Another flight of arrows from the Outlanders and another swarm of bolts. The pirates were using repeating crossbows, shooting darts faster than the archers could bend their bows. Against men lacking armour, the darts would have been devastating, but the crossbows were light and most of the bolts bounced off mail or broke.

Fifty yards to go and the commander of the junk knew something was wrong and shouted commands through a trumpet.

'Stay hidden until the last moment,' Vallon told Josselin. 'Concentrate our attack on the bow. Wulfstan, be ready.'

The junk's hull loomed up. More bolts fizzed. One of them glanced off Vallon's armour.

The raft struck the junk with a pneumatic sigh. Wulfstan and Gorka swung grapples over its side-rails.

'Give them hell!' Vallon shouted.

Josselin led the assault, covered by a squad of archers. He scrambled over the junk's side, swinging his sword like a flail until more Outlanders had boarded. Vallon didn't follow until his troops had secured the foredeck. From there they advanced towards the stern, each squad a cog in a mincing machine, driving the pirates back. The commander made a desperate counter and was hacked down with three of his men. The remaining pirates milled against the stern transom.

'Surrender or die,' Vallon cried. He looked for Shennu. 'Tell them.'

Vallon took more than thirty prisoners. On the other junk Hauk put every pirate to the sword.

Vallon tried to stop the butchery. 'You'll need some of them to show you how to handle the ship.'

Hauk dragged a hand across his brow, leaving a bloody smear. 'I don't need any damned Chinese pirate to tell me how to sail a ship.'

The Outlanders tied the raft to the junk's stern and Vallon set about learning what manner of craft he'd captured. A pirate only too willing to cooperate told him it was called *Jifeng*, meaning 'Auspicious Wind', while her sister ship bore the incongruous name 'Pleasant Clouds'. *Jifeng* was more than sixty feet long, her hull a narrow rectangle with a blunt bow, her aft deck canted up. She was equipped with a stern rudder, and amidships a board shaped like a flipper trailed from each side.

'What are they?' Vallon asked.

'Leeboards,' Wulfstan said. 'They're like adjustable keels that can be used in shallow water. The Arabs use them on their dhows.'

Vallon followed him below and found the captain's cabin – just large enough to accommodate a sleeping couch.

'Snug billet,' Wulfstan said. He turned. 'She's a stout craft, right enough. Look at that. Her hull's divided by partitions. They look watertight to me.'

Back on deck Vallon studied the sails. They were constructed of eight wooden battens lined with cotton and rigged in a fashion too complicated for him to work out.

'Do you think you can sail her?'

'Give me a day with a couple of Chinese mariners and I could sail her to Norway.'

'Mount the Greek Fire siphon at the bow and the trebuchet at the stern.'

They kept five of the pirates as crew and put the rest ashore. Most of them had been pressed into service and trotted off like prisoners released from jail. Three days later the river turned east through densely populated farmland dotted with peasants at work in fields already showing the pale green patina of approaching spring. The current had deposited so much sediment that it had raised the level of the river fifteen feet above the floodplain, giving Vallon the impression that he was floating on an elevated plane.

The Chinese caught up with them at Zhenzhong, throwing a barrage of junks and cables across the river. Vallon offered no resistance and allowed the commander to board. The officer, young and awkward, made a stiff bow.

'General, my orders are to escort you to Kaifeng.'

'I happen to be sailing there myself. I'm delighted to complete my journey under your protection, though I must say it's come rather late.'

'This ship is now under my command.'

Vallon closed on the officer. 'If you want to take command of a pirate ship, you must first capture it. The ship is mine.'

'General, I must warn you ...'

'Yes? That you'll send us back to Lanzhou?'

'General ...'

'Gorka.'

490

The corporal hurried up holding a small barrel. He opened it to display the pirate captain's head preserved in salt.

'He went by the name of "Mudfish",' Vallon said. 'An odd name for a pirate. I assume you know that I also killed the brigand Two-Swords Lu.'

The officer stared at the leprous head. His men craned to get a look.

Vallon followed up his advantage. 'Remove your soldiers from my ship and I'll be delighted to discuss matters further. Alternatively, you can arrest me and drive me into Kaifeng wearing irons like a common criminal. It's your decision.'

The officer conferred with advisors before answering. 'You may proceed to Kaifeng under my close supervision. The matter of the ship's ownership will be decided there.'

A knock at evening roused Vallon from troubled thoughts.

'Yes.'

Lucas opened the door and Vallon's innards tightened. No matter how many times he saw his son, it was like being confronted by a ghost.

'The capital's in sight,' Lucas mumbled, looking everywhere but at Vallon.

'I'll be right up.'

Lucas turned away and Vallon felt something tear around his heart. 'Wait a moment.'

Lucas paused, shoulders hunched as if anticipating a blow.

Vallon's mouth worked. His throat tightened. 'It doesn't matter. Now isn't the time.'

Lucas left and Vallon flopped forward, hands on knees, breathing in gasps. He'd been on the verge of trying to justify his crime. *Your mother was an adulteress who delighted in the company and caresses of a man who betrayed me and had me thrown into an oubliette lined with human bones. He even stole my sword.* Vallon unsheathed the blade and placed his brow against the cold steel. His breathing steadied. No, Lucas was an innocent and innocence

491

was holy. Realisation that he could never seek redemption from his son made him feel sick.

He dashed water over his face before going on deck to take his first view of Kaifeng. He stared across ten miles of flat farmland at a smoky stain on a dun-coloured plain under a dingy sky.

'Don't judge it on first impressions,' Hero said beside him. 'Kaifeng is home to more people than the whole of the Byzantine empire.'

Vallon rested his hands on the rail. 'It's not that.'

'I know. It's Lucas.'

'Having him in my company is torture. I've got nothing to say to him – nothing I dare say. I find myself opening my mouth to share with Lucas memories of him as a child – the first toy sword I gave him, the day I led him around the garden on a goat. Then I remember that all memories lead to one event and I want to gag.'

'You have blood in common.'

'Yes, the only thing we have in common is my wife's blood.'

'I've told him what terrible circumstances led to that murder. Give him time and he'll find it in himself to forgive.'

Vallon slapped the rail. 'You don't understand. I don't want his forgiveness. I'm not a merchant trying to profit from a gullible customer.'

'You're being too hard on yourself.'

'Am I? I'm a thrice-failed father. After Lucas I adopted Aiken and he couldn't wait to escape my care.'

'Thanks to you he's content and brighter than he's ever been in his life.'

Vallon hardly heard. 'And by now, my Lady Caitlin will have given birth to our third child, yet days pass without me giving a thought to wife or children.'

'On this side of the world, all of us find the places we left remote. Your men regard you as their father. Look behind you if you don't believe me. You promised to bring them to China, and you kept your pledge.'

492

XXXVIII

Orders must have been given to bring the Outlanders to heel as soon as possible because soon after *Jifeng* made fast, a column of officials borne in litters and flanked by a troop of cavalry and puffing infantry clattered onto the jetty. Vallon and his leading men went ashore to pay their respects.

Out from a gilt and lacquer palanquin stepped a gentleman wearing a purple gown that identified him as an official in the top three ranks of the Chinese civil service. Dark, bearded and hook-nosed, he didn't look like a native of the country. He managed to suggest a bow without moving his head. Vallon returned the compliment with more conviction.

Evidently he hadn't shown sufficient deference because one of the official's attendants upbraided him in a tone that set his teeth on edge. Shennu fell to his knees and began to knock his head on the ground. Vallon dragged him up.

'Remember your dignity.'

'He's a very important official – Chamberlain of the Court of Diplomatic Reception in the Bureau of Receptions, under the Ministry of Rites, a division of the Department of State Affairs. He heads a team of twenty scholars who act as interpreters for foreign envoys. That official behind him represents the Secretariat, which translates letters carried by foreign envoys. They'll be responsible for us during our stay.'

'Welcome to the Middle Kingdom,' the chamberlain said. 'News of your arrival outran you. I have prepared lodging where you will reside while we examine your credentials.'

'How did you know I spoke Arabic?'

'Because it's my job to learn everything I can about foreign visitors before they set foot on Chinese soil. Unfortunately, due to errors committed elsewhere, I have only skimpy information regarding your status and motives. In the next few days my officials will examine them in every detail. If you're wondering where

I learned to speak Arabic, my ancestors came from Baghdad. Most of the officials in my department have foreign roots. Their families were Koreans, Japanese, Khitans, Uighurs ...' The chamberlain pointed. 'Who are those men?'

Vallon looked over his shoulder and saw Hauk and his crew leaning splay-armed against the rail of *Pleasant Clouds*. 'Viking traders who joined forces with us. They're not members of my delegation and it was always our agreement that we would separate once we reached Kaifeng.'

'Very well.' The chamberlain indicated a squad of cavalry holding a string of spare horses.

'I'd rather ride my own mount,' Vallon said. 'And I need to make arrangements concerning my ship.' He heard murmurs of disapproval from the officials. 'This journey has taken the best part of a year. I trust you won't begrudge me a little time to compose myself.'

The chamberlain made a scissoring gesture. *Make it quick.*

The horses were already saddled, the troopers scrubbed and buffed for the parade ground. It didn't take long to get them ashore. Vallon detailed Wulfstan and four troopers to remain on *Jifeng*. 'You'll be relieved in a few days. Meantime, don't let anyone on board without my permission.'

'Over my dead body.'

Hauk hailed Vallon as he walked ashore. 'What's going to happen to us?'

Vallon turned. 'I don't know and I don't particularly care.'

'Bad cess to you, Vallon. Without our help you wouldn't have reached China.'

Vallon didn't look back. 'Without your interference, Otia and four other troopers would still be alive.' He mounted his Ferghana and rode away accompanied by the catcalls of the Vikings and a cacophony of drums, gongs and trumpets. Ahead of the Outlanders a soldier carried a pennant inscribed with Chinese writing.

'What does that say?' Vallon asked Shennu.

'Nothing important.'

'What does it say?'

'Foreigners carrying tribute to the emperor.'

Vallon gathered his reins. 'I guessed it would be something like that.'

Three walls defended Kaifeng. Inside the first lay a zone as much agricultural as urban. Beyond the second sprawled a slum with houses packed together as closely as teeth on a comb. Alerted by the drums and gongs, its citizens flocked to view the foreigners. Vallon caught the occasional remark, invariably phrased in tones of wonder mingled with disgust.

'See how long the barbarians' noses are.'

'Urgh! Look at their red hair.'

The inner wall was broached by a massive gatehouse constructed in the form of a truncated pyramid, with flights of steps rising to a concave-roofed tower and battlements lined with soldiers. As the Outlanders passed through the square arch, they had to give way to a train of camels shuffling in the opposite direction. Seeing the haughty indifference of the beasts, the casual yet determined strides of their handlers, Vallon felt an odd nostalgia for the desert that he'd laboured so long to escape.

On the other side of the gate the road broadened into a thoroughfare more than an arrow-shot wide – so broad that the citizens strolling beside the merchants' arcades on the far side looked tiny. Black-and-red-painted barriers divided the road, leaving an empty central passage that Shennu said was reserved for the emperor. Tier upon tier of upturned tiled roofs created a low skyline as undulating as the sea, broken at intervals by firefighters' watchtowers and pagodas topped with yellow tiles.

They crossed canals planted with lotuses, the banks lined by fruit trees, and clopped over an arched bridge spanning a river busy with vessels of all sizes. The escort turned right down a lively avenue crammed with stalls, shops, taverns and eating houses.

'That's ingenious,' Hero said.

Vallon couldn't see what he was referring to.

'That handcart,' Hero said. 'The single wheel at the front makes it easy to manoeuvre in tight spaces. Why didn't we think of it?'

Vallon smiled. 'I suspect an interesting time awaits you.'

Another turning brought them into a quiet residential quarter. The escort halted outside a high-walled compound overhung by trees. Soldiers swung open stout gates and Vallon passed through. He reined in, astonished. He'd been expecting a barracks with rough-and-ready accommodation.

'It's a palace,' he said.

The compound must have been more than three hundred yards square, subdivided into walled enclosures occupied by two-storey houses that were more windows than walls, with lattice screens to admit the weak winter sun. Under the chamberlain's supervision, Vallon's squadron peeled off into their allotted quarters until only he was left.

The last gate opened and he rode into a garden laid out on formal lines – an orchard of plum and peach trees in one quarter, a bamboo grove behind a rock feature contrived to resemble a mountain, a water garden with a pond spanned by a zigzag ornamental bridge, an area of lawn with a belvedere artfully sited to offer views of the different landscapes.

The sun was settling behind the tamped-earth walls, its rays lighting up a fairy-tale pavilion walled and roofed in vermilion and gold.

The chamberlain leaned out of his litter. 'The Palace of Peace and Friendship, reserved for honoured foreign delegations. You are the first guests to occupy it in eight years, so please forgive me if the arrangements don't meet your satisfaction. If anything displeases you, tell the steward and he will endeavour to correct shortcomings.'

'I'm sure it will meet my needs.'

An army of servants stood outside the house and flung themselves down, banging their foreheads on the ground when the chamberlain alighted. He ignored them and led Vallon into the house, pointing out this room and that, explaining the functions of the various lackeys who scuttled at his side with expressions almost demented by the wish to please.

Screens painted with landscapes and nature scenes decorated the rooms. Vallon felt too large and coarse for the house. He could imagine bringing down its walls with one clumsy movement. The last glow of sunset lit a window glazed with oiled paper. Fumes from a charcoal brazier made him light-headed. He took a short step to recover his balance and put a hand to his brow.

'It's been a long time since I slept under a roof.'

The chamberlain laid a hand on Vallon's arm. 'Take all the rest you need. No one will disturb you until you've recovered from your travels.'

Vallon missed a whole day in sleep and woke feeling soggy to the core under the anxious gazes of four servants.

'What are you doing here?'

'Your spirit was floating. We thought it might leave you.'

Vallon sat up. His tongue was furred and arid, his stomach hollow. 'Bring me water.'

A scullion darted off and returned with a bronze ewer. Vallon drank his fill, observed by the servants who apparently hadn't seen a man drink before.

Vallon wiped his chin. 'Leave me while I dress.'

They took some getting rid of, and even then they went only as far as the door, peering around it as if scared that Vallon might vanish in their absence.

'I need some fresh air.'

Trailed by retainers, he strolled through the gardens, stopping to listen to a bird whose familiar song sounded as if it came from the other end of the world. He was ravenous when he returned to the house and asked if he could eat.

The steward took charge. 'What food would give you most pleasure?'

For the last four months Vallon had been subsisting on broth, tsampa and noodles. 'I'm not fussy. Whatever you have ready.'

An age passed before a relay of servants entered bearing trays laden with delicacies. The steward lifted each cover in turn – bear's pads marinated in fermented soybean paste, bamboo rats stewed with jujubes, hornet larvae roasted with salt …

Vallon settled for mutton and turnips.

He slept again before dusk fell and rose at dawn and practised swordsmanship until he'd worked up a sweat. He returned to the ever-attentive household.

'I need a bath.'

The servants looked at each other. 'A bath?'

Vallon scanned their faces. 'You do bathe in China?'

After insisting that he could wash himself without help, he was allowed to soak in a tub scented with sandalwood and ginseng. Another thing he discovered about Chinese personal hygiene: they relieved themselves in privies and wiped themselves with paper pinned in sheets to the wall.

Next evening he heard carriages draw up outside the house. The steward pulled him back from the window and settled him in a throne-like chair. The entire establishment crammed the antechambers. From their giggles and nudges, Vallon guessed that his visitors weren't officials of state.

Into the room glided or teetered a dozen women with downcast faces – tall and short, plump and slender, fair and dark. This one had plucked her eyebrows and created artificial ones like the wings of a butterfly on her forehead. That one had caked herself with so much white and red makeup that her face resembled an actor's mask. Balsam, cloves and aloes scented the air.

'What the hell's going on?' said Vallon, knowing the answer all too well.

The steward bowed. 'A virile lord needs a consort to maintain harmony of mind and body.' Or words to that effect. 'Please make your choice – one or several.'

'I don't want a woman.'

Consternation ensued. At a command from the steward, a servant drove out the concubines and another lackey ushered in half a dozen simpering youths.

Vallon's eyes narrowed to quartz slivers. 'Get them out of here.

I don't want women. I don't want men or boys. All I want is peace.'

On the Chinese side, spirits sank. The steward despatched a servant and after a fretful interval Shennu showed up. 'General, it would be impolite to refuse a concubine. Your men have already taken partners. Whatever your proclivities, don't be shy in your demands.'

Vallon flushed with anger. 'The devil take it. They keep swearing to satisfy my every desire – except my wish to be left alone.'

'If you take a consort, she'll protect you from the pestering. You don't have to lie with her.'

Vallon stalked across the chamber. 'Very well, supply me with a quiet lady who can converse in my own tongue.' Seeing the steward's look of alarm, Vallon followed up. 'Don't tell me that in the whole of the Song empire, there isn't a single woman who speaks Greek.'

'We have mastered all known languages.'

'Then bring me a woman I can converse with. Only beasts couple without exchanging words. I'm not a dog in want of a bitch.'

A failure of translation caused confusion. 'You want a dog?' the steward said with polite disgust.

Vallon's roar made everyone jump. 'Bring me a woman who can speak Greek.' At the last moment he decided he'd pitched his demands too low. 'Preferably a lady not too ill-favoured.'

He was asleep in his chair when the steward returned, shooing in three women as if they were mice. Vallon blinked at them. One was squat and pitted with pox, one almost catatonic with fright. Setting eyes on the third, Vallon stood. Tall and slim, she had the high cheekbones, short upturned nose and almond eyes of the Turkmen, but her chiselled features and the delicate oval of her face suggested that her ancestry lay to the west, in Persia perhaps, or Circassia. Her skin was fairer than Vallon's – a luminous golden hue, set off by sleek blue-black hair piled high on her head and secured with ivory combs.

'*Hellenika legete?*' he asked. 'Do you speak Greek?'

'*Eulogemenos ho erchomenos en onamati kyriou.*'

Vallon recognised the biblical quote with some surprise. 'Blessed is he who comes in the name of the Lord.'

He turned to the steward. 'This lady will make an excellent companion. Thank you for your assistance and now leave us.'

Eyes rolling in relief, the steward swept his staff away. Vallon stood looking at the woman, aware that the walls were too thin to shield conversation from eavesdroppers.

'I expect you've been sent to report everything I say and do,' he said in Greek.

Her face took on a hunted expression.

'*Ti esti to onoma sou?*' he said.

She cast desperate looks about as if searching for a way out. '*Eulogemenos ho erchomenos en . . .*'

He tried again and received the same response. 'That's the only Greek you know,' he said. He flopped into his chair, cupped one cheek in his hand and began to twitch with husky laughter. He stopped when he saw tears highlighting the concubine's eyes. He pushed up and took her hands.

'You don't speak Greek, so we'll have to try to get by with my atrocious Chinese. I asked you your name.'

'Qiuylue,' she whispered.

'Autumn Moon,' Vallon said. 'It suits you.' He thought of a harvest moon rising through evening mist.

Qiuylue blushed. 'You are very gracious to ignore my hideous disfigurements.'

Vallon stepped back. 'Disfigurements?'

'My age and height. My clumsy hands and ungainly feet. I'm surprised you didn't choose one of the maidens from the Willow Quarter.'

'How old are you?'

Qiuylue hesitated. 'Twenty-six.'

Vallon would have guessed several years younger and assumed she had shaved as many years again off her real age. Her fine bone structure would preserve her beauty into old age.

'You're no taller than many women in my own country and your hands are very elegant. As for feet, whatever size yours are, I prefer them to the stumps and tottering gait of those women whose feet have been bound from birth. It's me who should apologise for inflicting a grizzled soldier on a young and beautiful woman.'

She spoke as if by rote. 'Youth passes. Beauty fades. Wisdom and courage never die.'

'You don't have anything to fear. I have no intention of imposing myself on you. I'm married with children. In my country we stay true to our spouses. Or try to. Now, if you would excuse me, I wish to take a bath.'

Her hand flew to her mouth. 'You bathe in water?'

'Of course I do. At home I have a bath house that I use every two or three days. Why do you look surprised?'

'I was told Western barbarians never bathe. My own people, the Khitans, are strangers to water from birth. It was only when I came to China that I learned the salubrious benefits of water.'

Vallon slung a towel over his shoulder. 'How often do you bathe?'

'Every ten days, on the official holidays.' Qiuylue must have noticed Vallon's frown. 'I bathed today when I was ordered ...' Her face crumpled. 'When I learned what honour the chamberlain had bestowed on me.'

'What circumstances brought you to China?'

She looked down, apparently ashamed. Vallon raised her chin. 'We're strangers, so let's be open with each other.' He poured a cup of wine. 'Here. It will help you relax.'

She ignored the cup. 'I was the youngest daughter of a clan chief who served at the Khitan Liao court. Seven years ago a Chinese military delegation arrived at court. Among them was an officer who admired me and wished to take me for his wife. My parents thought it would be a good match. Only when I arrived at my husband's home did I discover that he was already married. His wife resented me. She had good connections and forced her husband to drive me out of the house. After that—'

'You don't need to tell me any more,' Vallon said. 'We'll talk of other matters when I've bathed.'

She followed him into the bathroom and chased out three servants waiting to attend Vallon. When they had left, she remained.

'You can leave too,' Vallon said.

'But my duty is to serve you at all times.'

'Your duty doesn't extend to watching me wash myself.'

'If you don't want my hands to touch you, allow me to sing while you bathe.'

'I'd prefer to be left alone.'

Qiuylue grew agitated. 'If you send me away, the servants will think I disgust you and I'll lose face.'

Vallon was losing interest in taking a bath. 'All right. Sit over there.'

He unrobed and slipped into the tub. Qiuylue composed herself on a chair in the corner and plucked at a lute. She began to sing some wistful air. The song and the warm scented water lulled him. He lay back, holding the sides of the tub, eyes closed.

When he opened them Qiuylue was looking down at him.

'You're very thin. Your body scarcely casts a shadow.'

Taking this as an aspersion on his physique, Vallon became defensive. 'What do you expect? I've been travelling without rest for a year.'

'Under my care you'll grow fat.'

'Yes ... well ... we'll see.'

'Your crimson bird is very large,' she said in a matter-of-fact tone.

'My what?'

She pointed. 'So much of you.'

Vallon covered his groin. 'I hope it doesn't offend you.'

'You should be proud of it. It will father many sons.'

'Both my children are girls,' Vallon said. 'By God's mercy, there will be another child when I return home.' Then he remembered Lucas. 'No, I have a son too. He's serving in my company.'

'Ah.'

*

502

They ate supper together in silence.

Vallon cast aside his chopsticks. 'I can't use these things. They seem designed to come between a man and his food.'

Qiuylue rose. 'Let me help you.'

'Sit down!'

Qiuylue sat as if he'd struck her.

Vallon took a deep breath. 'I apologise for raising my voice. Let me try to make something clear. I'm not a child who needs to be dressed, washed and spoonfed. Please respect my mature years, as I respect ... well, as I respect you.' He hauled the conversation onto another tack. 'I travelled through Khitan territory on my journey down the Yellow River. I'd like to hear more about your people.'

From Qiuylue he learned that the Khitans had carved out an empire called Liao north of the Yellow River. They had adopted the Chinese system of government and gone along with the pretence that they were tributaries of the Middle Kingdom while accepting lavish bribes in return for not marauding in the Chinese frontier territories.

Supper over, the problem of bed had to be dealt with. Vallon asserted himself. 'I'm still tired from my journey and wish to sleep on my own. Please don't take offence. There's another bed next door.'

Qiuylue placed her hands together and backed out.

Five nights later Vallon retired to his night chamber to find moonlight filtering through the window and a girl in his bed with the cover up to her chin. She gave a coquettish smile. Vallon managed to contain his annoyance.

'What do you think you're doing?'

The girl exposed her breasts. 'Lady Qiuylue sent me. She says it's not fitting that a man should lie on his own.'

Vallon kept his tone gentle. 'Get dressed and go to the lady. Thank her for her consideration and ask her to call on me.'

He was staring out of the window at the hoary light on the tiles of the other buildings when Qiuylue entered.

'Are you angry with me?'

'No,' he said. He indicated the moonlight. 'How peaceful it is.'

She joined him. He could smell her scent. She spoke as if to herself.

> Seeing a gleam at the foot of my bed,
> I took it for frost on the ground.
> Lifting myself to look, I found that it was moonlight.
> Sinking back again, I found myself thinking of home.

'You're a poet,' Vallon said.

'Oh, no. I didn't compose that verse.'

Vallon left the shutters open. 'If I'm going to have to share my bed, I'd rather share it with you.'

They contrived to undress and slip between the covers without observing each other's nakedness. Lying next to Qiuylue, not touching her, Vallon felt as if he'd been put through a wringer. Gradually his muscles relaxed.

'Do the Chinese kiss?'

'Kiss?'

'You know – when a man and woman put their lips together as a prelude to making love. I ask because I saw more than one Tibetan man and woman rubbing noses. I can't see much pleasure in that.'

'Of course we kiss. Do you want me to kiss you?'

'For once, let me take the initiative.'

He slid his hand under her shoulder and eased her round.

'Let down your hair.'

She unpinned her coiffure and shook out her hair. The caress of her tresses on his chest made him close his eyes. He drew her face towards his. Their lips met, adjusted, pressed harder and melted into each other.

XXXIX

Each morning officials from the Court of Diplomatic Reception visited the Palace of Peace to question Vallon and Hero about Byzantium. How many people lived in Constantinople? How was Byzantine society ordered? Did it have a dress code? What did people eat? Who were the empire's allies, who its enemies?

If it wasn't the Court of Diplomatic Reception, it was the Department of Arms, responsible for making maps and demanding to be told every detail of the topography and conditions the expedition had encountered.

Within days of arriving at Kaifeng, ice had frozen *Jifeng* to her mooring. Now the ice began to break up, floating away in dirty yellow blocks. Buds appeared on the trees and the frozen streets turned to mud. When the chamberlain next visited, Vallon vented his impatience.

'We've been in Kaifeng two months. When are we going to meet the emperor?'

'Soon, I trust. The arrangements are proceeding smoothly.'

Vallon would have been driven mad by the procrastination if Qiuylue hadn't been there to soothe him. No matter how frustrating his day had been, his spirits lifted when he closed the door on the officials and found himself alone in her company.

'Why are you looking at me like that?' she asked one evening.

'I was thinking how fond I am of you.'

'I'm glad I make you happy.'

'More than fond.'

She shivered. 'Please don't say such things.'

On the first warm day of the year he was escorting Qiuylue around the garden, admiring the peach blossoms, when he saw coming the other way Lucas accompanied by a pretty Chinese girl who barely came up to his chest. Both parties stopped. By tacit agreement, Vallon and Lucas had contrived to avoid each other since arriving at the capital.

Vallon took the first step. 'Good morning.'

'Good morning, sir. Forgive me for trespassing. The gate was open and I—'

'That's all right. I trust you find your lodgings satisfactory.'

Lucas didn't quite succeed in suppressing a glance at the girl. 'I couldn't ask for better accommodation.'

They stood in awkward opposition, the two women covertly eyeing each other.

Vallon coughed. 'Allow me to introduce Lady Qiuylue. She's helping me learn the Chinese language and customs. My lady, this is my son, Lucas.'

Qiuylue made a graceful acknowledgement and Lucas gave a gentlemanly bow.

'May I present Xiao-Xing – "Morning Star". I, too, am trying to get on better terms with the Chinese.'

Vallon was sure that Xiao-Xing was the girl he'd found in his bed by moonlight. 'Excellent, yes, well . . . ' He rubbed his hands. 'Spring is definitely in the air.'

'Yes, sir.'

'The chamberlain called yesterday with the news we've been waiting for. In three days the emperor Shenzong will receive us at the palace. You will attend me.'

'Honoured, sir.'

'As my son.'

'Yes, sir.'

'Hero and Aiken will also be in the party. Since a mere general won't command the emperor's respect, I've conferred a dukedom on myself and bestowed appropriate titles on the other officers. I'm promoting you to count. Make sure your appearance reflects your rank. Have your servant polish your armour to mirror brightness. I need hardly tell you how important it is to make a dazzling impression.'

'No, sir.'

'There's no need to be so formal in your address. If you can't bring yourself to call me "father", I'm quite happy for you to call me by name.'

506

Lucas's face betrayed turmoil. 'I can't.' He turned about and led the girl away.

'We're going to have to face up to the past sometime,' Vallon called.

Lucas hurried the girl through the gate.

'What's wrong?' Qiuylue said. 'Why do you grow pale?'

Vallon emptied his lungs. 'I murdered his mother in front of him.'

Qiuylue hissed in shock. Vallon groped for her arm and led her to the belvedere. Looking out over the garden, he told her.

When he'd finished, she was quiet for a while. 'I see no reason why you should torment yourself.'

Vallon shook his head. 'Until Lucas appeared, I'd more or less buried the past. Seeing him is like watching a grave heave open. What torments me is the foul thought that I'd feel more at peace today if I'd killed Lucas too.'

Qiuylue kissed his cheek. 'He wouldn't be here unless he wanted to make peace with you.'

'You think so?'

'Yes. He takes after you.'

Vallon shook his head. 'No, and that's what rubs the wound raw. He has his mother's eyes. Every time I meet him, it's her I see.'

The chamberlain and his officials spent the next two days coaching the envoys on imperial protocol.

'On the day of presentation I will usher you into the palace and lead you to the west chamber outside the throne room. When the emperor has taken his seat, I will lead you into His Majesty's presence. You will stand in dignified silence while the vice-director of the Secretariat and his officials approach to receive your letters of credentials and state. They will place them on trays and read them to the throne. If the emperor makes no objection, I will receive your tribute and lay it on a table for the emperor to examine if he so chooses.'

'Wait a moment,' Vallon said. 'Did I hear the word "tribute"?'

'Tribute, gifts – the distinction is not important.'

'Yes, it is. Tributes are offered by subject states. Gifts are exchanged between equals. The treasures we brought are gifts from His Imperial Majesty Alexius I Comnenus.'

'I will give the emperor all the relevant facts.'

'Make sure you tell him it was a Byzantine expedition that first found its way to China, and not the other way around.'

'China has no need to go looking for Byzantium.'

Hero tugged Vallon's sleeve. 'You have many skills. Diplomacy isn't one of them.'

'Now, then,' the chamberlain continued. 'After the emperor has received your letters and gifts, you will be invited to approach. When you reach the appointed spot, you will kow tow.'

One of his juniors demonstrated, kneeling three times from a standing position, touching his forehead to the ground three times at each prostration.

'I'm not going down on hands and knees like a dog,' Vallon said to Hero. He set his face at the chamberlain. 'I will honour your emperor as I would my own – by kneeling with head bowed in respect.'

Gasps of dismay. The chamberlain and his entourage withdrew for discussion and returned quite adamant. 'No ambassador from a foreign country can approach the emperor without kow towing.'

'If my ruler was here in person, would you expect him to abase himself in that servile way?'

'You are not the Byzantine emperor.'

'I represent my sovereign. Your emperor should accord me as much respect as if it were Alexius himself who stood before him.'

'Does Alexius treat you as an equal?'

Vallon couldn't avoid the trap. 'No, of course not.'

'Then why should our emperor not treat you in a similar manner? You are not the embodiment of your sovereign. You are merely his honoured messenger.'

Vallon had begun to sweat. 'If I lower my dignity, I lower the Byzantine emperor's.'

'You cannot regulate the etiquette of the palace of Kaifeng by that of Constantinople. Our princes of the blood kow tow before their emperor. My children show me the same respect. Therefore you should do likewise. If you don't, you are raising yourself above us.'

'Suppose the positions were reversed and you'd sent Chinese envoys to Byzantium.'

'Not only would they kow tow to your emperor, they would also burn incense before him as they would do before their gods.'

'Has any foreign envoy refused to kow tow?'

'Several have resisted. Without exception, right thinking has convinced them of their error.' The chamberlain held out a hand and an official placed a scroll in it. The chamberlain unrolled it. 'In the second reign year of the Emperor Xuan Zong – that is to say, three hundred and seventy years ago – an Arab envoy from the Caliph insisted that he abased himself only before his god. After gentle persuasion he prostrated himself in the prescribed manner.' The chamberlain took another scroll. 'Here we have another precedent more closely touching your own situation.'

'How so?'

'You say that the Byzantines are the legitimate heirs of the Romans. You call yourselves citizens of Rome.'

'By direct descent.'

'Then you will be interested to know that one thousand years ago, ambassadors sent by a Roman sovereign called Anton performed the necessary obeisance before the Chinese emperor.'

Vallon looked at Hero. 'A thousand years ago? That can't be true.'

'My knowledge of Roman imperial succession is patchy, but I recall that an Emperor Antoninus ruled about that time. If we can reach China, there's no reason why the Romans shouldn't have done the same.'

Vallon resumed his debate with the chamberlain on less certain ground. 'I lost many brave men on this journey. I won't debase their sacrifice by fawning.'

'Please. In paying respect to the customs of the Middle Kingdom, you make those of your own more sacred. Every homage you render to our sovereign is becoming and will be returned.'

Forced into a corner, Vallon made his last effort. 'Suppose I refuse?'

'Unless you agree to observe the protocol, I will cancel the audience and you will leave China forthwith.'

Vallon sought advice from his colleagues. 'What do I do?'

'Agree,' Hero said.

'I suppose that if they asked me to kiss Shenzong's arse, you'd say do it.'

Aiken rolled his eyes. He'd become more forthright since stepping out of Vallon's shadow. 'They're not asking you to kiss the emperor's arse.'

'As good as,' Josselin said. 'Call their bluff.'

'It isn't bluff,' Shennu said. 'Nobody can approach the emperor without kowtowing. His Majesty would lose face and that would be unthinkable.'

Vallon found himself looking at Lucas. 'What do you say?'

'I think you have little choice. Being expelled from China with nothing to show for it would be an even more bitter pill to swallow.'

'Alexius won't be pleased to hear that his ambassador grovelled in front of the Chinese emperor.'

'You don't have to tell him. Just say that you observed the necessary protocol.'

'I have a suggestion,' Aiken said. 'Perform the kow tow. At the same time, pray to Almighty God and conclude by making the figure of the cross.'

Shennu looked sick with anxiety. 'The chamberlain won't agree.'

Vallon glanced at the officials on the other side of the room. 'I won't tell him.'

*

510

Vallon managed to bid the officials a polite goodbye before retiring to his sleeping chamber, barking at the servants to leave him undisturbed. Head thumping, he lay on his bed.

Dusk filled the room when Qiuylue slipped in. 'I know you gave orders that no one was to enter, but I'm anxious about you.'

'For heaven's sake,' Vallon snapped. 'The order doesn't apply to you.' He saw Qiuylue flinch. 'Forgive my harsh tone. This ceremonial flim-flam drives me mad.'

Qiuylue held his hand. Since learning that the emperor would receive her lover, she'd treated Vallon as semi-divine.

'I can't believe that tomorrow you will meet the emperor. What an honour. You must tell me every detail of the audience.'

'If I had my way, you'd be at my side.'

Qiuylue gasped and covered her mouth.

Vallon found himself comparing her to Caitlin. They were so different from each other, yet he loved both, and with that realisation came a pang of sorrow. He knew with painful certainty that he'd already lost Caitlin, and he knew that he and Qiuylue would never have a chance to find lasting happiness.

The emperor was an early riser who began working on affairs of state long before daybreak. It wasn't much past dawn when the chamberlain swept up with a troop of cavalry and a fleet of palanquins to convey the envoys to the palace. Waiting outside the pavilion, Vallon glanced at Lucas and experienced another wrench. The youth was as tall as him and already broader, but it wasn't just his stature that impressed. In the last few months Lucas had shed his peasant clumsiness. Now, clad in glittering armour, he looked like a young god. Vallon's swell of paternal pride subsided into bitterness. Lucas would never treat him as his father except in the most formal terms. How else could it be?

Vallon climbed into the leading litter with Lucas. Eight uniformed bearers hoisted it onto their shoulders and jogged out of the compound. Vallon peered out at the workaday streets.

'It seems we're not worthy of a triumphal procession.'

'The emperor doesn't want us to stage a grand entrance before he knows how the audience will turn out.'

Vallon shifted his sword. 'You're growing a head on those broad shoulders.'

For the rest of the journey the space around them ached with words neither could bring themselves to deliver. Vallon alighted as if he'd been set free and looked up the flight of steps ascending to the palace doors, each step occupied by soldiers bearing banners.

The chamberlain and his officials formed up in front and preceded the envoys into an antechamber where everyone stood with gazes uplifted as if waiting for a clap of thunder.

'I don't mind admitting it,' Vallon said. 'I'm nervous.'

Booming gongs and a roll of tympani brought the officials to attention. 'The emperor has taken his throne,' the chamberlain told Vallon. 'I must emphasise that you observe the correct procedures.'

'Lead on.'

The doors drew open and Vallon advanced into the throne room through files of soldiers and aristocrats. At the other end the emperor glowed like the sun. Clad in yellow silk brocaded with gold, hands clasped, he sat on a red lacquer throne decorated with dragon head finials, his slippered feet set on a footstool. Instead of the crown that Vallon had been expecting, he wore a clerical black hat with a stiff upturned front brim and a horizontal rod protruding from the back.

The chamberlain halted twenty yards from the throne and he and his entourage bobbed and scraped. Vallon was close enough to see that Shenzong had a bottom-heavy face, jaw wider than his brow, a rather sad moustache and a wispy goatee. Impassivity had been bred into him. Four flunkeys held rectangular flags above his head. In front of him and at a lower level stood the imperial family and ministers of the first rank.

When the envoys' letters had been read out and their gifts laid on a yellow table, the chamberlain beckoned Vallon forward.

'The emperor has graciously consented to receive you. Please observe the protocol.'

Vallon glanced round at his men. 'You know what to do.'

In a move practised many times the Outlanders performed the kow tow, at the same time chanting the *Kyrie eleison* and ending by raising their eyes to heaven and crossing themselves.

Sharp intakes of breath from the court swelled into murmurs of indignation. The barbarians had insulted the emperor. The chamberlain stamped his feet in front of Vallon.

'You broke your word.'

'On the contrary. Since your emperor rules by the Mandate of Heaven, you can't object if we address prayers to the Almighty who blesses both our realms.'

The hall grew still. Vapours from bowls of incense wafted up. A tiny gesture from Shenzong made the chamberlain gasp in relief. 'The emperor has decided to overlook your crass behaviour on the grounds that you are not yet familiar with palace customs.'

Shenzong examined portraits of Alexius and the Byzantine empress. A flicker of amusement showed on his face.

'His Imperial Majesty says your ruler is very hairy.'

'In Byzantium a heavy beard is considered a mark of strength and virility.'

Tut-tuts of disapproval indicated that this might be taken as a slur on Shenzong's masculinity.

'His Imperial Majesty asks by what mandate does your emperor rule?'

'By right of unbroken descent from the Caesars, by affirmation of his nobles and citizens, and by the grace of Almighty God who has appointed him His representative on earth.'

A few more questions followed concerning the route Vallon had taken and then the chamberlain said, 'His Imperial Majesty is glad that your sovereign extends his friendship. He hopes that your stay will be a pleasant one and wishes you a safe return to your homeland.'

Vallon looked at Shenzong. The emperor's face had lapsed into abstraction. 'Is that it?'

'The audience is concluded,' the chamberlain said.

After backing out of the throne room, Vallon gave a hollow laugh. 'We cross the world and for what? A few moments grovelling before a man who looks bored out of his wits.'

'It's an assumed manner,' Hero said. 'I imagine it never changes in public. The Chinese call him "the solitary man" and I understand why. He must be the loneliest man on earth.'

An official bustled up. 'The chief minister wishes to have a word.'

Attended by a flock of officials, a rather unkempt gentleman in his sixties approached.

'That's Wang Anshi,' Hero said. 'The emperor's closest advisor.'

Vallon made a cautious bow. Wang Anshi bowed back. His drooping eyelids and the bags under his eyes gave him a careworn look. At the same time his face projected intelligence and good humour. He waved his attendants out of earshot.

'Your Grace,' he said. 'I would like to hear more about your country and the reasons for your mission. I would take it as an honour if you consented to receive me at your residence tomorrow.'

'My lodgings, though opulent for an ambassador, are far too humble to entertain a personage as distinguished as yourself.'

'My tastes and habits are simpler than you might imagine.'

Hero murmured in French. 'He wants to speak in private, away from eager ears and prying eyes.'

Vallon bowed. 'I suspect I will make a clumsy host, but if you are prepared to overlook my foreign ways, I will be delighted to receive you.'

'How kind you are,' Wang said. 'I'll call at the tenth hour if that isn't inconvenient.' Bowing, he returned to his staff.

'That's it,' Hero squeaked.

'That's what?'

'Don't you see? The emperor is far too exalted to engage in diplomatic chit-chat. He leaves that to his ministers, none of whom is more senior than Wang Anshi. Tomorrow we'll get down to matters of substance.'

*

Qiuylue bubbled with excitement when Vallon returned. She made him describe the audience a dozen times, each time from a different perspective. Her delight when he told her that the chief minister would be gracing their residence tumbled into shock and anxiety. Vallon only just managed to stop her rushing out to organise his reception.

'Leave that to the servants. Tell me what you know about the minister.'

As the concubine of a senior officer she'd had many dealings with palace officials whose tongues had loosened after cups of wine. What she had to say about the minister worried and encouraged Vallon in equal measure. Wang Anshi was an enigma – a man born of low-ranking officials who'd risen to the highest office through the brilliance of his intellect. A Confucist who respected tradition, he was also a root-and-branch reformer. His attempts to overhaul the tax system, reorganise the military and create a bureaucracy based on merit had provoked furious opposition from conservative landlords whose interests he challenged, as well as intellectuals who on Confucian grounds preferred moral leadership to direct interference by a centralised government. Six years before, he'd been ousted from office, only to be reinstated two years later. He found solace from affairs of state in writing poetry.

The minister arrived at the appointed time with a modest retinue, bearers carrying his palanquin through an honour guard headed by Vallon. The general offered the minister his arm and together they went into the house. Wang Anshi subsided with a sigh onto a cushioned daybed. He dismissed all his attendants except a young clerk and a massive bodyguard who took up position in the doorway.

'Will you take chai, Your Excellency?'

'I drink only watered wine I prepare myself. I have to take precautions against poisoning.'

After a few pleasantries, Wang got down to business, beginning by explaining China's situation. 'Our greatest external threat comes from the Khitans. We have a standing army of more than a million, yet we pay the Liao empire an annual tribute of two hundred thousand bolts of silk and one hundred thousand ounces of silver.' The minister smiled. 'I believe a Khitan lady has infiltrated your own defences.'

Vallon blushed for the first time in decades.

'Our army is composed mainly of foreign mercenaries, criminals and peasants forced off their land by extortionate taxes. I understand it's the same in Byzantium. Does your military strategy work?'

'It succeeds for the moment. Like China, Byzantium prefers to use bribes or diplomacy rather than warfare. It was different a century ago, when the empire was organised into *themes* – provinces governed by generals and defended by soldiers paid not in cash but by land grants. A soldier with his own patch of land will fight to the death to preserve it.'

'I tried to introduce a similar system of local militia. I failed.'

They talked until noon before Wang stood. 'It seems that China and Byzantium have many things in common – a costly army, an inefficient and iniquitous tax system, and a bureaucracy staffed largely by aristocrats selected regardless of character and merit.'

Vallon put the all-important question. 'In your discussions with His Majesty, will you recommend that he draw up a formal alliance between our two empires?'

'An alliance based on mutual weakness will assist neither side. Besides, China and Byzantium lie too far apart, separated not only by mountains and deserts, but also by at least three aggressive barbarian empires. Fine promises written on paper are worthless if they can't be matched by deeds.' Wang noticed Vallon's disappointment. 'At the very least you will return home carrying His Imperial Majesty's formal declaration of friendship. That is,' Wang said, 'if you do decide to return home. There will always be a senior position in the Chinese army should you wish to remain in the Middle Kingdom.'

Vallon didn't reject the suggestion out of hand. 'Since you touch on the matter, I would very much like to have a first-hand look at Chinese military tactics and weaponry.'

'I will arrange a field day.'

'Thank you. I've heard stories of a strange weapon deployed by your soldiers – a powerful incendiary called Fire Drug. I'd be most interested to see it in action.'

Wang stood with his hands loosely clasped, rotating his thumbs around each other. There wasn't much that escaped his sharp mind. 'I will have to talk to officials in the War Ministry.'

A few days later Vallon and his officers rode out to watch the military stage manoeuvres. First they demonstrated the storming of a castle – a real castle, built for training purposes. A troop of infantry crept up under the cover of portable screens and raked the ramparts with bolts shot from heavy brass and wood crossbows. Then a team of engineers moved into place dragging trebuchets. They were smaller than the catapult Vallon had lugged from Constantinople, and instead of being powered by a counterweight, they were swung by teams of men hauling down on ropes secured to the short end of the throwing arm.

'They don't have the range or destructive power of Byzantine ballistae,' Vallon said. 'I'm surprised they don't adopt our method.'

'Their traction trebuchets are more manoeuvrable,' Josselin said. 'And they can discharge three or four missiles in the time it takes us to hurl one.'

The Chinese turned their attention to a wooden tower at one corner of the castle.

'God curse it,' Wulfstan said. 'That's a fire siphon or I'm a Frenchman.'

He was right. The Chinese pressurised a tank very similar to the one the Outlanders had brought with them and directed a spray of burning fuel onto the tower, reducing it to a blazing wreck.

Vallon applauded. 'So much for our secret war-winner,' he said.

In the afternoon they were treated to a display by cavalry units. One demonstration involved heavily armoured horse soldiers galloping down on an infantry position. From a distance the foot soldiers looked as if they were armed with nothing more than poleaxes, their position defended by thin, blunt-headed stakes fixed in the ground at an angle.

'Those aren't stakes,' Vallon said. 'The infantry are carrying fire-pots. Gentlemen, I think—'

Brazen blasts cut him short. The cavalry launched their charge. Fifty yards from their target, the infantry lit the heads of their staves. They exploded with pops and bangs, discharging invisible missiles that stung the horses into wild disarray.

Vallon rode through the stinking smoke and found the infantry commander. 'I was sure the cavalry would sweep you aside like chaff,' he said. He pointed at the smouldering staves. 'What manner of weapons are those?'

'Fire spears, your Grace. They shoot lead balls, pebbles and glass.'

Vallon rode back to his men. 'It's not a fiction. Fire Drug works.'

'That was play-acting,' Josselin said. 'A quarter of the spears didn't ignite, another quarter discharged too early or too late, and those cries you can hear tell us that some of the weapons injured their own side.'

Vallon's eyes narrowed. 'Nevertheless, Fire Drug is worth having.'

'How will you obtain it?'

Vallon sucked in his cheeks. 'I don't know, but I'm damned if I'll leave China without achieving at least one of our goals.'

XL

For Hero and Aiken, every day in Kaifeng brought new discoveries and delights. Escorted by officials they took in all the sights. They visited the two-hundred-foot-high Iron Pagoda and were only mildly disappointed to discover it was made of brick fired to the colour of metal. They were given a tour of a cast-iron foundry and made an excursion to the Grand Canal where they watched barges being lowered from one level to another by means of double-gated locks. They spent a day studying the mechanism of a thirty-foot-tall cosmic engine that told the time by puppet figures on revolving platforms, and which showed the movements of the heavenly bodies on a rotating globe. Its accuracy could be checked by actual observation of the sun, moon and planets with the aid of an armillary sphere supported by bronze dragons on the top of the tower.

All three instruments were driven by a single water-powered mechanism inside the tower. Hero's guides allowed him to inspect the workings and even make notes and drawings. A constant-level tank fed water at uniform pressure into thirty-six scoops evenly spaced on the rim of a great escapement wheel. As each scoop filled and dropped down, it tipped a pair of levers that pulled down an upper beam and released a gate, allowing the wheel to move round for the next scoop to be filled. So simple and so ingenious.

The only thing that clouded Hero's pleasure was his deteriorating eyesight. His right eye saw everything through a fog. Within days of arriving in Kaifeng he'd told the chamberlain about his condition and asked if anyone could cure it. The official sent him to three different hospitals, but at each one the physicians offered little hope, telling him that cataract surgery rarely worked and usually impaired vision even further.

'They don't want to take the risk of operating on a foreign guest,' Aiken said. 'If the procedure fails, they'll lose face.'

'And if I can't find someone to operate, I'll lose my sight.'

It wasn't until some weeks later, at a banquet, that an official suggested Hero consult an oculist who had successfully treated his own eye ailment. The physician was a third-generation immigrant from India, where cataract surgery had been pioneered.

Accompanied by the inevitable escort, Hero and Aiken visited the oculist a few days later. Their bearers carried them into a street crammed with medical practices that offered to cure everything from baldness to impotence, indigestion to infertility.

'Rapid Recovery Assured' promised one sign. To Hero the whole place smelt of quackery, so he was reassured when he saw that the oculist's surgery carried no advertising except for a painting of an eye.

A servant let them into a waiting room. Hero fidgeted on the edge of his seat. 'Nothing will come of it,' he told Aiken.

'Your servant, gentlemen.'

A dark and gentle-looking man had entered the room.

Hero stood. 'A palace official I met recommended you as a specialist in afflictions of the eye.'

'You have cataracts,' the oculist said, making the diagnosis from a distance of seven or eight feet. 'May I examine you?'

Hero stood rigid with nerves while the oculist peered into his eyes. 'The occlusion in your left eye is still at an early stage, but the one in your right eye is beginning to harden.'

'Too advanced to treat, I expect,' Hero said. He wanted to hear the worst and leave as soon as he could.

'Obviously the thinner and softer the phlegmatic matter, the greater the chances of success. But it's not too late to remove the cataract from your right eye.'

'You mean you can restore my vision?'

'There's a good chance I can improve it. I cannot restore perfect sight.'

Hero was reassured that the oculist didn't claim to be a miracle worker. 'I ought to tell you that I myself am a physician, though not a specialist in eye ailments.' He produced his copy of Hunayn ibn Ishaq's *Ten Treatises of the Eye*. 'Although the text is in Arabic, it contains many informative drawings.'

The oculist leafed through the pages. 'The author has a good working knowledge of the eye,' he said, suggesting that it didn't quite match his own. He handed the book back. 'As a physician, you will know what surgical techniques are involved.'

'I've been told about the couching procedure, where the surgeon punctures the eyeball with a curved needle and pushes the opaque matter out of the line of vision.'

The oculist went to a table containing his instruments. 'This is the type of needle you're referring to. I no longer use it.' He picked up a needle with a thicker, more flattened end. 'It's designed to penetrate the lens membrane and push the cataract into the vitreous body. I found it gave better and longer-lasting results. However, in many cases neither method corrects the condition, and in some they make it worse.'

'To the point of blindness?'

'Yes.' The oculist put the needle down and returned with a lancet. 'I prefer to use more extensive surgery. I make an incision in the eyeball about so long,' he said, holding thumb and forefinger about one-third of an inch apart.

Hero swallowed. 'You cut the cataract out?'

'I suck it out. I used to employ an assistant with remarkable lung capacity to perform the task. Sadly he passed away some years ago. Unable to find anyone as good, I devised a machine that would do the job.' The oculist showed Hero a suction pump with a narrow parchment tube at one end.

Hero and Aiken exchanged squeamish glances.

'What are the chances of success?'

'Every case is different. I can show you testimonials from grateful patients. Of course I won't show you the letters from patients I've blinded. All I will say is that I have had more successes than failures.'

Hero linked his hands to stop them shaking. 'And if I don't have the operation?'

'In two or three years, you will lose effective vision in your right eye. A few more years and the world will be just a blur. Let me suggest one possible course. The phlegmata in your left eye is soft and so can be removed more easily. Should you choose surgery, I can operate on that eye first. If my work is successful, we can consider removing the cataract from your right eye.'

Horrid calculations coursed through Hero's mind. He could still see tolerably well with his left eye. If the operation was unsuccessful, vision would be restricted to his right eye, which could barely decipher writing held to his nose. Since his right eye was already in such a bad state, perhaps it would be better to start with that one. If the operation didn't succeed . . . He strained his mouth, casting a desperate appeal at Aiken.

The youth spoke quietly. 'Only you can make the decision.'

'You don't have to decide now,' the oculist said. 'Reflect on what I've told you. Consult me if you have any further questions. Perhaps you'd care for some chai.'

He led the way into a snug chamber. A bronze statue of Shiva, Hindu god of destruction and renewal, stood on a table next to an inkstone and other writing materials. Examples of calligraphy hung on the wall.

Hero pointed at one. 'Your own work?'

'My amateur scribblings are not worthy of your attention. I do them to keep my fingers deft for surgery.'

'I think they're wonderful,' said Aiken. 'Particularly that one.'

The oculist removed it from the wall. 'You do me great honour and you will do me even greater honour by accepting my worthless scrawl.' He sat head bowed, covered in embarrassment.

A young woman entering with the chai things broke the awkward silence. 'My daughter,' the oculist said when she'd retired. 'My wife died last year.'

It did occur to Hero that if the surgeon couldn't save those closest to him, he might not be the best person to carry out a risky operation. Hero dismissed the unworthy thought, soothed by the fragrant tea and the room's calm atmosphere. Evening was beginning to dim the light outside the window. A faint breeze carried the smell of rain-damped earth, transporting him back to an early spring day in England. He marvelled at how far he'd travelled and how much he'd seen since then. He'd stored up enough memories to pore over for a lifetime, thousands of images to revisit long after blindness had brought a veil down on the world. He hardly heard the oculist's words of encouragement and farewell.

'Take your time deciding. Even if you decide against the operation, please visit me again. I would very much like to hear about the medical techniques you practise in the West.'

'I've reached my decision,' said Hero. 'I wish you to perform the operation.'

'Are you sure?'

'No. I'm acting out of blind faith. Begin with my left eye.'

The oculist took his hands. 'Tomorrow is an inauspicious day. Return the following morning. Come prepared for a three- or four-day stay. Abstain from solid food tomorrow.'

Rain was pelting the streets into slurry when Hero set off in a covered rickshaw for his operation. He watched porters dashing through the downpour holding makeshift canopies over their heads, and he wondered if they would be among the last sights he saw. His mood had see-sawed between optimism and despair. Now he was mired in a sludge of fatalism.

Aiken squeezed his arm. 'I know it's cold comfort, but by the time this storm has passed, your ordeal will be over.'

'Or just beginning.'

The oculist's warm welcome raised Hero's spirits. He regarded with approval the warm, clean and sweetly scented operating room. The rain drummed on the tiled roof.

As the oculist led him to a couch, Hero had just one question. 'Do you sedate your patients? If you don't, I have a mixture guaranteed to dull pain. Where such a delicate procedure is involved, it would help if the patient didn't flinch or toss about.'

The oculist indicated a mortar placed on a table beside a brazier. 'I try to reduce pain as much as possible. If you wish to apply your own relief, please do so.'

Hero was now lying on the couch, a serious-looking assistant standing behind the oculist.

'I can't trust in one of your methods while rejecting another. Let it be done your way.'

'Lie back and close your eyes,' the oculist said. 'Try to empty your mind.'

'Hold my hand,' Hero said to Aiken.

'Breathe deep,' the oculist said.

Hero inhaled heady vapours, and when the oculist spoke again, his voice reached him from far away.

'Open your eyes.'

The room swam.

'Good. As you've probably discovered yourself, physicians rarely make good patients. Try to look at your nose and stay quite still.'

A hand clamped over Hero's forehead. He saw the oculist lean over, the blade bright in his hand. Moments later he heard and felt a snick as the oculist slit his left eyeball.

'Excellent. You didn't move a muscle. The success of that first procedure determines the outcome above all others.'

Hero was only dimly aware of what followed. Something was applied to his left eye. The grip on his head tightened. Pain lanced his eye and he jerked.

'It's done,' said the oculist. 'I judge it a success.'

Hero's tongue was thick in his mouth, making it hard to speak. 'In that case, do the other eye.'

'Are you sure? Don't you want to wait to determine the outcome?'

'If the first cut failed, the second won't remedy it. I'm resigned to a cure or blindness. If the latter, I attach no blame to you.'

Once more the fumes made his head spin. The world dissolved in a spiral that sucked him into a white void. He didn't feel the second cut.

He woke in darkness, the taste of vomit in his mouth.

'Aiken?'

'I'm beside you.'

'I can't see.'

Aiken laughed. 'That's because your eyes are bandaged.'

'They hurt.'

'Of course they do,' the oculist said. 'I've applied healing poultices. I'll change them tomorrow. Try not to laugh or sneeze or cough.'

Hero floated in and out of consciousness. In his more lucid states, he was convinced that the operation had been a failure. Aiken remained with him the whole time, reading to him or reminiscing about their journey.

'What time is it?' Hero asked.

'It's late. Well past midnight.'

'I wonder how a blind man tells the time. I expect he uses his other senses.'

'You're not blind.'

'I might be.'

'If you are, I'll be your eyes.'

'That's what Wayland said before leaving us. I wonder where he is now.'

'Back home, I hope.

'Dear Aiken, thank you for your kind support. Leave me now and get some sleep.'

'I'm not tired.'

'But I am.'

Hero lay awake for the rest of the night and heard the first cock herald dawn and the growing buzz of traffic outside his window. In mid-morning the oculist arrived to remove the bandages.

'Don't expect too much,' he said. 'The incisions will still be inflamed. It will be another week before we can assess the strength of your vision.'

Light scalded Hero's eyes when the oculist peeled away the poultices.

'What do you see?'

'Shadows swimming in bright fog.'

'That's as much as I would expect at this stage. Tomorrow I'm confident we'll see an improvement.'

Three more times the oculist dressed Hero's eyes. The last time he removed the poultices, Hero sat up with Aiken's assistance. Vallon, Lucas and Wulfstan stood at the foot of his bed, their expressions straining between anxiety and desperate expectation.

'It's me,' Vallon said. 'Can you see me?'

'I can see you,' Hero said. 'I can see all of you as bright as day. Or at least I could if it wasn't for these tears.'

XLI

Vallon and Qiuylue were taking a night-time stroll in the garden when Josselin found them. He saluted and bowed. 'Forgive my intrusion, sir. Trooper Stefan has just reported something strange.'

'In French, please,' Vallon said. He knew that Qiuylue must report all his doings and it wasn't beyond the bounds of possibility that she understood Greek. 'My dear, will you excuse us for a moment?'

Qiuylue left them.

'Well?' Vallon said.

'Some of the troopers went out on the town this evening. They were drinking in a tavern when a Chinese man speaking in Arabic approached Stefan and asked him to pass on a message to you. He spoke of you by name. You and Hero are requested to go to the Golden Phoenix eating house tomorrow at noon. The man said you must make sure no one follows you.'

'Any idea who we're supposed to be meeting?'

'None at all, sir.'

'Strange indeed,' Vallon said. He could tell from Josselin's manner that something more was called for. He'd rather neglected his military responsibilities the last few weeks. 'Are the men content?'

'Too content. It will be a devil of a job to tear them away from this Lotus-land. Half of them are planning to marry their Chinese doxies.'

Vallon was familiar with the story of the travellers who, having eaten of the lotus tree, forgot their families and homes and lost all desire to return to their native country. 'I dare say you think I've set a bad example.'

'I won't quarrel with that, sir. Can I ask when you intend leading us home? That is, if you do intend to leave. There are rumours that you've accepted a commission in the Chinese army.'

'Nonsense,' Vallon said, smarting at the criticism. 'We'll leave in the autumn, when the cooler weather makes for easier travelling.'

'I think by then it will be too late,' Josselin said.

Vallon watched the centurion walk away into the darkness and stood for a long time thinking about what he'd said. He started at Qiuylue's voice.

'Did the officer bring bad news?'

'No, just routine business. I have to pay a call on Hero. I won't be long.'

He found the physician reading in his quarters. 'How are your eyes?'

'The soreness has quite gone and my vision is sharper than it's been for years.'

'Wonderful. Do you know the Golden Phoenix eating house?'

'It's on the corner of Beer Fountain Road and Toad Tumulus Street. It's one of the most popular eating establishments in Kaifeng.'

'We've been invited to dine there at noon tomorrow.'

'Who by?'

'I don't know,' Vallon said. He explained how the invitation had reached him.

'Will you go?'

'I suppose so. It might have something to do with Fire Drug. The messenger stressed that we keep our visit secret.'

'That might prove difficult.'

Whenever any of the Outlanders left the compound, they were followed by not-so-secret agents. Their surveillance was quite blatant, the trackers staying in plain view and sometimes intervening to point out interesting sights to their charges or assist with bargaining at a food stall or shop. It was the authorities' way of letting the foreigners know that their every move was watched, every contact reported. Vallon had experienced the all-pervasive power of the state when he tried to purchase firecrackers in an attempt to lay his hands on Fire Drug. His shadow had thwarted the attempt, telling him that fireworks weren't allowed in the compound. To test how far state control went, Vallon had sent troopers to two more establishments whose proprietors had flatly refused to serve them.

Allowing plenty of time to reach the rendezvous, Vallon and Hero left the compound and headed south. The day was mild and the streets bustling. They reached the river that flowed through the city from east to west and turned right.

'Are they following us?' Hero asked.

'Two of them,' said Vallon. 'Don't look back.'

A high arched bridge congested by stalls and traffic crossed the river. A grain ship with lowered mast had misjudged the headroom and stuck halfway under the span. Vallon and Hero dawdled along the bank, pausing to examine stalls selling everything from horoscopes to steamed buns, jewellery to toys.

'Beware that rogue,' one of the agents hissed in Vallon's ear. 'If you want to buy gifts for your lady, I can take you to a far superior place.'

'Thank you,' Vallon said. 'I don't know what we'd do without you.'

He and Hero resumed their passage, the two agents dogging their footsteps. Vallon paused on the embankment and pretended he'd seen something interesting on the other side.

'That's what we want.'

'Where?'

'Down there.'

Beneath them a man lay dozing in a skiff. Vallon dropped into it and thrust a string of coins at the startled boatman. 'A thousand cash to take us across the river.'

The agents didn't shirk their duty. One of them tried to fling himself into the boat and fell into the river a foot short. The other sprinted back toward the bridge, its roadway now blocked by a crowd yelling advice and encouragement to the crew labouring to free their ship.

Vallon and Hero disembarked on the other side with time to spare and made several false turns before reaching the Golden Phoenix just as distant drummers announced noon by beating a long tattoo. The restaurant stood on the corner of a busy junction criss-crossed by peasants shouldering bamboo poles strung with produce, sweating coolies carrying officials and ladies in litters, high-wheeled ox and donkey carts laden with wine tuns and sacks of millet ... A group of scholars had chosen to hold a disputation at the centre of the crossroads. Children bowled hoops through the traffic. To one side of the restaurant, a crowd had gathered around a professional storyteller.

Vallon and Hero picked their way through the streams and eddies of humanity. The restaurant stood three storeys tall, its two upper floors projecting in galleries so that diners could observe the street theatre. A doorman ushered the guests through the brightly painted entrance.

They stopped, taken aback by the scale of the establishment. At least a hundred diners occupied the central banqueting hall and as many again sat in booths on each side. The din of conversation and busy chopsticks was deafening. An army of waiters darted about.

A manager appeared in front of them.

'Do you have a reservation?'

'No. Our host made the reservation.'

'Name.'

'Ah, that's the problem. It's a surprise—'

'Your name?'

'Vallon.'

The manager consulted a pad and clicked a finger at a hovering menial, who took charge of the guests. 'Follow me, honoured sirs.'

'This is rather exciting,' Hero said, climbing a flight of stairs.

On the top floor the servant led them to a nook on a balcony overlooking the crossroads and partly screened from below by fruit trees planted in tubs.

'A good place to speak in private,' Hero said.

Vallon watched the comings and goings at ground level. 'Or assassinate us.'

He kept one eye on the road, the other on the entrance to the balcony. Beyond it the activity was frenzied. This diner wanted a hot and spicy dish, his companion something mild and cooling. One diner asked for his pork to be fried; his companion, after much dithering, preferred his meat to be grilled. When a table had decided, the waiter darted to the kitchen, singing out the whole list of orders.

'Extraordinary,' said Hero. 'They don't write anything down.'

One of these memory artists came bustling up to their table. 'Ready?'

'We're waiting for our host. He must have been delayed by traffic.'

'Very busy day,' the waiter said. 'You order now.'

Vallon noticed a tall Arab crossing the street, dodging a Taoist procession. He wore a blue turban with one end veiling the lower part of his face.

'Let's go ahead,' said Vallon. 'The whole thing might be some kind of hoax.'

The waiter teetered with impatience while Hero tried to make sense of the menu. 'What do you recommend?'

'You have hundred flavours soup and lamb steamed over milk.'

'I'll have the same,' said Vallon.

'Make that three,' said the Arab, materialising behind the waiter.

Vallon's brain refused to believe his eyes. 'My God.'

Hero sprawled across the table. 'Wayland! Oh, Wayland!'

'Not so loud,' said Wayland. He slid into a seat and smiled at his comrades. 'Well, fate spares the undoomed man.'

Vallon and Hero spoke at once. How had he arrived in China? What had happened on the journey through Tibet? Had he found the mysterious temple?

'All in good time,' Wayland said.

Vallon regarded him through stinging eyes. 'I thought I'd never see you again. I should have known that seas and mountains mean nothing to a passage hawk. You've lost weight.' He displaced his emotion by summoning a waiter and demanding a flagon of the finest wine.

A moment of hiatus followed, too many swirling questions to articulate.

'Here's my tale in brief,' Wayland said. 'I journeyed across Tibet and climbed the Himalayan passes into Nepal. I found the temple and learned something about its Christian hermit. Hero, I have a lot more to tell you about my discoveries when we have greater leisure. I reached India intending to turn west into Afghanistan, but found my way blocked by war and famine and ended up at a port near the mouth of the Ganges river. While I was there an Arab merchant ship put in with cargo bound for China. I was weary of wearing out shoe leather on foreign soil and I took employment as a sailor. After voyaging south around a great peninsula and passing through a strait, my ship sailed north until it arrived at a Chinese trading city called Canton. From there I continued north by sea and canal until I reached Kaifeng. I've been in the city for a month.'

'Why didn't you contact us sooner?' Vallon said.

'I judged that I'd be of more use if I hid our association. The Chinese think I'm a lowly Arab mariner and pay little heed to me. I can come and go as I please. The man who passed on the invitation is my spy, cocking an ear at conversations in this tavern and that gambling den. From what I've heard, the Chinese are holding you prisoner.'

'Hardly that,' said Hero. 'I've explored the city and seen wonders I never dreamed of.'

'Wayland's right,' said Vallon. 'The Chinese have penned us in a gilded cage, indulging our every wish. God knows, I've succumbed to their pampering. By the way, I'm sure we shook off our trackers.'

'I know. I followed you from the moment you left the compound.'

'What else have you learned?' Vallon asked. 'Do you know what the Chinese intend to do with us.'

'You've already answered the question. They're lulling you into a pleasant dream from which you'll never want to emerge. The tavern gossip is that the emperor doesn't want you to leave China. He hopes General Vallon will agree to command a regiment against the northern barbarians. He believes that Hero will choose to remain in the Heavenly Kingdom.'

The news sobered Vallon. 'Do they know about our interest in Fire Drug?'

'From the day you arrived, they knew what you were after and determined you would never find it.' Wayland looked up. 'Your concubine reports on your activities. Every servant is a spy.'

Vallon flushed. 'Let's eat.'

Hero took a few spoonfuls of soup. 'Do you notice anything different about me?'

Wayland studied him. 'Something about your eyes?'

'A surgeon removed my cataracts. The operation was successful. I can see again – not as well as you, but well enough to read without discomfort. And I no longer walk past friends in the street without recognising them.'

'That's wonderful.'

'And it's wonderful that one of the first sights to greet my eyes is our beloved friend Wayland.'

Vallon laid a hand on Wayland's. 'I too have gained more from our journey than I could ever have hoped for.'

Wayland looked at Hero. 'You told him?'

Hero beamed. 'Lucas told Vallon himself – not without a great deal of encouragement and arm-twisting.'

Wayland hesitated. 'And are father and son reconciled?'

Vallon pretended to give his attention to the food. 'I pray we will be in God's good time.' He gave a desperate laugh. 'My head's still spinning. So much news to catch up on.'

'My lodgings aren't far from here,' Wayland said. 'We can talk at leisure after we've eaten.'

'I'm afraid my curiosity must go unsatisfied a little longer,' Vallon said. 'I have a meeting with the deputy minister of war.'

'Actually, what I wanted to discuss would interest Hero more than you. It concerns something I found in the temple in Nepal.'

'Tell me,' Hero said.

'Later,' Vallon insisted. He raised a beaker. 'To old comrades.'

'It's best if we don't leave together,' Wayland told Hero. 'Give me time to get clear then turn right at the entrance and stop at the first corner. My Chinese friend will be waiting for you.'

Vallon and Hero went their separate ways, Hero turning right as directed. At the corner where the storyteller had been holding forth, a crowd had gathered to watch a wrestling match. Hero stood on tiptoe to view the contest. On the other side of the crowd, two country boys spectated from the back of a buffalo.

Hero waved away a ruffian vending fake money for use at funerals and scanned the periphery of the crowd for someone who looked like Wayland's agent.

The currency vendor gestured across the junction. 'You see the merchant selling archery equipment?' he said in Arabic.

Hero spotted a gentleman bending a bow on a veranda set up as a shooting gallery.

'I see it.'

'Wait until I've turned the corner. Stay well back.'

Hero watched him make his way across the street before following. His guide set a brisk pace heading along Beer Fountain Road and then turning into a side street. Hero had difficulty keeping him in sight. The lane was packed with off-duty soldiers, foreign seamen and young civil service candidates celebrating after examinations. Red silk lanterns hung above the doors of numerous wineshops, and heavily made-up women and a few effete boys struck provocative poses in the upper windows.

A gaggle of drunken students blocked his path, inviting him to take a cup of wine with them. When he'd struggled through, his guide had disappeared.

'Sss!'

Hero glimpsed the guide at the entrance to an alley. He

followed through a slum of ramshackle houses and courts. He reached a dead end. A door opened and he went in, the guide leading him up rickety stairs to a room where Wayland stood waiting.

'I never expected to meet you in the Willow Quarter,' Hero said. 'Every second house is a brothel.'

'It's the foreign quarter. I blend in. Can I offer you chai? Wine?'

Hero was still stupefied by Wayland's resurrection. 'Nothing, thank you. I was so amazed to see you that I forgot to ask after your companions.'

Wayland poured himself a beaker of wine. 'The Turkmen are dead. Two drowned in a flooded river. Toghan was killed by a wild yak.'

'Zuleyka?'

Wayland closed his eyes and drank. 'We parted in Nepal. She took my dog with her.'

A girl wandered into the room, her gown half undone, her make-up smudged. Wayland said something to her and she yawned and left.

Hero sat and composed his hands on his knees. It seemed to him that Wayland had changed during his absence. Hero had never seen him drink wine during the day. And the casual way he'd spoken to that whore . . .

'You said you found the temple.'

'It stands at the head of a valley above the treeline, overlooking a deserted village destroyed in an earthquake. Everything had been left just as it was, including the lama's body seated before the altar. I found a sacristan who had stayed on as guardian. He confirmed that a Christian hermit called Oussu studied at the temple a thousand years ago.'

Hero smiled. 'Even our most learned historians sometimes muddle chronology, and I suspect that untutored men in such a remote place would have a very hazy sense of time.'

'That's what I thought. But when I challenged the sacristan, he showed me a book listing all the lamas from the time the temple was built. Oussu arrived in the reign of the second lama. There have been at least fifty more since then. I counted.'

'You said you found something there.'

'Several things. The sacristan showed me the cave where Oussu meditated. On the walls were Christian symbols made by pilgrims who visited the temple a hundred years after Oussu left.'

'Crosses?'

'The outline of a fish. Does that mean anything to you?'

'A fish was one of the earliest Christian symbols.'

'Which suggests the sacristan was telling the truth.'

Hero hid his disappointment. 'I was hoping you'd discovered something more tangible.'

Wayland picked up a bamboo tube and uncapped one end. 'I took away a *thanka* and a scroll.' He removed the painting and passed it across. 'It's a portrait of Oussu.'

Hero studied it. 'The figure certainly has a Western countenance. How do you know it's Oussu?'

'It seemed different from all the other paintings. That's why I picked it out. It wasn't until later that the sacristan confirmed it was a portrait of Oussu.'

'It doesn't look very old. The colours are still fresh.'

'They were even brighter the day I first saw it. Nothing fades in that dry cold atmosphere. The lama had been dead for two years yet his body was perfectly preserved.'

'You said you took a scroll.'

Wayland handed it over. 'It was one of many I found in the cave where Oussu spent many days and nights meditating. I don't know what language it's written in.'

Hero unrolled it. He brushed back his hair. 'It's Aramaic.'

'Who uses that tongue?'

'It's widely used in the empire of the Arabs. The Jews use it more than they use their native Hebrew. It was the language of Jesus.'

'I thought the early Christians wrote in Greek.'

'Most did, but for many their mother tongue would have been Aramaic.'

'Can you read it?'

'No, but I know someone who can. There's a Jewish community in Kaifeng. They came from Persia more than five hundred years ago. I'm sure one of their rabbis or scholars will be able to translate the scroll. I'll arrange a visit.'

'Why don't we go now?'

'This moment?'

'I've been hugging that scroll close for the last five months, protecting it against tempests and thieves, all the while wondering what it means.'

XLII

The synagogue or *kenesa* called the Temple of Purity and Goodness stood behind high walls on Teaching Torah Lane, an affluent thoroughfare close to the imperial palace. Hero jangled a bell at the double-doored entrance and after a while a wicket opened and a man gave the callers a guarded appraisal.

'You're Westerners,' he said in Chinese.

'We're members of an imperial embassy sent from Constantinople.'

'Are you Jews?'

'No.'

'Then what do you want?'

Hero made his tone as pleasant as possible. 'On our journey through the Taklamakan we acquired a scroll at a Buddhist temple. What excited my interest was the fact that it's written in Aramaic. I was hoping that someone in your temple could translate it for me.'

The gatekeeper didn't soften his stance. 'We don't use Aramaic. We never have. Our native tongue was Persian and the last Persian speaker died generations ago.'

Hero's face fell. 'No one can help?'

The gatekeeper held out a hand. 'Give me the scroll. I'll enquire if anyone knows of a scholar who understands Aramaic script.'

'Don't part with it,' Wayland said.

'He's not going to run away with it,' Hero said. He smiled at the gatekeeper. 'Of course we would pay the translator a fee.'

'Wait here,' the gatekeeper said, shutting the wicket behind him.

'You obviously think the scroll is important,' Hero said.

'I nearly killed myself getting it.'

The gatekeeper returned, his manner somewhat softened. 'The rabbi will see you.'

The synagogue complex was built in Chinese style, the temple set in a pleasant garden. The gatekeeper ushered them in. Hero had visited several synagogues and found it strange to see the traditional layout grafted on to Chinese architecture. Beyond the entrance stood a table equipped with censer, candlesticks and bowls of oil. Behind it, enclosed in latticework, rose the pulpit-like Chair of Moses, on which the Torah had been placed for ceremonial reading. Two black lacquered columns flanking the chair rose to a dome in the roof – the only non-oriental feature in the building.

An elderly gentleman wholly Chinese in dress and appearance apart from a skull cap received the visitors.

'Forgive the porter's brusque reception. We rarely receive visits from anyone outside our community.'

'Do the Chinese persecute Jews?' Hero asked.

The rabbi's waxy face relaxed. 'They tolerate all faiths so long as they don't challenge the state. After all, the Chinese themselves can't agree if they're Confucists, Buddhists or Taoists. We Jews, together with Nestorians and Zoroastrians, are minnows in an ocean.'

He led them into a chamber hung with inscriptions in Chinese.

'Are those Jewish texts?' Hero asked.

'Yes, they are. That one is from the Book of Job. But I believe the text you have is written in Aramaic.'

Hero presented the scroll. The rabbi began to unroll it. 'My companion at the gate wasn't being entirely honest when he told you no one could read Aramaic. Realising that the fount of all things holy was drying up, I made it my business to learn Aramaic and Hebrew from the few souls who preserved those languages. My understanding of both scripts is poor.'

'Keep a close eye on his face,' Wayland said in French.

'When I'm gone,' the rabbi continued, 'even that tentative link with our roots will be severed.' His lips moved as he struggled to translate the text. He unrolled another section, holding it to the light. Then his brow furrowed, his eyes blinked and he gasped.

'I told you,' Wayland murmured.

'Has something engaged your interest?' Hero asked.

The rabbi forced his features into impassivity. 'You said you acquired the scroll in the Taklamakan. Where precisely?'

Hero had prepared a story both plausible and simple. 'On our Silk Road journey we visited the Buddhist cave complex at Dunhuang. Seeing that we were Westerners, a monk offered to sell me the scroll. He claimed it was a Christian text and therefore of no interest to him.'

The rabbi fingered his throat. 'I imagine not.'

'Can you tell us what it is?' Hero said. 'Perhaps you could read the first few lines.'

'I told you my grasp of Aramaic is weak. I don't want to confuse you with a garbled translation. It will take me at least a month to work my way through the text.'

Hero made a muted sound of disappointment. 'As a scholar myself, I understand the need for an accurate rendering, but if you could just give us a précis ...'

'I'm not happy leaving it in his hands,' Wayland said.

'We won't find anyone else to translate it.'

The rabbi smiled. 'You're impatient to fathom the meaning and your curiosity excites mine. I'll give the scroll my urgent attention. Return in five days.'

The gatekeeper showed them out and bolted the entrance behind them

'We should have made a copy,' Wayland said.

'The rabbi isn't going to steal it.'

Wayland's eyes had an odd glint. 'He's Jewish. Oussu was a Christian. Whatever is in the scroll might conflict with his own beliefs. It might not be something he wants to share.'

'I've always found Jewish scholars tolerant of other religions of the book.'

The street was empty, the city settling down under the onset of evening. Wayland led the way. 'I still wish we'd made a copy. My fault. Eagerness overmastered caution.'

Hero hurried to catch up. 'It sounds to me as if you have an inkling of what the scroll contains.'

A hundred trumpets warned Kaifeng's citizens that the evening curfew was approaching. Wayland stopped and placed both hands on Hero's shoulders.

'If I told you what I suspect, you'd think my wits were stolen. Perhaps they are. I can tell you one thing. I'm not the same man you bade farewell to all those months ago.'

When Hero and Wayland returned to the synagogue, the rabbi greeted them warmly and offered them chai.

'Have you finished?' Hero asked.

The rabbi picked up the scroll and a translation on paper. 'I burned many a lamp on the task. The Buddhist who sold it to you was correct. It's the Gospel of Saint John.' His finger traced the first few lines. '"In the beginning was the Word, and the Word was God".' He smiled. 'Only God knows how the scroll found its way so far east. You must be very excited.'

'A remarkable find,' Hero said, looking at Wayland.

'Why would Oussu spend time writing out a gospel in the Himalayas?'

'You don't know he wrote it. Perhaps he brought it to spread the gospel of Jesus's sacrifice and resurrection to the people of Tibet.'

'To a tiny village high in the mountains? He wasn't evangelising. The sacristan told me he spent his time learning the law of Buddha and meditating. When he had achieved enlightenment, he left to return to the West.'

The rabbi intervened with tact. 'Your friend seems upset.'

'He was hoping the scroll contained an undiscovered text that would shed new light on the early history of Christianity.'

'I think finding a copy of a Christian gospel so far from the Holy Land is noteworthy.'

'So do I,' Hero said.

The rabbi smoothed his gown. 'I have to prepare for a wedding.' He held out the scroll and translation. 'For me it's been a most interesting exercise. Perhaps you might like to make a contribution to the synagogue.'

Hero could tell that Wayland was downcast and chatted of other things as they returned to his lodgings. Back in the shabby room, Wayland unrolled the *thanka* and placed it on a table, weighting the ends down with cups. He studied the enigmatic figure. 'You weren't a copyist or a preacher.'

'Who do you think he was, then?' Hero asked.

Wayland didn't answer. He took the scroll out of its tube and unrolled it. He gasped.

'What's the matter?'

'This isn't the scroll I found in the temple.'

'But you can't read Aramaic.'

'I carried the thing for long enough to remember the pattern of the words.'

'Give it to me,' Hero said. He studied the characters. 'You're right.'

Wayland kicked the table. 'I knew we should have made a copy.'

'But why would the rabbi substitute a fake? The Gospel of Saint John wouldn't be of much interest to a devout Jew.'

'It wasn't John's gospel.'

'Then what?'

540

'Sit down,' Wayland said. 'I'm going to take a drink of wine and I suggest you do the same.'

Hero sat holding his cup on his knees. Wayland drank half his in one gulp.

'The sacristan told me Oussu had come to the temple a thousand years ago and showed me evidence to support the claim. Like you, I was sceptical. I remember saying that if it were true, Oussu would have lived around the same time as Jesus.'

'Several of his disciples carried the word of God abroad in their own lifetimes. St Thomas established churches as far away as India.'

'And the sacristan told me that within a hundred years of Oussu's departure, a group of Christian pilgrims came to worship at the site. It was they who left the fish symbol on the walls of the cave. The only reason they did that is because they venerated him.'

'I'm not sure where this is leading.'

'Oussu. Think about the name.'

When Hero made the connection, he spilled his wine. 'That's impossible.'

'Is it? That Gospel of Thomas you found in Anatolia. You believed it contained an account of Jesus's life before he began teaching and working miracles.'

'I didn't have a chance to read more than a few lines before the emir's secretary snatched it away.'

'I remember you telling me that nothing was known about Jesus's life between his boyhood and the time he was baptised at the age of about thirty.'

'That's true. Most of his life was passed in obscurity.'

'During that period he could have travelled anywhere. He could have travelled as far as Nepal. Why not? I did, and on my journey to China I had plenty of time to reflect. One thing that struck me was how much Buddhism and Christianity have in common. Show compassion for all livings things. Forgive your enemies. Turn the other cheek.'

'Most of the great religions teach similar precepts, and they're honoured more in the breach than the observance.'

'I knew you'd think I was crazy. The rabbi doesn't. That's why he stole the scroll. It contains Jesus's writings, his thoughts.' Wayland made for the door. 'I'm going to get it back.'

Hero caught him. 'Suppose you're right. The rabbi won't return it.'

'Yes, he will.'

Hero struggled to hold Wayland back. 'He'll deny it. You have no evidence. The rabbi is a well-respected citizen. He'll summon a magistrate. You'll be arrested. At the very least the authorities will uncover your connection with Vallon.' Hero eased Wayland away from the door. 'Have another drink.' He managed to seat Wayland and put a cup into his hand.

'I could have established proof if I'd had more time in the temple.'

'Perhaps one day you'll return.'

Wayland shivered. 'I lost three friends on that journey. I lost Zuleyka and I lost my dog. For what? All I wanted was to return to my family and instead I'm further from home than ever, living in a whorehouse with nothing to show for it.'

He knocked back his wine and stood looking at the *thanka*. His back was turned and Hero couldn't tell if he was laughing or weeping. Hero had never seen Wayland drunk before, not even tipsy.

'I possess the only portrait of Jesus in existence, and no one – not even you – believes me.'

XLIII

Hero entered Vallon's quarters fizzing with excitement. 'See what I've got.'

Vallon watched as Hero set a small rectangular iron plate on the table. He brushed the plate with a sticky resin then placed a frame over it.

'Does this have anything to do with Fire Drug?' Vallon asked.

'This,' said Hero, 'is far more interesting.'

From a box he took small squares of clay each carved with a Chinese character on one face and fitted them into the frame, wedging them tight with strips of bamboo. When the frame was full, he coated the characters with gummy ink, pressed a sheet of paper over the form and rubbed the surface with a pad. Grinning like a conjuror about to perform a thrilling sleight of hand, he took one corner of the paper, peeled it off and showed Vallon the impression of the inked characters printed on the other side.

'What does it say?' Vallon asked.

'I don't know. I placed the pieces at random.'

'What's it for?'

Hero inked the character again and made a second print. 'You see, once I've positioned the characters I can produce a copy in a fraction of the time it would take to write a page. I could produce a book in less than a day.'

Vallon wasn't impressed. 'Judging by how long it took you to put those pieces together, assembling an entire book would be a week's work. In fact a month might not be long enough. Besides, you were playing with only a few dozen characters and the Chinese language contains thousands.'

'That's why they continue to use wood-block printing. It's faster than the moveable-type system.'

'You're beginning to confuse me.'

'Don't you see? The technique isn't restricted to Chinese. The Greek alphabet contains only twenty-four letters. Carve enough of them and you could set a page in a morning, a book in a week. It will revolutionise the way books are produced.'

'Professional scribes will never adopt the method.'

'There won't be any need for scribes with my printing set.'

'You know, Hero, sometimes your enthusiasm for newfangled gadgets runs ahead of what's practical.'

'You're in a grumpy mood this morning.'

'Sit down,' Vallon said. He went to the window and pointed at the cherry trees in full blossom. 'We've been in Kaifeng four months and we're no nearer persuading the emperor to draw up an alliance. A meaningful alliance was always a fantasy. Byzantium and China lie so far apart they could be on different planets. Duke Phocas was right. The expedition was simply the emperor's way of ridding himself of a traitor and an embarrassment. All we've got are some presents and a message to Alexius that will be a talking point in Constantinople for a day and then forgotten. It's time to return home.'

Hero's chest went hollow with dismay. 'Considering how long it took us to reach China, four months isn't a lengthy stay.'

'If we don't leave soon, we'll find ourselves travelling through the winter.'

'Wait until the new year, when we'll have the whole of spring and summer to make the journey. I'd be happy to stay even longer.'

'You're not the only one. My troopers think they've made landfall on the Happy Isles, and the longer they remain, the more difficult it will be to prise them away from their paramours and wine cups.'

'We still haven't obtained the formula for Fire Drug.'

'And I doubt we ever will. Failure to find it isn't a calamity. From what I saw at the demonstration, its power has been exaggerated, the damage it causes being due to its incendiary qualities rather than explosive effects.'

'I think I know a way of concentrating its power. As you know, I was named after the engineer Hero of Alexandria, who made an engine powered by steam under pressure. If Fire Drug were to be enclosed in a tight casing and then heated, it would release all its energy—'

Vallon cut him off. 'I haven't given up all hope of discovering the secret. If I can't find a way to it by other means, I'll resort to bribery. The worst that will happen if I'm found out will be summary deportation. In any case, our stay in China is coming to an end.'

Hero probed uncertain ground. 'What will happen to Qiuylue?'

'She won't be coming with me.'

Hero ventured further into treacherous territory. 'It's clear that you hold each other in great affection.'

'The liaison could never last. You seem to forget that I'm betrothed to another with stronger claims on my heart.'

'Of course I'll never mention Qiuylue to Lady Caitlin.'

'It makes no difference. When I return to Constantinople, I intend to resign my commission and enter a monastery.'

Hero was staggered. 'But you're still in your prime.'

'The emperor effectively ended my career by sending me on this mission. Returning empty-handed will seal my fate. At best I can expect a posting to another dreary frontier.'

Hero rose in a pall of misery. 'Aiken and I have been invited to visit the imperial porcelain factory this afternoon. Perhaps you'd care to accompany us.'

Vallon pulled a face. 'I'm not interested in how dishes and cups are made.' He saw Hero's face fall even further and sweetened his tone. 'Don't let my troubles cloud your day. Enjoy your visit and call on me when you return.'

Hero said nothing of this conversation to Aiken as they travelled by litter through Kaifeng. He suspected that Vallon's decision to leave China ran counter to his real desires. He'd fallen in love with Qiuylue and the only way he could return to the path of fidelity was by giving up what he held most dear.

The imperial porcelain factory lay within the city's outer walls, in a secure compound that also housed an armoury and barracks. The factory superintendent showed the visitors round himself. First he took them to the site where the special clay was left to weather for fifty years. Then he showed them the kilns and the furnaces designed to generate the very high temperatures required to fire the porcelain body. Finally he took Hero and Aiken to a warehouse where the finished goods were stockpiled.

Depressed by his conversation with Vallon, Hero couldn't summon up more than tepid interest. The pieces were exquisitely crafted and beautifully decorated. Held to the sun, they admitted light and rang like a bell if tapped with a pebble. But after seeing yet another bowl glazed in a subtle shade of green, a sense of ennui began to set in. Hero was used to Arab lustreware and Seljuk pottery, which though much cruder in body, enchanted the eye with their vibrant designs painted in brilliant reds, blues, greens and gold.

'Wonderful workmanship,' he said, handling a ceramic pillow glazed to resemble jade. 'Do you ever decorate your wares with brighter pigments?'

The superintendent showed him a vessel with a mouth rimmed in soft purple that flowed down to a brown base. Hero thought it ugly. 'Like a diner who takes too much salt, my taste has been blunted by a surfeit of colour.'

'We use a yellow pigment exclusively for imperial wares,' the superintendent said. He clicked a finger and a workman returned bearing a vase that seemed to have been distilled from sunlight.

Hero handled it with reverence. 'Remarkable. I haven't seen anything finer in my life. The glaze is so deep yet so transparent. It draws the eye in even as it reflects.'

'Mutton-fat glaze,' said the superintendent. 'Only one family knows how to achieve it. Even I don't know the secret.'

'What makes such a glorious yellow? Where does it come from?'

'If I told you, I would part company with my head. Not more than a dozen men know the formula. The materials are so rare and valuable that they're kept under lock and key in the armoury.'

Nervous of holding such a treasure, Hero handed it back. 'I'm surprised you don't decorate your wares with strong blues. The Muslims in Turkestan employ cobalt to brilliant effect on their holy places, sheathing whole domes with tiles that gleam like heaven's vault.'

'Cobalt is a rare commodity in China and what's available is of inferior quality, producing a muddy hue that I would never allow on the porcelain produced here. The mineral used by the Karakhanids is imported from Persia and too heavy to be transported overland. I've instructed one of the imperial shipping agents to order a consignment by sea. Return this time next year and you'll see what magic my potters can achieve with Persian blue.'

Hero spoke without any thought of gaining an advantage. 'Actually, our expedition carried a barrel of Persian cobalt to China. It was a last-minute addition on my part, and sometimes when the way grew hard and the loads heavy, I considered abandoning it. I would love to see how your potters use it.'

The superintendent's face went from excitement to indifference in a trice. 'I'll take the cobalt off your hands. It will serve for practice pieces until my order arrives. As payment . . . ' He picked up an ivory-glazed bowl decorated with incised lotus leaves. 'One of our finest pieces, fit for a palace.'

'I don't seek anything in return,' Hero said. 'The cobalt is a modest gift compared to the riches His Imperial Majesty has heaped on our embassy. I only wish—'

A sharp kick on the ankle shut him up. 'Don't give it away,' Aiken hissed. 'See if you can exchange it for Fire Drug.'

'What would a porcelain factory be doing with Fire Drug?'

'The armoury. You heard the superintendent. He keeps his precious pigments in the armoury, the same place where they store Fire Drug.'

'I can't offer cobalt in exchange for Fire Drug. The explosive is a state secret. The superintendent will have us arrested.'

'Try him. This could be our last chance.'

The superintendent's smile had worn thin during these exchanges. 'Do you wish to sell your Persian blue? If so, you can take your pick of any three pieces not reserved for the emperor's palace.'

Hero plucked up courage. 'I fear these fragile beauties would never survive the rigours of a camel train. Perhaps we could explore alternative trade goods. In private.'

The superintendent was a toper. The moment he'd dismissed his staff, he quaffed wine from a vessel that was decidedly earthy compared to the porcelain. He adopted a fake jolly tone. 'Now

547

then, I'm no market trader. I have nothing to offer in return for your Persian blue except my porcelain. Well, perhaps I could run to a thousand cash.'

Hero sipped his wine. 'If artistry was the measure of value, your most flawed piece would be worth fifty times more than my cobalt.'

'A connoisseur. I knew it.'

'Alas, no. My interests reside more in the realm of science. I'm a physician. One of the reasons I travelled to China was because my first master told me your alchemists had discovered the elixir of life.'

'Cursed Taoists,' said the superintendent. He was on his second cup. 'They claim that if you stand on a certain mountain on a certain day and chant the right spell, you'll become an Immortal. Rubbish. In the past emperors followed their instructions and constructed man-made mountains and meditated on them while their subjects starved below. Didn't make any difference. The emperors died as must all men. I follow the old ways. I'm a Confucist.' He upended his cup. 'Wine made from mare's-teat grapes. That's the elixir of life.'

'My master said that Chinese alchemists had perfected some sort of compound that if taken internally increased longevity. My enquiries have left me confused. It seems that this formula is now used to make bangs and flashes at festivals.'

The superintendent frowned in the act of pouring his second refill. His face cleared. 'You mean Fire Drug.' He laughed. 'I call it Dragon Fire. Whole wards have been razed to the ground by alchemists experimenting with its properties. The government tried to make me adopt it, claiming it would make the kilns burn hotter. At the first trial the kiln burst apart, killing or maiming its attendants.' The superintendent raised his vinous face. 'I forget your question.'

'I'll exchange my barrel of cobalt for a barrel of your Fire Drug.'

'I don't have any. I wouldn't allow it anywhere near the factory.'

'They probably store it in the armoury, where you keep your yellow glaze pigment.'

The superintendent put down his cup, slopping some of the wine. 'Are you suggesting I steal Fire Drug from the imperial armoury?'

'Lord no,' Hero said. 'I was just thinking that you might requisition some for experimenting with in your kilns. I know the first trials were disappointing, but it might be worth making a second attempt.'

Thoughtful now, the superintendent poured again and sipped. 'Fire Drug for cobalt. Hm. It will take weeks for the director of the armoury to consider the requisition. You can't imagine the amount of paperwork involved. Even then there's no guarantee that my request will be granted.'

'If there's anything I can do to expedite matters . . . '

The superintendent absorbed the meaning. 'One of my cousins is employed in the quartermaster's office as an inventory clerk. I'll consult him as to the best course of action.'

'If he's to be employed as a consultant, he should be reimbursed.'

'Your thoughtfulness does you credit. My cousin isn't a rich man and has five children and two elderly parents to care for.'

'Would three thousand cash ease his lot?'

'Seven thousand would be better.'

'Five thousand and it's a deal.'

Vallon was playing chess with Qiuylue when Hero and Aiken burst in, grinning like excited kids.

Hero waited for Qiuylue to leave. 'We've done it,' he said. 'One barrel of Fire Drug will soon be ours.'

'How?'

'Remember the cobalt I included in the cargo? It turns out to be a rare commodity in China. In exchange for Persian blue, the superintendent of the porcelain factory has promised a barrel of Fire Drug.'

'Are you sure it isn't a trap?'

'There was no guile on either side,' Aiken said. 'The superintendent mentioned that he kept certain valuable pigments in the imperial armoury and I immediately made the connection.'

'How will it be delivered? The guards check all goods entering the compound.'

'I arranged for the handover to be made at our ship.'

'They check there, too.'

'I think I know a way to smuggle it aboard.'

'Did you obtain the formula?'

'That would have been too much to hope for.'

'Then we're not much further forward.'

'Don't be so sure. If the Chinese can unpick the secrets of Greek Fire, we can unravel the mystery of Fire Drug.'

The sun was diffusing into the fog over Kaifeng when Vallon and his party reached the ship. Wulfstan hailed them from the stern deck and raised a hooked hand in greeting. He'd had the prosthetic fitted to make ship-handling easier. A squad of Chinese infantrymen on the jetty rose from their mah-jong and dice. Their captain saluted.

Vallon saluted back. 'I appreciate you guarding my ship so diligently.' He slipped a purse into the man's hand. 'In appreciation of your vigilance.'

'I can't accept gifts.'

'Come now. In my country it's considered a virtue to reward exemplary service.' The other guards had clustered around. 'Share it with your men.'

They were bickering over their portions when Vallon and company went aboard. 'You must be bored out here on your own,' he said to Wulfstan.

'Not really, sir. I've become mates with the soldiers and ... well, craving your indulgence, sir, I took the liberty of inviting some company aboard.'

'A woman?'

'What else. Actually, I was thinking of making her my wife. She's a lovely thing.'

'Well, we're all human. Even you.'

'Thank you, sir. What brings you here?'

'Business. I'll explain when the transaction's done. You know how the cargo is disposed. Fetch me the barrel of cobalt.'

Wulfstan disappeared into the hold and emerged lugging a smallish cask. 'God knows what it's for, but it makes good ballast. A hundred of these would keep a dromon on an even keel.'

Vallon turned to Gorka. 'You know what to do?'

'Yes, sir.'

Gorka placed the barrel in a backpack and went down the gangplank. The Chinese officer blocked his path as he made to mount his horse. The bribe had made him well disposed to the barbarians, but it hadn't lowered his guard.

'What's in there? Where are you taking it?'

Vallon answered from the ship's deck. 'It's a pigment used in the manufacture of ceramics and it's on the way to the imperial porcelain factory. Gorka, show him the bill of sale and the superintendent's seal.'

The officer examined both. 'I'll have to examine the contents.'

'Go ahead. Careful, it's heavy.'

Satisfied that the barrel didn't contain contraband, the officer painted a character on the cask to show that he'd inspected the goods. 'I apologise for the delay.'

'Not at all,' said Vallon. He gave an airy wave. 'I'm going to my cabin now.'

Down below he grabbed Wulfstan. 'Bring me a sack of sand, a funnel and a dry barrel the same size as the one Gorka's carrying.'

He was looking out over the river from his cabin when the guards cried out. He went on deck to see Gorka galloping back to the ship. 'What the hell are you doing?' he shouted. 'You should have been in Kaifeng by now.'

'Why are you angry?' the Chinese captain called. 'Why has the soldier come back?'

'The dolt forgot the letter he was supposed to take to the superintendent.' He smacked Gorka's shoulder as the trooper staggered up the gangplank, still burdened by the barrel. 'Idiot.'

He followed Gorka down to his cabin, where Wulfstan, Hero and Aiken were waiting. 'Did you make the exchange?' he asked the sweating trooper.

'Yes, sir.'

'Make it quick,' Vallon told Wulfstan.

The Viking took the barrel from Gorka and nearly dropped it in surprise. 'This isn't the—'

'Of course it isn't. Empty it.'

Wulfstan prised out the bung and began funnelling the contents into the spare barrel. 'Could do with some light in here.'

'No!' Vallon said. 'Christ!'

Wulfstan dribbled out the last of the contents.

'Fill Gorka's barrel with the sand. Hurry.'

The sun was a crimson glow in the pall over Kaifeng when Gorka emerged on deck, stooped under the original barrel now filled with sand. The captain of the guard was diligent to a fault and insisted on checking the load.

'For heaven's sake,' Vallon shouted. 'He'll miss the curfew.'

The officer satisfied himself that the barrel was the one he'd marked before waving Gorka past. The guards watched him galloping away into the dust and then went back to their cooking fire. Sweating with excitement, Vallon returned below.

'Is it the right stuff?' he asked.

Hero had decanted a sample of the black powder onto a dish. 'It looks like finely ground charcoal. There's only one way to find out.'

'We can't test it outside. Vast as China is, you're never more than a few yards from a peasant. Burn a small sample here. Wulfstan, bring a bucket of water and a hide blanket in case it burns too fiercely.'

Hero formed the powder into a small heap. 'Bring me a lamp and taper. Stand well back.'

Wulfstan thrust himself forward. 'I'm the master of ordnance. If anyone's going to get his eyebrows singed, it should be me.'

Hero gave way and Wulfstan lit a taper from the lamp and

brought it towards the powder. Vallon, Hero and Aiken pressed back against the walls of the cabin.

Poof.

Red and yellow flame flashed. Aiken choked on the fumes. Hero opened the window and fanned the smoke out. 'I recognise one of its ingredients. That Devil's breath is sulphur.'

Wulfstan laughed. 'And the other smell is my charred beard. That's powerful stuff.'

'You ignited only a spoonful,' Vallon said. 'Imagine the effect if we lit the entire barrel.'

They dwelt on the outcome of such an experiment before Aiken spoke. 'It would consume our ship and everyone on it.' He crossed himself. 'That's a hellish compound.'

'Stow it somewhere safe,' Vallon said.

XLIV

Xiao-Xing was a skilful lover who made it her business to educate Lucas out of his farmboy fumblings and clumsy couplings. With the aid of a lavishly illustrated pillow book, she taught him how to give her pleasure and enhance his own. Lucas learned the technique called 'Fish Playing in Spring Water', the position known as 'The Dragon in the Cave', and one night, well after midnight, was initiated into the strenuous delights of 'Taming the Demon Princess'.

Xiao-Xing's cunning grip she'd taken with arms and legs alike drew him inexorably into the realm of reflex. He tried to delay the climax by thinking of Gorka eating. It was little help. Reflexive spasms began, signalling the end. Beneath him Xiao-Xing convulsed, clinging with all her might, her breath panting.

'Are you in there, sir?'

He was over the edge and shooting down cascades when Gorka's shout cut through his orgasm.

'Sir, it's urgent. We have to get out of here.'

Swearing, Lucas unpicked his way out of Xiao-Xing's hold, covered himself with a towel and slid open the door. 'What the hell are you shouting about?'

Even in his desperation, Gorka couldn't resist sneaking a look at the girl sitting up with her hands over her breasts. 'Vallon's orders. We have to make a run for the ship. Take only arms and armour.'

'Why?'

'We must have upset our hosts. If we wait until morning, they'll arrest us.'

Lucas threw on his clothes. Xiao-Xing looked on distraught. He kissed her and held her face. 'I'm sorry, my love. I have to go.'

He buckled on his sword, slung his suit of armour over his shoulder and ran out. Men's curses and women's wails from all quarters announced an unwilling separation of cultures.

Gorka ran through the compound. Distant firecrackers popped somewhere in the city. Josselin was waiting at the gate. 'Make for the Gold Bird Guard Bridge.'

Lucas's gaze fixed on the body of a Chinese soldier sprawled a few yards beyond the entrance.

Josselin pushed him. 'Get going. Let no one stand in your way.'

Lucas and Gorka ran through the empty streets, the feet of the other Outlanders slapping behind them. Not long before, each of Kaifeng's wards would have been surrounded by walls with gates closed after the evening curfew and watchmen patrolling the avenues. Now the gates and walls were gone, but the curfew was still in force and night patrols still walked the streets on the look-out for anyone wandering outside their own ward. Twenty blows with the thin rod was the punishment for transgressors.

It wasn't long before Lucas and Gorka ran into a squad of watchmen. The soldiers challenged them, and when the runaways failed to stop, they twanged their bowstring to reinforce the command, then shot arrows at their feet. Lucas and Gorka swept past. A whistle blew behind them and was answered by more whistles.

Lucas clutched his side to ease a stitch. 'It's miles to open country. Three walls and gates block our escape. We'll never make it.'

'Vallon must have thought of a way.'

The bridge came in sight, deserted now, lights from a few oil lamps dappling the river.

'This way,' a voice called.

Lucas turned right and saw two large sampans moored, a turbaned figure waiting on the bank. He slapped Lucas past. 'Into the boats and stay quiet.'

Lucas scrambled into a boat already occupied by half a dozen confused and disgruntled Outlanders. 'What the fuck's going on?' one demanded. 'What's fucking Vallon playing at?'

Lucas arched up. 'Talk of the general like that again and I'll take the hide off you. He wouldn't order a breakout unless it was necessary. Now stay as quiet as a nest of mice.'

A fraught silence fell, broken by shrilling whistles and braying trumpets dissipating through the city. Windows opened and householders demanded to know what outrage had disturbed their rest. A three-quarters moon raced through a rack of clouds. Four more men pitched into Lucas's boat and another five found places in the craft alongside. Through their panting Lucas heard more urgent footsteps and then a voice that sounded familiar but unplaceable.

'Is that everyone?'

'Everyone who's coming,' Josselin said. 'Two refused to leave. One was too drunk to stand. The night patrols caught another.'

He clambered into the other boat and the turbaned man stepped into Lucas's craft and cast off.

'If you haven't plied an oar before, you'd better learn fast. We have to get beyond the last wall before the Chinese work out how we intend to breach it.'

Lucas picked up a paddle. 'You heard him. Dig hard, dig deep.'

The Outlanders found some semblance of rhythm and the city began to slide past. Lucas thought of Xiao-Xing, the lovely maid he would never see again. He reached out and prodded the orchestrator of this upheaval in the back.

'If someone rousts me from bed at dead of night, I want to know who he is.'

The man turned and smiled. 'Well met, Lucas. I'm glad you survived the journey and even gladder that you overcame the demons holding you apart from your father.'

'Wayland! How did you get here?'

'Later. Keep going.'

Confusion made Lucas obey for a while. 'They'll soon work out how we intend to escape and send cavalry to secure the ship. We won't outpace horses.'

'Vallon's put a lot of thought into our flight. If we escape the city we'll reach the ship.'

'Where is he?'

'Gone ahead with Hero and Aiken. Now stop pestering and row.'

Lights bobbing ahead made Lucas draw his sword. He sank back when he saw they were only floating lanterns placed on the water by nocturnal revellers. Watching them glide past, he thought again of Xiao-Xing. The pang of loss subsided into a clench of vague dread. Kaifeng had been a haven, the ultimate oasis. What would they do now? Where could they go?

Several times on their journey watchmen spotted them and raised the hue and cry, their shouts merging into the alarms spreading through the entire city. By this time the Outlanders had put thoughts of abandoned sweethearts and warm quarters behind them and were rowing for their lives, what was lost gone forever and an unknowable future ahead.

A squad of cavalry intercepted them and loosed arrows without mercy, wounding two rowers before a warehouse built on the waterfront in defiance of planning regulations blocked their pursuit. The city's outer wall bulked large. Soldiers carrying torches ran about on its ramparts. A tunnel through the barrier gaped.

An arrow thrummed in the thwart beside Lucas and then the tunnel closed around them. Moments later they slid clear, the landscape ahead empty and the Yellow River mirrored on the base of low-hanging clouds.

'Not far now,' Wayland said.

Lucas heard a whinny and spotted horses in a node of darkness on the right bank.

'Put in,' Wayland said.

Vallon stood on the bank. 'Mount up and ride for the ship.'

Lucas flung himself onto a horse. Quarter of a mile behind, a stream of torches emerged from the city wall.

'They're coming,' Vallon said. 'Don't spare your horses. We won't need them again.'

With that he spurred into the dark and Lucas followed, concentrating on extracting every last effort from his horse. The plain flew past, pools of shadow stretching out to the north. The river showed ahead in the light of the fleeting moon. A flame winked on its bank.

'Make for the torch,' Vallon shouted.

Lucas reached the jetty and threw himself off his horse. Gorka stood on *Jifeng*'s deck, urging the troopers to make haste. Lucas ran up the gangplank and turned to see the lights of the pursuing cavalry pricking the plain behind. Wayland was the last to board. The sweating horses they'd left behind gleamed in the dark.

'Cast off,' Wulfstan shouted.

Jifeng slipped her moorings and nosed away down the flaccid current. She was still close to shore when the Chinese reached the bank. They galloped along the dike, loosing arrows until the ship drifted out of range.

'That was close,' Lucas said.

'They ain't going to let us slip away that easy,' Wulfstan said.

Vallon stepped onto the stern deck. Qiuylue stood behind him, dressed in nomad fashion – tight tunic nipped at the waist and kid-skin leggings. Josselin clapped his hands for silence. The mutters of the trooper died. A hundred Outlanders had embarked at Constantinople and only fifty-four remained to hear Vallon announce their fate.

'You've probably heard the rumours that I've accepted a

commission as commander of a Chinese regiment. Who'll take service with me?'

Lucas looked around and raised his hand.

'Only a third of you,' Vallon said. 'Just as well, because I have no intention of joining the Chinese army. I'm going home. Who'll follow me back across the Taklamakan?'

'I think it's one of his trick questions,' Gorka murmured.

Vallon's gaze swept the troopers. 'Still only a third. What do the rest of you want to do?'

The soldiers maintained an obstinate silence.

'I know what you want,' Vallon said. 'You want to rest idle in the Palace of Friendship with your doxies, being served on hand and foot. Do you really think the Chinese would allow you to go on living in such luxury? I'll tell you what they'll do. They'll conscript you and post you to some frontier outpost like that shithole in the Tsaidam. Or they'll send you to work building walls on the Yellow River. I'm told the bones of a million men lie entombed in those fortifications.'

'What's the reason for our flight?' a trooper demanded.

'We were sent east to establish mutually respectful relations between Byzantium and China. Unfortunately, the Son of Heaven doesn't recognise any country as equal to his own. We leave with only a few flowery words of friendship.'

No one spoke. Kaifeng was just a reddish smudge out on the plain.

'I was taxed with another mission,' Vallon said. 'That was to obtain the formula of a Chinese incendiary called Fire Drug. I didn't discover the formula, but Hero and Aiken succeeded in obtaining a barrel of the compound. Unfortunately the man who provided it is a drunk whose mouth runs over when he's in his cups. The transaction was discovered, and if Wayland hadn't had an informer in the armoury, we would all have woken this morning with swords at our throats. That's about all. Any questions?'

'Where are we going?'

'How the hell did Wayland get here?'

'Both questions beget the same answer. Wayland sailed from India and I plan to return the same way. The prospect chills me less than the thought of retracing our steps across Asia. With fair winds we could reach India by mid-summer and be home by Christmas. You'll have plenty of opportunities to trade on the voyage, and you'll find no shortage of women in the ports where we put in. And think of the stories you'll have to tell when you're back in Constantinople. It will be free drinks in every tavern.'

Gorka hawked and spat. 'Hell, I was getting bored lying around doing nothing but eat, drink and fuck.'

A trooper pushed towards Vallon. 'How come you get to keep your woman while we were forced away without even time to say farewell?'

'I'll overlook your insolence,' Vallon said. 'If I'd left Qiuylue behind, the Chinese would have killed her. Dismiss.'

Vallon entered his cabin and embraced his mistress. 'I'm sorry I gave you no warning. There wasn't time.'

'You shouldn't have brought me.'

'Would you have preferred death?'

'You're going back to your family. You told me that in your country a man takes only one wife. There can be no place in your household for another woman. It would create disharmony.'

Vallon sank onto his cot. 'I'll put you ashore with enough gold for you to start a new life. You can't return to Kaifeng, but every-where else is open. You could go back to your homeland. If it's city life and comforts you desire, you could go south to Hangzhou. Whatever you choose, I'll do my utmost to grant.'

'My only wish is to remain at your side for as long as possible.'

No sign of pursuit at dawn. That didn't mean the Outlanders were in the clear. The state employed thousands of runners who could relay messages up to a hundred miles in a day and night. Even faster were the horse couriers who, galloping flat out between staging posts, were disciplined if they didn't cover more than a hundred and

559

fifty miles a day. Strategic routes were also linked by signal towers that transmitted messages by flags or mirrors. By now, Chinese garrisons downriver might be laying plans to intercept the fugitives.

It came as some relief when clouds built up and released a downpour that lasted all day, turning the low-lying roads along the banks into quagmires. Even under a light breeze, *Jifeng* maintained a good pace. At this time of year the Yellow River was at its highest, swollen by melting snows in its mountain headwaters. In places spring ice had gouged away the dikes, creating lakes twenty miles across, dark lines of willows and poplars the only indication of where the river ended and land began. Wulfstan had picked up a hazy knowledge of the river's lower course. It should take four or five days to reach the sea.

The third day broke clear. Vallon leaned out from the bow, peering at the rising sun through the surface reflections. Each side of the river the wet green of flat farmland merged into the misty blue of distance. Waders rose in swirling clouds from sandbars. Ducks beat up from reedbeds and whistled down the sky. Barelegged women bent over in long lines, setting seeds. A cart drawn by two oxen followed a pale ribbon of road towards a village.

Vallon had ordered the Greek Fire siphon to be mounted on the foredeck. Wulfstan had rigged up the trebuchet on the stern, reinforcing the deck against its weight and the force of its recoil. For ammunition he'd selected about forty ballast stones weighing between twenty and a hundred pounds apiece.

In the afternoon Vallon watched Hero and Wulfstan conducting experiments on Fire Drug to determine its combustible properties.

'It's too fierce,' Hero said. 'Even a spark sets it off. To be of any use against an enemy, we'd need something to delay the ignition until the right moment.'

Wulfstan rubbed his forehead with his hooked stump. 'When I served in the Byzantine navy, we used Greek Fire to undermine city walls. To give themselves time to get clear, the sappers ignited the barrels with slow-burning tapers – a bit like Chinese incense sticks. Fuses, they called them.'

'How do you make one?'

'Piss. Boil a gallon of piss down to half a pint, soak a length of tow in it, let the tow dry. It smoulders without burning. Cut the tow to the size you need and you vary the time it sets off the incendiary.'

'Get pissing,' Vallon said.

They made a small raft. Wulfstan packed an earthenware pot three-quarters full with Fire Drug and tamped it with lint soaked in Greek Fire. Into the wadding he placed a tow wick.

'Someone will have to light it when it's clear of the ship.'

Vallon cast about. 'Gorka.'

'I knew you'd pick me.'

They tied a rope to the raft and paid it out astern. Gorka and another trooper lowered themselves into the ship's boat and drifted down the wake until the raft came within reach. While the other trooper held onto the rope, Gorka lit the fuse. They rowed back to the ship and joined Vallon, Wulfstan and Hero in the stern. There they waited.

And waited.

'You sure you lit it properly?' Wulfstan said.

Gorka bristled. 'If I light something, it stays lit.'

Vallon gave it a while longer. 'It must have gone out. Tow it in.'

The troopers had dragged the raft back to within twenty yards when the pot exploded, showering the spectators with clay fragments.

'I must have made the fuse too long,' Wulfstan said.

Gorka plucked a shard from his forehead. Blood trickled. 'Or else your piss is too weak.'

Lucas ran down to Vallon's cabin and stopped outside, checked by the sound of his father's easy laughter. Resentment made him wrench open the door.

Vallon looked up, one arm draped about Qiuylue. 'You might have knocked.'

'Wayland's spotted ships astern.'

Vallon took his arm away from Qiuylue. Sensitive to the tensions

561

between father and son, she slipped away. Lucas stayed where he was.

'Yes?' Vallon said.

'You lied to us. The Chinese weren't going to arrest us. You made up that story to panic us into flight.'

'What makes you think that?'

'Wayland said you'd given a lot of thought to arranging our escape. You couldn't have organised the horses and boats at short notice. You must have planned it over days.'

'It was the only way to keep my men together. You saw how reluctant they were to quit their billets. Given the choice, only a third would have followed me.'

Lucas gritted his teeth. 'I raised my hand.'

'Out of military duty rather than filial devotion, I suspect.' Vallon rose and touched his son's shoulder. 'One day you'll command a squadron. When you do, you'll learn that it's sometimes necessary to lie.' He reached for his sword. 'I'm sorry you had to leave that girl behind.'

Lucas's laugh was bitter.

'You'll soon forget her.'

'You don't forget your first love. I left a piece of my heart when I left Xiao-Xing.'

'I tore mine to pieces when I killed your mother.'

Hearing Vallon's admission rocked Lucas. His eyes filled. 'That didn't stop you marrying Caitlin. And now you've taken another lover.'

'I can't bring your mother back. If there was only one person meant for each of us, life would be a long and lonely search. Fortunately it offers second chances.'

Lucas's throat worked. 'In all the months since I told you I was your son, you've never tried to justify your crime.'

'It's not my place to justify or explain the unforgivable.'

'So you expect me to do it for you.'

'No. I would never lay that burden on my son. The weight is all mine to bear.'

562

Lucas clenched his hands. 'I've tried. I mean, Wayland and Hero told me how Roland betrayed you and left you to rot in a Moorish prison. I know my mother was unfaithful. It's just that . . .'

'She was your beloved mother and I killed her. Don't torment yourself. Leave that to me. I don't seek forgiveness. That's why I've never sought a confessor.'

Lucas looked at Vallon through tear-smudged eyes. 'I've kept close watch on you since we left Constantinople. Sometimes I thought you acted like a monster; sometimes I marvelled at the way you managed to slide through perils without shedding blood.'

Vallon appeared not to hear him. He buckled on his sword belt. 'I seem to have put on weight. Let's go up and face our doom.'

XLV

Far behind, many miles astern, three shapes broke the flat and empty riverscape.

Vallon waited, measuring their progress. 'They don't seem to be gaining on us.'

'They don't have to press hard,' Wulfstan said. 'The sea's still a couple of days away.'

By noon the enemy convoy was close enough for the Outlanders to see what they were up against. One of the ships was a four-masted three-decker twice the size of *Jifeng*. The second had three masts. The third vessel, more like a floating tower than a ship, had no sail at all yet was keeping station without any obvious means of propulsion.

'I saw ships like that in the south,' Wayland said. 'It's driven by paddle wheels, like the waterwheels in a mill. Some ships have half a dozen or more, each pair connected by axles with pedals sticking out like flat spokes – one set of pedals for each poor sod who has to tread them.'

'How many soldiers are we facing?'

Wulfstan answered. 'That four-master alone is probably carrying a hundred soldiers, and they'll be armed with all kinds of weaponry – heavy crossbows, traction catapults, flame-throwers, incendiary grenades ... One sailor I met in Kaifeng said the Chinese navy ain't quick to grapple with the enemy. Instead they have these long poles hinged at the base and with a spiked hammer at the top. When they get within range, they drop the hammer end onto the enemy ship, holding it at a safe distance while they bombard it.'

'We might as well give up now.'

'What the Chinese ain't got is a counterweight trebuchet. I can land a dozen rocks on their decks before their catapults get in range. Their incendiary ain't a patch on ours, either. Burns hot, burns fast, but it doesn't stick and burn to the bone like Greek Fire.'

Vallon turned to the troopers. 'Reposition the siphon at the stern.'

While they went about their task, he appraised the ship and saw how vulnerable it was to fire – a huge piece of floating kindling. 'What happened to the hides from the rafts?'

'Stored below,' Wulfstan said. 'Two hundred of them, enough to cover the entire deck.'

'Do it.'

Evening came and the sun set behind the enemy ships, now only a mile astern. The Outlanders toiled into the night sheathing the junk in hides, draping the stern with two layers. When the skins were in place, they soaked them with water. The slat-and-cotton sails couldn't be fireproofed and Vallon ordered his men to strike the mainsail and stow it below deck. The moon, only a day off full, shone on the Chinese warships shadowing *Jifeng* so closely that the Outlanders could hear the beat of drums and shouted messages between the vessels.

'Why don't they attack?' Lucas asked Vallon.

'Night attacks are risky. I'm going to take a nap. I suggest you do the same.'

'I'm too tense to sleep.'

Vallon walked off then walked back. 'I'd like you to stay close to me tomorrow.'

'I don't need mollycoddling.'

Vallon laughed. 'I wasn't thinking about your protection. I'm getting too old for combat. I'll feel more secure with a strong and skilled right hand at my side.'

Lucas flushed. 'Goodnight ...' he said, leaving a word unspoken.

Vallon stopped, his skin prickling. Say it, he prayed. There might not be another chance and if I die tomorrow I'll quit this world more peacefully knowing that my son acknowledged me as his father.

'Goodnight, sir.'

Vallon was back on deck in full armour before dawn, the warships still tagging in their wake, moonlight cupped in their sails. What little breeze there was blew from the south, almost at right angles to *Jifeng*'s progress. The moon was sinking into mist steaming off the river as the sun rose. The vapours soon burned off and the sun struck hot. The current had slowed and was so thick with silt that it resembled soup. Within a day of the sea the river seemed to have become indifferent about reaching it, branches wandering fitfully through a wilderness of reeds. Wayland, appointed sailing master, sought Vallon's advice.

'Which channel should we take?'

The river forked around a sand bar, the left-hand channel half the width of the right, less than two hundred yards wide and only navigable for a third of that.

'Take the narrow stream. We draw less water than the enemy. They won't be able to get past us without risk of grounding.'

Jifeng nosed into the channel between walls of reeds. The Outlanders waited, sweating in full armour. Vallon moved among them, exhorting them to be of good heart. He paid a brief visit to Qiuylue before taking up position on the stern deck.

Wulfstan shambled out from below, lurching from hold to hold, cowled and clad in heavy, full-length white robes like a member of some diabolical sect. Vallon grabbed him.

'You're drunk.'

Wulfstan hiccupped. 'And you're scared, but I'll be sober soon enough.'

'What the hell are you wearing?'

Wulfstan eyed his drapes with pride. 'Asbestos. *Hajar al-fatila*, the Arabs call it – "wick-stone", because flame can't touch it. In these togs I could walk through hell and step out the other side without a scorch.'

'They're coming,' Lucas said.

The drumbeats had quickened. War cries panicked flocks of wildfowl into flight. The four-master bore down on *Jifeng*, fire-pots glowing on its foredeck and the sun flaring off its iron-sheathed bow.

The first volley of heavy crossbow bolts struck.

'Everyone take cover,' Vallon ordered. He dropped below the stern transom with half a dozen other men.

Only the trebuchet team and steersman remained on deck, partly protected by bales and wicker screens. With his good hand, Wulfstan loaded one of the lightest stones into the trebuchet's sling. In stepping back to check the range and aim, he tripped and fell. Vallon rushed at him.

'I'll kill you for this.'

Wulfstan reached up. 'Give me a hand. This outfit weighs a ton.'

He was wearing armour beneath his fireproof drapes and it took two men to hoist him to his feet. He cracked his knuckles and squinted at the oncoming battleship.

'Not yet,' he crooned. 'Wait for my word.'

A dozen men working the enemy warship's catapult dragged down on ropes and launched the first missile. It fell well short. Wulfstan reached into the capacious folds of his robe and pulled out a bottle. He unstoppered it with his teeth and drank.

Vallon hefted his sword. 'Wulfstan, if you survive the battle, I'm going to flog you myself.'

Wulfstan capped the bottle and turned a sleazy leer on the general. 'Hush. You're disturbing my concentration.'

Another stone from the enemy catapult splashed into *Jifeng*'s wake. Wulfstan crouched, assessing the range.

'Wait ... Wait ... Launch!'

The throwing arm tilted skywards, the sling extended like a whip and the missile hurtled in a high parabola before crashing onto the warship's stern deck.

'Use that one next,' Wulfstan shouted, pointing with his good hand at another stone.

Five times the team manning the trebuchet dropped stones on the warship before the Chinese catapulters came within range. Vallon flinched as a stone bounced off the deck beside him. The enemy was within a hundred yards, their commander directing teams of crossbowmen who loosed droves of bolts so heavy that they splintered through the two-inch thick transom.

Outnumbered and under-armed, the Outlander archers could only respond with snap shots before ducking back behind cover. Indifferent to the lethal darts, Wulfstan continued calling the shots between slugs of liquor. 'Load that big bastard,' he said, pointing at the heaviest stone in the heap.

Two men struggled to lift the boulder and one of them fell dead as he rose, pierced through by a bolt that still had enough energy to bury itself in the mainmast.

The boulder trundled down the stern deck. Gorka sprang forward and threw himself on it before it rolled off. Between him and the other loader they managed to scoop it into the sling,

'I call this one the cuckoo's egg,' Wulfstan said. 'On account of you wouldn't want it in your nest.' He brought down his arm. 'Release.'

Crouched below the transom, Vallon watched as the throwing arm flicked up then slowed almost to a stop, arrested by its burden. The rope attached to the sling extended lazily before it tautened and the missile launched into space. A lob rather than a hurl. Vallon heard something terminal break on the trebuchet, but his attention was on the little black planet describing a shallow arc extending for no more than a hundred feet before it smashed through the warship's foredeck with a hollow crack. Another crash as it tumbled through the lower deck

Wulfstan abandoned the trebuchet and crawled over to Vallon. The warship was only fifty feet from grappling and lines of soldiers were jogging onto the foredeck, packing its bow in readiness to board.

Looking along the transom, Vallon tried to encourage his men. 'Your lives are precious to me, so don't sell them at discount.' He addressed the rear. 'Archers, make every shot count.'

He slid down. Wulfstan offered him his bottle. Vallon batted it away and would have struck the sot if he hadn't noticed the blood staining Wulfstan's moustache.

'You're wounded.'

Someone shouted. It was Wayland.

'What?' Vallon cried.

He couldn't hear the answer through the hubbub from the Chinese ship. The orderly commands had given way to an anxious caterwauling. He stuck his head up.

'Hell's teeth.'

Where only moments earlier the bow of the Chinese battleship had reared above *Jifeng*'s stern, it now dipped nose heavy, sinking lower. The ship was falling back, taking in water. The soldiers on the foredeck milled in confusion.

Vallon looked down at Wulfstan. 'Your last shot did it. Have another bottle.'

Wulfstan coughed blood. 'I've taken my last drink.'

Vallon didn't have time to find out how badly the Viking was injured. The bow-heavy battleship was steering for shore, making way for the second junk. Wulfstan clawed himself to his feet and leaned on the transom.

'The ropes fixing the trebuchet's axle have bust. We might just have time to prime the siphon.'

The brazier was already glowing and Wulfstan positioned it

under the oil reservoir. The wind had died and both ships drifted downriver at the same speed, a furlong separating them.

'Save your arrows,' Vallon ordered.

A buzz of activity on each side of the enemy junk drew his attention.

'They're rigging oars,' he shouted. 'Can we do the same?'

Wayland threw up his hands.

'My brew needs more cooking,' Wulfstan said through stertorous breaths. 'Tell your archers to put a crimp in the Chinese advance.'

With more time to aim, the Outlanders' bowmen launched volley after volley at the rowers. For every man they killed or wounded, another took his place. Vallon couldn't help but admire their courage and discipline.

'We're running low on arrows,' Gorka cried.

'Save them for the boarding party.'

The junk was gaining. Under his armour, Vallon was soaked in sweat. He'd ordered his men to take up battle stations not long after dawn and now the sun was almost at its meridian. The tank of Greek Fire clicked on a rising note.

'How much more time do you need?'

'I'd say it's done to a turn. In fact if we wait much longer we'll blow ourselves up.'

'How can we slow ourselves?'

Wulfstan wiped blood from his mouth. 'Drop a makeshift anchor astern.'

Within minutes the soldiers placed two hundredweight of ballast in a net secured with a rope to the mainmast. Six men heaved it over the stern and as soon as it hit bottom it dragged, halving *Jifeng*'s speed.

Something exploded on her foredeck. Fire broke out and two men howled from their burns. Their companions wrapped them in hides to suffocate the flames.

'Quicklime,' Wulfstan said.

The abrupt slowing of *Jifeng* flat-footed the commander of the junk. The oarsmen tried to back water, but the vessel had too much momentum behind it. *Jifeng* was almost stationary when the enemy junk slid to within ten yards and Wulfstan opened the valve on the siphon.

Crouched only ten feet away, Vallon felt the singeing heat of the incendiary as it sprayed the junk's bow. Through the pressurised roar, he heard screams. Next moment he was thrown down as the junk collided with *Jifeng*'s stern. Globules of Greek Fire sizzled on the wet hides.

Squinting through the smoke, he saw that the incendiary had taken hold on the junk's bow. Flames ran up shrouds like fiery squirrels. A patch of foresail flashed into flame, fire feeding fire until the junk's foredeck dissolved in an inferno.

Vallon's eyebrows charred in the heat. Holding his breath to preserve his lungs, he slashed the anchor rope. Slowly *Jifeng* separated from the enemy junk, flames six feet high rising from the leather drapes hung over the stern. Wulfstan in his fireproof suit walked into the blaze and cut the hides away. They fell into the river and continued burning. Pockets of flame danced on *Jifeng*'s deck. The Outlanders swatted them as if they were rats or goblins, only to see them spring back to life.

'Use sand and vinegar,' Wulfstan ordered.

When the fires were out, Vallon removed his helmet and splashed water over his scalded brow. The enemy junk was ablaze from bow to midships and its complement of sailors and soldiers had retreated to the stern and were stripping off their armour. Vallon saw figures leaping into the river clutching kegs and planks, anything buoyant.

Wulfstan spat blood. 'Two down.'

Through the noxious billows of smoke the third ship came churning, froth kicking up from paddle wheels hidden behind a false hull protected by a heavy fender or bulwark. It was the ugliest and most pointless vessel Vallon had ever seen. Where a junk had a bluff bow and low tapering foredeck, this monstrosity had a square tower twenty feet high, its wooden parapet loopholed for archers and crossbowmen. Behind the tower and taking up almost the rest of the hull was a superstructure shaped like a house, with a pitched roof and walls that had no windows, only doors – a dozen of them ten feet high, each one painted with a snarling tiger.

Vallon looked for Wulfstan. 'What the hell is it?'

Clasping his chest with his hooked left arm, Wulfstan lurched up. 'Those doors are hatches and boarding ramps hinged at the bottom. Behind each tiger half a dozen men are waiting for the ship to come alongside. When it does, they drop the hatches and as soon as the ramps hit our side-rail, over they pour.'

'Can you turn the siphon on them?'

'I emptied the tank. I've got only one barrel left and there ain't time to cook it.'

The paddle-wheeler took an erratic course, scooting like an aquatic insect well wide of *Jifeng*'s starboard side and holding position while its invisible commander weighed up the opposition and calculated how and when to attack. The absence of any visible threat unnerved the Outlanders and they drifted back to *Jifeng*'s port side, putting maximum distance between themselves and the hidden enemy.

Vallon stood at the starboard rail and bellowed at his troops. 'Why are you hanging back like maidens at their first dance? You're not virgins. They're not demons. They're soldiers the same as you, and they've seen us destroy two ships and kill dozens of their comrades.' He lashed a hand at Josselin. 'Two squads to form up in line with me. One squad of archers at the rear.'

The Outlanders shuffled into formation. Lucas approached Vallon. 'Where do you want me to stand?'

'My left ankle is weak. On that side if you would.'

Lucas took up position, breathing in deep but controlled gasps. Vallon glanced at him and all the fetters around his heart broke. In one quick movement he embraced Lucas. 'Whatever our fate, I want you to know how proud I am to have my son standing at my side.'

'I wouldn't choose to stand anywhere else. I've found my place, even though the journey has been painful.'

'How can I ease your pain? Tell me. We don't have much time.'

Lucas hunched his shoulders. 'Your sword. Every time I see it, it reminds me of that night.'

Vallon hissed. 'Of course. I should have thought of it myself.' He began to turn. 'Josselin, fetch me another—'

Lucas pulled him back. 'I don't mean now. Not with the enemy about to attack.'

Vallon turned to face the foe. 'You're an excellent swordsman but you lack combat experience. Here's my last lesson. Killing is a mortal sin, to be avoided unless absolutely necessary. But when there's no other resort, killing is all that matters. Nothing must intervene between intention and execution – not thought, anger or conscience. The soldier who kills without hesitation will triumph nine times out of ten. Kill your enemy and leave God to do the judging.

For all that the paddle-wheeler had the grace of a privy, it was surprisingly nimble, able to change direction within its own length. It fell behind *Jifeng* before putting on a burst of speed that brought it level, only twenty feet separating the two ships. Vallon looked along his line of soldiers and was dismayed to see how flimsy it was.

Wulfstan staggered up. 'I've got an idea. Use Fire Drug.'

'How? We don't have time to light it. Even if we had, it will probably blow us up.'

'Leave that to me.'

Vallon's eyes darted. 'Someone fetch the barrel of Fire Drug.'

A trooper ran below and returned with the barrel. 'Wrap it in a net and tie it to my hook,' Wulfstan said.

While a soldier lashed the barrel to his claw, Wulfstan picked up the last keg of Greek Fire. 'That's the problem of having only one hand. Someone else will have to pour it over me and set it alight.'

Vallon gaped. 'Wulfstan!'

The Viking touched a small blood-rimmed hole in his asbestos

572

suit. 'A bolt has stuck me through the vitals. I'm going to die whatever happens, so I might as well make my death count.'

Vallon swallowed. He looked around and his eye fell on Gorka. 'Do as he says.'

'Sir, I can't.'

'That's a direct order. Soak his suit with Greek Fire and stand ready to ignite it.'

While Gorka was pouring the incendiary over Wulfstan, the paddle-wheeler nudged closer. A dozen crossbowmen sprang up on the bow castle and triggered darts, dropping three Outlanders where they stood.

Wulfstan coughed up a gobbet of blood and tissue. 'As soon as they grapple, I'll run for the stern hatch. Have your archers clear the way.'

Vallon swung round. 'Hear that? Concentrate your aim on the two stern hatches.'

The paddle-wheeler sidled into boarding range. Vallon cleared his throat. 'You know what I'm going to say next so you might as well say it for me.'

The Outlanders struck their shields with their sword hilts. 'Here or in the hereafter!'

Only twelve feet separated Vallon from the snarling tigers. Ten feet... eight ...

The hatches swung open and clattered onto *Jifeng*'s rail. Down each ramp surged a file of soldiers wielding poleaxes and swords. Before the first one leaped onto the deck, Vallon registered his soldiers on each side dropping under a hail of bolts from the tower, Gorka holding a lamp to Wulfstan's robes and – Vallon could hardly credit his eyes – Hauk Eiriksson and his Vikings in the forefront of the assault.

Vallon pointed his sword. 'Traitor! Villain!'

He had no more time to consider Hauk's treachery. The first wave of soldiers leaped onto the deck. First to confront him was a Chinese infantryman swinging a poleaxe. Vallon ducked under the blade and skewered his attacker from groin to chest. Before the man had fallen he'd withdrawn the sword and was looking for the next target. From the corner of his eye he saw Wulfstan erupt in a ball of flame and greasy black smoke. The human torch ran across the deck and paused at the rail before climbing onto the ramp. Two soldiers tumbled backwards to get out the way of the frightful apparition, and Wulfstan disappeared into the paddle-wheeler's hull.

Vallon was embroiled in a mêlée. He sidestepped a soldier wielding a halberd and slashed down at the junction of the man's head and shoulder. The space occupied by the dead man filled with Rorik, the giant Viking who'd defied all natural law by recovering from a gangrenous leg back in Turkestan. Vallon led him left, led him right, right again, and when the man didn't know which way to move next, Vallon killed him with a quick thrust to his heart.

Jumping back, Vallon saw Lucas hard-pressed by two swordsmen. He dealt with one of them with one stroke and the other sprang away in search of easier opposition. Lucas's mouth twisted.

'Hot and heavy work.'

'Stay close.'

One sweeping glance told Vallon that the battle was lost. Knots of Chinese infantry had closed around his Outlanders, cutting them down one by one. He saw Hauk kill Josselin the centurion, a gentle man who'd always dealt courteously with the Vikings.

'You'll pay for that in hell,' Vallon shouted.

Hauk heard him. 'I'm saving you until last.'

Vallon didn't have time to respond. Two more men assailed him and he forgot his own injunction, so enraged that he cut the sword arms off both enemies with a single stroke. Lucas had drifted away and Vallon sprang towards him. 'Back to back.'

A mob of soldiers forced them to give ground. Vallon thrust, swung and hacked, but for every man he killed another two stood ready to fill the space. His suspect left ankle gave way and he buckled.

'Father!'

Vallon regained his feet. 'Don't worry about me.' He fended off

574

another attack, knowing that the next or the one after that would be the end.

'Behind you!' someone shouted.

Swinging round, Vallon turned headfirst into the path of a mace that smashed into his helmet. The world went white and then black.

He was sprawled on the deck, trying to regain control of his limbs when a hand wrenched the helmet off his head and he found himself looking into the smiling face of Hauk Eiriksson.

The Viking's voice seemed to reach him from far away. 'We never bade each other a proper farewell, Vallon the Far-Farer.'

Vallon coughed. 'I said goodbye to you two or three times, and always you returned like a cur in want of a master.'

'Not this time,' Hauk said. He raised his sword. 'So close to the grave, so far from heaven.'

Vallon was dimly aware of the clash of arms continuing around him. 'If Lucas is alive, spare him. Spare Qiuylue.'

'I'm on commission and can't afford to be lenient. Lucas will join you in hell. As for your tart, we'll use her tonight and discard her in the morning. When we've finished with her, no man will want to come near her again.'

'Why so much hatred?' Vallon groaned. 'After all we did for you. After everything we went through together.'

Hauk stood and drew back his sword. 'Do a proud man a favour that's to your own advantage and you make an enemy for life.'

Vallon saw the sword fall. Everything dissolved in a roaring red light, a hurricane that smashed the universe into pieces and sent them pinwheeling into a black vortex.

From very far away Vallon heard shouting, one voice closer and more insistent than the others. Something was pulling at his hand. He blinked and saw a smoke-blackened face. It was Lucas, dragging him out from under a dead weight. He struggled free and managed to kneel. It was Hauk's body that had fallen onto him, a

575

jagged piece of timber sticking out of the back of the Viking's head. Vallon used his sword to lever himself upright. The paddle-wheeler was drifting apart from *Jifeng* in a cloud of fumes, most of its superstructure blown open.

The explosion had taken the fight out of the Chinese. They tried to leap back onto their vessel, offering no resistance to the Outlanders, who followed up raining blows like tired drunks. The gap between the two ships was growing and many of the enemy soldiers fell short, their armour pulling them straight under.

Vallon riddled his ears. The screams of men being burned alive carried from the hull of the paddle-wheeler. He looked around at the carnage on his own deck and saw Lucas. He held out his hands and both men fell wordless into each other's arms, tears mingling on their sooty and blood-spattered faces.

Vallon broke the clinch and stood holding Lucas at arm's length. 'You called me "Father".'

'Look to the fires,' Gorka shouted.

A dozen flames had taken hold and would probably have devoured the ship if it hadn't been sheathed in hides. When the last blaze had been extinguished, Vallon looked at the paddle-wheeler blazing in their wake.

'God keep you, Wulfstan. You gave yourself a funeral any Viking would have been proud of.'

He turned with heavy heart to count his other casualties. The toll robbed him of any satisfaction in his victory. Seventeen dead. He looked around, still fuddled by the explosion.

'Where's Wayland?'

'Over here,' Aiken called.

Wayland sat propped against the port side, holding his upper arm. A dart from a repeating crossbow was lodged in it.

Vallon breathed a sigh of relief. 'Thank God it's not worse.'

Hero looked up. 'It's poisoned.'

Vallon didn't take it in. 'Poison? What poison?'

Wayland's grin was a rictus. 'The fatal kind.' He removed his hand to show viscous black blood leaking from the wound.

From a state of fogged consciousness Vallon was hurled into a reality too stark to bear. 'Can't you do anything? What about water? Try bleeding him. Keep him moving.' He reached down to lift Wayland to his feet.

'Don't,' Wayland said

'Where does it afflict you?'

Wayland's breath came in rapid gasps. 'It feels like an icy hand is squeezing my heart.'

'No,' Vallon cried. 'You're not going to die.' He dropped to his knees and clasped Wayland to his chest.

'I'm sorry,' Hero said. 'There's nothing I can do.'

Vallon watched Wayland die by degrees, the blood draining from his face and his eyes dulling over. Close as he was, Vallon couldn't make out Wayland's words except the last – 'Syth', delivered on an expiring note of love, guilt and sorrow.

His head arched back and his body convulsed before relaxing into death.

Hero stood wet-eyed but composed and pronounced the *Te Deum*. Lucas sobbed openly and the other Outlanders looked on bereft. Vallon cradled Wayland's head against his chest and raised grief-sodden eyes.

'Leave me alone with him.'

He rocked Wayland's corpse as if lulling a child to sleep. 'Not you, Wayland. Everybody else, but not you. You shone like the sun, with a light I thought could never be extinguished. On our first journey I came to look on you as a son, so talented and so contrary. And then you found my real son and on the day he called me father you slip into the void. Oh Wayland. What will I tell Syth?'

The surviving Outlanders committed the bodies of their comrades to the sea where it turned from muddy yellow to clear blue. The sun's dying rays spread like a golden fan over the receding coast. After the last rites, Vallon stood alone at the rail. He unsheathed his sword for the last time, looked at it for a few moments, then hurled it end over end. It disappeared into the ocean with hardly a splash.

The last of the Outlanders stood on the foredeck. Vallon hobbled over.

Hero held out a compass. 'Do you recognise this?'

'Oh yes. The south-pointing mysterious direction-finder that made me turn in my tracks when we met all those years ago. If I'd known then where it would lead me, I would have ridden on.'

'It doesn't dictate fate,' Hero said. 'All it does is show directions. You have to decide which one to take.'

Vallon screwed a knuckle into his eye. 'Wayland has shown us the way. South, then west. Back home.'

'This breeze is carrying us east,' Lucas said.

'What lies out there?' Gorka asked.

'If we continue east, we'll come to Korea,' Aiken said. 'Beyond that is an island called Nippon. "The land where the sun rises".'

'Sir.'

Vallon turned. Everyone turned. Qiuylue had come on deck dressed as Vallon had first seen her, wearing a gown decorated with cranes and pines – symbols of longevity and fidelity. She had made up her face and arranged her hair in the conch style.

She walked towards the stern. Nobody else moved.

'Qiuylue?'

She turned at the stern rail, faced him, brought her hands together and bowed.

'Someone stop her!' Vallon shouted.

The nearest man was still feet away when she gathered the folds of her gown, stepped onto the transom, spread her arms like a bird taking flight and jumped.

ACKNOWLEDGEMENTS

I drew some of the Kaifeng street scenes from Zhang Zeduan's *Spring Festival on the River*, an early twelfth-century scroll painting depicting society in the Chinese capital. This remarkable work, more than seventeen feet long, is unmatched in the amount of information it gives about a medieval city anywhere in the world. As well as showing the architectural details, it presents a pageant of everyday life in the metropolis, including scenes of traders and storytellers, caravans and cargo boats, fishermen and scholars, wrestlers and garden designers, conjurors and musicians, students and stevedores ...

As ever, I'm grateful to my agent Anthony Goff and his colleagues at David Higham Associates. Thanks, too, to Ed Wood and Iain Hunt, my editors at Sphere for their invaluable input.

With the delivery deadline approaching, my daughter Lily offered to read the first half of the typescript. Her corrections and suggestions were greatly appreciated – not least for what she implied rather than stated.

Deborah, my wife, provided the Latin and Greek, including the translation from Virgil's *Aeneid*. For her support and encouragement, I am more grateful than I can say.